BOYS OF KING ACADEMY

LOUISE ROSE

Contents

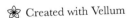 Created with Vellum

Description

They might be the elite of King Academy, but I am here for my own damn crown and I will do whatever it takes to get it.

Like in all the pretty pictures, King Town looks perfect. But underneath the cracks, that a painting can never altogether hide, lies and sins rule the town with the Academy right in the middle of it.

Kidnapped and forced from my latest foster home into the dangerous world of King Academy and the games they play, I find out I'm from here and now there is no escaping this world.

I'm born to play the same games they do.

Four houses rule this small gated town, and they always have done, poisoning the waters with their sins and darkness. And their heirs?

Well, they think they rule everything and everyone. They use their money and good looks to charm the academy into calling them their kings.

But I'm not falling for that bullshit.

Romeo Navarre, Archer Knight and Declan Dauphin may think

they own the academy, own the town, and get everything they want…but then they have *just* met me.

They will soon find out I'm not falling for the sexy boys of King Academy.

Recommend for 18+ readers due to content. This is a full-length book and the first of five books in this series.

Included in this collection-
Take My Crown
Take My Place
Take My Throne
Be My Traitor

Quote

"FROM THE DEEPEST DESIRES OFTEN COME THE DEADLIEST HATE." -SOCRATES.

Prologue

"*W*hen you're older, little dove, you will love four men."

Mum's smooth, calm voice whispers to me as I try to drift off to sleep in her arms. Her peppermint and tulips perfume comforts me, the familiar smell reminding me I am safe and loved. My pink fluffy blanket is wrapped around us, keeping us warm while a storm rages outside. Rain pounds against the windows while flashes of lightning sporadically light up the shadows in my room.

"Why four?" I ask around a yawn.

"The first is a knight who will be a mistake, but everyone needs those to help their heart blossom." Mum counted them off on her fingers. "The second is your first true love, but it won't last because the prince is promised to someone else. The third is a joker who never should have been more than a friend..." Her voice trails off, a look of sadness briefly crossing her face.

I don't know if I like this story. Mum usually tells me fairy tales about princes and princesses, brave women who save king-

1

doms from bad men, weaving a world of fantasy for me to escape into. This seems a little too… real.

I play with a strand of mum's soft, blonde hair, enjoying the feel between my fingers. "And the fourth?"

"That's the man you'll do anything for, the man you'd die for if it protected him. He's the king who'll steal your soul, wrap it in an ivy called love and never let you go," she smiles, lightly caressing my cheek with the back of her hand.

In that moment my mind is made up. I don't want a prince, or a knight, or a joker. I want to love a king.

"Is that why my name is Ivy, mummy?" I ask. "Am I the princess in the story?"

She drops a gentle kiss onto my forehead. "No. You're the queen in the story and no one will ever take that from you. Queens don't need kings, but a king always needs his queen."

It is the last story she ever tells me.

Chapter One

IVY ARCHAIC

"*Take me away,*
Make me pay,
'Cos you chase the grey away,
You're the one who makes me smile,
Even when I want to run a mile,
I'm always running, always-
I... I... I... Ugh!"

I throw my pen down on the paper, watching it bounce a few times before flying off the desk. I have been working on this song all day and I still can't figure out how the chorus should go. Music is my usual escape from the world, but for some reason, I can't get into the zone.

Running my fingers through my long, wavy ash blonde hair, I stare out the window at the nicer houses on the other side of the road. They are those fancy new builds with super eco everything and fake grass in their gardens to boot. I wonder for a single moment if they look at this side of the road at the old cottage I live in. It needs a new roof and the grass outside grows every single day. I bet they look over and think: 'the grass is definitely not greener on the other side'.

"Ivy!"

I put my guitar to one side, the sound of my foster mum Katy's voice giving me a welcome excuse to walk away from a song which simply isn't working and my thoughts on rich people's houses.

"It lives!" Katy deadpans as I walk into the small kitchen. She is chopping onions and the smell instantly makes my eyes water.

"Yeah, yeah." I roll my eyes.

Katy is all right as foster parents go, and I should know. I have had more than my fair share of them and most I pretend I don't remember for my own sanity. In the three years I have lived with her, she has treated me like family, which is a refreshing change compared to the ones who are in it for the monthly paycheque. Still, I am counting down the days until I can escape the system and strike out on my own. As soon as I finish school, I'm outta here. I don't care if I have to work dead-end jobs and study my butt off at college, I won't force Katy to keep me when she can foster another kid and actually get paid. This place is sweet, and another kid deserves her love.

And her fantastic cooking skills.

"It's okay," Katy says. "I enjoy hearing you play your guitar. But I'm going to need you to pop to the shop for me. I'm making cauliflower cheese and I realized I haven't got enough milk."

"Oops."

"Yeah, I know," Katy laughs. "You'd think I would've checked before I started grating the cheese. There's a ten-pound note in my purse, bring me back the receipt and change. And if you'd like to get yourself a little something while you're there, feel free. Just don't go nuts, okay?"

"Sure thing, Katy."

After taking the money from her purse, I head out and look up at the cloudy skies above. Knowing my luck, it's going to pour down before I get back from the shop. I can get a coat, but what's a little rain?

"Love you, Ivy!" I hear my foster mum call as I leave.

"Love you too, Katy!" I yell back.

The sun peeking out of the dark skies shines down on my skin as I walk down the road toward Sketchy's, the nearest corner shop. We lived in one of those downmarket suburbs where the terraced houses all look the same, with a tiny scrap of land in the front. Every now and then, I have to walk past a house where the owner has made an effort to plant a few flowers in the front garden, but their meagre attempts can't cover up the fact that this is a rough area where most people are more concerned about clinging to what little they had than keeping up with the Joneses. The new builds opposite our houses are built by a clueless contractor who doesn't know how bad the area is. Yet, they somehow still sold the houses, judging by the signs outside.

Sketchy's is a ten-minute walk away and the fresh air seems to fire up my creative thoughts. As I walk, I play with different combinations of lyrics in my mind. I'm pretty certain I will come up with something which can fix the problems with the song.

At last, I reach the shop and check my phone, seeing it's a few minutes from five pm when the shop closes. Heading over to the chiller cabinet, I pick up a couple of pints of milk. Then I crossed to the magazine stand, looking for the latest edition of *Kerrang!* I can't see it, so instead I pick up a couple packs of gum before heading over to the counter to pay.

"Morning, Ivy." Mrs Singh greets me from behind the counter. "And how are you doing this fine day?"

"Not too bad," I reply. "Katy's making her infamous cauliflower cheese for dinner…"

"Can you squeeze in another mouth to feed?"

I grin and shake my head. Everyone loves Katy's cooking and I've always wondered why she doesn't try to do anything professional with her skills.

"Just remember that if you get hungry, there's always a place for you at my table," Mrs Singh tells me.

"Thanks, Mrs Singh," I smile, taking the change she gave me. Hating the pity in her eyes which is like a knife to my soul. I'm always the foster kid of the town. The kid who lost her mum, no dad or family and now is getting too old to be considered the cute foster kid. I'm now the lost teenager, I see it in their eyes. When I finally leave, I'm leaving my past and the foster kid title with it. I put the milk in my rucksack, popping a stick of gum into my mouth and head back outside.

Humming the tune I have been working on, my fingers instinctively form the shape of the chords I would be playing if I had my guitar in hand. Yes, I think I might have finally figured out where I am going wrong. I need to switch the D minor for an F sliding to a G and then it should work.

I'm so caught up in thought that I don't hear the motorbike roaring up behind me until it's practically on top of me, the heat from the engine blowing against my lower legs. I can feel the vibration of the bike on the concrete under my feet.

"You've dropped something."

It takes a moment for me to realise the biker is talking to me. I frown, wondering what the hell I just dropped. I turn around, searching the empty footpath before finally looking at the stranger on a bike.

"Where?"

I can't see the face of the biker because he keeps the mirrored visor of his helmet down. Clad in black leather from head to toe, he gives off a bad boy vibe for miles. I can't help but wonder what he looks like underneath it all. Is the leather padded or he is just that muscular? The sidecar attached to his bike on the other side of him takes a little away from the edgy look he had going on, but I don't care. Boys are not my game right now. I can date when I'm older and hopefully *wiser*.

I tell myself that...but my body harshly disagrees and misses sex. We are in a permanent disagreement which I'm sure "she" will win. *Damn teenage hormones.*

"Are you Ivy Archaic?"

I frown. Now that's more than a little creepy. Thankfully my hormones fuck off real quick and the fact I'm alone in an empty street with a man on a bike who knows my name lets fear take over. "Who wants to know?"

Leaving the engine running, he kicks the bike stand down and gets off.

Shit. Shit. Shit.

"Someone wants to meet you," he says, his gravelly and somewhat sexy under different circumstances voice makes that statement sound unappealing.

"I'm good. Don't want to meet anyone right now. So, see ya!" I turn to run as fast as I can even before all my words have left my mouth.

Without warning, he grabs me around the waist and throws me over his shoulder like I weigh nothing more than a bag of sugar. My rucksack falls to the ground, as he heads back to his bike.

"Hey!" I scream, flailing around, trying to kick or punch him, anything to make him let me go but the guy is built like a damn rock and every hit does nothing more than hurt my own hands and knees.

"Fight me and it'll go very badly for you," he warns, as he dumps me in the sidecar. I growl at him, shoving his hands away from me as I try to escape the damn sidecar, but he is too quick. In seconds he has handcuffs all ready and waiting. Quickly he snaps them around my wrists, tying me to metal loops in the sidecar so it is impossible for me to get away.

Deftly, he jumps back on his bike, looking around quickly. I wonder what the hell he was going to do if anyone saw him. Fear lodges in my throat when I spot the gun in his back pocket. I'm so screwed. Screaming won't help me escape a lunatic on a bike with a fucking gun.

Revving up the engine, he speeds away too quickly for me to react.

I twist my head, looking back in the hope that someone had

seen me being kidnapped, but all I can see is the milk oozing out of my abandoned rucksack like a puddle of blood, sweeping down the street into the road.

Fuck.

Chapter Two

IVY ARCHAIC

The mysterious biker zooms off in the opposite direction of Katy's house and that doesn't surprise me, but every minute we get further away, the more I start to panic. If I don't get help now, I'm screwed.

Up ahead, I can see a family out for a walk. I had to get their attention, knowing if he gets us out of the town and into the country lanes, there won't be another chance.

Opening my mouth, I inhaled deeply, ready to scream at the top of my lungs but a leather-covered hand clams tightly over my mouth but the bike never slows down. I follow the hand to my kidnapper, wishing I could see his face, see if he is as cruel as he sounds.

"I will tell you this once, and fair warning, you don't want to piss me off," he warns, his loud voice coming to me from speakers in the sidecar. "My orders are to bring you back alive and I don't fail at anything. Scream and I will make sure those people never speak a word about you. Try to escape and I will kill anyone in my way to get to you. Your life is over, Ivy Archaic, and for now, you belong to me."

"I belong to fucking no one," I spit back the second he lets my mouth go, the anger in my voice hazing over the fear pounding through my body. I don't know if he heard me, he doesn't react if he did. All I know is that I believe him and I won't get anyone innocent killed for me.

I slump back in my seat, defeated. For now. If my kidnapper thinks he has beaten my fighting spirit out of me, he has another thing coming. I just have to bide my time. There is bound to be another opportunity for me to get help and I'm going to be ready to take it.

We wind through backstreets and roads next to a few motorways. I guess the biker is trying to avoid any cameras so no one would be able to trace our journey. If he had bothered to ask, I would have told him not to bother. I have run away from plenty of foster homes in the past. I had a history with the police, and the older I got, the less they seemed to care about bringing me back. Now I'm almost 18, there is no way they are going to waste time looking for me.

Gradually, the tired council houses give way to more expensive properties. My curiosity piqued, I start to pay more attention to where we were going. We seem to be heading into the posh side of town, which seems to be a weird place to go. Surely any kidnapper worth their salt would take me to some abandoned warehouse somewhere or an old farmhouse in the middle of nowhere. Okay, maybe I have watched a few too many Hollywood movies, but it still seemed strange that we seemed to be going in the direction of where the rich people lived.

The biker slows his pace a little, letting the engine die down so he can talk to me. Not that I want to hear a thing this idiot has to say. The second I'm out of this sidecar, I'm going to kick him. He didn't tie my legs up and I swear he is going to pay for that.

I haven't made a plan for what to do after I kick him, but I figure something might come up.

"We're about to go into a gated community," he tells me. "Which means going past the security guard on duty. I'm warning you now—he's a good friend of mine, so if you think you can get him to help you, you can forget about it. Nod if you're going to behave like a good girl."

I nod with gritted teeth, my body shaking with anger. I fucking hate this idiot. Not for the first time in our long journey I wonder why he is doing this. Why me? I'm seventeen and other than being a girl, I'm pretty useless. I'm not even a kidnap worthy girl. I hide my body under baggy hoodies and jeans… because they are comfy. I wear black combat boots and my blonde hair is always up in a messy bun. I don't even wear makeup. Not for lack of wanting to, but makeup costs money and I'd prefer to spend my money on my guitar.

Driving past a high wall, I notice a few trees which might make it easy for me to climb over. Yes, the most sensible thing right now seemed to be to keep my head down and figure out a way to escape later. Whatever is going on, they can't keep me locked up forever.

The bike swerves to the left, drawing up next to a security booth in front of a high, ornate, metal gate. A large sign announces that this is Kings Town. Great, never heard of it.

"Hey! Steve!" The biker calls out. "It's me."

He lifts his visor, but he is looking away from me so I'm not able to get a look at his face.

The security guard slides the window of his booth open and pokes his head out.

"I see you got the package," he says. "Nice work. I don't see your brothers making an effort to pay off that debt to the Archaic's. You're a good kid. Any problems picking it up?"

"Nah. Everything ran smoothly," the biker tells him.

Bullshit.

"Solomon's going to reward you big time for this one. Might even cancel the debt the Knight's owe," the guard says, pressing the button that opened the gate. It swings open silently and my kidnapper slowly drives the bike forward and into this supposed Kings Town.

My jaw drops as I see what is behind the walls. Each property is protected by further walls, but going by their length, they all have enormous gardens. I can see rooftops set far back from the road, suggesting that each house is more like a mansion.

There is some serious money here.

We turn onto a road signposted 'King Street' and at last, the biker pulls up by a large, carved gate obscuring whatever is behind. He presses a buzzer set into a column to the right of the gate. There is a nameplate next to it, but I can't make out the name carved into it as it is covered with overgrown ivy. Figures.

"It's me," he says into the intercom. "I've got a delivery for Solomon."

Whoever is on the other end of the intercom opens the gates and they swing open to reveal the most beautiful house I have ever seen. It is like something out of a dream, large and regal with a porch held up by pillars and the porches wrap around the entire mansion. There are too many windows to count–there had to be at least six bedrooms, if not more. I notice right away the cameras and bars lining the downstairs windows that look rather new. This only gets worse. Apparently being kidnapped was something someone rich planned out for me.

But why fucking me?

There are certainly worse places to be held prisoner, that's the only good thing I can come up with.

The biker slowly eases his vehicle over a gravel path, but instead of pulling up in front of the house, he turns off and follows the road out to the side, back to where there is a large garage. He drives in and switches off the engine.

Taking off his helmet I'm finally able to see what my kidnapper looks like and damn, he is as good looking as I thought. He is younger than I expected, not much older than me if I had to guess. Thick brown locks cover his deeply tanned skin and pearly grey-blue eyes. With dimples that appear when he smiles, like he knows I'm checking him out. This guy is as dangerous as he is good looking. I'm truly fucked.

Just my type. If we'd met under different circumstances, I would have been more than happy to go for a ride on the back of his bike. As it is, he's just an idiot.

"Welcome to your new home," he sarcastically points out while taking a set of keys from his pocket. Prick. He unlocks one set of handcuffs and does them back up again around both my wrists before releasing me from the other metal loop.

"You're not going to fight me are you?" he asks with a sadistic smile.

I shake my head, hoping I look weak and innocent for a moment. Enough to fool him.

"Out you come then." He helps me climb out of the sidecar. I wait until we have walked a few steps away from the bike. When we are next to a large tree, I swing my foot out and kick him hard in his leg. He stumbles and turns on me, picking me up by my shoulders and pushing my back into the tree. He covers my body with his and grabs my chin with his large hand.

"Don't fucking push me," he growls and I smile.

"Fucking do something about it then!" I provoke him. I don't know why I do it, it's not smart, and he has all the cards. He could hurt me if he wanted...but a small part of me doesn't think he will.

"Do you really want that, crazy girl?" he questions me like I'm insane and I might just be. With his body pressed against mine, I can feel how turned on he is against my thigh, even without meeting his eyes. His eyes burn with passion and lust, something I'm not that well versed in. For some fucked up reason, I'm not exactly put off by him either.

We stare each other down and I get the feeling he is enjoying this almost as much as me. With one more sneer, he drops me and then guides me by the elbow towards a small door in the side of the house. Pushing it open, he leads me into a corridor.

I stumble a little as he pulls me along, wanting to take my time to examine the inside of the house to get a feel for who I am meeting next.

"Move it along," he snaps in my ear, his hot breath warming my cheek. "Solomon's been waiting long enough as it is."

Solomon. That is the second time I have heard the name, and it is completely meaningless. I have never heard of anyone by that name and certainly don't know what they might want with me. What kind of name is Solomon, anyway?

We stop outside a closed door, the biker finally releases me from the handcuffs. I rub my sore wrists as my kidnapper knocks on the door.

"Come!"

The voice which beckoned us in is deep and gravelly, filled with the confidence of an alpha male and I grumble internally. Not another dickhead.

Pushing the door open, the biker gestures to me to go in first, so I step in to be presented to a man sitting behind a desk. He has black hair cut short with flashes of white at the temple, and a beard which had more streaks of white amongst the black. There is something familiar about his eyes, but I can't put my finger on what.

"Ivy!" he exclaims as soon as I walk in, getting up from his seat and walking around to greet me with arms outstretched.

I cringe, stepping back when it becomes clear he is coming in for a hug. No, thank you.

"Now, my child," he says with a mock pout. "Is that any way to welcome your father?"

"My *father*?" I shake my head and laugh. I keep laughing until I realise I'm the only one who is finding this funny.

Biker asshole dude is looking at me like I'm crackers and fake father man is mimicking that expression. Oddly, I feel relieved for a long moment. They must have kidnapped the wrong person because they don't want me.

Phew. "I don't know who you think I am, but I am *not* your daughter and I pity her if this is how you treat her. All your thug had to do was ask and I would have told him my dad died in an accident when I was a baby."

"Was that the story your mother told you?" Solomon shook his head and clicks his tongue. "The poor woman always loved making up fantasies."

"Don't you speak about her like that!" I protest. "She loved me. She was always there for me. If what you're saying is true, you abandoned me, left me to grow up in foster care. If you're my father, you've got a funny way of showing it."

Solomon sighs heavily. "We have a lot to talk about. Please. Take a seat and I'll tell you everything your mother should have told you years ago."

He indicates a chair opposite his desk, going back to take his seat, assuming I will do as I'm told.

Stuff that.

"Sit down," the biker snarls, shoving me forward to the chair.

I stumble a little but remain standing as I spin around and glare at him.

He smirks, pulling the chair out and raising one eyebrow.

"Now, now, Archer," says Solomon almost humorlessly. "There's no need for that. I'm sure Ivy will soon come to her senses when she realises that good behaviour will win her the right to contact her foster mother, while bad behaviour..." He shrugs expansively. "Let's just say I know where she lives."

Katy! I would never forgive myself if anything happened to her. Not that I believe this guy is my father at all. Either way, I'm stuck here until he figures out I'm not his daughter. I don't move and the room soon becomes even more thick with tension.

Solomon watches me and then he turns a photo frame around on his desk. My knees feel weak as I see my mother, a young version of her with long blonde hair, a light blue dress and heels on...looking so much like her that it makes my heart pang. I don't have many photos of her anymore and sometimes when I look at them, I can't even remember when it was taken, making me feel guilty for forgetting. This one is new to me, and the younger man in the photo is Solomon, his arm wrapped around my mum's waist. A bump under her dress that means I was in the photo.

Holy fuckcakes. I have a parent who is alive.

"Now take a seat. We have a lot to catch up on." My father's tone makes it clear he isn't in the mood for any more rebellion, so I do as I'm told and sit.

"Good girl." The way my father's eyes crinkle when he smiles is like looking in a mirror. "Oh, my child. You have no idea how long I've waited for this moment."

"Really?" I raise an eyebrow. "Given that I've spent almost ten years bouncing from one foster home to another until Katy took me in, I find that hard to believe."

"I am sorry about that." It is hard to tell from his expression if he is sincere. "Perhaps if you hear the whole story, you'll understand why I've done what I've done. Would you like some refreshments? A drink, perhaps, something to eat?"

As soon as he says it, my tummy rumbles, reminding me that I should have been sitting down to Katy's cauliflower cheese right now.

"Okay."

"Bring my daughter a coke and a grilled cheese sandwich," Solomon orders.

How does he know my favourite comfort food?

Archer nods and leaves to follow orders like the good little lap dog he is. I watch him until he gets to the door and looks back. The smug expression in his eyes is something I'm desperate to smack off his face.

Bye, bye, Archer.

"When you were born, I was the proudest man alive," Solomon sorry, *dad*—tells me. "I have always wanted a little girl, the first of a large family of Archaics. Sadly, your mother and I were not to be blessed with any more children, so instead, I devoted myself to you."

I nod my head once, unsure of what to say to that.

"Not long after your second birthday, my father died, leaving me the sole heir to the Archaic fortune. Unfortunately, with great power comes great responsibility. You see, the Archaics are one of the four houses who own Kings Town. Until recently, this place was practically a war zone as the houses vied for dominance. We tried to topple the Kings who transformed this town into a slum overrun by junkies and gangsters. Then we converted it to one which is civilised and offers wealth and riches to those who are willing to work for it. The King family lives far away and their father died, therefore the town was left to its own devices. The truce between our four houses and families is everything, but I have failed as a leader of my family in the sense of having children. Around the time your mother left with you, I suffered a bad accident that left me incapable of having more children. Therefore, you are the only heir and that is a danger." He stopped here for a moment, taking a sip of his brandy (Or water) before he continued.

"Nobody could know I had a daughter. As my sole heir, you are a prime target for kidnapping. I can't risk my enemies getting their hands on you, but your mother and I were so much in love. There is no way she would agree to staying away from me to keep you safe, so I had no choice. I had to fake my death to take up the Archaic mantle, securing your safety."

"*Had* to fake your death?" I scoffed. "You couldn't, like, hire bodyguards? Mum wouldn't have done anything to put me in danger. All you had to do was tell her what was going on. I'm sure you could have figured something out."

My father stands up and lifts his shirt to reveal a nasty scar running from his belly button up to his chest. "I got that when one of the Dauphins ambushed me. And I was surrounded by bodyguards. It is thanks to them I survived the fight, but if they'd known about you, there's no doubt in my mind you would have been taken and subjected to horrific torture. The only way I could keep you safe was if I disappeared from your lives until things had changed enough that you could join me by my side."

Archer comes back into the room bringing my coke and a sandwich.

Opening the bottle, I take a deep swig, struggling to process everything I'm hearing. This is nuts!

"Thank you, Archer," my father says. "Your help is much appreciated. You may leave now."

Archer nods briskly and leaves without looking back once.

"All these years, I've been watching you from afar, observing your progress," my father continues after Archer shut the door behind him. "I was devastated when I heard of your mother's diagnosis. In fact, I went to see her, wanting to offer my help."

"You saw my mother?" I laugh bitterly. "I bet that went well."

Dad smiles ruefully. "Yeah. She wouldn't forgive me for walking out, even though I explained how I was only trying to keep her safe."

"Wonder why?" I mutter.

"I offered her money for private healthcare," Dad continues, ignoring my remark. "But she wouldn't accept a penny from me. She told me she had done fine without me and she didn't need me anymore. If we'd had more time, maybe I could have talked her round, brought her to Kings Town where we have the best medics in the world. But sadly, she passed before I could get her to change her mind."

"So why didn't you come to get me then?"

"Because right when your mother died, a huge fight broke out between the four houses. The Kings had been forced out of the town, leaving the houses of Navarre, Knight, Dauphin and of course Archaic to battle for supremacy. I hated thinking of you going into foster care, but it was the best place for you. Now we've settled into an uneasy truce and the time has come for you to learn about your heritage. As my only heir, it's crucial you learn about your true place in the world so you're ready to take on the responsibility of leading the house when I'm no longer here."

An awkward silence descended, as I considered everything my father had said.

"If all of this is true, why haven't I read about it in the papers?" I ask eventually. "I mean, this seems like something out of a film, different houses fighting each other to rule the town. Surely someone would have reported on all the violence here?"

"Oh my dear, sweet, naïve Ivy," my father laughs. "Look around you. The world is a violent place. There's nothing going on here that doesn't happen outside the walls of our town.

There's nothing special going on here. I guarantee you that your disappearance will barely register with the media. Perhaps a photo in the local newspaper, a brief mention on social media. And for those rare occasions when a journalist has decided to stick their nose where it's not wanted..." He shrugs with one shoulder. "We have very effective lawyers who know how to squash a story before it begins, not to mention other ways of persuading people round to our way of thinking. Kings Town is one of the country's best kept secrets, and we like it that way. Only the elite can enjoy what we have here."

"I see." I take a bite of my grilled cheese, chewing slowly. It had to be said that whoever made it is a master chef. It still wasn't as nice as Katy's meal would have been. For that reason alone, the sandwich tastes like bitter poison in my mouth.

If my father thought a good cheese sandwich is going to make up for a lifetime of abandonment, he is the naïve one, not me.

"I know. It's a lot to take in," my father says. "I think that's enough for now."

He presses a buzzer on his desk and a moment later, the door opens and a woman wearing a simple black dress walks in. She is pretty with lighter blonde hair than me, a tiny button nose and she can't be more than five or six years older than I am. Her heels are high and sharp, clicking on the tiles as she walks.

"Sir?" She nods her head in a little gesture of respect.

"Isabella will show you to your room," my father tells me. "I've taken the liberty of buying you a brand new wardrobe. My shopping assistant has a good eye for detail and she has a daughter about your age, so I think you'll like everything she's picked out for you. You'll also find your new school uniform."

"School uniform?" I gasp. "You expect me to go to some shitty school and play happy family? Katy home schooled me because of issues at my last school."

The memories from my last school haunt my mind, making my hands sweat.

"Oh, yes you will go," my father tells me. "I've enrolled you at King Academy and I think you'll find it a very different experience to the establishments you've frequented in the past. My chauffeur will drive you there in the morning, so be ready for him by 8:15. They frown on tardiness at the Academy. However, you'll be pleased to hear that they also have a zero tolerance for bullying. You won't have to suffer anything like you did in your old school."

Bullying was a nice word for the shit that went down in my old school. I still have the scars on my back to remind me what being a victim to rich bullies is really like.

"But I don't want to go," I angrily snap. "I'll stay here, I won't be any trouble. I'll stay in my room. You won't even know I'm there."

"I'm afraid this is not up for discussion," my father tells me. "It is essential that you mix with your peers from the other houses so you can learn their strengths and weaknesses. This is a crucial part of your education and not something you can escape."

"Fine," I huffed, standing to follow Isabella. I'm older now and apparently have a rich dad. I won't let myself get into the same situation I once did four years ago. Four years ago I was naïve and desperate to make friends. Now I'm just angry but I do know how to protect myself thanks to self-defence lessons Katy took me to. One of the many reasons I will never put Katy in danger by trying to run away.

"Let me be clear, Ivy," father warns, no doubt seeing the resistance in my eyes. "I will not stand disobedience. As an Archaic, you're strong willed and headstrong, traits which will stand you in good stead when your turn comes to rule the House, but can get you into trouble in the meantime. If you rebel against me, you'll find I can make your life a living hell. But if you do as you're told and follow all my instructions, you'll discover that being an Archaic is a wonderful privilege which brings with it many advantages. The finer things in life are all yours now. All you have to do is ask and your wish will be carried out by one of my servants.

"Have a good day at school tomorrow and if I get positive feedback from the Head Master, you will be able to call your foster mother at the end of the day."

He turns his attention to some paperwork on his desk, making it clear our time together is over. I have no choice but to follow Isabella and see what my new room is like, while making sure to remind myself that this is just the start.

And my "Dad" might have all the cards right now, but he won't for long.

Chapter Three

IVY ARCHAIC

"When Solomon says the finer things in life are all mine, he isn't kidding, is he?"

My jaw drops when I see the room that my father had given to me. And by room, I actually mean a full on suite, with bathroom, walk in wardrobe, living area and bedroom. It's ridiculously nice and expensive, nothing like I have ever had in my entire life. A part of me doesn't want it all, knowing I don't deserve any of this shit. I wish my mum was here to tell me what to do, how to get through this, and if my father isn't the snake he seems to be.

Why did you leave all this, mum?

"He hired the best interior decorator to furnish it for you," Isabella tells me, "but if there's anything you don't like, all you have to do is say, and we'll change it."

"No, no. Don't be silly. This is fine. More than fine."

And it really is. For a girl who'd grown up on the wrong side of the tracks, this is unbelievable. Going into the wardrobe, I can see my father had spared no expense to get everything he thought a girl my age would like. The scary thing is that the clothes hanging up are just my style—sassy tees with funny slogans, cargo pants and black denim jeans, slouchy jumpers made from the softest materials.

It is quite spooky, really. He must have been watching me for a long time before he sent Archer in to snatch me.

Laid out on a low table in the middle of the wardrobe area is what I supposed is my school uniform. Picking it up, I can't avoid letting out a grunt of disgust.

"Really? They can't have designed something better than this?"

I'm being forced into wearing a black pleated skirt and black V neck jumper with a crest embroidered on the left hand side. Above are the words 'King Academy' and underneath 'House Archaic.' There are also some long black socks, a white shirt and a black and white striped tie.

The only good thing about it are the funky black Doc Martens. I have always wanted a pair, but Katy said they were too expensive. She was right. These have my name on the inside, and last name in a small font down the outside edges so they must be custom made. As it is, they are a small consolation for the fact I'm going to look like an idiot.

"Is there anything else I can get you?" Isabella asks with an overly sweet voice. I don't trust her or anyone for that matter. "More food, perhaps? There's a small fridge in your lounge with a supply of soft drinks, but if there's anything in particular you want, let me know and I'll arrange for it to be sent up."

"No, I'm fine for now, thanks," I tell her. "To be honest, I would like to be alone for a while. It's been a bit of a day." I pause. "Wait, can you send up some bells on a string or rope of some kind. I lost my bag and it's a comfort thing."

"Of course," Isabella nods, looking a little confused. "I'll leave you be then. But if you do need anything else, pick up that phone on the wall and press the button for the person you want to speak to. Solomon has asked me to be your personal assistant, so most of the time you should call me, but you've also got a direct line to the kitchen and chauffeur should you need them."

"O-okay."

Isabella leaves, closing my bedroom doors behind her. I hear the distinct sound of a key turning in the lock and even though I don't feel that threatened here, I still panic. Rushing over to the door, I try the handle. Sure enough, she locked me in.

I try to suck in deep breaths, pushing back all the memories of that one foster parent who loved to lock me in my tiny room and not come back for days, forgetting about me. I sink down to the floor, taking a long time to remind myself I'm not there anymore before I hear the lock being turned. I climb to my feet as a woman in her late fifties and soft eyes brings a tray of tiny blue bells and blue string, placing them on the small table by the door.

"For you," she claims in what I think is a Spanish accent.

I nod and she leaves the room quickly, the lock turning once more. I make quick work of tying bells to all the doors and windows like I do in every home I've lived in since I was fourteen.

Finally, I feel like I can breathe again. I slump down on the bed, knowing I'm stuck here for the foreseeable future.

Then something caught my eye, which made me sit up and take notice.

"Hol-ee crap!"

In the corner of the room is a guitar on a stand. Crossing over to it, I pick it up. Running my hands over the wood, I can scarcely believe my luck.

It is a Gibson Montana Hummingbird!

Placing the strap over my head, I strum a few chords and feel like I am in Heaven. It is the most beautiful sound I have ever heard.

Dad certainly had taste in guitars, but I had to keep sight of the fact that he seemed to be planning on keeping me prisoner for the indefinite future, perhaps the rest of my life. I have to stay strong, stay focused, and not let his money turn my head.

It is a gorgeous guitar though…

Sitting on the bed, I pick out notes at random, a song practically writing itself as I play. I have to get this written down.

Opening a few drawers, I eventually find pen and paper and start scribbling out what I have played so I wouldn't forget.

"Any other day and I would have noticed you,
Any other time and I might have forgotten you.
Forgetting is easy, cos my heart is taken.
But after what you did, how can I dare care?
After you.
Before you,
Who knows what I might dare?"

Not bad. With a bit of polish, this can be one of my best songs.

I spend the next few hours playing and singing, music becoming my escape from reality once more like it always has. I'm a bird in a gilded cage, Katy once told me, but boy can I sing.

"Ivy, wake up. Come on, wake up Ivy."

I'm woken by Isabella shaking on my shoulder and I jolt, shoving her away and wondering why I didn't hear the bells. In fact…when did I fall to sleep or get into bed? I must have been tired. I glance around the room, seeing the bells are still in place and it relaxes me. It's only Isabella. Apparently she moves like a cat.

"Sorry, Ivy. You've got to go to school. I've brought you some breakfast. Eat up and get dressed. Your car's leaving in half an hour and your father will not be happy if you're late. Trust me. You wouldn't like to see what happens when he's angry."

A shadow crosses her face that makes me wonder what my father had done to her in the past. But there is no time for questions if I only had half an hour to get ready. Isabella is right. Now is not the time to push boundaries. I need to play the game and get to grips with my new life so I can figure out the best way to escape.

Never a morning person, I ignore the food, chugging down the glass of orange juice instead before I get dressed in my new school uniform. It looks as bad as I thought it would, but I do my best to improve things with makeup. Someone had bought me a wide selection of the top brands, so I gave myself a smokey eye and choosing a dark lipstick to make a statement. Nobody is going to mess with me today. I don't care what my dad says—all schools have a problem with bullying. It goes with the territory. But if anyone tries to take advantage of me, I will hit back so hard they won't have time to blink. I won't be a victim for the rich boys of King Academy.

If dad wants me to play princess...then King Academy has no idea who they are letting through their doors.

And if I get expelled for defending myself against a bully, I won't be able to go back to school and it wouldn't be my fault. Let's see what dad does then.

Isabella is waiting outside for me, when she sees my appearance, she smiles. "A little rebel, just like your father. Come on. The car's ready and waiting."

She leads me through a warren of corridors and finally to the front of the house. I'm grateful for her help, I would get lost without her, especially since it looks like I'm going to be confined to my room for a while, and the last thing I want is to be late for school because I can't find my way round the mansion.

A large limo is waiting for me, a chauffeur standing silently by the open door waiting for me to get in. As I climb inside, he shuts the door behind me.

"Have a good day." Isabella waves me off as the car pulls away.

I wiggle my fingers in return, not wanting to alienate her. Right now, I can do with all the allies I can get.

There is a rucksack lying on the seat next to me, I open it up to see brand new exercise books and a pencil case filled with supplies. Dad really had thought of everything.

"How long have you worked for my dad?" I ask the driver, but he ignores me. There is a screen separating us and I tap on it, but he still doesn't reply.

There is a slight buzzing, and I hear someone speak over the intercom.

"Your father would prefer if we don't talk unless there's an emergency," the chauffeur tells me. "If you do need to contact me, press the orange button set in the armrest, but I would request you only do so if you really have something important to say. Otherwise, I need to focus on the road and be alert for any danger. In the event of an ambush, I will need to take extreme evasive manoeuvres, so I advise you to sit back, buckle up your seatbelt and let me do my job. Thank you, miss."

That tells me.

After about ten minutes' driving, we turn into the driveway leading to the school. A large sign by the gates announced that this is King Academy, Headmaster Mr Pilkington, Cantab. We join a queue of equally impressive limos, all there to deliver their precious cargos to the school. I assume that the gates would close once the school day starts. This is just as much a prison as the one I left at "home".

We slowly nudge forward, patiently waiting our turn to pull up outside the entrance. I'm glad for the tinted glass making it impossible for anyone outside to see me. Now that we are at the Academy, school is all too real and the butterflies performing an Irish jig in my stomach refuse to be still.

My dad is rich enough to hire a tutor for me. He doesn't *have* to send me here. Doesn't he know that home educated students performed better academically than those who went to school? And it isn't like I'm going to fit in with all these rich snobs. They'd take one look at me and know I came from the wrong side of the tracks. I will never fit in here. This is a disaster waiting to happen.

At last, we reach the front of the queue. I try to open the door to get out, but it is locked. Surprise, surprise. I have to wait for the chauffeur to come and let me out.

Embarrassing.

Hefting the rucksack on my shoulder, I take a deep breath and walk up the steps leading to the entrance. As I make my way up, a couple of younger boys run past, knocking my shoulder and making me trip up the stairs. My rucksack falls down and books spill everywhere.

Brilliant way to start the first day.

"Are you okay?" A girl around my age kneels down to help me pick up my things.

"Yeah, I'm fine."

I don't look at her, ashamed of the tears pricking at the corners of my eyes. I'm not going to let anyone see any sign of weakness. I'm an Archaic and while that hadn't meant an awful lot to me up until now, if we are some big powerful family, that makes me a target, whether I like it or not. If there is one thing I have learned from the last time I went to school, it is how to avoid drawing attention to yourself. If bullies got even a hint of blood, they'd go for the jugular.

"Here." The girl passes me a stack of books. "I'm Milly."

I take the books from her and shove them in my bag with a soft smile. "Ivy," I reply.

"I know," Milly says with a mischievous twinkle in her eyes. This girl looks like one of the popular girls who lived near me. Pretty, dark luminous hair and bright blue eyes. She must be rich, based on her designer bag and watch. Her uniform fits her tightly, just like mine, and I can't help notice that all the girls here look the same. The guys are far more casual. Typical. "It's all anyone can talk about—Ivy Archaic coming to King Academy at last!"

"Gee. I always wanted to be famous," I sarcastically reply.

"You're funny." Milly laughs, and it brightens up her face. Now I get a closer look at her, there is something familiar about her, but I'm sure we have never met. "Let me take you to Mr Pilkington's office. He'll want to see you before you go to class and he'll tell you everything you need to know about this place. Or at least, everything *he* thinks you need to know. If you want to know what *really* goes on here, we should talk. I can fill you in on all the gossip, let you know who's cool and who you need to avoid, especially since you're an Archaic."

Milly continues to talk as she escorts me to the Headmaster's office. I barely have to say a word as she babbles on about how I hadn't missed much, even though I am joining in the middle of term. Apparently, the Academy is doing well in the football and hockey leagues but not so well in swimming. Like I care.

"And here we are. Headmaster Pilkington's office," she announced, coming to a halt outside a solid oak door. "I have to head over to English, but hopefully we'll be in some of the same classes. And maybe we can have lunch together?"

"Maybe," I say, inwardly planning to find somewhere private where I can eat alone. I had no intention of staying at the Academy for a minute longer than I needed. Friends don't fit into my escape plan.

Knocking on the door, I am immediately summoned inside. I walk in to see a weasel of a man sitting behind a large desk. Large glasses hugged a sharply pointed nose and a bald head shone through his comb-over.

"Ah." He smiles when he sees me enter. "You must be our new Archaic."

"Guess I must be," I shrug.

"We were delighted when your father contacted us to enroll you here," Headmaster Pilkington tells me. "We have a proud heritage of serving the four houses. In fact, the school itself is divided into four houses, each named after one of the families, and engaging in friendly competition with each other in sports and academic studies. As our only Archaic pupil, you will automatically be appointed Head Girl, an honour I'm sure you'll be proud to accept."

"Are you kidding?" I can't stop the words erupting from my mouth. "Why on earth would I want to do that?"

"Manners, Miss Archaic." The headmaster arches an eyebrow. "Head girl is a wonderful position, one which will stand you in good stead when the time comes to apply to university. You are an ambassador of the school, a role model to the other pupils. You will be required to give speeches, do readings at assembly…"

"Oh hell, no!" This is the worst possible thing that can

happen. "Don't you already have a Head Girl? Let her keep the position."

"Miss Archaic!" The headmaster's tone is sharp. "I would hate to give you a detention on your first day with us and I'm sure your father wouldn't like to hear of your behaviour either." He fixes me with a pointed look and I know I am beat.

"Fine," I mutter. "I'll be your Head Girl."

"Wonderful!" Headmaster Pilkington smiles in approval. "You are correct. There is another girl who you will be replacing, but she fully understands the situation and is more than happy to step aside. We all appreciate the importance of having an actual Archaic heading up the school's House of Archaic. Right. Now that's settled, it's time to determine your timetable. Coming to us so late in your school career, particularly from a home-educated background, somewhat limits your options when it comes to A levels. But your father has made it clear that he has no issue with you remaining here an extra year should it be required in order for you to complete your studies to an acceptable level. What subjects are you interested in?"

"Katy signed me up for online courses in art, music, and graphic design," I tell him. "My work is marked by tutors and I've predicted good grades in all of them."

"An artist, eh?" Headmaster Pilkington nods slowly. "Well, I think we can get you onto either an art or a music course, but not both, I'm afraid. Your father is quite insistent that you are to study politics and business, so there's little room for more creative subjects in that mix."

"Seriously?" My heart sank. There is nothing more boring than politics and now I am supposed to do it at A level?

"Oh yes. One of our duties at King Academy is to prepare our charges for the reality of their lives when they leave our hallowed halls. Since you will be taking up the mantle of House Archaic, it is vital you learn the skills you will need to take over from your father."

Yeah, right. Like that will ever happen.

"So which is it to be? Music or art?"

"That's like asking me to choose a favourite child!" I protested. "Can't I do both? People do four A levels don't they?"

"The more gifted students do, yes," Headmaster Pilkington says. "But I'm afraid that with no history in the school system, we have to make allowances for you adjusting to a new way of doing things. I cannot allow you to overburden yourself. You must choose whether you prefer to do music or art. Unless you'd like me to call your father and see what third subject he would choose for you?"

"No!" I yelped as the headmaster reaches for the phone. "Music. I'll do music."

"Excellent choice," he beams. "I think you'll love the music department here. We have some of the top teachers in the country."

He turns to his computer and taps a few keys. A moment later, the printer on the other side of the room whirls into life and spits out a piece of paper. Headmaster Pilkington fetches it and passes it to me.

"I took the liberty of preparing your timetable when your father told me your choices," he says. "Those are your classes. You'll note that you have plenty of free periods. Do not take that as an opportunity to slack off. We set our standards high here and I expect to see you spending plenty of time in the library working on your assignments. Now I've arranged for the Head Girl of House Navarre to give you a tour of the facilities so you know where you need to be before your first class." He presses a button on an intercom. "Please tell Nicola Navarre to come in."

A moment later the door opens, and a perfectly pretty girl walks in. Her hair is styled pristinely, with subtle streaks of blue and green breaking up her natural auburn. Her makeup is flawless, that natural kind of look which accentuates her features without looking like she is wearing any makeup. A badge pinned to her jumper announces her Head Girl status.

"Nicola. Prompt as always. Excellent. Please show Ivy around and make sure she knows where she needs to be for each of her classes."

"Of course, Headmaster Pilkington. Hi, Ivy. It's good to meet you." She smiles, but there is no warmth to it. Great. I had an enemy already, and I hadn't even done anything. I wonder if she is an heir to one of the other houses? Or just a distant cousin or something? "If you can follow me?"

I pick up my rucksack and follow her to the door.

"Miss Archaic?" I turn back as Headmaster Pilkington says my name. He stands up and offers his hand out to me. "Welcome to the King Academy family and as a woman in your position, do know my allegiance falls heavily on the Archaic house. Come to me for anything."

I had no choice but to make nice and shake his hand. It is like holding on to a wet fish, his palm all sticky, his grip limp.

"So what are you doing?" Nicola asks after we leave the Headmaster's office.

"Music, politics, and business, apparently," I sighed, showing her my timetable.

"It's not so bad," she says. "You've got Mr Ronson for politics and he's great. And you're with me for business, so if you need to see my notes on the classes you've missed, you're more than welcome to them."

"Really?" *Pardon me if I don't believe you.*

"Sure." Nicola sighed. "Look, none of us were happy when we heard an Archaic was coming to the school. We had no idea you existed and if I'm honest, we are all waiting for the day when your family dies out. But regardless of the history between our families, the one thing we all learn when we come to this school is that we need to work together if we're going to continue to run this town. Obviously, you missed all the history classes which went over what happened when the four houses fought each other for dominance. Nobody wants to return to that, especially not the poor people like us that actually live in this town and need the main houses not to be at war. I'm just a descendant, like super thinned out from Navarre blood, but shit, we protect our own. Now, it's unlikely the rivalries between the families will ever fully disappear, but if we can maintain the truce, there's no limit to what we can achieve together." She sighs again. "Besides, my dad would kill me if he heard I missed out on an opportunity to suck up to Solomon's daughter."

"Well, you're honest," I laugh. "I'll give you that, Nicola."

She rolls her eyes. "Nikki, please. The only person who calls me Nicola is Pilkington."

"Okay... Nikki."

The Navarre Head Girl takes me all over the school, filling me in on all the gossip I need to know while she takes me from one department to the next. There is no way I am going to remember where everything is, so in the end, I give up trying to memorise the routes to my classes and focus on mining Nikki for information. This is a whole new world and information is clearly power. The more I can find out about the people I'm dealing with, the sooner I will be able to figure out a way to escape and go back to my old life. Or at least avoid the worst of the school.

"And that's pretty much it," Nikki announces as we go through a pair of doors which take us into a hallway lined with lockers. "That door down there leads to the sixth form common room. Forget what Pilkington says about spending all your spare time in the library—this is where we all hang out between lessons. This whole area is reserved for A level students and you'll end up being grateful for the opportunity to escape from the plebs in lower school. There are a few lockers left, so find one without a padlock and claim it as yours. You'll need to bring your own padlock or you can buy one from the office."

"Okay." That explains why there is one in the side pocket of my rucksack.

"Now-" Whatever it is Nikki is about to say is interrupted by the sound of jeering coming from the common room.

"What's going on?" I ask, unsure of what to do.

"Oh, that'll be Milly getting her daily dose of medicine," Nikki tells me. I'm stunned by how matter of fact she sounds. "She thinks she's all that because her brother's the football captain and heir to the Knight house, so every now and then we make sure to bring her back down to earth. You'd think she has to know by now she's nothing special."

"Milly?" The girl who'd been kind to me when I first arrived. "No way."

Dumping my bag, I raced down the corridor and burst into the common room without even thinking about it. I'm shocked to see three girls surrounding Milly, pushing her between them, chanting "Stupid! Stupid! Stupid!" as she cries out for them to stop.

"Hey!" I yell, running into the middle of the group and putting my arm around Milly. They stop instantly, which I didn't expect. "What the hell do you think you're doing?"

"Oh. It's the *new* girl," sneered one of the bullies. "Don't poke your nose into other people's business if you know what's good for you. You've got a lot to learn about what it takes to survive at King Academy. Let this be your first lesson–turn round, walk out that door and don't look back."

"I don't think so." I shake my head and push up my sleeves, ready for action. I see a Head Girl badge on her jumper, right under the House name Archaic.

"I think you'll find that belongs to me," I say, pointing to the badge.

The girl is beautiful in a plastic, oh-so-not-real-under-her-skin way. The sneer she gives me makes her look ugly though. Dammit, I don't want the badge, but I want them to leave Milly alone. "Oh yeah? Come take it, bitch."

"Fine." I shrug my shoulders then launch myself at the girl before she can brace herself. There is an audible gasp from everyone else in the room as I punch her straight in the face, knocking her to the floor. I jump on top of her, giving her no chance to get up as I slap her hard and wrap my hand around her throat.

"Don't. Be. A. Bully," I lean down and warn her, she struggles to push me off her. "And if you need me to teach you another lesson, I'll be right here."

"That's enough, Ivy." Milly tentatively reaches down and grabs hold of my shoulder. "I think she got the message."

"Not quite." Reaching down, I pull the Head Girl badge off the bully's chest, not caring that I have ripped her jumper in the process.

It is only then I get up and let the other girl go free. There is a stunned silence, but then someone starts clapping. Another pupil joins in, then another and another and soon the whole room is cheering me. Well, that's one way to make sure the entire school knows I'm here.

Crap.

The former Head Girl of Archaic is helped to her feet by her two cronies and the three of them storm out of the common room. The head girl looks back once at me, and when her eyes meet mine, I know I have a new enemy. When I'm not looking, she is going to stab me in the back and dig the knife in.

"You're amazing!" squeals Milly, giving me a huge hug and distracting me from the head girl.

"I hate bullies," I shrug, trying to break free with no luck.

"You certainly know how to make an entrance, Archaic," says Nikki. Is it my imagination or is there a look of respect in her eyes?

"What's all the noise?"

I nearly jump at the familiar voice. I kinda hoped I wouldn't hear his voice again and then the part of me that doesn't lie to myself knows I wanted to hear him. Milly squeals again and runs across the room to throw herself into the arms of the boy who'd just walk in.

"Oh, my god! You have to meet my new best friend, Ivy. She saved me from Ally!"

I look into the clear blue eyes I have only just seen the day before. Now I know why Milly looks so familiar.

"We've already met," Archer says with a condescending smirk. Damn my heart for beating quicker from just the sound of his voice.

I'm so screwed.

Chapter Four

IVY ARCHAIC

"*R*eally?" Milly is positively skipping with excitement. "Then you know how cool she is!"

"Oh yeah. Ivy's cool all right," smirks my kidnapper. "I *really* enjoyed hanging out with her yesterday."

"I bet you did." My eyes narrow, fingers itching to slap the smile off his face. I'm not usually so violent, but there is something about being kidnapped and having people dictate how to run my life that changes me.

Milly looks from me to her brother and back again, a confused frown wrinkling her forehead.

"Is something wrong?" she asks.

"Nothing's wrong, little sister," Archer says with a cheeky grin. "Ivy's just a little tired after all the excitement yesterday. Only an Archaic would have the energy to come to school the day after they are reunited with their long-lost father."

"That must have been so exciting for you," Milly gushed. "I bet you are so happy to meet your dad after all that time apart."

"That's one way of putting it," I say, deciding now isn't the time to go into the details of my abduction. "But look at you two. I should have guessed you are related. You've got the same eyes. Are you twins or something?"

"Irish twins," Milly corrects me. "Archer's ten months older than me, which is why we're in the same year at school. We've also got another brother in the year below and a sister the year below that. And our step mum's pregnant now, so there's another Knight coming into the world in a few months."

"Wow. You guys sure have a big family."

"It's pretty normal for the four houses," Milly shrugs. "In fact, House Archaic is unusual in only having one heir. Our families are big in case of any... accidents. If anything does happen to you, that would be the end of your house and your father would have to watch his back because someone would be bound to stage a coup."

"I see." It looks like my father had been telling the truth about keeping his distance to protect me.

But that doesn't excuse the way he is treating me now. Why can't he have just spoken to me like a normal person? He didn't have to *kidnap* me and treat me like a prisoner. Maybe he thought what he was doing was for the best, but if this is what having a family is like, I'm better off back in foster care.

A bell rang, interrupting our conversation.

"That'll be lunch. You wanna eat with me, Ivy? I can fill you in on all the gossip. Call it a thank you for rescuing me." Milly is ridiculously perky, but there is something endearing about her constant positivity, especially now I have seen the way the other kids treat her.

"Actually, Mills, do you mind if I grab Ivy for a second?" Archer sweetly asks. "I just want to see how she's settling in."

"Sure. Do you want to bring her to the cafeteria when you're done? I'll grab a table for us."

"Sounds like a plan," Archer smiles.

"Actually, can you do me a favour?" I ask. "I dropped my rucksack in the hallway by the lockers when I heard what was going on in the common room. Can you pick it up for me?"

"Of course. I'll take it to the cafeteria for you." Milly practically skips out of the room, seemingly overjoyed to be able to do this little thing for me.

Now that his sister is gone, I don't have to pretend to be civil to Archer anymore. "You've got some nerve," I hiss.

Archer shrugs with a cocky grin. "What can I say? I owed your father a favour."

"So he claps and you follow him like a puppy dog?" I mockingly ask, keeping my voice low so the other students won't overhear. My business is private. I'm already going to be the subject of school gossip after my fight with Ally. I'm not going to give them anything else to talk about. "There are a million different ways you could have handled the situation. God, Archer, all you had to do is ask and-"

I caught myself before I could put my foot in it any further, but it is too late.

"And what?" There is a little twinkle of amusement in Archer's eyes.

"Nothing?" I shrug, a little embarrassed and hoping he will drop it.

"Nothing, huh?" He steps closer and I take one step backwards, only making him look more amused. "Let me guess... foster kid so desperate for attention you would have fallen for a few pretty words whispered in your ear and a space on my bike?"

"Fuck you," I snap.

"Nah, I don't fuck my sister's friends," he replies. "Considering she has so little of them."

"I wouldn't say we are friends exactly..."

"That's not how Milly's going to see it," Archer tells me. "In case you hadn't noticed, Milly's not like most people at the Academy. She's a sweetheart. That girl doesn't have an evil bone in her body. It makes her an incredible human being, but it also means she's nothing but prey to the Houses. You standing up for her like that will have won her undying loyalty. You've got a friend for life in my sister, whether you like it or not. But it would mean a great deal to me if you don't break her heart by turning your back on her. I might even watch your back for you. Trust me, you need some help."

"I don't owe you anything or want anything," I remind him, but even as I speak, I knew I wasn't going to ditch Milly. Much as I hate her brother, I need all the allies I can get, especially now I have seen first-hand the cutthroat nature of this place.

"Make your mind up, sweetheart," Archer teases.

"Fine," I nod. "Maybe you can do my detention for me when I get busted for beating up Ally."

"Detention?" Archer laughs. "Don't worry about that. I think you'll find the teachers will be secretly applauding you for taking on Ally. They understand the politics of the houses. And Ally would be far too ashamed of losing to a noob to tell on you. You have no idea how important it is you established your presence with a show of violence. You're more Archaic than you know. Trust me—no one's going to challenge you."

"I guess I just have to watch out for the knife in my back, huh?"

Archer grinned, making a little dimple appear in his left cheek. "See? You're already learning how things work round here. Now come on, Milly's waiting for us in the cafeteria. Leave her too long and someone's bound to steal the table from her."

"How is she your sister?"

He smirks over his shoulder, and it's too sexy for my own good. "Milly will snap one day. You best be on her good side when she does. Knights never get knocked down for long."

Chapter Five

IVY ARCHAIC

*W*alking into the cafeteria, it's like one of those movies where someone walks into a bar out in the middle of nowhere and everyone goes silent and stares at the intruder.

Yeah. My first time walking into the cafeteria at King Academy is exactly like that. I feel like doing a huge bow or flipping everyone the bird, something to justify all the attention I am getting. Instead, I try to ignore them all, or at least focus on the people I do know in the crowd.

My eyes catch a pair of green ones. His remind me of an evergreen forest, deep and dark where you can hardly see the green in their depths. A guy with messy blonde hair and golden skin and reminding me of statues of Greek Gods. His body fills out his seat and two girls sit at his sides, trying to get his attention as he stares me down.

There aren't just kings at this academy, turns out there is a god.

And he looks more dangerous than anyone I have ever seen in my life.

"Just go and pick up a tray and join the queue," Archer

whispers to me, his hot breath blowing against my ear. "Keep your head high and don't let them see they're getting to you. Now laugh as if I'm the funniest person you know."

I laugh like he just told me the funniest joke I've ever heard and the chatter of the teenagers suddenly picks up once again. Realising I'm not going to be of any real entertainment, the other pupils slowly turn their attention back to their conversations, leaving me and Archer to get our lunch. Shaking my head, I head over to a stack of trays. Picking one up, I go to stand behind the last person waiting to be served, Archer following close behind.

"I recommend the curry," Archer says. "Although our parents pay a fortune to send us here, Pilkington clearly doesn't spend much of the fees on catering. It's mystery meat, but it usually tastes pretty good, unlike the soggy lettuce in the salad or slimy mash."

"How can you mess up a salad?"

Archer shrugs. "I have no idea. It takes a certain kind of talent to be that bad, but the King Academy chefs have it in spades. Even rich chefs can fuck stuff up. Eat at home, that's what most do."

"What'll it be today?" The cook smiles at me when it is my turn to choose.

Gazing over the options, they all look about as bad as Archer warned me.

"I think I'll take the curry, please," I say.

"Here you go. And a double helping 'cos it's your first day here."

I gulp as the cook dumps a second load of slop on my plate. "Err... thanks."

Deciding against the stodgy looking sponge with lumpy custard, I take an apple for dessert and turn to look for Milly. I spot her right at the back on the opposite side of the dining hall, bouncing up and down and waving to get my attention.

As I approach my new BFF, I feel my foot catch on something. Stumbling, I barely manage to save myself from eternal embarrassment that would have been caused by falling flat on my face on my first day at a new school. Turning to see what I tripped on, I see Ally slowly bringing her foot back under the table and brush her blonde hair over her shoulder.

"Oops." She smiles as if a thousand tiny angels are hovering around her pretty head. "Guess I didn't see you there. Sorry about that."

The only thing you're sorry for is that I didn't fall, I think, treating her to an equally insincere smile.

"You wanna watch yourself," Archer advises Ally with a zero bullshit tone. "I'd hate to see you have an accident of your own."

Ally's smile fades in the face of an obvious threat.

"Aww, come on Archer. Don't be like that," the girl sitting next to her seductively whispers, and she reaches out, placing her hand on his thigh. Way too high for a stranger. "It's just a bit of fun, you know? We all went through it when we first started at the Academy. We only want to know what Ivy's like, find out if the new Archaic Head Girl is worthy of the position."

"She is born to lead," Archer says, picking her hand off his thigh like it's poisonous. "Not her fault you're jealous, Taylor."

He turns and kisses me full on the lips like he owns me. Too stunned to react, I stand there, the tray in my hands making it difficult for me to do much else as his lips move across mine. Demanding. Craving. Possessing. He takes everything with one single kiss. Making it impossible for me to forget him. Archer gives me another light peck, winking at me before he pulls away.

"Let's go, sweetheart," he says, walking over to sit opposite Milly in one of the spaces she has saved for us.

I tightly smile one last time at Ally and her friend before following after him. I can't help but enjoy the sick look on both their faces. Like a bug has flown into their garden of perfect flowers. I don't know what Archer's issue is with them, but clearly he knew the kiss is the best way to get under their skin. While I don't appreciate someone taking advantage of me like that, I loved the effect it had.

I loved the kiss.

Fuck my life, no one has ever kissed me like that. And I suspect no one ever will.

"Wow, Ivy," says Milly, as I sit next to Archer in a bid to maintain the charade there is something going on between us. "I didn't realise you are dating my brother. You kept that quiet, Archer. How did you two meet?"

"We're not-"

"It's a long story-"

Archer and I start to speak at the same time before he gestures to me to go ahead.

"We're not dating," I tell Milly. Her face falls.

"Really? But you two would make such a cute couple. And Archer deserves someone like you after the way Ally treated him. Oh, and Taylor. Really, I should make a list of girls-"

She jolts as no doubt Archer kicks her under the table.

"Ahhh." I nod slowly. "So *that's* why you kissed me. You wanted to get back at your ex."

Archer shrugs expansively. "Can you blame a guy, especially now I've got the honour of being the first one to taste you? I figured you'd enjoy seeing Ally and Taylor being put in their place. You're swimming with sharks at the Academy. It's eat or be eaten here and I aim to be a top predator. Tell me you don't love seeing how pissed off they look."

"It *is* fun," I grin.

"Something tells me you and I are going to have a lot more fun together." Archer looks at me as if he is hungry for more than the food being served up. A desire bounces between us as we stare at each other. I will admit it might be fun and dangerous to start something with Archer.

But right now? I need to focus on surviving King Academy and not letting my hormones take Archer for a ride.

"See?" Milly claps her hands, breaking the mood. "I *said* you'd make a cute couple! So how *did* you two meet? You didn't actually say."

"No, I didn't." I take a sip of my lemonade, side eying

43

Archer. "Why don't you tell your sister the story? I think you'd tell it better than me."

"If you're sure…"

"Of course," I smile. "I think Milly should hear it from you."

"Okay, well, I was out on my bike when I saw Ivy. I didn't know who she was at the time, but there was something about her, so I pulled over to talk to her and things moved quickly from there. I suppose you can say I swept her off her feet."

"That's certainly one way of describing it," I agreed, impressed by Archer's audacity. The way he tells it is almost exactly what had really happened but spun to make him look like a charismatic charmer instead of the kidnapping sleaze he really is.

"That's so romantic," Milly sighed, tilting her head to one side. "I wish someone would sweep me off my feet."

"They will one day, little sister. You wait—once you get out of this place, you'll have men falling over themselves to date you."

"You really think so?" The sad hope in Milly's eyes almost breaks my heart.

"Absolutely. Don't you agree, Ivy?"

"Sure," I nod. "I mean, look at you, Milly. You've got those gorgeous big blue eyes and a figure most girls would kill for. Once you're out of that crappy uniform and in something more flattering, I reckon you'll have boys throwing themselves at you. I will help you however I can."

Glancing at her brother I think, boy problems are something I know a little about.

"You'd do that for me?"

"Of course. That's what friends are for, isn't it?"

And just like that, Milly became my first true friend at King Academy.

Chapter Six

IVY ARCHAIC

*S*omehow, I survive my first day of school. When the final bell rings to signal our release from confinement, hundreds of pupils stream out of classrooms and out to the front of the building where drivers are waiting to ferry all the rich kids home to their mansions.

It is a very different world to what I am used to. What would my life have been like if my father hadn't faked his death? Would I be as jaded and spiteful as girls like Ally and Taylor? Or would I somehow have managed to stay as innocent as Milly seems to be?

Standing in front of the entrance to the Academy, I'm not sure how to tell which one is my car and driver. They all look exactly the same. All black, shiny, and expensive.

I bite my lip, scanning the line of cars to see if I can pick out which one of the identically uniformed drivers is mine.

A car pulls up in front of me and the rear window rolls down to reveal a boy with floppy blond hair and a smattering of freckles over his nose. The boy from earlier with the girls.

"Hey, Ivy," he smiles, running a hand through his hair to push it out of his face. "You seem a little lost. Need a ride?"

"I'm sorry," I say with a frown. "Do I know you? You certainly seem to know me."

"Everyone knows who you are, Ivy," he tells me with a smirk on his pretty bowed lips. "You're Ivy Archaic, Slayer of Bullies, Champion of the Weak. Even if being the new girl isn't enough to make you the centre of attention right now, everyone's talking about how you stood up to Ally. Remind me never to get on the wrong side of you."

"Maybe I would if I had a clue who you are," I reply coldly. I have about reached my fill of being nice to people, even attractive boys with enchanting green eyes.

"Sorry. It's terribly rude of me not to have introduced myself. I'm Romeo Navarre, but everyone calls me Romy. I'm the Head Boy of House Navarre, so we'll be working closely together on speeches and presentations."

"Sounds like fun." I roll my eyes. I'm sure he plays this game with every girl. I'm not stupid enough to fall for a guy that looks like a damn Greek god and clearly has the charm to match.

I hope.

"Can I give you a lift home?" he offers, undeterred by my attitude. "You look like you've had about enough of this place for one day. I can get my driver to take the long route back, show you all the sights of Kings Town, not that there's all that much to see."

"Tempting as that is, I suspect my father would kill me if I disappeared off with some boy I've only just met," I say, just as my driver pulls up behind Romy's car with his head stuck out the window, glaring at me for not magically finding him. "And my ride's here, so thanks anyway, but I'll pass this time."

"Not a problem. Maybe next time, then, Ivy. Something tells me you and I are going to be friends. Good friends."

He pushes the button to close his window, the mirrored glass sliding up to hide him again. His car drives off, clearing the way for my driver to come and pick me up. The driver gets out of the car and comes to open my door for me, a gesture which is always going to weird me out. Can't rich people open their own doors?

Climbing in, I jump when I realise there is someone already sitting in the car waiting for me.

"Dad!" I gasp as our driver started the engine to take us home. Sitting in a crisp grey suit, a whiskey glass in his hand, he smiles at me.

"Hello, Ivy," he says. "How was your first day at school? No major incidents I need to know about?"

"No. Not that I can think of." I shake my head slowly, sticking out my bottom lip as if I have considered his question seriously.

"So you didn't bitch slap another Archaic then? Your very distant, bastard cousin who would be happy to rival the house for the place of heir if you disappeared?"

My eyes widen. How did he know about my fight with Ally? And I'm related to that bitch? Fucking great.

My father laughs. "I have spies *everywhere* so you better get used to it. This is your life now. You represent House Archaic at all times and everything you do sends out a signal about who and what we are. Given that, I have to commend you for tackling a potential threat so quickly. I always knew you'd have the Archaic instincts, and this confirms it. A girl like Ally needs to be shown who's boss right from the start or she'll only take advantage of you. I don't think you'll have any problems with her now that she knows you're not afraid to exercise your authority. However, I'm not convinced that your alliance with Millicent Knight is wise. She is of little value to us. I would rather you focus your attention on Archer. A union between our two houses would be of immense strategic value and Archer has other brothers who can lead his house when he becomes your consort."

"Wait—are you telling me you're marrying me off already?" Talk about bat shit crazy parenting.

"Not at all, my child." My father pats me on the hand, a gesture which I think he means to be reassuring but feels awkward and forced, only reinforcing the fact we barely know each other. We have a long way to go before any real dad/daughter bonding can happen.

"But as the sole Archaic heir, it behoves you to consider all angles," he continues. "As a woman, many will view you as weak and seek to take advantage of you. Someone like Archer can act as a guardian, letting would-be assassins know that if they are to come after you, it's not just House Archaic they'd have to worry about but House Knight as well. There's a good reason I asked him to bring you to me. I figured the two of you would be able to bond over a shared experience. Are you telling me you don't feel a connection with him?"

With my kidnapper? Sure, Dad. I got instant Stockholm Syndrome the second I saw those baby blue eyes and that sexy, sexy ass.

"I don't think I have a connection with anyone right now," I say. "I mean, my whole life I thought you were dead and not only were you here all along, you're the head of some weird gangster cartel."

"I'm not a gangster nor do I run a cartel." My father is quick to correct me. "My business interests are completely legitimate until proven otherwise. However, I'll let your attitude slide—once. The way this town works is a little unorthodox, I'll grant you. But I think you'll soon find yourself fitting in. It's in your blood after all. It won't be long before you discover your ruthless side. Now if I recall, we had a deal. I am happy with the reports I've received about your behaviour, so true to my word you may speak to your foster mother."

"You're giving me my phone back?" I sit up a little straighter, excited at the thought of being able to contact the outside world again.

"Oh, no," my father chuckles. "I think we're a long way away from my being able to trust you with your phone. No, you may use this burner to have a brief conversation with your foster mother. Tell her you're staying with friends but do not mention anything about me or I'll be forced to take action. If I'm happy with the way you speak to her, we can make it a regular event."

He passes me a phone with Katy's number already programmed into it. He nods, encouraging me to press the button to make the call, like he is doing me a huge favour instead of giving me the bare minimum.

Still, Katy must be going out of her mind with worry by now. Much as I wanted to defy my father and throw the phone out of the window, I owed it to her to let her know I was okay.

She answers the phone within three rings.

"Katy?"

"Ivy! Oh, thank goodness. Where are you? Why did you disappear like that? When I went looking for you, I found your rucksack near the shop and I was imagining all sorts of terrible things. I called the police, but they said you are old enough to do what you want and to come back to them in a few days if I hadn't heard anything."

"I'm sorry, Katy." She sounds terrible, like she had been crying for hours. "I didn't mean to scare you. I met up with some friends and lost track of time." I cringe as soon as the words leave my mouth. Katy knows me better than that. She knows I don't have many friends, and certainly not any I am close enough to want to run away with them. *But what else was I supposed to say?*

"Really?" I can hear the disbelief oozing out of every pore. "And what are the names of these 'friends'?"

"Err... Jane and Jo."

"All right, Ivy. I've never heard of a Jane or a Jo. I know when you're lying to me, so tell the truth. It'll be okay. I promise. What's really going on? Are you in some kind of trouble?"

"No... not really." I didn't want to say too much in case my father had set up recording software. If he listened to this call later, I don't want him to think I have been sending Katy hidden messages.

"There's something wrong. You might think you can fool me, but I know you too well. Tell me where you are, Ivy. I'll come get you, no matter how far away you are."

"I'm really sorry, Katy, but I'm not coming home. It's my

49

eighteenth birthday soon which means I'll be out of the care system and I have to stand on my own two feet. I've been given the chance to start a new life and I think it's best if I give it a go rather than being a burden on you. I'll call you soon to let you know I'm okay. You've been an awesome foster mum, but it's time to say goodbye and move on."

"Ivy! Tell me what's really going on! Ivy!"

"Bye, Katy." I hung up.

"Good girl." My father beams his approval. "Speaking of your eighteenth birthday, I want you to start thinking about what you'd like from me. Money's no object, so you can have a car, a couple of weeks in the Maldives…"

"What about my own home far, far away from here?"

My father laughs. "I really do admire your sense of humour, my child. But I mean it. Have a serious think about what I can do for you. Meanwhile, I want you to start planning your party with Isabella. She is an exceptional event planner and she'll make sure everything runs smoothly. I was thinking a mask ball might be a good idea, give you an excuse to get dressed up, make a display of power."

"A masked ball?" That sounded like my idea of Hell. I have been planning on spending my eighteenth at the local pub with Katy, enjoying my first legal taste of alcohol. "Who would I invite to a ball? I barely know anyone in this town and I'm not exactly Miss Popularity."

"Oh, you don't need to worry about the guest list." My father waves away my concerns. "I'll make sure everyone who needs to be is invited. You just have to focus on making it the best eighteenth birthday party a girl can want. We need to show the other houses Ivy Archaic has arrived."

"So it's my party, but I don't get a say in who's invited?"

"My girl learns fast." My father has an air of smugness about him. "This is why I want you to be sure you choose a present you really want. That's for you. The party is for everyone else. This is our opportunity to remind everyone that House Archaic is on the rise. We have to make the right impression on the right people. I'll have Isabella coach you in advance to make sure you don't do anything foolish."

With that, our conversation appears to be at an end. My father pulls out his phone and starts talking in some language I can't identify, let alone speak. So, I gazed glumly out the window for the remainder of the journey until we get home and I am able to escape to my room.

All in all, day one wasn't too bad.

Chapter Seven

IVY ARCHAIC

*M*y first class the next morning is music with Mr Metcalf, the one bright thing about my life right now. I didn't want to risk bringing in my precious new Gibson just in case someone like Ally decides to have an 'accident.' While I was sure my father would just buy me a replacement, I don't think I will ever get into the mentality of spending money for the sake of it. Besides, guitars are like children. You look after them your whole life. I don't want anything bad to happen to my baby.

Despite the tour of the Academy the day before, I get hopelessly lost looking for the music department, so I am fifteen minutes late by the time I find the right classroom. I burst through the door, apologising profusely, only to have half the class turn round and angrily shush me.

Blushing, I slip into a chair at the back of the room, while the boy who is at the front continues to sing, seemingly not noticing the interruption. His voice is amazing, husky and sexy, but with the kind of control that spoke of years of vocal training. It is kind of like a mash up between Shawn Mendes, Harry Styles, and Hozier. It helped that he has the looks to match;

long, shaggy brown hair and big brown eyes that are so dark they are almost black. The guy has star quality all right.

I don't recognise the song he is singing, but it is beautiful; soulful and haunting. It makes my heart ache to hear it and as the final few notes die away, the whole class sits in stunned silence for a moment, held captive by the spell of his music.

"Well done, Declan." The teacher finally speaks. "I love how you take on board the notes I gave you after your last composition. Your song writing ability is coming along nicely, but I would like to see you push yourself even further. I think the next assignment will do just that. You may go back to your seat."

Girls are practically swooning as Declan picks up his guitar and comes to sit next to me at the back.

"Hi," he whispers to me and I turn to see his face super close to mine. His brown eyes almost have streaks of green and blue in them, like a paintbrush has lightly skimmed those colours across his eyes. "Good to see a new face to brighten up the place."

I am about to reply when Mr Metcalf calls my name.

"And our disruptive newcomer must be Ivy Archaic."

I feel my face go an even deeper red than before as everyone turns in their seats to stare at me.

"Y-yes. That's me," I say, clearing my throat. "Sorry. I got lost."

"Well, see that it doesn't happen again." He tuts disapprovingly. "We have a lot to get through and if you're late again, I will request you leave the class so as not to disturb the more dedicated students. Be more organised in the future."

"Yes, sir." I slide down in my chair, wishing the ground would open up and swallow me whole as some of the other students laugh at my misfortune.

"Now, it is my understanding that you have already done some study for this course. Is that right, Ivy?" he asks.

"Yes," I reply. "I was doing an online course before I came to the Academy."

"Hmmm." It is clear Mr Metcalf is less than impressed by

the concept of online tuition. "I think you'll find my standards are a little more rigorous than some internet teachers. I warn you now, if you cannot keep up, you'll need to transfer to an easier subject. I don't tolerate any slacking off in my class. So I think it best that you show me what you've got. If you're not good enough to be here, it's better we all know now so we don't waste anyone's time, wouldn't you agree?"

"I guess." I was beginning to regret not choosing art.

"So come on up. We've been working on original composi-tions. I would like to hear something of yours."

"But I didn't bring my guitar," I confess.

"You can borrow mine," Declan offers, holding it out to me with curious eyes. "Show me what you got, new girl."

"There you go, Miss Archaic. You have no excuse. Let's see whether you are good enough to be one of my students."

Taking Declan's guitar with a grateful smile, I make my way to the front of the class and sit where he had been sitting. I strum a couple of random chords to get a feel for his instrument while I debate what to sing. Something tells me this is the toughest audience I would ever face and right now all of my songs seem utterly inadequate.

"Come on, Ivy. We haven't got all day," barks Mr Metcalf. "There's the door if you'd prefer to give up now."

Taking a deep breath, I close my eyes and let my fingers run over the strings in a complicated melody. This is a song which always got a good reaction whenever I performed it—it sounds way more impressive than it actually is. Years of practise means it is very easy to play, but to the untrained ear, it sounds like I was pretty damn good.

The complex accompaniment is offset by a relatively simple tune which showcases the best of my vocal ability. I don't have the biggest range, but I know how to work with what I had.

Swaying, I lost myself in words which had been inspired by the fear I felt knowing I wouldn't be in the care system for much longer and would have to take responsibility for my own life.

Most people thought I was singing about a boy who'd broken my heart, but it's about me.

"You say we should fly away
When my heart tells me I should stay
And now I'm on my own, pretending I'm alright.
You say I will be okay.
That I will always find the best way,
And I suppose that you are right.
Now I'm on my own tonight."

When I finish, I wince as I open my eyes, bracing myself for Mr Metcalf's reaction.

"Not bad," he conceded. "Perhaps you have some promise tucked away underneath all that pretension."

"Pretension?" I try to stay respectful to a teacher who is clearly looking for any excuse to throw me out of his class, but I had just laid my soul bare to a room full of hostile strangers and this is his reaction? "I wrote that song from my *heart*."

"And that's exactly the attitude you need to move past," Mr Metcalf states. "When we create music, we are expressing our soul, yes, but all too often we allow our emotions to cloud our judgement. We fool ourselves that because something has meaning to *us*, it therefore has meaning to our listeners. This is not always the case. I'm going to give you the same advice I gave Declan a moment ago. Push yourself outside your comfort zone. You can go a lot deeper than those superficial lyrics and you're going to need to if you want to excel. You may return to your seat."

Grateful to be out of the spotlight, I head back to my seat, handing back Declan's guitar with a whispered thank you.

"Now then," says Mr Metcalf. "For your next composition assignment, I want you to find a partner. You're going to work together to create a piece of music. It can be a song or purely instrumental in any style of your choosing, whether that be classical or contemporary. But I want it to be completely collaborative, the pair of you working together to bring out the best in each other. I am familiar enough with all your styles to be able to identify if one of you slacks off, with the exception of Miss Archaic, but I'm sure as Head Girl we can trust her to respect the requirements of the assignment.

"What you are aiming for is to deliver something which is greater than the sum of its parts, the pair of you working to both your strengths to create something neither of you can come up with alone. You will spend the rest of this lesson planning out your ideas and then your homework will be to finish the composition. I leave it to you to decide who you'd like to work with."

Great. Just what I need—having to work with one of these stuck-up preppy snobs. I am going to be the last one picked, just like in PE class yesterday. Not that throwing a ball between two people really needed much skill, nor was it enjoyable.

"Hey, Declan. Want to team up?" I roll my eyes as a blonde girl turns in her chair and drapes herself over his desk in a way which just happened to thrust her rather ample bosom in his general direction.

"No, thanks. I thought I would work with Ivy this time."

My eyebrows shoot up when I hear Declan say my name. "Seriously?"

"I never kid about something as serious as music," Declan tells me. "You need to ignore anything Metcalf says. That song of yours is dope. I think we'll write something amazing together—if you're up for it."

"Sure."

I smile sweetly at the blonde girl who looks like she has just sucked on a lemon as she turns away to find someone else to team up with.

Declan shuffles his chair along, pulling out a notebook and placing it on the table so I can see his notes. As he moves, I notice the Head Boy badge pinned to his jumper, right underneath 'House Dauphin' – the people my father claimed ambushed him and gave him that impressive scar.

"Dauphin?" I ask innocently. "Are you actually part of that family or are you just Head Boy?"

"I'm a Dauphin through and through. The Dauphin heir," Declan says. "Which means you've probably heard terrible things about me."

"Not you specifically," I answer honestly.

"Look, there's a history between our houses and you've probably only heard one side of the story," he says. "But there's always more going on than meets the eye when it comes to House politics. Who knows? Maybe our generation can be the one to heal the rift between our families."

"Maybe," I murmur. At the moment, I'm not going to take anyone's word at face value, but Declan certainly seemed sincere and meant what he said. Possibly. It's hard to trust the sexy music dude.

"In fact, that can be the theme for our song," he suggested. "It would fit the brief of doing something which is better than either of us can achieve on our own."

"That's not a bad idea," I nod, as Declan starts scribbling down some notes.

I lose track of time as we start to bounce ideas off each other. I can't believe my luck in getting the Dauphin Head Boy as my partner on this project. He had a really interesting approach to lyric writing, freestyling and recording himself so that he had a record of those moments of genius which flowed out. I am more of a sit and agonise over every single word kind of writer, so his way of doing things gave us a foundation to build upon while I work on tweaking and improving things.

"All right, everyone." Mr Metcalf claps his hands to get our attention. "I hope you enjoyed working with each other."

"Yes, sir," everyone choruses, some more enthusiastically than others. Declan and I exchange a grin. We really *had* had fun together.

"Glad to hear it," Mr Metcalf says. "Because you're going to be partnered together for the rest of the term. I expect you to support your partner and work together to improve both your grades. If one of you fails, you both fail. Do you understand?"

"Yes, sir."

"I guess we're going to be having some homework dates then," Declan says.

My stomach clenches with excitement. Suddenly, things are looking up.

Chapter Eight

ARCHER KNIGHT

*W*alking into the deadbeat bar, I find the rich assholes I am looking for right away. You can't miss them in this shitty place with broken chairs lining the floor around creaky tables. The bar itself looks clean enough, but no one has painted anything in here in a long time. I eye a talking fish statue on the wall that is playing some shitty music.

This place is shitty and crazy. Nice fucking mix.

The assholes I'm meeting are wearing high-end designer clothes, expensive watches and they actually look clean unlike half the people in this place who stare at them like fucking gods have walked into their bar.

They are close.

We are kings instead.

Declan looks back at me like he can sense my arrival as I walk over and take the stool in the middle of him and Romeo Navarre. We never talk like this, the whole thing is ridiculously awkward but now more than ever we need to meet up.

This conversation has been coming for a long time.

"One beer," I tell the middle-aged bartender with a white long beard and a tattoo on his left cheek. He eyes my thousand-pound designer leather jacket like it's a piece of shit compared to his very worn down one on his shoulders.

"Coming up," he grumbles back, looking disgusted with his new customers.

I might end up liking this place after all.

"Why this dive?" I eventually ask, stretching my arms out in front of me.

"No one will recognise us here," Romeo answers. "Now to business, I want Ivy Archaic. So. Back. The. Fuck. Off."

"Make me, pretty boy," I sneer. "She won't be another notch on your belt."

"We will see," he answers with a cocky grin. I humourlessly laugh before grabbing the collar of his jacket and slamming his face onto the bar. He kicks me hard in the chest, making me stumble and lose my grip, my ass nearly slipping off the seat.

"Calm it down or you all need to fucking leave," the bartender shouts as I straighten up and Romeo climbs up off the bar.

"Why don't we let Ivy choose who she wants?" Declan suggests, looking too pristine as he picks his whiskey tumbler up and downs it in one go. "Now, why don't we figure out where she has been all this time?"

"What do you mean?" Romeo asks, clicking his fingers at the bartender for another drink as he places my beer on the side. I drop a few hundred pounds in cash on the bar for the trouble and pick up my drink, taking a long sip as I look at Romeo. Turns out he is as fucking stupid as his face looks.

Declan laughs. "No fucking way was that hellcat in some posh boarding school all this time."

"Do you think she scratches?" Romeo jests. "Because I could get on board with that."

"I will punch you if you don't shut the fuck up," I warn him and he smirks.

Fucking hate this guy.

Declan clears his throat and steps close to me with a knowing grin. I might not like these fuckers, but we grew up together as kids. Our parents want us to get along, therefore we all went to the same schools and were forced to interact with each other. Eventually we drifted apart, girls and parties being the main distractions. "A little birdy told me you drove her into our little town. Now, are you so sure you don't know anything?"

"I never said I didn't know anything."

"What does Solomon have over your family that is worth helping him with her?" Declan asks me curiously, no judgement in his voice. I narrow my eyes though. The Dauphins do have ears everywhere, it seems.

"I'm going to warn you two just this once, and next time it won't be pretty. Stay away from Ivy," I snap, slamming my glass on the bar and walking away before I start a house war by trying to kill these two.

"If you think you can control a girl like Ivy Archaic, you're mad," Romeo calls after me. "She is too wild for you!"

I shake my head, gritting my teeth as I go outside and breathe in the cold crisp air. I don't waste much time getting on my bike and driving the fuck out of here.

Ivy Archaic was meant to be mine, and Romeo is right.

She is wild.

But fucking hell, I'm going to enjoy taming her.

Chapter Nine

IVY ARCHAIC

"Hey, Ivy." Milly practically skips over to me when she sees me walk into the common room. I can't help but admire the way she now wears her long hair down and a single braid hangs on the one side. "How are your classes this morning?"

"It's official. I *hate* politics." I dump my bag on one of the sofas and slump down next to it. "My father will never let me drop it, though. We spent an entire two hours debating whether the result of the Brexit referendum is valid or whether there needed to be a larger majority to trigger the process. It is *soooo* boring. Like, who cares? It's not like I'm going to be allowed to leave my father's house *ever*, let alone live abroad."

"You shouldn't speak about your father like that. He's only doing his best." Milly's response surprised me, but then she doesn't know the truth about my complicated family history. I can hardly tell her I didn't know my dad from Adam until he hired her asshole brother to kidnap my stupid ass and drag me here.

"Yeah, well, if his best means I have to suffer through more classes like this morning I can do without it, thanks."

"Look." Milly dropped down on the sofa next to me. "I know we've only known each other a couple days and I'm not exactly top of the class when it comes to the Academy, but if there's one thing I *do* know about, it's what it's like being a daughter of one of the most powerful men in King Town. Your father sent you away to that boarding school to keep you safe and only brought you back to make sure you can build the connections you need for when you take over his business. As his only heir, as well as being a girl, he's got to take extra special care of you."

"Boarding school?" I did a double take.

"Yes. Before you started here, we were told that you were transferring from an exclusive boarding school in Switzerland."

"Seriously?" It is all I can do not to burst out laughing. "Is that what you all think?"

"Well, yes." Milly frowned. "Why? Isn't it true? Were you not homeschooled by a governess, hidden away in your father's mansion until he thought you were old enough to take care of yourself?"

So close.

"N-no." I laugh nervously, realising that much as I liked Milly, I don't know her well enough to be able to trust her yet. "You're right. I did go to boarding school. I just didn't think Dad would tell you all where I was since it was all such a big secret."

"So what was it like?" Milly asks. "I always wanted to go to boarding school, but Daddy wouldn't let me out of his sight for a moment. He said I needed to stay close to home where he can keep me safe. Is it like those Enid Blyton books, you know, St Malory's and Clare Towers?"

"Malory Towers and St Clare's," I correct her. "And no, it isn't. I had a lot more freedom. I could pretty much study what-ever I liked." *Katy always said you learned best when you are excited about the subject.* "We were able to put together our own curriculum and choose when we wanted to work."

"Wow," breathed Milly, hanging off my every word. "That

sounds incredible. It must have been one of those progressive type schools. I wish we were able to do that here. I'd be able to study dress design and business studies so I can set up my own fashion label one day instead of Daddy making me do 'useful' subjects like French and German so I can take over the family business abroad one day." She pales and put her hand over her mouth. "I wasn't supposed to tell anyone that. *Please* don't mention I said anything."

"Of course not, Milly," I say. "Your secret's safe with me."

Though I'm interested in what she said. So, they have business outside of King Town? What exactly do they all do there?

"What are you two talking about that's so serious?"

Archer leans over the back of our sofa, his head suddenly between ours, making me jump. His hair looks wild today and I like the look on him. He grins, stretching his muscular arms out as he looks at me.

Dammit, his smile could stop my reckless beating heart.

"Where did you spring from?" I gasp.

"I saw my two favorite girls, and I wanted to hang out," he explains, coming around to squeeze himself between the two of us. He smells so good too. "So, come on. What are you talking about that has you looking so concerned?"

"Oh, I was just explaining to Milly the horrors of boarding school," I reply. "You know, the place I went to before my dad whisked me away…"

"Ah. I see." And of course, he really did. Archer knew full well I have never been to boarding school, so he can tell I was lying to him, but he can't call me out on it without exposing the details of my kidnapping to his beloved sister who saw him as an innocent teddy bear. "Is it like they say it is, you know, all lesbian orgies and romps with the stable boy?"

"That stable boy is the happiest guy alive," I shrug, as Milly giggled, eyes wide as she tried to decide if I was being serious or not.

The room goes oddly silent and I look up to see Romy walking in with a girl I don't know clinging to his arm. His eyes are on me, well, more like how close I am to Archer. His eyes narrow and I look over to see Archer smirking at him. "Are you two friends?" I question as Romy walks off to the seats on the other side.

"No," Archer's reply is sour at best.

"They are the kings of the academy. They don't like each other but they have to get along or there would be riots," Milly informs me and I chuckle until I realize neither one of them are joking.

"Kings?"

"My brother, Romeo Navarre and Declan Dauphin are the kings of the academy and hold it all with a tight balance. Nothing goes on here without them knowing about it," Milly tells me.

"Like you being bullied?"

Archer narrows his eyes at me as Milly answers. "I asked Archer not to get involved. I wanted to be brave and deal with it on my own. I'm a Knight and I can't let everyone push me around or expect my brother to save me."

"You should have let me help," he all but growls at her.

"No," she sticks out her chin.

"Stubborn brat," he mutters, running a hand through his hair.

"Well, you're a dickhead," she huffs and it makes me smile a little to see Archer's playful side with his sister. A peaceful silence falls between us all.

"So, are you going to Romy's party?" Archer asks me.

"What party? And will there be stable boys? I don't want to go if there aren't."

That is it. Milly erupted into fits of laughter. Even the oh-so-cool Archer can't stop himself from smiling at my sarcasm.

"Silly Ivy," Milly finally replies. "Romy doesn't have a stable!"

Archer and I exchange a look. Sometimes I wish I grew up in a world like Milly did where you didn't have to search for the seriousness in everything people said. To search for the lies.

Milly has been sheltered from everything in this school, in this town. The darkness hasn't corrupted her yet.

King Town soaked my soul in sin the moment I arrived.

"Seriously, though, Ivy, you should come," Archer suggests with a secretive smirk.

"But I haven't been invited," I point out.

"It's one of Romy's many, many parties," Archer explains. "You don't need a specific invite. Anyone who's anyone is welcome and you're the embodiment of House Archaic. It's practically compulsory for you to go. I think your father would approve—it's always good to see what people are like outside of the Academy."

"Well, if you think Dad would want me to go…" I sarcastically sigh and Archer raises one of his eyebrows. Shit, I need to get better at acting like I want my dad's blessing. "Fine. I guess I'm going to a party then. Just what I need—an evening sitting in the corner while everyone ignores me."

"No one will ignore you," Milly reassures me. "Besides, you'll have me to talk to. I can fill you in on all the gossip. We'll sit in that corner together and make fun of everyone."

"That can work," I nod slowly, coming round to the idea.

"Awesome! Why don't I come to your house before the party to help you pick out the perfect outfit?"

I thought about the bars on my windows and my permanently locked bedroom door. Archer catches my eye and gives a very subtle shake of his head. Yep, my "home" is not going to work.

"Maybe Ivy should come to ours instead?" Archer suggests. "You two look about the same size. You can lend her something of yours."

"Ooooh, yes! It'll be so much fun! Come to my house, Ivy. I'll put together the perfect outfit for you. It'll be a chance for me to practice my design skills. Please say you'll let me dress you."

"Sure," I say. "If my father will let me, I'll come to your house before the party."

Chapter Ten

IVY ARCHAIC

*B*efore the 'fun' of the party that now everyone is suddenly talking about, there is still the rest of the school week to get through and the one thing that makes the Academy bearable is that I get to spend lots of time with Declan. He is as serious about music as I am and the pair of us are determined to write the best song Mr Metcalf has ever heard.

He inspires me to be my best, so when we aren't working together, I spend all my spare periods in one of the music rooms practising our song. Declan is such an amazing guitarist and I don't want to let him down by making any mistakes when it is our turn to perform. I have mentioned to my dad about not wanting to risk damaging the Gibson by taking it to school, so he has bought me a second Gibson. I don't think he really understands that the guitars are so expensive that having two of them doesn't really solve the problem–it just means I have two guitars to worry about. Having grown up with foster parents who made it clear there was no spare money for luxuries, I don't think I will ever adjust to having more money than I could possibly count.

It is pretty clear that if one of the Gibsons is damaged at school, Dad would just buy me a replacement, but that seemed sacrilegious to me. Guitars are my life, each one of them having a unique personality. I can tell the difference between my two Gibsons by the way they played, even though they are exactly the same to look at. If anything happened to the one I kept at school, I would be heartbroken. A new one wouldn't be the same.

Wanting to mix things up a little, I started strumming one of my older songs. It has been a long time since I played it and I realise I can't remember the words to the second verse.

"Ugh! This is stupid!" I play the chorus again, hoping that if I run into the verse, the words would magically come to my mind, but they are stubbornly elusive.

"What's up?"

I look up to see Declan standing in the doorway, leaning against the door frame. My heart pounds in my chest every time I see him, even when I'm aware how dangerous he is. Declan doesn't allude danger, but his name and title at this damn academy gives him away. Under his playboy charm and elusive attitude, lies a hunter who gets everything he wants.

Declan is a king at the academy for a reason…but my heart doesn't listen one bit. It just sings him a damn song and makes me far too aware of him.

"Nothing." I wasn't going to admit I can't remember my own song to him. He is a god at music and I doubt he forgot a single note to anything he wrote.

"Do you want to play it to me? Maybe I can help."

Nope.

"Okay."

He grins before he comes to sit opposite me and gestures for me to start playing. Our eyes meet as I strum the guitar, like two magnets dead set on finding each other. I have to admit to myself…I'm attracted to Declan Dauphin and I think he feels the same way. I tuck my blonde hair behind my ear, wondering exactly what he sees when he looks at me.

I close my eyes when I have to sing, his gaze way too intense for me to cope with and remember any of the words at the same time.

"Let it keep,
I'm strong, but I can't stand,
The deceit, the games, your dishonest ways,
I'll still love you.
'Cos under the blanket of lies
I see you.
And you are always haunting me."

Just like last time, although I know the chorus, I can't remember the second verse, so I stop playing and open my eyes.

Declan stares at me intently, something I can't figure out shining in his eyes. Understanding, perhaps?

"That's all I've got." I shrug awkwardly. I'm shocked silent when he moves closer, placing us inches away from each other.

"I'm a fucking monster and a liar. You should tell me to leave, Ivy," he murmurs against my lips. Damn, I'm a traitor to myself because there is no way I want to push him away.

I don't care. I lean closer and kiss him, gently at first and then with more urgency as he kisses me back like a man without a soul. Like I can somehow pour my soul into his, we battle against each other with each kiss, the connection I felt between us blasting to life and weaving this kiss into my mind forever.

We break apart, but Declan stays close, leaning his forehead against mine. He sinks his hands into my hair and closes his eyes as he takes a deep breath.

"I never do anything for me. It's always for my family...except for this," he whispers to me.

"Then own your own crown and do whatever you want, Declan," I suggest. His eyes look pained as he stares back at me. I know it's not that simple...this town isn't simple and I've only cracked the surface with all the lies and evil that it owns.

"I'm so glad we teamed up for music," he tells me, back to his playful self, the guy I briefly saw washed away like a sandcastle on the beach.

"Me too," I smile. "You're one of the few people in the Academy who's actually nice to me."

"The other girls are just jealous and the boys are mad they can't get into your pants," Declan replies with a cheeky grin. "I mean, look at you, Ivy. You're smart, funny, talented and one day rich. And you will be head of House Archaic one day. Who wouldn't want to be with you?"

Declan lets me go and I miss his touch right away, like someone just cut the air supply off and I can't get it back.

"Can I borrow your guitar? Mine's at home," Declan asks me and I stare at my baby. Well, it's Declan...I can share it. I try not to look nervous as I take the strap off and hand it to him. He looks amused.

To my surprise, Declan starts playing my song, the song he has heard just *once*. It has a strange poignancy being sung by a man. I can really feel the heartbreak in every note.

After the chorus, he went straight into a second verse as if the song is an old favourite of his. Improvising lyrics, what he came up with is way better than anything I could have written. Frantically, I scramble about in my bag for a pen and paper so I can note down his words and use them as inspiration later.

"What do you think?" he asks after finishing.

"It's amazing," I breathe, and I mean it. "Just what the song needed."

"We can submit it to Metcalf instead of the one we've been working on if you want," Declan suggests.

I blushed. "No, we can't. It's something I wrote years ago. I was trying to remember how it went when you walked in. I was just too embarrassed to tell you I can't remember my own stupid song in case you thought I might let you down when it's time to perform our song to the class."

"Don't be daft," Declan laughs. "Everyone forgets stuff. It's no biggie. And I really like that song. Nobody would know it is something you wrote before you came to the Academy."

"But that would be cheating."

Declan laughs again, but something like guilt flickers across his eyes. "Don't you get it, Ivy? This is King Academy and you're the first queen it's ever had. You can do whatever you want."

Being called the Queen of King Academy reminds me of my mother telling me an odd story about kings and queens once. I wonder if when she walked around in this school she was someone or no one until a king like my father noticed her.

I want to ask my dad about my mum but I feel like I couldn't trust anything he told me.

"I still think we should focus on our new song," I suggest, clearing my throat. "I'm not really comfortable lying about something as important as music."

"If you say so." There is a twinkle in his eye that suggests he is mocking me but with his charm, I soon forget it.

Somewhere in the depths of my heart, a warning bell rings clear. Declan is dangerous to me after all.

Chapter Eleven

IVY ARCHAIC

*J*ust as Archer had predicted, my father thought it was a great idea for me to go to Romy's party when I got brave and asked him if I could go. He said it would be a perfect opportunity for me to "assess the opposition."

So now my driver is pulling up outside The Knight mansion and it is very different from my father's house, all boxy with big windows. I think it is the ugliest building I have ever seen, but I don't plan on telling that to whoever the woman and man are waiting in the door frame. Gathering from their age, I would guess they are Milly and Archer's parents. Well, one of them is. I remember Milly telling me her step mum was pregnant with twins, but I never did ask what happened to their actual mother.

Milly's stepmum has thick black hair, gathered up in a bun on top of her head and slim black glasses rest on her nose. Her cream dress screams designer as well as her tall heels. Her baby bump is quite large, and she keeps her hands rested on top of the bump.

I focus on their dad as the car comes to a stop and my driver gets out.

The head of the Knight house is an imposing man who looks just like an older version of Archer. His skin is a tad darker, possibly from spending more time in the sun, and his suit is a dark blue colour, which makes his eyes almost brighter.

"Miss Ivy," my driver says, holding a hand out for me. I ignore his hand as I climb out on my own.

"Thanks," I tell him and walk up to Mr and Mrs Knight with my head held high. I won't bow down to them because they run this goddamn town.

At some point I have to accept I'm Ivy Archaic and I have my own damn crown in waiting. And when I get it? I'm not going to be pushed over and commanded around like a slave.

"Ivy Archaic. We are happy to welcome you to our home," Mr Knight speaks first and holds his hand out for me to shake. Every moment with him I get the sense I am being highly scrutinised. I shake his hand as hard as I can to make a point, but he doesn't let go. "I remember your mother well and she was a great woman. I am truly sorry for her loss and I wish she had come to me in the end."

"You knew my mum?" I ask as he lets my hand go and stares at me.

"Well enough to see her in you. We should talk when you wish to know where your mother came from and how she changed King Town," he suggests and not giving me a moment to get over my shock, he takes his wife's hand and they walk back into the house. I stumble after them into a giant hallway with a monstrosity of a winding glass staircase in the middle of it. The walls are all white and the bright lights in here hurt my eyes.

"Wait!" I call and they halt. Mr Knight turns back to me, his eyes meeting mine.

"You are not ready to hear what I have to say," he warns and then he leaves me in the hallway, my head full of a million more questions about my mum than I had to begin with.

"Ivy! You came!" Milly squeals, running down the stairs and jogging to me. She hugs me tightly.

"I said I would," I tell her as she lets me go. "Did you really think I'd ditch you?"

"It's happened a few times before," she shrugs like that's nothing.

Making sure she sees how serious I am, I tell her the truth. "Well, it won't with me."

"You're a good friend," she softly smiles, tugging me to the stairs.

"What is with this place? It's an odd house," I whisper to her in case her parents are somehow listening.

"Daddy chose an architect who builds safety houses. This place could be blown up and still stand at the end, but it's... different," she replies. "Luckily, it won the eco-friendly category at some random architecture festival, otherwise Daddy would have had to cut the architect's career short."

I had a feeling it isn't the career which would have been cut.

"Anyway," says Milly as we get to an open door and she pulls me into her bedroom. It's a mess of dresses laying over a white framed bed and a big white fur rug takes up the floor. There is a cute modern fireplace on the one wall and a board with dozens of different bits of fabrics and drawings.

"I was thinking that we should put you in something which would really make a statement, you know, make all those bitches at school realise they've got competition. Something like this. " She holds up a yellow dress which is barely legal. Short with cutouts in the side, I would be exposing more flesh than material in the whole thing.

"Yeah. That'll be a hard no on that," I say. "I'm more of a jeans and slouchy tees kind of girl. There's no way you'll ever catch me in something like that."

"Come on, Ivy," Milly pleads. "You'll look amazing. Your figure's perfect. You'd have everyone's eyes on you for all the right reasons."

I fold my arms and glare at her.

"Fine," Milly sighs. "Maybe next time... All right. If you prefer a more casual look, why don't we go with a classic black outfit? I've got a few options for you. There's this one…"

She holds up a black dress that is hardly better than the yellow one. Seeing my face, Milly swiftly moves on.

"Or if you want to go with a more covered look but still keep it sexy, I've got these black leather jeans. Why don't you try those on and if they work, I've got a few ideas for what to team them with."

Now that is more like it.

I take the jeans and go into Milly's bathroom to get changed. They fit so tight they look like they'd been painted on, but I have to admit they do make my butt look amazing, all perky.

Coming out of the bathroom, Milly squeals with delight when she sees me.

"YEEEESS! Right. I've got the *perfect* tee to go with that."

She disappears into her walk-in wardrobe and returns a moment later with a scrap of fabric. She holds it out in front of her so I can see that rather than a rag; it is in fact, a crop top with a print of the Harley Davidson logo.

Beaming with pride, she says, "I remember you saying you liked motorbikes, so this shows off your personality *and* your figure!"

"Nu-uh." I shake my head. "There's no way I'm wearing that. What's wrong with the T-shirt I was wearing when I got here?"

"Oh, Ivy. So naïve."

That's rich, coming from Milly.

"You have to play the game," she tells me. "These parties are just as much about showing everyone how powerful you are in every way possible. For us girls, that includes showing off what our mamas gave us."

The phrase sounds ridiculous the way she says it, but she is so earnest, it is obvious she meant what she said.

"Trust me," she says. "If you don't wear this, or at least something like it, you'll stick out like a sore thumb. Everyone will be wondering what you've got to hide. There'll be rumours about hideous birthmarks or a misshapen belly button."

"So?" I scoff.

"So, any sign of weakness leaves you open to attack," Milly explains patiently. "Make life easy on yourself, Ivy. Wear the top."

In the end, we compromise. I wear the top but team it with a black leather jacket with studs Milly happened to have lying around. Although she insists I leave it open to show off my tummy, I have every intention of doing it up as soon as we get to the party.

"Do you need any help with your makeup?" she offers. "I do a mean smoky eye."

"No, I've got that covered," I reply, and I really do. I've always loved watching makeup tutorials on Youtube, but I never had the money to buy the things to actually do them. "Is it okay to use the mirror in your bathroom?"

"Sure," Milly says. "I'll go get changed."

Standing in front of her mirror, I had to acknowledge that Milly knew what she was doing. Much as I was a little uncomfortable exposing my navel, I *did* have a good body and the clothes she has lent me makes me look sexy without going too far.

I have a deep red lipstick with me and I keep the makeup around my eyes light to draw attention to my pouting lips. A little shiver of excitement runs through me as I imagine Declan kissing it off later if I can find him at the party. I mean nothing has happened since that one kiss, but I want tonight to change that. Finally, happy with my appearance, I walk out of the bathroom and stop dead in my tracks when I see Milly.

"Wow."

"Do you like it?" Milly stands on her tiptoes and does a little twirl, showing off all angles of an outfit that left nothing to the imagination. I think she looks like Jessie J in her *Do It Like a Dude* video, all legs and attitude. She is wearing black lipstick with a metallic sheen and just like she says she can, she is sporting a mean smoky eye.

"You look…amazing."

She really does. I have always thought of Milly as a wall-flower, but seeing her like this brings out a whole new side of her. There is an air of confidence to her that is missing while she is at school. Maybe Archer is right, Milly is a Knight and one day she will snap at school and show them who's boss.

"Thank you," she smiles. "Do you see what I mean now? These parties are an opportunity for us to show off who we *really* are. Outside of school, I'm Milly Knight and *nobody* messes with the Knights."

There is a knock on the door.

"Yes?" Milly shouts.

Archer walks in, his eyes fixing on me. I blush under his scrutiny and I can't help but notice how he looks sexy as hell, too in a tight blue shirt with a few buttons undone and dark jeans. He has to clear his throat and pull his eyes from me to his sister. "You two look amazing. I take it you're ready to go?"

Milly and I look at each other and nod.

Archer turns around and walks out, but Milly catches my arm to stop me from following.

"If you like my brother, he definitely likes you. Just saying, there are worse men than him."

Maybe Milly is right…but Archer has a lot to make up for before I'd ever trust him with my heart.

Chapter Twelve

DECLAN DAUPHIN

*L*ooking at the guitar in the corner of my room, I can't fucking stop thinking about Ivy. It only serves to remind me of her. Of her sweet lips, how she smells like the fucking best thing in the world and she breathed more life into me in just one kiss than anyone has ever done.

And I'm lying to her.

Fuck, I've messed up.

"Hey handsome. Your servant guy let me in," Ally states, and I turn to see her drop her bag onto the wood floor of my bedroom.

"His name is Philip, not servant," I all but growl at her. Another thing I hate about my girlfriend, Ally, is how she doesn't see the people who work here as people. She treats them like toys and whereas the other houses might be shit to their people, we are not.

My parents look after their staff and brought me up to do the same.

"Whatever," she dramatically sighs, climbing over me on the bed.

I freeze as she presses her lips to mine, but only for a second before pushing her away from me and climbing off the bed. I run my hands through my hair as she stares up at me in shock.

And a lot of burning anger.

"It's fucking Ivy Archaic, isn't it?" she snaps, kneeling upon the bed. "You want to dump me for

her, don't you?"

"Come on, Ally. We are just fucking and you know it. You sleep with five other guys, that I know of, and we have never been serious. What the fuck did you expect to happen long term with us?" I question her. "I just want to end whatever this was."

"Is," she corrects. "And fine, but then I'm going to tell your parents about August the fifteenth and everything I saw. I will make them hate you, and you will be all alone."

Fuck no. No. No.

I didn't think she had seen what I did, what Archer helped me hide in the end. My parents are good people, they have been in love since high school and they might rule the house but they do it with kindness and ruthlessness mixed into one. Nothing my parents ever do gets back to them. They just pay for it to go away. The only thing they couldn't fix with money and threats were my brothers lives. After my brothers died years ago, they gave up with this town and trying to fix things. I swore to them I would not do anything that could get me killed. And days later, I did just that.

Shaking with anger, I stare at her in disgust. "You know why I had to do that, you total bitch. That's a low move, black-mailing me to fuck you."

"You are mine or everyone knows. Make your choice, Declan," she suggests, leaning back on the bed and pushing up her tiny skirt. "I know which choice makes me and you really happy right now."

I glance away from her as she undresses. I look down at my guitar, wishing the world would swallow me up.

Ivy can do so much fucking better than me. And soon she will know it.

Chapter Thirteen

IVY ARCHAIC

*T*here is no way Milly is going to risk messing up her hair on the back of Archer's motorbike or sitting in the sidecar, so instead we all climb into his black convertible BMW. Milly and I sit in the back together, leaving Archer on his own in the front to program the satnav.

"Don't you dare," warns Milly, as he reaches out to push the button to make the roof slide back. "Do you know how long I had to work with the straighteners to get this look?"

Archer laughs, but wisely pulls his hand back and focuses on his driving.

"You're going to have the *best* time," Milly gushes to me. "Romy's parties are legendary. Someone always gets naked and goes streaking."

"Yeah, usually one of the Dauphins," Archer dryly says. "They're the only ones stupid enough to show everyone how tiny their dicks are!"

"Don't be like that," Milly tuts and her cheeks brighten for a moment. "Declan is a good guy. I think so anyway."

"Uh-huh," laughs Archer. "Just don't let dad hear you say that or you'll end up married to him…"

I can feel my face flushing when they mention Declan and in the corner of my eye I see how red Milly's cheeks are. Does she have a crush on him? Would her dad seriously expect a marriage if she liked him? What kind of crazy thing is that?

Archer cranks up the music in his car and Milly and I start dancing in our seats, making little dance moves as we get into a party mood.

I can quickly feel myself relaxing and unwinding. I feel normal for the first time since my father had kidnapped me, like I am any other teen girl without a care in the world.

The Navarre's live on the other side of town to the Dauphins. In my brief time living in King Town, my father had filled me in a little on the politics of the place. Each house had their own distinct business so they didn't step on each other's toes. Dad told me their businesses are all completely legit, but I had a feeling he isn't being entirely honest with me. Not that I cared–I wasn't going to tell him, but I have already planned to get as far away from this place as possible as soon as he died. I don't care where his money came from. It isn't like I wanted any of it.

That separation of business extended to carving out the town between them all as well. The Archaics and their supporters lived in the west, the Navarres in the north, the Dauphins in the east and the Knights in the south.

This is my first time going into Navarre territory and it had a completely different feel to the Knight and Archaic areas. As we entered the section controlled by the Navarres we drove past a number of industrial units, many with lights on. The Navarres did business twenty-four hours a day, it seemed.

Up ahead, I could see coloured lights flaring off into the night sky and the booming sound of a bassline countered the rhythm of Archer's sound system. He drives up to a wire fence manned by security guards. Rolling down his window so they can identify him, they rush to open the gates for him the second they see the Knight heir behind the wheel.

"Romy's dad lets him hold parties in his warehouses," Milly

explains. "It's a different one each time, and he goes all out with themed decorations and music. One time he even had an underground pool built!"

"Yeah, because nothing screams nouveau riche more than spending money just for the sake of it," Archer mutters.

"Jealous, are we?" I ask innocently.

"No one with any sense would want to be a Navarre," Archer sourly replies, as another security guard motions to him to turn left and park in front of a building pulsing with loud rock music.

"So you *are* jealous of pretty boy Romy, " I reply with a laugh. "What's the matter–did Romy steal your girlfriend?"

"Oh my god, Ivy!" Milly giggles while Archer's look could kill. "Are you psychic or something?"

"She wasn't my girlfriend," Archer replies through gritted teeth. "Steph and I got off with each other a few times, that's all. It isn't like we are actually going out. She's free to sleep with whoever she likes, even if she does have crappy taste in men."

"I don't know," I say. "I don't think there's *anything* wrong with her taste."

Milly frowns a little. "Okay, you guys. I don't know what's going on between you two, but if this is some kind of lover's tiff, you need to kiss and make up."

"Oh, we're not dating." I rush to correct her.

"But the other day? In the cafeteria? You kissed!"

"That is all for Ally's benefit," I explain once again. "Your brother took advantage of me to make a point."

"And you loved every moment," Archer reminds me. "Don't be a little liar now, Ivy."

"You keep telling yourself that," I retort with bright cheeks, glaring right back at him.

To be fair, he *is* a good kisser, but like I was going to tell him that.

"Okay, well I guess that makes sense. I really thought you guys were dating though. There's definite electricity between the two of you. Are you *sure* you're not seeing each other? You can tell me. I know how to keep a secret if you don't want anyone else to know."

"We're *not* dating." We speak in unison and that is the end of it.

"If you say so." Milly obviously doesn't believe us, but she wisely let it drop as the three of us walk into the warehouse where the party is being held.

A guard opens the door for us, and I am hit by a wall of sound straight away. Coloured disco lights created psychedelic patterns against the walls while teens jumped about the dance floor.

Archer immediately disappears into the middle of the dancing crowd, leaving me and Milly to fend for ourselves.

"Is that-?" I gasp when I catch sight of the live band playing.

"Deep Space 69?" Milly nods, naming the group which had been top of the charts for the past two months. Turns out, they are crazy good. "Yep. I told you–Romy really knows how to put on a party. Come on, let's go get something to drink." She grabs me by the hand and pulls me over to the side where a temporary bar had been set up.

"Two vodkas and coke," she orders and the bartender immediately sets to making our drinks without asking for ID. I supposed normal rules don't apply when you are at a gangster's son's party. Whatever my dad tells me, I know this isn't all above board. Something is wrong with King's Town and it doesn't take a genius to work out there are secrets buried far deeper than I want to find out.

As I wait for my drink, I gaze out across the dance floor. Suddenly, I see something which makes me feel sick and shock makes my heart pound hard in my chest.

"Is that Declan... and *Ally*? Kissing?"

Milly glances over her shoulder and shrugs with a strange look of annoyance in her eyes. "Oh yeah. They're dating on and off. Didn't you know? You'd think their tonsils would be sparkly clean by now with the amount they stick their tongues down each other's throats in public."

Suddenly I'm not in a party mood anymore as I watch them. He kisses her like he kissed me.

The slimy fucker.

Ignoring the drink the bartender offers me, I put a hand to my forehead.

"Do you think Archer would mind taking me home?" I ask.

"Why? We only just got here," Milly replies, but her eyes are on Declan.

"I think I've got a migraine coming on," I lie to her. "It must be the flashing lights or something. I don't want to spoil the party for anyone. I think I should just leave."

"If you're sure. But the party won't be nearly as much fun without you." Milly looks like she is about to cry as I stand on tiptoe, scanning the dance floor to see if I can catch sight of Archer's distinctive buzz cut.

"Looking for someone? He's right here."

I turn to see Romy standing next to me. Romy's blonde hair is brushed to the side tonight, and somehow he looks too sexy to be real. I can't help but breathe in how he smells so flipping nice, and his gravelly deep voice does things to me.

"Didn't anyone ever tell you that's a really bad pick-up line?" I say, going back to my game of Spot Archer.

His hand moves to rest on my lower back, tugging me closer to him and pulling all my attention his way. I want to tell him to let go, but I don't.

"Loads of times," shrugs Romy. "I figure that my charming personality will make it work one day."

"Oookay." Just what I needed. Another Academy arsehole. "Have you seen Archer? I need to leave."

"My dumb pick-up line isn't that bad, is it?" Romy asks, looking crestfallen. "Shit. The whole point of my throwing this party is so I had an excuse to talk to you. If you're going to leave, I might as well tell everyone else to go home too."

I did a double take. "You threw this party for me? Isn't that a bit over the top? We go to the same school. Why don't you just talk to me there?"

"I tried, remember?" Romy replies. "You made it very clear you weren't interested. I wanted a chance, any fucking chance, to get you to look my way. Hell, I would make the whole of King Town into a circus if that's what it takes."

I laugh despite myself. "For someone called Romeo, you've got a lot to learn about women."

"Why don't you teach me?"

The twinkle in his eye tells me maybe I am the one about to learn something.

Chapter Fourteen

IVY ARCHAIC

*R*omy takes my hand and leads me away from the dance floor to a door with a security guard standing in front of it. The guard nods at Romy, opening the door for us and closing it again once we have walked through. The second it shut the music became muffled, suggesting the door is a lot thicker and heavier than it looks.

We walk together down a short corridor and through another door which opens up to a large room. There is a bar to one side which looks even better stocked than the one in the main hall. In the middle of the room is a conversation pit lined with sofas and lots of scattered cushions.

"Drink?" Romy offers. "And then maybe you can tell me what has pissed you off?"

Realising I have left mine back at the bar, I nod. I could use a drink. I have no intention of telling Romy anything about Declan and really, it's my fault. Declan and I aren't dating, we have no claim on each other and I have no right to be mad.

But my heart calls him a traitor and thinks differently.

"Make yourself comfortable. I'll fix you one of my special cocktails."

Romy goes behind the bar and grabs a few bottles, liberally pouring liquid into a mixer.

I go to the conversation pit and sit down, sinking into luxurious, soft cushions.

"Here you go." Romy sits next to me, handing me a glass with a multi-coloured drink in it, a layer of yellow turning green and then blue. He holds up his own drink, and we knock the glasses together. "To the start of a beautiful friendship."

"We'll see about that," I murmur, keeping my gaze on his as I take a sip. Romy is really a sexy guy. A sensation of flavour explodes on my tongue from the first sip. "Oh. My. God. This is incredible! What's in it?"

"That would be telling." Romy tapped the side of his nose with a cheeky grin. "Let's just say I put a few things in that I had a feeling you might like. I invented it just for you. I will call it a Beautiful Ivy."

"You had to do it, didn't you? You had to fall back into cheesy." I shake my head, secretly flattered he is going to so much trouble.

"What can I say?" Romy shrugs. "Most chicks dig it."

"I think you'll find most 'chicks' are humouring you," I correct him. "I mean, anyone who can throw a party like this whenever they like is bound to have gold diggers throwing themselves at them. Add in your sexy ass and pretty face...you could say anything and girls would still jump into bed with you."

"It's so hard being me." Romy dramatically places the back of his hand against his forehead. "Having to sleep with all those gorgeous women, never knowing whether they want me for my money or my enormous cock. It's a tough burden, but I do my best to bear it."

I laugh despite myself. Yes, he is cheesy and arrogant, but there is also something very charming about Mr Navarre.

"But enough about me," says Romy. "I want to know about you, Ivy Archaic, woman of mystery. No one even knew there was an Archaic heir and suddenly you show up at the Academy, all sexy and alluring."

"Sexy? Me? Hardly."

"Oh, Ivy. You shouldn't put yourself down. You've got eyes a man can lose himself in and a body…" He lightly runs the back of his hand across my exposed tummy. "Legs for days is not the word. The moment I saw you, I knew I wanted to get to know you better, but do you have any idea how intimidating you are, Ivy?"

"Right. I'm supposed to believe the school's literal Romeo is too afraid to approach me?"

"That first day of school, when I saw you standing outside waiting for your driver, I felt like my life had changed forever. You had an aura about you that spoke of power, confidence, a self-assurance the other girls at school like to pretend they have, but inside they're just scared little girls. Not you. You're all woman. You know exactly what you want and you're going to get it. Why would I kid myself you'd want someone like me? With my reputation, you'd be forgiven for thinking I would break your heart, but I promise you, Ivy. I only want to possess it. Take it as mine."

I know he is spinning me a line. I know he can't possibly mean what he is saying, but when Romy takes the glass from my hand and sets it to one side, I let him. When he leans forward to kiss me, I feel like he is doing exactly what he says he would–taking my heart as his.

All thoughts of Declan and his girlfriend are gone. My complicated feelings about Archer are the last thing on my mind as Romy gently kisses me, lightly nibbling my lips and then working his way across my jawline to kiss me behind the ear. Whereas Declan and Archer kissed me like they wanted to claim me, Romy kisses me like he wants to treasure me.

And I don't know which is better.

But I don't want him to stop.

I lightly moan as he carries on dropping light butterfly kisses all over my face and neck, making me feel crazy with need for him. I desperately wanted to kiss him, but when I try, he puts a finger over my lips.

"Not yet, my beautiful Ivy," he smiles. "I want to show you how you make me feel, drive you as wild as you drive me. This is *your* time."

He caresses the back of my head, suddenly grabbing a handful of my hair. Pulling my head back, he continues to kiss my neck, as his other hand found its way under my top. Cupping my breast, he groans.

"Just as I suspected. No bra. You really are a wild one, Ivy."

I gasp, as he expertly plays with my nipple, running his thumb over it in erotic circles. I can feel myself becoming wet, my pussy clenching in anticipation.

I can't just lie back any longer. I have to have Romy and screw the consequences.

Sitting up, I push him away a little. Taking off my jacket and top, I casually toss them to one side and straddle him, loving how he grins. I feel his erection straining against his trousers as I lean forward and kiss him, hard. Our tongues meet, and I groan, rubbing my groin against his as I run my hands through his hair.

Maybe it's the alcohol. Maybe it's a rebellion against being locked up by my father. Maybe I am just pissed off that everyone is trying to control my life and nobody gives a damn about what *I* want. I was never this forward with guys, but right now, I want, no, I *need* to feel Romy inside me, to have something which is mine and mine alone.

To be wanted.

I reach down and start to undo his trousers, wanting to see every inch of him. Romy helps me, quickly struggling out of his trousers.

Wow.

He wasn't just saying it. He really does have a big cock. His erection stands proud, large, and firm, waiting for me to mount him.

I begin to undo my trousers, when we are interrupted by a loud banging on the door.

"Ivy! I know you're in there, Ivy! Let me in!"

"Archer!" I pale, feeling a guilt crawl up my chest even though it doesn't make sense. Crossing my arms, my father's minion bursts through the door to find me topless with Romy.

And if looks could kill, we would be dead.

Chapter Fifteen

IVY ARCHAIC

"*D*idn't anyone ever tell you it's rude to interrupt?"

Romy casually sits up as if this is just a normal conversation and we weren't half naked. Pulling his trousers up, he leans over and picks up my top, handing it to me so I can cover up.

Turning my back to Archer, I pull it on, running a hand through my hair in a vain attempt to tidy it up.

Archer ignores him, striding over to me. Grabbing my arm, he snarls, "Come on, Ivy. It's time to leave."

"Ow!" I pull away from him, he doesn't let me go. He doesn't hurt me, but the anger in his eyes frightens me for just a moment.

"You shouldn't treat a lady like that," Romy says. His tone is light, but there is a definite sense of underlying menace.

"Or what? You'll call your guards?" Archer shakes his head. "I'll deal with them like I did your friend on the door. Ivy is under my protection, not fucking yours."

"No need to call the guards. I can take care of things just fine by myself." Romy got out of the conversation pit and strode over to Archer, the two of them squaring up to each other in preparation for a fight with me right next to them both.

"Woah, woah, woah." I hurry to put myself between the men. "This is all getting out of hand really quickly. Archer, why don't you just get out of here? I didn't ask you to be here."

"No, but your father did and I'm duty bound to protect you, even from yourself if need be." Archer doesn't look at me, his gaze firmly squared on Romy, who seems to be finding everything hilarious. His amused grin never slips and I know this is more than just about me.

"Ivy's more than capable of taking care of herself as far as I can tell," Romy replies with a glance at me. "She needed a break from the noise of the party, so I offered to let her hang out somewhere quieter."

"I know. Milly told me Ivy had a headache, so I came to take her home. It's my job to protect her. Ivy, if you've got a headache, you're better off home in your own bed. Believe me, the last place you want to be is in *his*."

"I think that's up to Ivy to decide," Romy growls. "From what I can tell, she seemed perfectly happy with me."

"That's because she doesn't know you like I do."

Archer takes a step closer to Romy, practically stepping on my foot.

"E-*nough*! Both of you!" I put a hand out to both their chests, pushing them away from each other. "Jesus. Can you guys tone it down a little? You're like dogs fighting over a bone and neither of you seem to give a damn what I think."

Romy opens his mouth to say something and I glare at him.

"*Neither* of you." I repeat. "As it stands, I have to say the mood is well and truly ruined, wouldn't you, Romy?"

"Yeah. Thanks, Archer," Romy mutters sulkily.

"So why don't we take a rain check?" I reach out and squeeze his arm. Maybe it's a good thing Archer had interrupted us. Things had been moving pretty fast and it isn't a bad thing to take time to get to know Romy better before we take things to the next level. "It's my eighteenth birthday next week. Come to my party?"

"I wouldn't dream of missing it." That familiar twinkle comes back into Romy's eyes.

"Cool." I turn to Archer. "If you're ready to leave, I want to go home. You're right. I do have a bit of a headache."

"Everything all right, boss?" The security guard who'd been protecting the entrance to Romy's private room stumbles through the door, one of his eyes swollen shut and blood pouring from his lip. Glancing at Archer's hand, I see the bruises there and a bit of dried blood. Shit, he did that?

"For now," Romy coldly replies. "We'll discuss your failures later."

I narrow my eyes. There is an edge to Romy's voice that jars with his usual Casanova charm. Clearly, there is more to him than his womanising ways, and I really feel stupid for falling for it. I should know better. He is an heir.

And the heirs in this town are nothing short of ruthless.

"Let's get out of here." Archer takes my arm, gentler this time, and leads me out of the room. I turn to wave goodbye to Romy, who blows me a kiss before sketching an elaborate bow.

"Isn't Milly coming with us?" I ask, as Archer heads straight out of the building and towards where we'd left the car.

He shakes his head. "She's having fun. I'll come back for her later. If she needs a ride sooner than that, she can always call for a driver. Right now, you're my number one priority."

"How sweet," I sarcastically reply, as Archer holds the passenger car door open for me before going round to get behind the wheel. "I can almost believe you cared if it wasn't for the fact my father's got some weird hold over you."

"Actually, when it comes to Romy, it wouldn't matter who your father is. I would be warning you to steer clear anyway."

Archer avoids looking at me as he fires up the engine and reverses out of the space.

"Why?"

Archer ignores me, switching on the radio and turning it up

so loud conversation is impossible before speeding away from the warehouse and towards the Archaic part of town.

I lean over and switch off the music. Archer goes to put it back on again, but I put my hand over his to stop him. Even a simple touch of our hands sends goosebumps through me.

"I've got a headache, remember?"

Archer huffs, but leaves the radio off.

"Besides, I want to know what you've got against Romy. Surely it shouldn't matter to you who I hook up with? My father wants me to build connections with the other houses. If that means I have some fun along the way, what's it to you? I know he slept with your girlfriend, but it's not like there's anything going on between you and me."

"Steph *wasn't* my girlfriend," Archer insists. "But that's not why you should stay away from Romy."

"So why should I?"

Archer shakes his head. "Romy's got a habit of leaving broken hearts wherever he goes. I wouldn't want you to be another one of his conquests. You've been through enough already."

"Oh, Archer. Don't tell me you care? It's almost as though you're jealous," I joke.

A nerve in Archer's cheek twitches, but he doesn't say anything.

Maybe he *is* jealous.

"Tell me something about you growing up. I don't know you well and you're the only person who knows everything about me," I reply.

"I don't know everything about you," he counters, but he sighs. "What do you want to know?"

"Anything. Everything," I honestly reply.

"I've lived in King Town my entire life and Milly is my only full-blooded sister. I have three other siblings but none of them live with us," he starts to explain to me. "My dad loved my mum, and she made him a better person. I grew up in a house full of laughter and joy. We were always dancing, mum said not to dance when there was music was a waste."

He smiles, lost in the memory, and I smile with him.

"She died when I was thirteen when her car blew up with her inside of it," he softly tells me and my heart hurts for him.

"Archer...," I whisper.

"It took dad a year to find out it was one of his many lovers. She was jealous and wanted my mother's place," his voice is so cold and empty, spitting with anger. "She was taken out, of course, and I've never forgiven my dad for it. It was him that caused her death."

"Leaving King Town in a way caused my mum's death. If she had stayed, she could have gotten better treatment," I admit, and I'm so angry at her. Why didn't she come for help? What is so bad about this town that it is worth dying and leaving your daughter for? "I'm mad at her...she left me when she could have stayed. Even if it meant coming here."

"You didn't grow up here. For people like me, leaving here is a dream worth dying for," he tells me.

"Do you want to leave?"

He doesn't answer me even as we get close to my house. "I used to when there was not much here to stay and fight for. Things have changed."

I feel his eyes on me, but I can't reply to him. Things have changed for me, too.

Chapter Sixteen

IVY ARCHAIC

"*M*orning, Declan."

My music partner has the good grace to look embarrassed when I walk into class the Monday after the party. I made sure my hair is nice and wavy today, and I have a tiny bit of makeup on. I need to be confident to get through this.

"Oh, hey, Ivy. Look... about the other day..."

"It's okay." I shrug. "You wouldn't be the first guy to turn out a total waste of my time, but I'm working on you being the last."

The truth is, I cared. A lot.

After Archer took me home, I stayed up all night thinking about everything. I have been in King Town a week and already my life is way more complicated than it had ever been. Archer had done me a favour by walking in on me and Romy. Much as the guy is cute, I was on the rebound and if I had slept with him; I would have regretted it the next day. But there did seem to be a chemistry between us and I know I want to get to know him better so that if there is a next time, it is based on a deeper connection than a bit of alcohol and hurt feelings.

Thinking about Archer makes me wonder what is going on in his mind. The guy is moody and mean and working for my father. He is my kidnapper, for crying out loud. He is the whole reason I am here. Is some kind of sick Stockholm Syndrome making me have feelings for him?

Because I did. Looking back, I realised that when he walked in on me and Romy; it wasn't embarrassment I was feeling. It was shame. I don't want Archer seeing me like that. For some stupid reason, his opinion matters to me. I really wish it didn't. I want to hate him for always being there like some mad stalker, but the truth is, I like the fact someone cares what happens to me, even if it is only because my father is making him do it for some kind of debt he owed.

Something tells me Archer would still be there for me even if he wasn't in my father's employ. Milly adores him, which says a lot. Sure, he is her brother, but they don't seem to suffer from the kind of sibling rivalry you'd expect from families brought up to be cutthroat.

There is definitely a lot more to Archer Knight than I have learned so far.

One thing is for sure. I had a lot more options than Declan Dauphin.

"See, that's the thing," Declan says. "You're more than a distraction for me. You-"

"Settle down, everyone. Settle down." Declan is interrupted by the arrival of Mr Metcalf. "We've got a lot to get through today, so I don't want any distractions. We're going to be focusing on one of the set pieces you need to analyse. This is worth a lot of marks in the exam, so pay attention. I've got a 100% pass rate in my class and I won't hesitate to get rid of anyone I think will risk breaking my record." He sent a pointed glance in my direction before going over and putting on some classical music.

Declan nudges me with his foot, but I ignore him, closing my eyes to focus on the music. He nudges me again, harder this time. Opening my eyes, I scowl at him. He tosses a piece of paper on my desk.

I open it up and read it.

Sorry I didn't tell you about Ally.

I roll my eyes and scribble a reply.

What makes you think I care?

He wrote back.

We have a connection, Ivy. Don't pretend you can't feel it.

You're deluded. We wrote a song together and got carried away. It was a mistake.

Not for me.

So you're breaking up with Ally?

Declan takes his time thinking of what to write, which tells me everything I need to know. I stifle a bitter laugh, but I'm not quiet enough for Mr Metcalf.

He switches off Vivaldi's Concerto in D Minor. "Is there something you'd like to share with the class, Miss Archaic? I mean, it must be more important than your studies for you to be so distracted. Is that a note I see in front of you?"

"N-no."

"Bring it here." He snaps his fingers impatiently, beckoning me to go to the front of the class.

I don't have a choice unless I walk out of this class and never come back. I go to the front of the class, my heart pounding in my chest. I hand Mr Metcalf the note, who reads it.

"It's complicated, is it?"

I glanced over at Declan, who looks as though he wants the ground to open and swallow him up.

"I think it's really very straightforward," Mr Metcalf states. "Mr Dauphin. Miss Archaic. This is very disappointing behaviour from two Heads of House. The pair of you are in detention with me tomorrow evening. By the time I'm done with you, you'll be sick of Vivaldi, but you *will* be getting an A in your exam. Now sit back down and start focusing on your studies. If I catch the pair of you distracting each other with notes again, I'll be reassigning you to another partner. Go back to your seat, Ivy."

I ignore the whispers and giggles coming from some of the other girls as I go back to my place.

Sorry, Declan mouths. I shrug and turn in my chair so my back is towards him as much as possible.

I am done with cheating asshole boys with pretty faces.

Chapter Seventeen

IVY ARCHAIC

Somehow, I survived another week at the Academy and before I know it, it's Saturday and I am happy I didn't have to wear the stupid uniform this weekend.

I'm not so happy about what day it is.

My eighteenth birthday.

As I wake up, I lay in bed, staring up at the ceiling for a long time like the plain white paint can tell me the answers I've been searching for. If someone had told me I would spend my eighteenth birthday living in a mansion, the prisoner of my father who is a gangster of some kind, I would have wondered what they'd been smoking. But here I am, in a bed that probably cost more than Katy earned in a year. I have so many questions that all lie in the mind of my mother.

Oh, how I wish she was here.

There is a knock at the door that snaps me out of my thoughts.

"Come in!"

The door opens and Isabella walks in, followed by a servant pushing a food trolley. I pull myself up to a seated position, as the servant picks up a tray from the trolley and places it across my lap. There is a vase with brightly coloured gerberas to one side and a large cloche in the middle of the tray.

The servant picks up the cloche to reveal a large plate beautifully laid out with a variety of exotic fruits cut into delicate little flowers as well as a selection of Danish pastries. In addition, there are three glasses, each with a different type of juice – orange, cranberry, and apple.

"Tea or coffee, miss?" the servant asks, holding up a pot in each hand.

"Er... coffee, I guess."

The servant pours out a cup of coffee, placing it on the tray along with a little jug of cream and a dish with sugar lumps. Then they take the trolley and push it out of the room, leaving me alone with Isabella who I still don't trust.

"Do you want some of this?" I offer, trying to build a bridge between us. If I am going to see her every day until my dear dad dies and I can escape here, I might as well get to know her. "There's no way I'll be able to eat it all by myself."

"No, thank you," Isabella replies. "It would not be appropriate for me to share your food."

Better than letting it all go to waste, I mutter under my breath, but I knew not to push the aide by now. She is surprisingly strong willed, for all her calm demeanour.

"Now your father has asked me to tell you to take your time with breakfast," she tells me. "He says everyone should enjoy a lie-in on their birthday."

"How generous."

Isabella ignores my sarcasm. "But when you're ready, he asks that you join him in his study. He's got a surprise for you that I think you'll love."

"What is it?"

"Now if I told you, it wouldn't be a surprise, would it?"

Isabella smiles enigmatically and leaves me to eat my breakfast alone.

I take my time, happy to make my father wait for once. The pastries are amazing, no doubt home made in our kitchen. Just as I suspected, there is way too much food for me to eat on my own, so I placed the cloche back over the plate to keep the pastries fresh so I can snack on them later.

Eventually, I decide to go and see what this surprise is my father has lined up for me. No doubt it is some dumb present, another attempt to buy my affections.

I knock on his study door and wait to be summoned before going in to find my father and Isabella deep in conversation.

"Ah. Ivy. You live!" My father seems to be in a jovial mood, so I don't risk ruining it by responding to it with sarcasm. I have seen enough of him to know how mercurial he can be.

"Isabella says you had something for me?"

"First, let me take a good look at you."

My father gets up to stand in front of me, holding my shoulders to straighten me out.

"You're the spitting image of your mother." He smiles, a hint of a tear in the corner of his eye. The cynic in me wonders whether he has put in eye drops when he heard my knock to create the effect. "She would be so proud of the woman you're becoming." He looks into my eyes for a moment longer, his eyes glazing for the briefest of moments as if he is lost in a memory.

Starting to feel awkward, I clear my throat the tiniest bit. That seems to break him of whatever moment he was having in his mind.

"Isabella and I are just finalising the details for your mask ball tonight. I think you'll be very happy with what she's planned. She tells me you don't want to be involved in any of the decisions so she chose things she thought you'd like and I have to say, I think she's surpassed herself. It's not every day a girl turns eighteen, so you'll have to indulge a father for wanting to make a fuss over his little girl."

I was never your little girl. I bit my tongue, knowing it is best to play along with his delusion until I can escape back to my room.

"You never did tell me what you wanted for your birthday," my father says. "So I took the liberty of arranging a couple of little surprises for you. Here's the first."

He nods to Isabella, who brings over a top of the line iPad.

"Thanks, Dad," I say dutifully. "This will be really useful for my schoolwork."

"Oh, that's not the gift." He looks smug, as Isabella swiped the iPad to access the home screen then tapped on the Zoom icon.

"Katy!" I could cry with happiness when I see my foster mother's face appear on the screen.

"Ivy! At last! I've been waiting for you for ages!" I glance over at Isabella, who shrugs apologetically. Now I feel awful. I kept Katy waiting because I wanted to show my father he can't control me.

"You know how teenagers are, Katy," my father says, taking the iPad from Isabella so he can address my foster mother. "You can barely drag them out of bed for school at the best of times. Now I'll have to ask you to keep this relatively brief—I have some other things planned for Ivy today, but I knew she wouldn't want her birthday to pass without speaking to you."

He hand the iPad over to me. "You've got ten minutes," he tells me, before mouthing 'behave'.

I don't need to be told by this point. Now isn't the time to make my move.

"Hey, Katy," I say.

"Ivy," Katy sighs, her bright eyes watching me. "Why didn't you tell me you'd found your father?"

I shrug, trying to think of an explanation which might make sense of everything that has happened without giving away the truth.

Luckily, Katy saved me the trouble. "Your dad's been telling me all about how you'd been searching for him online and when you found him you didn't want to tell me because you were afraid of hurting me. You silly thing. You should have known you can trust me. If I had known you were looking for your dad, I'd have helped you."

"Yeah, well, I have been disappointed before," I shrug. "I suppose I didn't want to get my hopes up. If I told you what was really going on and then failed to find him, I didn't want to have to deal with your sympathy as well as being disappointed."

"I understand," Katy nods. "But you should know you can always come to me for help, no matter what. You're eighteen now, but just because you're no longer officially in my care doesn't mean you're not my daughter. You'll always be special to me."

"Thanks, Katy." My voice catches in my throat, tears threatening to spill out. "You've no idea how much that means to me. You've been the best foster parent ever."

"I try," she says. "I've got another child coming to stay with me in a couple weeks. They've had a really rough upbringing so I'm hoping I can give them some stability."

As Katy tells me about everything going on in her life, I wonder whether I would ever see her again. She has been amazing, but part of what makes a good foster parent is the ability not to become too emotionally engaged because the children you are looking after can be taken back to their parents at any time. Much as I knew she meant what she said, I was under no illusion. Now I was too old for the care system, her focus is going to shift to the next child who came to her and the next and the next. Soon, I would just be another one in a long line of children she has looked after for a while.

As if she can read my thoughts, Katy suddenly says, "You should come and visit. I think it would be good for Clara to meet you, see that it's not all bad being fostered. Perhaps in a few weeks after she's had a chance to settle in?"

"Maybe." Out of the corner of my eye, I catch my dad frowning. "But I'll have to see. Things are pretty busy here with my A levels and everything."

"Oh yes. You've gone to school. How is it?"

"It's okay," I shrug. "I mean, it's a school. They're all pretty much the same, aren't they?"

"And your dad tells me you're Head Girl. That's amazing!"

"It's not as impressive as it sounds," I say.

"Don't put yourself down like that, Ivy," Katy tells me. "You always did have a low opinion of yourself. I'm glad you're in an environment where you can thrive now. From what your dad tells me, he's really supportive of you. I'm so glad you've found him."

"Me too," I lie, more because I know it's what Katy needs to hear than because I mean it.

"I'm sorry to break up the reunion, but I've got some more surprises for Ivy," says my dad. Maybe my less than enthusiastic lie annoyed him. "Say your goodbyes."

"Have a wonderful birthday," says Katy. "Let me have your address so I can send over the present I bought for you."

My father reaches over and taps the button to end the call.

"It looks like the internet dropped out," he shrugs. "That is very good, Ivy. I am most impressed by how you dealt with that call. Continue to behave and we can make them a regular event if you like. Would you like that?"

"Yes, Dad."

"Excellent. Now in the absence of a list of things you wanted for your birthday, I've decided to let you go shopping with Isabella. She assures me that teenage girls enjoy the shopping experience and since you have a ball to go to tonight, she'll also take you for a manicure and pedicure while you're out so you look your very best. Choose an outfit which will make the other houses sit up and take notice."

"Yes, Dad."

His lips tighten at my reply, but he doesn't push on it. I will never be the obedient daughter he is looking for.

I will always be waiting for a single chance to run. This is not my home and he will never be my family.

Shopping with Isabella is more fun than I thought it would be. She knows a lot of cool shops. Although I have promised myself I wasn't going to take anything more from my father than the bare minimum, we somehow end up going home laden down with more bags than we can carry ourselves. We constantly call the driver to come and take them back to the car so we can buy more.

And I find the perfect outfit for my masked ball.

As I put it on, I finally find myself getting excited about my party. After everything that happened the past couple of weeks, it's going to be good to let my hair down and just have fun. My father's mansion has its own ballroom–of course it flipping does–and he has hired a party planner who'd spent the day decorating it in a moon and stars theme.

The theme is what inspired me to buy my dress. Isabella had taken me to a number of vintage clothing shops she knew and I found a designer dress which could have been made for me. A deep midnight blue, so dark it is almost black, the sleeveless bodice is incredibly figure hugging, pushing my breasts up to enhance my cleavage. Discrete sequins were added at carefully chosen intervals, so I sparkled when I moved. It enhanced my figure without being trashy or over the top. The skirt flared out at the waist, making me look like I had an hourglass figure, but without being stiff. I worried I wouldn't be able to sit in the dress, but it is deceptively free flowing.

Isabella had made an appointment for me at a hairdresser's at some point earlier in the week. Having already bought my dress, they are able to match the colour with streaks in my hair, which creates a subtle effect I absolutely love. Then they pile my hair on top of my head in curls upon curls upon curls which, combined with my dress, makes me look like an aristocrat from the French revolution. I love it.

My mask is white with tall feathers on one side. When I put it on, I barely recognise myself in the mirror. Maybe this party is going to be fun after all.

A loud noise comes from downstairs. The live band my dad hired are going through a last soundcheck. They start playing a song I recognise and my stomach tighten when I realise my dad hired Lost in Oblivion, my favourite band!

I wasn't going to forgive him for kidnapping me—ever—but this *is* pretty cool. I have wanted to see Lost in Oblivion play live again ever since the time I snuck out from Katy's and pretended I was 16 so I could get into a one-off gig they were playing in town. I was grounded for a month afterwards, but it was so worth it.

There is a knock on the door and Isabella comes in a moment later.

"By the look on your face, I take it you've guessed another one of your dad's surprises?" she asks with a big smile.

"Lost in Oblivion!" I practically squeal. "I can't believe it! How on earth did he manage to book them?"

"Your father knows people." Isabella shrugs enigmatically.

"You must have figured out by now your father believes in rewarding good behaviour," Isabella says. "Your eighteenth birthday is a chance for him to reassert Archaic authority. If things go as planned, he'll be more than happy to arrange for you to spend more time with the band. You'll like them a lot—they're good lads."

"Seriously?" I feel like I have died and gone to Heaven. "Wait, you've met them?"

"Someone had to make sure they knew where to set up. Their music isn't really to my taste, but I can see why you like them. I can definitely hear their influence in your music."

"You've been listening to my music?" I wasn't sure how to feel about that. I was supposed to have privacy in my room.

"Sound carries further than you think in this place," Isabella tells me. "My office is just down the hall, so I hear you singing sometimes. You have a lovely voice. Maybe your father can set up a session with a recording studio so you can put together a demo. I'm sure he will support your music until the time comes for you to take over the family business. You should talk to him about it."

"We'll see." If I make it in music, it will be despite my father, not because of him. Music is the one thing that is mine. I'm not going to taint my career with his influence.

"Anyway," Isabella continues. "Your father sent me to get you. He wants the two of you to make an entrance together."

Of course. I nod with a forced smile.

"Are you ready?"

I shrug. "As much as I'll ever be, I guess."

My father's face lights up as I walk into his study. He is wearing a tuxedo, and I have to admit he looks good.

"There's my beautiful girl," he says. "Or rather, beautiful woman. You're not a girl anymore. I wish your mother could be here to see you. She has to be so happy to know you are taking up the family business."

I am not so sure she would, but I don't bother to correct him.

He picks up a plain black mask and slips it over his face. With the mask on, he seems even more sinister than normal, as if he can do anything and get away with it. A shudder runs down my spine as I take the arm he offers me. He might be my father, but I have a feeling he wouldn't hesitate to deal with me as ruthlessly as he would anyone else if I rebelled against him.

This is why I was biding my time playing the game by his rules for now. I was only going to get one chance to escape, so I needed to take it when it came. Until then, knowledge is power. The more people think I am happy to go along with my father's ambitions, the more they let down their guard around me and I might learn something useful.

My father escorts me through the labyrinth of corridors, taking me upstairs to the first floor to where there is a landing overlooking the ballroom. Since I'm not allowed to explore the house by myself yet, I try to pay careful attention to where we are going, but I quickly get lost in the enormous building.

All thoughts of escape are gone when I see what is waiting for me in the ballroom. The place is filled with people in masks. Even the wait staff wear simple black and white masks as they smoothly weave in and out of the crowd to offer food and drinks to the guests. Even if they weren't wearing masks, I wouldn't know who most of the people are—there are simply more guests than people I know, even taking into account everyone I have met at the Academy. I can see a table that spreads the length of one side of the room absolutely filled with wrapped gifts. I can't imagine what can be inside—it isn't like anyone knew me well enough to know what to buy me. I suppose they must be expensive things chosen to show off their wealth and grovel to my father rather than anything bought with love.

My father leads me to the top of the stairs, where a man in an ornate frock coat is waiting, trumpet in hand. As we approach, he raises the trumpet to his lips and blows a fanfare. At the sound, the room falls quiet.

"I had the fanfare written especially for you," my father whispers to me, as the trumpeter clears his throat.

"Solomon Archaic presents his eighteen-year-old daughter, Ivy Archaic."

I find myself questioning the point of the masks if my father is going to just tell everyone who I am, but there is no time to wonder about things like that, as the room erupts into a hail of applause. There are whistles and cheers and shouts of 'happy birthday!' as we descend the stairs to join the crowd.

Masked guests reach out to pat me on the back as we walk past them and towards the stage. My father is clearly in his element, as he walks through the crowd, taking me up to where there is an elevated platform with the band's instruments waiting for them to play. He goes to the central microphone stand and taps the mic to see if it's on.

"Ladies and gentlemen, those of House Archaic and our allies in Navarre, Dauphin, and Knight," he begins. "Thank you all for coming to celebrate my beloved daughter Ivy's coming of age. As I'm sure you all know, Ivy and I were separated until very recently. You have no idea how much it means to me to have my daughter back by my side to ensure the future prosperity of House Archaic. I would ask you to raise your glasses and join me in a toast to wish my daughter a very happy birthday."

"Happy birthday, Ivy!" came the chorus, followed by more applause.

"And now I call upon Ivy to say a few words."

He steps back and gestures to me to take his place at the mic.

I gulp.

"I haven't prepared a speech!" I whisper, hating the thought of having to speak in front of all those people.

"Be a good girl and just say thank you." My father smiles through gritted teeth. "Now."

I step forward and adjusted the mic so I can speak into it.

"Er… I have to admit that this is all a little overwhelming," I begin. "I wasn't expecting to be celebrating my eighteenth birthday in such a grand manner. I'm used to quiet nights in with some birthday cake. So I'm very grateful to see you all. It means a lot to know you think so much of my father to be here for my birthday. Thank you all for coming and I hope you all have a great night."

"That's my girl," says my father, his words almost inaudible over the cheers. He takes over the mic again.

"One final announcement," he says. "We've been lucky enough to get an amazing band to play for us tonight. I would like you all to put your hands together and welcome to the stage; Lost in Oblivion!"

People don't just clap–they *scream!* I am too stunned to say anything as I see my favourite band walking towards me. Joey McIntyre, the lead singer, kisses me on the cheek.

"Happy birthday, Ivy," he says. "Any special requests you'd like us to play?"

"Y-you're so sweet?" I stammer, naming one of my favourite songs.

"Great choice!" Joey grins as he takes the mic from my father and we leave the stage. "Good evening, House Archaic!

We are Lost in Oblivion and as a personal favour to the birthday girl, this is *You're So Sweet!*"

Leo Grayson, the lead guitarist, starts strumming, the bass joining in to power through a rock riff that has kept the song at the top of the charts for three weeks. The teenagers in the room surge forward to crowd round the stage as Joey starts singing. Out of the corner of my eye I see my father disappearing off with another man in a suit. I should have known he was going to talk business at my birthday party. I suppose I should be grateful that he has given me as much attention as he had.

But I won't feel sorry for myself. Lost in Oblivion are playing at my freaking birthday party!

I dance, closing my eyes to drink in the music. Forget about being lost in oblivion—it is more like lost in the music, my body becoming one with every note.

I am under no illusion that this is my party. I know hardly anyone here, and this is more about my father making a state-ment than me having fun. Fortunately, as the bullied foster kid, I was used to going out by myself, so it doesn't bother me that I am on my own while dancing. Milly is probably around some-where, but with so many people desperate to get within touching distance of the band, I don't blame her for not coming to say hello.

As one song finishes, another begins and another, each one bringing me to the verge of tears with how powerful they are. Lost in Oblivion are even better live than they are on their albums.

"Okay, we're going to take things down a notch now," announces Joey. "So if there's someone you've had your eye on, now's your chance to grab them and get up close and personal!"

Leo started playing the mournful opening notes of *I loved you just to lose you*, a ballad which had been Christmas' number one a couple of years ago. I decide that this is my cue to go and get something to eat, but as I turn to find a waiter, a masked man steps in front of me. He is wearing a hooded black mask which conceals his hair as well as most of his face. Silently, he holds out a hand, making it clear he wants to dance with me.

"I don't know. I was going to get some food…"

The man shakes his head and puts out his hand again.

"Okay. I guess I'm dancing!"

I take his hand and let him pull me close. There is something rather exciting about dancing with someone when you can't see what they look like. Tall, I was pretty certain this isn't Declan trying to make up for cheating on Ally with me, but beyond that, I don't have a clue who the stranger can be.

He sure smells good though. Closing my eyes, I inhale his aftershave, the musky scent that is all man and slightly familiar. I drift off into a fantasy that this is my boyfriend and we are having a romantic slow dance together alone in my suite. Whoever this man is, we fit perfectly together. My head rests against his chest while his arms around me make me feel secure, as if he would protect me against anything or anyone who might want to hurt me.

All too soon the song comes to an end, and the truth is? I am alone. I don't have anyone I can trust on my side. My life here will always be full of lies and secrets. Reluctantly, I pull away from my dance partner as Lost in Oblivion begins playing an upbeat number.

"Thank you," I say, wishing we could have danced for longer.

My regret must have shown on my face because the man held out his hand to me. Taking it, I follow him away from the stage. Passing a waiter, he stops to take a glass of champagne, handing it to me before taking another for himself. Then we carry on walking, leaving the ballroom and out through a set of double doors to the grounds outside.

We aren't alone, a few people dot about having conversations away from the loud music. My companion takes me past them, further away from the house. I begin to wonder whether it is a good idea to leave my party with a stranger like this. What if this is another kidnap attempt? It is a crazy thought, but then my life has been pretty crazy these past couple of weeks.

Just as I am about to suggest we go back, I realise we are heading towards a tall hedgerow. Without breaking his stride, the masked man takes me through a gap in the hedge and into a hedge-lined corridor.

"Is this... a *maze*?" I ask.

My companion doesn't reply, but he turns to face me and nods as he continues to lead me through the lanes. He must be familiar with the maze because he leads me through a number of junctions without hesitating before we eventually reach a clearing. In the middle is a water fountain with a statue in the centre, a bench next to it so you can sit and listen to the sound of water trickling into the pool.

"I guess that's one way to get a bit of privacy," I say. "I had no idea this was out here. But then there's a lot about this place I don't know."

Whoever my companion is, he smiles sadly, reaching out to tuck a stray tendril of blonde hair behind my ear.

"You're beautiful," he whispers in a low voice I can hardly hear. There is something about his voice which is familiar, but I can't quite place it. "May I kiss you to wish you a happy birthday?"

This is weird. I have no idea who this guy is or even what he looks like under that huge mask. But then again, it is my birthday, and I deserve a kiss at least.

I take a large mouthful of my champagne for Dutch courage.

"Sure. Why not?"

I don't know what I was expecting, but it isn't the tender, romantic gesture that came next.

The man lightly cups the back of my head, pulling me to him. He kisses me lightly, as if sounding out how I really feel about him kissing me. Just like our dance, there is something which felt intrinsically *right* about being here with him.

I opened my mouth slightly, letting him know it is okay to

take things further, and he deepens the kiss, making it more passionate, teasing me with his tongue. This is someone who really knows what he is doing. I feel like I can stay there for hours, losing myself in his kiss, but eventually he pulls away. I moan with disappointment, torn between wanting to reach out and pull him back but not wanting to seem too easy.

"You taste as good as I remember, Ivy," the man boldly says, and the blood runs cold in my veins.

"No!" I gasp, pulling away from him. He takes off his mask to reveal what I have only just realised.

I was kissing Archer.

And now he has stolen not just one, but two kisses from me.

Chapter Eighteen

IVY ARCHAIC

I go to slap him instinctively but he catches my hand and effortlessly tugs me against his hard body, a smirk on his face.

"How *dare* you!"

"Don't lie to me. I felt you, I see you. There is something between us."

"You took advantage of me! You- you-"

"I took advantage of an opportunity," Archer corrects. "If you remember, I asked your permission before I kissed you. I would never do anything against your will, not after..."

"Not after you kidnapped me," I finish. "It's a bit late to develop a conscience, don't you think?"

"And *this* is why I kissed you." Archer runs a hand over his cropped hair, his frustration palpable. "I knew you'd never let me get close if you knew who I was. Can you blame me for making the most of the situation? I like you, Ivy. Really like you. If I had known what you're like, I would have never taken you like that."

"You'd have stood up to my father? Really? Sorry, Archer. I *don't* believe you."

"Maybe not exactly, but I would have found another way to get you here. I would have talked to you. You're right. I should have just asked you to come for a ride on my bike, given you the chance to choose to leave and not just make the choice for you. I know I did the wrong thing, but I really want the chance to make it up to you. Can't you give me that chance?"

"So let me get this straight," I say. "You kidnap me because my Dad tells you to because of some kind of debt. Then, when you realize you've made a big mistake, instead of talking to me like a normal human being, you hide your identity and whisk me off to the middle of a maze after dark so I haven't got a hope of finding my way out again, kiss me and claim that this is your way of making things up to me?" I shake my head, laughing in disbelief. "Jeez. And I thought Romy was bad with women. You house guys have got a lot to learn about how to talk to us."

"It seemed to me like Romy knew exactly what he was doing," Archer reminds me with glaring jealousy burning in his eyes. "From what I can see, he is exceptionally good at persuading you to do what he wants."

"It was what *I* wanted," I protest. "And it sounds to me like you're just jealous. What's the matter, Archer? Jealous Romy can get the girls and you can't?"

"Romy's no threat to me," Archer snarls. "And once you've taken off those rose-tinted glasses you wear when you look at him, you'll see why. Ivy, unlike him, I don't just want you for one thing. I want to get to know you, take you out on a date, even. I've spoken to your father and-"

The minute he says it, he realises his mistake.

"So it's up to my father who I get to date? Is that it? You really are something else, you know that, Archer?"

"I don't mean it like that! Ivy, if you can just calm down for a second-"

"Oh, I am calm," I say. "Deadly calm. The really sad thing is that you're just my type. Romy? He's the kind of guy you hang out with for a bit of fun, but he's not someone I could ever be serious about. But you? You've got everything I look for in a guy. You're tall, sexy, and you have a cool motorbike."

I can see Archer positively preening himself with every compliment.

"There's only one problem, though. You're a dick. Worse, you're a dick who does what my father tells him. Dad says jump and you ask 'off a cliff?' How can I ever think about dating someone when for all I know, he's spying on me for my father? This can be your way of getting some fringe benefits while you do your job. My father makes you hang around me to 'keep me safe.'" I make ironic air quotes with my fingers. "You might as well have some fun while you're at it, right?"

"That's not how it is, Ivy," says Archer. "If you can get over yourself for a minute and listen-"

"Me? Get over *my*self?" I laugh. "That's funny. Because last I checked I am Ivy Archaic and that apparently means something in this crazy town. Which means I don't have to do anything I don't want to do. And that includes spending any more time with you. Now you got me here. You can get me the hell out."

"Ivy..." Archer moved towards me as if he wants to take me in his arms again.

"I mean it, Archer. I want to go back to my party."

"Fine."

Archer puts his mask back on and stands up. He holds his hand out to me, but I ignore it, folding my arms.

"Have it your way," he mutters, striding off so fast I practically have to run to keep up. Dammit, boys at parties are bad news for me.

Chapter Nineteen

IVY ARCHAIC

*W*hether he meant it to or not, my party certainly increased my standing at school. The next Monday everyone wanted to talk to me to say thanks for the invite or show off their Lost in Oblivion autograph.

I wished I had as much fun as they did. After Archer took me back to the party, he disappeared off into the crowd, leaving me alone again. I tried to get back into the music, but what had happened had ruined things for me a little. I can't stop thinking about what Archer had said. I can't help but think he meant what he said, but that is crazy. There is no way Archer wanted to date me–is there? It had to be some kind of sick game my father had put him up to.

Because the alternative doesn't bear thinking about. I don't want to think about Archer wanting me. I don't want to think about him kissing me.

Because the more I think about it, the more I want it.

I've never been happier of a free period than first thing that Monday morning. I need time to myself to prepare for the inevitable encounter with Archer. We have politics together and much as tempted as I am to skip class, I know Pilkington would tell my father and then I would be in serious trouble. I'm going to have to suck it up and pretend like nothing happened between us.

But it seems like I wasn't going to get that time out after all.

"Ivy!"

As soon as I walk into the usually quiet common room, Milly comes running at me from the other side of the room.

"Hey Milly." I try to smile like I mean it, but seeing my friend only reminds me of her brother and what might have been if things had been different.

"Your party was amazing," she gushes. "I tried to come and talk to you, but every time I got close, someone asked you to dance and I didn't want to get in the way. I'm really glad Archer got to have the first dance with you. I know how much it meant to him. He can't stop talking about it and how he hopes you enjoyed the party. He talks about you all the time, you know."

"He does?" It is hard to imagine the usually quiet Archer being so open about his feelings with his sister.

"He really likes you," Milly tells me. "I know you're still trying to get over the boy you dated at boarding school, but I really think you should give Archer a chance."

"The boy at boarding school?"

"Yes. Archer told me all about him, how you broke up with him when you knew you were coming to the Academy because you didn't want to do the long distance thing. That you aren't ready to date anyone else just yet. That's right, isn't it?"

I have to tell her the truth about her beloved brother, that he made a pass at me and I turned him down because of our history. But something in me wanted to let Archer keep some self-respect with an explanation of why I wasn't interested.

"I don't like to talk about it," I say.

"I understand," Milly smiles. "But honestly, you should give Archer a chance. He's so sweet. I know he has this big, mean exterior, but underneath it all he's just a romantic softie, believe it or not."

Thinking back to our kiss, I can believe it.

"Archer! Archer!"

I cringe, as Milly spots her brother coming into the room and beckons him to join us. Luckily, he sees Milly, but ignores her.

"Archer! *Archer*! Over here!"

Archer knows his sister well enough to know she isn't going to let it go, so he eventually comes over, avoiding looking at me as he sits next to Milly.

"I was just telling Ivy here that she should give you a chance and go out on a date with you," Milly says.

"What have I told you about interfering in my love life?" Archer coldly replies. "Ivy doesn't need you bothering her about me."

"It's okay," I say. "Milly's given me a different perspective on things and I was thinking that maybe the time's come for me to get over... Derek."

"Derek?" Archer raises an eyebrow.

"You know," says Milly impatiently. "The guy she was dating at boarding school, the one you were telling me about."

"Oh yes. Derek." Archer smirks and tries not to laugh. "Derek the loser. So you think you might be ready to move on?"

"Maybe," I shrug. "I was thinking about what you said last night and I guess the time's come for me to accept that my life's changed for good. I need to move on and accept how things are. Which means being the representative of House Archaic my dad wants me to be... and starting to date other guys."

"Is that so?" Archer tries to keep his tone casual, but he isn't a good enough actor to cover his obvious interest.

"It is," I nod, taking a deep breath. "Which is why I was thinking that if a certain someone were to ask me out on a date, maybe I would say yes this time."

"Oh, my god! We're going to be sisters!" squeals Milly before Archer can say anything, throwing her arms around my neck.

"We haven't even gone out on a date yet. Heck, Archer hasn't even *asked* me on a date yet." Gently, but firmly, I pull

Milly's arms away from me. "Don't go picking out that brides-maid dress just yet."

"Of course you're going to go on a date," she says. "And you're going to have the best time and fall in love and realise you two are perfect for each other."

Archer and I exchange an amused glance.

"Why don't we just start with a movie?" he suggests.

"Sounds like a plan," I smile.

Chapter Twenty

IVY ARCHAIC

*E*ver since I agreed to go on a date with Archer, I can't tell who is more excited about it—me or Milly. In fact, it is probably Milly, who went completely overboard on how great her brother is, how great I am, how great a couple we are, how great it is we had finally realised we are made for each other, great, great, great!

It seems my father shares Milly's opinion, although he isn't quite as over the top about it. When I ask his permission to go out with Archer, he nods his approval.

"You can do worse than ally with House Knight," he says. "Archer's a man with ambition. The two of you can be quite the power couple. Still, it's early days. If he tries anything inappropriate, let me know and I'll make sure he regrets it."

I guess that is my father's way of showing affection, but it's creepy. Whatever happens between me and Archer, there is no way my father is hearing about any of it.

Even Isabella appears to want to get involved in making sure my date with Archer goes well. She takes me on another one of our shopping trips and helps me pick out the right outfit.

It takes me ages to decide on the right look. I want casual but sexy, dressed up without looking like I am trying too hard.

In the end, I go for a pair of high-waisted black leather trousers with a bright red top which has straps criss crossing over the back. I find a lipstick in a matching shade and I love how it looks against my pale skin. I decide to leave my hair down, straightening it out so I look like I mean business.

Looking at my reflection in the mirror, I nod with satisfaction. Yep, I have hit just the right note. Archer is going to love the way I look, but it sends off an air of 'yes, I'm gorgeous, but push your luck and I'll bite your hand off.'

There is a knock on my door and Isabella pops her head round it when I tell her to come in. "Archer's here for you," she smiles.

Grabbing a small backpack with my phone and purse inside, I head downstairs to see my date and my father shaking hands, a smug grin on both their faces.

"Ah, Ivy. Good to see you being punctual." As I approach, my father strides towards me, arms outstretched to enfold me in a hug. Keeping his arm around my shoulders, he walks me back to where Archer is standing.

"As I was saying, Archer, my Ivy is the most precious thing in the world to me," my father tells him. "If I hear *anything* about you not treating her like the lady she is, anything at all, you will face the wrath of House Archaic."

"Don't worry, sir. Ivy means a lot to me. I'll take good care of her."

I feel like miming putting my fingers down my throat and puking at the way Archer is buddying up to my father, but, like a good girl, I just smile.

"You've got your phone with you, in case there's any problem?" Dad asks.

"I'm a teenager. Like I'm going to go anywhere without my phone." I pat my bag to reassure him. "Come on Archer. We're going to need to hustle if we want to catch that movie."

"Don't stay out too late," my father calls after us, as we head out. Archer held the door open for me and my jaw drops when I see what is waiting outside.

"We're going on your motorbike?"

Archer's pride and joy sits in the driveway, minus the sidecar this time.

"What—are you expecting a limo or something?"

"Well… yes. Isn't that what most boys use to get about this town?"

"I'm not like most boys." Archer goes and picks up the two helmets hanging from the handlebars, passing one to me. "So do you want a ride or do I need to call a limo?"

He doesn't need to ask twice. I send up a silent prayer of thanks that I hadn't done anything creative with my hair as I put on the helmet and hop on the bike behind him. I put my arms around his waist, enjoying the feel of his body against mine, as he turns on the engine and revs it.

"Hold on!" he calls back, as he kicks off the stand. Gravel spins up behind us as the wheels turn and the bike lurches forward.

I close my eyes, revelling in the sensation of freedom riding a bike always gives me. If I try hard, I can imagine we are heading out of this town and off to somewhere new, maybe even back to see Katy and tell her what really happened.

"You alright back there?" Archer calls over his shoulder.

"Oh, yeah." He can't see my grin, but I can't keep the happiness out of my voice. This is just what I needed after being little more than a prisoner for the past few weeks.

"I'll go the scenic route then."

I don't think it's possible for my smile to get any broader, but I can't help it as Archer takes us down winding country lanes, away from the town, to show me more of the area. King Town itself seemed quite small from a few miles away. Nobody seeing it from this distance would think there are four feuding families living in uneasy peace together.

All too soon, Archer turns the bike back towards the town and out to a section I hadn't visited before. However, instead of taking us to the local shopping centre where the cinema is, he drives us to a pair of electronic gates with a sign next to them which reads 'House Knight.'

"What are we doing here?" I ask, as he reaches forward and taps in a code on a keypad to open the gates. "I thought we were going to see a movie?"

"We are," Archer says as he drives through the gates and up a long driveway which ends in the middle of a sprawling complex of buildings.

Parking the bike in front of one of the houses, we climb off and take our helmets off.

"Welcome to my home," says Archer, stretching his arms out to indicate the whole complex.

"It's... nice." And it is. Unlike the other House leaders' homes which are large, impressive demonstrations of wealth, this is more like a mini village within the town. The houses are pretty redbrick dwellings laid out in such a way that each has a private little garden area with no other building overlooking them.

"My parents live in the main house which is further up the drive, which you've seen and visited through the other gate." Archer points vaguely in the direction he means. "They had this little complex built for the staff a few years back. There's a gym and a pool and even stables for the horses. I prefer to live here with the staff than up at the house like Milly does."

He takes out a set of keys and unlocks the door. Beckoning me to follow, he leads me into a very chic, modern home. The door opens straight into the lounge, which is minimally decorated. It looks more like something out of an interior design magazine than someone's home.

"Do you want a drink?" he offers. "Seeing as you're all legal now."

"Sure."

He walks over to the back of the lounge and through a door into what I assume is the kitchen area. He comes back a moment later with a couple of beers.

Passing one to me, he says, "So, you still want to see that movie? Or just hang out?"

I laugh. "Be honest, Archer. There is no movie, is there? We wouldn't be here if there was."

"Okay. Movie it is."

I frown a little, as Archer gestures for me to walk with him. To the left of the lounge area are stairs leading up. Heading past them, he opens up a door underneath to reveal more stairs leading down into the darkness.

"Like I'm going down to some creepy basement with you," I laugh.

"Come on, Ivy. You're perfectly safe with me."

Not so sure about that, but I know Archer wouldn't risk upsetting my father, so I went with him.

At the bottom of the stairs, Archer flicks a switch to turn on the lights and I gasp when I see what is waiting for us.

"Shocked?" Archer treats me to one of his rare smiles, making a dimple dance in and out of his left cheek, as I slowly walk into his home cinema.

There is a large screen covering most of one wall. A large bed with plenty of cushions is laid out opposite it with a well-stocked bar to the right. Next to the bar is a sweet trolley laid out with share bags of all my favourite sweets. There is even a popcorn maker and a candy floss machine.

"I don't know about you, but I hate going to the cinema and hearing all those people talking," says Archer. "I much rather watch a film in the comfort of my own home and not put up with listening to someone's running commentary about what they think's going to happen next and which character's going to die."

"True, true," I nod. "Not to be ungrateful, though, but I was really looking forward to seeing the latest Ryan Reynolds' movie. You can't get the latest releases at home."

"That's where you're wrong." Archer looks incredibly pleased with himself. "Dad's got a lot of connections within the movie industry. He can get me any film I like at the same time it's released, sometimes sooner. Help yourself to snacks. I'll go and start the film. Even better—you won't have to sit through the trailers."

"But the trailers are the best bit!" I protest. I am aware I am being deliberately ornery, looking for problems when really I should be grateful that someone is going out of their way to make this an amazing date. I am still adjusting to this new way of living. I mean, who gets to see the latest films like this?

"You want trailers? Sure. Help yourself to whatever you want and make yourself comfortable. I'll be with you in a sec."

Archer goes behind a screen which hides the projector while I grab a large bag of peanut M&Ms. A moment later the lights dim and the screen counts down from three to one.

I perch on the end of the bed as Archer comes out and casually jumps on it, legs outstretched. He pats the bed next to him with a grin that could melt hearts.

"Come join me, Ivy. I don't bite."

I lay back next to him, fluffing up the pillows before settling in. Ripping open the M&Ms, I place the bag between us.

We sit in silence as the trailers start up. There is a new Marvel movie coming out which looks good, and a thriller about a girl who is kidnapped and kept in luxury by a mysterious stranger with a hidden agenda.

As I watch the trailer, I shake, the plotline a little too close to the bone.

"Hey. Are you okay?" Archer puts his arm around me, pulling me towards him to comfort me.

"F-fine," I sniff, trying to hold back the tears. The last thing I want to do is to cry in front of Archer. Damn, I'm a really terrible date.

"It's okay to not be perfect and in control all of the time. We live in a fucked up world and we have to find peace where we can. You may be locked in that house and feel trapped...but so do I. So do all the kings of the academy. We are all as trapped as you. I've got you, Ivy."

Archer gently runs the back of his hand down my cheek,

placing it under my chin to lift my head up to face him. He kisses me lightly on the lips, then moves up to kiss away the single tear trickling down my cheek.

"You're safe with me," he whispers.

He may be telling the truth, but the last thing I want from Archer is safety. I want to be dangerous, push the boundaries, do what feels right, regardless of whether it is the right thing to do. When someone is trapped...pushing the barriers is the only way to escape.

Impulsively, I reach up to pull him towards me, kissing him hungrily. For a moment, he holds back, then he returns my kiss, holding me tightly.

But then he pushes me away.

"Ivy... We shouldn't do this."

"Why? Because you're scared of my father?"

"No." Archer grins sheepishly. "Well, a little. But no, it's more that I really like you, Ivy. I mean, *really* like you. You have no idea how much I regret the way we met. Sometimes I think about how things would have been if you'd just been a new girl at school. Everyone would want you. Romy would turn on the charm as usual, wanting to be the first notch on your bedpost. But I want to be the one to catch your eye and sweep you off your feet."

"Wow," I say. "Milly is right. You really are a romantic at heart."

"You got me." Archer shrugs. "I just don't want to do anything unless the timing's right. I think we can have something special together. I don't want to rush you. I'm no Romeo."

"No. You're really not." As he speaks, I see him in a new light. Gone is the tough guy image. This is the real Archer.

And I want him.

"Let me get you another beer and I'll restart the movie. I think we'll skip the trailers this time though, okay?"

"Sounds like a plan."

Archer puts the movie on again, coming back to the bed with a couple of beers. He holds his bottle up against mine.

"To us!"

"To us," I echo, taking a sip before snuggling down, resting my head against his chest to watch the film. The pair of us share the M&Ms, our hands sometimes touching when we reach for the bag. It's sweet—and the last thing I expected from someone like Archer.

The film is typical Ryan Reynolds, a comedy where he regularly breaks the fourth wall to talk to the audience about how dumb it is for him to be playing a dead guy trapped in the body of a hamster. It is popcorn for the brain, but it lets me escape the mess that is my life for a couple hours.

As the credits roll, Archer moves to go and switch the lights back on, but I reach out to him.

"No. Leave it like that."

Archer shrugs and comes back to where he has been lying a moment before. I rest my chin on his chest, looking up at him.

"Thank you," I say.

"It's just a movie," Archer replies.

"It might be just a movie to you, but it's been a breath of fresh air for me," I tell him truthfully. "This is just what I needed. It's funny. If you'd said to me even a week ago that I would go on a date with you and enjoy myself, I'd have laughed in your face. But now, all I'm wondering is…"

"What?"

"When can we do this again?"

Chapter Twenty-One

IVY ARCHAIC

"*T*ell me all about your date!" Milly is positively bouncing with excitement as she confronts me in the common room at school. "I want to know every little detail."

"Hasn't Archer already told you what happened?"

"No. Duh!" Milly rolls her eyes and shakes her head. "Archer doesn't kiss and tell. He has never told me what happened between the two of you. But you will, won't you? I mean, we are best friends and all."

"There's not an awful lot to tell," I say.

"Don't be like that," Milly pouts. "I know something happened. I've never seen Archer so happy."

"Yeah… well…" I smile shyly. "I kind of feel the same way."

"I *knew* it!" Milly claps her hands. "You two are perfect for each other."

"What's this?" Declan walks up next to us, interrupting our conversation. "You two seem really deep in conversation. Is there some juicy bit of gossip I should know about?"

"No," I say, just as Milly burst out with, "Ivy and Archer are dating!"

"Dating, huh?" Declan raises an eyebrow. Is it my imagination or does he look slightly disappointed and angry?

"It's not any of your business," I snap.

"*Au contraire,* my musical partner," Declan says. "We're working together on a really important project. I need to know if there's anything going on in your life which might impact on your ability to focus on your work."

"I'm perfectly focused, thank you very much," I reply. "And for the record, no, Archer and I *aren't* dating."

"You're not?" Milly's face falls.

"Or maybe we are." I shrug. "I don't know. We haven't had that conversation yet."

"If I were you, I wouldn't have that conversation at all," Declan advises. "The Knights are bad news. Archer's only using you."

"Says you? That's rich, Declan," Milly snaps.

He ignores Milly, looking straight at me. "Do yourself a favour, Ivy. Stay away from the Knights. You'll only get hurt."

"Don't listen to him," says Milly. "Declan's such an arsehole."

"I know," I say, thinking back to our kiss. Milly doesn't know what happened between us, so I can't tell her that Declan's comments came from jealousy. But he is the one with the girlfriend. It isn't my fault he cheated on her. I'm sure that if he thought he could get away with it, he would have taken things further with me.

Declan is the one who would hurt me if I let him, not Archer.

"So, do you still want to know what happened the other night?" I ask Milly, wanting to cheer her up.

"Obviously!"

"Okay, so we went for a ride on his bike before going back to his place to watch a movie."

"Did he take you down to his cinema?" Milly looks impressed. "He doesn't do that for many girls. He must really like you."

"Or maybe he just likes watching movies without having to put up with people all around. I mean, we're going to be the main source of gossip now that Declan knows I went out with Archer. An Archaic and a Knight dating? Everyone's going to be watching us like a hawk. Maybe Archer just wanted to give our relationship a chance to grow a little first without having an audience."

"And I've ruined it for you." Milly's face falls. "I'm sorry. I wasn't thinking. I was just so happy to see Archer finally find someone he is serious about. He hasn't had much luck with women and he's the sweetest guy."

"It's okay. Don't feel bad," I say. "You didn't know. And sooner or later people are going to find out we're seeing each other."

"So you *are* dating then?"

"It's early days," I remind her.

"I *knew* you guys were perfect for each other!" The look on Milly's face is the epitome of happiness. "So, what happened after the movie?"

"We fooled around a little, but Archer is the perfect gentleman," I say. "He says he wants us to get to know each other better before we take things further. So, he's taking me out again this week."

"Are you having another movie date?"

"No. He's taking me to something called the Bomber Derby. Says I can be his partner."

"The Bomber Derby?" Milly let out one of her infamous squeals. "Oh my god! It must be serious!"

"What do you mean? What's so important about the Bomber Derby?"

"It's a regular race between the four houses. Well, three for now. The heir to each house competes to race around the town. The losers have to buy the winner a crate of beer, but it's more about the kudos than the prize. Archer's been on a winning streak for months now and the others would love nothing more than to see him lose, but that's not going to happen. If you get asked to ride on the back of someone's bike for the race it's a big deal. Usually only girlfriends get to partner up for the race, so if Archer's asked you to ride with him, it means he genuinely cares about you and he doesn't care who knows it. Archer's usually so private about his love life. This is *huge*, Ivy!"

"I had no idea…"

I hadn't. Archer had been so casual about inviting me to ride with him. After the movie ended, we'd kissed a bit, but before things could go too far, Archer said he had to take me home because he didn't want my dad to worry. But he said there is a race coming up and if I wanted, I can ride on the back of his bike for it. Of course, he didn't need to ask me twice—there's nothing I love more than a bit of speed. I had no idea it was so significant.

And then Milly asks the really serious question.

"What are you going to wear?"

Chapter Twenty-Two

IVY ARCHAIC

The black leather trousers I had worn on our date come in handy again as I get ready for the race. If I'm going to be involved in a high-speed race, practicality mattered more than looks–but it doesn't hurt that the trousers hug my butt in a way that really flatters my curves.

I knew all too well what damage can be done if you came off a bike when you are going fast. One of my friends had been involved in a crash and the only thing that had stopped his injuries from being worse was the heavy biker gear he had been wearing. As it was, the friction from sliding along the road when he came off his bike had worn away the leather until there was practically nothing left.

I wasn't going to risk something like that happening to me for the sake of a cute short skirt. Anyway, something tells me Archer will appreciate the biker chick look more than me dressing up, and the look of approval on his face as I left the house to meet him told me I had made the right call.

I drop a quick kiss on his lips before putting on the helmet he holds out to me.

"Are you ready for this?" he asks with a classic Archer smirk that melts my heart and *other* places. "The speed limit doesn't apply when you're riding in the Bomber Derby."

"Ride or die? Right?" I laugh but something in his eyes sparks like danger. "The question is, can you ride fast enough for me?"

"I think you will be happy," Archer grins, as I climb behind him on the bike.

I have done a little digging into the history of the race after Milly told me what a big deal it was. Apparently, it is a long-standing tradition in the town. All the police know about it and stayed out of the way, not wanting to get on the wrong side of the Houses. They turn a blind eye to the Bomber Derby and in return, the Houses make very generous donations to local police charities. It is a win/win all round.

The Derby is seen as a relatively harmless way for young heirs to let off steam while jostling for dominance. Before the race started, there'd been a number of street fights and people had died. Since the introduction of the Derby, the only injuries had been when someone crashed their bike. I wonder if my mum and dad raced at some point?

As Milly had said, Archer had won most of the races he has participated in since he started doing them, so the pressure is on tonight. Both Romy and Declan would be desperate to take the crown from him. And something tells me that the pair of them would be doubly keen to win once they saw me sitting on the back of Archer's bike.

I hold on tight as Archer drives through the streets of King Town. The route of the race changes every time, rotating the start/finish line between each of the four Houses' territories to keep things fair. Wherever it started, that House had the responsibility for coming up with the route and this time it is the turn of House Navarre to decide the layout of the race. Kept secret until just before the race is due to start, in theory, it gives an advantage to the hosting House, but it still hasn't stopped Archer from winning.

Once more, I find myself travelling through the industrial

area filled with Navarre factories. As we draw nearer to the starting point of the race, I can hear loud music and cheering. Turning down another street, I see a large banner hung across the road to signify the starting point. A platform has been erected to one side of the road and a DJ is spinning discs to entertain the crowd waiting for the festivities to begin. Girls in literally nothing skirts and bras walk around with drinks and I recognise many of them from school. I see Nikki, and her eyes widen as she pats a girl's shoulder next to her.

As Archer pulls up just before the line painted across the road, there is a lull in sound. The music continues to play but everyone falls silent as they realise Archer isn't alone.

"Is that... *Ivy Archaic?*" I hear someone say.

Archer takes off his helmet and twists round in his seat to see me. Mischief flickers in his eyes, drawing me to him. "Shall we give them something to talk about?"

I take off my helmet, shaking my hair out. "Sounds like fun."

I lean forward and kiss him, and just like every other time, there is a spark of something there. He breathes life into me, like bringing back a bird to life but this bird is still trapped in a cage. He reaches back and caresses my thigh as we take our time exploring each other's mouths.

"Get a room!" someone jeers when we finally break apart. Archer and I simply look at each other and laugh.

"I guess you think the best man won?" Romy comes over to talk to us, his eyes stormy and his jaw almost ticking in anger. My heart pounds when I see him, not in the same way it reacts to Archer. The feelings I get around both of them are intense, to say the least.

"Like I always do," shrugs Archer.

"Yeah, well, I wouldn't be so sure about that," Romy bites out. "I've upgraded to a Dodge Tomahawk. You're not going to stand a chance out there."

"It's all about the rider, not the bike," Archer counters. "You wouldn't know how to handle something like that. If I were you, I would go back to the Yamaha."

"What's the matter, Archer? Worried you're going to lose?" Romy cruelly taunts.

"I could be riding a fucking Vespa and I would still beat you," Archer laughs. Romy looks inches away from punching him and I don't blame him at this point. The stupid side of me reaches out and touches Romy's arm and I see Archer's eyes narrow at the move.

Romy turns his attention to me, a small grin brightening up his handsome face. "There's always room on the back of my bike for you, Ivy," he suggests, his voice deep and sexy in all the right ways.

I always used to think girls who fell for boys like Romy where completely stupid. I mean he is a man whore with all the shiny perks. He might as well have a giant sign claiming that title as his…but now I know why girls fall for him. He's hard to resist, the problem is…*he knows it.*

"I'm saving a space just for you. Come talk to me when you've had enough of hanging round with losers. Archer Knight might win the Bomber Derby but he's still got a lot to learn when it comes to taking care of women."

With that, he goes over to his bike and makes a big show of starting to check it over.

I notice Archer frowning, he's watching Romy with caution.

"What's up?"

"It doesn't look like Romy's got someone on his bike today," he says, still gazing over at his rival.

"And?"

"Romy *never* rides on his own. He's always got to have a woman with him, thinks it makes him look cool. He might not be able to win the race but he can always win someone's heart. It's a cheesy line he uses but it always seems to work."

"Yes, Romy's pretty good with the cheesy one liners," I murmur, thinking back to how he had seduced me with words and his sexy face.

"If he's riding alone, he's doing it for show." Archer turns to face me. "Look, Ivy. You can make up your own mind about who you hang around with. I'm never going to try and control you or tell you what you can or can't do. But I'm warning you now—be careful around Romy. He's always hustling. He's the kind of guy who'd try to steal you from me just to prove he can. He's just like his father—he'll never settle down with one woman. Did you know Romy's got eight brothers and sisters, but Romy's the only legitimate heir?"

I laugh nervously. "It's the twenty-first century, Archer. The whole concept of a 'legitimate heir' went out with the ark."

"Not in King Town," Archer reminds me. "Who you are and where you come from matters here. Your blood equals your place in King Town. It's why your father needed you brought back. Without you, there's no House Archaic. Without Romy, there'd be a huge fight over who gets to take over House Navarre. It isn't as simple as who is born first. It can be argued that Navarre's favourite concubine should have precedence, only his favourite's constantly changing. It would be a nightmare for House Navarre and a golden opportunity for the rest of us. We can swoop in and take their territory—and business—while they're squabbling over who's in charge."

"You people are nuts," I say.

"You're one of us now," Archer reminds me. "And there are good parts to being an elite in King Town. You just need to look for them."

There is the blare of a loud horn at the end of his sentence.

"Can all racers proceed to the booth where the route is now available for viewing," announces the DJ.

"That's my cue," says Archer. "Now I get to see what Romy planned for us."

"Wait—are you meant to *memorise* the route?" I ask.

"No." Archer laughs. "The route's clearly marked and there are checkpoints along the way. This is just to give us advance warning of where we're supposed to be so we can strategize. I told you—the hosting House gets an advantage. Romy will have run this route multiple times because he thinks it'll give him a chance of winning. But it won't matter–I'm still going to be first across the finish line."

There is something undeniably sexy about Archer's confidence. I can't stop myself from kissing him before he went off to join the other competitors.

I watch his butt as he walks, loving the way it looks in his biker gear.

"So you think you've pinned down the elusive Archer Knight, do you?"

I turn to see Ally standing next to me.

"He'll break your heart, you know," she sneers. "He *always* does."

"Yeah, right," I dryly reply.

"Oh, you're in love with him!" She laughs. "You poor thing. You're in even more trouble than you think."

"Thank you for your concern, but I'm fine," I reply. "You're just jealous Archer's found someone better than you."

"Meow!" Ally tried to be sarcastic, but there is a tinge of hurt to her tone that tells me I have hit the mark. "I guess we'll see who's best when Declan races past the finish line and I'm waving at you while Archer tries to keep up."

"In your dreams," I say even when her comment hits home. As much as I've tried to push Declan from my thoughts and heart, he is still there. Therefore, every time I see him with Ally, I want to hit her. "From what I've heard, Declan hasn't got a chance of winning this thing. Speak of the devil…"

"Look at this! Two of my favourite people hanging out together." Declan comes over and puts his arm around Ally, but his eyes stay fixed on me. I look away first, needing to put space between us.

"Yes, I was just letting Ivy know she's backing the wrong guy." Ally smirks and puts her arms around Declan's neck, casting me a glance that tells me he is all hers.

She is welcome to him. I don't date cheaters.

"Well, I knew that, babe." Declan kissed Ally, but he is

looking at me all the while. Ally doesn't notice—she is utterly smitten.

"Are you ready to ride with a winner?" Archer came to join us, wrapping his arm around my waist. "I've looked at the course and nobody stands a chance. Romy's put in a lot of straights because he thinks it'll give him the advantage with his new bike, but there's a few tight turns he's going to struggle with. This one's a foregone conclusion."

"Cool!" I wiggle my fingers to wave goodbye to Ally and Declan. "We'll be waiting for you at the finish line."

My stomach clenches, my heart pounds, as I get up behind Archer on his bike. The three House heirs are lined up at a line painted on the ground, each revving their bikes. Romy's Tomahawk is an impressive beast, but I trust Archer when he says he can beat him.

Ally is perched behind Declan dressed in some ridiculous small skirt and bra with glitter all over her skin, but Romy is riding alone. When he sees me looking at him, he swivels in his seat and patted the space behind him before pointing at me.

I have no time to think about why he is making such a big deal out of wanting me because the DJ spoke into a loudhailer, announcing the start of the race.

"Here we are at the start of another Bomber Derby."

The crowd started cheering and whooping; the noise deafening.

"Will Archer win for an eighth time in a row or will one of the other Houses edge him out? It's time to find out. Everyone join me for the countdown." The spectators chant along with him. "Three… Two… One… They're off!"

I almost lose my grip as Archer's bike lurches forward. Three bikes roar as they all speed down the road and into the heart of the industrial estate. It's neck and neck until we come to the first bend, then suddenly Archer guns it, turning so sharply we almost slide along the floor.

As we pull out of the turn, we are ahead of Romy and

Declan. Archer opens up the throttle, sending the bike surging forward.

As Romy and Declan try to take over, Archer swerves across the road, making it impossible for them to get past.

Another turn comes and again Archer takes it so fast, I am worried we are going to skid, only for Archer's skill with the bike he is able to pull us out safely.

We are comfortably ahead of our two rivals when we hit the first long stretch. Just as Archer had predicted, this gave Romy an advantage and this time he manages to edge past us, taking the lead for the first time.

I feel rather than hear Archer swear as we fall into second place. He drops down a gear, pushing his bike to go even faster than before. His machine is no match for Romy's doped up Tomahawk though, and on the straight road Romy pulls ahead, putting more distance between us before he hits the next turn.

Archer's skills close the gap between us, but Romy chose a route which gave him another long, straight stretch to speed down and by the time he hits the next turn, he has a comfortable lead.

Declan is nowhere to be seen as Archer takes the next turn even tighter, desperate to shave off a few seconds from his time. There is no sign of Romy as we wind through a number of junctions, Archer desperately trying to catch up with his rival to no avail.

At last, we turn into the road that leads back to our starting point. I can hear the roar of the crowd even louder than the roar of the engines as Romy victoriously crosses the finish line. Archer isn't far behind, but the distance might as well have been miles.

"Looks like your girlfriend weighed you down," laughs Romy, as Archer pulls up alongside him.

"Looks like the only way you can win is by spending more of Daddy's money and setting up a course which a baby can navigate," Archer counters right in his face. "But it's my turn next to set the route. We'll see who's laughing then."

"Err… guys?" I wave a hand in front of their faces to get their attention. "I hate to interrupt all this important willy waving, but shouldn't Declan be somewhere near? At the very least, shouldn't we be able to hear his bike? He wasn't *that* far behind us."

"He's always the slowest," shrugs Archer.

One of Romy's crew comes running up to us. He whispers something in Romy's ear, and he pales slightly.

"We're going to have to cut short the celebrations," he says. "Declan's had an accident. Apparently, he came off his bike a couple of junctions back. I need to go with him to the hospital, make sure he's all right."

My hands shake and my heart instantly hurts. He can't be dead…not Declan. Holy fuckcakes, I really care about him.

"We'll come with you," offers Archer, seeing my expression and I don't think he is happy about it.

Romy hesitates for a moment before nodding. "Okay. I'll get someone to take your bike back to your home. We'll go in my car."

Chapter Twenty-Three

IVY ARCHAIC

*R*omy's driver is fast, and it isn't long before we pull up outside the private hospital reserved for important members of the Houses and we hurry into reception.

"I'm Romy Navarre," he says like that should explain everything. "My friend Declan Dauphin and his girlfriend Ally were just brought in. I need to know how they're doing."

"I'm afraid I can only talk to family members," the receptionist started, stumbling over her words.

"I'm. Romy. Navarre." Romy leans towards her, menace dripping from every word. "This is Archer Knight and Ivy Archaic. I suggest you tell us about the current status of Declan Dauphin or you'll have our fathers to deal with."

"Yes, sir. Of course." The receptionist gulps, sweat pouring down her forehead as she types a few things on her screen. "They're currently being assessed. If you'd like to go through those doors over there and follow the signs for family waiting, I'll get someone in to update you as soon as there's any news."

"Thank you very much…" Romy squints, making a big deal out of reading her name tag. "Hannah. I'll be sure to tell my father how helpful you were. Eventually. Have his parents been told?"

"Yes, sir, but they are currently not in the country. They are being kept up to date." Hannah nods nervously, as we leave to go find the family room.

I look at Romy with new eyes, seeing what Archer was warning about. I'm not used to seeing him being so forceful and commanding. Beneath his charming exterior lies a man who is going to be the head of a business empire one day.

The playful king of the academy has a dark side I should have seen coming.

The family room is clearly signposted and the three of us sit together on one of the comfortable sofas, Romy and Archer sitting on either side of me. There is something which felt right about having the two of them supporting me like this and all of us being here for Declan. *And Ally, I suppose.* They are so very different, but there is something about both of them which speaks to my soul.

Archer takes my hand, squeezing it tightly.

"It's all my fucking fault," Romy clears his throat. "If I hadn't put in those turns at the end right after that final straight, we wouldn't be here. Declan must have taken one of them too fast."

"It's not your fault," says Archer. "We've done more challenging routes. He was probably just showing off to his girlfriend."

"Or maybe he is so desperate to win he made a stupid mistake," I added. "You can't blame yourself, Romy. It was an accident. Accidents happen."

"Yeah, Romeo," says Archer. "This isn't your fault. It's one of those things."

They nod at each other, but the guilt is still in Romy's eyes.

We fall into an awkward silence. There is nothing left to say until we know how Declan and Ally are doing.

At last, the door opens and a doctor walks through to us.

"I understand you're representatives of the other Houses," he asks and his eyes stay on me a second too long.

"That's right," Romy nods, as the three of us stand up.

"It is most unorthodox for me to be speaking to you like this, but I appreciate your position and the agreement the Houses have to share information when consent is given," the doctor says. "Both Declan and Ally are awake and capable of giving said consent and they've asked me to tell you how they are."

"And? How are they?" I ask, anxious to know they are okay. Okay, well that *Declan* is okay.

"We will be keeping the pair of them in overnight for observation," the doctor says. "And Ally has fractured her arm, which will require setting. But it looks like they've got nothing more serious than cuts, scrapes and mild concussion. While I would advise *all of you* to stay off motorbikes, they should be back at school within a week or two."

"Thank goodness," I breathe out. I can feel Archer relaxing his grip on my hand, as Romy lets out a sigh of relief.

"Please send the bill for their treatment to my father," Romy says with a wave of his hand. "House Navarre will cover all expenses."

"Of course," the doctor nods. "Would you like to see your friends now?"

The three of us exchange a glance.

"That would be great," Romy says, already moving towards the room.

Declan is in a twin room, the other bed presumably set aside for Ally. He pulls himself up to sitting when we come in and my heart bangs in my chest when I see the dirt and dried blood on his cheek and forehead. Tiny scrapes cover his chest, which is bare, and I notice his six-pack and muscular body. *Jesus Christ, looking like that under clothes should be illegal.*

"Any excuse to make up for the fact you're a loser," joked Romy and he holds his hand out to Declan. He shakes it hard. "Did you really have to put yourself in the hospital to make yourself look better though?"

145

"It was such a stupid fucking mistake," Declan grumbles. "It was that first turn after the final straight. I went into it too fast and came off the bike into a bush which helped save us from really getting hurt."

"Don't beat yourself up," says Archer, his tone surprisingly gentle. "Mistakes happen. The important thing is you're both okay."

"Yeah," says Declan, looking at me as I awkwardly stand between Romy and Archer. "They're just setting Ally's arm now, but they say it's a simple fracture and should heal pretty quickly. It could have been a lot worse."

"Good." I smile at him, moving closer and placing my hand on his shoulder where there are no cuts. He covers my hand with his and my eyes burn with tears as I look down at him. "I'd hate to lose my favourite music partner without telling him I forgive him for everything."

The doors open as Declan is about to reply and a nurse comes in pushing Ally in a wheelchair, her arm in a cast.

"Come to gloat, have you Ivy?" Ally scorns when she sees me and I drop my hand from Declan like it's on fire. "I should have known."

"Actually, Ivy came to check on you," Romy interrupts. "We all did. We were worried about you."

"More like worried that I don't sue you," says Ally. "What idiot chooses a course with a sharp turn right after a long straight? I'm going to make sure you pay for everything I'm suffering."

"No lawyer in town is going to represent you against me," Romy coldly looks down on her. "And I'll remind you that the Bomber Derby is a well-known tradition. Anyone who participates does so at their own risk. Try to sue me and you'll find you're no longer welcome in this town and neither will your parents or your sister."

"I'm not under Navarre protection. I'm an Archaic," she holds her head up.

Romy humourlessly laughs.

146

I step closer to her and lean down. "And I am the *heir* to the house of Archaic. My family's protection will not help you if Romy decides to kick you out. If anything, I will open the fucking door. Don't. Fucking. Threaten. Him."

Ally opens her mouth to say something else, but the nurse interrupts and I step back." I think that's quite enough of all that," she all but whispers nervously.

I glance at Declan, Romy, and Archer to find them all looking at me in shock. I guess they never expected the heir of Archaic to claim her place. But I am now. I want my own crown. I will use it to protect whoever I want.

"Ally's had a nasty shock. She needs rest. I think the three of you should go." The nurse looks as nervous as the one out in reception.

"Yeah, Romy. Let's go," I say. "See you later, Declan."

On an impulse, I lean over and kiss him on the cheek. Ally's face is black as thunder as I wave goodbye to her. Archer, Romy and I walk out of the room. The moment the door shut behind us, I can hear Ally having a go at Declan about letting us in to talk.

"Poor guy." Romy shakes his head. "Ally's got a real temper."

"But it isn't like anyone put a gun to her head and forced her to get on his bike," Archer reminds him. "She chose to participate. We all know the risks. Just because this is the first time there's been an accident for a while doesn't mean there isn't a chance of one. She should count herself lucky she isn't badly injured."

"You're right," says Romy. "I guess I feel guilty because it was my turn to host."

"And it can just as easily happen when it's my turn or Declan's," Archer says.

"Or mine," I put in.

The two men look at me.

"I'm a head of House too," I point out. "So that means I should get a chance to host a race."

"I don't know-"

"You don't want to race-"

The two of them speak at once.

"What—because I'm a girl?" I laugh in disbelief. "I'm an *heir* and one of those places *belong*s to me. I'm claiming it. Try to stop me. See what happens."

I stare them down.

"No, Ivy." Archer runs his hand over his closely shaved head. "Because nobody wants to see you get hurt."

"Let's be honest, guys. I was never safe. I was cursed the second I got here and I might as well enjoy the perks that come with it," I reply before turning around and walking away.

Romy's driver takes me and Archer back to his place where his bike is already waiting for us by the door.

"I better take you home," Archer says, after waving off the car. "I'm sorry tonight turned out to be such a downer."

"It's not your fault," I say for what seemed like the millionth time. I have spent most of the journey over here reassuring Romy and Archer that neither of them should feel guilty about what happened. "Anyway, I'm not due home for a while yet. Why don't I come in for coffee? You look like you can do with the company."

"That would be good." Archer smiles sadly, taking out his keys and letting us into his home.

"Take a seat," he invites, pointing over to one of the couches. "I'll get some coffee on."

"Or we can leave the coffee for the moment," I suggest. "I don't know about you, but right now I can really do with a hug."

Archer's stormy expression softens before he comes over and sits next to me, putting an arm around my shoulder. I rest my head against him. Putting my hand over his heart, I can feel him trembling underneath my touch.

"Are you all right?" I softly ask.

"I just can't stop thinking about what might have happened," Archer says. "It could have been us in that hospital.

You could have been seriously hurt. If I had taken a corner too fast, hit a bump in the road at speed…"

"But you didn't," I soothe, reaching up to cup his cheek in my hand. "You're a good driver, Archer. I feel safe when I'm with you. You would never let anything happen to me."

"I never would have forgiven myself if I hurt you," Archer vows. "You're far too precious to me. I could have so easily fucked up the only light in my life."

He breaks off, looking away so I wouldn't see the anguish on his face.

Gently I pull him round to look at me and I kiss him, pushing everything I'm feeling into the kiss.

"Shhh," I whisper. "I'm here. I'm right here. And I'm fine."

I kiss him again, and he groans as he holds me tightly to his chest.

Grabbing my thighs, he pulls me over so I am straddling him. His hands run up my back, coming round to the front to take off my jacket as we continue to kiss.

I help him pull off my jacket before reaching forward to yank off his. I tug at his tee and Archer takes the hint, taking it off as I remove my top.

"Wow." I run a finger down his torso. He clearly works out on a regular basis–his six-pack is taut, while a tattoo of a knight on a horse gallops across his chest in beautiful detail.

It's official. He has the hottest body of anyone I have ever known, even better than Romy's.

"Wow yourself," smiles Archer, reaching up to run his finger beneath my lacy red bra strap and making me shiver.

I reach behind to undo my bra, holding it out to one side before deliberately letting go. It falls to the floor, leaving me topless.

"Are you sure you want to do this?" Archer asks, as I step back to undo my trousers.

"Very yes," I reply. He needs no further invitation to undo his trousers and the pair of us scramble to see who can get naked first.

The truth is that I am more shaken by Declan's accident than I let on. I need the reassurance of knowing we are okay and I want nothing more than to feel Archer's naked body against mine. Letting his hands, lips, and cock tell me that I am still alive. That I might be trapped, but this prison has everything I need to feel alive.

At last, Archer stands in front of me, completely naked. His cock is large, his erection impressive as he steps forward to embrace me. I jump up, wrapping my legs around him as he holds me in his arms. We kiss, Archer's strong arms holding me as if I'm weightless.

"You are so beautiful, Ivy," he murmurs in between kisses. "I wanted you from the moment I saw you."

He turns and gently lays me down on the sofa. With his hands, he holds my legs apart as he knelt down in front of me. No one has ever done this to me before…my very short relationship a year back just couldn't care less about me getting off, it was all about him.

"Oh god," I moan. "What are you doing?"

Archer shoots me a brief, knowing smile before burying his face between my legs, his hands digging into my ass.

"Oh god," I moan again, as his tongue flicks out, dancing over my clit. I sink into the couch, letting myself relax into him. Archer knows exactly what he is doing, and he massages my ass with his hands while he lets his tongue work on me.

I can feel myself heading towards orgasm, but Archer suddenly pulls away.

"What are you doing?" I plead, "Don't stop!"

"Don't worry," he tells me, kissing up my stomach. "I'll be right back."

Reaching into his trouser pocket, he takes out his wallet where he has some condoms. He swiftly puts one on, coming back to kiss me, cupping my chin as he kisses me. I moan into his mouth as he plunges his cock deep inside me. We fit together as if we'd been made for each other and this just makes it so much more real. He flips us over on the couch so I'm on top and

I sink down on him, loving this position. Sex was always blah to me…and I never knew it could be like this.

I'm officially ruined for all other men unless they can do it this well. Declan and Romy flicker over my mind as I ride Archer, and I feel guilty for even thinking of them.

I throw my head back, enjoying the feel of him inside me as I ride him.

He reaches up to play with my nipples, rubbing his thumb over them in tiny little circles that drives me wild.

I reach forward and grab his shoulders to keep my balance, my fingers digging into him as I bite my lip to hold back the screams I need to let out. This is the best sex I have ever had.

Archer moves his hands to grip my thighs, his movements become more urgent as he draws closer to climax. He holds me to him, thrusting up into me and I buck my hips to meet him, the pair of us moving as one.

I feel myself spiralling out of control and as Archer explodes into me, my body is taken over by a powerful orgasm that leaves me trembling.

Our movements slow, and I fall forward onto his chest, my breathing gradually returns to normal.

Archer strokes my hair. "That was incredible, Ivy. Has anyone ever told you how amazing you are? Because you are. You're the most amazing woman I've ever met."

I raise my head to look up at him, and he takes the opportunity to kiss me lovingly.

"Good. We are doing that again before I have to leave."

His grin is nothing short of sexy as he flips us over on the couch and grabs another condom.

Chapter Twenty-Four

IVY ARCHAIC

I don't want Archer to take me home. I want to spend the night with him, wake up in his arms and start the day with even more sex, but for him to keep me would mean my dad freaking the hell out. In Archer's arms, I almost forget the cage I'm trapped inside of.

"It's not worth risking," he tells me. "Your father can decide we're not allowed to see each other and I can't bear it if that happens."

"He can *try* to stop us seeing each other. Doesn't mean he will succeed," I point out.

"Oh, Ivy." Archer laughs. "Sometimes you're so naïve. Aside from the fact you live in a virtual fortress which would be almost impossible to escape, your father will stop at nothing to have his way. If we go against his wishes, he'll make sure we're both put in our place. I wouldn't put it past him to start a war between our Houses if I were to continue dating his little girl when he has forbidden it. It's not worth it. Let's just play the game his way for now until we're in a position to go our own way."

"You're right," I sigh, and let him drive me back to my father's house on the back of his bike, the night sky soothing to look up at. I kiss Archer goodbye outside my father's house as a guard opens the front door for me. I try walking as quickly as I can to the stairs but just as I lift my foot onto the first step, dad calls me from his office.

Fuckcakes.

"I trust you enjoyed yourself at the Bomber Derby?" he asks as I come into the room. Resting on his nose are a pair of smooth black glasses and he takes them off, placing them on the pile of paperwork on his desk.

"It was alright," I say, rubbing my arm. "I would rather compete than be a passenger though. Those boys all think they're so amazing. I would love the chance to put them in their place."

"From what I heard, you put one of them in hospital," my father points out with a sinister grin. "My daughter already taking out the Dauphin competition. I love it. Declan is the only heir they have after his three brothers died a few years back in a terrible plane crash."

The way he says 'terrible' makes me think he loves that it happened. Poor Declan. My heart hurts for him.

"That isn't quite what happened," I say, clearing my throat. "Declan misjudged a turn and came off his bike. No one is seriously hurt, although his girlfriend broke her arm—if anything, I have to say his pride took the biggest hit."

"Good. Those Dauphins always are too full of themselves." My father nods slowly, taking in the latest piece of information. "I called you in here to talk about Archer Knight."

"What about him?" I try to keep it casual, wondering if he somehow knew we'd slept together, but I'm not a good liar or good at hiding my feelings.

"As you may recall, Archer is working for me as part of an agreement between our two Houses to pay off a debt his dad owes me," my father states. "As you get older, I'll start introducing you to the nuances of the inter-House politics. As it currently stands, all you need to know is that things have changed and Archer is no longer working for me. The debt is paid."

"Oh." I had to work hard to hold back my smile. If Archer isn't working for my dad, we'd have a lot more freedom. We can spend more time together, maybe even work up to me staying at his place.

"That's not all," my father continues and my smile drops. "I'm afraid that due to current circumstances, you will no longer be permitted to see Archer. I cannot have you falling in love with a Knight anytime soon."

"What?!" My jaw drops. "You can't be serious!"

"Deadly," says my father. "I have already checked with Mr Pilkington, who assures me you do not have any classes with Archer, so it should be a simple matter to avoid him while at the Academy. And whilst I am sympathetic to your need to have a social life outside of school, you are to avoid Archer should you encounter him while at a party or another Bomber Derby."

"No way." I shake my head, resolute. "You can't stop me seeing him."

"I would have thought you'd be happy." There is a twinkle in my father's eye as he spoke that suggested he knew more about my relationship with Archer than he is letting on. "I mean, the boy did *kidnap* you, whisk you away from your old life without warning. He tied you up and brought you to me without question simply because I asked him to. I would have thought someone so weak-willed and willing to do anything to make a good impression on me would be someone you'd be more than happy to avoid."

"It's like you said. Circumstances change," I tell him. "I've had a chance to get to know Archer and he explained every-thing. He's not a bad person. He did what he thought was right. He looks up to you, respects you. He wants to build a strong connection between our Houses. Heck, I thought that's what *you* wanted."

"Circumstances change," my father smirks. "The tides are constantly shifting between our Houses as the balance of power waxes and wanes. Your loyalty is to our House, first and fore-most. And given that, I must insist that you keep your distance from the Knight boy or I will have to take further measures. And trust me, Ivy. You really don't want to push me on this. Don't the houses have two other young heirs you like? Pick one of them, they are agreeable."

"But-" I try and fail to think of a good counter argument, but I have nothing.

"Not buts. Honestly, you sound like your mother," he huffs, his eyes narrowing on me.

"Why did my mother leave you?" I ask and silence answers me.

"To protect you. She chose you over me," he eventually spits out. "She told me I was her king and nothing would ever get in the middle of us and then she chose *you*."

"She never moved on. I mean there was no one else for her..." I decide to tell him, hoping if I try to build bridges between us, he might not treat me so coldly. "She was beautiful and could have anyone she wanted, but she didn't."

His eyes look away from me to the cabinet on the wall, making me wonder what is in there. "Your mother was beau-tiful even from a young age. I remember seeing her for the first time and no riches my family had ever shown me compared to her."

"You knew her as a child?" I question and he turns to me, his expression cold once more.

"Yes, she worked with her mother as a maid in my father's house. When her mother died when she was fifteen, my father let her stay in the apartment on our lands," he explains to me. "I stabbed my father in the back when I was eighteen because he would not let me marry your mother."

Cold disgust shocks me silent.

"Do you now understand what lengths I will go to get what I want, Ivy?"

My shoulders fall, and my head droops in defeat. "All right," I say. "I'll stay away from Archer. But what about Milly? She's my best friend, and it's not like I have plenty of other friends to hang out with."

"You may continue to see Milly at school," my father says. "But you are to keep your conversations solely to matters of the academy. Should she try to talk to you about her brother, you are to walk away immediately, do you understand?"

"Yes."

Like you'd know what we talk about, anyway.

As if he could read my mind, my father goes on. "Don't even think about disobeying my orders while you're at the Academy," he warns. "I have eyes and ears everywhere. You might think you can defy me, but I will know what's going on and I *will* take drastic measures if I have to."

"Yes, Dad." I keep my gaze low, not wanting to look him in the face. I may be too tempted to slap that smirk away. "I'll stay away from Archer and I'll only talk to Milly about school stuff."

"Good girl." My father nods his approval. "You can go to your room now. After all the excitement you've been through tonight, you must be exhausted."

"Yes, Dad. Good night."

I turn and go to my room feeling like my heart is breaking. How can my father take away the one good thing in the cage he has put me in?

In that moment, I knew I was going to escape the first chance I got. I have been lulled into a false sense of security in the mistaken belief that maybe I can make the most of being in this crazy town. But there is no future for me here.

There is no way I am going to live with a crazed megalomaniac for a second longer than I have to. I have to find some way to get a message to Archer without my father knowing. Maybe we can get on the back of his bike and drive off into the sunset together.

Yeah, right.

Chapter Twenty-Five

IVY ARCHAIC

I sleepwalk my way through the rest of that week at school. Clearly, Archer received the same warning I had because he kept his distance. On the one hand, I am glad he is making it easy for me to obey my father, but part of me wishes he had fought harder for me. We'd slept together, shared something really special, dammit. How can anyone simply turn their back on that?

Milly is distant, too, which saddens me. I know I am her only true friend. Her father must have done a real number on her to make her stay away from me.

Seeing her walk past me, I reach out and grab her arm, pulling her behind the lockers.

"Come on, Milly," I say, exasperated. "Don't be like this. Talk to me. We don't have to play by our father's stupid rules."

"Spoken like someone who never grew up here." Milly is cold, and for the first time I get the sense that there is a backbone in there after all, which makes me wonder why she let those other girls bully her all the time. "Ivy, if we don't have our House, we have *nothing*. I'm a Knight and Knights stick together, no matter what. I'm sorry if your feelings have been hurt, but that's not my problem. It's best for both of us if we just keep our distance."

"Fine." My jaw clenches and I don't know whether to cry, slap her, or both.

Milly turns to leave, but she stops and lowers her gaze. "If it's worth anything," she says, "Archer really does-*did* care about you. He's sorry things had to end this way. But you have to understand, Ivy, that if our families don't want a union between two heirs, there's nothing you can do about it."

I frown. "There's *always* something you can do if you want someone bad enough."

"Not in King Town."

Suddenly, Milly threw her arms around my neck, squeezing me tight.

"Pretend you're doing as you're told," she whispers in my ear. "Archer's working on a solution. Trust him, okay? He knows way more than you about working things out between the Houses."

She steps back and this time she really does walk away, leaving me more confused than ever.

Taylor, Ally's BFF, comes over to get something from her locker. "What's up?" she asks. "Worried your boyfriend's going to lose the race this weekend again?"

"He's not my boyfriend," I say. "And if there's a race this weekend, he's the one who needs to be worried."

With Declan still recovering from his injuries, the regular Bomber Derby is put on hold until he is ready to participate again. With Romy in no mood to host parties and everyone needing a distraction from school, we decide to hold a regular street race. No holds barred, anyone who wants to is allowed to participate.

And I want to.

My father raises an eyebrow when I ask him for a motorbike, but he seems pleased I am finally asking him for something. Much as I have sworn to never take advantage of his money, I'm determined to prove myself equal to the boys.

I have ridden pillion plenty of times—but I have also had lessons from one of my boyfriends while I was living with Katy. What none of the other Houses know is that I am pretty good on a bike myself. Having had a chance to watch Romy and Archer in action, I'm confident I can beat the pair of them in a race—and I am seriously looking forward to it.

As I pull up to the starting line on my Honda Blackbird, I can't help but laugh at the astonished looks on everyone's faces.

"What's the matter?" I ask. "You do know girls can ride motorbikes, right? This is the twenty-first century!"

Romy recovers from the shock first. "I'd hate to see that pretty face all messed up from an accident," he says.

"Worry about your own pretty face," I counter. "What about you, Archer? Think you can handle being beaten by a girl?"

"Bring it on," he shrugs, but his eyes can't stop roaming over my tight leather clothes.

Carly, one of the girls from my politics class, comes over, helmet in hand.

"Ready, Archer?"

"Sure."

My stomach clenches as I watch Carly climb up behind Archer to ride pillion in the race. If he is trying to come up with a way to let us be together, he has a funny way of going about it.

"Cheer up, Buttercup," says Romy. "Archer isn't worth mooning over. People say I'm the Casanova of the Academy, but the truth is Archer has broken way more hearts than I have. At least with me, everyone knows where they stand. Archer likes to pretend he's in love, when really he's just a player."

"Is that right?" I rev my Honda. "Well, the player's about to get played."

A horn blares, the signal for all the competitors to line up at the start.

"Ladies first!" jeers one of the lads, deliberately pulling his bike back to let me go to the front.

"Take care of yourself, little girl. Don't want you getting hurt racing with the big boys," adds another.

"Thanks for your concern," I drawl. I don't to need a head start, but if they are stupid enough to give me one, I'm not going to say no.

The street is a lot more crowded than at the Bomber Derby because of the lesser House members desperate to take advantage of the opportunity to gain some street cred by placing well in the race. There is no doubt going to be more than a few crashes tonight as bikers jostle for pole position, but I have no intention of getting caught up in any of them. I plan on being too busy winning to care what happens to anyone else.

"Are you all ready?" Taylor cries, the self-appointed referee. "Three... two... one... GO!"

A horn blares again. Tires screech as they fight to get traction and as one, we all lurch forward.

Romy comes up next to me, matching my speed.

"It's not too late to drop out!" he yells over at me. "There's no shame in staying safe."

"Take your own advice," I shout back, opening up the throttle and pulling ahead of him. I wish I could see his look of surprise when I take the first bend way ahead of him, but I'm too focused on the road ahead to risk it.

I hit a straight stretch of road and push the bike as hard as I can, dust flying everywhere. It has been a while since I've ridden and I'm loving the sensation of the powerful beast between my legs, completely under my control. This is way more fun than riding pillion.

"Watch your back!"

Suddenly, Archer speeds past me. His shouted warning breaks my concentration and I wobble a little, but I quickly get the bike back on track. Hunching forward, I urge more speed out of the bike, as we get to another corner.

Archer takes it at high speed, leaning so far to the side his passenger could put her hand down to feel the pavement beneath them.

I slow a little, knowing there are a couple more tight turns to follow and wanting a little space between us so I can take advantage of any potential gaps.

Being in front is Archer's comfort zone, but I am used to biding my time and waiting for an opportunity, so I fall back a little more, lulling him into a false sense of security. Then, as we come out onto another straight, I kick things up a notch, coming up on Archer's inside so tight I can feel the rush of air as I pass him and then cut in front of him, ready for the next turn.

"Bitch!" Carly yells, as I raise my hand to flip them off.

I can feel Archer hot on my heels as I take the next corner. The finish line is up ahead and I give it everything I have, desperate to prove I have what it takes to win.

Archer edges closer and closer, pushing his bike to its limits, but I cross the finish line just before him.

"Yes!" I pull the bike up to a screeching halt. Pulling off my helmet, I fist bump the air in celebration as Archer pulls in behind me, face black as thunder.

"What are you celebrating for?" asks Taylor.

"I just won," I reply. "That'll show all those misogynist arseholes who think a woman shouldn't be able to compete."

"I hate to break it to you, but you haven't won anything," says Taylor smugly.

"What are you talking about? I crossed the finish line before Archer. Nobody else is anywhere near us."

"You've been disqualified," Taylor says. "You cut in front of Archer. That's a clear case of bad sportsmanship and we don't allow that in our races."

"Don't be stupid." I laugh, unable to believe what I was being told. "I've seen the way they all race. Everyone's in front of everyone else."

"After Declan's accident, we decided to make the race a little safer," Taylor says. "It's not my fault you can't be bothered to stay up to date with what everyone agreed." She turns to address the crowd. "I declare Archer Knight the winner of this race."

I narrow my eyes and shake my head in disgust. "This is

crap." My hands itch to slap that smug look off her face. I should have known she'd come up with any excuse to make me lose.

I get back on my bike and start the engine, not wanting to stick around for the after-race party. I have had enough of these people and their petty power games.

I'm out of here.

Chapter Twenty-Six

IVY ARCHAIC

*A*s I drive away from the race site, the sound of the crowd fades into the distance and with it my stress. For just this little while, I can pretend nothing has changed. That I am going home to Katy and one of her home-cooked meals before we watch the evening soaps together. When we are done, I will go to my room and work on my songs, recording them for YouTube once I'm happy with them.

If only I had known then how good I had it.

Part of me is tempted to turn the bike in the direction of the town limits and figure out my way back to my foster mother's, but I am under no illusions. They may be well hidden, but I know I am under surveillance by my father's men at all times. The second he got a hint I might be trying to run away, I would be dragged back to his house and lose what little privilege I have been granted.

For now, I am simply going to go on a ride before heading home. It is a small consolation, but it is better than nothing.

I hear the sound of another bike coming up behind me. Looking in my rear-view mirror, I realise I recognise the vehicle, so I slow a little, pulling to one side so he can ride alongside me.

"What do you want, Romy?" I ask, flipping up my visor.

"To offer you my commiserations," he says. "I heard what happened. You were robbed. Taylor knew full well you won the race fair and square and so does everyone else."

"Yeah, I know. But it didn't stop Archer being happy to take the glory away from me, did it?"

"Fancy drowning your sorrows? There's a really nice little pub not far from here."

I think about it for a moment. "Oh, what the heck. Sure."

The pub Romy takes me to is as nice as he says. More like a country cottage than a pub, there is a little garden with views overlooking a river. Romy gets us both a pint and we go outside to sit at one of the tables.

"I mean it when I say I am sorry you didn't win," he tells me. "While I can't say it won't sting to be beaten so badly by a girl, a win's a win. Archer should have stood up for you."

"Yeah, he should have." I take a large swig of my beer, which takes the edge off my disappointment.

"Clearly there's something going on between the two of you. Want to talk about it?"

"There's not an awful lot to talk about, at least not anymore," I sigh. "I thought we had something. Turns out I was wrong. Family politics matter more than feelings."

"Welcome to King Town," Romy sourly chuckles. "It's a fucked up town filled with fucked up families. All you can do is grab what happiness you can when it comes your way and let everything else pass you by."

"Is that why you're such a terrible flirt? You're trying to escape reality?"

"I'll have you know I'm an *excellent* flirt," Romy smiles at me. "But seriously, you've got a point. It's not so much that I'm trying to escape reality as it is trying to pretend I can have a normal life and still be the heir to one of the Houses. I know you've got it hard being the sole female heir, but it's just as tough being male, albeit in a different way. I can have as many girl-friends as I like, but when it comes to settling down, any woman

I'm with *has* to be approved by my family. When I marry, it'll be for business, not for love."

"So don't marry then," I shrug. "I know I'm not intending to get hitched. Ever."

"You may well find you don't have much of a choice in the matter," Romy warns.

"My dad can't tell me what to do." The moment I say it, I realise how hollow my words are. Of course he can, and the chances are high he is going to want to approve my partner, if not choose them outright. And if dad wants his little girl to get married, get married she must.

"Oh Ivy. You're such a wonderful combination of naive and worldliness." Romy reaches up to brush a strand of hair away from my face. "It's one of the reasons why I'm so drawn to you. You intrigue me like no one else ever has. And you are most definitely someone my father would approve of."

"Is that a good or a bad thing?" I murmur as Romy leaned in to kiss me.

This time, his kiss is full of tender promise without demand. It isn't the prelude to sex his other passes had been; this is someone telling me he cares and letting his body do the talking.

I moan in disappointment as he pulls away.

"You deserve better than... this, Ivy." Romy gestures to himself and the town all around. "I'm sorry, but I don't buy that story about you having been at boarding school all this time."

I open my mouth to lie and tell him how wrong he is, but he puts a finger up to shush me.

"I don't care where you really are from," he says. "But I sure as hell know it isn't anywhere the Houses have an influence. It's why you have no idea how to navigate everything going on around you. I watch you and I want nothing more than to protect you. You bring out that side of me that wants to keep you safe from all the threats an heir has to deal with. I really, really like you, Ivy. More than any girl I've ever been with. I saw your face when Archer hooked up with Carly and I need you to know I would never treat you like that. You're special and you deserve the world. I know the time isn't right for us right now, but when you're ready, I want you to let me take you out. I think we'd have a lot of fun together and I would really love to get to know you better, the real you–and for you to get to know me. Think about it."

I don't need to.

"I would like that too."

Chapter Twenty-Seven

IVY ARCHAIC

Going back to school on Monday is the worst. I've gone from having a boyfriend and a best friend and building a social network back to total zero. Being forced to do subjects I hate doesn't exactly help. Even though I have music first thing, I can't even get excited about it since Declan is off school with his broken leg.

So when I walk into the music room to see him sitting in his usual place, I can't stop the smile spreading across my face. He might be a cheating arsehole, but he is one of the few allies I have left at the Academy. I don't feel quite so alone now.

"Hey, stranger," he grins as I take my seat next to him. "Fancy seeing you here."

"Fancy seeing *you* here, more like. What happened? Did you bribe the doctor to set you free?"

"Something like that," came his enigmatic reply. "Did I miss anything exciting while I was away?"

I think about breaking up with Archer, and of Romy asking me out.

"Nope." I shake my head.

"That's not what the rumour mill is saying," Declan says, a

twinkle in his eye. "I hear you are getting close to a certain Knight, only your parents broke up the party."

"Wow. Is *that* what they're saying?"

"Yep. Are they wrong?"

I sigh. "No. If you really must know, Archer and I were getting close, but my father suddenly told me that I wasn't allowed to have anything to do with the Knights, having encouraged me to get to know him before. It makes no sense to me and I was happy to figure something out on the QT, but Archer went all weird on me and then he took Carly with him for the race on Saturday. He has hinted he might be working something out for us, but if it involves sneaking around behind everyone's back while he plays happy family with Carly, he can forget about it. I'm not being anyone's bit on the side."

I glare at Declan pointedly and he has the good grace to look embarrassed.

"I *am* sorry about that," he says. "I can't help myself though. There you are, looking all gorgeous and kissable. We have a connection. You can't deny that. With Ally, it's complicated."

I can't–but I'm not going to give him the satisfaction of saying it, so I simply stare him down.

"What does your girlfriend say about our 'connection'?" I ask.

"She's not happy," Declan admits. "Can I tell you a secret?"

"I guess."

"The reason I had my accident is because Ally wouldn't shut up about you while I was driving. She kept going on about how you are a bad influence on everyone and it was so much better before you came to the Academy. It's like all she cared about was making me tell her you meant nothing to me while we were doing sixty in a thirty zone. I tried to tune her out, but she kept going on and on about it, so I turn my head to tell her to shut up, which is when the bike hit a bump in the road and you know the rest."

"So she knows we kissed?"

"I don't know." Declan shrugs, keeping his voice low. The

other students are a good distance away so as long as we keep quiet, I'm not worried that they could hear our conversation. "It's possible she's guessed, but I certainly haven't told anyone about what happened between us—unlike some people I can mention."

"Has Archer been shooting his mouth off?"

My day is getting better and better. Not.

"Not Archer."

My jaw drops. "*Romy*? He's been talking about what happened between us?"

"I thought you would have known better," Declan says, confirming my worst fears. "Romy's all about the notches on his bedpost. He once boasted how he intended to sleep with every single girl in our year and from what he's says, he's made good progress in making that ambition come true.

"Ivy, you've got to be more careful about the company you keep. The House heirs are ruthless—and yes, I include myself in that. It's how we're brought up. The law of the jungle rules at the Academy. It's kill or be killed, metaphorically speaking. Something tells me you aren't like the rest of us, even with your boarding school background. I don't want to see you getting hurt because you don't know how we do things round here."

"But you still kissed me," I point out.

"I know." Declan runs a hand through his hair with frustration. "And while I don't regret it, I wish it hadn't panned out the way it did. I should have broken up with Ally before making a move on you. I care about you, Ivy. That's why I'm warning you now—stay away from Romy and Archer. They're both bad news. They'll break your heart and stomp on the pieces."

"Thanks for the warning," I say. "Pity it's a few weeks too late."

Declan looks like he is about to say something, but he is stopped by the entrance of Mr Metcalf.

"Ah. Mr Dauphin. My star pupil returns. I trust your injuries will not prevent you from full participation in my class?"

"Of course not, sir," says Declan. "My legs and arms can all be broken and I will still find a way of keeping up."

"That's what I like to hear." He turns to address the whole class. "Get your notebooks out. We're going to be going over some music theory today, and I expect you all to have cramped hands with all the note taking you'll be doing by the end of this class."

We groan, but all did what we were told. I did a good impression of being an attentive student, but in reality my mind is elsewhere. After what Declan just told me, I am beginning to wonder whether it would be better if I swore off men for good.

Chapter Twenty-Eight

IVY ARCHAIC

The week dragged past slowly, as does the next. My new policy of keeping to myself means my heart isn't in danger of being broken, but I am so, so lonely. None of the girls want to talk to me and since they can't date me, I have nothing to offer in terms of political gain and nobody trusts the heir to House Archaic. And Romy continues to try and worm his way into my pants, I'm done with being the plaything for bored rich boys.

That's why, when I hear that there is going to be a party at Declan's house, I decide I am going to stay at home, even though Declan begs me to go.

"Come on, Ivy. Let your hair down," he says, as I pack my things, ready to go home for the weekend. "I know I said you should keep your distance from Romy and Archer, but I don't mean you should cut ties with everyone."

"Things are easier this way," I tell him. "Anyway, I've got a big project due for politics and if I don't spend all weekend working on it, I haven't got a chance of passing, let alone the A my father demands."

"All work and no play makes Ivy a dull girl," Declan says.

"Good," I reply. "Dull is how I like it."

"Don't be like that," Declan replies, catching my arm. "*Please* come to my party. For me?"

"Sorry." I shake my head. "Unless we're working on a music project, it's home and homework all the way until I'm done with school."

I quickly leave him in the classroom and head to the car park, finding my car easy because my driver holds his hand out the window for me. I'm about to step down when Romy slides in front of me.

"Want a lift to the party tonight?"

"Nope, I'm not going," I tell him, stepping around to go down the steps. He catches up with me.

"Why not? What's going on with you?" he asks.

"Why do you want to know? Want to brag to the entire academy everything I tell you?" I ask, meeting his eyes. He frowns, but he looks slightly guilty.

"It wasn't like that. Ivy, wait-," he calls after me, but I'm done. I get into the car and lock the doors for good effect. On the trip home my phone beeps a few times and I glance at it to see messages from both Declan and Romy, but I ignore them.

"What's this I hear about you turning down an invitation to party with the Dauphins?" Dad says, his tone making it *very* clear how unhappy he is with me the moment I step into my "home".

"I've got a politics project to do," I tell him. "You are the one who tells me I need to get straight As. The only way that's going to happen is if I spend all my spare time working on it."

"There are other routes to an A," my father waves his hand, looking relieved that it is the only problem and not that I actually didn't want to go. "Isabella will arrange it. Now, about this party…"

"Wait–you want me to *cheat*?" I can't believe what I'm hearing. "I thought the Archaics are honourable? You always tell me how there are certain standards to uphold, certain ways of doing things."

172

"And there are," my father says. "Which includes the ability to recognise the best use of your time and energy. Right now, the most important thing is for you to build connections with the other houses, especially with the current situation with the Knights. A levels will soon be a dim and distant memory, but you will be head of your House for the rest of your life. Get your priorities straight, child. Go and get dressed for the party."

I must be the only teenager whose parent wants her to party instead of study.

I stomp upstairs, exasperated. All I'm trying to do is make it through school without heartache. I can just about predict what is going to happen tonight. Archer would disappear off to the nearest bedroom with Carly. Romy would spend most of the night trying to seduce me and when that doesn't work, he'll make do with the nearest willing female. And Declan would stick his tongue down Ally's throat all evening.

Yeah. Sounds like my idea of fun all right.

I can't be bothered making a big deal of my appearance, so I throw on my favourite Lost in Oblivion T-shirt with a pair of ripped jeans. I keep my makeup light. It's not that I am going for the understated, can't-care-less look; I genuinely can't care less.

When I am done, I head back downstairs where Isabella is waiting for me by the door.

"You look nice," she says. "I bet you'll be fighting off the boys all night."

"Uh-huh." I'm *really not* in the mood for small talk.

"Anyway, your dad wants me to make sure you leave out the details of your politics assignment so I can deal with it for you."

"They're on my desk," I say. "But I really don't think I'm comfortable with getting someone else to write it for me."

"Everyone does it," Isabella assures me. "And our writers are already aware of your style. By the time they're done, no one will know it isn't all your own work."

"That's not the point," I say. "It's cheating."

"I told you—everyone does it. It's only cheating if it gives you an unfair advantage. As it is, you're putting yourself at a *dis*advantage if you don't accept help once in a while. Besides, it's important to your father that you go to this party. I'm sure he's already had a discussion with you about priorities—it's about time you started to act more like an Archaic instead of a spoilt little girl."

Seriously? Isabella had always been nice to me. What is with the attitude now?

"Whatever," I huff. "Can I take my bike to the party?"

"No." Isabella shakes her head. "Your father wants a driver to take you. He's waiting outside. He'll stay outside the Dauphin's place while you have fun and when you're ready to leave, he'll bring you back here. Just make sure you're not ready to leave until midnight at the latest, okay?"

"Fine."

There is something very weird going on tonight, but I know no one is going to tell me what, so I go outside and get into the waiting car.

Loud music blares as I walk up the drive towards Declan's house. Out of all the main houses in King Town, this one is the best. It's like a big cottage with ivy crawling up around the white stone and next to it is two more modern houses. The rest of the area is covered in thick trees, making it impossible to see much further. Expensive cars line the driveway around the naked Greek goddess statue, water fountain in the middle, water pouring from her open hands. Teenagers are spilled all over the place and my driver has to stop further away when it's clear a passed out teenager isn't going to move.

"Thanks!"

"Ivy, be careful," my driver tells me, and I don't recognise his voice. I look into the screen, wishing I could see who the new driver is before getting out. I'm sure my dad will not let him be nice to me for long. God help anyone who is nice to his heir. Kindness is a sin in King Town. Going inside, Ally pushes past me, tears streaming down her face and we both nearly tumble over.

"Ally! What's wrong?"

"You are *so* welcome to him!" she sobs. "I'm going to ruin you both for this! I'm glad he doesn't care about the consequences anymore because they are going to hurt him bad. You. Did. This."

"What do you mean, Ally? Ally?"

She ignores me, running off into the night and for a moment I feel bad for her, if not a little confused. If we were friends, I would have gone after her, made sure she is okay, but Ally has made it very clear we are rivals, so I leave it to someone else to deal with her.

Instead, I head off in the direction of what I think is the kitchen so I can fix myself a drink. If I am not driving, I am going to hide in a corner and get absolutely off my face and try to puke on my dad's expensive shoes when I get home. Whatever the reason is behind my father wanting me to be here, I don't care. I am going to stick around until midnight and get the hell out of here the moment I am allowed.

Declan's house is jam-packed with teenagers, most of them from the Academy, although there are a few faces I don't recognise. Inside it looks like a regular home, quaint and kinda cute. Pictures of Declan and three other guys who could have been his twins are above a stone fireplace. They must be his dead brothers.

I soon spot Carly kissing some guy I don't recognise as someone bumps into me and I step to the side. It looks like her romance with Archer was as short lived as mine.

Leaving the dancers, I find myself in the kitchen. It is as big as the whole ground floor of Katy's house, with a breakfast bar and two hobs. A trestle table had been set up along one side of the room, heavily laden with food. My stomach rumbles and I realise I hadn't eaten since lunch and then it had only been a sandwich.

I go over to the table and fill a plate with snacks before getting myself a glass of punch. Then I go through the double doors to one side of the room and out to the back garden.

There is a large pool and there are a few people skinny dipping.

Better them than me.

I perch on the edge of a lounger and take a large swig of the punch. It is sweet, a combination of fruit juices I can't completely identify, but it certainly packs a kick. There is more than a little vodka mixed in with a couple other spirits.

"Ivy! I'm so glad you came. I was hoping you'd change your mind."

Declan sits down next to me and I breathe in his scent. Masculine with a mix of lemon and it's comforting as well as sexy.

"I wasn't given much of a choice. How did you manage to persuade my father to make me come?"

"Your father?" Declan looks genuinely confused. "What's he got to do with this?"

"Don't play dumb with me," I say. "My father basically ordered me to be here. I have no idea why, but he made it very clear that I had to be at this party, so here I am. But if you think I'm going to do anything more than sit here and get quietly drunk so I can ruin his shoes, you're very much mistaken. So why don't you go find your girlfriend and see what's got her so upset."

"I don't need to," Declan says quietly. "I already know. She's not my girlfriend anymore."

"Not your-? Why? What happened?"

"I stopped being an idiot. You are right. I shouldn't even have thought of kissing you while I was seeing Ally, but ever since that moment, our kiss is the only thing on my mind. I can't stay with Ally when the only girl on my mind is you and I told her so."

"You *told* her that?" I shook my head. "Jeez, Declan. Nobody can accuse you of having Romy's charm."

"I figured honesty is the best policy," Declan says. "I've had enough of all the lies. There's so many secrets in this town and there's just no need. If the Houses are upfront with each other, we can work together and we'd all benefit."

Gazing into his eyes, I can see he meant every word.

"She said something weird to me. Something about ruining you," I tell him, wanting him to be prepared. "What secrets do you have, Declan?"

"I'm an heir. I swim in a pool of fucked up secrets for breakfast and claim them all as my own," he counters. "Let her spill a few. I don't give a fuck anymore."

"This is so messed up," I whisper, as Declan leans into me.

This kiss is so different to any other time I have been kissed. It speaks of love and romance, caresses and tenderness. It makes me wonder what making love would be like with Declan—and it would be making love. There is a chemistry between us that is like nothing else. This is why we wrote such powerful songs together. Our souls speak to each other.

I kiss him back, my hand resting on his thigh. I love the feel of him beneath me. He is surprisingly muscular and I wonder what he looks like naked. I can't get the image of his chest out of my mind. God he is so ripped.

He leans into me, his hand brushing against my breast as he moves his hand round to my back, pulling me towards him.

"That's one of the reasons why I want to get close to you," he tells me. "We're the next generation. We can change things if we want. We don't have to do things the way our parents did. We can come up with a new way, a *better* way. What do you think?"

"I think..." I wave my glass in his direction. "I need another drink."

"Coming right up."

Declan takes the glass from my hand and heads back inside.

After he leaves, I slump back on the lounger. What was I thinking? This isn't my father's twisted attempt to play Cupid, is it? Am I playing straight into his hands?

Now that Declan is gone, my thoughts are a little clearer. I can't let myself be confused by his body, his scent, oh dear god, his incredible scent. The guy is so sexy...

No, Ivy! Wake up!

I'm not falling for the sexy boys of King Academy. *They will ruin me.*

Declan might be single, but I am not interested. If he has cheated on Ally with me, he will cheat on me the second someone more interesting comes along.

Nothing has changed. I am done with men and my stupid treacherous heart for loving them all.

BANG! BANG! BANG!

Suddenly, there are screams as gunshots interrupt my reverie. Teens flood out of the house, running in all directions and making it impossible to see what is going on. My body shakes as I try to block out the screaming and hold onto the chair as so many teens run around me.

"He's been shot! He's been shot!" I hear someone yell. "Call an ambulance!"

My blood runs cold. Is Declan hurt?

I race into the house, pushing against the tide of people trying to escape, not caring what they think or how crazy this is. I have to know he is okay.

"Declan!" I cry. "Declan!"

"I'm out front!" came his strained reply.

I run out to the front of the house to find Declan cradling someone in his arms.

"Archer!" I gasp, paralysed with shock at the sight of my former lover covered in blood. I lied to myself. I care *too* much about the boys of King Academy.

I've fallen for them...and I could lose everything tonight.

Chapter Twenty-Nine

IVY ARCHAIC

"**D**on't just stand there, Ivy. I need you!"

I snap out of it, rushing over to help Declan.

"Here," he says, grabbing my shaky hands. "Press down on the wound. We have to stop the bleeding."

"Has anyone called an ambulance yet?" I ask, as I do what I was told. Archer looks so damn pale and his whole body shakes as he lifts a hand, placing it on my cheek. Tears mix with the blood he leaves on my cheek and I see the reflection of myself in his eyes.

Oh god.

"No... hospital..." croaks Archer.

"Save your energy," says Declan. "We can talk later. I won't let you fucking die. We need to change shit in the future so this doesn't keep happening. So stay fucking alive!"

Romy comes hurrying over. "I tried to get the license plate of the shooter's car, but they covered it in mud. It can have been anyone," he says.

"Worry about that later," I say. "We have to get Archer to the hospital before he bleeds out."

"I said. No. Hospital." Each word clearly pains him, but he insists on speaking. "This is a set up."

"He's right," nods Romy. "Whoever did this is a pro. They waited for Archer to arrive, then they whacked him before he came inside."

"Which means that if we take him to the hospital, whoever organised this is likely to be waiting there to finish the job," Declan finishes.

"So we take him to a different hospital," I desperately say. "You told me the place you are in is just for the House families. There'll be other hospitals for everyone else."

"No can do." Romy shook his head. "It's a gunshot wound. They'll contact the Houses as well as the police and it'll be game over. Archer's right. We can't take him to a hospital."

"We can't leave him here. He'll die!" I can't believe what I am hearing. "If we don't get him help, we're doing the assassin's job for him."

We all sink into depressed silence.

"I've got it!" I snap my fingers. "We can go back to mine. My dad has a private doctor who comes to give him regular check-ups for his heart. I'll get him to come round. He won't tell anyone and Archer can stay at our house while he gets better. I know there's been a fallout between our Houses, but my dad keeps saying he'll do anything for me. He'll get Archer the help he needs and since no one else will know he's at my place, he'll be safe from the assassin."

Romy and Declan look at each other and nod.

"I don't see that we have much choice, to be honest," Romy grimly states. "What do you think, Archer?"

Archer nods weakly, lifting up his thumb to show his approval.

"I'll get a car then." Declan scrambles to his feet and hurries away, leaving a dying Archer in my arms.

"Hold on, Archer," I whisper, taking his hand in mine and hating how cold he feels. "We're going to get you the help you need."

The doctor is already waiting for us, my father standing next to him as we pull up outside my house.

Declan and Romy open the door and help Archer out. He can still walk, but it is a struggle. At least the bleeding seemed to have stopped and I hope that means good things.

"Bring him in here." My father motions to the boys to go into a room to the back of the house. I try to follow them, but my father steps in front of me. "Not you, Ivy. I need to speak to you."

"But I want to be with Archer!" I protest. "I need to know he'll be okay."

"He'll be fine," Dad reassures me. "You can see him later. What I've got to tell you is important."

Reluctantly, I leave the boys with the doctor and follow my father into his study, trying not to be worried about the fact that two armed guards are taking up positions outside the room the boys are in.

"I owe you a huge thank you, Ivy," my father begins once we are sitting in his study. "My plans have been years in the making, but if it wasn't for you, I would never have been able to get the three heirs together in the same place. It seems their fondness for you has worked in my favour in ways I could never have anticipated."

"What do you mean?"

"Who do you think sent the shooter?"

My father laughs at the look of shock on my face. "Oh, my dear child. It seems there's still so much for you to learn. Still, don't worry. There's plenty of time for you to come into your own as a true Archaic. One day you'll thank me for all of this."

I narrow my eyes and shake my head. "No, I won't. You disgust me."

"You're being silly."

"No, I'm not." Filled with a rage the likes of which I have never experienced, I can't stop shaking. "You kidnap me, use me, manipulate me, and then expect me to be *grateful*? You're sick in the head and my mother must have been so horrified. No wonder she ran away and chose me! You likely made it so easy by being crazy!"

"Calm down, Ivy." He demands, his eyes burning with anger.

"Calm down? Calm down?" It is the worst thing he could say. I'm not a child and I won't let him kill my guys. "Go on, make me, old man. I'm so sick of being scared of you!"

With a roar of rage I throw myself at him, wanting to scratch his eyes out and do any damage I can. At that moment, I wanted my father dead.

"If anything happens to Archer, I'll *kill* you!" I scream. "If you touch Romy or Declan, I will kill you fucking slowly!"

My father is almost too stunned to defend himself as I slap him hard, but he quickly recovers, grabbing my wrists with impressive strength. That doesn't stop me as I start kicking him getting hits in wherever I can. I don't care how I hurt him. I just want him to feel the same kind of pain Archer is in.

"E-*nough*!"

With a deft movement, my father spins me round, pinning me down so I can't move.

"I. Hate. You," I scream as my eyes burn with tears. "I wish you weren't my father!"

"If you feel like that now, you *really* won't enjoy what's going to happen next," says my father with a coarse laugh. "I need you alive because you're my heir, but that doesn't mean I owe you anything. You are a resource for me to use as I see fit, nothing more. Your mother knew this, which is why she stole you away from me. She swore I would never get my hands on you.

"The foolish woman had no idea that the *only* reason I left you alone is because it suited me. All I needed to do was give the word, and you'd have been back here in a heartbeat. Know your place, Ivy. You are my property, nothing more, nothing less."

"I'm your daughter, you sick psycho!" I cry, but my father just laughs.

"And as my daughter, you get the privilege of choosing the

nature of how each of your friends die. I hear some of them have treated you rather badly, so if you would like them to suffer for their crimes that can easily be arranged. Once I'm done with them, we'll be the only House in a position to rule the town, which unfortunately makes you a very, very precious resource to be protected. Isabella!"

My father's aide had clearly been waiting nearby because she appears only a few moments later.

"Yes, Solomon?"

"Escort my daughter to her room and lock the door. Make sure she is comfortable and has whatever food and drink she requires, but she is not to leave her chambers under any circumstances or I will hold you personally responsible. Do you understand?"

"Of course, Solomon. She won't be going anywhere."

"And if she gives you any trouble, feel free to tase her," my father instructs and lowers his voice for me. "I'm protecting you and knocking out all the chess pieces in the way so you can rule like the queen you were born to be. One day, you will thank me as you rule the town."

"It would be my pleasure." The smile on Isabella's face sent chills through me just as much as my dad's words.

She steps forward, a set of handcuffs in her hands. She snaps them around my wrists, making sure they are super tight. Roughly grabbing my arm, she shoves me in front of her.

"Come on, Ivy. You know the way."

"I'm going to get you for this," I say over my shoulder as we walk away.

"Try little girl," my father grins. "Try."

Chapter Thirty

IVY ARCHAIC

*I*sabella shoves me into my room, making me fall to the floor and scrape my hands across the carpet.

"Get up," she coldly orders.

"Why are you being like this?" I ask, clumsily pulling myself to my feet.

"Like what?" Isabella asks.

"Like a bitch," I say.

Isabella laughs. "I serve your father, not you. He wanted me to befriend you, so I did what I was told. See, your dad found me in London using my body to pay for my life and I wanted to die. I hated myself and he showed me I could be so much more. You were so wrapped up in yourself, you never thought to ask anything about me or see how loyal I was to your father. That's what a real heir would do...you are just a silly girl who one day might be turned into someone important. Or you'll have a kid who will be."

"Yeah, like a good little lapdog," I sneer, even though what she said is so true. I didn't ask Isabella anything about herself and there is a good chance my dad does want me for the kid I might give him one day. He never wanted me to rule.

"Give me an excuse to tase you. I dare you," says Isabella, pulling me towards her to undo my handcuffs.

Like I was going to do anything to play into her hands.

She undoes my cuffs and I rub my wrists, more instinctively than because they are hurting.

"Now if you're a good girl, I'll bring you some breakfast in the morning," Isabella says. "If not... I know just how long someone can survive without food. Your father wants you alive, but right now I don't think he really cares what condition you're in."

"You're *sick*!" I snap.

Isabella lifts her taser. "Now, now. I must advise you to behave yourself. I have the authority to make the next few days very uncomfortable."

"I'm not afraid of you."

"That's the Archaic spirit!" she sarcastically replies.

Isabella retreats and I hear the familiar sound of the door locking behind her.

I run up and kick the door, knowing full well it isn't going to do anything, but it makes me feel a teeny bit better.

"You think you've won," I mutter. "There's no way you're getting away with this."

I stare at myself in the mirror, seeing the utter mess I am. On my one cheek, three lines of blood streak my pale skin and my tears look like puddles under my eyes.

My eyes...they look broken. I look broken.

But I can't be.

Romy, Archer, and Declan need me. My dad might think I'm just a tool for him to boss around, but I am my mother's daughter. Apparently she was good at running away with precious things of his, like me. I can run away with the guys, too.

He has underestimated me...he might not see me coming because of that. I grin to myself in the mirror, not seeing a broken girl anymore. I see an heir, a warrior, a woman who won't give up.

I see my mother.

I stuff my bed in that old classic way that is meant to fool people into thinking I am asleep and switch off the lights. It is unlikely to fool anyone, but maybe it might buy me a few extra minutes.

Ducking down on my hands and knees, I crawl over to the window, keeping to the shadows. What no one knows is that I have secretly been working away at the bars that are meant to trap me inside until they are loose enough for me to pull them out. I have left them in place until the time came for me to escape. I knew I would only get one shot, so I have been waiting for the perfect moment to escape.

That moment is now.

Cautiously, I pull back the curtains, trying not to let any extra light into the room as I sneak behind it. I softly take the bells off, leaving them on the floor. Carefully, ever so carefully, I open the window, thanking my lucky stars it is always kept well-greased, so it doesn't squeak as I push it up.

I reach out and grab a bar, gently twisting it until it finally comes free. Slowly, I place it on the floor and take hold of the bar next to it. A few moments later, I pull that one out of the wall too. I do the same over and over until the window is completely clear. I pull myself up onto the windowsill, leaving my legs on the inside as I lean out towards the drainpipe.

Stretching out as far as I can, my fingertips only just brush the metal. Looking down at the ground, it looks further away than I remembered. It is a good thing the doctor is in the house–I might need his help once he is done with Archer.

Taking a deep breath for courage, I pull myself out a little further, trying to press myself into the wall as if I were Spiderman to give myself the illusion of security. This time I manage to get hold of the drainpipe with one hand. Clinging on for dear life, I twist my body so my other hand can also catch the drainpipe.

I stay where I am for a moment, heart pounding. Then, I

pull myself out, bracing myself against the wall as I walk my feet along until I am wrapped around the drainpipe.

"All right, Ivy. You've got this," I whisper to myself, as I slowly shimmy down to the bottom of the pipe.

After what felt like forever, my feet eventually touch solid ground. I am safe. I rest my head against the drainpipe, sending up a silent prayer to whoever is listening to thank them for watching over me.

But I don't have time to waste. Isabella can go back to my room at any time. I have to get the boys and get us all out of here. For all I know, the 'doctor' my father had called in might be a torturer or an assassin and he could be doing terrible things to all three of my friends.

I creep along the side of the house, trying to make my outline as small as possible. The problem is that since I have never been given free reign of the house, I have no idea where my room is in relation to anywhere else. All I can do is go from window to window and briefly pop my head up, hoping no one inside spots me.

There is so much wrong with what I am doing that a real assassin might laugh at me. I wish I had time to come up with a decent plan, something which had half a chance of succeeding, but I could already be too late.

The first room I check is empty. The second seems to be a security room. Two guards are sitting in front of a number of screens, but they don't seem to be paying any attention to them, their card game being far more interesting. My heart leaps into my throat when I see Declan and Romy on their own in a room together, both unharmed. Archer is on another screen. The doctor is just finishing up with him and from what I can make out; he is still alive.

Thank goodness.

I also see my room. I was right. My father has been keeping tabs on me. Still, on the upside, I have done a good job of stuffing my bed. It definitely looks like I am asleep or sulking at how badly I've been treated.

There is still time for me to find the boys and set them free. The only problem I still have is that I have no idea where they are. Archer looks like he is in the same room he was taken in when we arrived home, so he is on the ground floor, but if the other two are on another level, I don't have a chance of finding them.

I move on past a few more rooms which are empty until I come to my father's study. He is on the phone with his back to me, so I decide to listen in for a minute.

"I know, I know. It's terrible to think that they have the audacity to strike at the Houses in the heart of our own territory. Whoever is behind this has just declared war on all of us and I swear that when we uncover the culprits, they will feel the full force of my wrath. They've kidnapped all our heirs and we have no idea whether any of them are dead or alive. I've only just been reunited with my beloved Ivy. To have her snatched away from us so cruelly is breaking my heart. I will not rest until she's back where she belongs with her loving family."

It takes every ounce of willpower not to let loose a tirade of swearing at what I thought of that. But my father could wait. I will make sure he gets what is coming to him when the time is right. First, it is the boys who need to be reunited with their families.

IF THAT IS my father's study, then I know I'm not far from the room where Archer is being kept. Sure enough, it isn't long before I see him sitting all on his own. He looks so defeated it practically breaks my heart.

I put my hand through the bars and tap on the window.

"Archer! Archer!"

Archer looks back, his eyes widening, and he slowly walks over to the window. He pulls it up so we can talk.

"Ivy! What are you doing here? Come to gloat?"

"What? I don't know what you're talking about."

"This is all your plan, isn't it? Your sick idea of getting back at me for seeing Carly. I thought Milly told you, I had it all worked out. Carly is just a decoy. I had it all figured out so we can see each other without our families suspecting. Why couldn't you have trusted me, Ivy?"

"Wait! You've got it all wrong," I say. "I don't know anything about this. It is all my father. He's got some mad scheme to take over the town and pin the blame on someone else. He locked me up in my room. I put some pillows in my bed, but I don't know how long they're going to fool anyone. We have to find Romy and Declan and get all of you as far away from here as possible."

"Really?"

The look of hopeful hurt on Archer's face tells me everything I need to know about how he feels about me. Impulsively, I reach through the bars and pull his face to mine. The metal pressing against our cheeks is cold as I kiss him passionately.

"I'm going to save you," I promise. "All of you. I just need to figure out where Declan and Romy are and find my way inside the house without anyone seeing me and get you out."

I turn to leave, but Archer reaches through the bars to grab me.

"Ivy, I need you to swear that if you find yourself in danger, you'll run away. Save yourself, no matter what. Romy, Declan, and I are big boys. We can take care of ourselves."

"Archer, you were shot a couple hours ago," I remind him. "You're in no position to take care of anything. There's no way I'm leaving you here. Besides, my father needs me. I'm his heir. There's no way he will do anything to really hurt me. He is just throwing threats around to try and intimidate me."

"You really think so?"

"Yes."

No. Not after the way Isabella was toward me.

Archer looks like he wants to say something else, but whatever it is, he decides against it.

"Look after yourself, Ivy. You're far too important to me, to all of us, for us to stand by and let you get hurt. Protect yourself.

If you need, go to my father and tell him everything. He'll look after you. He…"

"He what?"

"He knows how important you are to me. Whatever happens, he'll take care of you."

"Okay." I bite my lip as I consider everything he says. "If I can't free you, I'll go to your father for reinforcements. One way or another, I'm going to get you out of here."

I quickly peck him on the lips one last time and leave. Five rooms later, I find Declan and Romy in a room and I nearly sag with relief.

I rap on the window.

"Hey guys!"

They both rush over and open the window.

"Ivy! Thank God you're okay," Romy whispers. "We heard your dad's creepy aide talking outside our room about how she enjoyed pushing you around. We were so worried."

"She's all talk," I say. "For all her threats, I don't think she would risk damaging me in case my father thought she had gone too far."

"I mean this in the nicest possible way, but your father's a complete psycho," Declan deadpans.

"That's what I told him," I grimly reply. "He's got some crazy scheme to take over the town and pinning the blame on someone else. I don't know what he's got planned for the three of you, but whatever it is, it won't be good."

"So Archer's still alive?" Romy asks.

"For now," I say. "And I'm assuming that my father has a reason to keep him alive a while longer, otherwise he would have just let him die and not had the doctor remove the bullet. Whatever that reason is, it won't be good though."

"I hear that," Declan nods. "Can you get us out of here?"

"I don't know where you are in the house. My father never let me leave my room apart from when we threw that party. I can't find my way around without getting lost and with all the guards he's got stationed everywhere, they can find me at any time."

"What about if you are able to get the bars off the window?" Romy suggests. "We can just climb out."

"No chance. They're not going anywhere." I tugged on the bars, but I am surprised to see brick dust floating down. "Hang on a minute. They're not as solid as I thought. Maybe if you push from that side and I pull from here we can get them out together."

Romy and Declan start banging on the bars while I tug at them, bracing myself against the wall to get more leverage.

"We'd better stop," Declan holds his hand up. "We're getting a bit too noisy."

I look around for something I can use as a lever and spot a metal pole lying on the ground not too far away.

"Hold on a sec." I get the pole. Placing it near the base of the loose bar, I braced myself against the wall again, pulling with all my might.

"Cough," I say to Declan. He coughs to cover the noise I was making as I yank on the pole and suddenly the bottom of the bar broke free.

"Can you squeeze out if I push the bar to one side?" I ask. "I don't think we can risk pulling any of the other bars out. It's too noisy."

"I can try." Declan climbs up onto the windowsill. It takes a little bit of wriggling around, but he finally gets his head and shoulders through. I help pull him out, as Romy pushes him from the other side until he is finally free. Then it is Romy's turn. Slightly smaller than Declan, it is a little easier for him to escape.

"Archer's just over here," I tell them, picking up the pole to use it to free my other boyfriend.

Other boyfriend? As we race to get Archer, I realise that I have strong feelings about all three of the boys and if I read them right; they felt the same way about me. Maybe we weren't dating exactly, but there is definitely something here we are going to have to work out when all this is over.

With Romy and Declan's help, we are able to get the bars loose pretty quickly. We have to be extra careful because of Archer's injuries, but it isn't long before the four of us are standing outside.

"Okay, guys. You all need to get back to your families and tell them what really happened," I say. "My dad's already spreading lies about what's going on, so if he finds out you've escaped, he'll be coming after you all guns blazing."

"The garage is over there," Archer points. "I know where the keys are kept. We can all go together—safety in numbers."

"Good call," Romy agrees. The four of us run to the garage, well Archer more like fast walks. I half expect someone to sound the alarm at any moment, but luck is still on our side and nobody seems to notice we are gone. I guess the security guards are having too much fun with their card game.

"Yes!" Declan and Romy are both excited when they see my father's car collection. That is until two guards step around the corner, stopping when they see us. Declan and Romy run at them, throwing punches before they can blink. In seconds there are two passed out guards on the floor and the guys nod at each other like it was nothing.

Am I the only heir who can't fight?

"Don't get carried away," Archer says as Declan follows him to the keys. "We're going to take the Bimmer. It's the least showy so we're less likely to draw attention to ourselves—the faster cars all have custom plates so it'll be obvious we've stolen them."

"Good call," Declan answers.

Romy casts a longing glance in the direction of a nifty little sports car but follows the other three in the direction of the BMW.

"Wait!" I say, just as they are about to climb in.

"Can't it wait, Ivy? We've gotta get out of here," Archer suggests.

"I'm not coming with you," I say. "It's too dangerous. The

way my father behaved, any of the other Houses might try to use me against him. I have to go into hiding for my own protection."

"No, you don't," Declan snaps. "You can come to mine. I'll make sure you're taken care of. You never have to see your father again. You belong in King Town with us."

"I'm sorry, Declan. I can't risk it. I care about you but I don't know your family and they don't know me. It's best if I go somewhere nobody knows me."

"But Ivy —"

"Let me go," I whisper, pleading with him. "Please don't put me in another cage. This is my chance to be free."

"If you need to go…then go." Declan steps away, a troubled look on his face, his words bitter.

I turn to Romy. "I wish we had more time together. There's so much I want to say to you."

"It's okay," Romy treats me to one of his sexy smiles. "Just try and keep me away from you. Running won't always work."

"Wouldn't dream of it." I blink away tears as I stretch tiptoes to kiss him goodbye.

Finally, it's Archer's turn.

"I wish I had trusted you," I say.

"*I* wish you'd trusted me." He smiles sadly.

"Sorry," I whisper, standing on tiptoe to kiss him tenderly.

We lean into each other, taking a few moments of comfort.

"You need to leave," I say at last. "And I've got to go."

"Take the Audi," Archer advises, but he doesn't look happy about it.

"Oh, no." I shake my head. "I'm not bothering with a car."

I went over to where my beautiful new Honda is waiting, keys left in the ignition, helmet hooked over the handlebars. Straddling it, I pull the helmet over my head before I put my hand on the key.

"You guys better get out of here," I say. "Because the second I fire her up, everyone's going to know we've escaped."

Archer gives me one more look, and he gets into the

Bimmer. Romy starts the engine and the garage door rolls up automatically.

I turn the key and the Honda bursts into life. Clicking the visor into place, I kick the stand out of the way and speed out of the garage.

Guards come running out of the house, firing warning shots into the air. But it is too late. My beloved boys are already well on their way to safety and nobody is going to catch up with me on my bike.

My father is going to regret buying it for me. But that isn't the only thing he is going to regret. I will make sure of it.

Epilogue

ARCHER KNIGHT

Six months later...

*R*omy and Declan gather together in my front room, neither one of them saying a word for a long time. I don't know why we fucking bother with these meetings every week, nothing changes. It's not safe to get Ivy and we all fucking know it. We live off photos taken at a distance, off whispers from the guards who stalk her without her knowing.

We are the heirs to the most powerful town in the world.

And we can't save her.

"How's the shoulder healing?" Romy asks.

"It's okay," I say. "Dad hired a top physio to make sure I don't lose any movement. And when I'm signed off by the medic, I'm starting shooting lessons. I want to be the one to put a bullet between Archaic's eyes."

"You'll have to beat me to it," Declan replies grimly. "I'm not letting him get away with the way he treated Ivy."

"Speaking of Ivy," Romy says. "Have any of you heard anything we need to cover up about where she is?"

"No."

"Not a word."

"My dad hired a private detective, but he hasn't found anything yet," Romy fills in. "He was paid to not find anything by me."

"Same here," added Declan with a smirk. "It's like she vanished into thin air according to our parents. Funny that."

"I'm glad she's safe, but she can't stay under the radar forever," I add. "What happens if Solomon finds her before us? I hate to think what he would have done to her after she ruined his plans. I'm worried hiding her isn't always going to work."

"Yeah, there's no way I'm going to let him get his hands on her," Romy growls, picking up his beer and having a long drink. "We have to find Ivy before he does. It's the only way we can protect her."

The three of us fall into an awkward silence.

"I need her back," Romy adds.

"Ivy's special," Declan murmurs. "I've never met anyone like her. She's so talented, so pretty."

"And that body…" Romy sighs. "The feel of her against me is just… Mmm-mmm."

"Tell me about it," I reply, our one night haunting me all the fucking time. I can't sleep, can't do anything without craving more of her.

A knock at the door makes us all halt. No one should be here.

I quickly pick up the statue on the side table and grab a gun I left in here. I might be a shitty shot, but I won't let anyone get the one up on me again.

The door bangs open as I raise the gun and no other than Solomon Archaic himself walks in…and he isn't alone.

Behind him are our fathers. I lower the gun, eyeing my father with caution.

"We all owe Ivy's mother a debt and we can't pay it back to her any other way than this. Get Ivy back and she will be protected by us all,"

"And you?" I ask Solomon.

"I just want my daughter home. Then it's her choice what happens next. There is a lot I haven't told her."

"There is a lot none of us have told you all," Declan's dad says.

I eye Romy and Declan, seeing the same suspicion in their eyes.

The truth is...Ivy can't hide forever, and it looks like the rulers of King Town are bowing down.

No better time to strike...*if the queen wants to.*

"Let's get our girl."

CONTINUE READING THIS SERIES BY CLICKING HERE FOR TAKE MY PLACE (BOYS OF KING ACADEMY #2)

Description

The elite of King Academy have declared war...and I'm going to win.

Sometimes picture frames can be broken, shattered into a hundred tiny little pieces, and then no one can see the darkness under the cracks. King Town and its heirs couldn't save me from their sins. Instead, they pulled me in and even when I tried to run, I couldn't escape them.
And now I think no one can.

But maybe I'm not alone this time. Maybe the three heirs who challenge my heart can save me?

Archer, Romy and Declan own the academy, the town, and they call me their queen. They promise to protect me, if that is even possible.

But everyone falls. Especially those who have a secret.

And in this town, history repeats itself, creating the same chaos that ruined so many lives only nineteen years before. This time, will it be any different?

Recommend for 18+ readers due to content. This is a full-length book and the first of five books in this series and a reverse harem romance which means the main characters have more than one love interest.

Chapter Thirty-One

"Time keeps escaping me,
Cos I keep sitting under this oak tree.
Thinking of you,
Dreaming us true.
But dreaming is sleeping.
And I will never really find you."

I sing a newly made up song as I finish cleaning up the last of the mess left after one of the residents accidentally knocked over her tea. She is so apologetic, but it isn't her fault–Ethel has Parkinson's and has recently had a stroke. The poor woman is fiercely independent, but she doesn't have the physical capability to do everything she wants. It is becoming a habit of having to clean up after her, but I don't mind.

Ethel is such a sweetheart and has so many stories to tell about her time as a groupie during the Swinging Sixties. I'm not sure how much of what she told me is true–she claimed to have partied with Brian Jones and done LSD with David Bowie before he became famous. But if they weren't, she has an incredible imagination, and I love sitting with her to keep her company. She only has one son, and he lives on the other side of the country, so she rarely has any visitors.

Once I am done, I give the rest of the communal lounge another final check, making sure everything is clean and tidy, before taking the cleaning trolley and locking it up in the store-room. Heading out to the back of the retirement home where I now live, I walk past Leticia, the night nurse.

"Everything all right, Beth?"

"Fine, thanks, Leticia. I've finished up cleaning the lounge, so I'm done for the day. I'm going out now, but if there's anything you need me to do, text me and I'll get straight on it first thing in the morning. I didn't get time to put up that painting for Stan, but I'll make sure I do it tomorrow."

"Thanks, Beth. We got really lucky when you started work here. Not all our caretakers have been as diligent as you. You really care about the residents."

"It's no biggie." I shrug. "They're all really interesting people. I could listen to them talk for hours."

"Keep this up and you could find yourself getting promoted," Leticia tells me. "You've got a bright future here if you want it."

"Thanks." I couldn't help but glow with pride. For the first time in my life, I really felt like I belonged somewhere. This might not be the life my father wanted for me, but it certainly suited me and most importantly, I am safe from him.

Even if it means running from *them*.

As I go into my room, I feel my phone vibrate with a text. Pulling it out, I smile sadly at the photo I am using for my home page. Taken at the first Bomber Derby, Archer is tinkering with his bike, Romy and Declan are standing nearby offering 'help.' The three of them are grinning, but you can see the competitive undertone between them. The photo makes my heart beat fast and long to be near them once again.

Leaving was the right thing to do, to get away from my father, but I miss them.

This photo sums up the dynamic between the three of them.

In different circumstances, the three of them would probably have been best friends, but the politics between their families meant they would never be able to fully trust each other. They were always going to vie for dominance over King Town.

It is strange to think that I love each of them in my own way. I'm not quite *in* love with the boys, but if I hadn't been forced to flee, who knew what could have happened?

The three of them couldn't be more different. Take Romy Navarre. Short for Romeo, he is the school Lothario, fully living up to his name. But beneath the flirting lay a man who is fiercely loyal, with a strong sense of justice.

Declan Dauphin had been dating someone else when we first kissed. If I'd known he had a girlfriend, I'd never have gone there, but I was new to the school and he was just sexy as fuck, not to mention talented. We'd been partnered in music class and we'd been working on a song when I had to flee my father. It was the best song I have ever written, and I wished we'd been able to finish it before I left.

After our kiss, he split up with his girlfriend because he wanted to explore what we had together and I hated my father for denying me the chance of discovering what a relationship with Declan would have been like.

And last but not least, there is Archer Knight. The classic bad boy who stole my heart easier than I was willing to let it go. He was the one my father sent to kidnap me, but I soon forgave him for that. As I learned more about him, I found out what an impossible situation he'd been placed in. My father had some kind of hold over him that meant he had no choice but to do what he was told As I got to know him better, I learned that Archer is sweet, caring, and incredible in many ways.

Any one of them would be the perfect boyfriend, but I am going to have to forget about them. They are my past. I am building a new future, one which doesn't include my father. Which meant I had to say goodbye to the boys too. As many times as I tell myself that, it never sinks in. My heart just says no and demands that I figure out a way to get back to them.

Without letting King Town destroy me.

The text notification shows it is from Katy, my foster mum who has been a rock to me. I know I shouldn't be in contact with her, it's the first place my father would look, but I need someone. Being alone is harder than it seems.

Just checking we're still on for tonight K. x

Of course! Wouldn't miss it for the world. x

Great. What time do you think you'll be here? K. x

Give me half an hour to freshen up. I'll see you soon. x

My room is small, but it has its own en suite bathroom, so I have a quick shower, scrubbing off the grime from a day spent cleaning and fixing things. I throw on my red and white plaid shirt and jeans. Tying up my dyed blonde hair in a ponytail, I look nothing like the Ivy Archaic who'd attended King Academy. Call me twitchy, but after my father tracked me down before, I am always looking over my shoulder to make sure he hasn't found me a second time. I've changed my name, found a job with accommodation and board so I don't have to go out very often, and the only person who knows my new identity is Katy—and even she doesn't know where I live. I have taken every precaution I could think of to stay safe.

But tonight, I am taking a chance and going to visit my foster mum. She has been so supportive since I showed up on her doorstep after running away. She is the one who helped me set up a new identity and helped me plan out my new life. I owe everything I have to her and I fully intend to pay her back as soon as I have earned enough.

My phone beeped again.

Are you on your way yet? x

"Jeez, Katy! Impatient much?" I laugh as I tap out a reply to let her know I am leaving.

I didn't keep the Honda my dad bought me, as much as I wanted to. Not only did I need the money I got from selling it for a fraction of its worth, it's way too distinctive a vehicle. It would have been too easy for my dad to track me down if I still had it.

Instead, I traded down for a little Vespa. It doesn't have the oomph of a proper bike, but it has enough to get me from A to B and I can't bring myself to give up the freedom two wheels give me. There is something about the feel of the wind in your hair, being exposed to the elements instead of cooped up in a car.

My Vespa might not be winning any races anytime soon, but didn't attract any unwanted attention, which is just how I liked it.

As I buzz down the road towards Katy's home, I think about how lucky I am to have a job so close to her. She has no idea I am only in the next town, but I figure that being this close means I am hiding in plain sight. It is far enough away that I wouldn't run into her when I'm out doing errands for the care home, but close enough I could see her every six months or so.

And if I sometimes drive past her house and imagine the two of us sitting down together, gossiping over a cup of tea, I'm not doing any harm, am I?

At last, I arrive at Katy's house. I push my Vespa round the back, looping a chain through the wheels and padlocking it tightly shut. Katy doesn't live in the best of areas and if someone took my Vespa, I would be stuck without transport. The care home didn't pay enough for me to buy a replacement. Much as I love the job, the pay sucks, but at least they provide me with free food and accommodation.

Once my bike is secure, I go through the back door which is unlocked, as always.

"Hello?" I call out, walking into the kitchen. "It's me."

"Hi, Ivy."

I stop dead in my tracks when I see who is sitting at the kitchen table with Katy.

"Romy!"

Chapter Thirty-Two

"*J*vy! It's so good to see you."

Romy moves over to give me a hug, but I push him away, stepping back as my hands shake. What the living fuck is he doing here?

"What's he doing here?" I ask Katy. "Did you tell him where I was?"

"Of course not!"

"Don't blame Katy," Romy gently says, taking a step closer to me once more. Damn he smells nice, whatever aftershave he has on floods my system.

I close my eyes for a moment, pretending that if I keep them closed long enough, he wouldn't be here when I open them. It doesn't work, of course. Romy is here, looking sexier than ever, and my heart hurts because I really did miss him.

"My father has an excellent private investigator on his payroll and we always knew exactly where you were. You can't escape us. You belong to King Town, Ivy."

A million questions fill my head, but the panic over the slight chance my father could find me scares me out of asking any of them. "Which means that if you've found me, so will my father. Thanks for the heads up. I'm out of here."

I turn to leave, my head whirring with plans. Luckily, I've prepped for something like this, so most of my things are kept packed up, ready to run at a moment's notice. It is going to be heartbreaking abandoning my friends at the care home, but it isn't like they couldn't get another caretaker.

Get back to the care home. Grab my stuff. Run.

"Ivy, wait." Romy reaches out and softly grabs my arm, before pulling me against his chest.

I breathlessly stare up at him, remembering what it's like to kiss him. Wondering if he is thinking the same thing I am. The way his eyes seem to darken suggest he does.

"You don't have to leave."

"Of course I do. There's no way I'm going back to my father."

"Things have changed," Romy says. "Sit down and let's talk about it. I can explain everything. If you still want to go after I've finished talking, I'll give you a hundred grand of my own money to get started somewhere else. You could even leave the country. But I don't think you'll do that once you hear what happened."

"Please, Ivy. At least hear the man out." Katy pulls out the spare chair at the table.

Nervously, I sit down. "I suppose it wouldn't hurt to hear what you've got to say."

"Great!" Romy's smile sends a stab of emotion through my heart. I've *really* missed him. I had no idea how much until this moment. "As you can probably imagine, the shit really hit the fan when Archer, Declan and I managed to get back to our families. When Archer's dad saw the state of him, he wanted to start a full-on war in the town. But when we told him how we'd taken him to your father because we knew it was the best way to get him fast treatment and how he'd brought in his very best doctor to take care of him, he calmed down."

"Wait." I frown. "What do you mean, you told him my father looked after you? You *lied* about what happened?"

"It's how things work in King Town," Romy says simply. "We have a real chance of making peace. Believe it or not, our fathers have come to an agreement over you. Because of you. Something that has never happened before."

"But you're going to let him get away with it?" I shake my head in disgust. "I can't believe you people."

"Oh no." Romy reaches out and takes my hand. "We're not going to let him get away with it. I promise. Life in King Town is like a dance. Sometimes you take a few steps forward, sometimes you go back, and sometimes you sidestep. Your father tried to take over. But fuck, so has my dad. So have all our fathers at some point.

"If he'd succeeded in keeping us all hostage, he would have been able to wield his power over our families. He would have made us look weak, positioning himself as the only person strong enough to lead the town. Instead, he played right into our hands. Thanks to you, he's the one who looks weak. Archer, Declan and I all have material on him that he wouldn't want to be made public. How do you think he'd like it if it were public knowledge that his own daughter betrayed him to save the other Houses? It would be a devastating blow to his reputation."

"So you're going to *blackmail* him?" The more I hear, the less I like it.

"Not exactly," Romy replies with a cheeky grin. "For now, your father's secret is safe with us. He's got nothing to give us. It's not like we need money. But knowing how we outsmarted him means he'll be a lot more cautious in the future."

"Or sneaky," I correct him.

"Of course," Romy agrees. "But then sneaky is a way of life in King Town. We're used to dealing with that. Your escape dealt him a devastating blow, but it's time for you to come back."

"I don't think so." I shake my head. "If my father's suffering because I'm gone, let him continue to suffer. I never want to see that place again."

"Don't be like that," Katy interjects. "I know he's done some terrible things, but he's still your family."

"No, he's not." I grimace in disgust. "As far as I'm concerned, my father died when I was a child, just like my mother always said. I don't want anything to do with him. There's no way I'm going back to his house."

"I'm not asking you to," Romy tells me. "I've spoken to my parents, and you're welcome to stay with my family for as long as you like. You can even have your own little apartment so you have some privacy. Your father even agreed to pay you an allowance so you don't have to worry about money."

"That's big of him," I huff. "Thanks, but no thanks. I'm not taking the risk. I've listened to what you had to say, but I'm not changing my mind. I'm never going back to King Town. So if we're done here, I need to go home, collect my things, and hit the road."

"Please don't go." Romy says the words so quietly, I almost didn't hear him.

"What?"

"Look, there are so many reasons why I need you to come back, and a lot of them are personal," he tells me. "I've missed you so much, Ivy. We all have. You're not like the other girls at the Academy. You're not afraid of anything and I fucking love that about you. You know exactly who you are and who you want to be.

"Ivy, we've got plans for King Town, *big* plans which we need your help with. Archer, Declan, and I all want to drag the place into the 21st century, kicking and screaming if we have to. King Town needs to change and you're the only one who can make it happen. Thanks to your influence, the heirs are already starting to work together to make things better for everyone. We would never have done that without you to bring us all together. Do you know how much Archer hates my guts? It's not my fault I'm better looking than he is, but jealousy's a terrible thing."

"Romy…" I try to make my tone a warning, but the way Romy bats his eyelids and plays up to me makes me laugh, spoiling the effect.

"Look, I promise you. Things are different now." He takes my hand between his, holding it against his heart. "You'll be safe at my home. We can get you an armed guard if it makes you feel better. Heck, we can even arm *you* if that's what you want. And if you don't want to take up the offer of an apartment, there's always room in my bed for you…"

"I don't think so." I smile despite myself. Romy is so terribly charming. I can see why he is the one who'd been sent to persuade me to go back to King Town. I can feel myself warming to him, wondering whether there is some truth to what he says.

"What about the others?" I ask. "How do Declan and Archer feel about your offer?"

"We talked things through before I came down. They agree with me—you're safest staying at my place. They want you to move in with me. Fuck, they don't care as long as you come back."

"Is that so?" I arch an eyebrow. "Why do I get the feeling that's not quite how they put it?"

"It's not my fault you have a suspicious mind," Romy shrugs with a smile. "But if you don't believe me, there's one very easy way to find out what Declan and Archer think."

"What?"

"Come back with me and see for yourself."

I bite my lip. If I went back with him, my father would be way too close for comfort. It didn't matter how many promises Romy made me. My father is a psychopath, and I didn't want anything to do with him.

At the same time, I missed the heirs. The damn Kings of the Academy had made me fall for them, and I don't see a way of clawing my heart from their hands. And it sounded like they'd thought through every angle.

"Go with him," Katy urged. "If you don't like what you see,

you can always leave again. Romy's told me everything, and it sounds like you've got unfinished business with your father. If nothing else, look at this as an opportunity to get closure. I really think you should accept Romy's offer. What's the worst that could happen?"

A lot, I thought. Whatever Romy told her, there's no way it's the full story.

Still, gazing at the hopeful expression on both their faces, I can see how much they both care about me and how they think this is the right thing to do.

"Fine," I huff against my better judgement. "I guess I'm going back to King Town."

"Yes!" Romy jumps up and fist pumps the air. "I knew you'd see sense."

"Don't get too excited," I warn. "If I see anything, anything at all, which makes me feel uncomfortable, you won't see me for dust. I won't wait for money and I won't wait for any explanation. I'll be gone, and it doesn't matter how good your private investigator is, you'll never find me again. Okay?"

"Okay." Romy agrees with a smug grin. Asshole.

Katy gets up and gives me a hug. "You're doing the right thing, Ivy," she says. "Now you've all had a chance to calm down, I think you'll find going back to King Town is the best decision you've ever made."

"Maybe."

The truth is, the moment I was forced into King Town, it took my heart. And it won't give it back.

The sad reality is…I'm not sure I want it back now.

Chapter Thirty-Three

he drive back to King Town is quiet, the only sound is the quiet purr of Romy's Mercedes. I am torn between questioning whether I am doing the right thing in going with him and being excited at the thought of seeing Declan and Archer again. To his credit, Romy seems to understand I need some time to think, so he doesn't keep up his usual charm offensive, leaving me to think.

My heartbeat speeds up as we drive into King Town, the glossy and perfect sign not being honest about the sins that lie inside waiting.

"You okay?" Romy glances over, noticing I am getting a little agitated.

"Fine," I lie.

"It's me you're talking to, remember?" Romy gently squeezes my knee. "I know you. You don't have to be strong around me. If I were you, I'd be nervous right now. But I'm here for you. I won't let anyone hurt you. Not your father, not the other Houses. You're under Navarre protection now. You're safe."

"Thanks, Romy."

But what if you're the one I should be afraid of? What if you break my heart?

I wasn't ready to talk to him. Not yet. So I turn away, gazing out of the window at the place I had sworn I would never come back to.

"Here we are," Romy says, as he indicates to turn off the main road. "Home sweet home."

He waves at the security guard sitting in a booth by the electric gate. The guard nods and opens the gate, as Romy slowly pulls forward to go up the drive. We make our way up the winding drive, going for a few more minutes before we finally catch our first sight of Navarre mansion.

I couldn't help myself. My jaw drops.

Romy's house is like something out of *Downton Abbey*. Large and sprawling. From the outside it looks like I could have an entire wing to myself, let alone an apartment.

As he pulls up outside the steps leading up to the house, a butler comes out to greet us. Well, I guess a butler from his clothing.

"Welcome, Miss Archaic." He bows as I stand awkwardly, unsure of how to respond to him. "Are your bags in the car?"

"Ivy will need some overnight things for today, Johnson," Romy tells him. "She'll be going shopping tomorrow. We thought it prudent for her to be here sooner rather than later, so didn't want to go on a detour to collect her stuff. If I am able to find her, it is only a matter of time before her father did, so I wanted to bring her under Navarre protection as quickly as possible."

"Very wise, Master Romy," Johnson says. "In that case, Miss Archaic, let me show you to your suite."

I glance nervously at Romy, who gestures to me to follow Johnson.

"I need to tell my parents you're here," he explains. "Once you've freshened up, Johnson will bring you to meet us, won't you Johnson?"

"Of course, Master Romy."

I don't have much of a choice. I follow the butler inside to be greeted by a lavishly large reception room. There are a number of doors and corridors leading away from the reception area, no doubt creating a rabbit warren of a house I'd quickly lose myself in. This looks even more complicated than my father's house.

Stairs wind down either side of the room, leading up to the first floor. Johnson takes the left hand set, turning right at the top. We walk down a long, straight corridor, going past other corridors leading into the depths of the house until we stop outside some double doors. Johnson pulls a key out of his pocket and unlocks the doors. He pushes them open and steps to one side, gesturing to me to go first.

I shake my head, getting flashbacks to being locked in my room by Isabella.

"Oh, of course. My apologies, Miss Archaic." Johnson hands me the key. "These are your rooms to do with as you will. You are the only person with a key to this door. Master Romy thought you would feel safer if you had control over who can get in. Please, come in."

After a moment's hesitation, I walk into the apartment I will be calling home for the foreseeable future.

"Let me talk you through the features of your suite," Johnson suggests. "If you look on the wall here, you will see an intercom. This will allow you to see outside your room should you have any guests. In addition, you will note that there are a number of locations clearly marked next to different numbers. Simply dial that number and you will be able to speak to someone in those rooms.

"Should you require food to be served in your rooms, call the kitchen and they will prepare whatever you desire, although I should warn you that Mr and Mrs Navarre will expect you to join them for dinner every evening unless you have excused yourself by prior arrangement. In addition, you have your own kitchen, so should you wish to prepare your own food, all you need to do is tell me what supplies you need."

I follow as he walks to one of the doors in my suite. "Your bathroom is through there. You will find everything you need in the cabinet, but should you prefer different products, simply prepare a list and I will arrange for them to be delivered. Your living area is at the end of this hall with the bedroom through the door on the right. You'll find everything you need for an overnight stay in your rooms.

"While Master Romy has said you'll be shopping tomorrow, do please let me know if there's anything I can do to make your time with us more comfortable. If you dial nine-eight on the intercom, you'll be diverted straight to me regardless of where I am in the house. Of course, you are also free to come and go as you will. Should you need any assistance while you are out and about, you'll find intercoms mounted in all the rooms and any member of staff will be more than happy to help you."

I smile at his kind demeanor, and a little surprised he isn't out of breath.

"Finally, although the cleaning staff usually maintain the chambers, out of respect for your situation, they will not enter your rooms unless explicitly invited. If you prefer to clean your rooms yourself, we can provide you with appropriate supplies, as well as bedding to change your bed. If you have any laundry you would like us to deal with, place it outside your door and it will be collected and returned to you the next day. Alternatively, if you'd like the staff to attend to you, simply let us know when is convenient and someone will come and freshen up your room for you."

"Thank you, Johnson."

"I will leave you to get settled in," Johnson says. "When you are ready to meet Mr and Mrs Navarre, I will be waiting right outside to escort you." He backs out of the apartment, closing the doors behind him.

I step forward and immediately lock them. Much as Johnson seemed a sweetheart, he is still in the employ of the Navarres, which means I'll never be able to trust him completely. The same is true for anyone else I encounter while I am living here—

including Romy. Until I have a chance to assess what is really going on, I am going to be on my guard at all times.

Happy the doors are secure behind me, I walk down the corridor and into the sitting room.

Wow. This is so much nicer than the rooms my father had given me. For a start, there are no bars on the windows, which are large, letting plenty of sunlight stream through. There is a large couch and a few beanbags strewn around the room. A large flatscreen TV is hung on the wall opposite the couch. To one side is a large cabinet. Opening it up, I find a state-of-the-art digital sound system. There is a remote control sitting on top of it along with a note which reads *I've programmed in some of your favourite bands. Feel free to download anything else you want to listen to. R x*

I smile at the thoughtful gesture before going to take a look at my new bedroom.

It. Is. *Stunning!*

There is a large four-poster bed made up like a posh hotel. Lying across it is...

"My guitar!"

I run across the room and pick up my baby. Cradling her in my arms, I strum a few chords. She sounds as good as when I'd first played her. I didn't know who was responsible for bringing her here from my father's, but whoever it was they were clearly the best person in the whole wide world. The one thing I'd missed while I was working at the rest home is having a decent guitar to play. I had so many songs to write. Now I might finally get the chance to get them out of my head and down on paper.

Opposite the bed is a set of double doors which open out to a balcony. Carefully putting my guitar down, I go over to take a closer look. The key is in the lock, so I open up the doors and step out to see more of where I am staying.

The Navarre gardens seem to go on forever. I can see gardeners working and when one of them spot me standing on the balcony, he waves. I wave back before turning and going inside again. If I need to make my escape, it would be easy to get away from here.

This is a breath of fresh air compared to the first time I'd come to King Town. Maybe Romy is right. Maybe things are different here.

Now that I've seen my new living quarters, I decide the time has come to meet my hosts. It is getting late, and I'm tired. The sooner I thank Mr and Mrs Navarre for their hospitality, the sooner I can shower and go to bed.

Locking up the balcony doors, I head back out of the suite. Johnson is patiently waiting by the doors for me, just as he says he'd be.

"Is everything to your satisfaction, Miss Archaic?"

"It's lovely, thanks," I nod. "But please. Call me Ivy." I hate any reminder of my relationship to my father.

"I'm afraid that would not be appropriate. But I could call you Miss Ivy if you would prefer?"

"That would work," I smile.

"Then, Miss Ivy, I must ask: are you ready to meet Mr and Mrs Navarre?" Johnson asked.

"Ready as I'll ever be. Also, could you find some bells and string and have them sent to my room?"

"Of course, they will be there when you return," he replies and waves a hand down the corridor. "This way."

Swallowing the nervousness I feel, I make my way to meet one of the Kings of this little town I just tried to escape.

Chapter Thirty-Four

I was right. The Navarre mansion is a veritable rabbit hole. There is no way I was going to be able to find my way around without a map. But, unlike when I was at my father's, Johnson seems keen to help me learn where things are, and he takes the time while we're walking to meet Romy's parents to tell me where corridors lead, what is behind closed doors, and how I could figure out where I was if I got lost.

At last, we come to a halt in front of a solid oak door. Johnson raps smartly on the door before pushing it open.

"Miss Ivy Archaic," he announces, bowing and gesturing for me to go in. As I walk past, he closes the door behind me, going off to do whatever it is butlers do about the house.

I am in what must be the library, going by all the books lining the walls. In the middle of the room is a large coffee table, with a couple of leather sofas and a reclining leather chair around it. Romy and a woman are sitting on one of the sofas. I assume she is his mother.

There is no doubt that the man sitting on the recliner is Romy's father. He looks just like Romy, only older.

"Ivy! How wonderful to meet you at last."Mr Navarre stands

up and comes over to shake my hand, as does the woman. "I'm Ben Navarre and this is my wife, Kate."

"Pleased to meet you Mr Navarre… Mrs Navarre."

"Oh, let's not be so formal. You must call us Ben and Kate."

"Okay… Ben."

Ben sits back down, Kate taking her place next to Romy, who smiles encouragingly at me. "Take a seat, Ivy. Make yourself comfortable. This is your home now."

I sit on the empty sofa so I can see all the Navarres. Maybe I am being paranoid, but it is going to be a long time before I am going to be able to relax. I'm on high alert for anything which doesn't seem right. In my experience, if anything is too good to be true, there is no probably about it. It definitely is.

"Romy told us you were pretty," Kate says first. "I have to say my boy certainly has good taste."

"Er… thanks." I blush. God, this awkward. *Do I tell her she is pretty too?*

"You two make such a cute couple," she continues. "I always hoped he would find someone like you to settle down with."

I frown, tilting my head to one side. "What do you mean, settle down?"

"Romy! Do you mean you didn't tell the poor girl?" Kate lightly swats his shoulder.

"She just got back. Maybe we could wait for a better moment?"

"What is going on?" I ask, narrowing my eyes.

"It's nothing to worry about," Romy replies, glaring at his parents.

"I'll handle this son," says Ben. "Ivy, I understand you're having some problems at home."

You could say that.

"I'm not interested in seeing my father, if that's what you mean," I say.

"Understandable," Ben agrees. "Romy has told us a little about how he treated you.

Much as I would like to say I'm shocked, sadly I'm not.

Little surprises me about Solomon Archaic. He always is…
unscrupulous, shall we say? Romy asked us if we could offer you
sanctuary, and of course we were willing to oblige. For a price."

Here it comes. The catch.

"How much?" I sigh.

"Oh, we don't want your money," Ben laughs. "As you can
see, we have no need for it. No, what we want from you is something that will benefit both our families and make sure your
father can never hurt you again."

"And that is?"

"Isn't it obvious? You and Romy are getting married."

I blink a few times. Of all the things Ben Navarre could have
said, that was the last thing I expected. "We're *what?*"

Romy blushes and looks down at his feet, refusing to look me
in the eye.

"Romy…"

"It really is quite simple, Ivy," Ben interjects. "We are willing
to offer you the full protection of House Navarre. Our resources
are extensive and we can make sure your father does nothing to
hurt you. But you have to see there needs to be some quid pro
quo. A union between our two Houses would be of significant
benefit to both our empires."

"I don't have an empire!" I protest.

"You will when your father is no longer with us," Ben points
out with a smug grin that makes him look too much like Romy.
"And that may well be sooner than you'd expect. A young
woman like you needs to be careful, and combining our forces
would mean that neither the Dauphins nor the Knights would
ever dare take us on. Marry Romy and you will be safe for the
rest of your life."

"That's a very kind offer, but I can take care of myself."

"There seems to be a misunderstanding here." Ben's smile
lost a little of its sparkle.

"I'm not asking if you agree with me. You *will* marry my
son. From all accounts the two of you are highly compatible,
but even if you were not, this would not be the first marriage

for political and financial reasons and I'm sure it won't be the last."

"And what if I say no?"

"If you really insist on being so obstinate, you are of course perfectly free to refuse my son," Ben replies. "However, should that be the case, I would be obliged to place you in the care of my guards who will deliver you to your father forthwith. Whatever he chooses to do with you after that will be entirely up to him. My understanding is that he is most displeased when you ran away. I suspect that any punishment he chooses to mete out will be harsh, albeit fair to ensure you do not leave again.

"So, it is your choice, my dear. Will we be welcoming you to the Navarre family or would you prefer to return to your ever-loving father?"

"When do we go wedding dress shopping?"

***

Ben insisted on toasting our engagement with champagne, and it is late by the time I finally manage to excuse myself. My head spinning, I stumble as I stand up.

Romy rushes over to help me. "Let me take you to your room," he offers, and lowers his voice. "And let me explain. This isn't what it seems."

"No, I'm fine," I say, wanting to get as far away from him as possible.

"Do you know how to get back to your apartment?"

"...No."

"So, let me take you to your room."

"Whatever," I mutter, pushing him away as he tries to take my arm. Realising I'm not interested in any physical contact, he lets me walk ahead, as his parents chuckle over our first 'lover's tiff'.

I wait until I think we are out of earshot of his parents before I turn on him.

"What the hell was that all about?"

"I'm sorry, Ivy. I didn't think they'd bring up the engagement so soon."

"Why wouldn't they? Apparently, that's what it takes to get some sanctuary in this town. Jeez, Romy. Why didn't you mention this sooner? You had plenty of opportunity to let me know the real deal. It's not like we weren't stuck in a car together when you brought me back."

"I didn't think you'd come with me if I told you my dad expected us to get married. Being truthful, you would have run a mile. So stubborn."

"Ya think?" I laugh bitterly. "*This*. This right here is exactly why I didn't want to come back to this town. It's so messed up. It's like something out of the Middle Ages."

"Would it really be so bad being married to me?" Romy asks, taking a step closer. His chest brushes against mine as he runs a finger down my cheek. I shiver, almost closing my eyes from how much I enjoy his touch. "You can't deny there's a spark between us."

"Romy, I'm eighteen. I wasn't planning on even *thinking* about getting married for at least another ten years, if ever. It's not like marriage worked out too well for my parents. We may well have a spark, but-"

"You basically just admitted you have feelings for me," he points out with a happy smirk.

My shoulders slump. "Yes, I have feelings for you. But they're more the 'wonder if he's as good in bed as he says he is' kind of feelings rather than 'oooh. Let me spend the rest of my life with the man who's slept with half the girls in town.' And right now, there's no way I'm ever going to let you see me naked again, so you'd better prepare yourself for many decades of celibacy because if we're married and you cheat on me, we're heading to the divorce courts faster than you can say 'I blackmailed her into marrying me.'"

"Ouch." Romy mimes being shot in the heart, but I'm in no mood to fall for his charms.

"I'm serious, Romy. You have no idea how angry I am with

you right now. I thought you were different, but it turns out you're just as bad as my father. Worse-—at least he doesn't pretend to be a nice guy."

"Don't be like that, Ivy," he counters, lifting my chin with his finger. "You know I'm not that bad. I don't want to trick you. I just want you. Period."

"Still a trick, Romy."

"I can see you're in no mood to be reasonable, so maybe it's best if we talk about this in the morning."

"You think I will want to talk to you in the morning?" I smile sweetly. "Oh, Romy. You really don't know me at all." Burning with anger, I walk away, not giving one shit that I'm going to get lost in this house. No one is tricking me into marrying them.

Not even Romy with all his charms.

Chapter Thirty-Five

I was so angry the night before that I didn't think I'd ever go to sleep, but I must have drifted off at some point, because I am woken up the next morning by the sun streaming through the windows. I'm still wearing the clothes I wore last night and my head feels like a hundred tiny little people are hammering at my skull. I don't know what was in the champagne I'd had last night, but whatever it was, I am paying for it now.

Dragging myself into the bathroom, I turn on the shower, letting the water warm a little before stepping in.

"Oh my god," I practically moan as powerful jets of water massaged my aching body. This certainly beat the trickle of water I'd had to make do with when I was living in the care home. The luxurious shower helps chase away some of the fog from my mind as I think about how crazy the past twenty-four hours have been.

One thing is for sure. There is no way I am marrying Romy. Sure, I'd play along with his father's little game for as long as it suited me, but I would be long gone before the time came to walk down the aisle.

Yet again, I find myself planning my escape from King Town.

And yet again, my heart hurts at the thought of leaving Romy or Archer or Declan. I don't even know if Declan or Archer want to see me again. They could have moved on, got lost in the secrets of this place, but I hope they didn't. A part of me just wants to see them again.

The same part of me that doesn't question the feelings I have for three guys.

I lose track of how long I spend in the shower, loving the endless supply of hot water. Eventually I know I have to get out though. Much as I am tempted to lock myself in my room and never come out again, Romy said we are going to go shopping and I intended to milk his father's card for everything I could get today. If they want to keep me here and marry me off to their son, I'm not going to make it cheap. A part of me feels a little guilty, but then again, trapped people do insane things.

And I'm so tired of being trapped.

When exactly do I escape this hell town?

Wrapping myself in the softest, largest towel I'd ever seen, I go to the walk-in wardrobe to see if there are any fresh clothes for me to wear. Although most of the drawers are empty, I find some brand-new underwear in my size, as well as some jeans and a few T-shirts. None of them are very exciting, and I prefer black to the reds and blues that have been left out for me, but it is better than nothing. I can pick out some things which are more my style later today.

Picking up my old clothes, it feels wrong leaving them for someone else to clean, so I put them on a chair in my bedroom. I decide to ask Johnson where the laundry room is and do it myself once Romy and I are back from our shopping spree.

A strange buzzing sound catches my attention. For a moment, I wonder whether someone has messed with the ring-tone on my phone, but then realise it's the intercom. Going to answer, Romy's face comes up on the screen.

Damn, he looks more sexy than yesterday.

"Morning, Ivy. How are you feeling today?"

"I'm still mad at you, if that's what you're asking."

"Well hopefully you'll give me a chance to redeem myself," he suggests. "You still happy to go shopping with me?"

"What–and miss out on the chance of maxing out your daddy's credit card? I wouldn't miss it for the world."

"Good," Romy smiles, although I think he thinks I'm joking. The prince of this castle hasn't seen anything yet. I can shop like a princess if I need to prove a point. "Have you had breakfast yet? Do you want me to get the cook to fix something for you?"

The thought of food made my stomach lurch. I wasn't great at eating when I got up at the best of times, but when I am hungover, the last thing I want to do is have breakfast.

"Can we get something while we're out?" I ask.

"Of course. Anything you want. Do you need me to come and get you or can you find your way to the front of the house?"

"I'll be fine. I'll meet you in a few minutes."

I might have been drunk last night, but I still remember that all I have to do is head straight down the corridor leading away from my room and I'd eventually hit the stairs down to the entrance. It isn't long before I am outside where Romy is leaning against his Mercedes waiting for me.

"You look good," he says when I'm closer, his eyes running over me.

"Save it." I hold up a hand for him to talk to. "I'm not inter-ested in your sweet talk. You can speak when you're spoken to, otherwise I don't want to hear a word. You had your chance when you decided not to tell me about our engagement. You kept quiet then, so you can keep quiet now."

"Whatever you say." Romy mimes zipping his mouth shut, locking it, and throwing away the key.

Dammit, he is too charming for his own good.

"Ugh." I shake my head, trying to hide the fact that it is impossible for me to stay mad with him for long. He is right–we do have a spark. There is something about him that melts my heart, so even though it is going to take me a long time to forgive him—if I ever did—I still want to feel his lips against mine, run my hands down that incredible body, lose myself in him...

"Ivy?"

"What?" I shake my head to snap out of it.

"I said, do you mind if we do a brief detour before we head to the mall?" Romy asks. "I've got an errand I need to run."

"Do what you like," I reply, getting into the passenger side.

"Did you sleep all right?" Romy went on, starting the engine and pulling away from the house. "I hated the thought of you sleeping on your own when I was so close. I don't like fighting with you, Ivy. I-"

"Romy?"

"Yes?"

"I don't want to talk about this right now."

"Alright. But we *are* having this conversation at some point." He bit his lip to stay quiet, and I stifled a grin, turning away so he wouldn't see my face.

Although I'm not familiar with this part of town, I have a pretty good idea about which direction the mall is and that's not where we were going.

In fact, I'd bet good money we were heading in the opposite direction.

"Where are we going, Romy?"

"I thought you didn't want me to talk?"

"Don't be a smart ass."

"You'll see," came the enigmatic reply. "Anyway, we're very nearly there. You might as well sit back and enjoy the ride."

"Haven't you learned anything from last night? I don't like not being told what's going on. Where are you taking me?"

"Almost there... almost there... and here we are!" Romy pulled into the car park of a quaint little cottage with a sign over the door that simply says *Weaver's*. Parking in a space close to the entrance, Romy says to me, "This place makes one of the best cooked breakfasts you'll ever have. I figured you're going to need the energy for a long day of shopping, and you can't do better than some delicious crispy bacon, cooked to perfection."

As we walk into the café, I see something which makes me come to a halt, even though the sight brings my mood skyrocketing to exhilarated.

My mouth goes dry as my heart beats happily in my chest as I stare at them. Archer looks too good as he sits on a stool, his leather jacket covered arms resting on the sides of his seat. Tight jeans, navy tee-shirt and heavy boots finish off his bad boy look that has me completely lost in him for a moment.

But my gaze drifts to Declan at his side, looking his exact opposite in style and looks. The blonde, pretty boy has black trousers and a clearly designer white shirt on, tucked into the trousers. His sleeves are rolled up, making him look incredible in so many ways. I clear my throat as he runs a hand through his hair and stands up.

"Oh yeah," Romy says. "Archer and Declan both thought this was a good place to meet."

I run over to where Archer and Declan are sitting, falling into their arms in a crazy, three-way hug. "You guys! Why didn't you tell me they were going to be here, Romy?"

"What–and miss that look on your face?" Romy leaves me to sit down with the other two as he heads over to the corner of the counter to order food for us.

"How have you been?" I ask. "It feels like forever since I saw you." *And I've thought of both at least twenty times a day.*

"Seven months, two weeks and four days," Declan grumbles. "Not that I'm keeping track or anything like that."

We stare at each other, a thousand words going unsaid. I pull my gaze to Archer, who hasn't answered me.

"And how are you healing, Archer? Did my father's doctor do a good job at least?" I ask as I take a seat and they both sit back down in theirs.

Archer's leg presses against mine, and I almost gasp from the contact. "He did." Archer pulls the neck of his shirt to one side to reveal an impressive scar. "I've got full mobility back in my arm, although it still aches when the weather's about to change.

The one thing I'll say for your father is that he always did know how to find good help."

"So, am I forgiven for keeping this little secret?" Romy asks, coming to sit in the empty chair next to me, his arm wrapping around the back. It doesn't escape my notice when Archer and Declan both look at his arm like they want to chop it off.

"*This* one, yes," I say. "But that doesn't excuse you for our engagement."

"Your engagement?" Archer tightly asks.

"Wanna explain this one, Romeo?" Declan growls.

"Oh, didn't Romy tell you?" I say lightly. "It's the condition for looking after me. His father is insisting we get married, otherwise he's sending me straight back to my father."

"That is not fucking happening," Archer snaps, leaning across the table into Romy's face. "I will not let you marry my girl. Asshole."

"Your girl? Huh, funny that," Romy replies with a cocky smile.

"Enough!" Declan shouts, grabbing Archer's jacket and roughly pulling him back into his seat.

I glance around the room, noticing how we are being watched by everyone. It takes a few moments for the room to pick up its chatter once again.

Romy's confident smile loses a little of its brightness as Archer looks like he is about to kill him—literally.

"I want Ivy safe. That's all I care about, and I assume you both want the same." He turns to me. "I know you thought you had done a good job of flying under the radar, but you should never have stayed in touch with Katy, let alone live so close to her.

"I honestly believe the only reason your dad didn't get to you before I did is because he's been fixated on control after his failed coup attempt. I had to get you out of there before he started looking. The only way my dad would allow an Archaic to stay with us is if it benefited him. I tried to argue with him, but once Dad's got an idea in his mind, there's no shifting it. He can be really stubborn. I figured the important thing is to make sure you were safe. We could work out the details later."

"Details like the colour my bouquet should be?" I sarcastically ask.

"Well, if you want me to be the best man, you can forget about it," Declan snaps. "You can't expect Ivy to swap one controlling father for another. Grow some balls and stand up to your Dad for once. Oh, but you wouldn't do that. Can't risk losing Daddy's money, can we?"

"You should talk," Romy counters. "How many expensive guitars does one man need? And when are you going to realise, it doesn't matter how many fast bikes you have, you're not a good enough driver to ever win against me or Archer? But no. You have to get your father to shell out for a new one after every race you lose because you kid yourself that if you can just find the right vehicle, you'll miraculously be able to ride it. Face it. You're just jealous I got to Ivy first. Don't pretend you wouldn't have done exactly the same thing in my position."

"I know I wouldn't," Archer shouts. There goes the chatter in the room again. "I've seen first-hand the way Ivy's father treated her. She deserves better and if you cared about her the way you claim to, you'd have come up with some other way of making sure she is safe."

"You can move in with me," Declan offers me. "We've got a little guesthouse we save for visitors. It's completely private, out of the way. Nobody would know you were there. You can move in this afternoon. My parents are never home, therefore no one would make you do anything."

"That would be-"

"No, she can't." Romy interrupts before I could accept Declan's offer. "Do I need to remind you guys about what Solomon Archaic did to Archer? What he is planning to do to us? He is willing to kill us if he needs, and he won't lose any sleep over it. He's happy to take this town into an out-and-out war. We just have to give him the slightest excuse and he'll be there." He pauses to catch his breath.

I look at him with my mouth agape. Snapping my jaw closed, I am about to say...something...anything when he continues.

"Ivy, I'm sorry I didn't talk to you about it, but being engaged to me makes it less likely your father will try anything. He's not going to take on House Navarre while his reputation is still recovering. You go and stay in an isolated house and he could snatch you back at any time. Tell me I'm wrong, Archer. Tell me you wouldn't have been able to get to her if she is living alone in this town."

"You're not wrong," Archer concedes reluctantly.

"So she doesn't stay in the guesthouse," Declan nods. "We'll make room for her in the main house."

"And your parents would be happy to do that, would they? Protect an Archaic without getting anything in return?" Archer asks. "They might not be there but they must check in with the staff. The staff are never going to keep that secret."

"Well..." Declan's voice trails off uncomfortably.

"Exactly. For all you know, they would have demanded something even worse from her. And there's no way Archer's family would look after her, not when there's a feud between the two Houses. Ivy would be in even more danger staying with the Knights. No, I know it's not ideal, but Ivy's safest with me as my fiancé."

"Fine, but I don't fucking like it," Declan growls. "And if you marry my girl, I will kill you."

I shiver as I meet Declan's eyes. I don't doubt him, not one little bit.

Now that Romy has laid things out like that, I hate to admit he has a point. But that doesn't mean I am going to go through with his father's crazy plan. Let him think he's won my heart for now. It seems like everyone is out for themselves in King Town. It's about time I start playing them at their own game.

Romy had ordered food for everyone and the waitress brings over our breakfast not long after, looking terrified of us all. I try to smile at her but it only makes her look more nervous and the plates shake in her hands. The conversation lulls as we all focus on our food. Romy is right—the bacon is the best I'd ever had, and it really takes the edge off my hangover.

It isn't until I begin eating that I realise I haven't had anything since lunch yesterday and I'm starving. I wolf down my food, pushing my empty plate away long before any of the boys.

"So, what's the plan for the rest of the day?" I ask. "Are the four of us going shopping? I can't imagine you'd all enjoy sitting around changing rooms while I try on endless outfits."

"Oh, I don't know," Declan replies, a flirtatious smile playing about his lips. "I can see there being a certain charm about seeing you take your clothes off…"

"You don't actually watch me change." I roll my eyes, laughing. "But I've got a lot of Romy's Dad's money to spend and I intend to max out at least one of his credit cards. If I'm marrying into the family, I'll make darned sure they pay for it."

"Good for you." Archer nods his approval with a classic bad boy smirk. "But much as I'd love to come along with you, I've got a few things I need to do. Maybe you could come over to my place when you're free?"

"I don't know." I answer, glancing at Romy and see nothing but rage shimmering in his eyes. I imagine he thinks he is hiding it well. He isn't. When an heir is angry, the whole of King Town can feel it. And me? I feel it in my heart. "Will my fiancé let me?"

"You're not a prisoner," he tells me. "You can go wherever you like, see whoever you want. But I would recommend you tell either me or my Dad where you are, just so we can make sure you're properly protected. But don't worry—the guards are very discrete. You won't even know they're there unless you need them."

"That's nice," I say. However you dress it up, it still sounds to me like I am a prisoner in everything but name.

"And we've still got a song to finish," Declan reminds me. "Unless you've dropped out of the Academy?"

"Dad wants her to finish her education," Romy says before I have a chance to answer. "He's already spoken to Pilkington. She can come back to the Academy and it's her choice whether she repeats a year or has extra tutoring to stay in our year."

"What if I don't want to go back at all?"

"Not an option," Romy says, shrugging apologetically. "Like I said, Dad wants you to finish your studies. He says it's important that the mother of the next generation of Navarres has brains as well as beauty."

"Well, in that case, I'll take the tutors," I say. "I'm not spending a day longer at that place than I have to."

"Which means we have to finish our song," Declan says, not giving up. And I don't want him to. "You should come over to mine and we can work on it together. I did try to finish it without you, but it wouldn't come together. It really needs your brilliance to make it work. Maybe you could come over tomorrow?"

"I'd love to," I say.

"Okay, well if you've finished making plans to see everyone except me, maybe we can get on with our shopping." Romy all but snaps.

I place my hand on his under the table without thinking about it.

Romy is used to clicking his fingers and having girls flocking to him and I imagine he doesn't know what to do with me, but I still don't want to see him hurt. I just can't.

I'm born and bred for King Town, for an heir, and I have three to choose from.

But what happens if I just can't choose?

Will I start a war?

Chapter Thirty-Six

*A*fter we say our goodbyes, Archer and Declan leave me and Romy to our shopping. He takes me back to the same place Isabella had taken me to, and I had a lot of fun taking outfits I had no intention of buying into the changing rooms, just because I wanted to make Romy sit around waiting for me.

To his credit, he is very patient and even when I deliberately put on clothes I knew would look awful; he is wonderfully complimentary, finding something nice to say about everything.

Much as I wanted to spend his father's money, when it came to actually buying anything, I really struggled. Having grown up bouncing from one foster home to another, it felt wrong to spend money for the sake of it, so in the end I found myself picking out a few things I really needed without going overboard and putting the rest back.

However, when it comes to finding a ring, Romy insists on making sure I have something special.

"Everyone needs to look at you and know you're engaged to a Navarre," he tells me. "This ring symbolises our two Houses coming together for a brighter future."

"Not to mention you want everyone to know I belong to you, right?"

"You look at Archer and Declan like they are yours and they look at you like you are theirs. I don't want to share you," Romy says unapologetically, making my cheeks redden. "I want you to know I'm not going to forbid you from seeing them. We're all heirs, and it's important to maintain ties between the Houses. But you're my fiancée and they need to respect that. A ring sends out a signal to everyone that you're off the market. Besides, my father will expect you to have something which shows off the Navarre fortune. He'd be very disappointed if you didn't come home with something appropriately impressive on your ring finger."

I try not to wince when I see the price tags on the engagement rings Romy picks out for me to choose from. Reminding myself that this is an investment in my escape plan, I decide to go for a cluster of diamonds around a black sapphire. Set in a platinum band, it will surely broadcast to the world I am an engaged woman.

After he paid for it, Romy insists on placing it on my hand and it all feels so wrong.

"What—you're not going to propose to me in some romantic set up to make it all official?" I jokingly ask.

"Do you want me to?" Romy looks surprised.

"Believe it or not, I always thought the man I was going to spend the rest of my life with would care enough to plan a beautiful proposal," I honestly say. I didn't spend all my childhood thinking about it, but a good amount of my childhood I pretended to be a bride and dreamed of my fairy-tale ending. I dreamed of princes and kings. Knights and jokers. And somehow the joker of the bunch is the one I'm engaged to.

Even though he is the joker of the story, he is so much more than it seems. "Even if it is just taking me out to dinner and bringing the ring out with dessert, I figured he'd take the time to make me feel wanted."

"Why Ivy Archaic. I do believe you're quite the romantic at

heart," Romy teases, but honestly looks surprised. "I had no idea."

"There's a lot you don't know about me," I remind him. "Maybe if you knew me better, you wouldn't be so keen to rush me down the aisle."

"I don't think there's anything I could learn about you that would put me off marrying you," Romy tells me. "In fact, I'm looking forward to a lifetime of learning all about you. You strike me as the kind of woman who's always going to surprise me, and that sounds like the perfect recipe for a successful marriage if you ask me."

"Hmm." Part of me hoped Romy would see this marriage as being as much of a game as I did, but by the sound of it he is actually taking it seriously. I'll have to tread carefully over the coming months while I figure out how to get myself out of this mess. I might not be in love with Romy, but I like him a lot. The last thing I want to do is hurt him.

I fiddle with the ring on my finger, which feels like it shouldn't be there.

"All right. Take it off," Romy says.

"What?"

"Take it off," he insists. "You want a romantic proposal, you're going to get one. You're right. If this is going to work, we need to start as we mean to go on. I'm going to spend the rest of my life treating you like the queen you are, which means a proper proposal."

Oddly, my heart beats hard in my chest, and I find myself smiling. "What are you going to do?"

Romy taps the side of his nose. "That would be telling. Leave it with me. I think you're going to be pleasantly surprised."

"MASTER ROMY, Miss Ivy. Mr Navarre wishes to see you in his study immediately," Johnson says, coming out to greet us as we arrive back at Romy's house. I refuse to think of it as my home, even temporarily. I'm not planning on spending a second more here than I have to.

"I'll just take my bags up to my room, then I'll go see him," I say.

"No need, Miss Ivy. I'll have them brought up for you," Johnson kindly tells me. "Mr Navarre is most insistent you were to go see him without delay."

"Fine. Thank you," I sigh.

Romy takes my hand as we walk along the long corridor that led to Ben Navarre's study. My instinct is to pull away, but I don't, knowing I am going to have to keep up this charade for a while yet.

Romy gives my hand a reassuring squeeze before knocking on his father's door.

"Come!" Ben looks up from his computer, smiling as he sees us coming towards him. "There's my favourite young couple," he says. "I trust you now have a wardrobe suitable for a Navarre bride?"

"I've got what I need," I say.

"Excellent." Ben nods his approval. "Make sure you wear something suitably striking when you go to dinner with your father this evening."

"Dinner? With my father? This evening?" My blood runs cold and my stomach lurches at the thought of being in the same room as that man, let alone having dinner with him.

"Yes. While I can appreciate you may not wish to see your father at this moment in time, it is important he sees that you're healthy and being taken care of. He cares about you, Ivy."

"Ha!" I choke back a laugh. "That man cares about no one but himself."

"He may not have a conventional way of showing affection, but trust me. You are very important to him."

Yeah, as a bargaining chip in the sick games people play in this town.

"Plus, of course, if he doesn't see that you are here of your own free will and happily engaged to Romy, your father would be perfectly entitled to see your residency as an act of aggression and take appropriate retaliatory action."

"What?"

"Your dad could take revenge on us in the name of rescuing you," Romy translates.

"Yes, I understood that, thanks. But my father lost any rights over me the moment he made me prisoner in his house and attacked R-"

Romy squeezes my hand, warning me to keep my mouth shut.

"It's all about appearances in this town," he reminds me, his eyes drifting to his son. "As long as everything looks okay, it is, regardless of what's really going on."

"You'll be heartened to hear that Romy sought your father's approval before agreeing to marry you," Ben says. "As soon as we discovered your whereabouts, we put everything in place for you to enjoy Navarre protection. Remember—you owe us for putting a roof over your head. Once you have met with your father, you won't ever have to see him again unless you choose to. You have my word."

"So if I meet him tonight, that's it?" I want to be sure before I say yes.

"That's it," Ben nods.

"Okay. But I'm not going to his house. I'm not risking him doing anything. We go for dinner in a crowded restaurant and I want Romy with me."

"I will book two tables, one for you and one for Romy," Ben partly agrees. "Your father is very clear that he wanted time alone with you, but he cannot complain if Romy happens to choose to eat in the same place. In addition, I'll have guards stationed about the place, so if your father does try something foolish, he'll regret it. We're here to protect you, Ivy. Nothing bad is going to happen."

I am sure Ben means what he says, but my father is bad to the bone. Wherever he goes, trouble follows.

"Now, what type of food would you like? Italian? Chinese? Mexican?"

"Surprise me." Something told me I won't have much of an appetite if I am dining with my father.

I SPEND the rest of the day a nervous mess, dreading the confrontation with my father after escaping his mansion. I have a bath to relax, but it's impossible. With nothing to do but lie in the water, my mind is free to run through countless scenarios of what might happen tonight, none of them good.

Going through my new purchases a little later, I am glad I'd listened to Romy when he suggested I buy a couple of power suits for House business meetings. As Romy's fiancée and representative of House Archaic, it is expected for me to be involved in plans and discussions about the future of the town and how we would work together as we move forward.

Now it seems the most sensible thing to wear to send out a signal to my father I am not to be messed with.

I decide to put on a black trouser suit with a white blouse. The cut of the jacket emphasized my waist, flattering my figure without being revealing. Romy had thought of everything during our trip, including a brand-new pair of high-heeled Jimmy Choos to go with the suit, the extra height making me feel strong and powerful.

Putting the finishing touches to my makeup, the bright red lipstick I'd selected made me look like I was out for blood. My father isn't going to know what hit him.

The intercom buzzed with a message from Romy asking if I'm ready yet.

"I'll be right down." I take one final look at myself in the mirror.

Not bad, Ivy. Not bad.

As I strut out to Romy's Mercedes, he wolf whistles and makes me smile. "Wow, Ivy. I loved that on you when you tried it on, but the way you've put it all together." He shakes his head admiringly. "I'm one lucky guy."

"Yes, you are." I get into the passenger seat and Romy takes off.I stare out of the window, nervously nibbling at a hangnail.

"You okay?" Romy reaches over and gives my thigh a gentle squeeze. "It'll be alright, you know. I'll be right there, and so will the guards. If your father tries to do anything, anything at all, we'll put him down, but he won't. He's not stupid."

"It's not that." I sigh. "It's just that…"

"What?"

"This is going to be the first time my father and I have sat down as civilised human beings to have dinner together. What will we even talk about? I don't know the man and I don't want to know him. Can't we pretend I've got a migraine or something?"

"We *can*," Romy says slowly.

"Let's do that then."

"If you really want, I'll turn the car round right now," Romy replies. "But if you miss this dinner, it'll cause more problems than it would solve."

"Why?"

"Your father would automatically assume you're not really unwell."

"And he'd be right."

"But he would argue that it's a Navarre plot to keep you away from him."

"That's crazy! It should be obvious I don't want to see him."

"Maybe." Romy nods. "But the way things work in this town, that doesn't matter. You should have figured that out by now. It's all about how you can spin it and, in this instance, your father could use your failure to show up for dinner to launch an offensive against us and insist on us handing you over to his custody. It could get very nasty very quickly. He'll withdraw his consent for our marriage."

"So what if he does? It's not like his opinion matters. If he is going to be like that, I'd marry you as soon as we can arrange it. Heck, we could elope."

"Much as I'd love to do that, there's a number of reasons why it wouldn't work," Romy explains patiently. "Tradition matters in this town. A wedding like ours is a chance to make a political statement and consolidate our Houses' power. But if your father isn't supportive, he could disown you and name a new heir."

"I thought the whole point of kidnapping me in the first place is because I am the only true heir."

"And you are," Romy agrees. "And that is why he brought you here. But if you don't play by the rules, your father would be perfectly entitled to decide you no longer hold any value for him and fall back on Plan B. Choosing a new heir who isn't related to him isn't ideal, but it's an option. If he does that, it puts you in danger. You're no longer useful to House Navarre, so my father would want to get rid of you."

"So we get divorced. So what?"

"No, Ivy." Romy briefly takes his eyes off the road to look me straight in the eye.

"He'd want to *get rid of you*. Permanently."

"Oh." I gulp.

"I will protect you, but there's only so much I'd be able to do against the might of my father's empire. Honestly, I think we would both end up dead," Romy explains. "And while I'm not the only potential Navarre heir, my father has invested a lot in grooming me to succeed him. If we were to run away together to escape our families, he'd hunt us down. We'd spend the rest of our lives looking over our shoulders, and that's no way to live."

"You people are so messed up." I go back to looking out of the window. There is nothing left to say.

"We're here," Romy finally announces, pulling up outside Gazpacho's, a Spanish restaurant. "What do you want me to do? I can take you home if you really want."

"What—you'd deal with all the backlash if I stood my

father up?"

"Of course." Romy smiles. "I care about you, Ivy. If that's what you really want to do, I'll take you back right now. I will fight for you, protect you. Die for you, if that is what is needed. I knew the second you kissed me that you were the first girl I would let myself fall for. I'm here and not leaving."

Oh my god, how am I meant to walk away from him when he tells me things like this?

"No." I sigh. "We're here now. I might as well get it over and done with."Impulsively, I lean forward and kiss Romy. Taken by surprise, it takes him a moment to react, but his natural instincts take over and he kisses me back, gently nibbling at my lower lip as I feel so much more than I can explain. Kissing Romy is seductive and natural all at the same time. He is addictive, and I forgot how good it was to be in his arms.

"Crap, my lipstick!" I laugh, pulling away to see a red smear across Romy's mouth. I run my finger over his lips to wipe away the lipstick, and Romy turns his head to take it into his mouth. Teasing my fingertip with his tongue, I gasp at the sudden sensation.

"Maybe you could come to my room for a nightcap after dinner?" he suggests when he finally lets me go.

"Mm-hmm." I was a little too aroused to be able to speak. It's funny how such a simple little gesture could have such a powerful effect on me. I can't deny the sexual chemistry I share with Romy. He sure knows how to make a girl feel good.

"You might want to touch up your makeup," Romy suggests.

I pull out a mirror from my bag and see he managed to kiss away a lot of my lipstick. Quickly, I repair the damage.

"Gorgeous," Romy says, as I look to him for approval. "Come on. The sooner you finish your meal, the sooner we can be alone together."

"I like the sound of that."

I really did.

Romy takes my hand and we walk into the restaurant together. I see my father straight away, sitting on his own at a table laid for two towards the back of the room where we would have some privacy.

"I'll leave the two of you to it," murmurs Romy, letting go of my hand and giving me a gentle nudge of encouragement. "Remember—I'm right here if you need me."

My father stands up when he sees me approaching, spreading his arms wide to hug me.

"Ivy!" he smiles. "You have no idea how good it is to see you, my child. I've been so worried about you. When I heard you were staying with the Navarres, I had to see for myself that you were okay. You are okay, aren't you? They're looking after you properly?"

"Yep." *No thanks to you.*

My father pulls out a chair for me and waits for me to sit before going back to his seat.

"I've already ordered for us so we don't waste time," he tells me, clicking his fingers to summon a waiter.

"Of course you have," I say. Not sure why I expected anything else.

The waiter pours me a generous glass of red wine, before topping up my father's drink and leaving the rest of the bottle behind for us to help ourselves.

"Your food will be brought out shortly," he says, bowing to my father before leaving us alone again.

"A toast." My father raises his glass. "To my beautiful little girl who is becoming an even more beautiful woman."

I say nothing as I lift my glass to meet his and take a little sip of wine. Much as I want the comfort of alcohol to numb our encounter, I need to keep a clear head tonight.

"I can't believe this is the first time I've sat down to a proper, grown-up meal with my daughter," my father says. It is weird. He is acting as though we were a normal father and daughter instead of him being a psychopath who'd abused and manipulated me.

"Well, make the most of it," I warn him. "It's not like we're going to make a habit of this."

"We'll see." My father smiles enigmatically as our food arrives.

"You'll be enjoying a grass fed, 28-day aged ribeye," the waiter tells me. "Your father has also selected some of our most popular tapas, including pan fried octopus and confit pork with a chipotle mayonnaise and fresh herbs grown in our very own garden. Should you desire anything else, please let me know and it will be my pleasure to serve you."

"Yes, it will," my father says. "But she'll be fine."

"Of course, sir." The waiter bows as he leaves again and I shake my head. No wonder my father is such a jerk with so many people brown nosing him.

"Eat, eat." My father gestures with his knife and fork before he tucks into his ribeye.

I did as I was told and cut a small piece of meat. My appetite has completely deserted me, which is a shame. The food really did smell good and is cooked to perfection, clearly prepared by a skilled chef.

"I must admit I am delighted to hear you'd been working in a care home," my father tells me. "That sense of compassion will stand you in good stead when you are ruling the House."

"What–like yours does?" I snort. "No, wait. You don't even know what compassion means."

My father shrugs his shoulders, seemingly good-natured in the face of my hostility.

"I do what is appropriate in any given situation," he says. "It took a great deal of compassion to let those three boys live when I had them in my control. It is only my love for you that enabled me to be so restrained."

I want to throw my wine at his smug face. He thinks he knows what restraint is? It is nothing compared to what I am going through right now. "That is kind of you."

"Indeed." My father nods, my sarcasm seemingly going over his head. "And it turned out to be the right choice. When young Navarre came to me and requested your hand in marriage, I immediately saw what an opportunity it is for both of us to consolidate our position in this town. Had I executed the Navarre heir, it would have closed a window of opportunity which will prove very lucrative for all of us. I trust his family are treating you in a manner befitting your station?"

"They're treating me better than you ever did, if that's what you're asking," I reply. "I have my own apartment within the mansion, but there are no bars on the windows and I have the only key to the door."

"Is that right?" My father chuckles. "If you believe that, you're more naïve than I thought. Any freedoms you have are nothing but an illusion. Mark my words, you're a prisoner of the Navarres as much as you were mine, only you don't have a father's love to protect you there. You might want to consider coming back home."

"Might I?" I raise an eyebrow. "I don't think so. I'm staying where I am."

"Well, I'm sure young Romeo Navarre has something to do with that," says my father. "I must admit, I was a little surprised when he came to ask for your hand. Of all the young men in town, I thought you would have gone for someone who didn't have such a wandering eye."

"Like Archer, you mean?"

My father shakes his head. "That boy disappointed me," he clicks his tongue. "I had high hopes for him, but after a while in my employ, it became clear he didn't have what it takes to be a leader. He's more of a follower."

"If you say so."

"Still, I can see plenty of advantages in you becoming a Navarre," my father says. "Although I must insist you keep the Archaic name. It would undermine your authority to be a Navarre when the time comes for you to take over from me."

"Insist all you like," I say. "I'll make up my own mind when it comes to the name I go by. And I rather like the idea of having a name, any name, that isn't yours."

My father bursts into fits of raucous laughter. "That's my little spitfire. I've always loved your attitude. We can figure out those details later. For now, you have my permission to marry the Navarre boy."

"For now?"

"Permission granted can always be taken away." My father leans back nonchalantly. "You still have a lot to learn when it comes to playing the games in this town. It suits me to have you engaged for the moment. Should that change, you *will* break it off or I cannot be held responsible for the consequences."

"Of course you can't." This is so typical of him. "Nothing's ever your fault, is it?"

"I've made mistakes in my time." My father sighs heavily. "I wish I had never let your mother get away from me."

Right. Because you wanted to continue to control and dominate her.

"I wish I'd had a more active role in your upbringing, but I wanted to respect your mother's wishes that I keep my distance. I wish I'd come back for you before she died. I hate the idea of her being alone those final few months without my support. I could have given her the best possible medical care, but she refused to accept my help."

I wonder why?

"But all those things are in the past and I'm not a believer in dwelling on things I can't change," my father continues. "I keep my focus firmly on the future and I have every faith that you and I will achieve great things together. Now please, Ivy. Try the octopus. It truly is delicious."

I do as I am told. It is easier that way.

The rest of the meal passes fairly uneventfully. My father spends the whole time talking about himself, seemingly not caring about my life. Part of me is grateful—it means I don't have to come up with any lies to avoid telling him anything he might use against me later. But part of me wishes he cared about me, just a little bit.

Most fathers would be proud to see their daughter get engaged, want to plan the wedding with them. Something tells me that if I let my father get involved with mine, it would become the Solomon show with him dictating everything and ignoring what I wanted. Still, it would have been nice for him to show some interest.

As the waiter clears away our plates, he asks if we want to see the dessert menu.

"No," says my father, before I had a chance to even think about it. "Ivy needs to watch her figure. She's got a designer wedding dress to fit into. Just the bill will be fine."

"Very good, sir." The waiter performs another one of his obsequious bows, leaving to fetch the bill.

"What's that face for?" my father asks as I scowl. Yet again, he's made my decision for me. "Don't tell me you actually wanted more food? Good thing I turned it down then. You need to be looking your best when you walk down the aisle. You're representing House Archaic, remember."

"Yep." I stand up, ready to go.

Seeing me move, Romy comes over to join us. "Everything all right, Ivy?"

"Why wouldn't it be?" my father asks. "My daughter is back where she belongs. But since you're here, I might as well warn you that if anything were to happen to her while in your care, anything at all, you will face the wrath of House Archaic. I will burn this town to the ground if that's what it takes. Don't you dare hurt my daughter."

"I wouldn't dream of it," Romy says smoothly, putting his arm around me and not fearing my father one bit. I kinda like that he protects me and doesn't seem to fear a man who kidnapped him and could have killed him not that long ago. "I love Ivy and I plan on spending the rest of my life putting her happiness first. You can trust me."

"We'll see."

"Anyway, Dad, we've got to go," I say. "We told Romy's parents we wouldn't be late back. It was good to catch up."

"Yes, it was." My father stands up and comes to hug me goodbye. Kissing me on both cheeks, he whispers so Romy wouldn't hear. "Be on your guard at all times. You can't trust the Navarres."

Chapter Thirty-Seven

"That man!" I stomp across the carpark, steam practically coming out of my ears. "I hate him *so* much!"

"I would never have guessed," Romy laughs. "You should have seen your face while he was talking. You looked bored out of your brain."

"That's because I was," I say. "He did nothing but drone on and on about himself and all the incredible things he's doing right now. He didn't seem to care that I'd spent months on the run. He is more interested in telling me how much money he's made. Shame he didn't want to spend any of it on dessert. After all that time listening to him speak, I deserve chocolate cake!"

"Would ice cream do?" Romy offers. "There's a parlour not far from here that does a mean sundae."

"Sounds wonderful."

It's funny how an evening with my father helped put things in perspective. My engagement to Romy is a problem I was going to have to fix at some point, but for now, it offered me some protection while I figured out how I could break free from my father forever.

Running and hiding isn't a permanent solution. I know that now.

The atmosphere in the car is a lot more relaxed as Romy drives us to the ice cream parlour. I survived the meeting with my father, and Romy respects the fact I have a lot to think about, so he doesn't badger me with questions about our discussion, giving me time to unwind.

Romy switches on the radio to a rock channel. Closing my eyes, I lay back in the seat, dozing. It has been a long night.

"Arse!" Romy's sudden curse woke me.

"What?"

"The ice cream parlour's closed. We must have just missed it."

I look out of the window. We are outside a parade of shops. The ice cream parlour is right in the middle, but the lights are dim and I can make out a single server sweeping up inside.

"That about sums up my life right now." I sigh. "Oh well. I guess I can do without ice cream tonight."

"Wait here."

Romy pulls the car into a space right in front of the shop and nips out of the car. I watch as he dashes over to the shop and taps on the door. The server opens it and the two of them have a brief discussion which ends in Romy coming back to the car, a large tub of ice cream in his hands and a smug grin on his face.

"Here you go. The lady wants ice cream. The lady gets ice cream." He passes the tub to me before starting the car and heading back home.

"It's not quite the same as having one of their freshly made sundaes, but their ice cream is amazing, however you eat it," he tells me. "And if it's okay with you, I thought we could maybe go to my room and eat together?"

"That sounds nice." I smile and realize I mean it. It has been too long since I'd allowed myself to enjoy myself without any pressure. When I was working in the care home, I always had one eye open for my father to come and snatch me away.

Since being back in King Town, I'd been consumed with House politics. I'd earned an evening off.

ROMY'S ROOMS were in a different wing than my apartment. This is the first time I've been in his living space, so I don't bother to hide my curiosity as I stare around.

The main room is tastefully decorated in light greys and blues, framed landscape photos hung at strategic points.

"These pictures are amazing. Did you take them?"

Romy smiles shyly, for once not being his usual confident self. "Yeah. Photography is a passion of mine, but it doesn't exactly fit in with the playboy image I've carefully cultivated. Not many people know, but I often go away for the weekend to the countryside, just me and my camera, looking for the perfect shot."

"Sounds blissful," I say. "I love the idea of being out in the middle of nowhere with my guitar and no one to hear me as I write and sing."

"Maybe you and I could go away for the weekend soon then?" Romy suggests.

"I'd like that."

"Great! Now we'd better get started on this ice cream before it melts. "Romy goes through a door to the side, and I can make out a small private kitchen. He comes back with a couple of spoons.

"Where do you want to eat? We can stay in here or…" He pouts seductively. "We could take it into the bedroom."

"Wherever's most comfortable," I reply, knowing exactly where Romy would want to go.

"Bedroom it is!"

I follow Romy through to his bedroom. It is huge, and like mine, has double doors leading out to a balcony. The main feature, of course, is the bed, a massive super king four poster made up like a hotel bed with more pillows and cushions than anyone could ever need.

More of Romy's photos are hanging around the walls, along with a large flat screen TV suspended opposite the bed so you could watch in comfort. There were two bean bag chairs at the foot of the bed and Romy flops down on one, patting the other for me to come and join him.

"A spoon for you and a spoon for me," he says, handing it to me before peeling open the lid of the ice cream tub. He scoops out a generous helping and holds it out to me to eat from his spoon. After a brief hesitation, I lean forward and open my mouth so Romy can feed me.

"Oh. My. God. That is *divine!*" I exclaim as silky milk chocolate explodes on my tongue.

"I told you it's the best," says Romy, taking a spoonful for himself.

I took another spoonful, lying back on the beanbag as I sucked the ice cream off the spoon. "Why can't it always be like this?"

"What do you mean?" Romy settles himself more comfortably.

"Life. Why can't it always be this simple? You, me, ice cream. We don't need anything more than this. We should just buy a lifetime's supply of ice cream and disappear off to some deserted island in the middle of the ocean."

"Tempting. Very tempting." Romy nods slowly. "You in a bikini. Yeah, it could work."

"I'll do that if you wear nothing but a palm frond to protect your manhood," I counter.

"Who says I need to wear anything at all?" Romy waggles his eyebrows suggestively, making me laugh. "I mean, if it'll make you happy, I'll make the sacrifice and go without clothes. For the greater good."

"I don't know." I tut and shake my head. "I'm not sure I can believe you."

"I'd do anything for you, Ivy," Romy says. "Tell me what you want me to do and I'll do it."

"Well…" A slow, wicked smile spreads across my face. "If you really are so happy to go without clothes, prove it."

"Your wish is my command." Romy hands me the ice cream tub and stands up. I sit there, lazily enjoying the ice cream as he strides over to a chest of drawers. Picking up a remote control that is lying on the top, he presses a button. A sexy beat starts pulsing as he puts the remote down and turns to face me. Grabbing the bottom of his shirt, he starts playing with it, pretending to lift it, then dropping it again as he sways in time with the music.

At last, he reaches up and slowly unclasps his buttons, one by one, moving down until his shirt is completely undone. With one swift move, he pulls it off, swinging it over his head before throwing it across the room.

"Woo!" I cheer as Romy dances around, doing a casual little hair toss that made his floppy blond hair cover his face in a way he clearly knows is incredibly sexy. "More! More!"

Romy turns to face me, his hand at his fly. Grinning, he pops the top button and slowly slides down the zipper.

Not many men could have made wriggling out of their jeans seductive, but Romy manages it, turning round to wave his perfectly defined butt at me.

"And the rest!" I cry in laughter, as Romy plays around with the waistband of his boxers, pulling it down just enough to reveal the top of his groin and pulling it up again while he dances around.

His back to me, he looks over his shoulder and does a skillful shimmy that sends his underwear falling down to the ground. Deftly, he hooks them up with his foot and kicks them up to catch them in one hand and throws them to join the rest of his clothes at the side of the room.

Turning to face me, he strides across the room to stand over me. He is fully erect, his beautiful cock standing proud.

"See?" he says. "I told you I'd do anything for you."

"But you're not naked," I point out. "You've still got your socks on."

"Picky, picky!" Romy made a show of huffing as he pulls off his socks, completely naked at last. "Is that better?" He puts his hands on his hips. Confident. Proud.

"Oh, yes." I put the tub of ice cream down and reach up to grab his cock. I love the way it feels in my hand, so firm and strong, promising a good time if I want it.

I start moving my hand up and down.

Romy closes his eyes and throws his head back, groaning a little."Are you sure you want to do this?" he asks. "It's not too late to stop. I don't want you to do anything you'll regret in the morning."

"I'd regret it if we *didn't* do this," I tell him. "Ever since we were interrupted by Archer, I've wondered what it would have been like between us if we hadn't been stopped. You have an effect on me I've never experienced with anyone else. I need to know what you feel like inside me."

I stand and step towards him. Grabbing a handful of his hair, I pull him towards me and kiss him deeply. I can feel his erection against me, and my body clenches in anticipation.

"You can have anything you want. You're the queen of King Town," he reminds me.

"I want to feel you," I whisper, as we break apart. "I want to feel every inch of you inside me. I want your hands all over my body as you make me come over and over. I want-"

"I know what you want, Ivy," growls Romy, pushing me back onto the bed and climbing on top of me. "And I'm going to give it to you, all night long."He kisses me, his tongue running over mine as he puts his hands to either side of my head to play with my hair.

I wrap my legs around him, wanting to pull him closer as he runs light kisses down the side of my neck, tickling and teasing me.

"I think you need to be naked, don't you?" he murmurs against my skin.

I nod, not trusting my voice, as he moves back to help me take my jacket and blouse off.

"Nice bra." Romy smiles in approval at the sight of one of the new bras we'd bought on our shopping trip. "It looks better on you than I imagined."

"The matching panties aren't bad either," I tell him, as he undoes my trousers and pulls them off. When he is done, he is kneeling before me, as I sit on the edge of the bed. He looks me up and down, admiration in his eyes as he massages my thighs with his hands.

"Exquisite. You're a work of art, Ivy."

I reach behind me to unhook my bra, wanting Romy to see all of me.

He reaches up to pull down my panties, helping me to get out of the last of my clothes so I am as naked as he is.

Then he pushes my legs apart, leaning forward so he can kiss and nibble at the inside of my thighs, getting closer and closer to my pussy. His hands are working as much as his mouth, fondling me, his thumb rubbing my clit, making me clench with anticipation. I am dripping wet, desperate to have him inside me.

"Oh my god, Romy." I arch my back, grabbing handfuls of the bedcovers as Romy works his magic on me. "I need you inside me. Now."

Romy lifts his head up to grin at me. "Good. But you're going to have to wait awhile. I want to make sure you're really ready for me."

"How much more ready do you need?" I moan. "I can't wait any longer."

"I think you can."

Romy quickly comes up to kiss me lightly on the mouth before going back to between my legs.

I am filled with the most intense sensation, torn between needing to fuck Romy and loving everything he is doing to me.

He slips a couple of fingers inside me, finding my sweet spot with them as he licks my clit with the flat of his tongue.

I raise my hips, helping him to get the perfect angle to send me soaring towards orgasm. I can feel it building inside me as he continues to love me, knowing exactly what to do with his hands and mouth to make me feel good.

His thumb replaces his tongue at my clit, his hands skilfully working my body as he kisses his way up my body until he reaches my breasts. He continues to touch me as he takes my nipple in his mouth, lightly nibbling it and licking it. The feel of him at my breasts and between my legs is overpowering.

I am lost before him. In that moment, I would have done anything he asked, anything at all. I need Romy like I've never needed a man before.

I can feel myself edging towards climax and Romy reads the signals my body is sending him, working with my natural rhythm to nudge me closer and closer.

"Romy... I'm coming... Don't stop. Please, don't stop!"

As my body is engulfed by waves of pleasure, Romy suddenly stops touching me, replacing his hand with his cock. As he slides into me, the feeling of him inside me sends me to a place of ecstasy I've never experienced before. I feel like I could die from how intense the feelings are.

As one orgasm ends, another one hits, coming one after the other in a tsunami of desire, leaving me panting and moaning for more.

At last, I come back down. Romy is still inside me, but he slows his movement, recognising it is a little too much for me to take right now.

"You all right?" he asks, brushing my hair out of my face.

"Oh, my god." I roll my eyes. "I am *more* than all right."

"Good. So, are you fully satisfied?"

I can feel his cock twitching inside me. I know he hasn't come yet, but all he seems to care about is whether I've enjoyed myself.

"I'm not satisfied until you are," I tell him, wrapping my legs around his waist and drawing him into me.

He takes the hint and starts thrusting again, hitting my

cervix as he moves in a way that drives me crazy. I might have just had the biggest multiple orgasm of my life, but my body isn't done yet. I respond to his movements, my hips bucking to meet his as we become more and more frenzied.

Romy cries out, coming hard as I ride off his energies to orgasm with him.

When he is done, he stays lying on top of me, the two of us connected as our breathing gradually slows to normal.

"If I thought I was addicted to you before…this just made it worse," Romy tells me, brushing his lips across mine.

"Good, as I think I'm getting addicted to you too," I reply and kiss him before he can say anything else. I don't need to hear those three words, and my heart can't give away another piece to Romy just yet.

If the heirs of King Town steal my heart anymore, I will never be able to leave this place.

Chapter Thirty-Eight

*W*hen I wake up the next morning, I am snuggled up against Romy's chest, his arm tightly wrapped around me.

"Hello, beautiful."

I look up to see him smiling down at me. "How long have you been watching me?"

"A while," Romy says. "I woke up ages ago, but you looked so cute and peaceful lying there I didn't want to disturb you. But now you're awake, do you want some breakfast? I can order something up from the kitchen or if you prefer, I can cook something for you right here."

"Would you mind making me something?" I hate asking, but if we ordered something from the kitchen, they'd know I'd spent the night here and I'm not comfortable with the idea of everyone knowing my business.

"Anything for you." Romy kisses me on the top of my head before getting up.

I roll over to my side, watching him as he gets dressed. I love the lines of his body, the well-defined muscles calling for me to run my hands over them.

"I'll be right back," he says. "Eggs and bacon okay?"

"Great." I nod, lying back in bed as a smile plays about my lips. Memories of last night come into my mind and I can feel myself getting wet again at the thought. Romy might have played the field, but unlike some of my past encounters, he'd really learned from his experience to know his way around a woman's body.

It makes me jealous to think of him with anyone else, but we all have a past.

Maybe we should go and disappear off to that deserted island and spend the rest of our lives making each other feel good. Although it's hard to imagine that sex between us could be better than it was last night. If that is just the start of things, I wonder what our connection will be like once we have a chance to get to know each other's bodies better and learn what really set us off.

"You look deep in thought," Romy says, coming back into the room carrying a tray. "What's on your mind?"

"You," I reply honestly, as I push myself up to a seated position. The blankets fall down, revealing my breasts, but I don't care. It isn't anything Romy hasn't seen before.

"Glad to hear it," Romy grumbles, as he put the tray on my lap and moves to sit next to me. Not only has he made me bacon with scrambled eggs, there were sausages, mushrooms and fried tomatoes. To the side of the tray is a vase with a single white rose and a newspaper is tucked by the plate.

"Wow. You've really gone overboard," I say, tucking into a perfectly cooked sausage. "I had no idea you could cook. How did you get the rose?"

Romy shrugs. "I put a quick call in to Johnson." Seeing my frown, he hurries to reassure me. "Don't worry. He doesn't know you slept in my room. I told him I wanted to surprise you, so when he brought up my morning paper, he brought roses as well. I want to bring you flowers every day and breakfast in bed every morning."

I raise an eyebrow. "Why do I get the feeling you're just

saying that? You don't have to go so over the top to impress me, Romy. Just be yourself. That's more than enough for me."

"Sorry," Romy shrugs. "I'm used to turning on the charm with women. Sometimes I forget you're not like the other girls. And just so you know, if you *were* like the others at the Academy, I'd never have agreed to my father's plan. It's not just you who has the right to say no to a proposal, you know. Anyway, why don't you read the paper? Tell me what's going on in the world."

I unfold the paper and lay it out flat on the bed next to the tray so I can read it.

"*King Town Express*," I say. "There's a surprise. This town has got so much going on, it needs an entire paper to itself to cover it all. Let's see... There's a fundraiser at the Academy in a couple of weeks to raise money for charity."

"More like an excuse for all the Houses to one up each other to see who can be the biggest donor," Romy nods.

"Sounds about right." I reply as I turn the page. "Hmm. That's interesting."

"What?"

"In the gossip column there are some photos of my dad boarding his private jet and a commentary asking why he's been spending so much time in Italy recently. He didn't mention Italy last night, and he certainly had plenty of opportunity considering all he talked about was himself. I wonder what's going on?"

"He's probably got a mistress out there," Romy says. "That column's notorious for trying to make something out of nothing. I don't know why they print it–the news is interesting enough without all these cryptic hints about who's having an affair or who's argued with whom. Find something more interesting to print, why don't you?"

I laugh and turn the page, only to gasp when I see what is written there.

In simple, bold print were the words, "Ivy Archaic. Will you marry me?"

"Romy? What's this?" I hold up the paper to show him the full-page ad, although he obviously already knows what is there.

"You said you wanted a romantic proposal," he shrugs. "I figured what's more romantic than telling the whole town how I feel about you?"

He gets off the bed and down on one knee. He takes a small box out of his pocket and opens it to reveal the ring we'd picked out together. "Ivy Archaic, you're an incredible person and someone I admire more and more as I get to know you. I want to spend the rest of my life learning what makes you happy and doing my best to make all your dreams come true. I want to be your knight in shining armour, your protector, the man you turn to because you know I'll keep you safe and always be there for you. Will you marry me?"

There is only one answer I could give, but where the last time I agreed to marry him because his father hadn't given me any choice, I am starting to think that maybe, just maybe, we could make a marriage work.

"Yes."

Romy takes my hand and slips the ring on. I look at it on my finger, admiring the way it catches the light.

"It's really happening, isn't it?" I say. "We're really going to get married."

"We really are," Romy agrees with a grin. "In fact, Dad asked if you could go see him later today. He wants to talk about wedding plans."

"You mean tell me what I'm going to wear and how it's going to go?" I roll my eyes.

"It won't be like that," Romy reassures me. "My dad's not like yours. Although obviously he's head of House Navarre so he has to make decisions based on furthering our position, he also cares about other people. I know he pressured you into this, but he wouldn't have suggested it if he didn't think we could make it work. He'll want to make sure you're happy with every-thing. After all, you only get married once, so you need to get it right."

"Okay. In that case, let me finish my breakfast and I'll go and see him. Might as well get that out of the way and then you and I can hang out and do… something."

"Something?" Romy raises an eyebrow. "You mean..?"

"Uh-huh." I grab a fistful of his t-shirt and pull him over to me for a kiss. "I need to be sure last night wasn't just a fluke."

I SURREPTITIOUSLY RUB my hands against my jeans, trying to cover up how badly I'm sweating as I stand outside Ben Navarre's study, working up the courage to knock on the door. Romy made it clear his father wanted to see me on my own, but I'd much rather have my fiancé with me for support.

Fiancé. It is going to take a while for me to get my brain around the thought.

Come on, Ivy. The sooner you do this, the sooner you can leave.

I knock on the door before I can change my mind and run away.

"Come in!"

As I walk in, Ben gets up from behind his desk and comes round to meet me. He kisses me on both cheeks before grabbing hold of my left hand. "Let me see the ring."

I stand passively as Ben runs his thumb over the stones set in my engagement ring, twisting it from side to side to examine it.

"My boy has good taste." He nods his approval.

"We chose it together," I tell him.

"Who says I was talking about the ring?"

I blush, as Ben goes back to his chair. "Please. Take a seat." He gestures to the chair opposite him and I do as I'm told.

"I think it's time we got to know each other a little better, Ivy, don't you? After all, you are going to be an important member of the family. I feel we ought to establish a few ground rules, so there's no misunderstanding between us."

"Okay." I shrug. Ben can be as polite as he likes and dress

things up so they look good, but we both know that whatever he wants, he gets.

"I remember your mother, you know," he says, surprising me.

"Really? You knew my mother?" I sat up a little straighter.

"Oh yes. She was an incredible woman. I was very sad to hear of her passing. I often wondered what would have happened if she'd made better choices."

"What do you mean?" I narrow my eyes.

"I loved your mother," Ben says. "We all did. There was something about her which lit up the room whenever she came in. Even though she wasn't an heir to a house, we all wanted her.

"Your mother lost her parents and brother in a car accident when she was eleven and inherited a small house on the edge of town and enough money to go to King Academy. Me, Gabriel Knight, Claude Dauphin, and of course, Solomon, soon became her closest friends. We were all alone in our own ways, of course," he pauses as I stare in shock.

"I was devastated when I heard she'd fallen pregnant and decided to marry Solomon. To this day, I wonder whether there was more coercion involved in that decision than she'd ever let on. If only she'd come to me, I'd have been more than happy to protect her. I would have taken you on as my own, offered you the same courtesy as if you were blood. It's one of the reasons why I agreed to invite you into the family. If I couldn't save your mother, I can at least honour her memory by saving you from your father. I know he's your parent, but that man is evil. He's always got some kind of scheme going on. He never does anything which doesn't serve himself first and foremost. It's no surprise he left you in foster care until you were old enough to use to further his ambitions. I'm just glad I am able to offer you sanctuary from him."

"And use me to further *your* ambitions instead?" The moment I say the words I regret them, but Ben takes them in good grace.

"That's a fair accusation," he agrees. "But no. There's a lot more going on behind my wanting you to marry my son than gaining an advantage for my house, although I won't deny that it's a factor. I know you have a lot to learn when it comes to the nuances of House politics, and I fear that your time spent elsewhere means you'll never fully understand what it takes to be successful in this town. As an Archaic, I can only protect you to a certain extent. If your father were to insist I send you back to him, I would have to comply or risk starting a civil war. Much as I know my son is fond of you, I couldn't do that for just any young girl who caught his fancy. But my future daughter-in-law? The woman who will bear the next generation of Navarre heirs? *Her* I can protect. I'm sorry I came across all heavy-handed when we first met, but it was crucial you agreed to be married then and there, otherwise I might as well have sent you back to your father's."

"So why didn't you just say that?"

"I couldn't take the risk you would say no. Your mother could be stubborn. Once she got an idea in her head, nothing would shift it. She'd never admit she made a mistake in marrying Solomon, even though it was clear to all of us that he was making her miserable. I didn't want you to say no out of some misguided, naïve sense of independence. You did a good job taking care of yourself when you were working at the care home, but the fact you thought you could hide there indefinitely shows how much you've got to learn about how the world works. The only reason your father didn't come after you before we did is because his attention has been elsewhere."

"On what?"

"I don't know." Ben frowns. "My sources can't tell me. All I know is that he's spending a lot of time travelling to Italy, but there doesn't seem to be anything to show for it."

"Romy thinks he's got a mistress there," I say.

"If he does, it'll only be out of convenience," Ben tells me. "No, there's something more going on, but I don't know what. But while he's been focused on his business, he hasn't had time to come after you. That could change at any time, which is why I had to bring you under Navarre protection. But I want you to believe me when I say that I wouldn't have done this for just anyone, heir or not. Romy's told me a lot about you and how you're just as incredible a woman as your mother. He cares for you deeply, Ivy. He's serious about making this marriage work. I hope you are too."

"I am," I assure him, even if my mind wanders to Archer and Declan. Guilt settles in my stomach thanks to that thought.

"Good. Now, let's start making some wedding plans. This is going to be an event everyone will be talking about for years to come. First, we need to choose a date. I was thinking this summer would be good."

"This summer?" My jaw drops. "I was thinking more like a couple years' engagement, maybe even longer. We're only eighteen."

"I was the head of my House at eighteen after my father died," Ben tells me. "Your mother was engaged at eighteen and married before she turned nineteen. You're old enough to accept the responsibility of your birthright. A long engagement would give your father an excuse to argue you have no intention of getting married. He'd be perfectly entitled to demand we hand you over to his custody if he thought this was all a game. No, you will be getting married this summer. It's the only way to secure your safety. Your father won't have time to try anything if you walk down the aisle as soon as possible."

"Could we at least push it back to the autumn?" I ask, desperate to reclaim some semblance of control over my life. I think quickly, coming up with an excuse that might make sense. "I always dreamed of an autumn wedding. I think it's so romantic, all those falling leaves turning orange and red. I want an outdoor wedding. Imagine how beautiful it would look with all those brightly coloured trees in the background."

Ben nods slowly though he is reading me like a book. I wonder if he sees my mother when he looks at me, and not me at all. Now I know they all loved her, but am I just a ghost to them? A ghost of a woman they could never control? Am I making the same mistakes she did?

"Hmm. Yes, I think that could work. I am in the process of registering one of the barns as a wedding venue for you to hold the wedding here."

"Really? But I thought you could only register a property for weddings if it is open to anyone to get married there."

"A mere formality." Ben waves aside my remark. "I have friends on the council who are fully understanding that if someone wanted to get married here, they would have to find an available date in our calendar and unfortunately, that is going to prove to be difficult."

Why am I not surprised that Ben is as corrupt as my father in his own way?

"Now, while it is tradition for the father of the bride to pay for the wedding costs, I am willing to ignore that particular custom and cover all the costs myself," Ben went on. "I don't think any of us like the idea of you being beholden to your father for anything. This will be my gift to you, along with a few other little surprises."

"That's very generous of you," I murmur.

"Your dress will be handmade for you," Ben says. "I have the portfolios of a number of designers for you to decide. Have a look and choose the one you like best and we'll make an appointment for them to consult with you." He hands me a stack of folders.

That is my bedtime reading sorted out for the next few nights.

"I have retained the services of a wedding planner," Ben continues. "She'll be handling all the little details so you don't have to worry about a thing. All you have to do is let her know any specific requests you have and she'll take care of the rest."

"But I was hoping I could get Katy to arrange things," I say. "She's really good at organising and I know it would mean a lot to her to be involved. She's been almost like a mother to me these past few years. It would break her heart not to be able to help."

"I'm sure we'll be able to find something for her to do on the day," Ben says. "But until that time comes, I'm going to have to insist you work with the planner. Whilst I'm sure Katy is a lovely person and highly competent, she won't have the experience of arranging a high-end wedding. There are certain standards to be upheld, etiquette to be observed. With only a few months to sort everything out, I'm not going to trust such an important event to the hands of an amateur."

"But-"

Ben holds up a hand to silence me. "I'm afraid there will be no further discussion on the matter," he says. "Whilst I appreciate this is your wedding and will allow you a lot of freedom in your choices, I must insist you use the planner I have hired. That way we can be sure you have the wedding you deserve. It's what your mother would have wanted."

But Ben, my mother didn't choose you and you clearly never knew what she wanted.

"I guess I'm using a wedding planner then." A fake smile plasters across my face hurts my cheeks. Let Ben think he'd won me over. If I'm going to have to do things his way, I'll do things his way. I just hope that he doesn't have a heart attack when he sees the cost of this wedding. If that's how he wants to play it, he'll soon discover I'm not nearly as naïve as he thinks.

"Excellent. Oh, Ivy, you have no idea how excited we all are to have you join our family. Your engagement party will give us an opportunity to show the whole town how happy we are."

"Engagement party?" *Of course there is an engagement party.*

"Yes. We've planned it for the end of the month. That will give you a chance to get used to being back at the Academy and invite all your friends."

Great.

Chapter Thirty-Nine

"*I*t'll be okay, you know. You don't have anything to be nervous about."

Romy places a hand on my knee to stop my leg bouncing up and down with stress. I manage to talk my way out of going back to the Academy for another week, claiming I need time to adjust to being back in King Town, but Ben puts his foot down when I ask for another extension.

"You're an Archaic," he reminds me. "You need to live up to the name. Go back to the Academy and establish your authority. You and Romy are engaged. You're a power couple. You should be ruling that school, but you can't do that while you're hiding away. It's time you stepped out and showed everyone what you're made of. If not, we'll have to rethink your living arrangements. Perhaps some time with your father is what you need to teach you appropriate behaviour." The second Ben mentions my father I knew I was out of options.

So here I am, sitting in the back of a bulletproof limo with Romy, joining the queue of expensive cars waiting to pull up outside the Academy to drop off students.

"I just never thought I'd be coming back here, you know?" I

say. "I only came to the Academy because my father insisted. He even picked my subjects for me. This place symbolises everything I ran from. Now I'm going to have to deal with the snide comments, pointed glances and whispers behind my back. I haven't got any friends in this place."

"You're not alone. You got me," Romy says. "If anyone tries to give you any grief, they'll have me to answer to."

"Thanks, but I'd rather fight my own battles," I tell him. "I don't like the idea of hiding behind some man."

"I'm not just 'some man.' I'm your fiancé," Romy reminds me. "But it's not like that. We're together now. If someone comes for you, they come for me and vice versa. If I was in trouble you'd come and help, wouldn't you?"

"Well, yes…"

"Right. It's the same for me."

But it isn't. Much as I appreciate Romy trying to support me, he doesn't understand. He isn't the stranger. He grew up in this town and understood its strange ways. He'd never put himself in a position where he needed me to back him up. As an heir, and a particularly charming one at that, he has power and status.

I don't. I am a nobody, someone who is used to fighting for every little scrap she has. I have always been on the alert for a fight because in my experience, someone always wanted to try and take away what is mine. Add into the mix the fact that I'd been away for a few months, I was under no illusions I was going to be welcomed back with open arms. With the exception of Archer and Declan, no one is going to be happy to see me walk through those doors.

"Are you ready?" Romy smiles reassuringly as our driver pulls up in front of the steps and comes round to open the door for us.

I take a deep breath and nod at him.

Romy gets out first, then turns to offer me his hand to help me out. I am perfectly capable of getting out of a car by myself, but appearances matter, here more than anywhere else, so I take his hand and gaze at him as if he were the most beautiful thing I'd ever seen as I step out and stand next to him.

Impulsively, Romy leans over and kisses me, cupping the back of my head.

"Get a room!" someone jeers, deliberately shoving me in the back as they walk past.

"Hey!" I protest, turning to see who pushed me, but whoever it was, they knew how to blend into a crowd. It could have been anyone.

"They're just jealous assholes," Romy says, taking my hand and holding it tight. "They wish they could have you."

I raise an eyebrow. "Really?"

"You're a catch, Ivy Archaic," Romy grins. "And don't you ever forget it. I know I'll always be grateful you said yes."

We walk up the steps to the Academy, and I lean into him. If I'm honest, it feels good having someone on my side, even though I can't fully trust Romy. If I'd learned one thing over the past few months, it is that everyone has an agenda.

Even attractive young men who profess undying love.

"Hey! Ivy!"

I turn to see Declan hurrying towards me, guitar case in hand.

"Hi, Declan. Good to see you."

"Ivy! You're back!" He dumps his guitar on the floor and draws me into a giant hug that takes my breath away. "Music class hasn't been the same without you."

"Yeah, well, I still don't know if I'm going to be allowed back into class with you or if I've missed so much I'll have to redo the year," I admit, ignoring the dark look Romy is sending at Declan for daring to hug me in public. "I've been told I'm going to have to sit through a load of assessments and then they'll decide what to do with me."

"If they don't let you stay in my class, they're nuts," Declan agrees. "You have a natural understanding for how music works that I can only dream of."

"Thanks. Let's hope Mr Metcalf agrees with you."

"Ivy!" An ear-piercing scream that could split the sky streaks across the quad as Milly runs towards me and practically throws herself into my arms.

"So you're talking to me again are you?" I ask, surprised with how much I missed Milly now that she is here.

"I never stopped," she replies. "I had to figure out how to do it without getting into trouble with my family. You know what it's like."

"Not really." I shrug. "Where I come from, we don't play stupid games. You don't have to spend all your time wondering who's going to stick a knife in your back."

"Don't be like that, Ivy," Milly pleads, tears in the corner of her eyes. "You've no idea what it's been like while you've been gone. Ally and Taylor have been total bitches. Archer's been horrible, too. He's missed you so much. I thought he'd be happier now you're back, but he's as grumpy as ever."

"He's probably just jealous." Romy possessively put his arm around me, marking me as his. "You can't blame the poor guy. I'd feel the same if I knew I'd lost Ivy to a better man."

"I wouldn't say 'better'," Declan growls. "I think we all know about marriages of convenience. And just because you're engaged doesn't mean you're going to stay that way."

"All right, guys. That's enough." I shake my head. I am tired already and the day has barely begun. "If you all care about me as much as you say you do, you'll at least pretend you get on when you're around me. I've got enough on my mind."

"Sorry, Ivy." Declan didn't look sorry at all.

Romy says nothing.

The bell rings, signifying the start of lessons.

"Meet me for lunch, Ivy?" Milly asks, looking between us three.

I think about it for a moment. "Okay." Milly is about the only friend I had in this place. I needed every ally I could get if I'm going to survive the next few months unscathed.

Besides, she might be able to tell me more about what is really going on with my father. Milly might come across as being all naïve and innocent, but she is a lot more astute than she lets on.

"I'll let you two girls be alone, then," Romy says.

"Yeah. You do that."

Romy kisses me quickly before heading off to his economics class while I turn and walk off to Pilkington's office.

I remember when I first saw Mr Pilkington, the headmaster, on my first day at the Academy. He'd made it clear just how powerless I was when he told me two of my subjects had already been chosen for me. Now he has the power to make me endure another year in this place if I didn't meet up to his standards.

I knock on the door and wait to be summoned.

"Come in!"

I walk in and take a seat opposite Mr Pilkington.

"Ivy." He smiles warmly. "It's so good to have you back with us. I always knew you'd want to return to finish your education here."

I didn't exactly want to come back, but I nod as if he'd said something profound.

"Now I'm sure you're aware that we cannot just accept you back into your classes as if you'd never been away, especially given your grades in politics and business."

"Yeah. I know."

"I suppose it's too much to ask for you to have continued your studies during your absence?"

I look at him pointedly. "I wrote a few songs."

"I see. Well, we will have to give you some assessment tests to ascertain what classes you will be returning to. We cannot risk the reputation of the school by allowing you to take an exam you are unprepared for. We pride ourselves on our academic achievements and will not risk a pupil failing to live up to their potential. Not only do you let yourself down, you let the entire Academy down."

"Yeah. I know."

"Good." Mr Pilkington shuffles some papers. "I have arranged for all the instructors to assess you. You will be spending the rest of today sitting the tests and we will know by tomorrow what level you are best suited to. I hope you appreciate your teachers giving up their time to mark your papers so you can return to class without delay."

"It's very kind of them." I smile sarcastically. I'd be more than happy to hear that I wasn't going to be allowed to continue with politics or business.

"Excellent. Now I have a private room set up for you to sit your tests. I trust you will be able to cope for a day without your fiancé…"

I could feel my cheeks reddening. "News travels fast round here."

"An Archaic and a Navarre getting married? We haven't had such a momentous union for as long as I can remember," Mr Pilkington says. "I for one am very happy to see it. It's good to see old rivalries being set aside in the name of a more positive future. It isn't so long ago that the Archaics and Navarres would kill each other on sight. It made for quite a challenging academic environment, I can tell you." He chuckles and I politely let out a fake laugh.

"So, given your standing in the town, let's see if we can get your studies to where they need to be to reflect your position, shall we? You're an intelligent young woman. I'm sure with a little extra coaching we can get you to where you need to be, fill in the blanks, as it were."

"Thank you, Mr Pilkington."

"Right. Let's start the assessments. If you would follow me?"

Mr Pilkington leads me to a small room down the hall from his office. The walls are lined with filing cabinets, leaving barely enough room for a small table. Mr Metcalf is already waiting for us, a bored look on his face.

"I'll leave Ivy in your capable hands." Mr Pilkington says when he sees my music teacher. "Please report back to me as soon as you're done here." He walks out, closing the door behind him.

"Sit down, Ivy." Mr Metcalf gestures to the chair opposite

him. "Now, I don't want to waste either of our time. I have a good idea about what level I think you're suited to, so I'll just ask you a few questions and we'll see where you're at."

He picks up an iPad that is on the table in front of him and taps to play an excerpt of Ravel's Bolero. "What instrument takes over the tune from the clarinet?" he asks when it is done.

"The bassoon."

"And what is the main feature of the bassoon's melody?"

"Blue notes."

"Moving on to Bach's Brandenburg Concerto, how would you describe the texture of the opening passage?" He plays the piece to me so I can hear it before answering.

"Polyphonic."

"And what is the interval between the first two notes?"

I hummed the tune to myself, counting the number of notes between the first two. "It's a fifth."

We went on like that for half an hour, Mr Metcalf firing questions at me and giving no indication as to whether I had given a right or wrong answer.

Finally, after getting me to analyse Mike Oldfield's *Tubular Bells*, Mr Metcalf treats me to a rare smile. "Just as I suspected, Ivy. You remain one of the best students I've ever had."

"So I can come back to class?" I gasp, hardly daring to believe Mr Metcalf is complimenting me.

"Your presence has been sorely missed," he tells me. "Quite frankly, if some of your classmates had half your passion for the subject, I'd be a happy man. Maybe if you come back, you'll inspire the rest of them to up their game instead of mooning over Declan Dauphin." A blush covers my cheeks. "Oh yes, I notice the way you all look at him. I might be older than you, but I'm not stupid."

"Yeah, well, Declan's just my song writing partner," I say. "I'm engaged to Romy in case you haven't heard."

"Oh, I heard," Mr Metcalf tells me. "Like I said, I'm not stupid. But when you've been around teenagers for as long as I have, you soon learn that no matter how passionate you feel right now, tomorrow's a new day." He pauses and looks to the door before back at me. "This town can make you feel like there is nothing else in the world, but that isn't true. The world is a big place and full of people that are pressured into a lot every day. If you ever need to talk or need help, come to me. You shouldn't have to do something like get married if you don't want to."

For a second I think of my mother...was she forced into marriage? Was it never what she wanted?

"Romy and I are in love." I was lying, but I don't like the suggestion that my engagement is nothing but a passing phase and that I needed to escape.

There is no escaping King Town, not for someone like me. My hands are dirty, like everyone here, and my heart has been taken by the heirs. I can't leave.

"I'm sure you are," Mr Metcalf says. "And I don't mean for that to sound patronising. But as one of my favourite students, I would caution you to be on your guard. There isn't a single person in this Academy who doesn't have an ulterior motive."

"Including you?"

Mr Metcalf smiles sadly. "Touché, Ivy. Anyway, I've overstepped the mark. It's not my place to get involved in your personal life and I apologise for any offence I may have caused. Suffice to say that you are very welcome back in my class and maybe you might even consider performing a duet with Declan at the fundraiser."

"Duet? Fundraiser?"

"Yes. The charity fundraiser. A number of students are preparing acts for the evening and I know Declan would love to write a song with you just for the occasion. Perhaps you could view it as one last piece of homework before you rejoin my class. It'll earn you extra credit."

"Maybe. I'll have to see what Romy says."

"Let me give you a little piece of advice, Ivy." Mr Metcalf leans forward. "Take it from someone who knows. Never let a man tell you what you can or can't do. If you want to work with Declan, then work with Declan. The two of you create magic together. Many of the students at the academy used to call your mother the first Queen of King Academy. Your mother never let anyone tell her what to do. Don't you think there is a second now?"

"You knew my mum?"

He nods. "Yes, and I admired her. Like many did."

"I'll think about it," I say softly. The more I learn, the more I feel like King Town is smaller than I thought. Did everyone know my mum? Is there nothing but secrets in this place?

After acing Mr Metcalf's assessment, I am filled with optimism about my politics and business courses. But I'd never been that enthusiastic about the subjects, since my father had forced me to take them, and I hadn't made a particularly good impression on either of the teachers, so my good mood quickly evaporated when Ms Dupree starts quizzing me on Tony Blair's key policies, something I vaguely remembered but really couldn't care less about.

By the time I am released from my politics assessment, I am about ready to go home, bury myself under my duvet and never come out again. But I still had to meet with my business studies teacher after lunch. As the bell rings to announce the midday break, the corridors fill with swarms of students. The noise is overwhelming, and I felt like disappearing off to one of the music practice rooms for peace and quiet. Then I remember I'd agreed to meet up with Milly. If anyone can give me an insight into what has really happened while I was away, it's Milly.

As I walk into the cafeteria, I look around to find my friend. I don't see Milly anywhere, but Archer is sitting on his own at a table to the side.

Looking at how long the queue for food is, I decide I can't be bothered to stand in wait. I go over and sit opposite Archer.

"Hey. How're you doing?"

Archer looks up and smiles a rare, genuine smile.

"Better for seeing you," he says. "It's not been the same without you at the Academy—even though technically we're not supposed to talk to each other while our families are at war."

"That's my father's battle." I shrug. "He can be at war with whoever he likes. He can't stop me talking to you if I want. Heck, if he tries, it'll make me *more* likely to go out of my way to hang out with you. House politics are stupid if you ask me. I don't see why you can't all get along. There must be enough business for all of you. From what I understand, we've got complimentary businesses. If we worked together, we'd make more money. Instead, this in-fighting hurts *all* our bottom lines."

"Careful now, Ivy," Archer says. "You'll have me thinking your dad is right to insist you take a business class."

"I don't need a class," I counter. "That's just common sense. Make love, not war. You catch more flies with honey. Insert your choice of uplifting cliché here..."

Archer laughs. "Well, much as I admire your passion, aren't you going to have to check in with Romy before you go fraternising with the enemy?"

"You just had to go kill the mood, didn't you?" I sigh. "Romy's my fiancé, not my jailer."

"From where I'm sitting it is still pretty much the same thing," Archer says.

"It's not like that," I protest. "It's--" My voice trails off. I can't think of a good argument against what Archer is saying.

"Don't be taken in by Romy's pretty boy charm," Archer warns. "He's not what he appears. Romy's only ever cared about himself. The only reason he gets away with being such a womaniser is because he's charismatic with it. He gets the girls to beg him to use them. I wish I knew how he did it."

"Why? So you could do the same?" I snort and shake my head. "It sounds like you're jealous."

"No. It's not like that," Archer says. "The only thing I'm jealous of is-- Actually, you know what? Never mind. It's not important."

"I think it is, and I'd appreciate it if you told me what you were about to say."

"Fine." Archer ran a hand over his shaven head. "I'm

jealous he gets to be with you, okay? After everything, I thought we were starting something special. You know?"

"I do know," I say softly. "I felt the same way."

"Right. So having you come back and find that Romy's manipulated you so he's got you exactly where he wants you is a real kick in the teeth."

"I haven't been manipulated," I say.

"So you want to spend the rest of your life with Romy?"

I shrug. "I don't know. Right now, Archer, I'm focused on putting one foot in front of the other. Romy isn't my biggest problem. My father is. I have to figure out a way to get him off my back once and for all. If marrying Romy sets me free from Solomon Archaic, that's what I'll do. I can worry about the next step after that. Maybe I'll stay married to Romy. Maybe I won't. But that can't be what I think about right now. There are more important things at stake here."

"What if I told you I could get you free?" Archer says.

"I'd say keep talking."

"One of the reasons why your father arranged for me to work for him is so he could set me up to give him an excuse to declare war on the Knights," Archer told me. "He claimed I stole some documents from his safe. Of course I didn't, but it's not like your father needed any evidence to back up his claims. The accusation is enough to put the next stage of his plan in action. However, what he doesn't know is that I saw a lot more than he realised when I was working for him. I know more about his business than he would ever want his enemies to know. I don't know what I'm going to do with that information yet, but I reckon we could come up with a plan together that would bring him down for good."

"Interesting." I nod slowly. "What about these trips to Italy? Do you know what's going on there?"

"No." Archer frowns. "And it worries me. The last time he did a lot of travelling like this he was gearing up for a major assault on the Dauphins. He did an incredible amount of damage to their business and they're only now getting back on an even keel. If he attacks my family, we'll be forced to retaliate and although I would never do anything to hurt you, I can't say that all the Knights share my attitude. Your engagement to Romy won't be enough to protect you if someone gets it into their head that hurting you would hurt your father, and even after you're married, you'll still be the only heir to House Archaic."

He takes my hands and gazes earnestly into my eyes. "Ivy, you're in more danger than you realise. The fact you aren't aware of that tells you everything you need to know about Romy's true intentions. If he genuinely cared about you, he'd make sure you knew everything that is going on in this town. Knowledge is power. How can you protect yourself if you don't know what you're up against?"

"This is nuts," I mutter under my breath. I stand up abruptly, desperately needing some space.

"Ivy, I'm sorry, but I thought you deserved to know the truth," Archer says.

"Or maybe, just maybe, you thought you could break up my engagement in any way possible," I snap.

"It's not like that, Ivy. Ivy!"

I turn and storm out of the cafeteria. As I stomp through the doors, I run into Milly coming the other way.

"Ivy! I'm so sorry I'm late. I got stuck in my history class."

"It's fine. I just need to go."

I push past Milly, not caring about the hurt expression on her face. I have had enough of people for now. I just need to be alone where the heirs can't find me and my mother's past isn't haunting me.

But in King Town? Is that even possible?

Chapter Forty

*S*itting at the piano, I stare at the keys like they might hold all the answers as silent tears fall down my cheeks. It's all too much. Jealous boys, manipulative fiancés, devious fathers... It seems that all the men in my life want to take something from me and I have nothing left to give. Music is the one solace left to me, but right now, I feel too emotionally wrung out to even sing.

Look on the bright side, Ivy. All this misery will give you plenty of inspiration when you're ready to write again.

Oh yeah. I am going to have enough songs to last a lifetime at this rate.

I hear the door opening, but I don't look up.

"Oh. Sorry. I didn't know this room was in use."

I sniff and turn my head away so whoever it is won't see my tears. "That's okay."

"Ivy? What's wrong?" Declan comes over and sits beside me on the piano stool. He puts his arm around me, a simple act of kindness which makes me cry even harder.

"Shh. It's okay." Declan pulls me closer to him. "Whatever it is, we'll sort it out."

"I don't think anyone can clean up the mess that is my life,"

I sob. "I thought things sucked when I was in foster care, but I'd give anything to go back to being a poor nobody. At least I didn't have to worry about what people wanted from me. I'm scared that whatever I choose, someone is going to be hurt. And what if my father just decides he has had enough of me and tries to kill me?"

"You were never a nobody," Declan tells me, gently stroking my hair. "Someone like you shines wherever you are. You walk in and you light up the room." He pauses. "As for your father... he won't touch you. I will never let that happen. Neither will Romy nor Archer."

"You're only saying that because I'm an Archaic," I say.

"Nope." Declan firmly shakes his head. "It wouldn't matter who you were. I'd think you were beautiful... and talented... and funny... and smart..."With every compliment, he drops a kiss on top of my head. At the last one, I move so that he kisses me on the lips.

"I shouldn't have done that."

I don't answer him. I don't want to talk about how wrong and right his lips feel against mine.

"Shut up and kiss me." I put a hand on either side of his face and pull him to me, kissing him deeply.

He groans, pulling me harder against his chest and swirling his tongue around mine in a way that made my knees weak.

"We shouldn't do this." He gently pushes me away. "You're engaged."

"I know. We always seem to kiss at the wrong times."

"You didn't know about Ally and that was my fault. She blackmailed me into staying with her, if I'm being honest."

"How?"

Declan looks down, like he doesn't want to admit it. "I ran someone over. By accident but I was drunk and I just left him there on the road. I passed out later on, I was super out of it and I don't really remember it happening at all. Ally knew about it. She was in the car, and the man didn't survive. He had a wife and kid. He was innocent."

"Declan," I whisper.

He clears his throat. "I told his wife it was me. She slapped me but still let me give her a big check. My parents never found out. I was ashamed."

"You didn't do it on purpose. You should never have driven drunk though."

"I never have before or after that event. I can't remember driving, or getting to the party. I don't remember much, other than what Ally told me and flashbacks," he admits to me. "Anyway, Ally blackmailed me into staying with her and threatened to tell my parents. When I broke up with her, she told them. My mother hasn't spoken to me since and my dad is weird with me. I deserve it."

"It was an accident. I'm sorry though," I tell him. "Ally shouldn't have used that to keep you. That's not real."

"Like you and Romy are?"

"Declan, for once, I want something which is just mine. I want to be in control of my own life, make my own choices without someone making them for me. I want you, and right now I really couldn't give a shit about Romy, Archer, or anyone else who says they love me but are just using me. Is that clear enough for you?"

Declan sits back and looks at me. "Are you sure about this, Ivy? You have no idea how much I want to kiss you, but the last thing I want is for you to turn around later and say I was using you. I've learned from my mistakes. I don't want to be *that* guy."

"Declan, right now, you're about the only person I can trust. You seem to be the only person who doesn't have a hidden agenda, except maybe to write good songs with me. And that's not exactly hidden—we both want to be our best when it comes to music. So when I tell you I want you to kiss me, when I say I need you to hold me, I mean it. So will you quit jerking me around and kiss me already?"

My heart falls as Declan stands up and walks away. But then a huge grin spreads across my face as Declan turns the key in the door.

"If you're serious, then I don't want anyone to walk in and interrupt us," he says. He crosses over to the sound system. Every music room has one so you could listen to set pieces to practice. He hits play and ironically Ravel's *Bolero plays*.

"How appropriate," he smiles, loosening his tie and coming to sit next to me so that he is facing one way on the stool and I'm facing the other. "I always think the crescendo in this is vastly overrated when it comes to seduction…"

He leans forward to kiss me and for the first time in a long while I feel I am finally living in the moment without worrying about what else might happen. Romy couldn't be upset about me kissing someone else. Our engagement is a business arrangement. Yes, I am attracted to him, but I am starting to see that I am really too young to settle down. I need to experience more of the world before I am ready to say that any one person is the right man for me to settle down with.

And the way Declan's lips feel against mine tells me that I am right when I said I needed him to kiss me. I moan and lean into him, the physical reassurance of his body against mine telling me I deserve some happiness of my own.

Declan reaches up to brush the back of his hand against my cheek, running it down the front of my body to cup my breast. He squeezes lightly, running his thumb over my nipple. I arch my back, pushing up against him as I enjoy the way he caresses me. I can feel my pussy clench in anticipation of what is to come.

Declan continues to kiss me as he moves his hand away from my breast and down my body, squeezing and massaging my thigh before finding his way under my skirt. I open my legs to make it easier for him to touch me as he runs his hand over the outside of my panties before slipping inside them. He rubs at my clit, making me gasp.

"You're so wet," he murmurs.

"That's the effect you have on me," I say, moving to take my knickers off.

Sitting on the piano bench with no underwear is such a turn

on. I love the idea that I am fully clothed, yet completely exposed, as Declan moves to slide his fingers inside me. I grab his shoulders, my fingers digging into his flesh as he starts to move. I throw my head back, losing myself in the sensation as he finds the perfect angle to hit my G spot with every touch. He finds the perfect rhythm to drive me wild, and I bite my lip to hold back my cries, not trusting that the music would cover the sound of my orgasm.

"Oh… my… God… Yes! Yes! Don't stop!" I open my legs even wider as Declan continues to work his magic.

He pulls his fingers out and plays with my clit some more.

"Turn around," he whispers in my ear, moving his hand away to let me swivel around on the stool. He moved so that he is on his knees between my legs. Putting his hands behind my thighs, he pulled me close, burying his face between my legs. I lean back, thankful the piano lid is shut so I wouldn't randomly bash the keys and give away the fact that the only instrument being played right now is my body.

His tongue flicks across my clit, teasing and tantalising me. I grab a handful of his hair, holding his head in place as I urge him to keep doing what he is doing.

Putting his hand between my legs, he slides his finger in and out of me. I can't keep quiet any more. (OR I struggle to keep quiet)

"Yes!" My cries mingle with the music, and as *Bolero comes* to its inevitable conclusion, I explode into bliss, coming harder than I ever thought possible.

"Oh fuck," I murmur, as Declan emerges from between my legs, a smug smile on his face.

"I take it that's what you needed?" He grins.

"And then some." I pull him to me and kiss him passionately. His cock is hard and I can feel the bulge in his trousers rubbing against me. "We need to fuck."

"I think that can be arranged."

I fumble at his fly, but we are interrupted by the bell giving the signal that afternoon registration is about to start.

"Oh, shit!" I say, my head dropping against his chest as Declan puts his arms around me and laughs. "We have to skip class. There's no way I can focus on anything when I'm still so worked up."

"What—you mean that orgasm wasn't enough for you?" Declan shakes his head in wonder. "Wow, Ivy. I had no idea you were so insatiable."

"It's all you," I tell him. "This is how you make me feel."

"Well, much as I definitely need to finish," Declan gestures to his erection, "you've got another assessment to sit through this afternoon if I'm not mistaken and I can't afford to miss my math class. I'm struggling enough as it is."

"And you think you'll be able to focus on the teacher when you're all worked up?"

"I need to try," Declan groans apologetically, bending to retrieve my underwear from the floor. "But we're not done. Not by a long shot. There's no way that's the last time I get to make you come."

He kisses me again and I moan in frustration. "You're right." I sigh. "Pilkington will kill me if I don't show up for that assessment. Why is it everyone else it seems to care more about my education than I do?"

"Because we see your potential," Declan says. "Now, come on. We better go. If anyone spots us leaving, we were working on a song. And since we *do* have to write something for the fundraiser, what say we set another date for music 'practice'?"

I grin, knowing exactly what he is suggesting. "Works for me."

MY BUSINESS STUDIES assessment goes about as well as can be expected. Not only do I hate the subject anyway, memories of Declan between my legs haunt me. Mr Robson asks me a question and a flashback of Declan touching me comes flooding back.

"I can see you're as focused as ever, Ms Archaic," Mr Robson says grimly at the end of the session. "It's a pity. Nothing bothers me more than wasted potential. If you would only apply yourself, you could pass this subject standing on your head. As it currently stands, you'll be lucky to scrape a pass—and that's with the extra year's tutoring I'm advising."

"You can't be serious!" I gasp.

"Of course I can. I would be doing you a disservice as well as whoever is currently paying your school fees. A place at the Academy does not come cheap, and you'd do well to remember that. If you cannot be motivated to work on your own behalf, perhaps you might consider who it is that's working so hard to put you through your exams to give you the best possible future. You cannot rely on being an Archaic to coast through life. Not all of us had your privileged start."

I could laugh in his face, but I know it isn't worth the grief, so instead, I cast my gaze to the floor so he wouldn't notice me rolling my eyes so hard they practically fell out of their sockets.

"Yes, Mr Robson. But I really don't want to have to repeat a year. Mr Metcalf said I can continue in his class. If I promise to work extra hard to catch up, would you reconsider putting me back? It would be horrible to be a year behind all my friends."

"I'm afraid a little last minute on your part will be too little too late," says Mr Robson. "However, out of sympathy for your position and not in the slightest bit because the head has emphasized how generous a donor your father is to the Academy, I am willing to allow you to continue in your current position."

"Thank you!" I could have hugged him.

"On one condition." Mr Robson holds up one finger to warn me not to celebrate too soon. "Your place in my class is on a probationary basis. You will attend extra revision classes with me and I will subject you to regular testing. If over the next two months I do not see sufficient progress, I will have no choice but to put you back a year. So it is entirely up to you what happens next, Ivy. Your future is in your hands."

Ms Dupree has offered me a similar deal which is the best I could hope for, so I smile and nod.

"I won't let you down," I promise.

"I am entirely indifferent whether you do or don't," says Mr Robson. "The only person you'll be letting down is yourself. But that would be hardly surprising given your bloodline. The Archaics aren't exactly known for their high standards." With that he turned and stalked out of the room, leaving me gaping after him, practically picking my jaw off the floor.

I wanted to yell after him that I'd tell Mr Pilkington what he'd said, but it wouldn't make any difference. It would be his word against mine, and I knew all too well how that dance goes. When I was growing up in foster care, it didn't matter how many times I told the truth about who'd started a fight; it was always me who got the blame. Now I knew when to pick my battles. This one isn't worth it.

But I am going to have to work doubly hard to keep my place in Robson's class. I am under no illusion now that he'd take great delight in chucking me out if I give him the slightest excuse.

Romy is waiting for me by the entrance to the Academy, he smiles when he sees me. "How was your day?"

"Okay." I shrug. I thought I'd feel guilty when I saw him after what happened with Declan, but I'm surprised to discover I didn't care. After all, it isn't like Romy didn't play the field himself. There is no way he is going to stay faithful to me for the rest of his life. I am just taking something for myself for once.

Yeah, right, Ivy. You keep telling yourself that. That justifies cheating on someone who's been nothing but nice to you the entire time you've known him.

"What about the assessments? Do you have to repeat a year?"

"Not at the moment. But I've got to keep my grades up and have extra tutoring in politics and business studies." I sigh. "That's just what I need. Wasting more time in the two subjects I detest. But on the bright side, Mr Metcalf told me I'm one of his best students and he's really happy to have me back in his class. That's nice to hear."

"I'm unsurprised. My fiancée is so talented." Romy beams with pride, and I smile weakly. Would I still be his fiancée if he knew what I'd done?

"Isn't that our driver?" I point at a car edging up the drive, a black limo in a sea of identical black limos. I have no idea if it really is our car, but it gives me an excuse to change the subject.

"No. But the car behind it is." Romy reaches out and takes my hand, and we descend the steps together to meet the car.

"What do you want to do tonight?" Romy asks when we are settled in the back seat.

"I really ought to study." I think about all the catching up I have to do and sigh. It is a mammoth task, but all my teachers have told me I have the intellectual ability to get the grades, I'm simply not motivated enough about most of my subjects to want to do the work.

"So why do I hear a 'but' in there?" asked Romy.

"Because I've been back at the Academy five minutes and already I want to leave again. If it wasn't for my music class, there's no way you'd be able to get me to finish my A levels."

"Have any of your teachers set you homework to do yet?"

"No." I shook my head. "Other than Mr Metcalf telling me I need to write a song with Declan for the fundraiser, but I can't really do that by myself."

I feel my cheeks turning red at the mention of Declan's name, but Romy doesn't seem to notice.

"Which means you can take tonight off," says Romy. "Some guys are having a race and I thought you might like to ride pillion. It's not as intense as the Bomber Derby and something tells me having you riding behind me will bring me luck."

"Don't I get to compete as well?"

"What? And make me look bad?" Romy jokes, but I get the sense there is more than a little truth mixed in with the sentiment. "No, I don't think that would be a good idea, Ivy."

"Why not? Is it because I'm female?"

"No." Romy looked awkward. "Well, yes, but not for the reasons you think. I know you're incredible on a bike. I've seen you ride and I don't doubt for a second you'd win most of the races round here. But you're the only Archaic heir and the mother of my children one day. My father made it very clear that he doesn't want you competing. It took all my powers of persuasion to convince him to let you have your own bike to go for a buzz around town, so you can take it to the race if you like, but there's no way you can actually compete."

"But we don't have to tell your father," I point out. "How's he going to know what we do when we're out?"

"You know better than that, Ivy." Romy sighed. "He's got eyes and ears everywhere. That doesn't mean we can't bend the rules a little, but if he finds out you did something as dangerous as race, we'll both be in serious trouble and you wouldn't like my father when he's angry. Think Jack Nicholson from *The Shining* crossed with Sonny Corleone from *The Godfather*."

"I'd rather not." *Great. Just what I need in my life. Another psychopathic father figure.*

"But riding pillion's almost as good as competing, isn't it?" says Romy, a pleading tone to his voice that needs me to agree with him. "You'll be my lucky charm and imagine the look on Archer and Declan's faces when we cross the finish line and they're eating our dirt. Wouldn't that be more fun than staying home sulking because you've got a ton of homework?"

"I guess." The way I'm feeling right now, I'd rather lock myself in my apartment with my guitar, but I feel guilty for letting Declan get so close to me, so I end up agreeing to ride with Romy.

For a girl who prided herself on being independent, I seem to be doing an awful lot of bending over backwards to make the men in my life happy—and not in a good way.

Chapter Forty-One

"*Y*ou're not still sulking, are you?" asks Romy, as he makes a few last-minute checks to his bike before we drive to the rendezvous for tonight's race. "Come on, Ivy. I explained to you how my father feels about you racing. If it were up to me, I'd let you race."

"'Let' me?" I haven't been in the best of moods and Romy's poor choice of words make me feel even worse. As soon as we'd arrived home after school, I'd gone straight to my apartment, ignoring Romy's suggestion we have dinner together. I needed time to get my head together, figure out why it is I'd let Declan lead me astray. I mean, I am the one who seduced him. I know that. But why did I take that step? What is it about Declan that made me cross the line?

I'd always thought of myself as monogamous. Sure, I'm happy to have fun and fool around when the opportunity arose, but once I was in a relationship, I'd always been faithful. But ever since my father has first brought me to King Town, it is like I'm a different person and I'm not sure I like who I am becoming.

I know I am being a bitch taking out my emotional angst on

Romy and it isn't fair, but who says life has to be fair? I am tired of feeling powerless. Racing is the one time I feel in control, and now even that is being taken away from me.

"You look amazing, by the way," says Romy, coming over to kiss me. He tries to put his hand around my waist, but I pull away.

"I know." I'd gone overboard to make sure I looked good for tonight. I might be mad at Romy but that didn't mean I wasn't going to support him when we were out in public. We are a power couple and we have to present a united front—which includes looking my best in front of our friends and rivals.

I'm wearing skin tight black leather trousers with bright red Doc Martens. As well as my favourite leather jacket, the one Katy bought for my birthday last year. To complete the badass ensemble, I am wearing a studded dog collar, bright red lipstick and I'd followed a YouTube tutorial to create a powerful effect with red and black eye makeup.

My whole look screams *fuck me but don't fuck with me.*

"Okay, Ivy. I get it." Romy inhales deeply, trying to stay on top of his temper. "You're pissed off with me and I under-stand. I'd be annoyed if I were in your place. Would it make you feel any better if I promise you could compete in your own race once we're married? I promise I won't tell you what you can and can't do once we've exchanged our vows. All you have to do is put your head down and survive the next few months, and you'll be free as soon as that wedding ring is on your finger."

"You've got a funny sense of what freedom means," I tell him, but I can feel my attitude softening. It's impossible to be cross with Romy for long. That's what makes him so dangerous. He's wormed his way into my heart and I care about him, even as I resent the politics which has thrown us together.

"Your happiness is the only thing that matters to me," Romy says, putting an arm around my waist and pulling me to him. This time I let him. "And I'm going to keep telling you that until you believe me."

"Pretty words, Romy Navarre," I say, as Romy kisses me on one cheek, then the other, before finally kissing me on the lips.

"I mean every single one of them," he tells me. "Promise. "Now do you want to go to the race or shall we head to my room instead? I don't mind either way."

"I bet you don't," I say. But the thought of sleeping with Romy after what happened this afternoon feels wrong, so that left me with only one choice. "Let's go race. Everyone's expecting us and we don't want to let them down, do we? They'll only start gossiping about why we didn't show. Before you know it, it'll be all over school that we're on the rocks. You'll have girls throwing themselves at you thinking they can steal you away, I'll get even more annoyed and it'll be one big disaster."

"I love your imagination. I'm not sure things will get that bad." Romy laughs. "But I get your point. We're the power couple of King Town and it's time we showed everyone that we really do rule. Your bike's in the garage and the keys are hanging up on the wall. You can follow me down."

"I don't think so." I shake my head. "If I'm going to ride pillion for the race, I might as well get some practice in."

"You mean-?" Romy's face lights up.

"Yep. I'll ride behind you on the way there as well. It's the best way for us to make a united entrance, don't you think?"

"You bet!"

Romy passes me one of the helmets which hung off the handlebars before putting the other one on. Then he climbs onto his bike and I get up behind him. He turns the key in the ignition and as the engine fires up, revs it to create a deafening roar.

There's something wonderfully primal about the feel of a motorbike between your legs. All that power, yet it is completely tamed and under the control of the rider—as long as they have the ability to stay on top of it. Romy might not be the best racer out there, but he certainly knows how to handle his bike. He kicks off the stand and heads off down the drive, away from the estate and over to the agreed location for that evening's race.

There is a festival feel to the race tonight. Someone set up a hog roast and the smell of cooking meat permeates the air, making my mouth water even though I'd already eaten. A band is playing on a temporary stage and there are a few booths set up selling clothes, snacks and random trinkets.

"Do you want a drink?" Romy offers.

"I'd love one, but I think it'd better wait until after the race," I reply. "I don't want to jeopardise your chances if I lose my balance."

"I don't think one drink will do that!" Romy laughs. "But I appreciate your caring. Come on. Let's go and see who else is going to race tonight."

He takes my hand, and we walk over to where Matt Knight, one of Archer's cousins, is in charge of the sign-up sheet.

"I told you. It's fifty pounds to compete or you don't get to race." Matt is in the middle of a heated conversation with someone I haven't seen before. The man looks to be a couple years older than me, with long, dark hair tied in a ponytail and striking grey eyes. Ordinarily I'd think he was attractive, but there is something about him that doesn't sit right. Maybe it is the arrogant twist to his mouth or the way he is looming over Matt in an attempt to intimidate him. Whatever it is, I'm not impressed.

"What's the point of paying? It's not like any of you spoilt rich kids even need the money. Charging money to race is just a way to keep out those who really deserve a break. Although I don't know why I expect any different from you lot. You don't even know you've been born."

The guy practically spits at Matt as he turns and storms off, roughly pushing past Romy as he leaves.

"Hey, Matt." Romy nodded at him as he wrote his name on the list. "That looked like fun."

"Tell me about it," says Matt, rolling his eyes. "Have you got the buy in?"

"What spoilt rich kid doesn't?" jokes Romy.

He hands over a fifty-pound note and Matt tucks it safely

away in his pocket. All the competitors have to pay to race tonight, with the winner taking all. Of course, the real prize is the kudos of winning and the winner is going to buy everyone else drinks with the money, so it is more of a symbolic gesture than anything else, but it seems weird that someone would get so bent out of shape at the idea.

And the moment I have the thought, I laugh at myself. It isn't so long ago that the idea of being able to find fifty pounds just to enter a street race would have been absurd. I guess I'm becoming one of those spoilt rich kids and I didn't even notice.

The guy has a point, even if he was a dick about how he made it.

I do a quick look down the list of competitors. All male, of course.

If Romy meant what he said about my having freedom to do what I liked once we were married, I am going to shake things up a bit. I couldn't be the only girl who would rather be on her own bike than be nothing more than a pretty side piece for her man. I'm going to drag King Town out of the Dark Ages, kicking and screaming if need be.

"I'm just going to say hi to a few people," Romy tells me. "Are you going to be alright on your own for a bit?"

"I think I'll survive," I deadpan, wiggling my fingers at him in a little wave as he walks off.

I wander over to have a look at some of the stalls. I see Milly examining a boho style coat hanging up on a rack and I turn to walk the other way before she spots me, not wanting to get into a discussion about what happened at lunch, but I'm too slow.

"Hi, Ivy. I'm so glad you came." Milly comes over and hugs me. "I wanted to say sorry I was so late. I don't blame you for being angry with me."

"You're not the one who should be apologising," I say. "I was in a bad mood and I took it out on you. *I'm* sorry."

"I don't blame you for being in a bad mood. I would be if I'd had to wait as long as you did. *I'm* sorry."

"Okay, Milly." I laugh and hold my hands up in a gesture of

surrender. "I get the feeling that if we keep this up, we're going to be apologising forever. Why don't we say we're both sorry and put it behind us? I haven't seen you for months. Haven't we got better things to discuss than who's behaved the worst?"

"You're right." Milly smiles. "I just missed you so much, you know? Things were weird between us before you disappeared. You're my only friend and I hated that I didn't get a chance to make sure we were okay."

"I wanted to message you," I told her. "I knew you'd be wondering what happened to me, but I couldn't risk it, not after Archer was shot. I didn't want to put you in danger. Who knows what might have happened if my father knew we were in contact? I couldn't take that chance. But if it helps, I missed you too. You've been the one person who's stood by me with everything I've been through. I hated not being able to talk to you about things."

"Things like your engagement?" Milly nudges me with her elbow. "I saw the ad Romy put in the papers. That must have been so romantic. How did you feel when you saw it?"

"I was surprised," I admit. "I mean, I knew Romy was going to propose, but I thought he'd do something like take me to a restaurant or maybe a long bike ride to a quiet place in the countryside. I wasn't expecting him to effectively propose in front of the entire town."

"I guess you don't know Romy as well as you thought," says Milly. "He's always been about grand gestures and when it comes down to something as important as a union of two Houses, of course he is going to do something everyone would see. I'm surprised he didn't hire a skywriter to put a message in the clouds like last time."

"Last time?" I frowned. "What do you mean?"

"Oh." Milly paled. "You didn't know? He was engaged a couple of years ago to an heiress who lives in London. They were going to have a long engagement because they were both so young, you know? It is pretty obvious they were only getting married because their parents wanted to build business connections between the two families, but Romy claimed to be in love. Then rumours started to spread that you were still alive when we all thought you and your mum had died in a car crash years ago and Romy broke it off."

"Because he thought I would be a better match?"

"I didn't mean it like that, Ivy." she sighs. "It's different with you and Romy. I'm sure it is. The way he looks at you, I've never seen him like that. I think he genuinely cares about you."

"Until an even bigger heiress comes along, right? You're not the one being stupid. But I guess you can't know what you don't know, huh?" I shrug as if I don't care and my heart doesn't feel like it is shattering into a million different pieces.

If Romy had been up front about things from the start, agreed with me this engagement is a sham, that would have been one thing. We could have worked together for both our benefits. But no. He has to pretend he cares about me, seduce me, make me feel like we have a connection. There is simply no need.

I hate being lied to.

"Hey, Ivy. Are you ready for the race?" Romy comes over to join us, that attractive smile on his face.

Milly looks nervously from me to him, but I act as if nothing is wrong.

"Yep," I reply. "Really looking forward to it. Can't wait to be riding right behind you when you beat Archer and Declan."

Romy holds out his hand, and I take it. As he leads me over to his bike, I turn to Milly.

We'll talk later, I mouth. Milly nods, eyes wide.

Just as Romy said, there are fewer competitors than there would be for a Bomber Derby, the entry fee presumably chasing away some of the poorer bikers. Of course, Archer and Declan are here, along with some of the more distant relatives of the Houses.

Races like these were an opportunity for the less powerful House members to climb the ranks and gain a little kudos. Although few of them stood a chance against Archer and Romy, a strong showing still made them look more important—and helped them make connections with the other Houses.

Interestingly, neither Archer nor Declan have someone riding pillion with them tonight.

Romy notices, too. "Looks like those guys are already embracing their loser status," he laughs. "I guess no one wants to ride with them."

"Or maybe *they* didn't want to ride with anyone?" I suggest lightly, hardly daring to believe that the reason why they were on their own might be because if they couldn't have me on the back of their motorbikes, they didn't want anyone else.

"I doubt it," Romy scoffs. "But it's going to make it all the sweeter when we pass the finish line first. I'll have the girl *and* the prize."

He turns the key in the ignition and his bike comes to life. "Come on, Ivy. Let's show them how it's done." He pats the space behind him and I climb up like the good little puppet I am pretending to be.

Matt speaks into a bullhorn as the competitors draw up to the starting line. "Are you all ready?"

Ten or so bikers rev their reply.

"Now, remember. Winner gets all the money and all the glory. So it's time to see which one of you has got what it takes to finish first. Ready... set... go!"

I cling tightly to Romy, my arms wrapped around his waist and my knees gripping his thighs as his bike lurchs forward. This race is more straightforward than a typical Bomber Derby. All we need to do is circle the block a few times. The one to do it fastest won.

Romy takes an early lead, vying with Archer for first place. "Give it up, Archer!" Romy yells over to him. "You're going to lose this race—just like you lost Ivy!"

I bristle at his words. I am not some trophy to gloat about. Sometimes Romy can be a real jerk.

Archer doesn't bother to reply, letting his riding speak for him. He kicks things up a gear and his bike pulls ahead.

Romy doesn't act phased, waiting for the first corner to undercut Archer and take the lead from him. We pass so close I could reach out and touch Archer. It isn't unknown for pillion passengers to sabotage rival racers, but I'm not going to do anything so sly. If Romy can't win the race on his own merit, he doesn't deserve to win.

Archer and Romy are so caught up in their personal vendetta against each other, they aren't paying any attention to the other riders. I can feel Romy start in surprise as the angry stranger who'd argued with Matt over the buy-in suddenly overtook all of us.

"What's he doing?" Romy exclaims.

I'm just as surprised. I know how these people work. If the youth hasn't paid his fee, it isn't going to go well for him after the race.

Romy and Archer exchange a look, the pair of them nodding at each other. I hold on even tighter to Romy, knowing the pair of them are going to work together to defeat the mysterious upstart.

Romy and Archer push their bikes to their limits, coming up behind the man on either side. Suddenly, they move in unison, veering off to the right. Although neither of them touched the man's bike, the unexpected move distracts him and he yanks the steering to the left to avoid an anticipated impact. He overcompensates, and his bike falls into a long slide, sending the man tumbling.

"Yes!"

Romy and Archer bring their bikes close enough to each other to high five. Then it is business as usual. With only a couple more turns left to the finish line, it is still anyone's race, but I'd lost interest in which of the two is going to come first. Their behaviour sickens me. It revealed everything that is wrong with this place—you could be deadly rivals, but anyone else threatens your position and suddenly everyone is best buddies. What is wrong with simply doing your best and seeing how it panned out?

As we took the final corner, Romy and Archer were neck and neck.

"Don't worry, Ivy!" Romy calls over his shoulder at me. "We're going to win this one."

Something comes over me, maybe it's resentment that two of the richest people I'd ever known conspired to make sure someone who really needed the prize money wouldn't get it. Whatever it is, a little mischievous imp takes over and I tap Romy on the shoulder.

"Over there!" I cry.

There is nothing to see, but the sudden distraction is enough to make Romy slow a little, giving Archer the advantage. He blasts his horn in victory as he crosses the finish line before us, the victor once more.

Romy screeches to a halt. Second place is not good enough. I get off the back and step away from him as he pulls off his helmet.

"What the hell was that about, Ivy?" he yells. "You cost me the race."

"I'm sorry." I shrug, doing my very best impression of an innocent airhead. "I thought I saw one of my father's spies and I was afraid."

"Oh." The second I mention my father, Romy's bad move evaporates. A look of concern comes over him. "Do you want me to go check him out? Your father has no right to stalk you. You're in the care of House Navarre. If he is following you, it's an insult to our ability to take care of you."

"No, no, it's fine." I shake my head. "Now that I have a better look, I realise I am mistaken. But it's very sweet of you to care."

I kiss him lightly on the lips and whatever irritation is left in Romy melts away.

"Hey! Let go of me! I just want to talk!"

We're interrupted by a scuffle and we turn to see the guy from earlier being restrained.

Romy glances over at Archer and the two of them nod.

"Let him go," says Archer, striding towards the group.

The stranger pulls himself free, and he crossly brushes himself off, trying to regain a little dignity.

"No hard feelings?" Archer extends a hand for him to shake. "We didn't mean to hurt you, but everyone knows that unauthorised riders are fair game."

"No hard feelings," the man agrees. "I should have known that you guys wouldn't play by the rules. But I wasn't an unauthorised rider."

Romy frowns. "But we saw you arguing with Matt. You left without paying."

"He did. But then I paid for him." Declan came over to join us. "I figured it would make things interesting to have an unknown quantity join in. I should have known your egos would have teased up to make sure he didn't stand a chance."

"It's okay, Declan," says the stranger. "I'll know better next time. I didn't think we were playing dirty, but now I know all's fair in love and motorbike races..." He gives me a look that is decidedly suggestive, but I didn't give him the satisfaction of letting him know how gross I thought it is.

"Yeah, sorry, Lucas," says Declan. "I should have known these guys would get all bent out of shape."

"So you two know each other?" I ask.

"No." Declan shakes his head. "We met just as he was storming off. I saw him riding round King Town earlier today and I knew he could handle a bike. I figured it was only fair to give him a chance to show us what he could do."

"I would have won if it wasn't for these two teaming up on me." Lucas gives a nod of respect. "But that's fine. I have a few ideas for next time. You won't be able to pull the same trick twice."

"We'll see." Romy laughs. "We'll see."

"Anyway," says Archer. "I think it's time to celebrate my victory. Who's up for a drink or two?" He holds up the wad of cash he'd just won. "You're welcome to join us, Lucas. You can drown your sorrows."

"Thanks for the offer, mate, but I've got somewhere I need to be," Lucas says. "Maybe next time—but it'll be me buying the drinks."

"In your dreams," Archer jeers as Lucas walks away.

"He's an interesting chap, that one," Declan says. "Have any of you seen him before?"

"No."

"Nope."

"I thought everyone went to the Academy," I say. "Even if he's too old for school, I would have thought one of you would have recognised him from the years above you. Wonder where he comes from, then?"

"Not everyone can afford Academy fees," Declan tells me. "And only the most academically gifted get scholarships. There's a state school on the other side of town. He must have gone there."

"Still, it's weird he's never been in a race before, don't you think?" I persist.

"Maybe it's taken him this long to save up for a bike worth riding," Romy suggests. "If his family doesn't have the money for the Academy, it's not likely they'd have enough to buy a halfway decent bike. But why are you so bothered by someone who isn't part of a House, Ivy? He's not worth your energy."

"I guess." I frown a little. There is something about Lucas that is bugging me, but I can't put my finger on it.

"Enough about him. Are you guys coming to celebrate or am I drinking alone?"

Archer waves his money at us and this time we follow him. Romy is right. Lucas isn't worth stressing over. It isn't as though I'm likely to see him again anytime soon.

Chapter Forty-Two

"*J*ust a little higher…"

I teeter at the top of a ladder. Milly stands on the ground, looking up at me as she gives instructions for pinning the banner straight.

"I don't think I can go much higher, Mills. Not without falling."

"There! That's perfect."

I push the pin in and climb back down the ladder, relieved I finally got it where Milly wanted. The girl is a serious perfectionist!

"Don't you think the hall looks beautiful?" she sighs. "The parents are going to be so impressed."

I gaze around at the school's main hall. Balloon arches and wreaths in the purple and yellow school colours are strung at regular intervals, while banners proudly declare that this is the 53rd annual charity fundraiser. This year we are raising money to support a local donkey shelter which needs to rebuild its stables after arsonists have done some serious damage to the old buildings. I have a feeling that with the general attitude of one-upmanship that pervaded the Houses, by the time we were done, the shelter wouldn't just have a new stable. They'd be able to buy acres of fields, soft, warm blankets, and all the carrots a donkey could get.

The school would also keep 25% of anything raised for "essential works." You'd think with the amount they charged in fees they would already have more than enough to pay for everything, but apparently not.

"You've done a really good job," I tell her. "You should be an interior designer after you leave the Academy."

"You really think so?" Milly beams with pride.

"Don't listen to her, Millicent," says Ally, overhearing our conversation. "The only reason you got to decorate the hall is because no one else wanted the job. A toddler could have done a better job than you."

"Yeah, yeah. You're just jealous," I retort. "You wish you had Milly's eye for design."

"When people see my performance at the show, nobody's going to be talking about a few balloons on the walls," Ally says. "They'll all be stunned by how good I am."

"Because a few slut drops are just *so* impressive." I yawn. "You keep telling yourself how great you are, Ally. Nobody else is going to do it, that's for sure."

Ally sniffs, but she doesn't have a snappy comeback, so she walks off.

"Are you all ready for the show?" Milly asks. "I hear you and Declan are going to do a duet."

"Yeah, it's one of our A level pieces. Mr Metcalf insisted we do it. Wouldn't take no for an answer."

"Good. I'm really looking forward to hearing you sing. I've never seen you perform."

"I wouldn't get your hopes up too much. It's nothing special."

"Don't say that." Milly lightly raps the back of her hand against my arm. "I know you're an amazing songwriter. Every-one's going to love you."

"Maybe. If it were up to me, I wouldn't be singing at this fundraiser."

"Why not?"

"My father is going to be sitting right at the front," I tell her. "He's going to be boasting to everyone that I'm his little girl and it's thanks to him that I'm as good as I am. My music is something that belongs to me, not him. I hate the thought that he's going to attempt to take credit for it. I tell you something, once I marry Romy, I'm going to take his name and then House Archaic will be gone forever."

Milly gasps. "You don't mean that!"

"Oh yes I do." I nod grimly. "It's the only way I can hurt my father the way he deserves. You all keep telling me how ruthless the Houses are. Well, I'm my father's daughter and I'm going to make darned sure he regrets everything he's done, including the way he treated my mother. By the time I'm done with him, he's going to wish he'd left me with Katy and adopted someone else to continue the family line."

"Remind me never to get on the wrong side of you!" Milly laughs.

I don't like to mention the way she'd treated me when our Houses declared war on each other. Milly seemed to only remember things when they were convenient for her. I supposed that if I had grown up in this messed up place, I'd probably develop a selective memory too.

Mr Pilkington came up to stand behind us. "Excellent work, girls," he says. "I think your parents will be very impressed with what you've done. Impressed enough to get out their cheque books and donate generously. Yes, you've done a very good job indeed."

"Thanks, Mr Pilkington." Milly beams. "I might not be as talented as some people, but I like to think I can still contribute." She cast a proud glance my way.

"I understand you're helping out with the front of house as well, Milly?" he asks.

She nods.

"Wonderful! That's just the kind of school spirit I like to see. Remember to sell as many raffle tickets as you can. Every little bit helps!"

He strides off, leaving Milly and me alone again.

"I guess I'd better go and tune my guitar," I say. "It's not long before the show's due to start."

"Okay. I need to go and sit out front anyway," Milly says. "Parents will start to arrive soon so I need to make sure the complimentary glasses of champagne are ready and waiting. Catch you later!"

She wiggles her fingers at me to say goodbye and heads off to take her place checking tickets. I turn and walk up the little steps to the stage. Heading behind the curtains, I go offstage and out to the corridors that lead to the music room where I'd left my guitar.

The room is empty, which is just what I need to clear my head. Helping Milly allowed me to forget my nerves for a while, but what I hadn't told her is that I suffered from crippling stage fright. While I'd been telling the truth when I said I didn't want to give my father anything to boast about, the real reason why I didn't want to perform is that I hated singing in front of an audience. I know it's something I have to get over, but I'd always preferred recording my material or performing it on YouTube. Online, potentially millions might discover me, but from a performance perspective it is just me on my own in a room with a camera. I could pretend nobody would ever see me and to be fair, so far, not many people have. Tonight, I am going to be singing in front of hundreds of strangers and the thought makes me want to hurl.

Although I haven't seen him yet today, Declan's guitar case is propped up next to mine. Seeing it there gives me a little reassurance I'm not going to be alone on stage.

I take my guitar out of its case and tune it. Once it's ready, I strum a few chords to make sure it is properly in tune. I don't think I'll ever get tired of the instrument's rich tone. There is something to be said for playing a good quality guitar.

I make a couple small adjustments and then pick out one of my favourite classical pieces. Katy insisted I take a few lessons once she saw how keen I was of music. I didn't last long. I much preferred playing my own material, and figuring out for myself how my favourite musicians did what they did. There are a few pieces I learned that I really love, and they were a good warm up before I start playing.

I close my eyes, enjoying the sound I'm making as my fingers dance over the strings. When I'm done, I am surprised by the sound of someone clapping. I look up to see Romy standing in the doorway.

"How long have you been listening?" I ask.

"I've been here a while," Romy says. "I saw you going into the practice room so I followed. I know you need time to get yourself together before a performance, so I figured I'd let you have a few moments alone before I came to wish you luck. Not that you're going to need it. I know how hard you've been practising. You're going to steal the show."

"I'm not performing on my own," I remind him. "Declan and I are doing a duet, remember?"

"No one's going to be listening to him." Romy waves away the mention of my music partner. "All eyes—and ears—are going to be on you. I'm so proud to be able to call you my fiancée. I'm a lucky man to have someone as talented as you."

He comes over and kisses me, my guitar forcing him to lean forward awkwardly to reach me where I'm sitting.

"This isn't going to work." He took my guitar out of my hands and put it to one side.

"That's better." He cups my face in his hands and kisses me. His tongue flicks between my lips and I instinctively open my legs to let him get closer.

I put my arms around him and hold him to me. He runs his hand over my hair tenderly. It's one of those sweet romantic gestures that makes me think he really does have feelings for me and isn't just going through the motions for the sake of a political marriage.

"A-hem."

We're interrupted by someone coughing. We break apart and I glance over to see Declan standing in the doorway. I blush at being caught like this. We were in the room where Declan and I had been intimate and I still felt guilty. Although not guilty enough to tell Romy what happened…

"Sorry to come between you two lovebirds," he says. "But Ivy and I need to start getting ready for the show."

"Of course." Romy kisses me one last time as if to mark his territory.

"Be as awesome as you always are," he whispers to me before leaving to take his seat out front with his family. Performance isn't his thing.

"Do you want to run through our song one more time?" Declan asks.

"Nah." I shake my head. "We've practised it enough and I feel too sick to sing right now."

"Are you okay?" Declan comes to my side and rubs my back, an anxious look on his face.

"I just get really bad stage fright."

"Well, you know what they say. If you feel nervous, imagine-_"

"Yeah, yeah. Imagine everyone in their underwear. But then I'm singing in front of a bunch of out of shape people wearing ugly underwear. It doesn't help, Declan. It doesn't help!"

"Okay, you got me." Declan laughs.

"I'll be fine once I get out on stage," I state. "It's just getting out there in the first place that's the problem."

"I'll be right by your side every step of the way," Declan says. "Come on. Let's go and sneak up to the back of the balcony. I want to see Ally's dance. I hear it's *really* bad!"

I laugh and follow him out to the corridor and up the stairs which leads to the balcony, giving us a good view over the entire hall. We creep around the back row of seats to stand in the middle where we can see everything.

My stomach lurches when I see just how many people are

crammed into the hall. I've never sang in front of such a large audience, and the thought terrifies me. What if I forget the words? What if I forget the chords? What if I forget the words *and* the chords? I'd die of embarrassment. I'd never be able to show my face in school again.

Sensing my thoughts, Declan grabs hold of my hand and squeezes it. "You're going to crush it," he whispers as the lights dim and a spotlight tracks Mr Pilkington's progress across the stage to a microphone stand ready and waiting for him.

"Good evening, everyone," he says. "And can I say how delighted I am to welcome so many of you here to our annual Academy fundraiser. I hope you've all brought your cheque books!"

Everyone laughs at the mere notion they wouldn't be ready to show off their wealth by splashing it about.

"As you are aware, this year's charity is the King Town Donkey Sanctuary which is so cruelly targeted by thugs. I hope they'll be apprehended very soon, but in the meantime, we can put a smile back on those donkey's faces by building them a brand-new luxury stable. Now, I know you don't want to hear me droning on all evening, so I'm going to make way for our very first act, the Ally Alligators!"

The audience bursts into applause as the curtains pull back to reveal a group of four girls all wearing skin tight leotards with an alligator print on them. Ally has been boasting about how her father is paying to get a top body painter to work with them and they'd certainly been worth their money because the leotards flowed seamlessly from material to flesh, making it look like they'd been transformed into an alligator/human hybrid.

It is a shame the dance doesn't match up to the quality of the costume. Ever see any of the dances Gina did in *Brooklyn Nine Nine?* She is a first-class professional in comparison to this lot. Ally has been going on about how much rehearsal they'd been doing, but they are all over the place. When she goes left, everyone else goes right. At one point, she trips and knocks over one of the other dancers. A complete mess.

But Ally seems happy with it, running over to the mic to yell, "Donate, everyone!"

"If that's the standard we're up against, maybe I really don't have anything to worry about," I murmur to Declan.

"There's a reason Mr Metcalf wanted us to perform," he replies. "I told you we'd be fine."

We stay there for the first half, watching comedians, magicians, singers, dancers, and even someone who'd brought their toy poodle along to do tricks. Unfortunately, the dog seems more interested in licking something off the stage floor than doing what it is told, but it's so cute that nobody cared.

By the time the curtain comes down for the interval, I lose my nerve, but as the lights come up, they flood back with a vengeance. It isn't long before it will be our turn to take the stage.

From my vantage point up high, I see my father get up from his seat in the front row and go over to talk to Romy's family. They all seem to be smiling and laughing. Whatever they are talking about, the discussion seems to be going well.

"Come on, Ivy. Let's go and get a glass of Dutch courage."

Declan takes my hand, and I let him. It feels right, even though it might raise a few eyebrows.

He skilfully works his way through the crowd and down to the dining hall where refreshments are being served. Ignoring the queue, he goes around the side and behind a long table laid out with glasses. Grabbing a couple and a bottle of wine, he nods at the girl serving, who smiles back, before leading the way back to the music room where I'd left my guitar.

"Here you go." Declan unscrews the wine and pours me a small glass.

"Is that all?" I raise an eyebrow. "I think I might need a bit more than that."

"Sorry, Ivy. That's all you're getting," Declan says. "Too much alcohol before a performance can screw your vocal chords. Besides, we need to save the rest to celebrate with afterwards. We're going to be amazing, you know. There's a reason we've been scheduled to close the show."

"Yeah. It's to make sure I'm as nervous as possible," I joke.

"Stop putting yourself down," says Declan. "You're an amazing performer. Channel those nerves into your music. People will think the little wobble in your voice is vibrato! Besides, you saw the standard of the other performances. We could crash and burn and they'll still be impressed. And we're *not* going to crash and burn."

"We'll see." I take a sip of my wine. I can tell it's expensive, not just a standard supermarket plonk. If Pilkington is serious about raising money, I'd think he'd economise on things like this. A lot of donkey blankets could have been bought for the price of this wine.

This is how the other half lives.

The muffled sound of cheers filters through the walls. The second half of the show is starting.

I take a large swig of wine to drown out the butterflies dancing around in my stomach.

"Take it easy, Ivy!" warns Declan. "I don't want to have to carry you onstage."

"Why did I agree to do this?" I wail. "I should have told Mr Metcalf I lost my voice."

"Don't be silly. This is what you were born to do, Ivy. Everyone else can see it. You just need to relax."

He comes around behind me and massages my shoulders. I close my eyes and lean back into him. He certainly knows what he is doing, I can feel some of the tension melting away under his touch. My nerves aren't completely gone, but he certainly helped.

His hands move down my front, lightly caressing my breasts.

"Mmmm." I moan, loving the way he is making me feel.

"Does this take away the stress?" he asks.

"You know it does!"

I can sense Declan's grin as he fondles my breasts, lightly

running his thumbs over my nipples, teasing them into being erect.

"Oh, god…"

I arch my back, leaning into him to give him easier access as he continues to play with me through my clothes. There is something incredibly erotic about the thought that anyone could walk into the room at any time and catch us like this.

"Feeling better?"

I pout with disappointment, as Declan stops touching me and comes back around to take another sip of his wine.

"Why did you stop? I'm all frustrated now."

"Exactly." Declan clicks his fingers and points at me. "You're frustrated, not nervous. Your mind is a million miles away from the audience waiting for you and your channelling the sentiment of our lyrics. You're in the best possible place to give the audience what they want."

"But I'm *really* horny." I wriggle about in my chair, desperate for him to come back and finish what he started.

"Sorry, Ivy. I can't help you with that." Declan grins wickedly, clearly enjoying the fact I am desperate to be with him. "Or at least, not right now. There's nothing to say we can't hook up later…"

"I like the thought of that."

Yes, it is wrong. Yes, I have a fiancé and it should have been him I turned to when I needed my physical needs fulfilling. But I still haven't seen Declan naked. He has a hold over me that makes me want to know what it feels like to have him inside, filling me completely, sending me to ecstasy as he enjoys himself over and over…

"Ivy! Ivy!"

I snap myself out of it, having lost myself in a daydream where Declan and I spend all day in bed together.

"Sorry, Declan. What is it?"

"We need to go stage side. We're on soon."

I gulp down the last of my wine and grab my guitar while Declan fetches his. A little rush of nerves runs through me, but it isn't as bad as it was, thanks to Declan's unusual relaxation technique.

We take our places by the side of the stage, listening as Nate, one of the other students finishes up a dramatic monologue. He is actually pretty good, which is a change given how bad some of the acts have been.

When he is done, he takes a deep, dramatic bow before walking off stage towards us.

"I warmed them up for you," he grins. "You're welcome!"

"Nothing like an actor's ego to fill the room," laughs Declan.

He gives my hand a final reassuring squeeze as Pilkington announces us.

"We've saved the best for last," the Head says. "As you've seen, we've got a number of very talented students in our midst, but these two are something special. I have absolutely no doubt that we'll see them at the top of the charts someday very soon. Please put your hands together and give a big round of applause for Ivy Archaic and Declan Dauphin!"

"This is it," Declan whispers to me. "We've got this!"

We walk out together, guitars in hand, to where the stage-hands have put a couple of stools out for us. We each sit down and the stagehands put mic stands in front of us. I reach up to adjust the mic so it is in the right position for me to sing.

"Good evening, everyone." Declan speaks into his mic, waving to the crowd. "Are you all having a good time?"

The crowd roars their response.

"Glad to hear it. This is a song Ivy and I wrote together. It's called *All That You Knew.*"

He nods at me and I start playing the chords to the introduction. He pick out a little riff over them, taking the lead while I establish the rhythm.

I close my eyes, letting the music take control. Declan is right. Now that I'm on stage and doing what I do best, I didn't care about anything else.

I have the first line to sing, and I put my heart and soul into it.

"You thought you had it sorted. You thought you had it made."

Declan takes over the next line.

"But if only you had known you were the one who's being played."

We continue to take it in turn, singing a line until we come together for the chorus.

"For all that you knew, I really loved you. For all that you knew, I'd given you my heart. But now you know it's not like that and you were wrong from the start. I was the one in charge all along, and all that you knew is gone."

We sing that song the best we ever had, but as the last notes fade away, we are greeted with silence. I look over at Declan anxiously, but then the hall explodes into raucous cheers and whistles.

"I told you they'd love you." I read on Declan's lips. It's impossible to hear him over the standing ovation.

"More! More! More!" People are stomping the floor, pounding away as they demand we sing another song.

"New School, New Start?" Declan suggests. I shrug my shoulders and nod at the suggestion of one of my songs.

"Thank you, guys, thank you." Declan has to raise his hands to gesture for silence as the audience continues to yell their praises. "If you want another song, we'll give it to you, but you need to be quiet to hear it!"

At last the crowd calms down. Declan looks at me and smiles.

We start strumming together, an upbeat rhythm that soon has everyone clapping along. In contrast to the beautiful ballad of our first song, this is a fast-pace rock number, and I always love singing it because it is so much fun.

I don't think it's possible for the audience to get any louder, but I am wrong. Their cheers are deafening to the point I wish I'd worn earplugs.

I scan the front row. Just as I thought, my father has a smug grin on his face and I knew he'd be taking credit for my performance later. On the other hand, Romy looks so proud he could burst. Seeing me catch his eye, he mouths *I love you*, pointing to himself, drawing a heart in the air and then pointing to me. I smile and blow him a kiss.

"Okay, everyone, I've got one more song for you."

My head whips around to look at Declan.

"Don't worry, Ivy." He put his hand over the mic to address me directly. "I'm going to do this one solo." He turns back to speak to the audience. "This is a little number I've been working on by myself and I figured tonight would be a good change to test it out in front of an audience. It's called *Loving You From Afar.*"

He closes his eyes as he plays a delicate little tune. He sways from side to side as he weaves notes together in an interesting chord progression, moving from minor to major and back again.

And then he sings, and I wish the floor would open and swallow me up. The lyrics were about *me*. Nobody else would possibly know what the references to 'stolen kisses' and 'kidnapped sighs' could mean, but it is clear that Declan is telling me that he loved me in front of a crowded hall—with my fiancé watching!

My heart aches with the beauty of the music. I'm always the one to write the songs. Nobody has ever written one about me. It is gutting me that I can't throw myself at Declan and kiss him thank you. But how can I possibly acknowledge this thoughtful gift he's given me? Nobody knew about that time in the music room. Nobody could ever know about it.

I feel myself pale as I realise that after this, there is every chance Romy will guess what happened.

Declan looks over at me and winks. I realise he knows exactly what he is doing. He is probably hoping Romy would guess.

I'm not sure how I feel about that. If things were different, I'd leave Romy and see how things went with Declan. But they weren't different. I'm under House Navarre protection. Declan and I never seriously discussed relations between our Houses. I have no idea if his family would take me in the way Romy's has. I can't take that risk.

My mind in a whirl, I want to leave the stage and lose myself in the rest of that bottle of wine, but I know that would be the most suspicious thing I could possibly do. All I can do is sit here, a sick smile on my face, as I wait for the final chords.

"Thank you very much." Declan nods and waves to the crowd when he finishes singing. "I want to dedicate that song to a very special lady. It's early days in our relationship, so I don't want to name names, but she knows who she is."

As Declan walks backstage, I can only stare at him. His words, his song running over and over in my mind.

"Your song was beautiful," I say.

"And true," he replies, making my heart beat so fast. Everything hurts as I stare at Declan, wondering at what point he snuck into my soul and made himself home. The song just made everything so much clearer. I realise I don't know how to be away from Declan.

Romy walks around Declan to me, and I have to snap out of it.

"Hey." I say, clearing my throat. "I was just telling Declan how much I liked his song. What did you think of it?"

"It's all right," says Romy, casting a cold glance at Declan. "Not really my kind of music."

"Yeah, well, it's still a work in progress." Declan shrugs. "It needs a bit of tweaking to get it to where I really want, but the audience seemed to like it."

"Whatever." Romy turns to me. "Are you ready to go, Ivy? There's a party at Archer's if you want to check it out."

"I'd love to, but I think I've got a migraine coming on." I put a hand against my forehead. I'm not completely lying. The adrenaline rush from performing is wearing off and combined with the stress of the situation, my head is pounding. "If it's okay with you, I just want to go home and go to bed. You can go if you like. I wouldn't mind."

"You think I'd abandon you to party when you're not feeling well? I don't think so." Romy says. "You don't look too hot. Let's get you home. I'll get Johnson to make up one of his famous headache remedies. They really work."

"Okay." Romy puts his arm around me and we turn to leave.

"You were great tonight, Ivy," Declan calls after me. "See you on Monday."

Of course. I have music first thing on a Monday morning with a guy who just sang the most hauntingly beautiful love song to me.

A song I will never, ever forget because it stole my heart.

Chapter Forty-Three

I spend the whole weekend locked up in my apartment, ignoring Romy's attempts to talk. I know he knows something is up, but I'm not in the mood to deal with his reaction, not when I am still trying to work through my own complicated emotions.

No wonder I spent a couple of days in bed with my duvet pulled over my head. I barely emerged for long enough to make myself a bowl of cereal when I was hungry.

Romy knocked on my door a couple of times to see if I was okay, but he left me alone after I rang his mobile and treated him to a few cut words about being bothered when I'd locked myself away. After that, he took the hint.

But now it's Monday morning and I don't have any choice. I have to face the world and pretend everything is okay.

Putting on my makeup, I feel like I'm putting on war paint. The look is more aggressive than usual, with dark purple lipstick and heavy eye makeup. By the time I'm done, I know that nobody is going to mess with me today. Not if they don't want their head bitten off.

As I walk out to the car to take us to school, I see Romy is already there waiting for me.

"Wow, Ivy." He does a double take. "You look…"

"What?" I ask.

"A-amazing," he says with a grin. "Definitely amazing."

"Thanks."

I get into the car and Romy climbs in after me. "How are you feeling?" he asks. "I've been really worried about you."

"I told you. I had a migraine," I say. "I'm sorry if I was short with you. I just needed to be alone."

"Did I upset you?"

"You didn't do anything." I sigh. "I'm the one who should be apologising. I told you I get really bad stage fright. What I didn't mention is that after I come off stage, I always feel like crap because I've wound myself up so much. It takes a few days for me to recover, but I'm fine now."

God, I'm such a liar. But how can I tell him that I'm struggling with my feelings for him and two other guys?

"You can always talk to me, you know?"

Romy puts his arm around me. I stiffen a little, then allow myself to relax into his embrace.

"You should have told me. I'd have arranged for a massage for you. We've got an amazing masseur who comes to the house. He could have set up the table in your room and helped you relax. Or, if you don't like that idea, I could give you a massage…"

I laugh. "Any excuse to get your hands on my naked body."

"Can you blame me? It is pretty incredible."

"That's very sweet of you, but honestly, I am much better off in bed on my own, sleeping away the weekend."

"You certainly seem better now," Romy says. "But if you need a massage anyway, I'd be more than happy to oblige."

"I may well need one after the day I've got," I told him. "Mondays are bad enough at the best of times, but I've got double politics. Dull with a double dose of dull."

"At least you're not in pure maths with Dr Clyde," Romy

reminds me. "His voice is so monotonous it's almost impossible to keep my eyes open."

"Looks like we could both do with a pick-me-up after school," I say. "Maybe we could go to that ice cream place? They'd be open this time."

"I like that idea. We've got a date."

When we arrive at the Academy, Romy takes my hand, and we walk up the stairs together. Maybe everything is going to be all right after all. Whatever the truth is about Declan, it's pretty clear he wants to pretend like he doesn't have any feelings for me, and that's just fine. I'm pretty good at faking being okay. We could both lie about our feelings and everything would go back to normal.

The bell rang to warn us that our first class is about to start, and Romy kisses me. "You've got music first thing, right?"

"Uh-huh."

"Say hi to Declan for me."

"Okay." I frown as Romy turns and goes off in the direction of the economics department. What did he mean by that? Has he seen something happen between me and Declan after all?

I don't have time to think about it too deeply, as a second bell rings to let us know that we have five minutes to get to the classroom or risk a late penalty.

I hurry to the music department, getting to my seat next to Declan moments before Mr Metcalf walks through the door—and he isn't alone.

"Good morning, everyone. I'd like to introduce you to a late-comer to our class." Mr Metcalf indicates the youth standing next to him. "Lucas Donatello, would you like to tell everyone a bit about yourself and why you're here?"

My jaw drops as the angry stranger who'd competed in the bike race speaks. Looking around the class, I'm not the only one who is surprised by his being here.

"As Mr Metcalf says, my name's Lucas Donatello," Lucas began. "Some of you may remember me from when we met a week or so ago. I'm staying with Solomon Archaic, who is an old friend of my mother's."

I gasp at the mention of my father's name. Declan kicks me under the table, warning me not to make too big a deal out of it. He is right. I need to wait and find out more information before I open my mouth big enough to put my foot in it.

"My mother wanted me to experience the very best education for my final years of school and the Academy's reputation is renowned throughout the world. When Solomon said he could get me a place here, it was an offer too good to refuse. I'd been studying at a conservatory back home in Italy so Mr Metcalf here kindly agreed to let me audition for him to see whether I'd be able to enter his class at such a late stage. Luckily I was able to impress him enough to be able to study alongside you all. I feel very honoured to be here and I look forward to studying with you."

"Thank you, Lucas. Here's hoping you maintain the same standard of excellence you displayed at your audition. Ivy and Declan, you've got some real competition now. You're going to have to work hard if you're going to maintain your position at the top of the class. Lucas, why don't you go sit in that spare seat next to Ivy?"

"Yes sir." Lucas nods and comes to the back of the class to take the seat next to me.

"We meet again." He reaches his hand out to me and I reluctantly shake it. "It's nice to be formally introduced, Ivy. Your father's told me a lot about you."

"I wish I could say the same about you," I reply. "I've never heard of you, let alone anyone with the name Donatello other than a dead artist. For someone who is such a good friend of my father's, don't you think it's strange he never mentioned you?"

"From what I heard, you didn't exactly see much of your father growing up," Lucas replies smoothly. "I'm sure there's lots of things he hasn't mentioned to you. It doesn't mean they didn't happen or that his friends don't exist. But he did ask me to tell you that he hopes we become as close as he and my mother are. And I have to say I hope so too."

"Is that right?"

"Quiet at the back!" Mr Metcalf barks. "We've got a class to get through. Don't think you can get away with disrupting my lessons, Mr Donatello. I have every right to withdraw your place if you fail to maintain the standards I require."

"Sorry, sir. Won't happen again."

Lucas slinks down in his seat, a smug grin on his face. I get the feeling he is getting a real kick out of making me feel wrongfooted.

"Now before we get into the real meat of today's lesson, I'd like to say thank you to everyone who performed at the fundraiser. Becky—your piano playing is very much appreciated by the singers who needed accompanying. The orchestra is on point—your interpretation of Saint-Saens rivalled any professional performance and of course Ivy and Declan you were as great as I knew you would be. Mr Pilkington will be announcing the final figures for the fundraiser later this week, but I know it's been an exceptional year and there'll be a lot of very happy donkeys thanks to all your efforts. Now please open your textbooks to chapter seventeen. Josie, if you could please read the opening paragraphs for us?"

I never enjoyed music theory lessons much, but today I'm grateful for the excuse to bury my head in a textbook. I can look like I'm paying attention and working hard while I try to figure out what is really going on.

There is no way Lucas Donatello is who he says he is. Just last week he couldn't find fifty pounds to enter the race and is accusing us all of being spoilt rich kids, but now his family can afford to send him here?

Another thought occurs to me; maybe his family isn't rich. Maybe my father is covering his school fees. It would certainly make a lot more sense, but if that is the case, why? What possible reason could my father have for spending all that money on a nobody? He'd left my mother and me in poverty and I am his *daughter*. Why would he help out someone who isn't even related?

There is a lot which didn't stack up here, but there is no way I'm going to get the truth out of Lucas. I am going to have to be sneaky if I want to find out what is really going on.

Lucas did a good impression of a model student during Mr Metcalf's class, and when the bell went off to announce break, he takes out his timetable and shows it to me.

"Looks like I've got double politics next," he says. "Any chance you could point me in the direction of the class?"

"Are you kidding me?"

"No. It's here in black and white. Double. Politics. In room 3E. Where do I have to go?"

"I'll take you." I sigh. "I've got double politics as well. We're in the same class."

"Really? Well, my day just got a little brighter." Lucas smiles and for the first time I see why girls might find him attractive. He has the bad boy look going on, but it's more hidden than what Archer gives off naturally. Lucas hides who he is under freckles and a sexy smile, but I see the darkness in his eyes. The darkness he is trying so hard to make sure I don't see.

But there is something about him that creeps me out. I can't quite put my finger on what it is. Maybe it is the fact that he arrived out of nowhere and now he is suddenly in two of my classes. Maybe it's just that I can't trust anyone who is close to my father. Either way, I'm not going to be sitting next to him in politics. Someone else can have that honour.

"You okay, Ivy?" Declan says lightly as he puts his books in his bag, but I remember how he nudged me earlier. I don't think he trusts Lucas either.

"Yeah, fine." I subtly shake my head to let him know I'm lying.

"I'll be in the music rooms at lunchtime if you want to rehearse," he tells me. "I'll see you there?"

"Sounds good."

We can compare notes about Lucas. Knowledge is always power in this place.

Lucas strides along confidently as we go to the politics department.

"How did you get into the politics class?" I ask him. "Music I can understand, but we've covered a lot of material. You've got a lot of catching up to do."

"Not really," Lucas says. "I was in the advanced class at home and mum got me a tutor as well. She thought it was important I be aware of the British political system because of our business interests over here."

"Really? What kind of business?"

"Oh, a bit of this, a bit of that," says Lucas breezily. "I'm sure you don't know everything your father's involved in. Same deal with me."

"I don't *want* to know about everything my father's involved in," I retort.

"Ah yes. Solomon warned me you weren't exactly close right now." Lucas chuckles.

"What do you mean, right now?" That's it. I am getting annoyed. "Did he tell you about how he chased my mum away and then left me in foster care after she died? What about the way he kidnapped my friends and almost killed one of them?"

"From the way he told it, your families were at war at the time. Is that wrong?"

"Well, not exactly."

"Ivy, I know your father didn't bring you up and believe me, he's absolutely heartbroken about that."

"Pah!" I spit.

"But he wants to make up for it now. Whether you believe him or not, he's only ever had your best interests at heart."

"My father only cares about himself."

"It's very easy to think that and I'm sure if I were in your position, I'd want to think the worst about him too."

Ooh, I want to slap Lucas so bad. There is nothing I hate more than being patronised.

"But when you take over your father's business, you'll understand why he's done the things he has," Lucas continues. "It's one of the reasons why he wanted you to take politics as a subject. He thought that if you understood more about how the world works, you'd be able to appreciate all the things he's done for you."

"You really are a good little lapdog, aren't you?" I sneer. "Do you do tricks? Will you sit up and beg if I offer you a treat?"

"Maybe. If it's you asking."

I open my mouth to make a snappy comeback, but we've reached the politics class.

"Come on you two." Ms Dupree waves us in. "Don't stand around in the corridor gossiping. Thank you, Ivy, for showing our new student where to go. Mr Donatello—would you like to introduce yourself to the class?"

Lucas went to the front of the room to repeat the same little talk he'd given earlier while I find my seat.

This is going to be a long class.

"ARE YOU FREAKING KIDDING ME?" I exclaim when Lucas walk into my business class. "Are you stalking me or something?"

"Not at all," says Lucas. "I took the classes your father recommended. He says they would be most beneficial to me. The fact that I got to spend more time with his lovely daughter is just a fortunate side effect."

"Uh-huh. I believe you. Thousands wouldn't."

"No talking!" snapped Mr Robson. "We've got a lot to get through."

"Fine by me," I mutter, taking out my business notes. I spend most of the day being tailed by Lucas. Any excuse not to talk to him is just what I need right now.

There is no way this is a coincidence. He has to have been planted here by my father, but why? Is he spying on me? I wouldn't put it past my father to pay for someone to go to my classes just to find out what I am up to. He wouldn't have been able to infiltrate Romy's household. All the servants have worked there for years. It would be impossible to get a stranger in there to find out what I am up to. The next best thing has to be getting someone in my class.

The thought makes me sick, but it is just the sort of thing my father would do. It seems there were no depths that man wouldn't sink to.

Mr Robson lectures us on venture capitalists and I can feel my eyes glazing over. I suppose that this sort of stuff would be useful if I ever wanted to set up my own record label, which is something I'd considered doing at some point, but it is so much easier to pay someone else to worry about the money side of things. All I want to do is make music.

I've never been more relieved to hear the bell for the end of class. It isn't just that Mr Robson has taken dull to a whole new level, having Lucas in all my classes creeps me out. He hasn't done or said anything exactly to make me dislike him, but knowing he is close to my father is more than enough to get red flags waving all over the place.

I shove my books into my bag. I can not get out of the class quickly enough.

"Ivy! Wait up!" Lucas hurries after me.

"Can't," I snap over my shoulder. "I've got to go."

"But I was hoping I could borrow your class notes," Lucas says. "The teachers here are teaching a different syllabus to what I'm used to. I thought maybe we could get some coffee and you could go over the things I don't understand."

"I'm not the right person to ask," I tell him. "I'm not exactly a star pupil in politics or business. Ask Travis or Becky. They'd be more than happy to help you—especially Becky. She was giving you puppy dog eyes all the way through politics. I'm sure she'd love the chance to spend more time with you."

"I'm sure she would, but I'd rather be with you, thanks."

"Sorry. You're shit out of luck on that front. I'm busy."

"Come on, Ivy. Don't be like that." Lucas reaches out and

grabs my shoulder, forcing me to stop and face him. "You were the new girl here not so long ago. You must remember what it's like to come into the Academy and feel like everyone wants to stick a knife in your back because they don't like the thought you might be a threat to their standing. Wouldn't you have liked someone to help you out?"

"Yeah, I would've." It is annoying, but he has a point.

"So, why won't you do that for me?"

"I have a fiancé," I point out.

"So? It's coffee, not a date. Surely your fiancé isn't so insecure he has an issue with you getting coffee with another man?"

"He's not." I thought about Romy and how self-confident he is. He is almost *too* self-assured, knowing that his prowess in the bedroom is more than enough to keep any woman coming back for more. Romy would probably laugh at the thought that Lucas posed any kind of threat to him.

"Then have coffee with me. Help me figure out everything I've missed. And maybe I can fill you in on a few things your dad's been up to."

I don't know how he knew that is the one thing which would intrigue me enough to meet him, but if Lucas could help me figure out what is going on in my father's twisted mind, it is worth spending an hour or so with him in a coffee shop.

"Fine," I huffed. "I'll have coffee with you. We've got an early finish tomorrow so we can go out then.

"Great. I look forward to it." Lucas smiles. But if he thinks he has anything to be happy about, he is deluded. My notes aren't worth a dime. I am going to get way more out of this meeting than he will.

Chapter Forty-Four

"That new guy Lucas is an interesting chap, isn't he?" says Romy as we drove home together.

"That's one way of putting it. He's in all the same classes as me. I can't get away from him. And somehow, he managed to talk me into having coffee with him tomorrow after school," I say.

"Good call."

I frowned. That is *not* the reaction I was expecting. "Really?"

"Of course. The guy's a total unknown quantity. Knowledge is power in this town, so if you can figure out where he's coming from and how he fits in with your father's plans, we'll be able to work out how we can use him."

"Of course. Why didn't I think of that?" I laugh bitterly. I am never going to get used to this town. Everyone is always out for themselves and what they could get. Nobody could just be friends without thinking about how that friendship impacted on their status.

"It's okay, Ivy. That's what you have me for." I think Romy intended to be reassuring as he pats my knee, but it comes off as patronising.

"Anyway. Enough about me," I say. "How was your day?"

"Pretty typical for a Monday. I've got a major essay I need to finish tonight though, so do you mind if I get a few hours to myself to work on it?"

"I've got a lot of homework myself, so that's fine."

"We could work in the library together," Romy suggests. "We might not be able to talk much, but we can at least be together."

"Thanks for the offer, but no." I shake my head. "Part of my endless amount of homework is a piece to work on for music. I don't want to disturb you," I lie. I don't have much homework at all, but all I want to do is have a long bath and listen to music by myself.

"Fair enough. Maybe we can have dinner tomorrow night after your coffee then? I can get Cook to make us something special, get the dining room set up with candles and roses, open a bottle of wine while you tell me everything you learn from Lucas."

"Okay. That would be nice." It would be nicer if it was just a simple dinner without getting all caught up in the politics of the Houses, but beggars can't be choosers.

***

I take extra care over my appearance the next morning. It isn't that I want to impress Lucas, but if a hint of cleavage and pouty lips could persuade him to reveal a little more about what my father is up to, I am not afraid to use what feminine charms I have to figure out what the hell is going on.

"You look good today." Romy's eyes travel up and down my body when I get out to the car. "Poor Lucas won't know what's hit him. Just remember you come home to me, okay?"

"Like I could ever forget." I lightly kiss him before getting into the car.

"Do you know where you're going tonight?" Romy asks as we head off to school.

327

"I thought I'd take Lucas to that coffee shop around the corner from the Academy," I reply. "We can walk there and there'll be plenty of people around to make sure he behaves himself."

"I like the way you think," Romy says. "Do you want me to come and lurk in the background to keep an eye on you?"

"I think I can cope with having coffee with someone," I tell him. "Anyway, we're going during our free period this afternoon. I'll be back at the Academy in time for us to go home together so I won't be late for dinner, if that's what you're worried about."

"I'm only worried about *you*," Romy tells me, kissing me on the forehead. "This guy is a mystery to all of us. For all we know, he could have a wicked plan to kidnap you and whisk you off somewhere I'll never be able to find. It would kill me to lose you."

"Don't be daft."

"I'm not. When you're an heir to a House, you're always a target for kidnappers. And it's not like this would be the first time your father got caught up in something like this, remember?"

My stomach clenches as I think of how my father imprisoned Romy, Archer, and Declan just a few months ago. "You don't really think Lucas would do something like that, do you?"

"Anything's possible." Romy shrugs. "We don't know this man. Until we know what he's up to, it's always best to be on the safe side."

"Okay. I'll make sure the GPS tracker on my phone is on," I promise. "If it looks like we're going anywhere other than the coffee shop near school, send in the cavalry."

For the first time, I feel grateful Romy's dad has insisted we both install apps on our phones so he could track where we were. I'd rebelled and switched mine off at random times just to annoy him, but now it seemed like he had a good reason to keep tabs on us. I don't think my father would do anything to hurt me, but then again, he seemed to view me as more of a pawn in his games than his own flesh and blood. And, of course, there is always the chance Lucas would have a scheme of his own, possibly even wanting to use me against my father.

This is why I'd need time out by myself. Having to think three steps ahead all the time is exhausting.

When we get to the Academy, Romy kisses me before heading off in the direction of the economics department while I wander off to the music practice rooms. As I walk down the corridor, I see Archer heading towards me. My heart beats faster. Archer is just my type, and if I am honest with myself, if I'd met him in a less fucked up situation, he'd have been the one I'd have gone for out of the three men who complicated my life.

"Hey, Archer." I smile at him, but he ignores me. I frown, wondering what I'd done to make him be so rude, but as he walks past, he subtly presses a piece of paper into my hands. He glances at me and subtly shakes his head, warning me not to open it just yet.

I know when to take a hint, so I palm the paper, heading into the nearest bathroom to read the note. Locking myself in a cubicle, I open it up.

Meet me behind the gym at lunch. I have information you need to hear. Make sure no one follows you, and don't tell Romy.

I read the note a couple of times. What could he possibly have to tell me?

There is only one way to find out.

I tear the note up into little pieces and flush it down the toilet so no one would be able to read it. It is going to kill me having to wait for lunch to find out what is going on. I've never been good at being patient, and I am desperate to know what is so important it merited this kind of secret squirrel behaviour.

"EVERYTHING OKAY?" Lucas asks as the bell rings for lunch. "You've been jumpy all morning and you've paid more attention to the clock than the teacher."

"Isn't it a little creepy that you know that?" I point out. "I mean, shouldn't *you* have been focused on the teacher instead of watching me?"

"I can't help myself." Lucas shrugs affably. "You're much easier on the eye than Ms Dupree. So what's the matter? Didn't you have breakfast or something? Let's go to the cafeteria. I'll buy you lunch."

"You're buying me coffee later, remember?" I remind him. "You go on ahead. I've got to find Mr Metcalf. I need to check the details of the latest composition assignment."

"Okay. But we are definitely going for coffee, aren't we?"

"I said we were, didn't I? You go have lunch and I'll see you in business later. We'll go straight to the coffee house afterwards."

"Can't wait." Lucas smiles and heads off in the direction of the cafeteria. I waits until he turns the corner, then wait some more, wanting to be sure he isn't going to double back and follow me to check I really am going to see the music teacher.

Once I am absolutely certain no one is paying any attention to me, I walk to the gym, desperate to find out what Archer has to tell me.

The gym is a large, redbrick building which stands on its own away from the main building that houses most of the classes. Behind it is a small copse of trees which provides perfect cover for clandestine meetings. It is also out of bounds, since those same trees meant it would be easy for students to be snatched without anyone noticing, and the Academy is marketed as a safe environment for rich students. If we get caught, we'd be lucky not to be suspended.

I glance around, checking no one is watching before I walk around the side of the gym building and out to the back where Archer is already waiting for me.

When I see him, my stomach flips. Damn, the man looks fine.

"Archer! What's all this about?"

"Not here."

Archer puts his arm around me and guides me, moving further away from the school to where no one would be able to see or hear us. My skin tingles at the feel of him being so close to me. This man has always been a danger to me in more ways than one.

A horrible thought suddenly occurs to me, and I stop dead in my tracks.

"Where are you taking me, Archer? Is this your twisted way of getting revenge on me for what my father did to you? Are you going to take me somewhere you've got men waiting to hurt me?"

"What?" Archer looks at me, confused. "No. Of course not. I'd never hurt you. I can't believe you'd think that about me."

He looks so downcast I immediately regret what I said. "I'm sorry. But you can't blame me for thinking about all the possibilities. This town seems to run on a diet of vengeance. What are we doing out here?"

"There's a CCTV camera that monitors the back of the gym," Archer tells me. "I have to get you somewhere it wouldn't be able to see us. In case you haven't noticed, I am standing directly beneath it in the blind spot, but with both of us there, there is a chance it might have caught the edge of one of us and have the guards come check us out. We need to be somewhere completely safe."

"That makes sense. But haven't we gone far enough yet?"

"Not quite." Archer shakes his head. "We need to go deeper into the trees so no one can see us. The guards patrol the path round the back of the gym and they can still see us from here. If we go a little deeper into the woods, there's a large dead tree which has been hollowed out. We can sit inside it and no one will be able to see or hear us. Then I'll explain everything. I promise."

"Okay."

Archer reaches out his hand to me, and I take it, following him down a narrow path through the trees. It takes about five minutes to reach the hollow tree he told me about, but once we get there, it's obvious it's the perfect place for a secret meeting. A few cigarette butts dot the ground, evidence that some other students snuck out here when they wanted to do something which would be frowned upon by the faculty, but we are the only ones here as Archer leads me inside the tree.

The ground is soft and comfortable, the tree surprisingly large enough for the two of us to sit next to each other and stretch our legs out without being crisped.

"All right, Archer," I say. "So what's so important you had to bring me out here and risk us both getting suspended?"

"Jeez, Ivy. Nice to see you too."

"Of course it's nice to see you, Archer. We haven't really had a chance to spend much time together since I came back because I'm with Romy. But you made such a big deal about how we had to meet in private, I thought you'd want to skip the pleasantries and get straight down to business."

"I'm sorry, Ivy. I've just missed you. I didn't realise how much until we got out here. But you're right. I should just tell you the news and not expect you to be happy to spend time with me."

He looks so miserable. I want to pull him into my arms and let him know how much I've missed him, too, but I have a feeling anything I say would just dig me even further into the hole I am already in, so I say nothing and let him continue.

"What do you think about the new guy, Lucas?"

"Not an awful lot. Not yet. We're meeting for coffee later and I thought I'd pump him for information then."

"Good luck with that," Archer says.

"Why? What do you know?"

"The guy's a liar. Whatever he tells you won't be the truth."

"How can you know that?"

"Because his name's not Lucas Donatello."

"Seriously?" I gasp, my hand flying to my mouth. I feel sick. "But I thought he is supposed to be a friend of my father's?"

"I have no doubt he's in your father's back pocket," Archer tells me. "But he's not one of the Donatellos. I've had my family's spies on the case and they confirm he definitely isn't related to them."

"So, who is he then?"

"We're still trying to figure that out. There's no doubt your father has been in contact with the Donatello family. They're one of the most influential business families in Italy, so his time out there would make sense if he's trying to build links with them. But whoever this Lucas is, he's not one of them. He's something altogether different and when your father does something this shady, it's something we should all be worried about."

"We have to tell Pilkington about this." I scramble to my feet, ready to go marching into the head's office here and now.

"No, we can't." Archer reaches up and pulls me back down. "If your father's paying Lucas's school fees, he'll already have paid off Pilkington to keep his mouth shut. I bet he knows exactly who Lucas really is or, if he doesn't, he's been paid enough not to care. If we start throwing accusations around, we'll be the ones to get in trouble."

"But you must have proof that Lucas isn't who he says he is," I plead with him. "We get that, plaster it all over school. Stick it on social media. Tell everyone Lucas is a fraud. Pilkington can't keep him here if we do that."

"I understand why you'd want to do that, but we can't." Archer shakes his head. "Sure, we could get Lucas chucked out of school, but what good would that do? It would let your father know we know he's up to something, so he'd just fall back on Plan B and we have no idea what that might be."

"We have no idea what Plan A might be!"

"A few of us went to the pub with him last night to welcome him to the Academy and it was all he could talk about. Says he is really looking forward to getting to know you better and implied Romy isn't going to be on the scene for much longer once he worked his charms on you."

"Good luck with that." I snort. "I might be getting married to Romy under pressure, but I'd still choose him a million times over before I ever go near Lucas."

"Well, you might have to suck it up a bit and let Lucas think he's in with a chance," Archer says. "Out of all of us, you're the one who has the best chance of figuring out what he's really up to. You can get him to talk. All you need to do is bat your eyelashes at him and he'll be putty in your hands."

"Oh, puh-lease. I'm not that irresistible."

"Ivy, have you looked at yourself in the mirror recently?" Archer casts a pointed glance down at my chest.

I blush. "Okay, so I made sure the girls were on display today. Funnily enough, you weren't the only one to have the idea that I ought to pump Lucas for information. I didn't realise there is so much at stake though. Now I *really* don't want to go out with him. The thought of being anywhere near him gives me the creeps. He's in all my classes, Archer. Says my father advised him which ones to take. I don't even know how he managed to get into music. He can barely play an instrument and you don't want to hear him sing."

"That's what money can do for you." Archer shrugs. "But you don't have to be on your own. I can come to the coffee shop with you, sit nearby, make sure he doesn't do anything he shouldn't."

"Romy already offered, and I said no," I told him.

"That's because Romy's your fiancé and it would be weird to have him there. I'm no one special. Lucas isn't going to give me a second glance."

"Of course you're special. At least... you're special to me."

I bite my lip and look away. I shouldn't be talking like this, but Archer *is* special. My body responds to being around him in a way I've never known before. It is weird, but just sitting here makes me ache to be with him again. I want to kiss him, feel his hands on me...

"You're special to me, too." Archer reaches and gently guides my head around to face him. "You have no idea how special."

He kisses me, and I let him. As his lips meet mine, I moan.

This feels so right. Archer and I fit together perfectly, as if we were made for each other.

"I've missed you so much, Ivy," he says. "There isn't a day that didn't go past without my thinking about you and wanting to know where you were. I hated being apart from you and then when you came back and moved in with Romy-"

"Shhh." I place a finger on his lips. "Let's not talk about him right now. It's... complicated. I'd rather talk about you and forget about everything, every*one*, else."

"Who says we have to talk at all?" Archer grins at me and I grin back, knowing exactly what he is thinking.

I lean forward and kiss him, his lips warm and soft. His tongue probes my mouth and I feel my pussy clench with desire.

I am going to have him right here in the middle of the woods where anyone could walk in on us. This might be my last chance to enjoy his body and I am taking it with both hands.

"Are you sure about this, Ivy?" Archer asks when we break apart. His face is flushed and I can tell he wants me as much as I want him, but he is trying to be a gentleman.

"I couldn't be more sure," I reply, pulling him to me to kiss him again. He put his hand inside my blazer, cupping my breast to rub my nipples through my blouse. There is something truly erotic about having him touch me through my clothes, a promise of pleasures yet to come.

I reach down and caress his groin, feeling how hard he is through his trousers.

"I need you," I whisper. "I need to feel you inside me, even if this is the last time. I have to have you, Archer."

I pull off my blazer and Archer follows my lead, the two of us quickly stripping off our clothes. Archer lays them on the ground as a makeshift bed, and I sneakily watch his cock out of the corner of my eye, loving how large it is when it is standing to attention.

"I've got a condom in my wallet," he tells me.

"Good. We're going to need it. But right now, I need you to suck on my tits."

"I can do that." Archer smiles and winks at me.

He kisses me, cupping my left breast as he rained kisses down the side of my neck, down my front until he reaches my right breast. He takes my nipple in his mouth and sucks on it hard, letting his tongue flick over it. I gasp as my nipples become erect, sending shudders of electricity through my body.

I reach between his legs and grab his cock. Gripping it hard, I massage him and he moans, moving his body so I can hold on to him as he kisses his way down my body to my clit. He lays on top of me, his cock in my face as he licks my clit. I grab his butt with both hands as I take his cock in my mouth, sucking on him hard while he continues to eat me out.

I grip his bum harder, my nails digging into him as his tongue sends me spiralling off into ecstasy. My whole body shudders as I come hard, but Archer is nowhere near done with me yet.

"You taste so good," he says, as he pulls out of my mouth, his cock hard and slick. "But I think I'm going to need that condom now."

I am so not going to argue. I prop myself up on my elbows, watching him as he gets the condom and puts it on. He climbs between my legs, plunging into me with a single thrust. I cry out as Archer slams into me, lifting my hips to meet his every move. He pulls out until only the tip of his cock is inside me before going in deep, his balls slapping against me to add to the plea-sure. His pace is unrelenting. He is like a machine, determined to fuck me until I am beyond satisfied, and I am happy to take it.

Suddenly, Archer pulls out all the way, and I sigh with disap-pointment.

"Get on your knees," he orders, and I am more than happy to oblige, loving not having to think about anything other than enjoying myself. I think I hear a noise outside of the tree, but I am too lost in sensation to care if someone is out there.

Archer enters me from behind, his hands reaching around to play with my nipples. The extra stimulation makes me cry out, unable to keep quiet. I reach down for a handful of clothes and stuff them in my mouth, knowing that although we are a distance from the Academy, someone might still hear us.

Archer's cock seems to grow even larger as he fucks me, filling and stretching me as he pounds at my pussy. My body seems to dissolve into waves of pleasure as I come over and over again. I feel high and will never come down again as long as Archer is inside me.

Archer's movements become more urgent as his own need to come takes over, I push back against him, wanting to make him feel as good as he is making me. He cries out as his orgasm hits, collapsing against my back when he is done.

The two of us fall to the ground together, our legs intertwined, Archer's arm around me holds me to him, spooning me. His cock stays inside me and I love that feeling of intimacy. You can't get closer than we are in this moment.

"I told you that you were special, Ivy," Archer murmurs in my ear. "No one else could ever make me feel like this."

I'm beyond speech, but I know what he means. Archer has an effect on me that is unlike anything I'd ever experienced with anyone else. Romy is a skilled lover, amazing. Declan seems to care about nothing but making me feel good; but Archer and I have a connection you can't manufacture.

In the distance, I heard the sound of the school bell. Lunch is over and I am due back for a business class.

"Shit."

Archer and I break apart, scrambling to get our clothes back on so we won't be too late.

"Wait," says Archer, as I turn to leave the tree and go outside. He reaches up and plucks a leaf and a couple of twigs out of my hair. "I'm so sorry, Ivy. I've ruined your makeup and you most definitely look like you've just been having sex. Not exactly the kind of look you want when you've got a class to go to."

"I'll just have to detour via the cloakrooms on my way to business then," I say lightly. "I'll be a bit late, but it is worth it."

Archer grins when he hears that and kisses me again, taking my hand in his before leading the way out of the tree. As we stand up, we see a couple of younger students standing on the edge of the clearing, unlit cigarettes in hand.

"Hope you enjoyed the show," Archer jokes as we hurry off in the direction of the gym.

"Did you mean it when you offered to come to the coffee shop later?" I ask.

"Of course," he says. "I don't trust Lucas, even in a public place. If you want me there for backup, I'll skip class and be there. I'm acing maths, so it won't matter if I miss a lesson."

"Thanks, Archer. I really appreciate it." I kiss him one last time as we hit the gym. The two of us separate to go to our respective classes, running off before the CCTV alerted the guards we were there.

Chapter Forty-Five

*I*t is hard enough to focus in classes I hate at the best of times, but after Archer's revelation, I struggle to take in any of what Mr Robson is saying.

Why is Lucas lying about his identity? I suppose I shouldn't be surprised. This whole town is built on subterfuge and deceit, but this is taking things to a whole new level. Not only has Lucas lied about who he is, my father has placed him in my school to get close to me, or at least, that's how it looks.

"Everything okay?" Lucas asks, as the bell rings for the end of that session. "Still up for our coffee? We can always make it another day if you prefer."

"No, no. I'm fine. Might as well get it over and done with."

"Wow. Talk about making a guy feel welcome." Lucas's tone is light and he doesn't seem to take offence, but I feel bad about being rude.

"Sorry, Lucas. I've got a lot on my mind."

"Maybe you can tell me all about it over our coffee." We walk together out of the Academy and in the direction of the coffee shop that is a favourite among Academy students.

"I thought I was supposed to be helping you catch up in class?"

"I've got a high IQ." Lucas shrugs. "I'm sure I'll pick it up pretty quickly and then we can spend the rest of the time getting to know each other before you have to run back to your boyfriend."

"Fiancé," I correct.

"Ah yes. Don't you think you're a little young to be getting married?"

"When you know, you know," I tell him. "Why wait?"

"Because there's a world out there waiting to be experienced?"

"Like I'd get to see any of it. I'm the heir to House Archaic. I'm supposed to spend the rest of my life in this miserable town."

"It doesn't seem that bad to me," Lucas says. "And your dad's house is pretty impressive. I wouldn't mind inheriting it."

"You can have it then," I tell him. "I don't want any of my father's dirty money."

"So, that's why you're marrying Romy? To let him take care of you so you don't have to take anything from your dad?"

"No, I'm not marrying him for his money, if that's what you're trying to say," I say. "And if you're just going to insult me then you can forget about coffee."

"Hey, no offence intended." Lucas holds up his hands in a gesture of surrender. "I'm just trying to understand you better, Ivy. You're a real enigma. I've asked around about you and nobody knows much. You didn't grow up here, so you don't fit in, which is something I can relate to. We moved around a lot when I was younger."

"Really? Why?" I try not to make my curiosity too obvious, but this is the perfect opportunity for me to learn more about who Lucas really is. I just have to keep the focus on him and get him to open up.

"Mum has to travel for her work," he tells me. "And she didn't like the idea of leaving me with tutors or sending me to boarding school, so I had to go with her. It's cool though, I saw a lot of the world and now I'm fluent in French, German, Italian, Mandarin and Japanese because of all the places we went to. But the downside is that it got pretty lonely. We were never in one place long enough for me to make friends, so after a while I stopped bothering. It is easier to keep to myself than try to get close to people I'd never see again after we left."

"There is this thing called the internet you know," I say. "Why can't you speak to them on Zoom or stay in touch on social media?"

"Meh." Lucas shrugs. "It's hard to coordinate calls when you're in different time zones. And out of sight, out of mind. Once you've left the country, people forget about you pretty quickly. Besides, Mum doesn't like me to be on social media. She says it's uncouth to be in people's faces all the time and no one cares what you're having for dinner."

"Uncouth, huh?" I'm not sure I buy into Lucas' explanation, but we arrive at the coffee shop, so I push open the door and lead the way over to the counter.

Coffee, Coffee, Coffee is an independent coffee shop which prides itself on fast service with a smile and good quality. It is so close to the Academy it could have served rocket fuel and still done a roaring trade, but the drinks were delicious so the place is usually packed with students on a free period wanting to get a break from the common room.

"I'll have a hazelnut hot chocolate with marshmallows," I say. "Lucas?"

"Iced caramel latte, please." He takes out his wallet, but I wave him away.

"This one's on me," I tell him. "Call it a welcome to the Academy."

"Nope. That's nice of you, but I'm paying," he says. "Mum would never forgive me if she heard I went out for coffee with a lady and didn't pick up the bill."

"Fine." I'd been involved in enough of these male ego

driven conversations to know when it is best left alone. "If you want to pay, be my guest."

"We'll take a couple of blueberry muffins as well," Lucas says, handing his card to the barista.

I look around the room and spot an empty table at the back.

"I'll go grab a couple of seats," I tell Lucas, taking the muffins and going over to the table. Sitting down, I pick a blueberry off the muffin and eat it while I gaze idly around the room. I frown when I spot Declan on the other side of the coffee shop. I'm sure he has an art class at this time. He looks up from the book he is reading and I wave at him, but he ignores me.

Strange.

Lucas comes over with the drinks and sits opposite me. "Everything okay?"

"Yeah, yeah." I take the hot chocolate from Lucas and scoop off a bit of cries with a marshmallow, popping the whole thing in my mouth. "What I want to know is how come someone who couldn't afford to enter a race suddenly rocks on up at one of the most expensive schools in the country?"

"Would you believe I left my wallet at home?" Lucas smiles winningly.

"No. I wouldn't."

"Okay. I was undercover. I wanted to check you all out, you especially, before I started at the Academy. I figured that if I pretended to be poor, I'd get a feel for what you were really like, who were the spoilt brats and who were the halfway decent people worth hanging out with once I started school."

"So I guess that Declan's your new best buddy then?"

"Not quite." Lucas chuckles. "He's a decent guy and I appreciated him paying for me to ride, but he's too caught up with his music to be interested in making new friends. He seems to really like you though. Whenever I've spoken to him, he's always mentioned you and how cool you are. Is there something going on there Romy needs to know about?"

"No. Of course not. Declan's just my song writing partner.

Why would there be something going on? We have to spend time together to work on our music, but that's as far as it goes."

Lucas gives me a knowing smile and I realise I'd given myself away by babbling too much.

"The lady doth protest too much," he says. "But don't worry. Your secret's safe with me."

"I don't have a secret," I lie. "Romy knows everything about me and Declan and he's fine about it because he's secure in our relationship. Romy trusts me because he knows I'll always come home to him."

"Is that right?" Lucas sips his coffee. "I have a feeling that might not be the case for much longer."

"Look, are we here to talk about my love life which, quite frankly, is none of your business, or are we going to discuss what we came here to talk about? Because if you don't want to know about what we've been doing in business politics, I've got homework. I'd rather be home, working, than have you insult me."

I get up to go but Lucas puts a hand out to stop me.

"Sorry. Of course we're here to talk about class. You make me nervous, which is strange. Girls don't usually have that effect on me."

"What have you got to be nervous about?"

"I'm having coffee with Ivy Archaic. That's enough to make any man nervous."

"Are you serious?" My eyebrows shoot up so high they must have gotten lost in my hairline.

"Completely. Who do you think the guys talk about when we think no one's listening? Your name is on everyone's lips. Everyone wants to be the one to have you ride pillion. There's a sweepstake going on about how long your engagement to Romy is going to last."

"No way."

"Yes, way. Word on the street is that the two of you are never going to walk down the aisle together, so they're all biding their time for an opportunity to get inside your knickers."

"Is that right?" I murmur.

"Yep. Declan, Archer, Matt, Tyler, everyone. They're all talking about how they're going to be there to pick up the pieces when Romy moves on to his next conquest."

As Lucas continues to tell me all about what people were really saying about me behind my back, I forget all about trying to find out more about his background. I feel sick to my stomach. Did Archer seduce me this afternoon just so he could boast about it to the lads? How would Romy feel if he heard about what happened?

"I'm sorry. I can't do this."

"Ivy? Is it something I said? Ivy!"

I get up and practically ran out of the coffee shop, tears blinding me. I hear Lucas coming after me, but I am not going to stop so he can apologise. I've had enough.

As I leave the coffee shop, I run into someone. The impact is more of a surprise than anything else, but it is enough to make me stumble and drop my bag.

I kneel down to gather up my things and the person I'd run into bent over to help me.

"Ivy? What's wrong?"

I dash away the tears when I realise I bumped into Romy.

"Nothing. I'm fine."

"Don't even go there. You're clearly not."

"Ivy? Is it something I said?" Lucas comes out of the coffee shop.

"Stay away from me, Lucas," I say. "You've done enough already."

"Ivy? What's happened?"

I sigh heavily and roll my eyes as Declan comes out to join us, Archer hot on his heels. I didn't see Archer in the coffee shop, but I am not surprised he is there, given how good he is at sneaking up on me.

Great. All the boys are here and all I want is for the floor to open and swallow me up.

"What did you do to her?" Romy snaps at Lucas.

"Me? I didn't do anything."

"Ivy doesn't get upset like this over nothing," says Declan. "I saw you say something which made her run out. What is it?"

"It isn't important," I say hurriedly, not wanting to open up that particular can of worms. "It's been a long day, that's all. Romy, can you take me home?"

"Not until I've taught Lucas a lesson in what happens when you upset my fiancée."

Suddenly, he lunges at Lucas and punches him in the face.

"Romy!" I scream. "Stop!"

I tug at Romy's arm to pull him away, but he is a man on a mission, following the punch with another blow.

Lucas makes to hit Romy back, but Archer grabs his arm. Twisting it around, he gets Lucas's neck with his other hand, pushing him forward so that he can't move without breaking his arm.

"Nobody hurts Ivy," he says. "I suggest you suck this one up."

"Fine," Lucas spits angrily.

Archer lets him go and Lucas slowly stands up…

…and goes straight for Romy.

Declan sticks out his foot and Lucas trips before he can reach my fiancé. He falls to the floor and the three boys surround him, kicking him.

Is that..? Lucas is *laughing*?

Even though the others are beating the crap out of him, Lucas thinks it is *funny*?

The guy is even weirder than I thought.

"Stay away from Ivy if you know what's good for you." Romy jabs his finger at Lucas, panting with the exertion of the fight. "If I find you anywhere near her again, I'll put you in hospital–and you won't be coming out again."

"Oh, Romy, Romy, Romy." Lucas stays on the ground, getting his breath back. "Make the most of her while you can. She won't be yours for much longer."

"What did you just say?"

"Enough, Romy." I pull his arm and this time he listens to

me. "Let's just go home. Leave Lucas in the gutter where he belongs."

"Yeah. Stay on your knees," Archer says. "You're not fit to be anywhere near Ivy."

"Come on, guys," Declan says. "Ivy's right. We should leave him here. He won't be bothering anyone anytime soon."

Declan, Archer, Romy, and I walk off together in the direction of the Academy to get our ride home, leaving Lucas behind.

Hopefully, he'd take the hint and transfer out of all of my classes. The boy is trouble, and I want nothing to do with him.

Chapter Forty-Six

$\mathcal{T}$here is another Bomber Derby scheduled for the weekend and I am really looking forward to it. It has been one of the worst weeks I've had since my father brought me to King Town. All my teachers were piling on the work and I feel like I am falling behind in every subject, even music. The only good thing is that Lucas has been off school all week. Maybe he'd been more badly hurt than he seemed. If so, he deserved it. I am not one to usually wish ill of anyone, but Lucas is a creep. If he did anything to jeopardise my engagement, it isn't just Romy and the boys he'd have to worry about. He'd have me to deal with me, and I am a bitch when I'm angry.

This Bomber Derby is in the Dauphin district this time and Declan has promised us a particularly tricky route. For now, I am not making a big deal about not being allowed to compete. Once Romy and I are married, it would be a different matter.

Romy roars up to the meeting point. Loud music is playing and there seems to be more people than normal gathered to watch the race. Most of the crowd seems to be milling around one particular area, and after Romy has parked his bike, he takes my hand, and we go over to see what is going on.

"Are you freaking kidding me?" Romy gasps when he sees what everyone is so fascinated by.

Lucas is standing by a Kaisaki Ninja H2R, arms stretched wide to address the crowd.

"This bike does 0-60 in 2 seconds," he is saying. "It has a top speed of 248.5 mph. My very generous benefactor gifted it to me because he wanted to make a statement to you all, which is move over, slow coaches. There's a new champion in town."

I don't stick around to hear what else he has to say. Just the sight of him makes me sick. I don't like to think about how much my father must have spent on that bike, but it is another sign there is definitely something going on behind the scenes and it is killing me that I have no idea what it is.

"Hey, Ivy. You okay?" Milly sees me walking away, and she comes over. "Lucas's bike is pretty cool, isn't it?"

"It's okay." I shrug. "But we all know that it's the rider, not the bike, that counts. Romy's going to check out the route now, but Declan's territory is filled with windy country lanes. All that horsepower won't do him much good when he's trying to go round a number of hairpin bends."

"Lucas seems pretty confident though. He was saying earlier he is going to get back at the ones who sabotaged him in the last race."

"Good luck with that." I snort. "Neither Romy, Archer, nor Declan will let him get anywhere near the finish line. He can throw as much money as he likes at his vehicle. He's never going to win."

"I hope you're right. Quite a few people are betting on Lucas taking the crown this time."

My stomach clenches at the mention of betting. I haven't talked about what Lucas said with Romy yet. I don't want him to get into trouble for fighting and I know he'd go nuts if he heard what Lucas is claiming. I'd thought about asking Declan if Lucas is telling the truth. He is the one person I thought could trust to tell me without getting angry about it, but I decide against it in the end. Who can I really trust in this place?

I hang around with Milly, wanting a bit of normalcy. All anyone want to talk about is Lucas and his bike and I can't care less.

"Can I tell you a secret?" Milly asks.

"Of course."

"And you promise you won't tell anyone, especially not Archer?"

"I won't tell a soul, particularly not Archer."

"I've started dating." A shy smile spreads across Milly's face.

"Really? Who's the lucky guy? Anyone I know?"

"He's not at the Academy," Milly told me. "I met him at Coffee, Coffee, Coffee. He saw me sitting by the window and said he had to come in and talk to me because I intrigued him. We've been seeing each other in secret, but I can't let Archer know because I'm not supposed to date anyone without running them past my parents first."

"Don't worry. Your secret's safe with me." I mime zipping my mouth shut, locking it and throwing away the key. "Tell me more about this mysterious stranger."

"His name is Carl, and he's 24," Milly says. "He works in IT and he has nothing to do with any of the Houses, so my dad would hate him, but I really like him. He's so sweet and considerate."

She is about to tell me more, but Romy comes over, interrupting us. "You ready to race, Ivy? We're about to start."

"I think you should ride on your own," I tell him. "Not because I'm pissed off I'm not allowed to race, but because I want you to beat Lucas and you'll have a better chance of doing that if I'm not behind you weighing you down."

"You won't weigh me down," Romy protests.

"Even so. I think you should keep your full focus on the race. I'll be at the finish line to celebrate your victory with a kiss."

"If you're sure."

"I really am. I want Lucas to realise he's wasting his time hanging around like a bad smell."

"Okay."

Romy goes off to get on his bike and I turn to Milly. "Shall we go over to the starting line?"

"Sure." Her phone buzzes and she pulls it out. "Oh. It's Carl. He's nearby! He's asked me to go meet him. I'll try and persuade him to come and let me introduce him to you."

She hurries off, leaving me on my own. I head over to the starting line, where ten bikes are lined up ready to race. Romy is in the middle, flanked by Archer and Declan. Lucas is towards the end, and when he sees me standing by the starting point, he salutes me.

I roll my eyes and shake my head in disgust.

"Are you ready? Three... Two... One... Go!" Matt gives the signal for the race to start and the bikers surge forward.

Lucas takes an early lead and as they zoom round the first bend, he is already ahead by a couple metres, the acceleration of his vehicle proving to be a huge advantage.

Now there is nothing left to do but wait and hope the boys can find a way of bringing down Lucas. I don't care who wins, just as long as it isn't him.

The route is circular, finishing where it has started, and I kick at the ground, bored already. Milly hasn't come back, and I'm not interested in small talk with the other spectators.

It seems like an eternity before the sound of motorbikes can be heard in the distance. I lean forward, craning my neck to see around the people surrounding me to spot who is in the lead.

I can hear the bikes long before there is any sight of them and it is a while before I see a bike approaching us from a distance. A solitary rider is a long way ahead of the next competitor and unless there is an accident, there is no doubt who will win.

My heart sinks as he draws closer, and I see that it is Lucas in the lead. Apparently throwing money at a problem did solve it after all. As he roars over the finish line, no one cheers. It appears I'm not the only one who has an issue with the newcomer winning. King Town didn't like it when an outsider showed up our own.

Archer came in second, with Romy a respectable third.

"Sorry, Ivy," he says. "I guess you were my lucky charm. I shouldn't have left you behind after all. It's not like I could have done any worse with you riding pillion."

"Don't be sorry," I tell him. "It is what it is. But now I really need to know why my father is helping Lucas so much. None of this makes any sense."

"But how are you going to find out what he's got planned? My father doesn't have any spies in his inner circle, and it's not like you can go up and ask him what he's thinking."

"Maybe I can." I think for a moment. "Romy, could you do a detour and drop me off at my father's? I can sneak in and see what I can find. I've done it before when I rescued you guys. I might be able to find something which will let us know what he's up to, and we can figure out our next move based on that."

"I'll come with you," Romy offers. "I don't want you going in there by yourself."

"It's safer if I'm alone," I say. "I'm less likely to be spotted and if they do find me, I'm my father's daughter. They won't hurt me. But if they capture you, there's going to be all sorts of trouble."

"I'm not happy about this, Ivy," Romy says. "I should be there to protect you."

"I'll be fine," I tell him. "I've got my phone and I'll have the tracking switched on. I'll hit the speed dial if there's any trouble and you can storm the place to get me."

"All right. But I want you to know I'm not happy about this."

I climb on the back of his bike and Romy speeds off in the direction of my father's. He drives past the security guard at the entrance and around the corner, parking up by a large tree.

"Here. I'll give you a leg up." Romy leans forward and clasps his hands together so I could put my foot in them, and boosts me up the tree. I shimmy up the branches, climbing out and over the wall around my father's grounds, dropping down on the other side.

The sun is setting, providing me with plenty of shadows to hide in as I scurry towards the house. I remembered the layout from when I'd rescued the boys, so I went around the back, staying low as I try each of the windows, trying to find a way in.

"Bingo!" I find a small window which has been left open. Carefully, I push it open, trying not to make a sound, tumbling through it into a study. Picking myself up, I dust myself off, trying to get my bearings. If I'm right, my father's study is a couple of doors down. If he is in there, I am planning on listening at the door to see if I can hear anything useful. And if he isn't, then I am going to rifle through as many drawers as I could. Somewhere in this house lay the secret to what my father is up to with Lucas.

I tiptoe over to the door and put my ear up to it. I can't hear anything, so I slowly pull it open...

...walking straight into the arms of two guards.

I reach into my pocket for my phone to press the button that would call Romy, but one of the guards grabs my hand. Pulling out my phone, he yanks it out of my hand, throws it to the floor, and stomps on it.

So much for the cavalry.

"Hey!"

They hold tightly to my arms and roughly drag me down the hall to my father's study. I did my best to fight them, kicking and struggling, but they are way too strong for me.

They go into the study without knocking. My father is clearly waiting for me, leaning against his desk, Lucas by his side like the good little lap dog he is.

"Ah, my dear Ivy. How good to see you again. I've been expecting you. I must admit it is quite amusing watching you ninja your way across the lawn, thinking you were being discrete. Surely you must have realised I'd have stepped up my security since you helped my prisoners to escape? You didn't honestly think you'd be able to get anywhere near my house without my seeing you, did you?"

Yeah. I did.

"What are you up to?" I don't let any of my fear show, instead letting my hostility towards my father shine through. "Why is *he* here?"

"I'm so glad you asked." My father smiles smugly. "Meet your new fiancé."

"Fiancé?" I do a double take as Lucas grins.

"Although not for long," my father continues. "Now that you're here, we can step up plans for your wedding. How does tomorrow sound?"

"Tomorrow? Woah, woah, woah. Hold on. I'm not marrying *him*. Not tomorrow, not ever."

"I had a feeling you might say that." My father leans across and presses a button on his desk. "That's why I arranged for a little insurance."

"Let go of me, Carl!"

My blood runs cold as an attractive young man drags Milly into the room.

"Ivy! What are you doing here? Have you come to save me?"

"I suppose in a manner of speaking, she has," my father says. "You see, Ivy is going to marry young Lucas here."

"Lucas?" Milly frowns. "But she's marrying Romy."

"Not anymore. Ivy will marry Lucas tomorrow, otherwise we'll all be gathering to witness your execution."

"What?"

"No!"

Milly screams and I gasp.

"So, you see, it's all Ivy's choice. Marry Lucas or your best friend dies. Which is it to be?"

Epilogue

I look at my reflection in the mirror. My father's assistant Isabella certainly has good taste in wedding dresses. The ivory gown is figure hugging, just the right side of understated with delicate embroidery running around the hem with a high front and low back. My hair is caught up in a chignon, a long veil covering my face and hair.

Milly stands next to me, wringing her hands. "I'm so sorry, Ivy." She is on the verge of tears. Again. "I had no idea Carl was working for your father. I should have guessed. No one that attractive would want someone like me. I owe you my life for this, Ivy. I'm going to change, I'm not going to be the pushover any longer. I will figure out a way to make your father and Lucas pay for this."

"Stop it, Milly." I turn and put my hands on her shoulders, wanting to shake some sense into her. "You're beautiful. Any man would be lucky to have you. If Carl hadn't brought you here, my father would have found some other way of black-mailing me into doing what he wants. None of this is your fault, so don't beat yourself up about it. I'll get an annulment or something."

"But what about Romy? His heart will be broken when he finds out."

Neither of us mention the gunshots we'd heard the night before. I was in no doubt that Romy had tried to come get me, but my father's men fought him off. I could only hope that he'd managed to get away without being hurt.

And that he'd forgive me. How stupid I'd been, thinking I'd be able to figure out my plans so easily. This isn't Milly's fault. It is all mine.

There is the sound of someone unlocking the door. Milly and I look over to see Isabella come in.

"Are you ready to get married?" she asks with a fake smile just for me.

Never in a million years.

CLICK HERE *to find the next book in this series.*

Description

King Academy has fallen with its elite and I'm going to save them.

All towns have sins, most hide them well, but King Town?
The sins rule here.
And they each have a name.
Archer Knight, Romeo Navarre, and Declan Dauphin rule this little town. *And I am theirs.*
Together, we have come up with a plan to make sure our throne never ends.

My father has no idea what is coming next.

Some say our story started with a fairytale but it will end in blood and crowns.

Recommend for 18+ readers due to content. This is a full-length book and the first of five books in this series and a reverse harem romance which means the main characters has more than one love interest.

Chapter Forty-Seven

"Good morning, wifey."

I open my eyes to see Lucas smiling down at me, leaning against the side of the bed like he owns the entire world. I feel like throwing up. It's been a week since Lucas and I had exchanged vows, and I still am not used to being married to him. I didn't think I ever would be. It wasn't as though I'd done it because I wanted to. When you're faced with a choice of get married or see your best friend butchered before your eyes, you say 'I do,' even while your heart screams *I don't!*

The only good thing so far was that Lucas had behaved like a perfect gentleman since he put a ring on my finger. He hasn't even kissed me, other than an awkward peck on the lips once the priest declared us man and wife. Sure, we slept in the same bed and my father insisted on calling me Mrs Donatello every time we met, but for all intents and purposes, we might as well have been brother and sister for the lack of passion between us. Every time I see him, I only see them. The three kings who have my heart and nothing my father or Lucas can do will change that fact.

I stretch out, trying to act all nonchalant when the reality is that the thought of walking back into that school a married woman makes me feel like I have heavy rocks at the bottom of my stomach. How am I meant to explain this to Declan? And what about Romy? Poor Romy will be heartbroken. Our engagement might have been one of convenience, but at least the two of us had feelings for each other. It wasn't all fake.

Archer would know about it by now. My father had kept Milly under lock and key since the wedding. He called it insurance in case I decided I wasn't going to accept life as a married woman, but now we are going public with the news I'd married Lucas, he let Milly go home last night.

I hope against hope she would be at school today. I am going to need a sympathetic face, but something tells me her family would insist she stay home to recover from her ordeal and I can't blame them. The Knights had suffered enough thanks to my father.

"It's going to be okay, you know," Lucas says. "I'll be with you. I know you don't think much of me right now, but I want to make this marriage work. It's to both of our benefit if it does. It might be too much to ask for you to love me right now, but I think, no, I *know* that when you get to know me better, you'll find I'm not a bad person and maybe you'll change your mind."

"You keep telling yourself that," I say, getting up and grabbing some clothes before going to the bathroom to brush my teeth. I lock the door behind me. This is the only privacy I ever get, so I take my sweet time getting ready.

My father confiscated my phone, so I have had no contact with the outside world since my sham of a wedding ceremony. I can only imagine how many text messages Romy has sent me. The poor guy must be going out of his mind.

If I'd been allowed to wear whatever I liked to school, I'd have picked all black clothes, a signal that I was in mourning for the life I should have had. As it is, I go for a Goth look with my makeup, going as over the top as I dared without risking being told to wash it off by Pilkington. I am not going to glam myself up for Lucas. Anyone watching me will know I am angry with the world and my father in particular.

"Wow, Ivy." Lucas does a double take when he sees me stride out of the bathroom. "I wouldn't like to get in your way today. You look like someone seriously pissed you off."

"Someone did." I give him a look, and he smirks.

"Look, none of this is my fault," he protests, holding his hands in the air. "I've told you that so many times I'm sick of hearing it. I'm as much a victim here as you are."

"You keep saying that, but I've yet to see any evidence of it," I reply. "You're still as buddy-buddy with my dad as always. The pair of you are up late talking every night, no doubt plotting your next move to take over this town. Well done on preventing a marriage to Romy Navarre which would have given me independence from my father, but would *also* have benefited House Archaic. I don't know what you said to my father that persuaded him that a complete unknown was a better bet, but whatever it was, it must have been good. My father never does anything unless it benefits him. So, what was it, Lucas? What did you promise him? Or did you *buy* your way into my family?"

"We ought to go to the dining room," Lucas replies, sidestepping the question. "Your father wants us to have breakfast with him before we go to school."

"Probably wants to check I'm not wearing gloves to cover up my wedding ring," I snipe, but I follow Lucas out of our suite and down to the dining room where we've been having meals with my father three times a day since the wedding. Most couples would have been on honeymoon this past week, but not us. My father said he was going to pay for us to go away on our first anniversary. Until then, he wants to 'keep an eye on us', presumably to make sure that I am behaving the way he wants. Lucas has the father-in-law from hell, but what my father doesn't know is that I can be as stubborn as him and I am more than happy to wait for the perfect opportunity to get my revenge.

He won't know what hit him by the time I'm was done with him.

"Ah, the happy couple." My father beams at us as we walk into the dining room together. "So good to see you ready to announce your marriage to the world."

I scowl but say nothing as I cross over to my regular seat to the left of my father, Lucas coming to sit next to me. I bite down on my cheek as hard as I can to stop myself from screaming. The taste of my own blood settles me.

"Let me see your hand, I want to make sure everyone can see your commitment to Lucas," my father orders. Obediently, I hold out my left hand and he takes it, inspecting my engagement ring and wedding band. Even though Lucas and I hadn't had time for an engagement, my father had insisted on supplying me with a ridiculously over the top diamond solitaire and matching platinum wedding ring which had been engraved with Lucas and my names.

"Good." My father nods, satisfied. "Be sure to show that to everyone you meet, particularly Archer Knight and Romeo Navarre. Let no one say that your new husband doesn't know how to treat a lady. And while you're at it, be sure to mention how in love the two of you are. By the end of the day, no one at the Academy should be in any doubt that you are serious about this marriage and being with Lucas. I do not want to hear any rumours about you and Romeo rekindling your affections behind Lucas's back--nor do I want to be told that Archer is using you to get to me. Are we clear?"

"Clear," I mutter.

A maid comes and places a plate with a selection of Danish pastries in front of me as well as a large bowl of fresh fruit salad with a dollop of plain yogurt on the top, exactly how I like it. I have no appetite--hadn't wanted to eat since the wedding--but I know my father would be displeased if I didn't finish everything in front of me, so I force it down, every bite turning to ashes in my mouth.

"Now then," my father comments. "I want you both to

come straight home after school today. Ivy, I'm sure you'll have a lot of catching up to do with all the classes you missed. Your work has never been exemplary other than for music. Need I remind you that I allowed you to take that class on the condition you maintained a certain standard in your other subjects? I know you were able to scrape by the assessments on your return to the Academy, but you and I both know that if you do not remain diligent in your work, you'll soon slip behind your peers, which will not do. You've missed enough school this year without having to lose another week."

And whose fault is that?

I know better than to openly criticise my father, so I say nothing.

"Lucas," my father continues, "I want you to come see me as soon as you return home. We have a few matters to discuss after you've assessed the situation at the Academy. Of course, I know there's no need to worry about *your* grades. There's no doubt who has the brains in your relationship."

I narrow my eyes and bite harder on my cheek. If I'd been allowed to take the subjects I'd chosen, I'd be acing them. It isn't my fault I was being forced into doing something which didn't suit my skills and interests.

I force down the last of my fruit while Lucas finishes his bacon. He starts every day with a full English. He must have hollow legs to eat all that food and still be as skinny as he is, but I take a small satisfaction from thinking about the damage it is doing to his arteries in the long term. If I can't figure a way out of my sham of a marriage, maybe I'd get lucky and he'd keel over from a heart attack in his forties.

"I guess it's time for us to head off to the Academy." Lucas takes my hand and squeezes it, smiling at me. "Excited?"

"Yeah. I can't wait to show everyone my new bling." I fight hard to keep the sarcasm out of my voice.

"Have fun, you two!" My father waves as Lucas and I leave the dining room and go out to the car, our school bags already packed, sitting on the back seat ready for us.

Perfect for a trip to hell. Or in other words, King Academy.

LUCAS and I stood at the bottom of the stairs leading up to the Academy. He reached out and took my hand, and for once I didn't pull away.

"It's going to be all right, you know," he tells me. "Once the excitement over our wedding dies down, nobody will care about us. Today's news is tomorrow's chip wrappings, as they say. I know you're nervous, but it's going to be all right. Romy will understand. He knows how the politics of this place works. Love doesn't enter into the equation when you're heir to a House. He'll be happy for you. You wait and see."

I smile weakly, wishing I could share his optimism. I knew what things had been like between Romy and me. He isn't going to take this lying down.

"Come on." Lucas nods in the direction of the school. "The bell for first period is going to go in a minute. We might as well go up and hit the common room first. That way we can make sure as many people know as possible. After that, the rumour mill will spread the word way faster than we'll be able to."

"Okay."

I keep holding Lucas's hand as we walk up the stairs and into the entrance hall of the Academy.

"There they are."

I look over to the stairs leading up to the first floor. Romy, Archer, and Declan are standing by the bottom step, waiting for us. The three kings of the academy and each one of them look ready to kill.

And for some reason, it makes my heart pound that much more.

"Ivy!" Romy walks to me, but Lucas moves in front, stopping him from getting closer.

"Stay away from my wife if you know what's good for you," Lucas coldly warns.

"So it's true?" Romy looks at me, his face twisted with hurt and pain but mostly anger. So much anger. And it hurts me to see any of it. I never wanted to hurt him, I just pushed him away because I thought it was the best thing to do, but the truth of it is, I am in love with him. So in love with him. I just wish this wasn't the moment I realised my heart belongs to the kings of the academy.

I can't speak. I can't say a word as I move to Lucas' side and Lucas grabs my hand, showing off my ring.

Archer swears, his gaze flickering between me and Lucas. "I don't know how you managed it, but I know you don't love him."

Archer moves right into Lucas' face, basically spitting his words out. "How can you sleep at night?"

"Very well, thanks, with my beautiful wife to keep me warm." Lucas puts his arm around my waist and pulls me to him. I stand there limply, not knowing what to say, and I hate that this has made me so weak.

How can I fight my dad? How can I have the men I love in my life?

Either way, this all ends in heartbreak and I can't have my heart broken anymore.

"Can't you see she's not happy?" Declan asks, his hands shaking with anger.

"Who, Ivy?" Lucas kisses me on the top of the hand he is still tightly holding. "She's head over heels in love, aren't you?"

"Yes," I bite out.

"All right. That's enough," Archer says. "Ivy, you need to apply for an annulment. There's no way this sham of a marriage can be allowed to continue. Milly will sign an affidavit to say you got married under duress and this can be undone in no time. I'll give you the money for court fees. You'll be free to marry whoever you want. Romy. Me... it doesn't matter. You're *our* girl."

My heart feels like it is shattering into a million pieces at the intense look in his eyes. I'd love nothing more than to take him up on his offer, but I know my father would never let me get away with something like that. He'd threatened to kill Milly, and I hadn't doubted he would have carried through with it if I hadn't done what he wanted. I don't like to think what he'd do if I divorced Lucas to go off with someone else. Probably burn the whole town down.

"Back off. Ivy's married to me, so you're going to have to get used to it, because we're in it for life." Lucas pushes Archer in the middle of his chest to emphasise his point. *Big* mistake.

Archer doesn't budge an inch, so Lucas shoves him again with both hands this time. Archer doesn't even stumble as he pulls back his fist and punches Lucas in the face. I fall to the side as they start fighting and I crawl to my feet.

"Lucas! Archer! No!" I try to pull Lucas away, but he easily shakes me off.

"Leave them to it." Declan takes me to one side, safely away from the fight. "You've got to understand that we're all really upset about what's happened."

"But we've got to do something!" I desperately want to go over and separate the boys, but Declan's calming hand on my arm is enough to keep me away.

"Believe me, you don't want to get between those two," Declan advises. "I don't think Archer's ever going to forgive Lucas for endangering Milly and that's without him putting a ring on your finger. He's been practically climbing the walls this last week, wanting to know what's happened to his sister. There were all sorts of rumours flying around about where she was. The Knights were *this* close to putting together an army and going door to door in this town to find her. Then when she came home with the news that she'd been forced to witness your wedding to Lucas Donatello, well… This is exactly what he said he'd do."

I watch in horror as Archer lashes out at Lucas, raining down blows. Lucas is a good fighter but he has nothing on Archer. Archer is known for being a tough guy. Nobody messes with him. Not only does he spend hours in the gym, his father has made sure he's been trained in multiple martial arts, so he knows how to take care of himself. But if he thought this was going to be an easy fight, he's as surprised as the rest of us at Lucas' ferocity. The man fights like someone possessed. He takes everything Archer throws at him and gives it back tenfold.

"Somebody do something!" I cry out, unsure as to what exactly I wanted to see happen. I only know that someone has to stop this. As much as a small part of me is happy to see Lucas getting beaten on, I don't like Archer being hurt.

I meet Romy's eyes over the fight, seeing him leaning against the lockers and I beg him to help without saying a word.

Romy finally moves over to them. He grabs Lucas' jacket and pulls him back, shoving him against a locker.

"This has gone too far. If you want us to kill you, then we will, but not in front of her. What the fuck are you doing getting involved with Ivy's dad? Or Ivy, for that matter?" He slams him one more time into the locker. "You know she is ours and we will never, ever let her go. You fucked up, Lucas."

"Fuck off," he growls and punches Romy hard in the side of his face. Romy falls and Archer growls as he gets ready to attack Lucas again.

"That's enough! Break it up, you two, Break it up!"

At last, Mr Pilkington appears. Without hesitation, he strides over to the two boys and somehow manages to get between them. Some sort of self-preservation kicked in, Lucas and Archer recognising that hitting the principal isn't a good move and the two of them step back, panting.

"Romy!" I run over when it's safe, crouching down beside him. He is out cold.

"Ms Andrews. Call an ambulance, please," Mr Pilkington orders one of the staff members who'd come with him to break up the fight. She nods and pulls out her mobile, calling for one of the private ambulances which serviced the House hospital. "Now, would somebody care to tell me what's going on here?"

"I have no idea," Lucas growls.

"Yes, you do." Archer reaches around Mr Pilkington and shoves Lucas, who pushes back.

"I said, that's e-*nough*. Don't make me get the guards to restrain you."

Lucas and Archer keep their focus on each other, but they put down their hands, releasing their fists. Now that the fight is over, I can see that they'd both hurt each other. Archer is going to have a black eye, and Lucas is holding his left arm awkwardly.

"Mr Donatello. Tell me your version of what's just happened."

"Archer is jealous of the fact I married Ivy. He wouldn't leave my wife alone, so I had to defend her."

"Ah yes. I hear congratulations are in order." Mr Pilkington nods briefly in my direction. Was it my imagination, or did I detect a faint hint of disapproval? "And Mr Knight. What do you claim happened?"

"Lucas pushed me," Archer smoothly replies. "He thinks he's something just because he blackmailed Ivy into marrying him. I couldn't let him dishonour House Knight like that."

"You don't need me to dishonour the Knights," Lucas counters. "You can do that all by yourself."

"All right, all right." Mr Pilkington put his arms out to keep the pair of them apart. "I've heard enough. House politics are for you to figure out between you—*without* using your fists. You know our school policy on violence. The pair of you are suspended for the rest of the week. I want you to go to the hospital to get yourselves checked out. Make sure you haven't done any serious damage to each other while you're under my watch. I'll phone your parents to let them know the situation. Once the doctor signs you off, you'll be sent straight home. Now sit down over there and wait for the ambulance."

Lucas and Archer stride over to a bench down one side of the room and sit on opposite ends, casting filthy looks at each other. Mr Pilkington comes over to me to check on Romy, who'd just woken up.

"How are you doing, Mr Navarre?" he asks.

"What happened?" Romy struggles to pull himself up, the movement clearly hurting his head, so he falls back down again. I kneel down, gently supporting him. Putting his head in my lap, I stroke his hair, wishing I could do something more productive to help.

"Someone hit you and you fell over. You must have banged your head," I tell him. "You've been unconscious for a couple of minutes."

"There's an ambulance on the way," Mr Pilkington says. "Stay where you are until they get here."

Ms Andrews comes over with a blanket and drapes it over Romy, who closes his eyes.

"All right, you lot." Mr Pilkington addresses the crowd of students who've gathered round to watch the drama. "Move along now. You're late for class. Stick around here and I'll be giving detentions to each and every one of you."

There's a lot of grumbling and muttering as the students disperse to go off to their lessons. I stay where I am, worried about Romy.

"You can go in the ambulance with him if you like," offers Mr Pilkington gently. "I can imagine how you must be feeling right now. You've been through a lot this past week or so."

"That's one way of putting it," I mutter.

A siren can be heard wailing in the distance, getting louder and louder. Not longer after, a few paramedics come rushing through the Academy doors.

They worked efficiently, clearly used to cleaning up clashes between the Houses and knowing that there is more than their jobs on the line if anything happened to one of the heirs. As they bundle Romy onto a stretcher to get him into the ambulance, Romy's eyes open. He reaches out towards me.

"I love you, Ivy, and I will save you."

He passes out before I can reply. Before I can tell him I love him too.

Chapter Forty-Eight

I ride to the hospital with Archer; Romy and Lucas both in their own ambulances. I wanted to go with Romy, but he needed urgent medical care and they told me to stay out of the way. I know I should have gone with Lucas. As his wife, I am his next of kin so I should have stayed with him, but I just didn't want to be around him. If he'd hurt Romy, I don't care if we are married. I'll kill him myself.

When we arrive at the hospital, we are ushered into separate rooms to wait for a doctor to come and check the boys out. Archer and I are alone for the first time in over a week and I want to make the most of it.

"So…" I say.

"So…" Archer can't even look me in the eye.

"I am so sorry." I can't think of what else to say.

"Why? It's not your fault your father is an overbearing, controlling megalomaniac." Archer shrugs, but I still feel like I was to blame. "As long as you don't actually love him, we can fix this."

"You have no idea how bad I feel about all of this," I tell him. "I was being forced into marrying Romy, but at least I liked him and his parents didn't have to threaten anyone to get me to agree."

"No, they just threatened *you*," Archer points out. "Be honest, Ivy. You wouldn't be marrying *anyone* right now if we didn't have parents who like to control every aspect of our lives."

"I guess not." I sigh.

"Have you slept with him?" The question caught me off guard.

"Who? Lucas?"

Archer nods.

"No."

Archer visibly relaxes with relief.

"I know you all hate Lucas," I say. "But he's not too bad when you get to know him. He's been a perfect gentleman. He hasn't even laid a finger on me, even though we're sleeping in the same bed. We have to," I add quickly, seeing Archer's face darken. "My father told us that this is to be a real marriage, and he's forced us to share a room. I wouldn't put it past him to do something really messed up and spy on us to make sure we're sharing a bed. It's not something worth making a big deal about when Lucas is willing to keep his hands to himself."

"But for how long?" Archer clenches his fist, clearly still filled with anger. "Ivy, no man could sleep beside you and be happy with just sleeping. You need to watch yourself with Lucas. He's not like the rest of us. He's not one of the Houses. He's got his own agenda and none of us know what that is. My father's spies have been trying to find out information on him, but the man's like a ghost. Nobody has a clue where he's come from or what his motivation for being here might be. He's going to find a way to get whatever it is he wants from you, and you won't know you've been played until it's too late. If he takes you from me, *really* takes you, I don't know what I'll do."

There is no way of reassuring him with words, so I did the only thing I could think of. I kissed him, slow and deep.

"Lucas can't take me away from you," I whisper, as we pull apart. "My father's the one you need to be wary of."

Archer shakes his head. "You're wrong. I know all about your father and the kind of games he plays. We all do. He's a known quantity and my family has measures in place to make sure he doesn't overstep his bounds. But Lucas? None of us know anything about him, what he's capable of, the kinds of resources he has to hand."

"But Lucas is still at school," I protest. "How much of a threat can he really be?"

"Never judge by appearances," Archer says. "I'd have thought you'd have learnt that by now. Someone needs to put Lucas in his place, and I'm more than happy to be the one to do it."

"Are you sure that's such a good idea?" I gently run my hand over the bruising surrounding Archer's eye and he winces. "Maybe the two of you should talk. I know, I know. That's a very strange thing to do in this place. Talk instead of fight. But perhaps it's time to try a new way."

Archer reaches up and takes my hand in his. He is about to say something, but the door opens and Lucas strides in. I move to pull away from Archer, but he grips my hand tightly, sending a message to Lucas.

Lucas narrows his eyes. "Come on, Ivy. It's time to go home."

"She's staying with me," Archer replies. "Try and take her from me. See what happens."

"Is that right?" Lucas smirks, tilting his head to one side. "Ivy, while I appreciate you may have fooled around before we met, it's time to put those attachments aside. You made a commitment to me, to our marriage. Do you really want me to tell your father what you've been doing with *him*? Are you willing to see how far your dad would go to make sure you had no one but me left in your life? Stop playing princess, Ivy. We have a kingdom to rule and you belong at my side."

"This isn't your kingdom, Lucas," Archer growls out.

"Let me go, Archer." I have to leave with Lucas. I don't know what my father would do if Lucas told him I'd chosen Archer over my husband, but I know it won't be good. I am going to have to tread carefully around the boys if I want to keep Lucas--and my father--happy.

Archer squeezes my hand one last time, his eyes on mine, and I know he understands. This isn't the time or the place to stand our ground. The fight isn't over...it's just beginning. He slowly lets me go and my heart hurts the moment we aren't touching anymore. Lucas grabs my arm and roughly pulls me out of the room.

"What do you think you were doing in there?" he hisses. "Have you forgotten your wedding vows already? It's not just your life on the line here."

"You and I both know I said those words under duress," I remind him. "How valid can they really be?"

"As valid as Solomon wants them to be," Lucas replies. "This marriage is important to him. It's important to *me*. We need to make this work. Look, Ivy. You know I'm a reasonable guy. I've slept next to you and respected you all that time. I've never done anything you didn't want me to, and I never will. But you're going to have to accept the fact that this is for the long term and we need to make the best of it. Your father wouldn't like it if you cheated on me and neither would I. Yes, we barely know each other, but from what I've seen of you, I admire and respect. You're intelligent, feisty, strong willed, just the kind of woman who'd challenge me for the rest of my life and I love that. I *want* to love you. If you'll let me. Give our relationship a chance. You never know what it might become if we both work at it. Can't you say you'll at least try?"

I don't want to. I don't see how anyone forced into getting married could fall in love with their spouse. But there was a twisted kind of logic to what Lucas was saying. While my father is head of House Archaic, he could make life very unpleasant for me if I didn't fall in line. It *did* make sense to at least pretend to be happily married.

And if I want to see any of the boys, I am going to have to be a lot more discrete in how I go about it.

Screw being the princess of this kingdom, I'm the damn queen and I'm going to make my own happily ever after.

Lucas and my father be damned.

☐☐

Isabella waits for us when we arrive home. "Your father wants to see you in his study."

Lucas and I exchange glances. A summons from my father was never good news, and as we walk into his study, the look on his face tells us that he is *not* happy.

"First day back at the Academy and you couldn't stay out of trouble for five minutes."

"I'm sorry, Solomon." Lucas spreads his hands in a placating gesture. "It was a misunderstanding."

"No, I don't think it was." Solomon gets up from behind his desk and walks round to stand in front of us. "I've read the witness reports, and it's very clear that Ivy's been a busy girl. It would appear that not only did you manage to persuade the Navarres to protect you with that fake engagement to Romy--"

"It *wasn't* a fake engagement!" I protest. "Unlike *this* marriage."

"Do *not* interrupt me." My father's eyes flash with anger. "Do not *ever* interrupt me. That engagement was never going to end in a wedding. Your marriage will last for as long as you both live--assuming you don't have an accident if you persist with your willful disobedience."

"You wouldn't!" I gasp. "I'm your only heir."

"Don't test me," my father warns. "You'll discover that there's nothing I wouldn't do if I had to. And while you are more useful to me alive than dead, circumstances change and there's always more than one way to get what you want. Do you understand?"

"I understand." I speak through gritted teeth, but it's enough to satisfy him.

"So, as I was saying before I was so rudely interrupted, not only did you manage to manoeuvre yourself into an engagement with House Navarre, which was a rather bold move on your part, you've been developing connections with House Knight *and* House Dauphin."

"Declan's just my writing partner," I say.

"Now, now, Ivy." My father tuts. "You and I both know that's not true. You and Declan have a very... special connection."

I pale. How on earth had my father found out about me and Declan? *Nobody* knew about our times together.

"I commend you for your forward thinking," he continues. "It was very sensible of you to build alliances with the other Houses to keep your options open. But now you have only one option open to you: Lucas. He is your husband and you *will* be a faithful wife to him."

"Or what?"

The blow comes without warning, a slap to the side of the head which sends me sprawling. I cry out in pain, putting a hand to the side of my head where my father had hit me.

"Some women need firm discipline," he snarls, and the evil side of my father I hate to see comes out in full. I don't know how I am related to this monster. "Your mother was just the same. They won't listen to reason, so you have to make sure they get the message another way. You are to stay away from those boys. Do you understand me?"

"You really think you can *beat* me into doing what you want?" I know talking back to him is dangerous, but I don't care. He might have a temper, but I am my father's daughter. I am going to get back at him for this.

"I can have a darned good go." My father raises his arm to hit me again, but Lucas catches it.

"That's enough!" he snarls. "You've gone too far. Ivy might

be your daughter, but she's my wife and nobody lays a finger on her. Do you understand me?"

For a moment I think my father will hit him as well, but to my surprise, he lowers his arm, nodding.

"You're right," he says. "Ivy *is* your wife, and it's up to you to keep her in line. But I warn you now--do not let her make a fool of you with those other boys. A bit of fun is fine while you're young, but as a married couple, a married *Archaic* couple, you both have an image to uphold. If I hear you're allowing her to do anything to bring our name into disrepute, I will be holding you responsible for any consequences arising from that. Do I make myself clear?"

"Yes, sir." Lucas nods.

He comes over and reaches out his hand to help me up. I take it, never taking my eyes off my father as Lucas puts his arm around me in a reassuring hug.

"Now," my father went on as if nothing happened. "It's the King Town annual ball this weekend. You will both be attending and as your first major event as a married couple it is important you make the right impression. Ivy, this is your opportunity to prove you are a true Archaic. You have an uphill battle given your recent behaviour, so don't let me down."

"Don't worry. I won't," I snap. *I'll just stab you in the back the first second I get.*

Chapter Forty-Nine

Safely back in our rooms, Lucas turns to me, a worried look on his face. He brushes my hair out of my face, wanting to get a good look at where my father had hit me.

"Are you okay? Ivy, I'm so, so sorry. I had no idea he was going to do that."

"I know." I wave him away. His fussing irritates me. "And I'm fine. You don't need to stress about me. I can take care of myself."

"But you don't have to." Exasperated, Lucas runs a hand through his hair. "That's the whole point. That's what I've been trying to get through to you. You're not on your own anymore. You can rely on me. I'll look after you."

"You just don't get it, do you?" I shake my head. "I don't want or need you to look after me. I was never one of those girls who imagined a white wedding, a prince swooping in to rescue her from her life. I saw what my mother was like after she left my father. I swore I would never let a man affect me like that. If I can't stand on my own two feet without a man propping me up, then I'm a pretty sorry excuse for a woman. So if you're serious about making this marriage work, you've got to start giving me some space to make my own decisions."

"But what about--"

"My father?" I humourlessly laugh. "Don't worry about him. I know how to keep up appearances. Years of sneaking out of foster homes taught me a lot about leading a double life. I'll make sure he has the good little Archaic girl he wants me to be. But he doesn't get to control me, and neither do you. I'm going to do what I want and you can either support me in that as the husband you claim you want to be, or you can go telling tales to my father, in which case I'll know you're the spineless wonder the boys say you are. It's your choice. Now I'm going to take a shower. It's been a long day."

Lucas leaves me alone as I head off to the bathroom. I turn the water up as hot as I can take it and stand under it without washing. Letting the water cascade over me in a vain attempt to stop my mind racing at a thousand miles a minute.

It never gets any easier. It seems that everyone is determined to make my life as complicated as possible.

After the water begins to cool, I pick up the soap and scrub myself down. Sometimes it feels like a shower is the only time where I get any privacy...room to think. Shutting off the water, I put my PJs on. It's still early, but it has been a long day and I want nothing more than to flop into bed and binge some Netflix.

"You okay?" asks Lucas, who is already stretched out on the bed. "Want me to get some food brought up?"

"No." I sigh. "I'm not hungry. You get something if you want."

"No, I'm fine. Besides, it would be rude to eat in front of you if you're not having anything." He pats the bed beside him. Even sitting next to him feels like a betrayal. However, he did protect me and a part of me knows he isn't the bad guy.

"Anything in particular you want to watch?" Lucas asks. "There's a new game show where people have to figure out a way round a maze while dressed up like rats. Looks silly but fun. Or we can check out that zombie survival drama if you like."

"I don't mind. Whatever you want."

Lucas points the remote at the TV mounted opposite our bed and flicks through Netflix to find *Where's My Cheese?* The game show is as daft as it sounds, and just what I need to take my mind off everything that has happened.

After a few episodes, Lucas puts on a thriller. I've seen it before, so I close my eyes, listening to the sounds of a father desperately trying to rescue his kidnapped daughter before time runs out and her attackers kill her. If only my father would do something like that for me. My life would be so different.

I'm so comfortable I end up drifting off to sleep out, worn out and exhausted.

□□

When I wake up, it is dark and Lucas is asleep, the movie long since over. I throw on a pair of black jeans and a black polo neck jumper. I pull on a black beanie and carefully make my way across the room.

"Where are you going?" Lucas sits up in bed and I nearly scream.

"I just need some fresh air," I lie.

"Do you want some company?"

"No. I need some time out if that's okay."

"Sure." Lucas lays back down and rolls away from me. "Don't let the guards catch you and be back before sunrise."

I should have known he'd guess what I was up to. Still, it is sweet of him to let me go without making a big deal about it.

There are no bars on the windows of our apartment. Unlike when I lived here before, I assumed my father trusts Lucas to make sure I 'behave.' The window slides open quietly and easily, and I shimmy down the drainpipe to the ground floor. Staying close to the building, I make my way round to the back where the cars are kept. This is the most dangerous part of the building--there are more cameras because of the many expensive cars my father keeps in his garage. But if you know where they are, which I do, it's easy to stay out of their line of sight until you get to the other side. From there it is a straightforward run to Romy's.

I debate calling a cab, but decide it isn't worth the risk of word getting back to my father that I've gone over to the Navarres. Instead, I jog, making sure to keep to the shadows and backstreets so no one would see me. Fortunately, there is no one around at this time of night, so it isn't long before I am at the outskirts of Romy's estate.

Romy has taken me round his estate many times when I lived there, so I knew the places where he and his siblings used to sneak out at night when they were younger. It was an open secret between them and the guards, and everyone turned a blind eye as long as no one got into serious trouble.

I find the tree with low-hanging branches that Romy said was his favourite for getting in and out of the estate and start climbing. It is easy to get up with many strong, low branches which can support my weight. Romy says his dad kept threatening to cut them but he never did, another sign that he was more than aware of what his children were doing.

Once I am in the grounds, it is a little harder to evade detection. Romy's parents don't have my father's arrogance, so they have more guards and the patrols are set at random intervals so you never know when someone will be coming your way. Still, Romy had shown me a route which leads to his side of the house with plenty of places to duck and hide if a guard was coming. I thought one might have caught sight of me, but if he had, he let me go on my way, presumably because he remembers who I am and what I mean to Romy.

At last, I am standing on the ground beneath Romy's window.

"Romy! Hey, Romy!" I hiss, not wanting to call out too loudly in case I attract attention. Of course, it means that the chances of Romy actually hearing me are a lot lower that way, so I pick up a handful of gravel and throw it up at the window.

"What?" Romy snaps as he opens the window, but his bad mood melts away when he sees me standing there. "Ivy! What are you--? Don't worry. Tell me when you get up here."

He moves away from the window, and a moment later a rope ladder comes winding down for me. All the rooms on the first floor and above have one in case of a fire or an enemy attack so the family could escape to safety.

Romy helps me over the windowsill and into his room. Once in his room, he pulls me into the tightest hug I'd ever had.

"Ivy! Thank goodness you're okay." He takes my hand and leads me over to a couch where we sit down together.

"I could say the same about you. What did the doctors say?"

"I've got a mild concussion." Romy shrugs. "They wanted to keep me in for observation, but I said I'd rather be home, so my dad's hired a nurse to stay for a few days to make sure I'm okay."

"But you're feeling okay?"

"Yeah. I mean, my head's a bit sore, but that's to be expected. I'll be fine. It's a good excuse to take a few days off school. But what about you? How have you been? We were all so worried about you and when that fight blew up, I didn't get a chance to talk to you and find out what happened."

"It's pretty much as Milly says," I told him. "My dad used her to force me to marry Lucas. Now he wants me and Lucas to be properly married, an actual couple for the rest of our lives."

"Are you kidding me? Is he serious?"

"Deadly. And I mean that in every sense of the word."

"Oh, Ivy." Romy pulls me to him and I lean my head against his shoulder. "I'm so sorry. For all of this. I can't help but feel it's partly my fault. If my dad hadn't set up our engagement, your father probably wouldn't have been in such a rush to get you married to Lucas."

"You shouldn't blame yourself," I reply. "We're both victims of this messed up town. You did what you thought was best."

"Still. I feel responsible. And I promise I'll find a way to get you out of this. I'll save you, no matter what it takes."

I smile sadly, a single tear trickling down my cheek. "That's sweet of you, but maybe this is how things are meant to be. There are plenty of other girls out there who'd love to be with you. You could marry one of Archer's sisters, build an alliance with House Knight and form an unbeatable force to take down my father. I'm sure there are other women who'd be much better fits for your family's ambition."

"Don't you get it, Ivy?" Romy clenches and unclenches his fist, frustrated that there is nothing he can do. "It was never about ambition, not for me. I wanted to be with *you*. Selfishly, I went along with my father's plan because it meant I could have you all to myself without worrying about you going off with Archer or Declan."

"Declan? Why would you worry about him?"

"Ivy, *everyone's* noticed the way you look at him. I know the pair of you think you've been discrete, but we all know there's something going on between you, and that's okay. You're entitled to be with whoever you like. I'm not the jealous type. I believe that if you love someone, you want them to be happy and if he makes you happy, I don't mind you spending time with him--or Archer, for that matter. All I've ever wanted is for you to be happy and safe. And now it looks like I've screwed up the possibility of that ever happening."

He sighs heavily. I hate seeing him so miserable. I take his face between my hands and turn him to look at me, kissing him deeply.

"No, you haven't. I'm here now, aren't I? I'm happy with you. We have some time to be together."

"It won't be enough, though," says Romy. "It'll never be enough."

"So we better make the most of it while we can then, hadn't we?"

I reach up to his shoulder and give it a gentle massage.

Romy closes his eyes and inhales deeply, slowly releasing his breath.

"That's good," he says. "But I feel like it ought to be me reassuring you. Turn around."

I smile and do as he says, swivelling around on the couch so he can work on me. He kneads my shoulders and I throw my head back, loving the way he knows his way around my body.

"No, this isn't going to work." I frown as Romy takes his hands away, but I smile again when I realise what he has in mind. Romy pulls off my top. I hadn't bothered to put on a bra, wanting to get out as quickly as possible. His hands run down my back, his touch giving me goosebumps.

I'm practically purring like a kitten as Romy's hands find their way to my front. I lean into him, closing my eyes. He cups my breasts and starts playing with them, tweaking and pulling at my nipples. I reach behind me and grab a handful of his hair, loving the feel of it between my fingers as he nuzzles my neck.

One of Romy's hands works its way down my body, sliding beneath my waistband to tease me with the promise of delights to come. I reach down to undo my zipper, but Romy gently pushes my hands away, undoing my button and pulling down the zipper for me.

I stand and slowly slide down my trousers, looking over my shoulder with a sly grin at Romy as I step out of my jeans to reveal lacy underwear. I slip out of them, turning around to stand before Romy completely naked. I can see his erection straining against his trousers.

Romy reaches out and grabs me by the hips, pulling me closer to him. He looks up at me as he puts his hand between my legs and caresses my clit with his thumb. My legs tremble, and I put my hands on top of his head to keep my balance as he inserts a couple fingers inside me while his thumb rubs against my clit in slow, tantalising circles.

I close my eyes, losing myself in the moment as Romy's fingers thrust deep inside me, hitting the perfect spot every time to send me closer and closer to the edge until finally, I come with an orgasm that makes me want to scream. I stuff my hand in my mouth to stifle my cries as Romy continues to touch me, wanting to make sure I enjoy every last second of what he is doing. My legs buckle under me and Romy finally pulls his hand away to catch me. I fall into his lap, both of us laughing.

"See?" I say. "You know exactly how to make me feel better."

I kiss him, and Romy runs his hands all over my body. Despite the intensity of my orgasm, my body responds to him as if it were the first time.

He twists around, placing me on the couch. He spreads my legs wide. I lay back, feeling utterly wanton and loving it. He kneels in front of me and lowers his face between my legs. I let my legs rest over his shoulders as he licks me.

If I wasn't wet before, I am absolutely dripping now as he tortures me with his tongue. I am still sensitive from coming, too sensitive to have another orgasm like this, but that's what makes it such an exquisite pleasure. Romy keeps me on the edge, teasing my swollen clit with gentle loving, leaving me breathless.

At last, I can't take it anymore. I unlock my legs from around his neck and push him away.

He looks up at me quizzically as I gesture to him to take my place, incapable of speech just yet.

It's my turn to get on my knees, and I took him in my mouth. He groans as I put my hands underneath his buttocks, encouraging him to thrust into my mouth as my head bobs up and down, loving the way he fills me so completely.

"You better stop or I'm going to come," Romy warns, pulling away from me.

I nod, needing him inside me before we are both spent.

He helps me to my feet, taking me in his arms for a tender embrace. We stand there, simply enjoying being together for a while. This feels good. It feels *right*. Romy holds a piece of my heart in his hands, and I don't think I'll ever get it back.

"Do you want me to take you from behind?" Romy

murmurs in my ear and I can feel my pussy clenching at the thought.

I bite my lip, nodding. Romy takes my hand and leads me over to the end of the couch, leaning me over the arm so I am supported with my butt in the air. He enters me cleanly with one deep thrust. I am so wet he easily slips into me. We fit together as if we were made for each other. He pounds into me faster and harder, making me moan. We are both panting as he reaches beneath me, stroking my clit while he maintains his momentum.

I don't think I will be able to come again tonight. I'm wrong. I feel myself building towards another orgasm, even more overwhelming than the first. Romy moves his hand to grip my hips as his movements become more frantic.

I come before him, but he quickly follows, collapsing on top of me as he finally finds his release.

We stay where we are for a moment, his weight on top of me a comfort.

There's a knock at the door.

"Romy?"

"Shit! It's the nurse!" hisses Romy, pulling out of me. "Quick--hide in the bathroom."

Trying to stifle our giggles, we hurry around, scooping discarded clothes off the floor before I run into the bathroom and Romy pulls on a robe. I listen at the door as he lets the nurse in.

"Are you okay?" I hear her say. "You look a little flushed."

"Err... yeah," Romy replies. "I was asleep, and I fell out of bed when I heard you knock."

"Oh dear. You haven't hurt yourself, have you?"

Careful not to make any noise, I get dressed as the nurse guides Romy back to bed to check him over. When she is satisfied, she leaves him, promising to be back in another few hours.

"That was close," I say when Romy opens the bathroom door. "Do you think she suspected?"

"Possibly." Romy shrugs. "But staff here know to be discrete.

As long as my health doesn't suffer it's not a problem if I have a girl visiting me for a little TLC."

"I think we *both* had some TLC," I say. "I know I certainly needed that."

"Good. I'm glad I was able to help you feel better." He smiles sadly. "I meant it, you know. I fully intend to find a way to save you from your father *and* your husband. I don't know what I'm going to do, but I'll figure something out. One way or another, I'm going to set you free because I love you."

"I love you, too," I admit, knowing this is the first time I've really said it to him. His eyes widen before he kisses me and we both know whatever happens, we are going to fight for each other.

Chapter Fifty

he skies are getting lighter in the east as I finally climb back through the window to the rooms I share with Lucas.

"Ivy!" He rushes over to help me into the room. "I thought you were gone for good. I was trying to figure out what I was going to say to your father to explain your disappearance. I think he would have killed me—and that's not a figure of speech."

"Sorry, Lucas. I didn't mean to worry you." As I say it, I realise it was true. I thought I didn't care about Lucas and while it's true I don't feel about him the way I feel about Romy, Archer, and Declan, I certainly don't want anything bad to happen to him. He's been nothing but nice to me.

"How was Romy? I shouldn't have hit him that hard. I fucked up."

I blush. "How did you know I went to see him?"

"I didn't." Lucas grins. "I do now though. So, how is he? That bump on the head do any permanent damage?"

"No, he's going to be fine." *More than fine.*

"Good. The last thing this town needs is even more conflict.

Maybe now Archer's got the urge to punch me out of his system we can work together to find a way forward. They're going to have to accept our marriage sooner or later. I'd like to think we could eventually be friends."

"Mmm." I keep my tone noncommittal, but somehow, I can't see Archer ever being interested in befriending Lucas.

"You know, when I agreed to move to King Town to support your father, I really hoped you'd want to get to know me. I was really looking forward to being a regular teenager for a while, doing things that normal people do. I wanted to compete in the races, go to parties, meet girls, just be *normal*. I should have known that wouldn't happen. Like I would ever be that lucky."

"Sounds like there's a history there."

"You could say that." Lucas laughs bitterly. "My parents died in a car crash when I was three. I don't remember anything about them, although sometimes when a certain song comes on the radio or I smell a particular perfume I have vague memories of feeling loved and protected. I grew up in foster care."

"Seriously?" I look at Lucas with a new respect. "I had no idea. I was in the system too. Fun, isn't it?"

"That's one way of putting it," Lucas agrees. "You're part of a family, only not. I always got the impression that I was there under sufferance. The people I stayed with took me to classes with their own children where I got to sit on the side while they had fun. I was only little, but I remember always feeling like I was different, the odd one out."

"I know that feeling."

"It all changed when I was eight," Lucas went on. "That's when Penelope Donatello walked into my life. She was looking for a boy to adopt and I was exactly what she wanted. I looked like I could have been related to her, so she was able to claim I was her nephew, living with her after the tragic death of her sister. She made it very clear to me that I had to support her lies or I'd be sent straight back to the foster system. I might have been young, but I wasn't stupid, so I went along with her story. Whenever people asked me about my mother, I started crying so

I wouldn't have to give out any details that could give away the lie and it wasn't long before they learned not to ask.

"They weren't the only ones who learned not to ask questions. Penelope was rich. *Very* rich. We're talking houses in Monaco, Bermuda, Nice. I had a private tutor as we travelled the world, staying in one exotic location after another."

"That sounds idyllic," I say.

"I know, right?" Lucas shakes his head. "Looks can be deceiving. As you've seen yourself, money doesn't mean anything if the person who has it is evil, and that was Penelope. She was one of the nastiest people I've ever met. Maybe one day you'll see the scars on my back from the beating she gave me because I got a merit in my piano exam. She told me that the Donatellos were known for excellence and if I didn't get top marks in everything I did, she would leave a mark on my body for every grade I dropped. I'm sure you can imagine what my grades were like after that. It's why I was able to breeze into the Academy and know that I'd be able to keep up with whatever classes you were in. I'm used to being the best at everything because I had no choice. Penelope had her standards and I wasn't allowed to let them drop."

"That's awful!" I gasp.

"That was my life." Lucas shrugs. "I was Penelope's little fashion accessory, the one thing which demonstrated to the world that she was perfect. She couldn't deal with the fact that she wasn't capable of having children herself. She hated the idea that for all her ambition and money, she still couldn't have everything, so she took her resentment out on me. It was like she desperately wanted me but she despised me because I reminded her that not even the great Penelope Donatello could conquer Nature."

"So what happened?" I ask. "Where's Penelope now?"

"Dead." Lucas says it without feeling, but I was sure there was a world of conflicting emotions behind that reality. "She died a year ago after a long and painful battle with cancer, another fight she couldn't win, although she threw everything she had into it. She paid for expensive consultants, alternative therapists, even bought a pharmaceutical cannabis company. If something was supposed to cure cancer, she knew about it, but nothing worked. I always thought that it was her passion for winning that made her live longer than the twelve months the doctors predicted. She spent three years trying to cure herself, but in the end, the cancer took her--and it wasn't pleasant. She left everything to me. I have more money than I know what to do with and it's just as much yours as it is mine."

"I don't want your money." I shake my head.

"I know," says Lucas sadly. "I know you don't want anything from me. But I hope that will change in time. What's mine is yours." He inhales deeply. "I know you might not believe me, but I wasn't keen on this wedding either. I don't need Archaic money."

"So, why did you go ahead with it?"

"One of the conditions of Penelope's will was that I marry someone who would help grow the family business," Lucas says. "If I didn't, I'd lose everything."

"So?" I ask. "It's just money. If it were me, I wouldn't want anything from someone who'd treated me like that. I tell you something for nothing--I have absolutely no intention of picking up from where my father leaves off when he dies. I'll give it all to charity. I don't care."

"Don't you think he knows that?" Lucas asks. "It's one of the reasons why he approached me to marry you."

"Why would you care what happens to my father's fortune?"

"I don't." Lucas shrugs. "But I'm not like you. There's no way I'm going back to the kind of life I had before Penelope adopted me. Money might not buy you happiness but it can certainly rent it for a while. Working with your father, I have the opportunity to build a business which can change the world. When your father asked me if I'd be willing to help him keep you safe from the other Houses and showed me your photo, I had no hesitation. With Penelope's money and Solomon's mentorship I can do something which will really make a difference in people's lives and if that means I have to marry a beautiful woman to do it, I'm okay with that."

"Even if she's marrying you against her will?"

Lucas has nothing to say to that.

I don't know what to make of my new husband. He is such a curious mix of caring and cold. I love the idea of his doing something to help people, but can I believe he really means what he is saying? He could be lying, telling me what he thinks I want to hear to get me to fall for him.

While Lucas is saying all the right things, there is no way I am going to trust him. Not now, and maybe not ever.

Chapter Fifty-One

"*C*an you do me up, please?"

Lucas comes over to help do up the ballgown Isabella had picked out for me. I wanted to go dress shopping myself, but my father wouldn't let me. Yet another way he insisted on controlling every little aspect of my life.

Still, Isabella has beautiful taste even if I hate the bitch. The black dress she picked out for me is tight at the waist and flows out into a full skirt, enhancing my figure in an hourglass shape. The corset top pushes my breasts up, giving me impressive cleavage. A delicate lace overlaid on the black silk gives the dress an intriguing look from all sides. It is easily one of the most beautiful dresses I'd ever seen, let alone worn.

She also booked a professional makeup artist and a hairdresser to come and make me look my best for the ball. I prided myself on my makeup skills, but I had to admit that Nola really knew her stuff. Once she is done with me, I look like something out of *Vogue*. Once Becky finishes teasing my hair into an intricate updo, I can barely recognise myself.

Lucas wolf whistles as I do a little turn for him, showing off my complete look.

"You are stunning," he tells me. "I'm going to be the envy of every man there. I'm so proud to call you my wife."

"Thanks. You don't look so bad yourself."

And he doesn't. Lucas is wearing the traditional James Bond tuxedo, and it really suits him. Some men are uncomfortable in formalwear, but not Lucas. The suit had been tailored for him and it makes him look sharp. But he isn't *them.*

"Are you ready, m'lady?" Lucas does a little bow, offering me his arm with a cheeky smile. I take it and let him lead me out of our suite and downstairs to my father's study, where Isabella is helping him with his cufflinks.

He smiles when he sees us. "Lucas. Ivy. Don't you look elegant? You are truly doing House Archaic justice."

"You look pretty good yourself, Solomon," Lucas answers.

"How many times do I have to tell you, Lucas? Call me Dad."

"...Dad." Lucas tightly replies and nods to hide his expression, but I see it.

Isabella finishes with my father's cufflinks and steps away from him. "There you go, Solomon. I'll see you at the ball."

She smiles at us and leaves the study to go get ready for the ball. As my father's aide, she is entitled to a ticket to one of the most exclusive events of the year and she'd be following us there. Tickets cost upwards of a thousand each, meaning only the wealthiest families in town could afford to go. It is an opportunity to show off your wealth and vie for dominance as you network. While on the surface it is meant to be a purely fun event, a chance to let off some steam and party as a united town, just like everything else that went on here, there was more going on beneath the surface than you'd think.

"Are you two ready?" My father beams, looking between us. The urge to smack him in the face is strong.

"Ready as we'll ever be," Lucas replies for me.

"Then let's hit the road. I have a feeling tonight is going to be wild."

He claps his hands and rubs them together before leading

the way out to a massive stretch limo waiting outside for us. The driver opens the door and my father gestures for me to go in before him.

I step inside to be greeted by a bottle of champagne cooling in an ice bucket. There are seats lining three sides of the limo, across the back and down both sides. I sit down on the opposite side of the door. Lucas enters and sits next to me, while my father takes the rear seat, stretching out to take up as much space as possible. I knew he'd do it, which is why I left the space empty for him.

"Who's for a drink?" My father doesn't wait for our replies as he picks up the bottle of champagne. The cork pops and a little alcohol fizzes over the lip of the bottle before my father fills three flutes with champagne. He hands them out to us and holds his up in a toast.

"To House Archaic," he says.

"House Archaic," Lucas and I echo.

The limo driver starts the engine and pulls out smoothly as we all sip champagne, that smug smile of my father's never leaving his face.

I sit in silence during the drive across town to the hall where the ball is being held. This is one of the rare occasions where an event is held on neutral territory, in this instance a large club which has been commandeered for the night. It is one of the few places which is large enough to hold everyone, with a big dance floor and private rooms for the more expensive ticket holders. Naturally, my father has paid for one of these and when we arrive, we head straight up to our room for the night.

A number of my father's bodyguards are already there waiting for us. This night might be one of the most hotly anticipated of the year, but it's also one of the most dangerous.

My father booked the best room available, which has a balcony overlooking the dance floor as well as a more private area which no one can access without going through a number of guards first. As well as the main entrance, which we'd come through, there is a small door at the back which Lucas tells me leads to an escape route out back in case of any trouble.

Lucas and I go out on the balcony. Music is pounding and there are already a number of people dancing. I think I can make out Archer in the crowd, but I can't be sure from this distance.

"You okay?" Lucas squeezes my hand.

"Yeah." I smile at him. "It's just weird being out with my father, you know? I don't feel like I can really relax until I know what he's got planned."

"Why would he have anything planned? Why can't your father be here for some fun?"

"Because my father's idea of fun means someone always gets hurt," I say grimly.

"Don't be so negative. You never know—maybe he's turned over a new leaf."

"Ha! I wish."

"Come on. Let's go dance." Lucas holds out his hand to me and we head back into our room. Isabella has arrived and her and my father are deep in discussion already. There is no doubt in my mind that they are plotting something. I just wish I knew what.

Lucas caught my father's attention and made a gesture to let him know we were going downstairs to dance. My father nods and we leave the room to go down to the dance floor.

We walk into the hall, just as the DJ puts on a slow dance.

"Perfect timing." Lucas grins as he pulls me onto the dance floor and into his arms.

I close my eyes and rest my head against Lucas's shoulder as we sway together, knowing there is no way I can escape. This is the first time we've danced as a married couple, and it feels weird. We don't have the same kind of connection I do with Archer, Romy, or Declan, and I don't know if we ever would. There is no way I could even think of trying with him. I'm not a fool, I see how Lucas looks my way, but he doesn't know me. He never could.

"Mind if I cut in?"

As if he is able to read my mind, Romy appears next to us, tapping Lucas on the shoulder and my eyes lock onto his.

"Not at all." Lucas steps away with a tight jaw and Romy takes his place. Lucas walks off in the direction of the bar as Romy pulls me to him.

That's better.

"Won't your date mind you dancing with me?" I ask as we move in perfect synchronicity.

"Who says I have a date?"

I laugh. "Come on, Romeo. It's you we're talking about here. You've always got a woman on your arm."

"Not tonight." He shakes his head. "How could I be here with someone else when I'd be thinking about you."

"For real?" I laugh again, nervously this time.

"For real." Romy gazes at me intently. "Ivy, ever since I met you, you've changed me. I haven't wanted to be with anyone else. I haven't even kissed another girl, let alone anything more. If I can't be with you, I don't want to be with anyone."

For a moment I think he is going to kiss me, but the DJ puts on a more up-tempo song, killing the mood.

"Is this a private party or can anyone join?"

"Archer!" I give him a huge hug as Romy steps back to make way for Archer Knight. "It's so good to see you."

"It's good to see you too, Ivy," he replies. "I've been worried about you all week."

We start dancing together, Archer surprising me with how well he moves. There is a natural grace to his dancing, and he has an innate sense of rhythm that makes me see him in a new light.

"Where's your date?" I ask.

"Haven't got one," he replies. "There wasn't anyone who I wanted to bring, and it seemed pointless dragging a girl along just to keep up appearances. The one person I wanted to ask was already taken."

I blush, knowing exactly who he meant.

"I came with Milly instead," Archer went on. "By the looks of it, we've swapped partners." He nods over to one side of the dance floor and I look over to see Lucas and Milly dancing together. Milly looks pissed off, a rare sight on her, while Lucas seems amused.

"It's nice to see Lucas finally settling in," I say. "It's not been easy for him coming to the Academy with everyone so hostile towards him."

"Can you blame us?" Archer's eyes flash with anger. "We thought we'd found a way to keep you safe from your father. If he hadn't come along, you'd be with Romy right now. Tell me you wouldn't be happier engaged to him than married to Lucas."

I open my mouth to reply, but Archer talks over me.

"And if you were still engaged to Romy, I might have been able to find a way to get you out of that engagement. I was working on it, you know. I had plans. None of them matter now. Instead, I'm reduced to snatching what little time I can with you. It's not enough. It'll never be enough."

"I know," I whisper, knowing exactly how he feels. "But what can we do? I'm married and my father has me well and truly trapped."

"We'll just have to take each moment as it comes, I guess." Archer shrugs as the song comes to an end and the DJ puts on another slow song. Archer moves to get close, but someone pulls him back.

"I think it's my turn now, don't you?" Declan asks. "Unless Ivy has any objections?"

"No." I beam. "It's good to see you, Declan."

"See you later, Ivy." Archer bows and kisses my hand before disappearing off into the crowd, leaving me with Declan.

I put my arms around his neck, and he put his around my waist. Taller than me, I have to look up to talk as we dance. He really is gorgeous.

"Who did you bring to the ball?" I ask. "Won't she mind you slow dancing with me?"

"The only person who might mind is Lucas and I don't care about his opinion," Declan smoothly replies. "I decided not to bring a date with me tonight. I had a few people dropping some heavy hints, including Ally and Taylor, but I wasn't interested. Even though I knew you'd be here with Lucas, I wanted to be free to spend time with you if the opportunity came up and look at us now. Dancing like we haven't got a care in the world."

"I don't know that I'd go that far…" I smile up at Declan, feeling all warm inside. My boys are all here on their own, and I didn't have to cope with seeing them in someone else's arms. It's selfish of me when I am with Lucas, but I don't care. I love all my boys and it will kill me when the time eventually came for them to move on and find someone else. Someone who didn't come with my complications.

"Lucas seems to be having a good time." Declan nods over to where Milly and Lucas were slow dancing together. "Him and Milly look good together."

"They do, don't they?" I rest my head on Declan's shoulder as I watch my husband with Milly. He's acting like the perfect gentleman he always is; one arm around Milly's waist, their hands clasped, like they are ballroom dancing together. They seem deep in conversation. Knowing Lucas, he is likely pumping her for information about the Knights and sweet Milly is naïve enough to give it to him.

Declan runs his hand over my hair, kissing me gently on the top of my head. I close my eyes and lean into him more. I desperately want to leave with him, spend some quiet time together, but with my father here, not to mention all his guards, I have no choice but to stay at the dance until it's time to go back to the Archaic mansion.

Before I even realise it, a tear is trickling down my cheek. I dash it away with the back of my hand, hoping it hasn't ruined the beautiful makeup Nola had worked so hard on.

"Hey." Declan put his hand under my chin, tilting my head to make me look at him. "It's okay, Ivy. Everything's going to be okay."

He leans forward, kissing the tear away. Then he kisses the tip of my nose and I can't hold myself back any longer. I stand on tiptoes and kiss him. Properly. In front of the whole room.

But I don't care. I want to be with Declan. I want to be with Archer. I want to be with Romy. I want to be with all of them, men who aren't beholden to my father and who saw me for *me*, not a pawn to be used to further their own ambitions.

"What the hell's going on?"

Declan and I break apart as I feel someone grab my arm to pull me away.

"Lucas!" I gasp as I realise my husband has seen us and he is *not* happy.

"Hey, man. It's okay." Declan puts his arms out in a gesture of placation. "We weren't doing anything."

"Didn't look like it to me," snarls Lucas. "That's my wife, you had no right to kiss her."

"I'd say that was up to Ivy to decide, wouldn't you?" Declan gazes at him coolly, daring him to do something. "It's not like you weren't having fun with someone else."

"I was just dancing with Milly. I didn't kiss her," Lucas points out. "I would never kiss her."

"And you can never kiss Ivy. A piece of paper isn't going to make her fall for you. Sorry to break this to you, but her heart is taken," he replies with a cold glare. "and we are not fucking giving her back."

"How dare you!" Lucas pulls back a fist to punch Declan, but I get between them, yanking Lucas's arm down.

"Stop it!" I look at Declan over my shoulder. "The pair of you. Let's go to our private room to cool down, Lucas. It seems like we could all do with some time out."

Lucas glares at Declan, who smirks back, but he allows himself to be guided off the dance floor and back to my father's private room.

"What were you thinking, Ivy?" he asks, as we walk up the stairs. "You made me look stupid out there."

"I wasn't thinking at all," I told him. "I hoped you were

distracted with Milly."

"That was business," says Lucas, confirming what I'd suspected. "Milly can be a useful source of information if you know how to read between the lines. Anyway, this isn't about me. It's about you. You need to learn how to behave as a married woman. Don't make me talk to your father about teaching you appropriate behaviour."

"That sounds uncannily like a threat." I narrow my eyes.

"Just a promise, Ivy. It's just a promise."

The guards outside my father's private room step aside to let us in. My father is out on the balcony watching the action on the dance floor, so the room is practically empty other than a few guards.

Lucas immediately goes to the bar and orders a whiskey. He downs it in one gulp and grabs a bottle of beer before coming back to me.

"Where's mine?" I don't really care that he didn't get me a drink. I could get my own, but if Lucas is going to make a big deal about my behaviour, I am going to point out every little thing he is doing wrong too. I can be petty if I wanted.

"We're at a ball, Ivy," Lucas says. "Standing around with a bottle in your hand doesn't exactly fit with the sophisticated image you're supposed to project."

"Is that so?"

I stomp over to the bar and help myself to one of the bottles laid out.

"Put that back, Ivy."

I scowl as my father comes back in from the balcony.

"It's a party, *Dad*," I say. "I'm allowed to drink if I want. And I am eighteen, remember?"

"How could I forget?" My father smiles but his eyes are stone cold. "Still, you'll need a cool head and a steady hand for what I want you to do."

"Oh really? What's that?"

"Come with me."

Lucas slumps on a couch as I follow my father out to the

balcony. My cheeks redden as I realise there is a good chance he'd seen me dancing with the boys--and kissing Declan.

"Look down there, Ivy. Tell me what you see." He gestures expansively across the dance floor.

"People having fun?"

"That's the surface view. Look closer."

"I don't know." I shrug. "People talking. People dancing."

"I see opportunity," my father says. "I see networks. I see the chance to take things a step further without anyone even knowing what's about to hit them."

He nods to one of his guards who steps forward and hands him a gun. My father opens up the barrel to check it is loaded. Satisfied, he snaps it shut with a flick of the wrist and offers it to me, handle first.

"Take it," he says.

I frown and shake my head.

"It wasn't a suggestion," my father states, offering the gun to me.

Reluctantly, I take it.

My father stands behind me and grabs my shoulders. He turns me to face the crowd. Leaning forward, he speaks directly into my ear. "Can you see the man standing by the bar with brown hair going grey at the temples?"

I look in the direction of the bar and spot Claude Dauphin, Declan's father. I nod.

"Shoot him."

"What?" I try to turn but my father grips my shoulders, holding me in place.

"You heard."

"I'm not going to do that." I hold the gun away from me as far as I could. "Someone take this thing because I'm not using it."

"Oh, yes, you are."

"You're crazy. There's no way I'm shooting anyone, let alone Declan's dad. I'd rather die first."

A guard steps forward and grabs my other hand.

"That would be far too easy," my father tells me. "No, Ivy. What I have in mind is a much simpler solution. Either you shoot Claude Dauphin, or Martin here will run his knife right through your hand. I'd love to see you playing guitar when you've lost the use of your left hand."

"You wouldn't!" I gasp, as Martin pulls out a wicked looking blade and holds it up against the back of my hand, ready to run it through the moment my father gives the command.

"You and I both know I will," my father says. "Now do as I tell you and shoot Claude."

"I can't do it with Martin holding my hand." I fight hard to keep the quiver out of my voice, but I don't quite manage it.

"Fine." I feel rather than see my father nod at his guard, who lets go of my hand and steps away. "But if you don't shoot him, Martin *will* stab you."

Hands shaking, I grip the gun and point it at Claude. I close one eye, aiming at his chest, but lower the gun as I see Declan go over to talk to his dad.

"I can't," I say. "I can't risk hitting Declan."

"That's a shame." My father sighs. "All right, Martin. Do your thing."

Martin steps forward and, in that moment, I know I can't do it. I can't lose my hand.

Sorry, Declan.

I swing the gun up and pull the trigger.

It feels like time stands still for a moment. The shot is so loud, it can be heard over the music. The noise of the crowd falls silent for a moment before screams break out.

Claude crumples to the floor. Declan looks round for who is responsible, as people rush to help his father. Our eyes meet and I see the shock in his eyes. I feel the guilt like a knife to the heart.

"Come on, people. The party's over." Someone shouts but I don't see who.

Bodyguards crowd around my father, me, and Lucas as we hurry out to the back exit. The Dauphins will be out for blood, and if they catch up to us, we are dead.

Chapter Fifty-Two

"*I* can't do it. I *won't* do it."

I stay in my seat, secure in the safety of the car. My father insisted Lucas and I go to school the Monday after the ball and there is no way I am ever going to step foot in that place, not when everyone would know by now who was responsible for shooting Claude.

"Yes, you can." Lucas is patient, even after reassuring me a million times. "It won't be as bad as you think. Claude's okay."

"He's in a hospital wired up to a machine to keep him alive, Lucas," I wail. "How can you possibly think that's okay?"

"He's still alive," Lucas reminds me. "And he's in the hands of the best doctors in the country. He might be in bad shape now, but our intelligence tells us that he's going to pull through. Ivy, much as I know it hurt you to do what you did, that shot has raised your profile big time. You might hate your father for forcing you into it, but trust me. He did you a favour. He's established you as a force to be reckoned with." He smiles reassuringly. "No one's going to judge you. It's just business, another day in this crazy town. Come on. I'll be right by your side. I'm

402

in all your classes. You won't have to face anyone alone, not unless you want to."

He holds out a hand to me and I know I don't have a choice. My father has dictated that we go back to the Academy, so that's what we are going to do.

Hand in hand, Lucas and I slowly walk up the steps to the Academy. Is it my imagination, or are people giving me weird looks?

"Keep your head high, Ivy," Lucas whispers, squeezing my hand. "You haven't done anything wrong, not as far as the Houses are concerned. Everyone's going to respect you."

"Still." I shake my head. "I feel really uncomfortable being here."

"Why don't we go to one of the practice rooms?" Lucas suggests. "We can hide out there until classes start."

"Okay."

I feel a little more relaxed as Lucas leads the way to the practice rooms. A-level music students are allowed to go there whenever we like to work on our assignments, which means that we have keys to the rooms to unlock them—and lock them behind us. In the past, those locks had allowed me and Declan to have some privacy while we explored each other's bodies. Now I am grateful for that privacy for a completely different reason—it means I can delay the moment when I have to face Declan. How on earth am I going to look him in the eye knowing I am the one responsible for putting his father in the hospital.

The music rooms are fully soundproof, so you can't hear whether someone is practising inside. Instead, there are red and green lights mounted over the doors so you could immediately see which ones were available.

The first couple of rooms have their red lights lit, but the third one is green, so Lucas pushes the door open. The room should have been empty, but then I see who is sitting at the piano waiting for us.

"Declan!" I try to back out, but Lucas grips my hand tightly and practically drags me into the room to confront the one person I don't want to see.

"What's she doing here?" Declan stands up, fists clenched. "I thought you said *you* wanted to talk. If I'd known you were going to bring *her* along, I'd never have agreed to meet you."

"She's the one you need to talk to though," Lucas tells him.

"She shot my dad. I've got nothing to say to her."

My heart shatters into a million pieces as Declan turns away from me.

"It wasn't her fault," Lucas says. "Her father forced her to do it."

"She could have said no."

"Declan, her father was going to have his guard stick a knife in her hand. She would never have been able to play guitar again. And I don't think that would have been the end of it, either. She did what she did out of pure fear. You and I both know that Solomon would have found a way to punish her beyond that."

"Is this true, Ivy?" Declan finally looks at me.

"Yes." I drop my head, unable to meet his gaze. "I didn't want to do it, I really didn't. But Martin was about to shove a knife through my hand. My instincts took over and I pulled the trigger. I aimed to miss though. I'm such a bad shot, I hit the target, but I really didn't mean to. If I could turn back time, I would. I'd take a stabbing over hurting you, hurting your dad."

I burst into tears, burying my face in my hands to hide my shame. I hate myself for being so weak, but it's all too much. I hate my father for putting me in this situation.

I feel arms around me, I relax into the hug... thinking it's Lucas. But when I look up, I see Declan is the one comforting me.

"I'll leave you two alone," Lucas says.

Declan follows him to the door, and I am sure I hear him thank Lucas. As my husband leaves, Declan locks the door behind him so we won't be disturbed.

"Lucas arranged for us to meet here," he tells me, coming back to me. "But I thought it was going to be just me and him. I was prepared to give him the beating of his life for what you did to my father."

"None of this was Lucas's fault," I say. "He doesn't deserve that kind of treatment."

"I know," Declan says. "But you have no idea how much I hate him for taking you away from me. I knew the moment I saw you up on that balcony with your father behind you that you'd been forced to fire that gun. I never blamed you for one second. But Lucas? He married you, taking you away from the protection of Romy's family. Worse, he took you away from me. It drives me wild thinking about you with him. Ivy, I love you."

My breath catches in my throat when I hear those three little words.

"I mean it, Ivy," Declan goes on, mistaking my silence for doubt. "I can't stop thinking about you. Ever since I first saw you, I knew I wanted you, but I'm not like Romy or Archer. For all my confidence on stage, I've always been shy around women.

"Romy doesn't think twice about jumping from bed to bed. Archer doesn't hesitate when it comes to taking what he wants. But me? I was dating Ally for months before we slept together. It's why I've been taking my time with you, making you feel good in the hope that one day you'd want to give everything to me, your heart as well as your body. Now I wish I'd been more outgoing, made a play for you sooner. Maybe it would be my ring on your finger."

As he speaks, I know exactly what I have to do.

I put my finger on his lips to stop him talking and step back, pulling my blazer off and throwing it to one side of the room. My jumper follows soon after, along with my skirt. As I unbutton my blouse Declan moves around in his seat, adjusting for the growing bulge in his trousers.

There is no doubt in my mind that he wants me.

I look him straight in the eye, as I slowly undo each button, lightly running my hands down the exposed flesh to titillate him.

When my blouse is completely open, I take it off and toss it to join the rest of my clothes.

I smile slowly as I unhook the front clasp of my bra. I hold the two pieces together, moving my hands around in a little dance before slowly pulling them apart to reveal my breasts.

I finally take my bra off and throw it on top of the pile. Declan closes his eyes and gulps before opening them again. Feasting himself on the sight of me standing in front of him wearing nothing but my knickers and shin-high boots.

"What are you doing, Ivy?" he asks.

"It's awfully hot in here, don't you think?" I smile, batting my eyelids at him. "I figured I'd take off my clothes, you know, cool down a little."

I cup my breasts, tweaking my nipples between my thumbs and forefingers, teasing and caressing them until they are completely erect.

"Why don't you take your trousers off?" I suggest. "It looks like they're really uncomfortable. Don't you feel as hot as me?"

He doesn't need me to ask twice. He yanks down his jeans and boxers at the same time, revealing his magnificent erection.

"Hmmm." I am definitely enjoying the view, but there is something else that would make it even better. "I think you should take the rest of your clothes off. I'd hate for you to overheat…"

Declan grins and swiftly removes his jumper and shirt as I continue to play with my nipples. I was telling the truth when I said I was feeling hot, but it had nothing to do with the room temperature. I can feel my heartbeat speeding up as Declan sits in front of me, completely naked.

I slip my right hand inside my knickers and find my clit. I'm already soaking wet, and we haven't even started.

"Touch yourself," I order. "I want you to make yourself good and hard for me."

Declan grips his cock and firmly runs his hand up and down the shaft. "Keep playing with your tits," he tells me. "I love watching you do that."

I keep my hand inside my underwear while my other hand cups my breast, presenting it to him as I continue to touch myself. With one hand working on my nipple and the other rubbing my clit, I'd be turned on at the best of times. But doing this in front of Declan, putting on a show for him while he plays with his cock? I want to scream with how turned on I am.

It's a good thing the music rooms are soundproofed.

"Do you want me to take off my underwear?" I ask.

Declan nods, incapable of speech as his hand continues to pump his cock.

I take off my knickers, leaving my boots on as I step out of my underwear.

My clothes all bundled up together in a corner of the room, I slowly step towards Declan. Our eyes meet and we grin. We'd had fun together in the past, but we'd never gone all the way. The time has come to scratch that itch.

He pulls me to him and we kiss hungrily. I can feel his erection tapping against me, his hands playing with my hair while his tongue dances with mine. We are filled with need for each other. I am torn between wanting to fuck him hard so I could come quickly and wanting to take my time to enjoy him. With all the craziness in both our lives, who knew when we'd be able to do this again, if ever?

Declan pulls away from me, breaking our kiss. "You have no idea how many times I've fantasised about this moment," he tells me. "I've lain awake so many nights, imagining you with me, thinking of what it would be like to be in you."

He leans forward to take one of my breasts into his mouth. He sucks hard as he plays with my other nipple, mimicking my earlier caresses as he uses his thumb and forefinger to tweak it. My legs feel weak and I can barely stand. What he's doing is so erotic, I think I might die.

"Oh. My. God." I moan, suddenly feeling an orgasm building. I don't know what Declan's secret is, but the way he's fondling my breasts is like nothing I'd ever experienced.

I cry out as Declan's tongue and hands send me over the

edge. I practically see stars with the power of the orgasm that rushes through me. My nails dig into his shoulders, needing something to help me stay standing as I luxuriated in one of the most powerful orgasms I've ever had.

"Everything okay?" Declan smirks, knowing exactly what he's just done.

"Oh, yeah." I nod, feeling very satisfied. "But I'm nowhere near done with you. I need you inside me. Now."

"If you insist." He stands up and guides me to lean over the table he's just been sitting on. His cock as solid as a rock as he enters me in one powerful thrust, burying himself in me.

I gasp and cling to the edge of the table, grateful I have it to support me. There is no way I'd be able to stand for long the way Declan is making me feel.

Declan grips my waist as he pounds into me, thrusting into me over and over, driving me insane. I buck my hips, meeting every one of his movements to help him go even deeper. This is all I could have hoped for and more. Declan and I have a connection that makes our lovemaking positively electric.

I think he is nearing climax when he suddenly pulls out of me.

"I've waited too long not to take my time with you," he tells me. "I want you from all directions."

He helps me to turn round, sitting me on the edge of the table. I spread my legs wide, putting my arms behind me for support. I angle myself to make it easier for him to slide into me. He thrusts into me, hitting me in just the right place.

I wrap my legs around his waist, and he picks up his momentum again. This time, his movements have more urgency, and I know neither of us will be able to keep this up for much longer.

I cry out, unable to hold back as a second orgasm takes over. Declan closes his eyes, his own climax finally coming. He roars as he empties himself into me, my orgasm enough to tip him over the edge.

We fall back on the table, still connected as he lays on top of me. He brushes my hair away from my face, slick with sweat.

"I meant it, Ivy," he tells me. "I really do love you."

"I love you too."

Chapter Fifty-Three

*N*ow that Declan and I are on good terms again, no, *amazing* terms, I feel much happier being at the Academy. Starting the day with mind blowing sex is definitely the best. I breeze through my classes, a faraway smile permanently etched on my face.

Lucas isn't stupid. He must have noticed something was up. My hair is all tousled and my makeup is messy even though I'd touched it up in the cloakroom. But he doesn't say anything other than to comment on being happy that Declan and I are friends again.

After school, I'm surprised to not see our usual car rolling up to meet us. Instead, one of the drivers pulls up in a vintage convertible MG.

He gets out and leaves the driver's door open, stepping aside for Lucas to take his place.

I frown. "What's going on?"

"I'm taking you for a drive, Ivy," Lucas explains. "Think of it like your own private magical mystery tour."

The driver comes round and opens the passenger door for

me. Then he salutes us both and walks off to another car that is waiting to take him back to my father's estate.

Lucas fires up the engine and revs it a few times, the powerful V8 engine sending a very loud signal to everyone in the Academy that Lucas is a man to be reckoned with.

"Wait," I say as Lucas starts to pull away. He takes his foot off the gas and waits for me to rummage around in my bag.

At last I find my sunglasses. Putting them on, I lean back in the seat, luxuriating in the feel of the sun against my skin. "Okay, you can go now."

Lucas grins and pulls out. When he reaches the gates of the Academy, he turns in the opposite direction to home. Soon we're driving down winding country lanes, the wind running through my hair as Lucas takes the scenic route to wherever it is we are going.

"So, you sorted everything with Declan?" he asks.

"Yes." *That's one way of putting it.* I'm glad Lucas has to focus on the road because I'm sure I look guilty as hell.

"I'm glad. I want you to be happy, Ivy," Lucas says. "I wish you would believe me about that."

"I'm starting to," I tell him. "But it's going to take time. I mean, we barely know each other. Trust is something which comes through experience and you've been sending me mixed signals. I mean, someone who *really* wanted me to be happy wouldn't have forced me to marry them, but at the same time, you can be so sweet and thoughtful. I don't really know what to think, if I'm honest."

"That's fair." Lucas nods. "I'm doing my best to make it up to you, Ivy. I really am. That's why I arranged for you to meet up with Declan this morning and why we're going on this little drive."

"Where are we going?"

"You'll see." Lucas smiles enigmatically, but refuses to reveal anything else about our destination, simply telling me to wait until we get there.

All I can do is sit back and enjoy the views. The countryside around King Town really is pretty, and it gives me something to look at while I try to figure out where my head's at. Lucas seems to be making a huge effort to get into my good books, but the cynical part of me wonders whether this is just a ploy to get me on his side while whatever it is he had going on in the background comes to fruition.

In the end, I give up. My life's way too complicated right now even for me to figure out.

"Hang on." I sit up in my seat as I realise I'm *very* familiar with where we are headed. "Are we going where I think we're going?"

"I don't know." Lucas grins. "Where do you think we're going?"

He indicates and turns into the road where Archer's family has their estate.

"Are you taking me to see Archer?"

"Declan isn't the only one who's been worried about you. Archer asked if I would be okay with you visiting him without me. Since I'm your husband, not your jailer, I thought the easiest way of making it happen was to tell Solomon I wanted to take you out for a picnic in the countryside after school. That should buy you a few hours of time.

"I'll take the car for a drive. Solomon had Cook prepare us a picnic hamper, so I have plenty of food to have a picnic by myself. If you're happy grabbing a snack on the way back home, I'm happy to let you hang out with Archer for a while. Whatever he wanted to talk to you about, it seemed important. If you want to fill me in later, I'd love to know what you talk about, but if you don't want to tell me, that's totally fine as well. I just hope that one day you'll trust me enough to include me in your plans."

He pulls up outside Archer's house, leaving the engine running. Impulsively, I kiss him on the cheek before getting out and running over to knock on Archer's door.

Lucas revs the engine. He raises one arm to say goodbye, and I wave back at him as he drives off on his solitary picnic. I feel a little sorry for him that he's eating alone, but those feelings evaporate as soon as the door opens.

Seeing Archer standing in front of me, away from the stress of school, marriage, House politics, is just the tonic I need. First Declan made love to me this morning and now I'm getting some alone time with another man who holds a piece of my heart.

"Hey, Archer." I smile at him, genuinely happy for once.

"Hey, Ivy. Glad you could join us."

"Us?" A puzzled frown wrinkles my forehead as I follow Archer inside.

"Ivy!"

"Hi!"

I could squeal with delight when I see Declan and Romy sitting on the sofa waiting for me.

"What are you guys all doing here?"

The three men exchange glances.

"After you shot my dad, we decided something had to change," Declan says. "So, while Mum was at Dad's bedside, hoping he'd pull through, I got together with Romy and Archer to see what we could do about Solomon Archaic once and for all."

His tone is very matter of fact when he speaks about his father, but I can't help the wave of guilt that engulfs me at the mention of him being in hospital. Yes, my father had forced me, but I am still the one who'd pulled the trigger.

"And what did you come up with?"

Declan looks at Romy, signalling it's his turn to speak.

"We've looked at it from every angle and as far as we can make out there's only one way we can solve the problem of your dad. We kill him."

I should be shocked at the cavalier way in which he spoke about murdering my father, but the moment Romy says it, I know it makes perfect sense. My father is like a leech, sucking the life out of everyone around him. He's never happy unless he's hurting others.

There was a time when I would have been overjoyed to hear

that I had a father and wasn't an orphan. That was before I met him. Over the past few months, I haven't seen a single good thing my father has done. He doesn't have a single redeeming quality about him. He's a bug who needs to be squashed underfoot.

"I'm in." I went to sit with the guys on the sofas, Archer sitting next to me. "How are you thinking we do this?"

"That's where we need your input," Romy says. "You know his movements better than any of us. You can tell us what his weaknesses are, where we're most likely to hit him without warning."

"I don't know that I know any more than you do," I tell him. "My father has kept me at an arm's length the whole time I've been around him. He only lets me see what he wants me to see. I don't think I can help you come up with a plan. It's not like I've ever assassinated someone before."

"I thought that's what Saturday was all about." Declan spoke quietly, trying not to hurt me, but it's impossible not to feel upset about what I'd done.

"I don't think it was," says Archer. "Solomon would have known Ivy had never shot a gun before. I don't think he actually expected her to hit the target. It was simply his way of proving that he has ultimate power over her. Even as a married woman, it's still her father who owns her."

"Like any real man could ever own a woman." Romy shakes his head in disgust.

"But this is why we need to put Ivy in charge of House Archaic," Declan says. "With her at the helm, the four Houses would be able to work together for once instead of being locked in this permanent power game. I think the four of us all agree that we'd much rather be on the same side than at each other's throats."

"Yeah."

"Absolutely."

We all nod.

"But what about Lucas?" Romy asks. "While he's in the

picture, Ivy's never going to be free to make decisions on her own."

"So she gets a divorce the second her father's in the ground." Archer shrugs.

"Actually, I think I can get an annulment," I say.

"You mean-" Declan raises an eyebrow while Romy and Archer look at each other.

"Lucas and I haven't slept together," I confirm. "At least, not in the Biblical sense. My father makes us share a bed, but we've been keeping our hands to ourselves. As far as I'm concerned, that's what we're going to continue to do until I'm able to get out of this marriage. Add in the fact that I was forced to marry him and I'm pretty confident I'll be able to get the whole thing written off as some bad dream-—as long as we can get my father out of the picture as soon as possible."

"Which brings us back to the original question," Romy says. "How do we kill him?"

"Ivy could put poison in his food," Declan suggests.

"Won't work." I shake my head. "Everything's prepared by his cook under supervision. I can't get anywhere near his meals."

"Ivy shoots him," Declan suggests.

"I get where you're coming from," says Archer, "and I love the irony of her shooting him after he made her shoot Claude, but Ivy's already shown what a terrible shot she is. Even up close and personal, I don't think we can rely on her being able to take him out before the guards pile in on her. Best case scenario, they'll disarm her, but there's every chance they'll simply kill her to keep Solomon safe. I don't know about you, but I'm not willing to risk Ivy's life like that."

"I'd do it," I say. "It's the least I can do to make it up to Declan. But Archer's right. I'm a really bad shot. I'm not confident even holding a gun. I could barely take it from my father's hand. I hated the way it felt. I knew it was a lethal weapon and the thought of it made me feel sick. I just don't think I can pull it out and kill my father before the guards step in. Plus, I think my father would sense that something was up. No, you can forget about guns. Or knives, for that matter." I look around pointedly, making it clear I'm being serious. "I'm totally down with killing my father, but I'm not sure that I hate him enough to do it myself."

"Which means we need another way of getting to him," says Romy. "Ideally something from a distance."

"What about a bomb?" I suggest. "No, forget about it. That's a dumb idea. It's not like any of us know how to build one."

"I do," admits Archer, surprising us all. "My father wanted to be sure that all his children were well versed in a number of different ways of dealing with our enemies. It's one of the reasons Solomon wanted me working with him—to figure out just how much I knew so he could decide how big of a threat I was. I was wise to him, though. I only let him know what I wanted him to know."

"What are you thinking, Ivy?" Declan asks.

"My father's private plane," I say. "He's going on those trips to Italy all the time. If I can get a hold of his schedule, I can figure out when he's due to leave and we can plant something on his plane. It's heavily guarded, but if we are able to watch the guards for a few days, I'm sure we'd be able to figure out a way to get close to it."

Romy nods slowly. "That could work. How soon do you think you could get his schedule?"

"I'm not sure," I reply. "His study is like a fortress within a fortress. It's almost impossible for me to get in it."

"What if you didn't have to go into his study?" asks Archer.

"What do you mean?"

"Well, Isabella knows everything that's going on. She'd be able to tell you when he was due to travel. Can't you try sweet talking her?"

"Or even turn your charm on your father," Romy suggests. "Tell him something like you want him to bring you back something from Italy so it would be helpful to know when he was travelling next."

"I can do that." I feel an excited little tingle in my tummy. We are planning to take out my father and it might actually work.

"Do you think you can do it without Lucas figuring out what you're up to?"

Declan's question brings me back down to earth with a bump.

"I don't know." I bite my lip. "Lucas isn't stupid and I still haven't been able to figure him out. Sometimes I think he's an arsehole who's got his nose permanently fixed up my father's backside and other times he does sweet things like getting my favourite people in a room together and leaves me on my own with you. I'd like to think I could get away with finding out my father's schedule without him figuring out there's something going on, but I can't guarantee it. Nor can I promise that he wouldn't go to my father if he did hear about our plan. For all I know, he's being nice to lull me into a false sense of security. He could be plotting against me. I mean, we're married. If something were to happen to me, he'd be the new Archaic heir."

Declan pales at the thought. "You really think he could be planning something like that?"

"I'd like to say no, but I just don't know him well enough to be sure." I shrugged sadly.

"All right. So for now, we have to assume that Lucas would be against us if he found out we're going to make a move against Solomon," says Archer. "So we need to come at this from a number of angles. Ivy, you try and find out your father's schedule without raising any suspicions. We'll scout out the plane and see if we can figure out a way of getting a bomb on board without anyone noticing. Timing's crucial--if we put it on there too soon, they'll find it when they do a security sweep before the flight."

"Unless we can figure out a way of camouflaging it so no one notices it," Romy puts in.

"Maybe." Archer does a half nod, half shake of his head. "We don't want to over-complicate things though."

"What about if I could get the bomb in his luggage?" The thought suddenly hits me. "That way we don't have to know about his schedule or anything like that. Archer can just give me the bomb and I'll keep it until I see my father packing. I'll figure out a way of smuggling it into one of his suitcases and he'll take it onto the plane himself without realising he's carrying his own death in his hands. It's a private airport, so he doesn't have to go through the security checks you usually get, so his case will be right by his side when the bomb detonates."

"Ivy, you're a genius!" Archer kisses me full on the lips. "That's the perfect solution."

"Yeah, good idea, Ivy." Declan smiles. "Simple is best, and that's so simple nobody will suspect a thing."

"So, Archer, you need to make the bomb as soon as possible," Romy says.

"No problem," Archer replies. "I'll put a remote detonation on it with a timer, so we can control exactly when it goes off. I can make it so that once it gets far enough away from the trigger, it automatically explodes, and I'll give you the trigger, Ivy, so you know you're perfectly safe until then."

"Good." I don't like to show any nerves about having a bomb in my room until my father went away, but knowing there's no way it can go off until he's up in the air makes me feel a heck of a lot better about the plan.

"And you're sure you're happy to do this?" asks Declan. "I mean, I should be glad you're taking on the lead role in assassinating your father and making amends for what you did for mine, but if you're not comfortable, we'll figure out another way."

"I have a feeling that taking out the current Head of House is the Archaic way," I tell him. "If anything, my father should be proud that I'm following in his footsteps."

"Okay." Declan nods slowly, satisfied.

"Well, now we've finished planning, Ivy, send a text to Lucas and let him know he can come pick you up. While we're waiting for him to arrive, who's for some champagne to celebrate?"

I tap out a message on my phone as Archer went to get the bottle of champagne. He pours out four flutes and passes them out.

"To Ivy, soon to be a single woman and Head of House Archaic!"

"To Ivy!"

We clink our glasses together. As I sip my champagne, I gaze round at the three men standing with me. I am so lucky to have them on my side. I'd be utterly lost without them.

There's only one problem with the thought of being a single woman again. Which of these three would I choose? I love them all so much, I can't imagine picking one over the others.

I put the thought aside for the moment. One day, that will be the worst of my problems and it isn't a bad one to have. Many girls would be more than happy to have three gorgeous guys in love with them, and when the time comes, I'll just have to follow my heart.

For now, we need to deal with my father once and for all.

Chapter Fifty-Four

"Have fun?" asks Lucas, as I climb into the passenger seat next to him.

"Yeah, I did."

"What did you two talk about?"

I almost correct him, then think better of it. If he believes I was only hanging out with Archer, he's less likely to suspect there is a conspiracy against my father.

"It was like you said, he was worried about me," I tell him. "He wanted to know how I'd been over the weekend and if there was anything he could do to cheer me up. We ended up watching a few episodes of the latest season of *Brooklyn Nine Nine* and had some champagne. He called it a belated wedding toast."

"That was nice of him."

There doesn't seem to be any guile behind Lucas's words as he drives me back home.

As we pull into the garage, I see my father talking to Isabella in front of the garage while the staff loads suitcases into one of the limos.

"Ah, Ivy, Lucas. I'm glad you're back before I leave. I would have hated to go without saying goodbye."

My father strides towards us, arms outstretched, and I suffer an embrace.

"While I'm gone, you'll be the man of the house," my father continues. "This means you are the interim head of House Archaic."

"Aren't *I* supposed to be the head of House Archaic?" I point out.

"My dear Ivy." My father practically pats me on the head, his tone is beyond patronising. "I would love to leave you in charge, but I have yet to see evidence of your loyalty to your House and family. In comparison, Lucas has worked diligently for me, following my every command to the letter. Moreover, his upbringing means he has an innate understanding of what to do in any eventuality without needing to seek my approval first. At this moment in time, your husband is the best person to take care of House affairs. Perhaps when you have proven your worth, I will be able to trust you with the duties which are your birth right, but as it currently stands, you are nowhere near ready for such responsibilities. Sit back and let Lucas do the heavy lifting. Go play your guitar, get Isabella to arrange a visit from a masseur. You're far too uptight."

"I might just do that. Thanks, Dad." I do my best to sound grateful, but in my mind I am puking. Anyone would be uptight in my position. "Where are you going, anyway?"

"I'm off to Italy." He sighs dramatically. "My partners are insisting on an in person visit and it's a good opportunity to stock up on fine Italian wine. Would you like me to bring you back anything, Ivy? Lucas?"

"Surprise me," I say.

"I don't need anything, Dad," Lucas tells him. "But thanks for offering. Is there anything I need to know about while you're gone?"

"There are a few little details that would be useful for you to know. Walk with me."

My father leads Lucas away, out of earshot, leaving me and Isabella on our own together.

"How can you bear working for that sexist pig?" I ask.

"I have my own agenda." Isabella shrugs. "Besides, men like him think they're in charge, but you and I both know where the power really lies. There's always a woman behind the throne and we're always the ones pulling the strings."

"Is that right?" I look at Isabella with new respect. "So how would you advise I manage my father?"

"Simple," Isabella says. "Do exactly what he wants you to do--for now. While you were estranged, he always talked about his perfect little girl. He had an image in his mind about his princess, a girl who loved pink and unicorns, a girl who spent hours playing with her dolls. When his spies brought back reports of a tomboy who had a major rebellious streak running through her, he didn't want to believe it, so he continued in his fantasy of the girl he wanted you to be until the time came to bring you here. It was harder for him to keep up the picture perfect daughter with you standing right in front of him. So instead, he's done his utmost to force you into the vision he has for you."

"Tell me about it." I roll my eyes.

"I get it. I really do," Isabella says. "It's frustrating when we're forced into living up to someone else's idea of who we ought to be."

"It sounds like you have personal experience of that."

"We're not talking about me right now," Isabella snaps. I make a mental note to find out more about her background later. "We're talking about you and how you can manipulate your father into giving you more freedom. I'm not saying you have to jump to his whims permanently. Just do enough to create the illusion he has the daughter of his dreams. Once he buys into that, you'll be surprised at what you can get away with. For example, when he asked you to shoot Claude Dauphin, you didn't have to actually aim at him. You could have sent the shot way over his head. No one would have been hurt, but you would have demonstrated pure loyalty. Your father didn't have to know you missed deliberately. He was *expecting* you to miss. You have no experience with firearms. What he wanted to see was you obeying without question. Instead, you fought him--and make no mistake, he *would* have given the order for you to be stabbed. Anything less would have made him weak in the eyes of his men, and Solomon will never do anything to make himself look weak.

"But I promise you, it would have broken his heart."

"Somehow I doubt that." I laugh bitterly. "My father doesn't have a heart to break."

"Still, the things he does don't bring him any pleasure," Isabella tells me. "But that's what it takes to be head of House. Which is why he's left Lucas in charge. Do not underestimate that boy. He can be absolutely ruthless if need be. That's why your father likes him so much. He sees a lot of himself in Lucas. In many ways, he thinks of Lucas as more of an heir than you."

"Well, duh."

"But that's only because Lucas knows how to play the game," Isabella says. "If your father had asked him to shoot Claude Dauphin, he'd have done it in a heartbeat. And he'd probably have missed deliberately *and no one would care.* Ivy, haven't you figured it out yet? This town is nothing but a game. The players dance around each other, but it's all about appearances. Your father gave you good advice when he told you to relax. If you stop going around looking for reasons to be offended, you'll have a much easier time of it."

"If you say so."

I don't like to admit it, but I can see the wisdom in what Isabella is saying. I just hate the thought of sucking up to my father like that. I detest him, and that is never going to change.

Speak of the devil...

Lucas and my father come back to join us, a broad grin on both their faces.

"Isabella--I want you to treat Lucas as you would me. His word is your command, understood?"

"Yes, sir." Isabella nods.

"Ivy—be a good girl for once?"

Isabella and I exchange a quick glance.

"I'll do my best," I say.

"That's what I like to hear. Now I'll be back before you know it, so don't have too much fun while I'm gone."

My father turns and gets into the back of the limo. Lucas puts his arm around me as we wave him off.

I inhale deeply, blowing the air out in one long, relieved stream. "Thank goodness that bastard's gone and I don't have to see his smug little face anymore."

"Don't let his guards hear you talking like that," Lucas warns.

"I don't care," I say. "I've had enough. I tell you something, Lucas. You're welcome to House Archaic. If I could, I'd walk away from it all today. I'm done with all these mind games."

"Oh, boo hoo, Ivy," Isabella sneers. "Next you'll be saying you didn't ask to be born. We all get it. You've got it tough. We all know your father's treated you badly, but instead of focusing on what you don't have, look at what you do. You've got more money than most people can ever dream of. You've got a husband who is kind, caring and considerate. Who wants nothing more than to make you happy if only you'd let him. I've told you how to handle your father. It's not rocket science. But if you're not even willing to help yourself, then I'm done. Be miserable, Ivy. That's clearly what makes you happy."

She stalks off, leaving me gaping after her.

"I hate to say it, Ivy, but she does have a point," Lucas says, giving me a sheepish smile.

I glare at him and he steps back a little, putting his hands up in a gesture of surrender.

"Hear me out," he says. "I don't agree with what your father's done to you, but you can turn it around. It's like Isabella says. Play the game. Learn the rules and then bend them. Do that, and you could have the whole of King Town in your hand. Now, I've got to go and do something for your father, but I want you to think about what I've just said. If you want my help, you only have to ask and it's yours. It's time to stop feeling sorry for yourself and make a change."

If only he knew what I'd been discussing earlier tonight. I am going to make a change all right. And by the time I'm done, this town will be reeling.

Chapter Fifty-Five

"Are you looking forward to the Bomber Derby tonight?" Lucas asks me over breakfast.

"Sure. I want nothing more than to ride pillion while you do your best to win, only to come in behind Archer yet again."

"Actually, I was talking more about whether you were looking forward to competing in the Bomber Derby?" Lucas side-eyes me, grinning.

"What do you mean?" I don't dare to believe that he's actually telling me I'm allowed to compete.

"Well, since your father's away and I'm the interim head of House, what I say goes. You even heard him say that. And I say that my wife should be allowed to compete on her own terms as the amazing biker she is. Only heirs to a House are allowed to compete in the Bomber Derby, but technically we're both heirs, so I figure we might as well take advantage of the opportunity to give us two chances for House Archaic to take the crown."

"Thank you!" I squeal and throw my arms around his neck.

"Now, just because you get to compete doesn't mean you're going to win," Lucas warns me. "I'm not going to slow down to let you go ahead of me. Nobody's going to give you any slack. You'll be lucky to come in third."

"We'll see." I smile enigmatically, already running over the route in my head. Tonight, our House is in charge and Lucas and I spent ages plotting out the perfect route to challenge the racers. I knew it like the back of my hand, because we've ridden round it a few times to make sure it was as challenging as we wanted it to be. The others didn't stand a chance. If I'm competing, Lucas and I are going to take the first two spots-- and I am going to cross the finish line first.

"I'm going to oversee the preparations for the race tonight," Lucas says. "You can come with me if you like, but it's going to be pretty boring."

"Because sitting around in our suite all day is so exciting," I point out.

"True, but that's not the only option you've got."

"What do you mean?"

"I don't know how many times I have to tell you I'm not your father, but maybe actions speak louder than words. You can do whatever you like while he's away. If you want to go and see your friends, I don't care what House they belong to. They're your friends, and if you want to visit them, that's fine. Just because we're married doesn't mean we have to be joined at the hip. Why don't you go and see Milly? The two of you are well overdue for some chill time together. I'm sure she'd love to see you."

"Are you sure?" I like this side of Lucas, although the cynic in me wonders whether he is getting me out of the way so he can do something without me knowing. Those thoughts can drive you mad, though, and I am not going to look a gift horse in the mouth.

"If I wasn't, I wouldn't have suggested it."

"Thanks, Lucas." I lean over and kiss him on the cheek, unable to wipe the smile off my face as I polish off the rest of my breakfast burrito.

I AGREE to meet Lucas at the Bomber Derby later and get on my motorbike to go visit my best friend. Buzzing down the road, no guards looking over my shoulder, I feel free for the first time in I don't know how long. If I want, I could simply ride off into the distance, but where I might have been tempted to do that just a few days ago, now that I have a plan to depose my father, I need to stick around. I am not going to abandon the town to the evil machinations of Solomon Archaic. I don't know what's behind all his trips to Italy, but whatever it is, it can't be good. Someone has to stop him once and for all, and the only person who has a chance of doing that is me.

I am staying in this town for the time being.

Just like her brother, Milly has her own house on the grounds of the Knight estate. From the outside, it looks just like Archer's, so I wasn't expecting what greets me when I walk inside.

"Wow, Milly. This place is amazing!"

Archer's house is very much a typical bachelor pad, with simple furniture and sleek lines. But Milly's home is the complete opposite. The walls are painted with intricate murals, swirls of pastel colours sweeping across the surfaces. But over the murals are countless hand drawn images from manga comics, creating a mind-blowing montage I could look at for hours.

"Did you do all these?"

Milly nods. "Yeah. I wanted to take art A-level, but my dad wouldn't let me. He says there's no future in making comics and nobody wants to read my comics, anyway. I guess he's right. I mean, I'm supposed to be a representative of House Knight. Comic illustrator isn't exactly a popular career choice for my family."

"I had no idea you could draw like this," I say, still fascinated by the images surrounding me. "I wanted to do art as well, but my father made me choose between that and music."

"I'm not surprised you went with music," Milly says. "Your songs are so beautiful. And if you hadn't chosen that subject, you and Declan would never have started writing together. I loved that song you sang at the concert about forbidden love. It filled me with emotion—I've never had a boyfriend, let alone anyone who would look at me the way Declan was looking at you while you were singing."

"So you know about Declan too, huh?"

"Everyone does," Milly says. "I didn't want to say anything because I figured you'd talk to me when you were ready. And obviously, I knew you had a thing with Archer, so I wasn't sure if you wanted to discuss it with me in case I took my brother's side against you."

"And? Do you take his side?"

Milly shakes her head. "He's absolutely head over heels in love with you, Ivy, but just because he has strong feelings for you doesn't mean you have to reciprocate. I mean, I wouldn't say no to a date with Declan. The way he tosses his hair gives me goosebumps!"

"Declan is pretty darned gorgeous," I agree. "But then Archer's just my type. If you asked me to describe my dream man, I'd give you a photo of him and call it done. The problem is, I like them both. They're so different—how can I choose between them? Declan's really sweet. He's never pressured me to do anything I didn't want, and he really seems to care about my happiness. Like, if I choose Archer over him, he'd be sad, but he wouldn't do anything to change my mind. He'd rather I was happy with Archer than miserable with him. Not that he'd make me miserable. Argh!" I could tear my hair out with frustration.

"And then there's Romy. What's the deal with you guys? I thought he'd be devastated when you married Lucas, but he seems to be fine."

"That's because everyone thinks Romy's a player," I remind her. "He's good at putting up a front so no one knows how he really feels. That's what I like about him. He intrigues me. He puts up a huge front so people think he's nothing but a Casanova, but underneath all of that he's really sensitive. He *was* devastated when I married Lucas, but he understood it wasn't my fault. My marriage is a sham, so it's not like anybody should take it seriously. I know who I want to be with, even if I tried to push them away. They know it too."

"You don't think you can figure something out with Lucas and make it work?" Milly asks. "I mean, plenty of arranged marriages turn out perfectly fine and you've got to admit that Lucas is really good looking."

"You think?"

"Oh yes," Milly gushes. "All the girls at school think so. If he didn't have that ring on his finger, he'd have his pick. As it is, a few have tried to make a move on him."

"Really?" I am surprised by the little pang of jealousy which hits me when I hear that.

"Yeah. Ally tried to get him to kiss her at the ball. She was probably trying to get back at you for stealing Declan from her."

"I guess I can't blame her for that," I say. "Although, I didn't exactly steal Declan. It was a little more complicated than that. I had no idea he had a girlfriend when we kissed and nothing more than that happened until after they broke up."

"Lucas wasn't interested though," Milly told me. "He's so loyal to you. When we danced together at the ball, all he could talk about was how cool you were and how you were even better in real life than your picture."

"Is that right?"

"It was interesting though," Milly says. "I got the impression that although he likes you a lot, it wouldn't have mattered what you were like--he would have married you anyway. It's just that he likes you enough to see if you can make your marriage work right now. But there was a part of me that thought..."

Milly bites her lip and looks away.

"What is it, Mills? What did you think?"

"You'll think I'm being silly." Milly shakes her head and

waves me away. "It's not even appropriate for me to say. Forget I mentioned it."

"You know I can't do that, Mills. Just tell me. Whatever it is, it'll be fine, but you've got me all intrigued now."

Milly inhales deeply, not looking me in the eye. "I kind of got the impression he was flirting with me."

"Flirting with you?" That's the last thing I expected her to say.

"I know. It's silly of me to even think about it. Like someone like Lucas would be interested in someone like me. He's a great guy."

"Someone like you?" I scoff. "I've told you this before and I'll keep telling you until you believe it. You're beautiful. Anyone would be lucky to be with you. If you think Lucas was flirting with you, then I have no doubt that's what he was doing."

"And you're okay with that?"

I shrug. "Maybe if things were different I'd be annoyed, but with Lucas, not with you. You're my best friend. I know you'd never do anything to hurt me. But this isn't a real marriage and I'm planning on getting it annulled as soon as I possibly can. We haven't even slept together."

"Really? Not even once?" Milly's eyes boggle. "Aren't you curious to find out what he's like in bed?"

"Not really. I mean, I'm already juggling three guys. I really don't feel the need to complicate things but adding a fourth one into the mix. In fact, Milly, if Lucas does make a pass at you and you want to reciprocate, that would be fine by me."

"Are you kidding?"

"Nope. You deserve a little happiness, and so does Lucas. I'm not ever going to be interested in him in that way, and I don't expect him to live like a monk for however long we're married."

What I don't tell Milly is that if she did have an affair with Lucas, it would make it even easier for me to get my marriage annulled. Part of me feels bad for using my friend like this, but I know Milly well enough to know that it is unlikely she'd ever follow through with Lucas. She is simply too sweet.

"Well, I was probably imagining him flirting with me anyway," Milly says. "So, I don't think you're going to have to worry about that any time soon. Do you want a drink or something? I can make some coffee. My dad got me the most amazing coffee maker for my birthday."

I can tell Milly wants to change the subject, so I nod. "Sure. That would be great."

"I can add something stronger if you like," Milly offers. "Do you like Irish coffee?"

"I do, but I'd better not," I tell her. "Not if I want to win the Bomber Derby tonight?"

"Win?" Milly gasps, a delighted smile spreading across her face. "You're competing?"

I nod as she throws her arms around me, squeezing me tight in a hug.

"I'm so excited for you! I just *know* you're going to kick those boys' butt! It's about time a woman showed them how to compete. But how did you persuade your dad to let you ride?"

"I didn't have to," I say. "He's gone to Italy, leaving Lucas in charge. Lucas said that if I want to compete, I can. He isn't going to tell me what to do. What my dad doesn't know won't hurt him."

"That's so cool! I *told* you he's a great guy. But why do you think your dad keeps going to Italy? I overheard my parents discussing it. Nobody can figure out what he's doing there."

"Beats me." I shrug. "It's not like my father tells me anything about his plans, even if I ask. Maybe Lucas knows something-- his adoptive mother was Italian, and he's spent a lot of time there--but if he does, he's not say anything to me. It can't be anything good though. You know what my father's like. He never does anything without a million and one other plans going on behind the scenes. I wouldn't be surprised if he told Lucas one thing, but the truth was completely different."

"I feel sorry for your father." Milly's statement surprises me.

"Why would you feel sorry for *him*?"

"It must be so lonely not being able to trust anyone," she says. "All that money but he hasn't got anyone to curl up with at night. He can't hang out with his friends. He doesn't have any because he can't trust they're not trying to get close to him to hurt him."

"And whose fault is that?" I snap. "My mother adored him, but he was so abusive to her, she had no choice but to run away. He could have come for me after she died, but he chose to leave me in foster care. I mean, if I'd grown up with him, who knows what our relationship would be like now? We might be close."

"And you'd probably be a bitch, like Ally and Taylor," Milly points out. "Hasn't it ever occurred to you that your father did you a favour abandoning you like that? I know you had a hard childhood, but it's made you into the person you are today and she's pretty darned awesome."

"Thanks, Mills." I smile as Milly pours fresh cream into my coffee, just how I like it.

We take our drinks and step outside to sit on the deck. Her house has stunning views across the Knight estate and sitting there with my best friend, I have a brief moment of forgetting my messed-up life and simply enjoying the moment for what it was.

"Is that Archer over there?"

Milly nudges me and I beam when I see one of my favourite people walking towards us. He's wearing a wifebeater, the lack of sleeves showing off his well-defined muscles. I feel my cheeks reddening at the memory of those powerful arms pinning me down, while he...

"Hey, you two." He pulls out a chair and turns it round, sitting on it backwards. "You look like you're having a serious conversation."

"Just thinking about what might have been if my arsehole father had made different decisions," I tell him. "But I guess he's too full of himself to do things any other way. He's selfish to the core, and that's never going to change."

433

"I hear that," Archer says. "Still, I thought he was in Italy at the moment. That should give you a bit of a break."

"Yep, although he's left Lucas in charge instead of me. Sexist pig."

"Would you expect anything else?" Archer reminds me. "It's frustrating, but I don't think your father would ever let you take over the family business. I have a funny feeling that the only reason he made you marry Lucas is because he didn't want you to marry into House Navarre. If you hadn't been engaged to Romy, you probably would have had a little longer as a single woman, but sooner or later, he'd have forced you to marry the man of his choosing. He couldn't possibly trust you to make your own decisions when it came to important decisions like that, not with you being just a girl."

"You're probably right." I sigh. "There was no way my father was going to let me marry Romy unless it was his idea, and it fit into one of his nefarious schemes. I should have agreed to marry Romy sooner."

"I'm glad you didn't." Archer fixes me with a meaningful look. "None of us takes your marriage to Lucas seriously, which means you're free to be with whomever you like. And isn't it even more exciting knowing that every kiss, every caress, is a slap in the face for your father?"

"It does feel good to go against his wishes," I admit. "Although I feel sorry for Lucas."

"Why?" Archer's tone is sharp. "Unlike you, he could have said no. He didn't *have* to marry you. He's only got himself to blame if you cheat on him."

"I don't think it's quite that simple," I tell him. "Lucas has told me a bit about his upbringing and he hasn't had it easy either."

"So?" Archer sneers. "I've got no sympathy for the man. And I can't wait to rub his nose in it when I beat him in the Bomber Derby tonight."

"Is that right?" I smirk. "You'll have to get past me first."

"I didn't think you wanted to ride pillion."

"Who says I'm riding pillion?"

I love the look of delighted surprise which comes across Archer's face. "You don't mean-?"

"Yep. Since my father's away, I'm competing. And when I win, he can't exactly complain about me racing again. In fact, knowing my dad, he's likely to start boasting about how amazing I am and insisting I compete in every race going."

"You think you're going to win, huh?"

"I *know* I am."

Chapter Fifty-Six

rev my bike, the powerful roar of the engine mingling with the other bikes to create a deafening cacophony. Lucas is lined up next to me on my right, while Archer flanks me on the left. Romy is next to him, with Declan on the other side of Archer. Just like the last few races, none of them have a girl riding behind them.

Taylor volunteers to start the race tonight and she slowly walks up and down in front of the bikers, a loudhailer in her hands.

"You all know the rules," she says. "There aren't any! Just ride your fastest and your hardest, first across the finish line wins. If you want to team up with another rider to take someone out..." She glares at me. "Feel free, but remember—there's still only one winner. You have Lucas and Ivy to thank for tonight's route, so if you've got any problems with it, take it up with them. Now rev your engine if you're ready to race!"

I flip down the visor on my helmet and rev my bike. Adrenaline courses through me as Taylor makes her way to the side, safely out of the way of the bikes.

"Ready... Set... Go!"

The second she gives the word, I release the brakes and slam on the gas. My bike lurches forward, quickly picking up speed. I'd chosen my bike for its powerful acceleration, knowing that once I was out front, it would be easier for me to maintain my lead than try to take it from someone else.

I come up to the first bend, a sharp turn which takes me into the grounds of the Archaic estate. With my father being away for the foreseeable future, Lucas and I decided to make the race partly off road, knowing we had bikes in the garage which could cope with the difficult terrain better than most of our competitors. When we heard the groans as the others saw the course, we'd both grinned, knowing our decision had the impact we wanted it to have.

I take my bike across the grass, following the route which Lucas spent all afternoon marking out. Heading up a slope, my bike takes off when it reaches the top and I fly through the air for a few feet before coming back down to earth. I can hear the sound of bikes following me and there is a scream as someone crashes. I didn't dare risk looking back to see who it is. I have a race to win!

I lean into the next bend, my bike so close to the ground I almost fall, but I grip the handlebars tightly, determined to show the boys who's boss. The next bit of the race involves weaving through the trees in the small forest on the estate, requiring lightning fast reflexes. I'm forced to slow down a little, which allows Lucas to shoot past me. He raises his hand in salute and I narrow my eyes. There is no way I am going to let Lucas beat me.

He goes left round a tree, so I go right, hoping to gain some ground on him, but I realise I'd made a mistake as I see another tree looming right in front of me. I turn the handlebars sharply, kicking at the tree to make sure I get round it, but the error cost me. I emerge from the trees to see Lucas ahead of me, Romy and Archer close behind him.

There is a short lawn after the forest, and then we are back on the road. I grin, knowing that we are about to hit a straight, which will allow me to go full throttle and make up some ground. The boys' bikes have powerful engines too, and the noise is incredible as our speed creeps up.

70... 80... 90... 100.

I am closing on the three men ahead of me, but with the finish line looming, I'm not sure I'll be able to catch up to them. Darn it. Why didn't I just go after Lucas and overtake him as we hit the road? I *knew* the track. I'd helped design it! There was no excuse for making a mistake like this.

First Lucas is ahead, then Romy, then Archer, the three of them in a dance as they vied for victory. I'm not sure which one of the three I want to win. I am not even sure I care. *I* want to win.

We go round the final bend, Archer out front, Romy close behind him, Lucas snapping at their heels. I lean forward over my handlebars, willing my bike to go faster, even though I am pushing the limits of what it is capable of achieving.

I see Romy and Archer exchange a look, nodding at each other. Suddenly, they yank their handlebars to the side, braking and stopping in the middle of the road to create a barrier in front of Lucas. He has no choice but to pull on the brakes and veer off to the edge of the road.

The way is clear, and I speed past all three of them to cross the finish line first. I'd won!

Milly comes rushing over to me. "That was amazing!" she squeals. "I didn't see that coming. I'm so glad you won. You deserve it."

"Mmm." I want to share in her excitement, I really do, but the reality is that if it hadn't been for Romy's and Archer's intervention, I'd have come in a disappointing fourth. That wasn't anywhere near good enough. I should have done better.

"Well done, Ivy." Archer and Romy come over to congratulate me. "A well-deserved victory."

"Hardly," I say. "If it wasn't for the two of you, I wouldn't have even made it to third place."

"So?" Romy laughs. "That's how it works. You know that

anything goes and there are reasons why you might not want to win if it helps to have someone else win. If you want to get all deep and meaningful, the race is a metaphor for life in King Town. You may not be able to compete again in the Bomber Derby, so Archer and I agreed that you deserved to win, even if it's only this once."

"Yeah, well, you could have told me that's what you had planned. Maybe I wouldn't have almost run into a tree trying to overtake Lucas. Or maybe I would have told you to leave him alone and let him win. One of you could have been seriously injured with that stupid stunt you pulled."

"Nah." Romy laughs. "We've been doing this sort of thing for years. We know what we're doing. Nobody ever gets badly hurt. Well, not often, anyway." He and Archer exchange a glance and laugh, a rare moment of male bonding.

"What did I miss?" Declan joins us. "Sounds like there was some drama."

"Ivy won," Archer says. "And deservedly so."

"What about Lucas?"

"I didn't make it past the finish line." Lucas limps over to join us.

"Are you okay?" I'm surprised by how worried I am about him.

"I'm fine," he says. "I twisted my ankle when my bike went over, but it's nothing that won't be okay in a few days. The only thing that suffered any real damage was my male pride, but that'll recover as well." He reaches out his hand to Archer and Romy who each shake it in turn. "Nice move, guys. I should have seen it coming. But you won't be able to get me that way next time. I'll be first past the finish line, one way or another. Now come on. Ivy and I have a party planned which will blow you away."

He casually puts his arm around my shoulders to lead me away in the direction of our house where the party is being held, a signal that whatever the boys' feelings for me might be, I still belonged to him. At least for now.

Chapter Fifty-Seven

The heavy bass is thumping, the hall heaving with dancing bodies as we celebrate the latest Bomber Derby. I stand at the edge of the dance floor, sipping a cocktail, as I watch everyone else losing themselves in the music.

Over by the double doors leading outside, I see Lucas deep in conversation with Isabella. Whatever it is seems serious, because Lucas glances over at me, then takes Isabella by the elbow, hurrying her outside.

I frown and make to go after them, when Romy appears by my side.

"Where are you going?" he asks.

"I wanted to have a word with Lucas."

"Why would you want to talk to him when you could hang out with me?"

He treats me to one of his winning smiles and I am lost. Whatever Lucas is involved in can wait until later.

"It's a little too loud to talk in here," I tell him, having to yell to be heard.

"So let's go somewhere else."

I nod.

Romy takes my hand, leading me in the opposite direction to where Lucas and Isabella had gone. I know I shouldn't let him hold my hand in public, especially not when there are spies for my father everywhere, but I don't care. We're just holding hands. It is perfectly innocent.

As we walk out of the doors to the hall, we almost bump into a couple kissing.

"Looks like Ally's moved on," I murmur, as Romy leads me round the two teens and upstairs.

"Which one's your room?" he asks, faced with a number of identical looking doors.

"This way." It's my turn to lead as we head down the corridor to the suite I share with Lucas.

"This is nice," says Romy politely, looking round.

"I prefer the suite I had at yours," I tell him. "At least there I had some kind of say over the décor. This is all my father's idea of what a married couple would want in their home."

"I wasn't going to say anything…" Romy flops down on the couch and pats the space next to him. I move to sit next to him and he put his arm around me, drawing me close.

"This is nice." I sighed.

"Any time with you is nice," Romy says, dropping a light kiss on the top of my head. I close my eyes, trying to pretend we are just a normal couple, enjoying some alone time.

I turn to face Romy, wanting to tell him how I feel, but he anticipates the movement so his lips meet mine. He runs his hand down my front, lightly caressing my breast.

"No. Don't." I push his hand away.

"What's wrong?" Romy frowns. "Don't you like me kissing you anymore?"

"I love you kissing me," I confess. "But it doesn't seem right to do it right next to where Lucas and I share a bed. I know we're just keeping up appearances, but even so. It feels wrong to do anything here when I'm supposed to be married. I know that doesn't really make any sense, but I can't help it."

"And that's one of the reasons I love you." My heart

lurches when I hear Romy use the L word. "You put on this front like you're a tough girl, but you're one of the sweetest people I've ever met. You care so deeply about the people you love."

"Isn't it a big assumption that I love you?" I keep my tone light, but I know that this is a conversation that has been a long time coming and I can't put it off any longer. We are going to have *that* talk.

"Don't you?" Romy looks at me all vulnerable, and I can't risk hurting him by teasing him.

"Of course I do."

Romy can't help himself. He kisses me again. "I knew it!" He pumps his fist.

"Hold your horses, cowboy," I warn. "Just because I have feelings for you doesn't mean a thing. You're not the only man I love you know."

"I know." Romy shrugs. "And I can't say it doesn't bother me, but at the same time, I respect your choices. It's not like I haven't been with plenty of women. It would be wrong for me to judge you for doing the same. You've done your best to be discrete, but I know what's going on with Archer and Declan. They're good guys. If you chose one of them over me, I'd be upset, but I'd know you were with someone who really cares about you-—unlike Lucas."

"Why do you say Lucas doesn't care about me? It's thanks to him I was allowed to compete tonight."

"Have you listened to what you just say? 'Allowed'? Ivy, you're the Archaic heir. Nobody allows you to do anything. You do whatever the heck you like-—it's your birth right!"

I nod slowly, taking in what he said.

"You're right," I say. "And you know what I want to do right now? Have sex."

"That's my girl," Romy grins and moves to kiss me, but I put my hand up between our faces.

"But not here. Can we maybe go to your place instead? Lucas will be so caught up in hosting the party, which is going to go on for hours yet. Nobody will notice if we disappear for a while."

"We can do that." Romy smiles as we get up and hurry downstairs. But as we pass through the front door, Archer spots us and comes over to join us.

"You two look like you're up to something," he says. "Can I join in?"

Romy and I exchange a look. The thought of Archer being involved in our lovemaking is something I've daydreamed about before, but never imagined it would be a possibility. The two of them are such macho men, I didn't think they'd be comfortable being around another guy.

But if you don't ask, you never know what was possible. What's the worst that could happen? Archer says no and Romy and I leave together? That would still work. I'll just imagine Archer is with us, watching.

I stand on tiptoe and whisper in Archer's ear. "Romy and I are going over to his place to have sex. Want to join us?"

Archer looks over at Romy, who shrugs at him in a gesture that says *I'm up for it if you are.*

"Okay. But I think we ought to go to my place. We'll have more privacy there."

I can't believe my luck as we go to where Romy and Archer's bikes are parked. There is still no sign of Lucas as I put on my helmet and climb up behind Romy. I cling tightly around his waist as he starts up the bike. The vibration from the bike's engine added to the excitement I am feeling. By the time we reach Archer's house, I'm already soaking. All this time I wondered who I'd choose if I had to, and now I am discovering I don't have to make that decision.

Romy kicks down the stand on his bike, as Archer walks over to open the door to his house. I climb off, Romy close behind me. He turns to take me by the hand.

"Are you sure about this?" I ask him. "I don't want you to feel that you're being forced into anything."

"What—and miss out on a new experience?" he asks. "I've

always told you I want you to be happy and I know you have feelings for Archer. I'm not going to pretend this won't be a bit weird, but I'm here for you, Ivy. Besides, Archer's always claimed he's better in bed than I am. Now we're both going to find out how wrong he is."

"Are you two going to stand around talking all night?" asks Archer. "Because I thought we had other plans."

Romy squeezes my hand, and we follow Archer into his house and down into the basement where he has his home cinema and that enormous bed. The three of us stand there awkwardly for a moment, none of us knowing exactly how to start this.

In the end, I make the first move, taking off my jacket and tossing it to one side before climbing onto the bed.

"Come on, guys." I pat the bed on either side of me. "As Archer said, we have plans and I want to make the most of our time together before Lucas notices I left our party."

Romy and Archer crawl onto the bed after me. Romy kisses me, slow and lingering.

"Isn't Ivy the best kisser?" he asks Archer.

"I've always thought so," Archer agrees, coming to kiss me.

The two of them are very different in their technique and yet they both feel so right against my lips, Romy's tender loving contrasting with Archer's urgency. We sit there for a while, the two of them taking turns at kissing me. Whichever way I turn, there's a man, and I adore them both.

As I kiss Romy, Archer tugs at my top. I break away from Romy and the two of them help me out of my top, revealing a rather unflattering sports bra I'd chosen to protect myself during the race.

"I don't think you need that anymore," Romy says, unclipping it at the front. He and Archer pull it open between them, revealing my breasts.

The two of them lean forward, sucking and licking at the breast they are closest to. I close my eyes and throw my head back, running my hands through Romy's hair and over Archer's shaven head. The contrast in texture is another reminder that I have two men loving me and I wallow in the feel of them. My hands clench, tugging at Romy's hair as their tongues flick across my nipples, driving me wild.

"I have to get naked." I can barely speak, I am so aroused. I finally work up the strength to push them away so I can unbutton my leather trousers.

"Let us help you," Romy offers.

He takes one leg of my trousers and Archer takes the other, the pair of them pulling them off in one swift, smooth movement. They throw them to the floor, and I lean back on the bed as Romy and Archer both nuzzle against my neck. My hands fumble for their crotches, feeling a firm bulge. The boys are just as excited as I am. I spread my legs wide, wanting to expose myself to their touch.

They take the hint as they fondle my thighs, working their way up my legs until they slip their hands inside my underwear. I am so wet, their fingers easily slip inside me, one of them finger fucking me while the other rubs my clit in erotic, circular movements. Eyes tightly closed to focus on what was happening, I have no idea whose finger is whose, and I don't care. All I know is that I want this moment to last forever.

With a loud cry I come, the sudden orgasm taking me by surprise. I pout. "I wanted to go on for longer."

"Don't worry." Archer grins. "We're nowhere near done with you yet."

The two of them pull off my knickers, and I notice that they are stained with my juices before the boys throw them away. I am completely naked before them, completely vulnerable, yet I've never felt safer and taken care of.

"Your turn, guys," I say but kind of plead at the same time.

Romy and Archer look at each other and shrug. They stand on either side of the bed and unzip their trousers, revealing two very impressive erections.

"Come closer." I crook my finger, beckoning them to both

come within easy reach. They kneel on either side of me, giving me access to their gorgeous cocks.

I take Romy's cock into my mouth for a few sucks then suck on Archer for a while. I turn from one to the other then back again, doing just enough to arouse them both, only titillating them with promises of pleasure to come.

"I need one of you to fuck me. Now," I order.

"Go for it, Archer," says Romy.

"You're the guest," he counters. "You go first."

"I don't care who goes first," I say. "Just fuck me!"

Romy climbs between my legs as Archer goes to the side of the bed so I can suck on him while Romy slips inside me. I moan, feeling my pussy clench to hold Romy tight as he thrusts into me. I lift my hips to meet him. He knows my body well enough to find the perfect angle to make me cry out, and I feel myself heading towards another orgasm.

"I'm going to come," says Romy, pulling out. "But I don't want this to end just yet. Your turn, Archer."

Archer and Romy switch places, and I smile, loving the weight of Archer on top of me. I turn my head to take Romy's cock in my mouth, licking off the precum. I love the taste of him.

Archer pounds into me, his movements more urgent than Romy. It's like he's read my mind, knowing that this is what I need to come again. I suck eagerly on Romy, working him with my hand as well as my mouth, my desire for him increasing as I spiral towards another all-encompassing orgasm. As it takes over, I finally let go of Romy and let myself relax into the most powerful orgasm I've ever experienced and Romy comes on my chest.

Archer lay on top of me, not wanting to come yet but he soon speeds up, finishing not long after. He gives me time to recover my breath, his cock twitching inside me as I come back down to earth.

I collapse on top of Archer, feeling Romy against my back.

He kisses me on the shoulder, the three of us lying there intertwined, waiting for our breathing to return to normal.

"I don't know if I'll be able to walk any time soon," I say.

"You and me both," smiles Archer, as we tumble back onto the bed, me lying in the middle with the boys on either side of me.

"Have you ever done anything like that before?" I finally ask.

"No," says Archer.

"I've been with two women at the same time," Romy tells us.

"Now why doesn't that surprise me?" I say.

"They asked me to do it!" Romy protests. "It would have been rude for me to say no."

"Uh-huh." I laugh as the two of them cuddle up to me. I've often fantasized about being with two men—what girl hasn't? But I never imagined it would ever be possible. I'd always thought it would be disappointing or weird, but this was way better than anything I've ever imagined.

I guess that's what happens when you're in love with both of the men you've just fucked.

"So where does this leave us?" I ask.

"Beats me." Archer shrugs. "You're still married, so until we get you out of that relationship, all we can do is snatch some time together whenever the opportunity arises."

"Is that why you agreed to come with me and Romy?"

"Yes," Archer confesses. "I must admit, I've never really thought about being in a threesome with another man, but I'm never going to turn down the chance to see you naked. I focused on you and making you happy, and I enjoyed myself in the meantime. I'm never going to regret making you happy."

"So things aren't going to be weird between us all?"

"Not at my end," Archer says.

"I'm cool," says Romy. "It's like Archer said. It's all about making you happy."

"I suppose we ought to get back to the party before anyone notices I'm gone," I sigh. "The downsides of being the host."

"Can I suggest a shower before we go back?" Archer says. "You walk into the hall looking like that and *everyone* will know what you've been doing. My shower's big enough for the three of us."

We all exchange glances and grin.

"Yeah. A shower sounds like just what I need right now." I say what we are all thinking.

Chapter Fifty-Eight

$\mathcal{T}$he party is still in full swing as we pull up outside my
house.

"I don't think we needed to worry about anyone missing us,"
says Romy as we head back into the house.

He spoke too soon.

"Where did you guys go?" Lucas comes out to meet us as we
head towards the dance hall.

"Oh, it was getting a bit too stuffy, so I wanted some fresh
air," I lie. "Romy offered to take me for a buzz on his bike and
Archer said he fancied a break as well, so the three of us went
for a ride together. After my victory earlier today, I felt like a
break from riding."

"Speaking of your victory," says Lucas, seemingly buying my
story, "well played, guys. I should have known you'd pull something like that. I was planning on doing a sudden move, but I
saw Ivy coming up behind me, so if I'd pulled out in front of
her, it would have taken both of us out of the race. As it is, an
Archaic victory is still an Archaic victory, no matter which one
of us won. Well done, wife."

He puts a subtle emphasis on the word wife as he puts his

arm around my neck and kisses the top of my head, letting the others know who really owns me. I could laugh at his naivety. If only he knew what we'd been doing not so long ago, he wouldn't be anywhere near so smug.

"Anyway, I came to find you because I thought we should break open the champagne and formally toast your win, Ivy," Lucas says. "I would have done it earlier, but I had to deal with some business."

"Oh yes," I say lightly. "I saw you talking to Isabella earlier. Anything wrong?"

"No, no. Everything's fine." I've spent enough time with Lucas to know when he's lying and something is definitely up.

"Are you sure? Is everything okay with my father?"

"It's fine, although he's going to be staying away for a little longer than planned," Lucas tells me. "Something's come up that needs his personal attention, so he's going to be staying in Italy for a few more days to sort it out. Nothing you need to worry about though."

"Well, I am just the wife," I beam brightly, doing my best *Stepford Wife* impression.

"Glad you're finally accepting that," says Lucas, ignoring my sarcasm. "Now come and have some champagne with me."

He moves to take my hand, but Archer steps forward. "Actually, Lucas, do you mind if I have a very quick word with Ivy? I'll send her after you in a minute or two. Promise."

"Haven't you just been out on a ride together?" say Lucas grumpily. "Couldn't you have talked then?"

"Come off it, Lucas," says Archer. "You know it's impossible to have a conversation when you're speeding down the road. I guarantee it won't take long."

"Fine," Lucas huffs. "Ivy, I'll be in the main hall waiting for you. Make sure you don't take long--everyone will want to congratulate you."

He storms off to the hall, leaving me with Archer and Romy.

"What is it?" I ask. "Didn't you get enough of me earlier?"

"I'll never have enough of you," Archer confides. "But that's not what this is about. Have you had a chance to check out your father's schedule yet?"

"Are you kidding?" I say. "I haven't been able to get anywhere near his study. Whenever I've tried, Isabella pops up or Lucas suddenly decides we need to be spending quality time together. It's like they know what we're planning and they're deliberately trying to stop us."

"How could they know?" Archer asks.

"I have no idea," I reply. "I haven't talked about it with anyone. So unless one of you has said something, which I doubt, or I've been talking in my sleep, which I'm pretty certain I don't do, it's just the typical Archaic paranoia coming into play and they don't like me roaming round the house myself. My father's always kept me on a tight lead when I've been home, so it's no surprise that Lucas is continuing with that tradition while he's away. For all that he's been really nice to me, I wouldn't be surprised if he was still working with my father on some nefarious scheme."

"Okay," says Archer. "Let's assume you're not going to get any time to yourself any time soon. I'm going to try and break into Solomon's office."

"Don't." I shake my head. "It's too dangerous."

"I used to work for your father, remember?" Archer assures. "The guards know me, so I can sweet talk my way round them if they see me. And I know a lot of the security codes your father uses for his safes. Of course, he may well have changed them, but he's arrogant enough to think no one would get that close to him, so if we're lucky, everything will have stayed the same. I might be able to find something which will help us with our plans."

I hesitate for a moment, unsure whether I'm comfortable with Archer putting himself in danger like this. "Okay," I say finally. "I can't hang around here any longer. Lucas is expecting me. Do what you need. Just stay safe, okay?"

"Always."

I kiss the top of my fingers and waved goodbye as he turns and heads off in the direction of my father's study.

"What say you and I go get some champagne?" Romy says, offering me his arm. We walk into the dance hall together, to be greeted by a thunderous cheer.

"Ivy! Ivy! Ivy!"

Lucas walks over and wraps his arm around my waist. The whole touch is seriously uncomfortable for me.

"Congratulations, Ivy," he says, side-eying Romy, who simply smiles. "I'm so proud of you. You brought the title home for House Archaic."

"Time for your victory lap!" Romy suddenly bent down and picked me up. Lucas comes and stands by his side and I find myself perched on top of their shoulders as they parade me round the hall. Everywhere I looked there are happy faces, people cheering me on, glad that I'd taken the title away from the boys.

For the first time since my father kidnapped me, I feel like maybe, just maybe, I do belong here.

At last, Lucas and Romy set me down, and Lucas is the one who holds me close. Appearances are all that matter, and it is important Lucas and I maintain a united front. A win for one of us is a win for all of House Archaic.

"Mind if I interrupt?"

Lucas and I break apart as Ally taps me on the shoulder. I turn to face her and she hands me a glass of champagne.

"Can we talk?" she asks. "In private?"

"Sure." I follow her outside, away from the hustle and bustle of the party. From experience, it is going to go on until the wee hours of the morning, but I am not sure I am going to be able to last much longer. It has been such an eventful night and all I really want to do is curl up in bed with one of my boys. Instead, it seems like there is even more politicking to get through.

"Look, I know we got off on the wrong foot when we first met," Ally begins.

"You can say that again," I say coldly. "I don't like bullies."

"Yeah. You made that clear." Ally rubs her cheek, remembering the hard slaps I'd treated her to when I stopped her taunting Milly. "Although if you'd grown up here, you'd understand that's just how we do things."

"Maybe it's time you tried another way," I tell her. "Now if all you wanted to do is walk down memory lane together, I think I'd rather do that with someone who wasn't so much of a bitch."

I move to go back inside, but Ally grabs my arm.

"Ivy, wait. This isn't how I meant for this to go. We really need to talk."

I inhale deeply. "So talk and get it over with."

"You have no idea how much it meant to me, to Taylor, to all us girls to see you cross the finish line first," Ally says. "That's the first time a woman's been allowed to compete in the Bomber Derby and to see you win was incredible. This town has been living in the Dark Ages for too long. Us girls get to ride behind the boys while they take all the glory. Our job is to look pretty for them while they have all the fun. And I say enough. It's time for the women to stand up for ourselves and take action. I think you're right. It *is* time to try another way. Taylor and I have been talking and we want to set up a girl's House group. My family's affiliated with House Archaic, which is why I was Head Girl before you, but Taylor's connected to House Dauphin. If we could get Milly involved and maybe Nicola Navarre, we could create our own team. With you leading us, people would listen and we could make some real change in King Town. What do you think? Are you in?"

I look at her, considering what she just said. I like the sound of it, but this is Ally we are talking about here. How can I trust her?

"I'll talk to Milly about it and get back to you," I finally say.

Chapter Fifty-Nine

$\mathcal{T}$he day after the Bomber Derby I wake up late with a thumping headache. People kept refilling my champagne each time I emptied the glass. The cost of all the champagne I'd drunk would probably have been enough to keep Trudy in groceries for a month.

I get out of bed and stumble over to the bathroom. Looking at myself in the mirror, I look like death warmed up. I desperately need a shower.

Standing under the jet of hot water, I feel human again. I remember what Ally had said last night about a girl House group. Now that I've had a chance to sleep on it, it isn't such a bad idea. Not only had she bullied Milly for years, she'd been dating Declan before he broke up with her to be with me. How could I trust anything she says?

Shutting off the water, I decide I need to go over to see Milly. She's known Ally a lot longer than I have. She'll know whether this is a good idea or another twisted scheme.

I walk out of the bathroom and almost run into Lucas.

"It lives!" he jokes.

I roll my eyes and shake my head. "Not now, Lucas. I'm not in the mood."

"I didn't think you would be after the amount of champagne you were downing last night. That's why I've made you a full English breakfast, bacon, fried bread, bacon, beans, bacon, eggs, and did I mention bacon?"

"*You* made it?"

"Well, I got the cook to make it, but it was all my idea and the bacon is particularly crispy, just the way you like it. Come on. Baaaaa-cooooon!"

He finally coaxes a laugh out of me. "Fine. I don't really feel like eating right now, but since you've made the cooks go to so much trouble, I'll give it a go. I'll meet you in the dining room in five, okay?"

"See you there."

Lucas leaves to go downstairs, giving me some privacy to get dressed. I pull on a pair of frayed grey jeans and a T shirt with a picture of a grumpy hedgehog on it with the tagline *I'm sorry I'm late. I didn't want to come.* It pretty much sums up my feelings at the moment. I'd much rather be having coffee at Milly's than having to make small talk with Lucas, but I was taught never to waste food, so I was going to have to eat something.

Isabella sits with Lucas in the dining room, the two of them deep in conversation. When they see me walk in they immediately stop talking about whatever is so important.

"Have some food before it gets cold, Ivy," Lucas invites, pulling out the chair next to him.

I take the seat he offers, looking out at the spread laid out on the table in front of us. There's enough food to feed an army. I am going to have to disappoint my foster mother. No way am I going to be able to eat all this, not with how delicate I am feeling.

I pour myself a cup of coffee, thick and black. Just what I need. I close my eyes, inhaling the aroma. The caffeinated smell immediately perks me up.

"Isabella was just telling me that someone tried to break into your father's study last night," Lucas says. "You wouldn't have any idea who that would be, would you?"

"Me?" I shake my head, years of lying to foster families giving me the ability to be convincing. "I was too busy partying to care what happened in that part of the house."

"Well, your father will be back later today," Isabella informs me. "So he'll be able to review the security footage in his office for himself. After what happened with your three friends, he increased the number of cameras about the place, so there are a few in his office even the guards don't know about. You can't trust anyone, not even highly paid guards."

"He's coming back today?" It takes all my willpower not to show how nervous I am at the thought of Archer being caught on camera. It is more important than ever I get over to see him and Milly today.

"Yes," Isabella says. "He's finished with his business in Italy and he says he's been missing you too much to want to stay away any longer."

"How sweet of him." I'm proud of being able to keep almost all the sarcasm out of my voice. "What was he doing there again?"

"That's highly confidential," Isabella deflects.

"You mean, you don't know either?" I am being facetious, but the way Isabella's cheeks coloured tells me I hit a nerve.

"I mean that if your father wants you to know why he was in Italy, he'll tell you himself," she snaps. "Lucas, he's asked that you meet him at the airport. He has a few things he wants to talk about with you."

"But not with me?"

"He only requested Lucas's presence," Isabella confirms.

"Wow. He really did miss me then," I say. "Fine. I'll go and see Milly then."

"That sounds like a good idea," Lucas says, not reacting to my irritation. "But at least have some bacon first. You can't subsist on coffee."

I can. But I help myself to a few rashers of bacon, some mushrooms, and a generous dollop of scrambled eggs. Taking a bite of the bacon, I close my eyes and moan. It really is that good.

"I told you the bacon was amazing," Lucas grins. "It's the only cure for a hangover."

He's right. After a few mouthfuls of bacon, I'm feeling better. I even help myself to a bit more, loving the salty crispiness of it.

"Right. I'm heading over to Milly's," I say after I clear my plate. "I'm taking my bike and I'll be back later today, so don't worry about lunch for me."

"Are you sure? I can get cook to make you some bacon sandwiches?" Lucas offers.

"Much as the bacon is awesome, I've had enough for now," I tell him. "I'll see you later."

I push my chair back and get up to leave. As the dining room doors close behind me, I could have sworn I heard them mention Archer's name. The thought of what my father might do if he finds out that Archer tried to break into his study makes my blood run cold.

I want to go see Milly to discuss Ally's proposal, but now I have to get there to warn Archer he might be in danger.

□□

I pound on Archer's door, desperate to speak to him. It seems like forever before he answers it. He's clearly just woken up. He is wearing nothing but his pyjama bottoms, showing off his toned abs, but I can't appreciate how sexy he looks when my father is going to be home any minute and will see Archer on camera going through his things.

"Ivy! This is a rather pleasant surprise." He leans against the doorframe, looking me up and down in a way that makes it hard for me to focus on why I am there.

"You won't think that when you hear what I've got to say." I push past him and into his lounge. I'm too nervous to sit, so I pace up and down.

"Calm down, Ivy. Whatever it is, you're freaking me out."

Archer comes and stands in front of me, putting his hands on my shoulders to stop me moving.

"You *should* be freaked out," I say. "My father's coming home today and he's got new hidden cameras in his study. Isabella asked me if I knew who tried to break into his study last night, so whatever you did, you weren't careful enough. As soon as Dad gets home, he's going to see what you did and then all hell will break loose."

"No, it won't." Archer smiles.

"Of course it will." I can't believe Archer isn't worried. "Don't you get it, Archer? We're busted. They know you broke into his study. They're just stringing things out to see if I'll crack."

"They don't know anything," Archer tells me. "Maybe they suspect something, but that's as far as it goes."

"How do you know?"

"Because I didn't try to break into your father's study," he explains. "I couldn't get anywhere near it. There were too many guards, so I pretended I just wanted to say hi and let them know no hard feelings. They were just doing their job when they held me, Romy, and Declan. The thing your father doesn't realise is that money isn't enough when it comes to buying people's loyalty. I've seen first-hand how he treats his staff. He makes it easy for me to get them to talk to me. I didn't get to find out details of your father's schedule, but I did find out a few interesting things, which includes the fact that he's selling his plane."

"*Selling* it?" I frown. "But that makes no sense. He loves that plane. He always boasts about how important he is to have his own private plane and how it's kitted out to his precise specifications. He's not going to fly to Italy with a commercial airline."

"Yeah, well, whatever's going on, it's pretty clear we're going to have to change our plans," Archer says. "We can't bomb his plane if there's no plane to bomb."

"So we're back to square one." I sigh.

"Maybe," Archer says. "Now that I've reconnected with some of the guards, I might be able to persuade one of them to turn against your father. They're not happy with the way he's been treating them recently. I don't think it would take much to get one of them to give us some information we could use. It's not a complete loss."

"But how did Isabella and Lucas know you tried to break into my father's study?"

"They were just fishing." Archer shrugs. "It's the kind of thing people do at parties. We all try and see if we can look around each other's houses. It's an unspoken rule--any chance to gain an advantage over your rival *must* be taken. It's a matter of honour. So, they made an educated guess to see what your reaction would be. Did you tell them anything?"

"Of course not!" I can't believe Archer would even consider that. "I figured it was easier to pretend I didn't know anything than try and make up some story I'd forget later. I've gotten away with a *lot* of things over my years in foster care. I know how to cover my tracks--and cover for my friends. I didn't tell them anything."

"Good." Archer nods. "So it looks like we're in the clear. Now that that's settled, fancy a coffee? Or something else?"

He looks me meaningfully in the eyes and I catch my breath. Even though it has only been a few hours since I'd slept with him and Romy, I can't get enough of him. Of any of my boys.

He cups my cheek in his hand, tenderly stroking it with his thumb. "How about that coffee then?"

"Are you kidding me? Kiss me, Archer."

He doesn't need telling twice. He leans forward, his lips meeting mine. I close my eyes, my knees weak as I sink into his kiss. We fit together so perfectly, our bodies made for each other.

Archer rains kisses all over my face, on my nose, my cheeks, my lips, delicate little butterflies that drive me wild as he makes his way down to my neck. He nibbles and licks, an erotic mix of titillation and tickling that makes my whole body tense with anticipation.

"Archer…" I groan, as Archer reaches down to pull my T-shirt over my head. I'm glad I hadn't bothered with a bra this morning.

"It says you didn't want to come," he says, tossing it to one side. "Are you sure about that?"

"What do you think?" I sigh as Archer runs his hands over my breasts, squeezing my nipples to make them erect.

We tumble down onto the couch together, literally falling into each other's arms. I love the feel of his bare chest against me, our hands exploring each other, our legs intertwined. I can feel the bulge of Archer's erection against my thigh, promising delights yet to come.

I fumble at the zipper of my jeans and Archer helps me pull them off. Whipping off his PJ bottoms, we are naked in record time, desperate to be together.

I lay back on the couch, legs wide. His mouth meets mine and his hand is between my legs, the movement of his tongue mirroring the movement of his fingers as he plays with my clit. I am soaking wet, ready to take his cock inside me, but he's so skilled at touching me. I want this to go on forever.

My nails dig into his skin as I feel my body edging closer and closer to orgasm. I cry out as he finally tips me over the edge, but he isn't done. My body is still trembling with the force of my orgasm as he slams into me, his cock easily sliding in.

The soft cushions of the couch cradle me as he nuzzles my neck, his hips grinding against mine. I feel so safe, so loved in his arms. If I could stay in this moment, enjoying him possessing me for the rest of my life, I'd die a happy woman. Archer knows exactly how to please a woman and he's proven his devotion to me time and again with the way he makes me feel.

His movements slow and he kisses me on the lips. "Do you want to try something else?" he asks.

I nod, too lost in pleasure to speak.

Archer pulls himself off me and helps me up. He sits on the

couch and turns me so that my back is to him. He grips my hips and guides me back down onto his cock so I am sitting on him, facing away. Then, instead of thrusting into me, he moves my hips so that I'm grinding against him. He's balls deep in me, stretching me further than I ever thought possible. His balls rub against my clit, echoing the way he made me come with his fingers.

I grip his thighs with my hands, my nails scratching him hard enough to draw blood, but Archer doesn't care. He is so focused on keeping this going for as long as possible, wanting to make me come a second time.

And it isn't long before he achieves his goal.

The feel of my breasts bouncing with every movement, the knowledge I am completely in control, the sensation of his balls massaging against me all combine to push me over the edge. I cry out in pleasure as Archer finally allows himself to thrust up into me, a few strokes is all it takes to join me in the ultimate erotic experience.

Our movements slow, and I look over my shoulder at Archer, still panting. "That was just what I needed," I tell him.

"You and me both." He grins, running a finger down my spine. My body is so sensitive, it makes me shudder. "So, do you want that coffee now?"

"Sure. Do you mind if I quickly use your shower while you make it?"

"You know where it is."

I smile as I clean myself, thinking about the last time I'd been in this shower. Archer and Romy had made sure I was *thoroughly* cleaned. I've never had a threesome before and maybe never would again, but that's a memory I'll always treasure. It was probably thanks to the champagne that the three of us had wound up in bed together. There's no way the guys would have done that if they were completely sober.

Only we'd all come on bikes. They weren't that drunk...

I wonder whether Declan would ever be interested in doing something like that. It never ceases to amaze me how different men were in bed. Declan is the least confident of my lovers, but he has nothing to worry about. There is nothing wrong with his technique and he cares so much about making me happy, I am always guaranteed a good time with him. Imagine Declan joining in with Archer and Romy…

Enough, Ivy! I shake my head, trying not to be so greedy. I know the time is fast approaching when I'll have to choose one of the guys over the other. I can't continue to juggle them like this. Once I manage to get my marriage annulled, I'll have to pick one, and the thought breaks my heart, but it's the fair thing to do.

I am just going to have to make the most of the three of them while I still can.

I return downstairs, towel drying my hair. Archer is sitting at the dining table, two steaming mugs of coffee in front of him as well as a plate filled with pastries.

"Help yourself," he says as I sit down next to him. "Unless you fancy going downstairs to watch a movie? I've got a preview copy of the latest Liam Hemsworth film. It's an action adventure where he's having to race round the world solving a puzzle to save the life of his girlfriend."

"Sounds awesome, but I need to see Milly," I tell him. "I'd love to hang out with you, but Ally came to me with an interesting proposal last night and I want to discuss it with Mills."

"Oh, yeah?" Archer raises an eyebrow. "Sounds intriguing."

"Yeah, well, it's Ally, so I don't know if I can trust her, but I figured I could run it past Milly and see what she thinks. I mean, she's had to deal with Ally for years. If anyone knows whether it's worth making a deal with her or not, it'll be Mills."

"After the way Ally's treated Milly, I think I can predict what the answer will be," Archer says.

"Me too," I agree, "but I still want to talk about it with her. Besides, I told Lucas I was coming here to see her, so I should at least say hi before I head home to deal with my father. I don't know what time he's due back, so I probably shouldn't stay out too long. You know what he's like if I'm not there to jump the second he clicks his fingers."

Archer nods sympathetically.

The coffee is just what I need, the jolt of caffeine chasing away the final remnants of my hangover. Sitting there at the table with Archer is a reminder of what life might have been like if I hadn't been forced into marrying Lucas. He tries hard to make things nice, and he is considerate, but we simply don't have the connection I have with the boys. I can never fully relax around him because I can't quite trust him. Not the way I trust Archer with my life.

"Thanks for that." I lean over and kiss him. He tastes of coffee and the promise of sex. "Mmm, you are *way* too tempting, Archer Knight. You make me want to get naked all over again."

"I'm not stopping you," he points out.

"No," I sigh. "Much as I'd love to, I've got to see Milly and get home. If I walk in stinking of you I think my father will go nuts. As it is, since they suspect you are the one that's been snooping around, I'm going to have to tread carefully to make sure they think they have nothing to worry about. If they think I was with you instead of your sister, my father will probably call in the interrogators. He's made it very clear that just because I'm his daughter doesn't mean I can expect any special treatment."

"That's Solomon for you." Archer walks me to his door. "If he crosses the line, call me. I don't care where you are. I'll burn down the house to get to you if I have to."

"Thanks, Archer. I appreciate it." We kiss one last time and I get on my bike to travel the short distance to Milly's house.

Chapter Sixty

"*Eeeeeeee!*" Milly squeals and throws her arms around me when she sees me standing on her doorstep. "What are you doing here?"

"I need to talk to you. Something interesting happened."

"Sounds serious," Milly says. "Anything I need to worry about?"

"I don't *think* so," I reply. "But that's why I wanted to talk to you. I figure you'd know better than I would what's really going on."

"You better come in then."

I follow Milly into her quirkily decorated lounge. "Coffee?" she offers.

"No, thanks. I've just had some at Archer's."

"Oh, you went to see my brother before you came to see me?" She fixes me with a glare.

"I'm sorry, Mills."

"It's okay." She laughs. "I'm just kidding. If I were you, I'd take any opportunity to visit my boyfriend too."

"Archer's not my-" I break off. Who am I kidding? "Okay, but maybe he's not my boyfriend, so much as my lover, what with my being married. But I didn't come here to talk about my stupidly complicated love life."

"Oh yes. What's this interesting thing that's happened?"

"Ally came to me last night and suggested we come together to make a girls' House group."

"I see." Milly's face falls. "Well, I suppose you and Ally will make a powerful team."

"No, you don't understand. When she said we, she was talking about her, Taylor, Nicola maybe, me… and you."

"Me? Ally wants to be in an alliance with me?"

"Yeah. She says that the time has come to change how things are done in King Town and I agree with her. This place is archaic--and I should know. It's time the women stepped into their power. If we come together, we can stop the men running the show by themselves. We can compete in the Bomber Derby. I think anyone should be able to compete, regardless of gender or status. We can stop all the stupid secret squirrel stuff every-one's got going on and bring the Houses together. We can put an end to the mind games my dad's a master of, and get people to talk. I mean, can you imagine that? People actually communi-cating with each other?"

"That's pretty out there," Milly agrees.

"But it means working with Ally and Taylor, and I know they've made your life hell for years," I remind her. "I'm not going to do it without you, but I'm not going to force you to do anything you don't want to. If you think Ally and Taylor are up to something and this is just another scheme to get at us, then I'll tell Ally no, and that'll be the end of it."

"I think we should do it." Milly's reply surprises me.

"Really? Are you sure?"

"Very," Milly says.

"You're a better person than I am," I admit. "I don't think I could ever forgive Ally for treating me the way she treated you."

"It's not about forgiveness," Milly tells me. "It's about what we can achieve together. Ally doesn't have your status, but she *does* know how to play the social game of King Town better than anyone I know. It's why she made Head Girl. Pilkington knew that she was the best person to look after House Archaic's interests and she'd made sure that the Archaics were top of the House table because she's so ruthless."

"But aren't you worried she'll turn that ruthlessness on us?"

"It's always a possibility," Milly says. "But I don't think that's what's going on here. Ever since you came to King Town, you've changed things. I don't think you realise how much influence you have on the people around you. I'm not surprised you've got my brother tailing after you like a little puppy dog. I've never seen him like this with anyone. And it's not just him. Romy has suddenly stopped playing the field. He won't even look at another woman. Declan is clearly head over heels in love with you. Anyone with any sense would want to be on your team, and Ally's not stupid."

"But I stole Declan from her," I point out.

"No, you didn't." Milly shakes her head. "Ally's been cheating on him their entire relationship. It was only a matter of time before he found out and left her. I don't even think she really liked him. She was only with him because he was an heir and it helped boost her social standing. Everyone can see that Declan's head over heels in love with you. You're a much better match for him." Milly looks me straight in the eye. "If she's proposed a truce, she means it. And she's right. Us girls could start a revolution, make things better for everyone. It's not just the women who'll benefit from a more equal community. Don't you think the boys are just as tired of all the petty little games? I say we give her a chance. If she turns out to be playing us, we'll find a way to get back at her, but I don't think she is. Your victory last night did a lot to shake things up. Anyone with any sense would be on your side."

"All right." I never thought I'd say these words, but that was how weird my life is. "I guess we're going to work with Ally and Taylor. It's about time people saw what girl power can do."

"And you know what the first rule I want to introduce will be?" Milly asks.

"What?"

"No cheating or stealing boyfriends from each other. Not that I'm likely to have a boyfriend any time soon. The one guy I like is already taken. But if we're going to support each other, we have to *really* support each other. That means if a boy comes on to us and we know he's got a girlfriend we immediately tell her. Let's flush out the rats in this place. It would do a lot to stop all the bitchiness and bickering."

"I didn't know you liked someone."

Milly blushes. "It's just a dumb crush."

"Don't be silly, Mills. If you like someone, you like someone. There's nothing dumb about it. Who's the lucky guy?"

"Sorry, Ivy, but I can't say." She looks away. "Like I said, he's already in a relationship, so it's pointless talking about it. I'm never going to be the other woman, not for anyone."

"Good for you, Milly." I smile and nudge her with my elbow. "That's the kind of self-respect I'm talking about. If we work together with the other girls instead of against each other all the time, there's no limit to what we can achieve."

Chapter Sixty-One

$\mathcal{A}$s I walk through the door at home, Isabella comes out to meet me.

"You took your time, Ivy." She frowns disapprovingly.

"As I told Lucas, I went to see my best friend," I say. "I'm sorry that we lost track between girly giggles and gossip."

"Solomon's home," Isabella says. "And he's waiting for you. I suggest you go straight to his study and don't keep him waiting any longer."

"Yes, sir." I salute sarcastically and head in to see my father.

I knock on the door and wait for the command to enter. Nothing. I knock again. Still no reply. I knock one last time and am about to give up and go to my suite when the door suddenly swings open, the guard on the other side finally letting me in.

"Why so impatient, Ivy?" My father glares at me. "You know full well that I don't take kindly to people attempting to beat down my door. Knock *once* and wait for me to be ready to see you."

"I'm sorry, Dad. I just missed you so much, I couldn't wait to see you again."

I know I'm lying. He knows I was lying. But the appearance

of loyalty seems to mollify him a little, and he motions to me to take a seat at his desk opposite him.

"How was your trip?" I ask.

"It could have been better," my father replies, "but I got the business done I went out to do, which is all that matters."

"I guess you'll miss having all those trips to Italy," I say. "I've heard it's a beautiful country."

"It is," my father agrees. "And no doubt one day your husband will take you to see it. But why do you say I'll miss my trips to Italy?"

My heart sinks as I realise I'd put my foot in it. "Oh, just that if you're selling the plane, it's going to be difficult for you to keep going out there. Unless you're selling it to get an upgrade? It can't be that your business is in trouble. I know how good you are at what you do."

I am babbling, trying to cover my nerves, but it is no use. My father can see straight through me.

"Selling my plane? Interesting. How did you find out about that?"

"I can't quite remember. You must have told me," I say. "Either that or I overheard you and Isabella talking about it. I definitely got it from you."

"Is that right?" My father arches an eyebrow, motioning to the guard standing by the door. "Gary, go fetch Dave for me."

"Yes, sir." Gary nods curtly, turns and leaves the room.

"What's happening? Did I do something wrong?"

"No, no, Ivy." My father smiles, making a calm down gesture at me. "You haven't done anything wrong. In fact, you've behaved exactly as I'd hoped you would. I owe you a debt of gratitude."

This doesn't sound good.

A couple of minutes later Gary comes back in accompanied by Dave, one of my favourite guards. Whereas most of the guards would barely even look at me, Dave was always happy to say hello and tell me stories about his wife and two little girls.

"You wanted to see me, sir?"

469

"Yes, Dave. We have something important to discuss."

"Do you need me to do something for you?"

"Not anymore. You've already done it."

I frown and Dave looks a little worried as my father stands up and slowly walks round his desk to lean against it, facing Dave.

"You see, I have long suspected that I have a leak in my security," my father says. "But that can't be possible, can it? After all, my guards are all loyal to me. None of you would betray me, would you?"

"No, sir."

"So then why would you tell my enemies information I gave you in confidence?"

Without warning, my father lunges forward and grabs a fistful of Dave's hair. Pulling on it hard, he forces Dave down to his knees.

"Urgh!" Dave grunts. "I don't know what you're talking about, I swear! I haven't told anyone anything."

"Oh, Dave, Dave, Dave." My father tuts. "It's pointless trying to maintain this façade. I have irrefutable proof that you are the mole. The only thing I want to know is why? Why turn your back on me when I've treated you like one of my own, cared for you and your family? You'd have wanted for nothing if you only stayed loyal."

"But I have!" There are tears in Dave's eyes from the pain of my father twisting his hair.

"I suppose I'll have to spell it out." My father sighs dramatically. "I knew that someone was passing on my secrets, but I didn't know who, so I gave out a number of false stories to different people. Depending on which story made it out to the rumour mill, I'd know who couldn't keep their mouth shut." He casually slaps Dave across the face. "And it turns out that the lucky winner is you. You are the only person who thought I was going to sell my plane." He looks up at me with a smile on his face that says, *isn't that ridiculous?* "Like I would ever be without my plane when I've got so many more trips to Italy planned. I knew my darling daughter was still talking to my enemies, so I relied on her to let me know which story had made it back to them. The second she told me, I knew it was you. And I have to say, Dave, I'm disappointed. Of all my guards, you were the last I thought would betray."

"But I didn't, I promise." Dave is begging, and it breaks my heart to see him so pitiful. "All I did was have a chat with Archer Knight during the party. I didn't tell him anything he didn't seem to already know."

"And yet no one else thought I was selling my plane." My father shrugs. "But thank you for your honesty. I suspected Archer was still managing to weasel information out of my daughter and it doesn't surprise me he was able to play you like that, although I had hoped you had sense enough to resist."

He let go of Dave's hair and helps him up, kissing him on both cheeks.

"So I'm forgiven?" Hope shone in Dave's eyes.

"Of course." My father pulls out a gun from his shoulder holster and shoots Dave square in the forehead. "*Not.*"

I scream as Dave collapses to the floor.

"Let that be a lesson to you, Ivy." My father calmly returns to his chair as if nothing happened. "Be careful who you trust. Not everyone is who they appear to be. And now that you have a husband, I have a second heir, so be careful who you choose to associate with in the future. It would be better for you if you became pregnant sooner rather than later to guarantee the continuation of my line. Take that as a simple piece of fatherly advice. You may leave."

He waves me away, and I am glad for the opportunity to escape. I edge round Dave's body, trying not to get any blood on my shoes as I practically run to the door and up to my suite.

"Is everything okay, Ivy?" Lucas is already in our rooms and he immediately comes over to hug me when he sees my face.

"No, everything's *not* okay." I am shaking uncontrollably. "My father just shot Dave."

"Dave? Security guard Dave?"

"Yes, Dave. Dave with the two kids who was one of the few people in this prison who treated me like a half decent human being. *That* Dave." I am practically screaming hysterically. I know my father is a monster, but this is something else.

"Calm down, Ivy." Lucas holds me by the shoulders, looking me straight in the eye. "Breathe with me. Come on. In... and out... In... and out..."

I hate having to rely on Lucas, but without him there to bring me back down, I probably would have done something really stupid. As it was, although I am still traumatised by what I'd witnessed, I'm not as lost.

"Feeling better?"

I nod, still feeling shaky as Lucas guides me over to the couch.

"I'll get you a brandy." Lucas walks over to the fully stocked drinks cabinet we had in our room and pours me a generous dose of alcohol. He presses it into my hands, keeping hold of me, guiding it up to my mouth so I can take a large sip. "Now, tell me what happened."

"As soon as I came home, I went to see him," I say. "I made a stupid comment about him selling his plane and he called Dave in. Apparently, it was a story he'd made up to find out who he can trust, and because Dave told Archer about it, my father shot him right in front of me."

"Wow. That's rough. But Dave brought it on himself."

"Are you kidding?" I jerk away from Lucas. "He talked to someone he knew really well, someone who worked for my father for a while, and he deserved to be *shot?*"

"Solomon told me he was worried that someone was leaking his secrets, so he was going to set them up. This was going to happen sooner or later." Lucas shrugs. "With Dave out of the picture, your father has sent a very powerful message to the rest of his team. No one's going to be talking to anyone outside of the household now. I wonder what he would have done if you'd say anything."

"Me? My father was testing me?"

"Solomon was testing *everyone*," Lucas confides. "You, Isabella... me. I don't know what the tests were for us, but I knew we were being tested. Your father's paranoid and with good reason. You've got to understand what it's like for him, Ivy. He's under incredible pressure. He's had to cope with a number of assassination attempts over the years and he's trying to build a legacy which will last forever. Ivy, your father is going to eliminate all the other Houses and when he's achieved that, you and I will be the most powerful couple in the world. There's going to be a few bumps along the road, but we're all headed along a path to glory."

"You're crazy." I stand up and back away from him. "You're all crazy. Who cares if my father sells his plane or not? It's not important. A man lost his *life*. He has a wife, children. They're going to miss him for the rest of their lives. His daughters are only four and two, for Christ's sake. And you're defending my *father?*"

"Wake up, Ivy." Lucas stands up, raising his voice. "We aren't like normal people. We've got to think about the House. That's a *massive* responsibility and one you clearly aren't ready for. If you were, maybe we wouldn't be married. If you would face up to your legacy, your father wouldn't have had to get me involved to keep you on the straight and narrow. What happened to Dave is a tragedy, but if he'd kept his mouth shut, he'd still be with us. But now everyone else knows what will happen if they betray your father. Dave might have lost his life, but he's potentially saved many more. Try stepping back and seeing the big picture instead of thinking about yourself all the time. You're so selfish, Ivy."

"Selfish?" I've had enough. "You really are delusional. I'm outta here."

"Ivy..." Lucas reaches out to grab me, but I shake him off. I can't bear to be in the same room as him.

"Let me go, Lucas, or I swear I will not be responsible for what I do."

Lucas has enough sense to let me leave, and I practically run out to the garage and get on my bike. One of the advantages of being married is that I'm not kept locked in my room all the time, and I am glad for that freedom. If I have to be in that house a moment longer, I don't know what I'd do, but it wouldn't be pretty.

Chapter Sixty-Two

"I've called Declan and Romy. They'll be here in a minute."

Archer hands me another glass of brandy as I sit on his couch, shaking with rage and stress.

"I just can't believe he did that, Archer. How could he? He murdered a good man, a really sweet man, right in front of me just because he had a conversation with you."

I burst into tears, and Archer pulls me into his arms. He takes the brandy from me and places it on the coffee table so I can lean into him more.

"I'm sorry, Ivy," he says. "It's my fault. I shouldn't have tried to get information about your father from the guards."

"No, you absolutely *should*," I tell him. "We have to find a way to stop him before anyone else gets hurt. After what I saw today, it's clear my father will do anything to further his ambitions. The sooner we deal with him, the better. And I want Lucas gone as well. He thought that what my father did to Dave was justified."

"I can see where he's coming from." Archer's words stun me, and I look at him in disgust.

"Not you, too."

"No, no. I don't mean it like that," he says. "There were other ways of dealing with Dave that didn't involve shooting him in the head right in front of you. But for a new kid on the block like Lucas, someone who's still trying to establish himself in this town? It makes sense for him to align himself with Solomon. It's not like the House heirs are interested in dealing with him, not when he's taken you away from us."

He reaches out to pulls me into his arms. I resist a little at first, still feeling wary, but my attraction to Archer wins out and I let him hold me.

We sit in silence, waiting for the other two to arrive. I am grateful Archer isn't forcing me to talk. My mind is running at a million miles a minute. I am never going to forget what I've seen. I'm not sure what is more frightening. Seeing a man die, or the cold, dispassionate look on my father's face when he pulled the trigger.

There is no way I am going to get pregnant by Lucas, not now, not ever. Not only had I no interest in sleeping with him, the second that baby was born, I'd be expendable and I am not sure I can trust Lucas to keep me alive. His loyalties lay with my father, not his wife.

There's a knock at the door. As Archer goes to answer it, I pick up my brandy and take a sip. It feel like there isn't enough alcohol in the world to numb my feelings, but it takes the edge off a little.

"Ivy! Are you okay?"

Declan comes rushing over to my side, Archer sits back where he was while Romy perches on the edge of the coffee table sitting immediately in front of me.

"Not really." I take another large swig of brandy. "Although I shouldn't be all that surprised that my father's a murdering scumbag. The story about him selling the plane was a ruse put out there to flush out the mole my father thought he had in his security. The stupid thing is, I don't think Dave *was* a mole. I don't think there is a leak in security. My father's just stupidly paranoid. Dave wasn't feeding us information. He was simply making conversation with Archer. And what does it even matter if my father *was* selling his plane? That's not something you kill a man over. It's just too messed up to even think about it."

I finish the last of my brandy, grateful for its warmth, and flop back into the cushions.

"So, what are we going to do now?" I ask. "Maybe some of my father's paranoia is rubbing off on me, but I have a funny feeling he's aware of our plot to assassinate him."

"There's no way he could be," Declan says. "We're the only ones who've talked about it and none of us would have told Solomon. So, unless he's managed to bug us…"

We all look at each other, eyes wide. Of course! It made perfect sense. That's why my father knew so much about my life. He'd bugged me.

"That's impossible," Romy says, gesturing to the rest of us to pretend we agreed with him. "Solomon isn't intelligent enough to think of something like that."

I have to stifle a laugh at that. If my father was listening to us, he'd hate hearing Romy say that.

Archer gets up and leaves the room. He comes back with a pen and paper. He scribbles a note and holds it up.

Ivy—give me your phone. I'll get one of our security experts to check it over right now. And it's probably best if you strip off so we can check your clothes for bugs. Meantime, change the subject. Talk about school.

Take my clothes off? I grab the pen from Archer and scribble underneath his note.

Any excuse to get me naked…

Archer shrugs unapologetically. His suggestion *does* make sense. If my father is bugging us, we need to know now before we say anything else we don't want him to hear.

I immediately hand Archer my phone, but I decide to have a little fun with getting him my clothes. I gesture to Romy to get off the coffee table as I stand up. He takes my place on the couch as I climb onto the table to give the boys a show.

"So, have you finished the music homework, Declan?" I ask, gesturing to them to keep the conversation going.

"Almost," he replies, as I pull my T-shirt out of my jeans and play around with the hem pretending to lift it up, but then dropping it down before I expose my breasts.

I turn round, slowly lifting up my shirt to pull it over my head as the boys make small talk about an economics assignment. I look over my shoulder, covering my breasts with one arm as I spin my T-shirt over my head, dramatically throwing it off to one side before turning around.

Wearing nothing but jeans, I turn back to face the boys. Still covering my breasts, I slowly sink down to my knees, finally moving my arm so they can see everything. Leaning forward, I panther-crawl across the table, going over to Declan. I put my hands on his thighs to balance myself as I slowly kiss him.

The fake conversation falters as I move over to Romy and kiss him before finally kissing Archer. Faced with me half naked and kissing them hard, it is impossible for any of us to pretend we are just talking about school and I don't care. If my father hears me making love to my three men, I don't care.

I spin round on my butt, putting one foot on Romy's lap and the other on Declan. I wiggle my feet, making it clear I want them to undo my laces and pull off my boots. They're happy to oblige, as Archer sits forward and massages my thighs.

I feel incredibly brazen sitting there with my legs wide open in front of three men, even though I still have my jeans on. After the threesome, I never thought I'd be in a situation like this again, let alone with Declan here as well, but I am going to make the most of it. I am Ivy Archaic, and I *deserve* this.

Romy and Declan get my shoes and socks off pretty quickly, so I pull myself back to standing on the table again. Slowly, slowly, I unsnap my jeans button and then tug down the zipper, taking my time. The three boys each have clear bulges in their trousers. I carefully peel my jeans off, dropping them in Archer's lap.

I turn round and tuck my fingers in the elastic of my thong. I look over my shoulder.

"Ready?"

"Oh yeah!"

I lean forward as I pull my thong down, giving them a good view of my backside as I step out of my underwear. Then I slowly walk away from them, stepping off the other side of the table before coming round, giving them all a good view of me as I head towards Archer to give him my thong.

"Are you guys going to be all right here on your own?" Archer asks. "I've just remembered I need to go and see my dad about something. I won't be long."

Romy, Declan, and I exchange a glance. "I think we'll be okay," I say, as Archer gathers up all my clothes. We all know he isn't going to see his dad, but if anyone is listening, it is as good a cover as any.

"I'll be back soon," he says, heading outside, leaving me completely naked with Romy and Declan.

"I must admit, this wasn't what I was expecting when I came over today," I say, gesturing to my body.

"Same here, but I'm not complaining." Romy grins.

"Yeah, any day I get to see Ivy naked is always a good day," Declan says. "But I'm worried about you getting cold sitting there like that. Why don't you come over here so we can keep you warm?"

I don't need to be asked twice. I sit between Declan and Romy, putting my arms around them as the two men cozied up to me. It seems like the most natural thing in the world for them to start playing with my body, fondling my breasts and thighs.

"We have to do this," Declan says solemnly. "This is how we make sure you don't get too cold."

"Is that right?" I smile knowingly. "In that case, you'd better keep doing what you're doing."

I turn my head to kiss Declan, as Romy lowers himself to take one of my nipples in his mouth. I feel his tongue dancing around it as Declan's tongue explores my mouth, and I wriggle about, knowing I need to feel them both inside me in the not too distant future.

My eyes close, I am completely lost in the moment when I hear someone say, "Is this a private party or can anyone join in?"

I open my eyes to see Archer standing in front of us, an appreciative look on his face.

"Well, not just *anyone*," I purr, opening my legs to create space for him.

Archer takes the hint and pushes the coffee table back so he can kneel in front of me. I feel his hot breath against my pussy and I moan in anticipation. I'm done for, utterly helpless as three men kiss and lick me all over. I have no idea who is doing what to me and I don't care. My body dissolves into bliss. An orgasm would almost be a disappointment in comparison to how incredible I was feeling. I want this to go on forever, my body worshipped by adoring admirers.

"I love you all," I murmur, as someone puts their fingers inside me. The combination of being finger fucked and licked is too exquisite and I come almost immediately, crying out in pleasure.

"Have you had enough?"

I open my eyes to see Romy grinning at me as he brushes hair out of my face.

"Never." I shake my head. "But I think you all need to get naked. It's a little unfair I don't get to see you all, don't you think?"

The three men look at each other and shrug, quickly getting out of their clothes. It's practically a race to see who can get naked first, and I love it.

Three men stand before me, their cocks all standing proud. They are all such beautiful, stunning Greek gods, and they were all mine. I have no idea who I am going to fuck first, but I know I am going to have all of them inside me.

Archer is in the middle, so it makes the most sense to suck him off first. I sit up and take him in my mouth, reaching out to grab Declan and Romy's cocks with my hands so I can play with them. I've never felt so fulfilled as Archer gently holds onto the back of my head to keep his balance while Declan and Romy come in closer to make it easier for me.

I love the taste of Archer in my mouth. I could sit here for ages, but I am conscious that the other two also deserve attention, so I make sure to take it in turns with each of them in my mouth, every blowjob making them even harder than they were before. I hadn't thought it would be possible, but they seem to get bigger every time they were in my mouth.

I'm in for a treat.

Not able to wait any longer, I get up on all fours on the couch, close enough to the arm that someone can stand in front of me and be within easy reach.

I look at them, wiggling my backside. "Take it in turns, boys. Just as long as one of you is in my pussy and one is in my mouth, I'll be happy."

I don't see who enters me first. This is going to be one long marathon of fucking.

Romy comes round the side of the couch, lightly playing with himself. "Are you sure you're ready for this?"

"Oh, yeah." I can barely speak because whoever is fucking me certainly knows what he is doing, but I want the ultimate pleasure, and after the other day I knew just how much I enjoy being spit roasted.

I've been with each of them often enough to know the signs of when they are about to come, so every single time the guy in my mouth seems like he is too close to the edge, I make them all switch positions, wanting, no, *needing* them to go on for as long as possible.

I lose count of how many times I come before I finally let the boys have release. Declan is fucking me, Archer is in my mouth, and I am playing with Romy when I decide the time has come to let them have their own orgasms.

I adjust the angle of my butt, pushing against Declan in a way that I know is guaranteed to push him over the edge, as I suck hard on Archer, running my tongue over the head of his cock. Seeing the two of them on the verge is enough to take Romy with them. The guys all cry out, and knowing they are coming is enough to send me over the edge.

We collapse in a heap of bodies, all of us utterly spent.

"Wow," I say when I am finally able to speak again. "That was *intense.*"

"You can say that again," Romy agrees.

"It's pretty clear we need to talk, though," Declan says, bringing the mood right down.

"Trust you to spoil the moment," Romy sighs.

"Let's get cleaned up first, then we can talk," Archer suggests. "Ivy, you can borrow a dressing gown otherwise I can see us getting all... distracted again."

By unspoken agreement, I have the shower to myself while the boys give themselves a quick wash at the sink. Archer lends me a dressing gown to protect my modesty, not that there is an awful lot left to protect, and soon we were sitting back downstairs, waiting for someone to break the ice.

"The thing is, Ivy, the three of us kind of already talked about something like this happening." Romy says. "I mean, I don't know if you noticed, but we're all madly in love with you."

"And I love you all, too." It is the first time we say it openly, and it feels good to admit it. I've dreaded having to choose between them all because I feel so strongly about each of them. I have a completely different relationship with each of them and they all complete me in ways I can't put into words.

"So, we agreed that we were going to wait for you to make the choice," Declan tells me. "And until you do, we are all free to be with you in our own way. But it's become obvious we could never make you choose between us. It might be messed up and it might be complicated, but what we've all got together *works.*"

"We don't care what other people think," Archer says. "The only thing that matters is that you're happy. So if you want to, we're willing to make a go of *this.*" He moves his hand in a circle, a gesture indicating the four of us together.

"Are you serious?" I can't believe my luck.

"Never been more serious."

Archer kisses me as Declan and Romy both squeeze my thighs, sealing the deal.

Who knows what would have happened next if there hadn't been a knock at the door?

Archer goes to answer it. Whoever it is, Archer spent a few moments talking to them before closing the door behind him and coming back to join us.

"Do you want the good news or the bad news?" he asks.

"Hit me with the bad news," I say.

"Your phone is definitely bugged and my guys found another one tucked inside the heel of your shoe."

"Great." I slump back. It isn't that I am particularly surprised, but it is still disappointing to discover that my father is as much of an arsehole as I suspected.

"At the moment, my guys have your things in a sealed box so no signal can get out," Archer tells me. "It's up to you what you want to do next. We can disable the bugs if you want your privacy back."

"Let's do that," I say, without even thinking about it.

"Wait a moment before you make the decision," Archer says. "Otherwise, you'll miss out on the good news."

"Which is?"

"Right now, your father won't suspect anything," Archer tells me. "It's pretty standard practise for the Houses to have equipment which can cancel out bugs, so the fact that the signal will have died won't raise any alarms. If your father doesn't know we've found the bugs, we can use that against him. We can feed him false information."

"We can lure him somewhere to assassinate him." I nod slowly. "You're right. That *is* good news."

"Exactly," Romy says. "Now we don't have to worry about tiptoeing around trying to figure out his schedule. We're in charge now and we get to decide what happens and when."

"Just as long as I get to be the one to deliver the killing

blow," I say. "There's no way I can let him get away with murdering Dave. I want him to look me in the eye and know that I'm the reason he's dead. This will be my revenge for all the people he's hurt over the years-–including my mother."

"So, all we need to do is come up with a plausible story to get Solomon right where we want him," Declan says. "And I think I have the perfect cover."

Chapter Sixty-Three

*K*nowing that I was bugged changed everything. I can't ever relax, knowing that my father is listening to every aspect of my life. I have to watch every word I say, take care not to slip up and reveal anything about Declan's plan. It is harder than you'd think and I hate my father for forcing me to tread on eggshells all the time.

It makes me sick to think that my father might have heard me making love. What kind of creep did that to his daughter?

It makes it even harder for me to get involved in the girls' alliance because I have to be careful about what I say, but I can't tell my new best friends what's going on. I don't trust them enough yet. I'm still not sure about Ally's motives and she hasn't exactly proven herself to be a decent person. Until I have a chance to assess where she is coming from, she is on my *handle with caution* list.

I meet with Ally, Taylor, Milly, and Nicola during lunch break at school. Milly is practically dancing in her seat with excitement. Ever since I told her about Ally's idea, she hasn't been able to stop talking about how cool it is that we are going to be in a girl gang together. Poor kid. She's spent so much of her life being an outsider, this is the happiest moment of her life. I wish I had her enthusiasm about this project. I am still bracing myself for being stabbed in the back.

"So, Ally," I begin. "This was all your idea. How did you see this going?"

"Well, first of all, I want to say thank you all for coming here. Between us, we're the most powerful women in the Academy and it's about time we used that power and stopped letting the boys railroad us."

"Girl power!" whoops Milly.

Nicola shoots her a dark look and Milly immediately cringes away.

"And that's exactly the kind of thing we need to stop," I snap. "You guys have been horrible to Milly for as long as you've all been at the Academy. She's not the enemy! The more we fight and bicker between ourselves, the easier it is for others to take advantage of us. That's what's been wrong with this town for so long. The Houses are all so caught up with dragging each other down, none of you can see that there's plenty of space for all of us. If one of us wins, we all win. So if Milly wants to be excited, let her be excited. Heck, get excited with her! Stop being such a stuck-up bitch and accept Milly for who she is. If you can't do that, you should just walk out right now."

For a moment, I think Nicola is going to storm out, but then she nods.

"You're right. And I'm sorry, Milly. We need to build each other up. I don't know why I've always been so horrible to you. I guess I got caught up in thinking that I had to put you down so I could get ahead. Ivy's right. We can all be successful together. In fact, we can be *more* successful together than on our own. We can share class notes, revise together, help each other to be the best we can be. If we can show that the Houses can work together instead of against each other, it'll help make this town a much nicer place for all of us."

"Agreed." Taylor nods, but I'm not that bothered about her opinion. I know full well that Taylor is just Ally's puppet. Whatever Ally wanted her to do, she'd do it without question. Wherever Ally went, Taylor followed.

"Okay, so a few ground rules to get started," I say. "First, and most importantly, we support each other unconditionally. This alliance crosses House divides, so if you see someone attacking one of us and they're in your House, it doesn't matter. We support each other, no matter what."

"Okay."

"Sounds good."

Everyone agrees except Nicola. I glare at her.

"Fine. I've got your back, even if it's against someone from my House."

"Look at it this way," I say. "If someone hurt Milly, even if it was Lucas, they'd have to answer to me because she's my best friend. Our friendship matters more to me than a family I happened to be born into. And if we start enforcing this alliance across House boundaries, we'll start building stronger ties between the Houses. Which means that when we leave the Academy and get more involved in our family's businesses, we'll be used to working together so we can make decisions which benefit all of us instead of being selfish. I've found that when people only think about themselves, they often miss out on amazing opportunities because no one wants to deal with them. We need to change that way of thinking. It's like being in a band. If I sing really loudly because I want to be heard, it ruins all the harmonies. If I match my volume to the other vocalists, we make magic together. That's what I want us to do. Make magic."

"And no stealing each other's boyfriends!" Ally puts in suddenly. She blushes as soon as she says it, the glance she gives me makes it clear what she is talking about. I am not going to rise to the bait though. If I want us to be able to work together, I have to lead by example and not point out that Declan had kissed me first, nor that I hadn't known that Ally was dating him at the time.

Even though I really, really want to.

"Exactly," I say. "We don't steal each other's boyfriends. If someone's dating, they're completely off limits. And if someone's boyfriend makes a pass at us, we have a duty to tell them straight away. What they choose to do with that information is up to them and if they decide to stay with their boyfriend, *no judgement*. The heart wants what the heart wants and we all know how hard it is to walk away from someone when you love them. Which is why we also need to be there to pick up the pieces for each other when need be."

"I like it," says Nicola. "But what happens if one of us breaks the girl code? There's got to be some kind of punishment, otherwise why would anyone bother?"

I look at her. "Wow. You really have had a messed-up childhood, haven't you?"

"I don't know what you mean." Nicola frowns. "What's my childhood got to do with anything?"

"Don't you ever do anything because it's the right thing to do? Do you have to have the threat of punishment to make you be a decent human being?"

Nicola opens her mouth to say something, but closes it without speaking.

Ally and Taylor nudge each other, stifling a giggle.

"We're trying to do something different," I explain. "I guess I didn't realise just how different the thought of cooperating was for you. We don't need to have a punishment because when you discover how good it feels to do the right thing, you'll want to keep doing it. When you know you've got friends you can count on to be there, no matter what, nothing can beat it. Wouldn't you rather know I was there for *you*, just you, instead of supporting you because I was afraid of what would happen if I didn't?"

"I guess." Nicola shrugs.

"And the problem with using punishment as an incentive is that you have to be caught first. So, if you're relying on the threat of reprisals to make sure we all support each other, it'll just encourage us to be sneaky. Before you know it, things will be even worse than they have been because none of us will be able to trust each other. We'll be fighting between ourselves because we'll want to get an attack in first before we get hurt. No, if we're serious about making this work, we live up to the code because it's the right thing to do, not because we're afraid of the consequences. If you don't think you can do that, we might as well walk away now and not bother."

"I'm in!" Taylor surprises me by speaking up. "I think everything you've said is so true. I know that some of the things I've done have been because I was afraid of getting hurt. I made a pass at someone's boyfriend because I thought she was spreading rumours about me. She wasn't, but I figured that she might do it one day, so I made sure I got to her first."

"You didn't tell me about that," Ally says. "Whose boyfriend was it?"

"I'd rather not say." Taylor looks down at her hands as she fiddles with the hem of her blazer. "It's not something I'm proud of and I'd rather leave it in the past. It wasn't anyone in this room, though, so you don't have to worry about that. But Ivy's right. I felt terrible afterwards. If I'd just gone and talked to her instead and told her how I felt, we might have become friends. Instead, she takes any opportunity she can get to have a go at me."

"You should try talking to her now," I say gently. "It's never too late. Explain to her about our new girls' alliance, maybe even invite her to join. We'll need more than the five of us if we're going to change the culture of this place. We might be leading the way, but we'll have to get the other girls to follow if this thing is really going to work."

"I don't know," Taylor says. "We've both said and done some horrible things to each other. I'm not sure we can ever come back from that."

"You should still try," I advise. "What's the worst that can happen? Things carry on the way they are now, which isn't the end of the world, but at least you've tried. I reckon you'll be pleasantly surprised, though. You could gain a new friend. But if you don't say anything, you *know* things are going to continue the way they have been and you're going to continue to be miserable. I know which one I'd prefer."

"Okay." Taylor nods. "I'll talk to her. You're right. Even if she doesn't want to listen, I'll know I've tried."

"We all have to lead by example," I say. "Nicola, you're head of House Navarre. I'm head of House Archaic. Everything we do represents our House. We need to start showing people that we live honourably and we work together, not against each other. It might take a little time for people to realise we really do mean what we say, but if we back up our words with deeds, we'll get there in the end."

"Sounds like a plan." Ally beams and we all smile and nod.

I put my hand out into the middle of our group. "Come on, everyone. Girl power on three."

The others all put their hands on top of mine.

"One… two… three… *Girl power!*"

We all throw our arms up and yell at the top of our lungs.

I hope my father is listening. He'd be livid to hear that I have no intention of following in his footsteps.

The Houses are going to work together on an even footing. I am not going to let him wipe out the other Houses, because I'd figured out that's what all these trips to Italy were about. He was clearly building up connections with other Houses out there so they could help him grow his empire. Well, no more. Not if me and my girls have anything to say about it.

Chapter Sixty-Four

The boys and I all gather in Archer's place so we could plan what to do about my father. We regularly keep notepads with us so we can carry out conversations without my father being able to hear us. There is a definite skill to being able to say something verbally while writing something completely different, but we've had a bit of practise and it works for us.

Declan and Romy talk about a movie they'd recently seen, so if my father did listen in, there'd be nothing interesting for him to hear. It killed me not to be able to kiss any of them, but the thought of him or any of his guards hearing us creeps me out.

So, are you still okay about going forward with this? Archer writes. *I'll understand if you want to back out. We'll all respect your choice.*

Are you kidding? I reply. *I want that man gone. He and Lucas have been having a lot of meetings recently and Lucas won't tell me what they're about. I'm really worried about what they're planning together. The sooner we deal with my dad, the better.*

Good, Archer says. *Now the first thing we need to do is figure out how we can get him on his own. If we can just get him away from his guards, it'll be easy to take him out. Do you have any ideas about that?*

I thought about asking him to come out to dinner with me, I say. *He's so arrogant, he'd genuinely believe I want to spend time with him. But he'd insist on bringing his guards with him, and I can't think of a good reason why he should leave them behind. If I say I wanted some time alone with him, he'd just order them to the other side of the room. And then we've got the problem of being in a public place. I don't want any of you to get in trouble with the police.*

Don't worry about that, Archer says. *All our families have close connections with the police, and they'd be more than happy to see Solomon gone. I think you'll find that any evidence connected to his death will mysteriously go missing.*

Okay, I say. *So, we have the start of a plan. I don't really know the best places to eat in this town. Where would you recommend as the best place to stage an assassination?*

Declan motions for me to pass him the pen and paper. Archer takes over talking to Romy, the discussion turning to the best Netflix shows to binge watch.

My father owns a restaurant which would be perfect, Declan writes. *I can get him to seat you in a booth out of sight of the other diners. We can poison one of his dishes and bam, job done!*

No. I shake my head. *I want to kill him myself. Do you think you can get a gun to me?*

A gun? Are you sure? You're not exactly the best shot.

I blush at the memory of shooting Declan's father. *That's exactly why I want to shoot him. It's the perfect revenge. And there's no way I can miss from that distance.*

Archer glances over at what we've written and motions for the paper.

I'm not sure that's such a good idea, he says. *It's much harder than you'd think to shoot someone. If you can't pull the trigger, it'll spoil everything. Solomon will know you plotted against him. If he doesn't kill you, he'll lock you up for the rest of your life—and I don't even want to think about what he'll do to make sure he has another blood heir. It's not worth the risk.*

I shake my head violently. I want to be the one to kill my father. It is my birth right!

Romy takes the paper from Archer.

Listen to him, Ivy, he says. *More than anyone, Archer would know how hard it is to shoot someone at point blank range.*

How would he know?

I look at Archer, but he shakes his head. He isn't going to tell me that story right now, and maybe not ever.

Poison is a better option, Archer assures me.

But what if they get the plates mixed up? I ask. *How would you feel if I was the one who ended up poisoned? I don't feel safe doing that.*

Just don't order the same thing as Solomon. It'll be obvious.

What if he gets suspicious and makes me try his food? I shake my head. *No. This isn't a good plan. My father's way too sneaky for that to work. If it was easy to poison him in a restaurant, he'd have died years ago. You have to let me shoot him.*

No.

I sigh and slump back in my seat, arms folded. This is a debate that could go on for hours, both of us as stubborn as each other.

Romy picks up the paper. *I have another idea. If Ivy can get her dad to agree to go out to dinner with her, we'll know where he is, right?*

We all nod.

So we can arrange for an ambush on his way home, Romy says. *He'll be all relaxed after eating good food so he won't be expecting anything. My family's men will deal with his guards and if you want to be the one to take out your father, Ivy, we can make it happen. If it turns out you can't pull the trigger when the moment comes, that's okay. There'll be plenty of other people there who are willing to do it for you.*

I won't chicken out, I promise. *But that does sound like a great plan. Now all that remains is for me to ask my dad out to dinner.*

What about Lucas? Romy asks. *Do you want us to deal with him at the same time?*

I shake my head. *Just because I don't want to be married to him doesn't mean I want him dead. With my dad out of the picture, it'll be easy to convince him to agree to an annulment. I'll tell him to stay home that night because I want it to be a daddy/daughter dinner. He won't mind. For all his faults, Lucas is pretty laid back. I'd rather he wasn't there to see my father killed.*

"Thanks for the recommendation," Archer says, carrying on with the fake conversation he'd been having with Declan. "I'll check it out. Now I've got a massive essay to write which is due on Monday, so if you guys don't mind, I'm going to have to be rude and say goodbye."

"No problem."

He gets up and goes across the room, as the rest of us start to say goodbye to each other. He opens the front door, saying, "Hey, Ivy. Can I have a minute?" before he shuts it again, putting his finger to his lips to warn us to be quiet as he walks over to a switch on the wall. Flicking it, he grins at us.

"You can speak freely. I've switched on the anti-bug blocker."

"Anti-bug *what?*" I run over to swat him. "You mean all this time we've been writing down our conversation and we could have just been talking normally?"

"We could have," Archer says, "but this way it's less suspicious. As long as we don't take too long, your father will think you're on your way home and we've got a few moments to say a proper goodbye. I thought you might prefer it if Solomon didn't hear us kissing…"

"You read my mind." I smile as Archer pulls me into his arms for a long, deep kiss. I moan with disappointment when we break apart, but I can't be upset for long because Romy steps up to take his place. I have to fight the urge to pull his clothes off, but Archer is right. We shouldn't take too long while the bugs are offline, otherwise my father will realise we were conspiring against him.

Declan comes up behind me, sandwiching me between him and Romy. I love the feel of a man's body pressed against me from both sides. It won't be long before we can do this as often as we like without having to think about my father, and I can't wait.

494

I turn to kiss Declan. Romy plays with my breasts as my tongue plunges deep into Declan's mouth. I moan again, this time with excitement.

"Can't we fool around a little while longer?" I beg, as Declan breaks away.

"We all want to," Archer says, "but it's not worth the risk. Get that dinner booked this week and we'll be able to do this whenever we want. It'll be sex for breakfast, sex for lunch, and sex for dinner with as many of us as you like."

"I'll hold you to that," I say, grabbing one last quick kiss with each of them before heading outside to my bike.

For the first time in a long time, I feel hope. Our plan is solid and soon I will be free from my father once and for all.

Chapter Sixty-Five

*a*s soon as I get home, I head straight to my father's study. I figure there's no time like the present to get things moving. But before I can get there, Isabella intercepts me.

"A word, Ivy?"

The way she says it makes it clear that it is a command, not a question, so I follow her away from my father's room and into the little office set aside for her to use.

"Your father has been thinking," she begins.

Uh-oh. This could be dangerous.

"He feels bad that your wedding wasn't the grand affair it should have been," she tells me. "House Archaic weddings should be huge celebrations, a sign to everyone that we're flourishing, not the quiet ceremony you had. People will think we're ashamed of you being married to Lucas, which couldn't be further from the truth."

Speak for yourself. I know better than to say the words out loud, but I am sure my expression speaks volumes.

"So, your father has decided to throw a reception party for you and Lucas," Isabella informs me. "These are the people he would like you to invite."

She hands me a piece of paper with a list of names: Romy, Archer, Declan, Milly, Ben and Kate Navarre, Gabriel and Rebecca Knight, and Claude and Marie Dauphin.

"Is that all?" I ask. "I thought you said weddings should be a huge celebration?"

"They should." Isabella nods. "But this isn't a wedding. It's a formal presentation of you as a couple to the other Houses, and as such, this is a more intimate occasion. Your father thinks the end of this week would be a good time."

"The end of this week?" My heart sinks. "But I was going to ask him to go to dinner with me this weekend. He won't want to do that if we're supposed to be having this little soiree."

"You can have dinner with your father any time you like," Isabella tells me. "Although I'm sure he'll be delighted to hear that you want to spend more time with him. One of his biggest regrets is that you don't understand him better. If you would only sit down and talk to him, you'd understand why he left you with your mother instead of rescuing you earlier."

Rescuing me from her? Boy, did he have his priorities confused.

Isabella continues, oblivious to my disgust. "I know he'd love to include you more in his plans. Perhaps after we've celebrated your marriage, you and Lucas can take him out somewhere together."

"But I wanted some alone time with him," I say. "I see enough of Lucas as it is. I'd much rather just go out with my father."

"Nevertheless, you are a married woman now," Isabella reminds me. "You need to include Lucas in any discussions with your father. I think you'll find your husband has a lot of very valuable insights to share. It's about time you treated him as the partner he truly is instead of a mere accessory. Your father isn't the only one who feels like you keep him at arm's length. Perhaps you might like to make a point at your reception of letting everyone know that Lucas is the only man for you. I appreciate that you've enjoyed playing the field, but the time has come to get serious about your future. Many arranged marriages develop into love matches and I'm sure if you just put in a little effort, you'd find that you and Lucas have a lot more in common than you realise. You really have the potential to be a good partnership."

"If you say so." I roll my eyes, bored of this particular game. "If we're done here, I'll go and text everyone to tell them about the party. This Saturday, right?"

"Saturday it is," Isabella says. "But you won't be texting. That simply won't do. I've had these invitations prepared for you." She picks up a sheaf of paper from her desk and hands them to me. "Fill them out in your best handwriting and I'll get one of your father's men to hand deliver them later."

"Seriously?" I huff, snatching the invites from her. "Fine. I'll get on it now."

"Fill them in neatly, remember?" Isabella reminds me. "Don't make me ask you to redo them."

"Yes, ma'am." I mock salute her and head up to my suite. Lucas is already up there.

"Hey, Ivy," he says. "What's with the face?"

"Is this stupid party your idea?" I ask, waving the invites at him.

"Party?" Lucas frowns. "You mean the wedding reception? It wasn't my idea, but I think it's a good one. Your father's right. We should have made a bigger deal out of our wedding. This will be the perfect opportunity for us to network with the other Houses."

"But I see Archer, Romy, Declan and Milly all the time at school," I point out. "There's no need to drag their parents over here as well."

"Yes, there is," Lucas says. "While it's great you have close ties with the other Houses…" I can't believe he can say that without a hint of irony. "…It's the parents who are the real powers right now, and will be for some time to come. It's important they view us as the power couple we truly are."

"But I had other plans for this weekend."

"What other plans? Ivy, I've been very tolerant of you

spending time with your exes, but that doesn't mean I'm happy with you being with them every spare moment. At some point, you're going to have to prioritise your marriage over your friendships. I can be patient about that, but eventually my patience is going to wear thin."

"Actually, I was going to ask my father to have dinner with me," I say frostily. "It's like you've said—the time has come for me to start putting House Archaic first. I wanted to work on our relationship."

"That's great news, Ivy." Lucas smiles. "I'm sure Solomon would love that. Look, why don't you have dinner with him on Friday? You can go over the final arrangements for the reception so that everything's perfect on Saturday. From what he's said to me, he bitterly regrets not having a closer relationship with you. I think if you ask him to go out, he'll jump at the opportunity."

I think about it. Although the boys and I have planned the assassination for Saturday, there shouldn't be any problem with moving it to Friday instead.

"Okay. I'll see if he wants to go out on Friday," I say. "But first, I better get on and fill these out. Isabella made it very clear that I had to write the names in my very best handwriting. Honestly, she was talking to me like I was five. When we're in charge, promise me the first thing we'll do is fire her."

"That can be arranged." Lucas laughs, as I sit down at my desk to fill out the invitations. It seems pointless doing them, since my father will be dead and I am not going to be celebrating my wedding. But, like always, appearances have to be maintained. I'll play his little game until the moment comes to reveal he is really playing mine.

Chapter Sixty-Six

$\mathcal{I}$ sit opposite my father in a booth at Declan's family's restaurant, watching with disgust as he breaks apart a lobster, eating it with his bare hands. I *really* hate the man, but I plaster a bright smile on my face and pretend to be enjoying myself as I pick at my spaghetti.

"I must say, the Dauphin family chef has outdone himself this time." My father slowly licks juice from his fingers. "This lobster is truly divine. I wonder if he'd be open to a change in position? I can do with a new chef. I'm becoming rather bored with our current cook's efforts."

"Can't you just get a new chef without stealing someone else's?" I suggest. "Do you really have to undermine the Dauphin restaurant because you fancy a change of menu?"

"But where would be the fun in that, Ivy?" My father smirks. "Food tastes much better when it comes at the expense of my enemies."

"But the Dauphins don't have to be your enemies," I point out. "You could work with them, not against them. Think about how successful your business would be if you did that."

My father bursts out into raucous laughter. "Oh, my dear

sweet girl. So wonderfully naïve. So foolishly stupid. I couldn't possibly work with the Dauphins. They are nowhere near my level. If you want your business to fail, collaborate with the Dauphins, my child."

I bristle at the way he patronises me. His arrogance is outstanding. Every word he utters makes it easier for me to imagine pulling the trigger and permanently wiping that smile off his face.

"Would sir like to see the dessert menu?"

The waiter comes over to take away our plates, giving me a break from having to listen to my father blather on.

"No need. I'll have the cheese plate with a coffee and my daughter will just have a coffee. She needs to watch her weight."

Jeez. The man doesn't know when to shut up.

"Very good." The waiter gives a little bow as he collects our plates and disappears off to the kitchen.

I glare at my father, who laughs.

"What's your problem? Just because you're a married woman doesn't mean you can let yourself go," he says. "Lucas deserves an attractive wife. It's important that you maintain appearances for his sake. He'll need a beautiful woman to support him when he's negotiating business deals."

That is it. I almost regret not agreeing to let the Dauphins poison my father. It is like he is deliberately trying to annoy me. I swear that as soon as we finish with my father, I am going to get the boys to take me to the ice cream parlour, and I am going to stuff my face with every single flavour. I'll be the one smiling then.

When the waiter brings over the cheese plate, my mouth starts to water. I struggled to eat my spaghetti because being around my father has a negative effect on my appetite, but I feel like grabbing a huge hunk of brie and stuffing it in my mouth, just to prove to him I can do whatever I wanted.

Instead, I pick up my coffee cup and make a big show of inhaling the aroma.

"Mmm. You're right, dad. I needed this." I take a sip and

have to admit that the coffee is amazing. Rich and creamy, it perks me right up. I can imagine getting Declan to make me coffee every morning in bed with whatever blend his restaurant uses.

I can't help the slow smile that spreads across my face at the thought, but, of course, my father picks up on it.

"What are you thinking about, Ivy?"

"Oh, just enjoying my coffee," I reply lightly.

"Are you sure that's all? Don't think I haven't noticed how distracted you've been over the past couple of weeks."

"I've had a lot on my mind," I tell him, being completely honest for once.

"If you weren't so easily distracted by all the other House heirs, you might be able to think more clearly," my father says. "I do wish you'd listen to me more. I know what it takes to run a House. I thought your time in foster care would toughen you up, but instead it seems to have made you weak. If I'd have known that would happen, I'd have taken you out long ago."

"So, why didn't you?" I ask. "All I've heard from you is complaints about how things would have been different if you'd been in my life sooner, but from where I'm sitting, I can't see any good reason for you abandoning me for so long."

"It's like I told you," my father says. "I live a dangerous life. I thought foster care was the safest place for you. I had faith that your Archaic nature would see you through. It would appear that I underestimated the impact your weak mother would have on you."

"My mother wasn't weak," I say through gritted teeth. "She got away from you, didn't she?"

"Only because I let her." My father shrugs nonchalantly. "Believe me, if I hadn't wanted her gone, she'd have spent the rest of her days with me. Nobody walks out on me without my permission."

Oh, dear father. If only you knew what I have planned for you. You wouldn't be anywhere near so cocky.

My father picks up a large chunk of cheese and takes a bite, closing his eyes to savour the taste. "Oh my, but that's good. Would you like to try some?" He holds it out to me, but when I hesitantly reach for it, he snatches it away. "Of course, you wouldn't. You're watching your figure, remember?"

"Yes, father."

After that, there is nothing left to say, so I sit there, watching my father take his time to enjoy every single bite of cheese. Part of me wishes he'd choke on it, but then that would take away the fun of shooting him.

"Right, my child. How much of a tip shall we leave?" asks my father, when he is all done and the waiter brings the bill.

"At least 20%," I reply. "We can afford it, after all, and the food was amazing."

"It was all right," my father says. "But the service was slow and not of the standard I would expect from a place like this. I think a couple of pounds is fair. It's more than they deserve really, but leaving nothing would suggest we'd forgotten. This way, they understand their worth and will do better next time."

"Two pounds?" I shake my head. "You can't do that. The bill's over a hundred pounds. That's like a slap in the face."

"Like I say. More than they deserve."

My father scribbles his signature on the credit card slip. I peer across the table and see that he really did only tip a couple of pounds, but when the waiter sees the amount, he is as professional as ever, merely thanking my father for his generosity.

"Thank you for a delightful evening," my father says as we walk out to his waiting car. "We must do it more often. I've thoroughly enjoyed myself."

"Me too," I lie as the driver opens the door for us to climb in. "Maybe we can make it a regular Friday night event?"

"If it means you start to become more of an Archaic, then I think it would be a very good idea," my father agrees. "Who knows? If I start seeing an improvement in your behaviour, I might even take you with me to Italy one day. There are some wonderful designer shops in Milan. If you maintain your slim figure, I'd be more than happy to let you loose with my credit card."

"Thanks, Dad."

When we are settled in our seats, the driver pulls away for the short journey home. My heart starts pounding. There are three possible routes he can take back, and one of my lovers is supervising each of them. We agreed on a suitable ambush site and whichever way we went, my father was going to find himself caught up in a roadblock. Once the car had stopped, guards from the other Houses were going to capture my father and hold him until the other two Houses had a chance to reach us. Then I was going to make my father pay for his countless crimes.

The moment of justice is almost here.

Chapter Sixty-Seven

"Wh at's wrong, my dear?" asks my father, as we pull up outside his mansion. "You seem a little agitated."

"N-no, I'm fine," I say.

What the hell happened? Why weren't we ambushed?

"That's funny, because I could have sworn you looked like you were expecting something to happen."

"I have no idea what you're talking about," I say. "I am just missing Lucas and want to get home to him. In fact, if you don't mind, I'm going to head straight up to our suite and show him how much I missed him."

"How sweet of you," my father says, "but you're going to have to put your plans on hold, just for a little while. I've got a surprise for you."

"A surprise? For me?" I don't like the sound of this.

"Oh yes. And I think you're going to love it."

Confused, I follow my father into the house and through to the dining room.

"Oh no!"

Tightly tied to the chairs are Romy, Declan, Archer, and Milly along with all their parents, gags around their mouths.

"I thought we would bring your wedding reception forward a day," my father explains. "You see, after I discovered word of a plot to assassinate me, I realised I needed to accelerate some of my plans. I'm afraid I can't have anyone getting in my way, not when I'm so close to achieving everything I've dreamed of. I'd been willing to overlook your little dalliances as long as you were discrete, Ivy. But when you actively conspire to kill me? I'm afraid lessons need to be learned."

"I don't understand. How did you find out? Nobody knew except us and none of us would have said a word. Archer? Romy? Declan?"

The three boys all violently shake their heads, desperately trying to speak through their gags to let me know they weren't the ones who betrayed us.

"Much as I'd love to let you think that one of your sweethearts had turned against you, unlike some, I cannot tell a lie."

"Oh, please." All pretence of caring about my father is gone now that our plan has been exposed. "Just tell us already."

"Very well. Since very few will be leaving this room alive, I see no harm in letting you know where you slipped up. Young Archer there did well in finding the bugs in your clothing, and you did a good job of trying to feed me falsehoods by writing down your conversations. However, what you didn't realise was that I'd planted another bug inside your pen, one which came with a camera as well as a microphone. I anticipated your attempts to circumvent my surveillance. I saw every single word you wrote. I knew you wouldn't be able to resist making a move against me. All Archaics rebel at around this stage in their life. I myself took over the House by killing my father with my own bare hands, although I had the guts to do it in his study without running to the other Houses for help. So, I forgive you, Ivy. You couldn't help yourself. But now the time has come to put aside childish things, and since I can't kill your lovers without incurring the wrath of their parents, now's the time to eliminate all the competition and take over the whole town once and for all. Michael--go and fetch Lucas. He needs to be here for this."

"Yes, sir." One of the guards nods and leaves the room.

"I'm so sorry," I whisper, tears running down my face. "This wasn't supposed to happen."

"Of course it was," my father says. "Why do you think Isabella had you handwrite all those invitation cards? After I had my men gather up all your friends, it was a simple matter to contact all their parents and inform them we'd made a mistake with the date, hoping they'd be able to come out this evening. Fortunately for everyone, they were available. I'd hate to have had to use brute force to get them here for this special occasion."

"No!" I gasp.

"Yes, Ivy. *This* is your wedding reception. All these people came here in good faith, expecting to celebrate your nuptials. And in a way, we still are. I'm doing this for you, Ivy, for our House. Their deaths are my wedding gift to you, that you and Lucas will be able to enjoy the fruits of my ambition."

"You're a monster!"

"You think that now, but in time you'll be able to see that what I've done was for the best."

I want to slap him, but I am distracted by Lucas coming in.

"So you've started the party without me?"

"You knew?" I may be reluctant to attack my father, but I have no such qualms when it comes to my so-called husband. I throw myself at him, wanting to scratch his eyes out.

Out of the corner of my eye, I see my father make a gesture to one of his guards, who steps forward and grabs my arms. He pulls them behind my back, restraining me tightly.

"Now, now, Ivy," my father says. "Don't blame poor Lucas here. He was only following orders. He knows what it takes to be a true Archaic."

"What's Milly doing here?" Lucas asks.

"I decided that eliminating your competition wasn't enough to send a strong signal to my darling daughter," my father explains. "Ivy needs to learn that the only true friends she has in this world are her family. So now all that remains is for Ivy to make her choice. Who dies first? Friend or lover?"

"I'm not going to choose." I shake my head, desperately struggling to break free but the guard is too strong. "If you force me to pick someone, then I pick me. Kill me, dammit!"

"Your time will come no doubt, daughter," my father says. "But you are far too useful to me alive right now, although believe me, I *will* make sure to punish you for your insolence. No, I will be shooting every single one of our guests, the children first so the parents can watch." He turns to face the watching parents. "I bet you wish you'd accepted my offer to buy your businesses now, huh?"

To give them credit, not a single one of them rises to his bait, staring impassively at him.

My father turns to one of his guards and nods. The guard takes a gun out of his holster and passes it to my father.

"So, who dies first?" He walks slowly along behind each of my lovers. "Romy? Archer? Declan?" Such pretty faces. It'll be a shame to spoil them with a bullet, but that's how it goes. No open casket funerals for any of you. But no. I think it should be ladies first."

He stops next to Milly and holds the gun to the back of her head. My best friend screams through her gag, her desperate cries muffled by the cloth. She shakes her head, tears streaming down her face.

"Any last words, Milly?" my father asks. "Oh wait. You can't speak. Never mind. From what I hear, you never had anything worth listening to anyway."

He cocks the gun.

"Nooo!" Lucas launches himself at my father, who is so surprised, he doesn't resist.

Seeing my opportunity, I stamp on the foot of the guy holding me. The heel of my boot digs deep into his foot and his grip on me loosens enough for me to be able to elbow him in the stomach. As he doubles over, I spin round and kick him hard in the balls. As he collapses to the floor, I pull his gun out of his holster.

"Don't move!" I warn, keeping the gun trained on him, as I hurry over to set free the captives. The table had been laid out for dinner, so I grab a knife and quickly saw through Archer's bonds. Lucas keeps his gun pointed at my father as Archer starts to work on the others, and soon everyone is free.

"So what do we do now?" I ask, looking to Archer, Romy, and Declan for guidance.

"You leave." It is Ben Navarre who answers me. "None of you need be involved in this. This is a job we should have done years ago when Solomon married your mother and didn't look after her."

I open my mouth to argue that I have earned the right to take care of my father, but Romy subtly shakes his head.

"Fine." I hand my gun to Ben, while Lucas gives his to Claude.

The boys, Lucas, Milly, and I all walk out, going out of the house and into the grounds. None of us say a word. There isn't anything *to* say.

A few minutes later, a gunshot breaks the silence.

Epilogue

THREE MONTHS LATER

A peculiar mix of emotions washes over me as I watch the bulldozers flattening the site where my father's house once stood. After everything that happened there, all the tears and blood that had been shed, I can't live there anymore, and I can't stand the idea of anyone else living there, either.

Besides, it isn't like I don't have more than enough money to build my dream home in its stead.

"Hey, Ivy. Ed's made the changes to the plans you requested. Want to take a look?"

I turn to see Declan walking towards me, a large blueprint in his hands. He kisses me lightly as he passes it to me, and I roll it out to check it.

The new Archaic mansion is laid out around a square garden which is in the centre of the building and is going to be planted up with thousands of sweet-smelling wildflowers to attract butterflies and bees. There are four wings, one for each of my boys so they can have their own space. They've each been allowed to consult with the architect to have it designed to their specifications. The remaining wing is set aside for me including a recording studio filled with state-of-the-art equipment so I can start recording my own material. Declan and I are planning on launching our own record label, and I needed the architect to make a few changes to our studio. It is the only room in my wing I really care about, and now it is larger with more space for us to work with other musicians.

"Happy?"

"Happy." I roll up the blueprint as Declan stands behind me, putting his arms around my waist to hold me as we watch the wrecking team do their job. I lean into him, loving how well we fit together. Declan is my safe place, the one who makes me feel that I could do anything, as long as we were together.

"Have your parents come round to the idea of you being an Archaic?" I ask.

"They're about as okay with it as Archer and Romy's parents are," Declan replies. "Which is to say, they're not really okay with it at all. But it's not like they have any choice in the matter. I want to be with you and the only way to make sure House politics don't interfere in our relationship anymore is for me to be an Archaic with you. They've finally accepted I'm not going to change my mind, so they've named Nicola as the new heir. I think they've made the right choice. She's always been ambitious and loyal to House Navarre. Even with your little girl gang, if she had to throw you under the bus for the sake of the House, she'd do it without even blinking. But you've been a good influence on her, Ivy. She's realised that we can achieve more when we work together, and I think she's going to take House Navarre to even greater heights."

"No regrets then?"

"Never." Declan squeezes me tightly. "I'd walk through fire for you. Walking away from my family is nothing in comparison. Anyway, I was always a musician at heart. I don't have the ruthless streak needed to be the head of House. I'm much better suited as the chief of a record label."

"I agree."

There is a loud bang as one of the main walls from my

father's house comes crashing down. I hear a few whoops and cheers as Romy joins me and Declan.

"Sorry I'm late to the party," Archer says. "My parents had to make a last-ditch attempt to persuade me to change my mind. When they heard we were all going to be living in a caravan in the Archaic grounds while the new house is being built, they were shocked. They begged me to change my mind, even offered to set me up with a supermodel, but I told them no supermodel was half as beautiful as my Ivy."

He kisses me deeply, and I love the feel of being sandwiched between him and Declan, all safe and warm.

When we break apart, the boys move so that they are standing on either side of me, their arms around my waist while I put my arms around them. I put my head on Romy's shoulder as another part of the mansion collapses into rubble.

"How are you feeling?" Romy asks. "It must be weird seeing your father's legacy destroyed."

"Not really." I shrug. "It's not like I grew up here, so I don't have any positive associations with the place. A fresh start is what we all need. We're going to create brand new memories here, build something new and beautiful. Besides, I always thought my father's taste was tacky. Our home is going to be amazing. I can't wait for them to dig out our pool in the basement. We're going to have so much fun there."

"Oh yes." Declan and Romy exchange a grin as we imagine going skinny dipping together like promised.

"Special delivery!"

Milly walks up to join us. "I bumped into the postman, so I said I'd bring your post to you. Save him the walk." Milly passes me a large envelope. I tear it open and smile when I see what's in it.

I turn the paper round so everyone can see. "My marriage to Lucas has been annulled," I announce. "As far as the law's concerned, we were never married in the first place."

"Oh yay!" Milly squeals and throws her arms around my

neck. We jump around together, hugging each other. "You're free! You can marry whoever you like!"

"Hmmm." We break apart and I look at my three lovers. "Something tells me I'm not going to be getting married any time soon, at least, not until the law changes and I can have more than one husband. There's no way I could choose one of my guys over the others." None of the men hide the look of relief that crosses their faces, but it is true. It would be impossible for me to pick one of them for the sake of having a ring on my finger. "Maybe we can do some kind of commitment ceremony for the four of us, combine it with everyone changing their name to Archaic."

"So you're really going ahead with it?" Milly asks Archer. "You won't be a Knight anymore?"

"House Archaic all the way," Archer replies. "Besides, you're a much better heir than I could ever be. You've got the heart and compassion needed to lead the Knights to success. I know you're going to be amazing."

"You really think so?" Milly asks. "I don't know. Everyone always told me I was stupid at school."

"Because they were jealous of you," I tell her. "You shouldn't pay any attention to them. Archer's right. You're the perfect person to take over House Knight one day, and between the two of us, we'll make sure our Houses form an unbeatable alliance that keeps the peace in this town. This is the dawn of a new era. Things are going to be very different from now on."

"And it's all thanks to you, Ivy," Romy says. "You're the one who made all this possible."

He hugs me, the other two men coming in close for a group hug. It is still taking us a while to figure out the practicalities of our relationship. At the moment, if one guy has a hug or a kiss, the others need the same, and I don't want anyone to feel left out. But I have a feeling over time, it will be okay for me to hold hands with just one of them, spend an evening with just one of them, and everyone will know that I still love and want all of them with all my heart.

"Have you heard from Lucas?" Milly asks.

"See?" I pull away from the guys. "This is why you're perfect to be the Knight heir. You care about everyone, including my not-husband. Most people wouldn't give him a second thought, but you can't help worrying about him."

"He's all on his own," Milly says. "He's got no family now. Who's going to take care of him?"

"He's got more than enough money to take care of himself," I remind her. "I wouldn't worry about him too much. Lucas will land on his feet. He's just that kind of person."

"Still, if you hear from him, will you tell him I'm thinking about him?" Milly asks.

"I don't think I will, but if he does get in touch, I'll make sure to let him know," I say.

There is another crash so loud it shakes the ground, making me jump.

"I think that was your father's study," says Declan, putting his arm around me to steady me. "I don't even want to think about how many nefarious schemes he came up with in that room."

"That's why I wanted to plant a garden over that bit of land," I tell him. "I want it to be a symbol of peace and new beginnings. There's going to be nothing but smiles and peace there from now on."

"I hear that."

Archer stands behind me, resting his hands on my waist, while Romy comes up on the other side, holding my hand so that I am surrounded by my lovers. Milly is right next to us as we watch the steady demolition of the old Archaic mansion.

Tears prick at the corners of my eyes as a wave of happiness washes over me. This is not the life I'd ever envisaged for myself, yet it couldn't be more perfect. I have three gorgeous guys who are head over heels in love with me, and I adore them all with every part of my being.

I remember the story my mother told me as a child. She predicted I'd love three men, but they would be nothing in comparison to my one true love. She was almost right. I did indeed love three men, but the one man I'd been married to was not the one for me. I hope he finds love for himself, but he will never have my heart.

Mum was right about one thing. A Queen doesn't need a king. I need my knight, my joker, and my prince. They are the ones who fulfil me, and the four of us will conquer worlds, but in the right way--with love and compassion.

This is the start of a new life for us, a new life for the whole town. The future is bright and we will enjoy it together in our new home, our new house and a better town.

THE END.

CARRY ON READING WITH MILLY AND LUCAS' STORY NEXT- FIND THE LINK HERE.

Description

**Five years ago he walked into my town and created chaos.
But I didn't know he would take my heart with him when he left.**

Lucas Donatello is back in King Town but he is in for a surprise. I'm not a pushover anymore, I'm an heir to the House of Knight, and I've had to learn to be tough to survive this little town.
In King Town, happily ever afters don't exist, and there is always a villain waiting in the darkness.

My name is Milly Knight and this is my story of the boy who stole my heart.

18+ Enemies to Lovers standalone romance based in the Boys of King Academy world.

Prologue

"*C*areful now. A pretty little thing like you might get lost in here."

A creep whispers in my ear as I dance to the thick, heavy beat of the club music. I spin around, glaring at the stranger, who smirks like he just said something charming.

"Fuck off," I suggest, nerves rising as his face fills with anger.

Before he can say another word, two of my bodyguards are at his side and dragging him off through the crowd. They'll take him someplace quiet where they can teach him a lesson in respect.

There are some perks to being the heir to the Knight house at least.

Pushing all thoughts of the jerk aside, I carry on dancing, losing myself in my favourite song until it ends. The next song isn't as great, so I make my way back to my table. Reserved for me, it's as empty as it was when I left it. I sit down alone, just the way I like it.

"Would you like a drink, madam?" The bartender standing on the other side of the VIP rope waves an alcopop at me.

"I'm twenty-one, not fifty, so less of the madam," I snap, rubbing the spot between my eyes. "And no thank you."

The bartender looks like he might pass out as he looks behind me. Whatever he sees, it freaks him out, making him stumble. He turns and rushes off into the crowd to escape, leaving me alone to deal with it. I turn around and find bright blue eyes in the darkness, a look that draws me in and begs me not to look away.

Lucas Donatello.

As he steps into the light, walking right up to me, I take in the small changes a few years have made. He was always sexy, with his built shoulders, small waist and a face that looks like it came down from Olympus. Those dimples, the ones I adored in high school where I last saw him, appear when he looks straight at me and smiles.

A god looking down at a mortal girl.

I never could figure out what Lucas was thinking and he's as inscrutable as ever as he takes the time to examine me from head to toe.

"Milly Knight. Long time, no see." His gravelly voice is one I couldn't ignore, even if I tried. It's haunted my dreams for years, taunting me with thoughts of what might have been if only things had been different. A *lot* of things.

The problem is, Lucas comes with a lot of bad memories. He was there when I was kidnapped and let it happen. He married my best friend, knowing full well she didn't want to marry him. He confided in me once that he'd hoped the marriage would work out once she'd had a chance to get to know him.

He chose Ivy Archaic, for what good it did him.

I wasn't stupid. He'd never have chosen me, even if Ivy wasn't on the scene. I'm a no one in our world, even though I'm an heir.

I say nothing as Lucas sits next to me, his thigh pressing into my bare one. The tight white dress I'm wearing does little to cover my response to him, my body betraying my feelings the way it always does when he's around.

Lucas lifts his hand to take a strand of my blonde hair.

"You dyed it," he comments as he turns it about in his hand, getting a good look.

"I wanted a change," I reply, wishing I'd said yes to that drink after all. "Do you like it?"

He drops my hair and meets my eyes once more. I swear the entire club disappears as he looks at me.

"Yes."

"Oh," I whisper. "I Have tattoos now too."

Oh god. Why did I blurt that out?

"So do I. We'd have to go somewhere private if you wanted to see them though." He raises an eyebrow, an invitation as he runs his fingers down my arm.

I should say no. I should run a million miles from Lucas. He only means trouble for me.

But I lean in and kiss him anyway, taking what should have always been mine.

Chapter Sixty-Eight

Five years later

The bell rang to announce the end of the lesson.

"Okay everyone." I raise my voice to be heard over the clatter of pupils shoving books into bags and scraping back chairs, desperate to escape. "Read the next chapter. Tomorrow I'm going to want to hear your thoughts on the dynamics between Kathy and Heathcliff. Think about their relationship – is it healthy? Is it love? Is it obsession? Be prepared for a challenging discussion."

I couldn't be sure how many of them actually heard me as they hurried out of the room, more interested in what was on their phones than in analysing *Wuthering Heights*.

I slumped down into my chair, sighing. The Bronte sisters were about as close as I got to romance these days and given what happened to Kathy and Heathcliff, that wasn't saying much. Ivy kept telling me I needed to get out more, start dating, but I was nowhere near ready for that.

I let out another heavy sigh as I picked up my bag, ready to leave. I'd find out tomorrow if anyone had bothered to do the reading.

"Hey, Milly. Have you heard the news?"

I looked up to see Nigel Burge standing in the doorway. He'd started teaching at King Academy around the same time I had and he'd asked me a few times to go out with him, but I'd always said no. Ivy had urged me to have a drink with him, just one drink, but I didn't want to give him any ideas. Besides, I could never date someone called Nigel. Shallow? Yes, but I didn't care. I had my standards and unless they were chiselled like a Greek god and went by the name Lucas, no one was going to measure up. I didn't care that Ivy thought I was wasting my life. It wasn't like I was going to date Lucas even if he showed up on my doorstep with a dozen red roses. I was firmly dedicated to my single life and happy to stay that way. Besides, I had my reasons for keeping men at arm's length.

"What's happened?"

"They've finally appointed the new head."

"About time." I went over to join Nigel. I looked over the room to check that I hadn't left anything behind before switching off the lights and closing the door behind me. "The parents weren't going to be happy keeping Jenny as interim head for much longer. She was running the Academy into the ground."

None of the staff had liked it when Jenny Nour was given the position of interim head, but she was the only staff member vaguely qualified to take over when Mr Pilkington died suddenly of a heart attack. Self-important and frosty, two teachers had already left because of the way she'd treated them. I'd been seriously considering following them, but my options were limited, since my standing as Knight heir meant I had to stay local to help with House business.

"So, do you know who our new head is?" I asked as we started to walk down the corridor.

"No idea." Nigel shook his head. "They say there's going to

be a meeting on Friday to give us all the details, so I suppose we'll have to wait until then."

"Whoever it is, they can't be any worse than Jenny."

"I guess not." Nigel laughed. "Hey – do you fancy going out for a drink to celebrate our freedom from her?"

"I'd love to, but I can't. I have to get home." It was only half a lie. I *did* have to get out of here, but even if I didn't, I wouldn't have wanted to go out with Nigel. Although I had to admit that I was impressed by his perseverance. If he kept this up, maybe I might say yes one day – in a few years' time.

"Some other time then."

"Sure."

Nigel turned to go in the direction of the staff room, while I went off to the building which housed the kindergarten children.

"Mummy!" My four-year-old daughter's eyes lit up when she saw me walk into the room to collect her. She squealed and ran over to throw herself into my arms.

"Hey, baby." I kissed the top of her head as she squeezed me tightly. "Have you been a good girl?"

"Amber's been a pleasure, as always." Liz, one of the kindergarten teachers, came over to see us. "Do you want to show Mummy your painting?"

"Oh, yes!" Amber raced off. A minute later she was back waving a piece of paper covered with brightly coloured splotches and stripes. "This is you and me going to the zoo."

"That's amazing!" I gasped. "I love the colours you chose. And is that a lion there?"

"Silly Mummy." Amber pouted reprovingly. "That's *you!*"

"Of course it is. I *am* silly!"

Amber slipped her hand into mind and waved goodbye to Becky. "Bye bye, Auntie Becky!" she yelled.

"Bye, Amber. See you tomorrow."

I waved at the teacher and led Amber out to the staff car park where my driver was waiting. I could have driven myself to school, but I loved sitting in the back with Amber, hearing about her day. That little girl was my whole world and I hated being away from her during the day, but I'd made a decision when she was about a year old that I wanted to go back to work. We had more than enough money for me to be a full-time mum, but it was important to me to set a good example to Amber. She needed to know that she could have a career of her own and I loved teaching, even if not everyone in my classes shared my enthusiasm for the classics.

Besides, Amber gave me a good excuse to say no to Nigel. After my own kidnapping, I was very cautious about who I left my daughter with and I didn't like to ask my parents to take care of her too often. Much as they were always delighted to see her, I was trying to teach Amber a different way of living and my parents were still very much immersed in House politics. Ivy's example had shown it was possible to throw caution to the wind and ignore tradition. While I didn't see myself ever finding myself one man to love me, let alone three, I was rebelling in my own quiet little way. I'd resisted telling anyone who Amber's father was, despite the pressure from my parents, and I'd ignored their not-so-subtle hints that they could arrange a suitable marriage for me to bring respectability back to the Knights. They kept telling me how hard it was to raise a child, which was why I finally caved and hired a part time nanny to help me out. With Claire's help, I was fine. *We* were fine. Amber didn't need anyone else in her life and most definitely not a man who was only going to let me down sooner or later.

Amber chattered away about all the things she'd done at kindergarten that day. I was only half-listening, as I wondered who the new head was going to be. I'd seen some of the candidates coming in for interview and they all seemed to be from out of town. It was no real surprise it had taken so long to find the right person. Anyone leading the Academy needed to have an in depth understanding of the way the Houses worked and how they influenced the town. House affiliations affected friendships between pupils, their behaviour, their academic performance.

Unless a Head understood all those nuances, they weren't going to last long.

The Board had approached me to take over before they gave the interim position to Jenny, but I turned them down flat, knowing full well they were only asking me because I was Knight heir. I didn't have the experience to run the school and besides, I didn't want to do more hours. Right now, my days mirrored Amber's and she could stay at the after-school club when needed for those all-important staff meetings. If I'd taken on the headteacher position, it would mean I'd be away from my daughter for longer and that wasn't going to happen.

Amber came first. Now and for always.

***

That Friday, I squeezed into the last remaining chair next to Nigel in the staff room, late for the meeting after needing to break up a disagreement between two girls from different Houses. Jenny was standing at the front of the room, droning on about how much she'd enjoyed being head and how it had opened new horizons for her.

"Have I missed anything important?" I leaned over and whispered to Nigel.

"Nah," he whispered back. "Just Jenny going on about how amazing she is and how great her career is going to be now that she's got head of King Academy on her CV. I think it's actually a case that the Board were so unimpressed by her performance they've told her to find another school and she's trying to put a positive spin on it."

"So no sign of the new head then?"

"Not yet. You'd think he was headlining Glastonbury the way they're keeping us waiting!"

I sat patiently, waiting for Jenny to introduce the new head, but she loved the sound of her own voice too much and it was a good ten minutes before she finally got round to what we were all waiting to hear.

"I asked him to wait in the kitchen so I could tell you how much you've all meant to me during my time leading the Academy," Jenny said. "I want you to know that your support and encouragement has meant the world to me and helped me realise that it really is my true calling to lead. But the time has come to introduce you to the man who will be taking over the helm."

She got up to open the door that led to the staff kitchen where we made our teas and coffees and microwaved our lunches.

"Talk about milking it," Nigel muttered to me out of the corner of his mouth. "I bet she goes home and cries into her vodka about not getting the head position permanently. I heard she interviewed but the Board weren't interested."

"Yeah." I nodded. "I reckon she made the new head hide in the kitchen so she could have our undivided attention for as long as possible. I feel sorry for whatever school she ends up with after this."

"What's taking her so long?" Nigel frowned and peered at the kitchen door. The rest of the staff were getting restless as we were *still* waiting to find out who the new head was.

"Maybe she had him tied up so he wouldn't interrupt her speech," I suggested. "And now she can't undo the knots."

Nigel spluttered, as he tried to hold back laughter. I laughed with him, but my smile fell away when Jenny walked back into the room, a big fake grin plastered across her face, as a familiar man followed her.

"Everyone, I'd like you to give a warm King Academy welcome to Lucas Donatello, our new headmaster."

Chapter Sixty-Nine

Lucas

A polite smattering of applause greeted me as I walked into the staff room. The teachers looked about as bored as I'd been waiting around in that kitchen. Jenny's goodbye speech had filtered through and I could see why the Board had wanted to replace her. The woman was about as suited to being head as a dead fish.

"Thanks for the welcome." I looked round the room, smiling as I made contact with each and every one of the teachers. My smile lost a little of its lustre when I saw Milly sitting there, but I quickly moved on to the guy sitting next to her.

Damn, she looked as good as she always did. Better, even. Was that man her boyfriend? There was something in his body language that hinted at an attraction between the two of them.

If that was the case, good. Milly deserved some happiness in her life. Growing up in her brother's shadow and then having to take over as heir had done a real number on her. She never had appreciated how amazing she was.

But it wasn't my problem. Not now, and not in the past either.

"Look, I know you've all got homes to go to, so I'll keep this short." The sense of relief when I said that was palpable. I had planned a longer speech, but after the way Jenny had gone on, I knew that the best way to start building rapport with my new team was to respect their time and not give them some empty motivational speech I'd cribbed together from a quick Google. "I went to this Academy myself and I know what a special place it is. As some of you may know, I was briefly married to Ivy Archaic and was mentored by her father, so I have an under-standing of the kinds of things we have to deal with here that aren't an issue in other more traditional schools. I've been fully briefed on the current state of play as well as the ambitions the Board has for the Academy and I think you're going to be really excited about some of the initiatives I've got planned. I'll reveal more about them when the time is right, but for now I want you all to know that I have an open-door policy. If there's anything you need to talk to me about, anything at all, please just come and see me. I won't bite." I grinned, deliberately not looking anywhere near Milly. Knowing her the way I did, she was likely to be way too shy to approach me unless she absolutely had to and that was fine by me.

"But for now, all I want to say is that I'm honoured to have been appointed head of this fine establishment and I look forward to working with all of you to build a positive learning environment to support all our pupils to excel both while they're with us and after they leave. Thank you and see you all next week when I officially takeover."

I nodded an acknowledgement of the slightly more enthusi-astic applause before the teachers started to disperse, grateful I hadn't kept them there any longer.

Jenny appeared at my side, a frosty look on her face. "Why did you let them go? I thought you were going to brief them on all the changes we discussed," she said. "I was going to bring out a cake to celebrate my new job."

Something told me no one was really interested in cele-brating anything Jenny was doing, but I'd met people like her before and it was always best to smile, nod, and ignore.

"I'm sorry," I said. "I had no idea."

"That's because it was a *surprise*," Jenny huffed. "What am I supposed to do with it now?"

"Why don't we put it in the fridge?" I suggested. "I'm sure it'll keep over the weekend and everyone will love to start their Monday off with cake. I'll be sure to let them know it was your treat."

"See that you do," Jenny snapped before going off to the kitchen to put the cake away.

I rolled my eyes once I was sure she couldn't see me. I was glad I wasn't going to have to work alongside Jenny. I could just imagine what a nightmare she'd been for all the teachers while she was interim head.

Well, I was here now and things were going to be very different – at least until I'd found what I was looking for. Or rather, who.

As it was, after a day of listening to Jenny tell me all about the amazing systems she'd put in place, systems I knew I was going to have to throw out and replace with ones which actually worked and improved the academic attainment of the students, I was tired. I was glad I didn't know about the cake she'd bought. The last thing I needed was to stand around making small talk with people I knew wanted nothing more than to get home after a long week.

I walked out of the staff room, not bothering to say goodbye to Jenny. I'd had enough of her and now she'd officially handed over the reins to me, I was under no obligation to be polite to her.

It was weird walking through the halls of the Academy I'd last attended as a student under the mentorship of Solomon Archaic. It almost felt like Archer Knight was going to ambush me to confront me about my relationship with Ivy. Solomon never really appreciated the strength of her connection with the three men in her life. At first, I thought I'd be able to win Ivy over, but it soon became clear that I didn't stand a chance. Her heart was already filled by Archer, Romeo and Declan.

But that was the past. I was here to take care of my future and that started with the girl I'd come here to find: my sister. I had no idea she even existed until recently when my family lawyer had called me in for a meeting. My mother had left a letter with him with strict instructions not to give it to me until my 30th birthday. To say that that letter had turned my world upside would have been an understatement.

I'd always known I was adopted. My mother had always been very clear about that fact and how grateful I should be to her for rescuing me from the life of poverty I'd been born into. I'd always thought my biological mother was dead, but instead, I found out that she'd placed me in care at an early age with the intention of coming back for me when she'd cleaned her act up. Instead, when Penelope Donatello offered her a hefty sum to adopt me, my biological mother was happy to sign away all her parental rights and never attempt to contact me.

My mother had gone on to have another child, a daughter this time, my sister. A sister who was apparently attending King Academy and would be in her final year. I didn't know her name. I didn't know what House she was in. But I had a private investigator on the case and when the head teacher position came up, I knew it was the best way for me to find my sister. I'd have access to all the students' files and I'd be able to figure out who she was if the PI didn't come through.

It was time for me to build a real family, one based on ties of blood. One which came naturally and wasn't forced for the sake of House politics and a desire to crush my enemies. It was time for me to enjoy a normal life for the first time.

I left the Academy building by the staff exit which led straight out to the car park. As I went over to my Audi, I saw Milly on the other side of the car park talking to the man she'd been sitting next to in the staff room. As I walked, the two of them looked over at me. I raised my hand in greeting, but although the man waved back, Milly just glared at me.

Whatever. If she had a problem with me, she was going to have to get over it pretty damn quickly. It wasn't like I'd broken her heart or anything like that. What happened between us all those years ago was a one off, a bit of fun for both of us that let us release some of the sexual tension that had been brewing between us after my marriage to Ivy was annulled.

Oh, who was I kidding?

I got into my Audi, but paused before starting the engine, gazing over at Milly again. Part of me wished things had been different. If Solomon hadn't pushed me into marrying Ivy, maybe I would have gone after Milly. I'd always thought she was striking with a figure that I'd fantasized about many times.

But I was determined to make my relationship with Ivy work because I trusted Solomon knew what he was doing. If I was honest, I wasn't exactly thinking straight either. After my mother died, I had my first taste of freedom and a fortune to fund the lifestyle any young man would kill for. I was the perfect target for someone like Solomon to take advantage of. Presenting me with someone like Ivy on a plate? Yes please! I believed Solomon when he told me she'd fall in love with me given some time and patience.

Instead, I wasted my time on a woman who loved three other men and by the time I realised I was interested in Milly, she was dating someone else. Then I went back to Italy for a few years and it felt like the universe was telling me that we just weren't meant to be.

That night in the club could have changed everything. She looked so vulnerable, sitting on her own at that table. I wanted to take her in my arms, let her know that I was there for her if she needed. Instead, I played it cool, not wanting to let her know how I felt until I was sure she felt the same way.

We'd gone back to my place and made love until dawn. We had a sexual chemistry that was electrifying. The way she made me feel was like nothing I'd ever experienced – and I'd had quite a lot of experience by that point. When I woke up with her in my arms, it felt right, like this was the start of something special, something life changing.

And then Archer had to go and spoil everything.

Milly's brother had come round to see her and when he discovered me sitting at the kitchen table wearing nothing but my boxers, he wasn't happy. The cunning weasel that he was, he didn't say anything in front of Milly. Instead, he waited for me to leave and ambushed me as I was getting into my car.

He'd never really forgiven me for forcing Ivy to marry me, so maybe that's why he was so angry. I'd always wondered whether what he did was his way of getting revenge on me for that rather than it being an expression of brotherly love, but whatever his motivations, it didn't really matter.

He shoved me up against my car and got right in my face. I'll never forget his snarl as he warned me to leave unless I could promise Milly forever.

What could I say? Although I liked Milly, it had been one night, hardly enough to know whether we could have a strong relationship or not. After the mistake of marrying Ivy, I wasn't going to rush into anything, so I told Archer I would leave and that's exactly what I did. I left town and thought I'd never come back. If it wasn't for my sister, I'd have stayed away, but it's funny where life takes you.

Part of me wondered what would happen if I invited Milly out on a date. She'd probably say no, but maybe she still thought about me the way that I thought about her.

But I wasn't going to risk it. Archer had warned me to stay away from her unless I was ready to commit and I knew what he was like. He'd follow throw on his threat to put me in the ground if I abandoned his sister.

Milly Knight was more trouble than she was worth, even if she was more beautiful than ever. I couldn't promise her forever back then and I didn't think I could now either. No, I was going to have to keep things professional. If she was dating that other teacher, good luck to the pair of them. I hope he made her happy.

She deserved the happy ever after I could never give her.

Chapter Seventy

Milly

"Are you sure you don't want to come out for that drink?" Nigel asked, seeing the expression on my face when I saw Lucas coming out of the Academy. "You look like you could do with one."

"How many times do I have to say no?" I snapped. I instantly regretted it when I saw the wounded look in his eyes. "I'm sorry, Nige. I didn't mean it."

"It's okay." He shrugged and looked away. "You're right. I do keep asking when I should respect the word no. I'll do better in future."

He turned to leave and I put out a hand to stop him. "No, please keep asking," I told him. "Maybe one day I'll be in a position to say yes. It's just that life is… complicated."

"Isn't it always?" Nigel laughed and I felt a little better seeing him relax again.

"Yeah, but you're not the one with a history with our new

head." I could feel my cheeks reddening as the penny dropped for Nigel.

"Oh."

"Yeah." I tried to keep my tone nonchalant. "It was a long time ago and nothing serious, but even so. It's weird seeing him again after all this time. I just want to go home and hug my daughter, you know?"

"I completely get it." Nigel stroked my arm reassuringly. "But you know where I am if you ever need to talk, okay?"

"I do. Thanks, Nige."

Amber and I had a regular Friday night tradition. When I got home from work, the two of us would go into the kitchen and make dinner together. Sometimes it would be pizza, making faces out of the toppings. Other times it would be a stew, Amber handing me the ingredients to top. It was something we both looked forward to, that time together priceless.

There would be no cooking tonight, though. I was in no mood to deal with anything and I was so distracted I'd probably chop a finger off while preparing the dinner. Tonight called for girl talk and wine.

I pulled up outside my house, one of a number in the Knight family grounds. I lived in a small settlement which my parents had built especially for me and my siblings. When Amber was born, they'd extended my house, so I had plenty of space for her and the nanny as well as an office for me to work on the family business when I wasn't teaching. One day, I'd move into the mansion when it was time for me to take over, but that day was a long way off and I loved my home. It was the one place where I could relax and be myself without worrying about who I needed to impress.

"Claire! Amber! I'm home!"

I put my car keys in the bowl I kept on the table by the door and dropped my bag next to it.

"Mummy!" Amber came rushing out to meet me. I picked her up and swung her round in a big hug before dropping a kiss on the tip of her nose. "You're late." She pouted.

"I know, baby. And I'm sorry. I had an important meeting."

"*I'm* important." Amber played with my necklace, refusing to meet me in the eye.

"Yes, you are. The most important person in the whole wide world."

"Hi, Milly." Claire walked out of the kitchen to meet me. "Amber's been a bit tetchy today. Apparently she got into a disagreement with one of the other children at nursery and refused to apologise."

"That's because it wasn't my fault!" Amber protested. "Damien tipped his water over my painting so I hit him."

"You know you shouldn't hit," I reproached her.

"Damien shouldn't have spilt water over my picture," Amber said. "I was making it for you."

"You can always make me another painting," I told her. "And I bet it'll be even more beautiful."

"Amber and I were getting things together for dinner," Claire told me. "She wanted to have shepherd's pie, so we've been cutting shapes out of potato to put on the top."

"It's going to look so cool!" Amber beamed.

"I'm sorry, sweetie." I felt awful letting her down, but the last thing I felt like doing was making a shepherd's pie. "We've got to go and see Auntie Ivy. I thought we could have dinner with her. We can finish off making the pie tomorrow."

"But I want to do the pie *now!*" Amber's face crumpled up. She'd always had a temper and on a day like today, a tantrum was the last thing I needed.

"Claire, would you be able to stay with Amber?" I asked. "I've really got to go and see Ivy."

"Sorry, Milly," Claire replied. "Normally I wouldn't mind, but I've got a hot date tonight and having to cover your meeting has already made me late."

"In that case, kiddo, you're going to have to suck it up." I put Amber on the floor. "Go get your coat and I'll order a driver to take us. Maybe we can have some cookies on the journey."

Cookies were the magic cure to everything. I knew I shouldn't bribe her with food. Before she was born, I'd promised myself I was only going to feed my daughter organic food, no sugar, nothing but wholesome, healthy ingredients. That quickly went out the window as I discovered how exhausting solo parenting really was. Sometimes, it was easier to head off the tantrum before it started, particularly when I was reeling from Lucas's return.

"Chocolate chip cookies?" Amber side eyed me suspiciously.

"Sure," I replied, hoping we still had some tucked away in the cupboard.

"I'll get them for you," Claire offered, while Amber went to fetch her coat. I picked up the family intercom and pressed the button to order a driver. Soon, Amber was safely strapped into her car seat munching on a cookie, legs happily kicking away while the driver took us the short distance to the Archaic estate. Normally I'd drive myself, but I needed wine and what was the point in being the heir to House Knight if I couldn't indulge myself in a few little luxuries every now and then?

"Milly! This is an unexpected pleasure." Romeo answered the door to us. "And how's my favourite little girl?" He leaned forward to give Amber a high five.

"I got a cookie, Uncle Romy!" Amber held up the soggy mess that was what was left of her last cookie.

"Aren't you lucky? Can I have some?" Romy pretended to reach out for Amber's cookie and she snatched it away, giggling.

"Silly Uncle Romy! It's *my* cookie!"

"In that case, I'd better go and get some cookies of my own. Do you want to come with me?" He reached out a hand to Amber, who happily took it.

"Would you mind making sure she eats something a little healthier as well?" I asked Romy. "She hasn't had dinner yet."

"No problem. Chef was just starting on dinner for Louis. I'll get him to make an extra portion. Ivy's up in the nursery."

Romy took Amber in the direction of the kitchen, my

daughter chatting away nineteen to the dozen as she skipped along next to him. I smiled sadly, wondering whether her beautiful innocence would last once news of who her father was got out.

Ivy. Ivy would know what to do. My best friend always had the answer to everything. She'd gone against House tradition to live with three men, all of whom adored her. This would be an easy fix for her after everything she'd been through.

I went up the stairs to the nursery. When Ivy first found out she was pregnant, she'd spent hours consulting with interior designers, determined to create the most beautiful nursery possible for her child. When she found out she was expecting a boy, she'd covered the walls with murals of sea creatures, creating a soothing watery retreat. I had no idea she was such a talented artist – her dad had forced her to choose between music and art when she went to the Academy. I always wondered whether he realised exactly what he was making her give up. She could easily have gone professional with her art, but instead, she'd poured all her energies into transforming House Archaic from the corrupt organisation· her father had created into an altruistic company which did as much work to help struggling communities as it did its core money making activities.

"Annie Mimi!" Louis, Ivy's adorable one-year-old son, came running over to me as I entered the nursery. He'd only recently started walking, but since he'd mastered the use of his legs, he seemed determined to get everywhere as quickly as he could, like he was in a rush to cram in all the things life had to offer. He couldn't say *Auntie Milly* properly yet, but I loved the way he pronounced my name and hoped I'd always be Annie Mimi to him.

I had no idea which of Ivy's three lovers was Louis's father. I wasn't even sure if Ivy herself knew. But it didn't matter – the three men all doted on Louis and they were all happy to share parenting duties, regardless of whether they were known as Dad, Daddy, or Papa.

I knelt down and gave the little boy a huge hug as he threw himself at me. "Hey, Lou-Boy," I said. "How's my favourite little man?"

"Happy as ever." I stood up as Ivy came up to join us. I hugged my best friend hello, holding onto her for a little longer than usual. I needed the reassurance of the physical contact.

When we broke apart, Ivy put her hands on my waist and held me in place so she could get a good look at my face. "All right, Mills. Spill it. Something's happened. What is it?"

"Lucas." I could barely say the word without my voice cracking.

"Lucas?" Ivy frowned. "What's he done now?"

"He's taken over as head at the Academy."

"Mother-" Ivy caught herself just before she could say something she didn't want her son repeating. "Why on earth would he want to come back? He must know that nobody wants him here."

"I don't know, but there's something I haven't told you. Something about Lucas."

"You need wine, don't you?"

I nodded miserably as Ivy scooped up her son and blew a raspberry on his tummy. "Come on, munchkin. Let's find Papa."

"Romy's in the kitchen with Amber," I said as we went back downstairs. "He's going to try and feed her something a little more nutritious than cookies."

"Cookie?" Louis's ears pricked up at the word.

"No cookies. Dinner," Ivy said firmly. I admired how she was able to set boundaries with her son. I really needed to be more like Ivy in my parenting, especially since Louis didn't seem all that upset to hear that he wouldn't be getting a cookie right now.

When we entered the kitchen, I was pleased to see that Romy had managed to persuade Amber to help him put together some mac and cheese. As I watched, he tossed in some finely chopped broccoli, getting Amber to help him put each piece in the sauce. Maybe I should come round here for Friday dinners more often. He was easily sneaking in the vegetables Amber would never eat when it was just the two of us.

"Room for another little one?" Ivy asked, going over to the high chair by the kitchen table and strapping Louis in.

"Of course." Romy came over and affectionately ruffled Louis's hair before kissing Ivy. There was so much love between them. I always loved seeing them together. Anyone else and maybe I might have been jealous that they had three men to love them when I couldn't even hold onto one, but Ivy deserved all the love in the world and more.

"Amber and I will be in my office if you need me," Ivy said, as she crossed over to the wine rack and pulled out a bottle of red. She grabbed a couple of glasses from the cupboard and gestured with her head for me to follow her.

Ivy's office was more like a cosy little nest than a place of business, but anyone who thought this meant she was soft would be making a serious mistake. Despite the plush sofas, comfy chairs, and brightly colour blocked walls, Ivy ran her international business empire with an iron fist. She knew exactly what was going on in every little aspect of her corporation. She always said that she did her best thinking when she was comfortable, so she'd wanted to create a space which made her feel relaxed. Now I was grateful for the soft seating as I sank down onto one of the couches, Ivy sitting next to me. She poured two generous glasses of wine, placing the bottle on a low coffee table before tucking her feet under herself, getting comfortable.

"So, do you want to tell me what's wrong, Mills? Lucas is my ex, not yours. If you're upset on my behalf, you don't need to be. He's the distant past and I'm happy with my life now."

I took a large gulp of wine, needing all the Dutch courage I could muster before telling her the secret I'd kept for so long.

"Lucas and I hooked up once," I revealed.

Ivy's eyebrows shot up, but she pulled herself together

before speaking. "Okay. I didn't know that. I guess it must have been a fling if you didn't tell me about it?"

"Just the one night," I confirmed.

"Okay, but if it was just one night, why would you be upset about him coming back? Unless…" Ivy's eyes widened as she put two and two together. "*He's* Amber's dad?"

"Yeah." A tear rolled down my cheek and fell into my wine. "That's why I didn't tell you. I couldn't."

"Milly, you can tell me anything. You should know that." Ivy put a hand on my knee to reassure me. "No judgement from me. Ever."

"Thanks, Ivy." I smiled sadly.

"So what happened between the two of you?"

"I always liked him," I confessed. "I figured that after he'd been married to you there was no way he'd be interested in me."

"Oh Milly." Ivy sighed. "I wish you'd realise how gorgeous you are. You could have anyone you wanted. You just need a little more self-confidence."

"You know me. It takes a couple of drinks before I can get up the nerve to talk to a man, let alone anything else," I said. "That's why, when I met him in a club, I was able to flirt with him. I thought it was harmless, but then Lucas kissed me…" A wistful smile spread over my face at the memory. "I figured what the hell? He wasn't married to you anymore. A bit of harmless fun was all it was meant to be. He stayed the night at mine and it was amazing. I've never been with anyone who made me feel the way he did. We were up all night and what he did to me…" I bit my lip, not wanting to go into too much detail out of respect to my friend. "Anyway, the next morning, he stayed for breakfast and I really thought it was the start of something special, you know? Then Archer came over."

"Wait – Archer knew about the two of you?" I frowned.

"Don't be mad at him," I begged. "I asked him not to tell you until Lucas and I were an official couple. I wanted our relationship to have a chance to develop without letting history complicate things. Only Lucas left later that day and never came back. I never heard from him, not an email, not a text, not a DM, nothing. I thought that was it, but then I missed my period. I hadn't been with anyone else."

"So, Lucas walked out on you, leaving you with the baby?" Ivy clenched her fist. "I'm going to kill him. The *boys* are going to kill him."

"You can't. Lucas doesn't know," I told her, panicked by her strong reaction. "I thought about telling him, but I figured that if he couldn't be bothered to get back in touch with me, he probably wouldn't be interested in being a father."

"You can't know that though," Ivy pointed out. "For all that he went along with my father's plans, Lucas always seemed like he had certain standards. I'm sure he would have wanted to be involved with Amber if he'd known."

"I did try to tell him," I said. "I was about eight months pregnant and feeling hormonal, so I reached out to him, wanting to see if we could figure something out."

"And?"

"And nothing. None of the contact details I had for him worked. Or if they did, he wasn't answering. So, I took that as a sign that it wasn't meant to be. Anyway, Amber and I don't need him. Never have, never will."

"He has a right to know, though," Ivy said gently. "Maybe he won't want to have anything to do with his daughter, but that's his decision to make, not yours. And what about Amber? Don't you think she should get to know her father?"

"She's never asked about him," I said. "She doesn't need to know. The two of us are fine just as we are."

"Even so, Milly. As a mother, I can see how important a father figure is to Louis. I know how great a mum you are, how much you've always wanted to do your best for Amber. Don't you think you owe it to her to tell Lucas what happened? Maybe he's got a good explanation for why he walked out on you. You should give him a chance."

"You're a better person than I am, Ivy," I said. "You always have been. I don't know if I'm brave enough to even face Lucas, let alone tell him about Amber."

"Of course, you are," Ivy said. "And you've got me to support you. I mean, whatever you decide, I've got your back. But if I were you, I'd tell Lucas about his daughter sooner rather than later. It'll only get worse the longer you leave it."

Chapter Seventy-One

J'd always loved my job, but walking into the Academy the following Monday was the hardest thing I'd ever done. Knowing that Lucas was officially head meant that I was bound to have to deal with him and I still wasn't sure what I was going to do about Amber.

I'd thought about what Ivy had said all weekend. I'd barely been able to sleep because I was so stressed about what might happen if I told him about Amber. Would he want access to her? Would he fight me for custody? Amber and I were a perfect little family, just the two of us. Lucas had the power to ruin all of that.

Or what if he wanted nothing to do with us? I didn't know what would be worse – Lucas deciding he wanted Amber in his life or Lucas turning his back on us again. Whatever he did, nothing good could come from telling him he had a daughter. Ivy might be the person I turned to for advice all the time, but on this occasion she was wrong. I was keeping my secret. It was only a matter of time before Lucas got bored and left town again.

"Fight! Fight! Fight!"

I heard the sounds of an all-too-familiar chant filtering through the hallways and I hurried in the direction of the sound. I pushed my way through the crowd that had gathered in one of the classrooms to the clearing at the centre where two girls were trying to tear each other's hair out.

"That's enough!" I forced myself between the two of them, making them step back. "You are young ladies! This behaviour is unacceptable!"

I got my first good look at the two girls and shook my head in disappointment. "Fenella Knight. I expected better of one of my cousins. We are Knights. We don't lower ourselves to these petty squabbles."

"It's not my fault, miss," Fenella protested. "Chantal was bullying Daisy. You always told us that it's a Knight's duty to stand up for the underdog. Daisy's younger than Chantal. She can't stand up for herself."

"Is this right, Chantal?" I turned to the other girl in the fight. "Were you bullying Daisy?"

"No way, miss!" Chantal's eyes were overly wide in that trying to look innocent expression that told me Fenella was telling the truth. "Daisy and me are best friends, aren't we Daise?"

She reached over and grabbed a younger girl, pulling her towards us. I couldn't help but notice the way the girl winced and I wondered what exactly Chantal had been doing before Fenella stepped in.

"Daisy?" I spoke gently, hoping the girl would speak up for herself, but knowing it was highly unlikely she would.

"Chantal's right," Daisy said softly. "We're friends. We were just messing around when Fenella decided to interfere."

"Oh come *on!*" Fenella groaned. "Stand up for yourself, Daisy. You're a Knight too! We aren't afraid of anything."

If only, I thought.

"All right, girls," I said. "I've heard enough. Fenella and Chantal – you've both got detention for a week."

"But miss," wailed Fenella. "I've got hockey practice. I'll be kicked off the team if I miss it."

"You should have thought of that before you started fighting," I said. "The pair of you should consider yourselves lucky I'm not marching you into Mr Donatello's office to be suspended. But if I find you fighting again, make no mistake. I'll make sure you receive a very harsh punishment. Do you understand?"

"Yes, miss." Fenella and Chantal both looked miserable at the news, but they had no idea how lucky they were. King Academy had a zero-tolerance policy towards violence. If Jenny was still head, I'd be marching them both to her office where they'd be lucky if a suspension was all they got. It was only because I couldn't bear being around Lucas that I was giving them detention instead.

"All right, everyone." I clapped my hands, gazing round at the crowd which was still there, enjoying the drama. "Classes are about to start. You've all got places to be, so I suggest you go there before the bell rings and you're late."

Daisy made to follow the others out, but I pulled her to one side. "A quiet word, Daisy?"

"I've got class, miss." The girl looked incredibly uncomfortable, but I wasn't going to let her off. If she'd stood up for herself, Fenella wouldn't be risking her place on the hockey team.

"This won't take long."

I shooed away a couple of straggling students and closed the door to the classroom so we could talk in private.

"I don't believe for a second that you and Chantal are best friends," I said. "In fact, I think Fenella told me the truth about everything. Am I right?"

Daisy shrugged miserably.

"Look, I can't tell you what to do with your life, but take it from me: things get a lot easier if you learn to fight your own battles. Fenella is one of our star hockey players and she may well lose her spot on the team because she was defending you. Do you think that's right?"

"No, miss."

"You need to learn to live up to the Knight name," I said to her. "Doing what's right isn't always easy, but it is the best strategy in the long run. And if you ever need to talk, you can always come to me in confidence. I won't do anything you don't want me to do, but take it from someone who's been there – there are ways of dealing with people like Chantal that mean you don't have to rely on someone else to rescue you."

"Yes, miss."

I looked at her, shaking my head. I had no idea whether my little pep talk was going to make any difference, but I'd done my best. Maybe I could get Fenella to mentor the girl. She certainly wasn't afraid of doing what was right.

And now I supposed it was time to practice what I preached. Lucas needed to know about the fight, even if I didn't want to face him. I had a free period first thing. I might as well get that awkward first meeting over and done with and go see him now.

"All right. Go to your class," I said to Daisy. "The bell's going to go in a minute and it would be a shame if you got a detention for being late after Fenella tried so hard to keep you out of trouble."

"Yes, miss."

Daisy scurried away while I tried to quiet the nervous butterflies flapping up a storm in my stomach as I went over to the head's office. Maybe he'd forgotten that we'd slept together and we could just be two old friends catching up.

Yeah, right!

I stood outside the solid oak door which already bore a brass plaque with Lucas's name on it. Jenny must be pissed off that they'd acted so quickly to wipe out every trace of her. She'd dropped so many hints during her time as interim head that needing to interview for the position was only a formality. She was convinced that she was guaranteed the job, only to have

Lucas swoop in and turn her life upside down. Funny how he had a habit of doing that.

Taking a deep breath to quell my nerves, I knocked.

"Come in!"

I pushed open the door to see Nigel sitting opposite Lucas at his desk.

"Oh, I'm sorry." I blushed. "I needed to talk to you alone, but I can always come back later."

"No need. Nigel and I were just about done, weren't we?"

"Yep." Nigel got up and reached over to shake Lucas's hand, the two of them looking like they'd been best buddies for years.

As Nigel walked past me, he winked at me, making me smile despite myself. Maybe I was never going to say yes to that drink with him, but it felt good to know someone had my back while I dealt with having Lucas as my boss.

Nigel shut the door behind himself, leaving me with Lucas.

"Take a seat, Milly." My legs were quivering like jelly as I crossed over to sit where Nigel had just been.

For a moment, we sat in silence, gazing at each other. I wanted to look away, but I made myself keep eye contact, not wanting to give Lucas any sense that I might be afraid. I was the Knight heir, dammit! If I couldn't stand up to one man who didn't care enough about me to stick around, I had no right to take over the family business.

"You look good," I said at last, not sure what to say. How was I supposed to tell him about Amber? Already, I was regretting coming here.

"I'm glad you said that," Lucas told me. "Because I've been wondering how to approach you knowing our history."

"Uh-huh." Was he going to ask me *out*? I wasn't ready for this. I was *so* not ready for this!

"What happened between us was great, but it was a long time ago," Lucas went on. "I've moved on and now that I'm your boss, it wouldn't be appropriate for us to start anything. I'm going to respect your professional boundaries and I'd appreciate it if you did the same. So no flirting, no hitting on me, nothing that's not work related, okay?"

"Dammit, Lucas, I'm not flirting with you. You have a daughter." The words came out before I could stop them.

Lucas looked like a ten-tonne truck had just run over him. If he wasn't sitting already, I didn't doubt that he'd have collapsed.

"What did you say?"

"You have a little girl," I repeated. "Her name is Amber."

"But I thought we used protection?"

"We did." I shrugged. "We were unlucky."

"A daughter…" Lucas gazed off into the distance. "I had no idea."

"Yeah, well, I tried to tell you, but you disappeared. I guess falling into bed with me was a mistake, but you didn't have to run like that. I'm a grown up. I could have coped if you'd just told me you weren't interested in seeing me again."

"It wasn't like that," Lucas said.

"So, what was it like?"

He pursed his lips and shook his head. "It's not important. What's done is done."

Chapter Seventy-Two

Lucas

*I*t had been tough enough coming back here knowing that I'd have to face Milly after all these years. Archer had been very clear. I wasn't to tell her he'd warned me off and I'd respected that. After what I'd done to Ivy and the way I'd supported Solomon, I figured it was the least I could do.

But knowing I had a daughter? That changed everything.

"Do you have a photo of her?" I asked.

"Of course." Milly took her phone out and opened up the photos folder. Selecting one, she handed the phone over. The little girl in the picture was the cutest thing I'd ever seen. She looked a lot like Milly, but she had my grey eyes and the way she was holding herself reminded me a lot of photos of myself at that age.

"She's beautiful," I said, passing back the phone. "But then I guess any daughter of yours would be. Jeez, Milly, I wish I'd known. I'd have been there for you. For both of you, no matter what anyone else said."

Milly frowned. "Why would anyone else want to get involved?"

Damn. I'd almost put my foot in it. "You and I both know I was public enemy number one after what happened with Solomon," I said, smoothly covering. "Do you really think your family would be happy to see you play happy families with me?" A thought struck me. "Do they know I'm Amber's father?"

"Archer may have done the maths." I shrugged. "I mean, he knew we'd spent the night. But if he suspected you're Amber's father, he's never said anything. And I never told anyone else, not even Ivy. I was too ashamed."

"Of being with me?" I laughed bitterly. "That figures."

"No!" she protested. "I don't mean it like that. It's just that I'm supposed to be the heir to House Knight. I'm here to set an example and getting pregnant after a one-night stand isn't exactly in the business plan. But everyone was so supportive, after a while, I became used to the idea of bringing up my daughter by myself, even though my parents try to marry me off every now and then. They're starting to get the message that I prefer to be on my own."

So, Milly was single. That was good to know. I wasn't in the mood to square up to another alpha male to fight for my daughter. And if Archer tried to interfere again, this time I was going to let him know he couldn't push me around. I left because he was right – it wasn't fair to start something with Milly if I couldn't see it through. But knowing I had a daughter changed everything. I'd come back to find my sister. Now it turned out I had even more family here than I realised. I wasn't going anywhere, no matter how much Archer Knight tried to push me around.

I cut straight to the chase. "So, when can I see my daughter?"

Milly bit her lip, nervously shuffling around. "Do you really think that's such a good idea, Lucas? Amber's settled. Do you really want to disrupt her life? Is that fair on her?"

"Is it fair on her to deny her a relationship with her father?"

I countered. "You've had it your way for the past few years, but it takes two to make a child and a whole village to raise one. I'm part of Amber's family, whether you like it or not. But if you want to try to stop me seeing her, that's fine. I happen to have an excellent team of lawyers who I'm sure would be more than happy to take you on. And given that you've hidden my child's existence from me for so long, I think it would be only fair for me to go for full custody."

Milly paled.

"I'd rather not go that route," I continued. "Whether you believe it or not, I'll always act in Amber's best interests and I don't think it would be good for her to see her parents fighting it out in court. I know all too well what that sort of experience can do to a child's mental health. But make no mistake. If you keep me away from my daughter any longer, I'll bring the full force of my legal team down on you and we won't stop until Amber's living with me."

"You wouldn't," Milly whispered. "You can't possibly think you'd win. You're not the only one with good lawyers."

"Maybe I'll win, maybe I won't." I shrugged. "But at the very least, I'll get access to my child, so what good will it do to delay the inevitable?"

"You're right." Milly sighed. "Fine. You can see Amber. Why don't you come round to my place this weekend? I think it would be easiest for her to see you at home. And I'd appreciate it if you didn't say anything about being her father before then. Give me a chance to prepare her. I know her better than anyone. I'll explain who you are when the time is right."

"Okay." I nodded. "I can do that."

"Fair warning, I'm not the girl you left in that bed. I'm her mother and I will fight to the death for Amber. So hurt her, Lucas, and you will be dealing with a storm," she warns, fire burning her in eyes. I like that fire.

Way too much.

"I will never hurt her," I simply reply, smiling a little cockily.

She searches my eyes for a second before nodding. "Good. I'll see you at my place, say, Saturday at one?"

"Saturday at one would be perfect." A warm glow spread through me at the thought of having a daughter. I'd always dreamed of having a little girl, someone to spoil like the little princess she was born to be.

I couldn't wait to meet her.

Chapter Seventy-Three

Milly

I paced up and down my lounge, compulsively gnawing at my fingernails. What had I been thinking, agreeing to let Lucas see Amber? So, he threatened me with lawyers. So what? I was a Knight. I'd faced off bigger and nastier demons than Lucas Donatello.

He'd caught me off guard, but it wasn't going to happen again. I was going to make sure I was the strong, confident woman Ivy always told me I was. Lucas couldn't steamroller me into doing what he wanted. Nobody could.

"Are you okay, Mummy?" Amber came skipping into the room, stopping when she saw my expression.

"Of course I am, sweetie." I inhaled deeply, pulling myself together to put on a brave face for my child. I had to model the kind of behaviour I'd want to see in her. I'd hate it if Amber was intimidated by some man. "I'm just getting ready for our guest. You remember who's coming to visit, don't you?"

Amber frowned. "You said it was my daddy. But I don't have a daddy. I just have you and you're the best!"

She came and threw her arms around me, squeezing me in a tight bear hug.

"Oh, Amber." That kid practically broke me with how sweet she was. I closed my eyes as I leaned over to hug her back. I loved the way she smelled, the way she felt in my arms, everything about her. The way I loved Amber was fierce and all consuming. There was no room in my heart for anyone but her.

Still, I was going to have to share her from now on. Lucas was right. It had taken two of us to create this beautiful little person. All I could do was hope he'd get bored with playing happy families and disappear off into the sunset again, just like he always did.

I knelt down so I could look straight into her eyes. "I know I told you that you didn't have a daddy and I thought I was telling the truth. I didn't think I'd ever see him again. But you *do* have a daddy and he's coming to see you. He's very excited and he wants to get to know you. You're going to spend lots of time together and I know you're going to have so much fun."

"No, I won't." Amber stamped her foot and pouted. "I don't *want* a daddy. I only want you."

"Amber…" I frowned. "I need you to be a good girl and be nice to your daddy."

"I won't be nice!" Amber shouted. "I won't! I won't!"

She turned and ran out of the room, just as the doorbell rang.

"Great." I rolled my eyes, as I went to answer it. If that was Lucas, his timing couldn't have been worse.

I opened the door to find myself being faced by the biggest teddy bear I had ever seen.

"Hi!" came a squeaky voice from behind the bear. "My name is Tyrone and I'm here to see Amber! Is she here?"

"Come in, Lucas," I said. "But I warn you now. Amber's not in the best of moods. She may not come down from her room. She has a bit of a temper."

"I wonder where she gets that from?" Lucas grinned, as he followed me through to the lounge. He sat the bear down on one of the armchairs. It barely fitted, it was so large.

I went to the bottom of the stairs and yelled up. "Amber! Come down and say hello to your visitor!"

"No!" I knew exactly what Amber would be doing right now. She'd be sat on the end of her bed, arms folded, kicking her feet in the air, ready to kick out at anyone who dared come close.

I turned to Lucas, shrugging in frustration. "I'm really sorry, Lucas. I told her you were coming and you were her father. Unfortunately, she didn't take the news all that well. I guess she's so used to it being just the two of us, it's been more of a shock to her than I expected to discover she has a dad after all this time. If you hadn't left, maybe things would be different."

"Now don't you put this on me," Lucas warned, his expression darkening. "If you'd reached out to me, I'd have come straight back to support you. How was I supposed to know you were pregnant?"

"I know." Part of me wished that I had tried to contact Lucas when I'd first seen that little blue line, but dealing with him would have been one complication too many for me at the time. "I'm sorry."

Lucas's face softened. "Look, we've both done things we regret," he said. "How about we draw a line underneath the past and try to do better moving forward?"

"Okay." I nodded, smiling a little.

"Now if you tell me where I can find my daughter, I'll go and have a word with her."

"Her bedroom's upstairs, first on the left," I told him. "But I warn you – Amber can be very stubborn. I promise you that I tried to persuade her to be nice to you, but she didn't want to know. It might be better to leave it for today and try again some other time."

"I'm here now," Lucas said. "You might as well let me try to work my magic on her. I can be very charming when I want, you know."

Oh yes. I know.

He turned and went upstairs to find Amber. I waited a moment, then tiptoed up after him. My room was next to Amber's and I hid behind the door where I could hear their conversation.

"Hey, Amber," Lucas said. "How you doing?"

Silence.

"My name's Lucas." Lucas didn't seem perturbed by Amber ignoring him. "Do you know who I am?"

"Mummy says you're my daddy, but I don't believe her."

"Why?"

"Because I don't have a daddy. Only Mummy. And she's the best Mummy in the whole wide world."

"I bet she is," Lucas said. "I've always thought your Mummy was a very special person."

I smiled when I heard him say that. Maybe he didn't mean it and was just saying it to get Amber on side, but it still felt good to hear Lucas compliment me.

"So, you won't try to take me away from her?"

I could have cried when I heard Amber say that. So *that's* why she was so angry at the thought of meeting Lucas. She was worried he was going to make her leave me.

"Of course not." Lucas sounded shocked. "I would *never* want to take you away from your Mummy. I know how much you love her. Can I let you into a little secret?"

"Uh-huh."

Lucas lowered his voice to a whisper. "I love her too."

My heart skipped a beat. Lucas *loved* me?

"You do?"

"Of course! I love her because you love her. Anyone who is important to you is important to me."

I was surprised by how disappointed I felt when Lucas said that. I'd always thought I felt more strongly about Lucas than he did about me, but hearing him admit that he was only telling Amber what she wanted to hear hurt more than I'd have expected. I guessed those feelings I thought were long since gone weren't quite dead and buried after all.

"Now," Lucas went on. "I've got someone downstairs who really wants to meet you."

"Who?"

"His name is Tyrone," Lucas said. "And he's very excited about seeing you. Do you want to come and say hello?"

"Okay." I heard Amber scramble off the bed and thump her way downstairs, her running sounding more like a herd of elephants than a small child in her excitement to see this mysterious Tyrone.

I stayed where I was for a moment, wanting to give Lucas and Amber a few more minutes to connect. It seemed like Lucas had managed to work his way into Amber's affections, just like he did with every woman he met.

I wasn't sure how I felt about that. If Amber hadn't liked Lucas, it would give me a strong argument to stop him seeing her again. But if the pair of them were bonding already, I couldn't exactly stand between the two of them. It wouldn't be fair to Amber.

I supposed I was stuck with Lucas, for the time being at least.

Putting on a brave face, I went downstairs to find Lucas and Amber playing with Tyrone. Amber was using the giant teddy bear as a trampoline and Lucas was pretending to speak on behalf of the bear, begging her to stop, which only made her laugh and want to be even rougher.

"Okay, you two," I said. "Who would like some lemonade and cookies?"

"Cookies? Really?" Amber looked at Lucas. "Mummy says I shouldn't have too many cookies because it will spoil my appemite."

"It will spoil your appetite." I gently corrected her pronunciation. "But we can make an exception just this once. It's not every day a little girl gets to meet her daddy."

"I have the best daddy in the whole wide world." Amber gazed at Lucas adoringly, an expression she'd only used for me in the past. I hated that she was connecting with him so easily, but I had to think about what was best for her. Lucas was her father, after all. She deserved a good relationship with him.

"And I have the best daughter." Lucas reached out and ruffled her hair.

"Why don't you take Lucas out to the garden and I'll bring the cookies out to you?" I suggested. "You could show him your swings."

"Yay! Swings!" Amber ran off in the direction of the garden. Lucas pulled himself up, taking a little longer to drag himself to his feet.

"She's a real live wire," he remarked. "She's got so much energy. I don't know how you keep up with her. I'm exhausted already!"

"Yeah, it's tough being a single parent," I said. "But Amber's worth it. Even if some days, I'm counting down the hours until she goes to bed!"

"She's a great kid," Lucas said. "You've done a good job raising her."

"Thanks."

Lucas gazed at me, his expression inscrutable. He looked like he was about to say something, but we were interrupted by a little voice calling from the garden.

"Daddeee! Come and watch me swing! I can go really high!"

"You'd better go," I advised. "Amber doesn't have much patience."

"I'll be right there, honey!" Lucas grinned at me before heading outside to watch Amber on the swings.

I watched the two of them playing through the kitchen window as I poured out three glasses of lemonade and put some cookies on a plate. I put the glasses and plate on a tray and went outside to place them on the garden table.

"Cookies!" I called. Immediately, Amber started wriggling about on the swing, wanting it to stop so she could come and have a snack. A pang of nerves shot through me as I worried about the possibility of her falling off the swing, but Lucas was on it. He grabbed the swing and carefully brought it to a halt so Amber could jump off.

"Race you!" she cried, calling over her shoulder as she set off running as fast as she could.

"I'm going to get you!" roared Lucas, deliberately pacing himself so that he could almost catch her but would never overtake her.

"I won!" crowed Amber, flopping down into a chair and grabbing a handful of cookies.

"One at a time," I warned.

Amber pouted and looked at Lucas for support.

"Your mum says one at a time," Lucas said gently but firmly. "That doesn't mean you can't have more when you've finished that one."

"Okay."

I was stunned when Amber put the cookies back. Normally, she'd have argued, maybe even taken a quick, cheeky bite out of the extra ones. Clearly Lucas was a good influence on her. Wonders would never cease.

"So, what do you do, Daddy?" Amber asked, surprising me with how quickly she slipped into using the name.

"I'm Mummy's boss," he said.

Amber turned to me, eyes wide. "Really?" she gasped.

"That's right," I said. "Daddy is the new head at the Academy. Which means that in theory he gets to tell me what to do."

"Something tells me that's not really how it's going to work though." Lucas grinned at me and I smiled back.

"Yeah," said Amber. "Nobody tells Mummy what to do. She's the *real* boss round here!"

I laughed and Lucas and I exchanged a knowing glance. This was nice. It felt like we were a real family.

Careful, Milly. You don't want to let your guard down. You know what always happens. Don't let another man hurt you.

But I had a feeling it was too late. Being around Lucas felt right. I'd always felt like we were meant to be together, if only I could convince him. Maybe this time, things would be different.

Chapter Seventy-Four

"Can Daddy read my bedtime story?" Amber asked as we brushed her teeth together and got her ready for me.

"Sure." I plastered on a fake smile. Truth be told, I loved our bedtime routine. I loved snuggling up next to her in her bed, choosing a good book. We were working through *The House at Pooh Corner* at the moment and I loved putting on silly voices for all the characters. I was planning on reading Beatrix Potter to Amber once we'd finished. I was going to introduce her to all the best children's classics so that by the time she got too big for me to read to her, she'd be one of the most well-read kids in town.

After a bedtime story, we would sit and tell each other three things we were grateful for about that day. I always ended by saying that I was grateful she was in my life, because I was. My daughter was a blessing and I felt so privileged I got to be her mother. Then I'd kiss her on the top of the head, on the tip of her nose and on each cheek before Amber did the same to me.

It was a ritual we'd done every night for as long as I could remember. But my daughter had casually tossed it aside in favour of having Lucas read to her and I had to be the bigger person and be okay about it. The last thing I wanted was to make Amber feel like she had to choose between us. I was going to be a grown up and be supportive of Amber's relationship with her father, even if I felt like I was dying inside.

"Daddy! Daddy! Come read to me!" Amber ran out of her ensuite bathroom and called to Lucas from her bedroom door. A moment later, Lucas was there, carrying Tyrone with him.

"Can Tyrone listen to the bedtime story too?" he asked.

"Of course, silly." Amber giggled. "We're having a sleepover!"

I watched as Amber and Lucas tucked the gigantic stuffed toy up in bed before Amber climbed in next to him. She was lucky she had a room big enough for a double bed – if she was still in the small cot she'd had when she was younger, there'd be no room for the bear, let alone for her as well.

"What story are we reading?" Lucas asked, going over to the bookshelf.

"Pooh! Pooh!" Amber laughed again, the strange bear name always amusing her.

Lucas found *The House at Pooh Corner* and came over to perch on the edge of the bed. I tiptoed out of the room, as Amber helped him find the right page. Bigger person or not, I wasn't quite ready to watch Lucas usurp me.

I went downstairs and poured myself a generous glass of wine. I figured I'd earned it after the day I'd had. I took a large gulp before going to sit in my favourite comfy chair to wait for Lucas to finish the story.

Was this was it was going to be like from now on? Lucas gradually taking my place in Amber's life while I get shoved aside?

I tried to tell myself not to be so daft, but it was hard not to feel a little hurt when my daughter had ignored years of bedtime stories in favour of having some stranger read to her. Because that's who Lucas was to her – a stranger.

I took another large swig of wine. Everything was going to

be okay. Lucas was just a novelty to Amber. Once the excitement of someone new wore off, she'd be back to her regular clingy self, wanting me instead of some man who was just as likely to get tired of her as she was of him.

Yeah, right.

Watching the two of them together this afternoon, I could see that there was a definite bond between them. It wouldn't take many more afternoons like that for the two of them to develop an unbreakable connection. I just hoped that Lucas wouldn't suddenly abandon her. I didn't like the idea of picking up the pieces. I hated seeing Amber upset at the best of times. If she lost her father, she'd be devastated and if Lucas hurt her, I wouldn't rest until he paid the price.

"Whew!" Lucas came down and slumped onto the sofa. "Amber's full on, isn't she? She wanted me to read her three stories and then sing her a song. When I said I didn't know the words to *Baby Shark*, she insisted on teaching me. She point blank refused to settle down until I'd sung it to her word perfect, complete with a little dance."

"Ha!" I snorted, before taking another sip of wine. "If you think an afternoon's tough, you should try the last four years."

"I don't know how you've done it," Lucas said. "I take my hat off to you. Hey – is there any of that wine left? I could really use a glass."

"The bottle's on the side in the kitchen." I waved a hand, indicating he could help himself. I really wasn't in the mood to get up and serve him. He'd forced his way into my life again. He could get his own damn wine.

Lucas went and poured himself a small glass before coming back to sit with me. "I better not have too much. I've got to drive home."

An awkward silence descended. I'd run out of small talk for the day and it seemed that Lucas felt the same way.

Whatever. It wasn't my job to entertain him. Didn't he have wine in his own place? Did he *have* to stay here?

"So, what are your plans for the rest of the weekend?" he said at last.

"Nothing special," I replied. "We usually spend Sunday with my parents. They love Amber and she absolutely adores them and all her aunts and uncles. She's particularly close to Archer. She never could say his name properly, so she always called him Unky Woof when she was little. The nickname's stuck and everyone calls him Woof now." I caught the amused expression on Lucas's face. "I wouldn't call him that if I were you," I warned. "Archer will take it from cute four-year olds. Not so much from guys who abandon their family."

"That's low," Lucas said. "I didn't know you were pregnant. I've already told you I wouldn't stayed away so long if you'd said something."

"Whatever." I sighed heavily. "What's done is done. We need to figure out where we go from here."

"Well, if it's okay with you, I'd rather not involve the lawyers," he said. "If we can agree an arrangement between the two of us, I'd rather keep things informal. How about if I take Amber every weekend?"

"What – and leave me to have to deal with all the school runs and meltdowns when we get home without the fun of downtime at the end of the week?" I shook my head. "I don't think so."

"All right. What about if we have her alternate weeks? That way, we both have to deal with school and we both get to have fun with her at the weekend."

"That would be way too disruptive for Amber." I shook my head even more vehemently. "It's not going to work."

"All right. You make a suggestion then." Lucas was working to keep his tone light, but I could tell he was getting frustrated.

"You can have her every other Saturday," I said. "That way my parents can still keep our Sunday tradition."

"That's nowhere near enough time," Lucas protested. "I have to have her for at least the whole weekend."

"She still doesn't know you," I pointed out. "Give it some time. Sure, you had a good afternoon with her today, but you're a novelty and you came with a big present. When you become just another person in her life, she won't seem nearly as cute and she can push boundaries like nobody's business. I think you'll find one day a fortnight is more than enough for now. We can always change it later once she's had a chance to get to know you."

"What you say makes sense." Lucas nodded slowly. "But it's still not enough. What about if I have her on every Saturday?"

I had to work hard to keep the smug grin off my face. I'd been expecting Lucas to fight harder for more time. One day a week was okay for now. I hadn't had a chance to speak with the family lawyer yet, but I knew enough to know that if I made some concessions now, it would look good for me if we ever ended up in court.

"I think I can agree to that." I held up my glass in salute and Lucas leaned over to clink his against it.

"Good. There's a circus coming to town next week. I'd love to take Amber to it."

"Just be careful you don't set the bar too high," I warned. "You're her father, not her best friend, okay?"

"You don't want to be the bad parent, that's all." Lucas laughed. "If I want to be a fun dad, that's on me."

"Uh-huh. Well, when Amber starts acting up and you don't know how to deal with her, don't come crying to me."

"I'm the headmaster of the Academy, remember?" Lucas pointed out. "I handle hundreds of kids every day. I think I can tackle one iddy biddy four-year-old."

"We'll see." I lifted my wine glass to hide the smile on my face. Lucas might think he knew it all, but I knew from experience that teaching children and parenting them were two very different things.

Lucas finished up his wine. He looked in the empty glass, considering his next words.

"I suppose I ought to get going," he said at last. I'd been

expecting him to say something else, but he must have changed his mind. "I guess I'll see you at work on Monday."

"Okay." I stood up to walk him to the door. I opened it for him and stood there, waiting for him to leave, but he hesitated, again, looking like he wanted to say more.

"Yes?" I folded my arms, giving him my best teacher glare.

"Nothing. I'll see you at the Academy on Monday."

He went off to his car and I closed the door so I wouldn't have to watch him leave. I didn't want him to think I cared. Part of me wanted him to stick around, maybe even flirt a little. He looked even better than I remembered him and it had been a *long* time since I'd enjoyed any male company. But it wasn't worth the risk. Right now, Lucas was the enemy, someone who might try to take my daughter away from me.

If I forgot that, I'd only end up regretting it.

Chapter Seventy-Five

$\mathcal{I}$ sat there, trying to look like I was paying attention as Lucas moved on to the next item on the agenda in the weekly staff meeting. He was currently talking about his plans for the football team and how he wanted to get sponsorship from all the Houses so that they could go on a European tour playing against other Academies. As Knight heir, I should have been taking notes, but I just couldn't bring myself to care. I'd ask my father to write a cheque for however much Lucas wanted and forget about it. I wasn't interested in any of the details, but I knew better than to speak up and tell Lucas to move on to the next topic already. I didn't want anyone to think there was any kind of conflict between the two of us. I was determined to be a consummate professional, regardless of my personal feelings about the head.

"Unless anyone has got something to say, I think we're just about done." At last, Lucas said the magic words. I held my breath, praying no one would speak up and when no one did, I jumped up, ready to make the dash to my car and go home.

"Milly, can I have a word?" My heart sank when Lucas

called me over. Whatever he wanted couldn't it wait until tomorrow? I'd spent more than enough time here today.

Reluctantly, I mooched over to him as the other teachers hurried out. As he left, Nigel put a hand on my shoulder in sympathy. "Good luck," he whispered.

"Thanks." I smiled ruefully, as I went to stand by Lucas.

"Give me a minute," he said and it was all I could do not to roll my eyes in exasperation. He seemed to be shuffling round his papers for no real reason and it was annoying. Some of us had children to get home to. Out of everyone, he should have understood that.

Lucas looked up and watched the last teacher leave.

"What did you want?" I looked pointedly at my wrist as if I had a watch there. "Amber will get worried if I'm too late."

"Sorry." Lucas ran a hand through his hair. "I needed to talk to you about something and I've been struggling to think about the best way to approach it. The last thing I need is to be accused of sexual harassment in the workplace."

"Why would anyone do that?" I frowned.

"Because I want you to go out with me."

My face must have been a picture. When I heard him say that, my jaw dropped and my eyes boggled. "Are you serious?"

"Why wouldn't I be?" Lucas shrugged. "You and I had fun together in the past, didn't we?"

Fun wasn't how I'd describe it. Mind blowing sex, maybe. Life changing consequences, but fun..?

"You're right. This could open you up to being a sexual harassment case." I was stalling I knew, but this had thrown me for a loop. "But I don't see why that would matter. It's not like you need the money."

"No," Lucas conceded, "but there are other reasons why I need this job. So, I figured I'd ask you out without any pressure so we can get this out of the way. If you're not interested, say the word and I won't ever mention it again. We'll keep it strictly professional from now on. I'll come round to pick up Amber but keep conversation to a minimum when I do and I won't even think about what it would be like to spend time with you, get to know you better, discover the difference being a mother has made to you..."

He was saying all the right words, but the way he was looking at me suggested he had one thing on his mind: rekindling the fire we shared in bed.

I knew I should tell him no. I knew the best thing to do was to see if he could stay true to his word and be professional. I opened my mouth to turn him down.

"Yes."

"Great!" Lucas's smile lit up his face. "How does Thursday sound? That leaves us the weekend free to be with Amber."

"Thursday would be good." I nodded cautiously.

"I'll make a booking. Do you still like curries?"

"The hotter the better." I smiled.

"No problem. I'll pick you up from yours at seven, okay?"

"Looking forward to it."

Chapter Seventy-Six

"What on earth was I thinking, agreeing to go out with Lucas?" I wailed, tossing yet another outfit on my bed. The pile of clothes was impressive, but I couldn't find a single thing to wear that worked for a date with my baby daddy who I may or may not be interested in having a relationship with if only I could make up my mind.

"You were thinking that you deserved a little bit of fun after all these years living as a born-again virgin," Ivy said. Although Claire had offered to stay late to look after Amber, I'd asked Ivy so I could have a bit of moral support while I got ready for my date. It turned out to be the right decision, since I was having a total crisis of confidence.

"Maybe I should phone Lucas and tell him I've got a migraine. No, a tummy bug. No, the *plague!* He won't want to date a woman suffering from the plague, will he?"

"Milly..." Ivy shook her head pityingly. "It's just a date."

"A date with *Lucas*," I reminded her. "Your ex-husband and Amber's father. This could never be just a date."

"Why not? From what you've told me, Lucas sounds

genuinely interested in being a proper dad and I know you always had a crush on him."

I could feel myself blushing. "I thought I'd hidden it well."

"You did." Ivy rushed to reassure me. "But you forget I'm your best friend. I know when you're hiding something and it didn't take much to figure out what. I knew you'd never do anything you shouldn't but I always got the vibe Lucas liked you back."

"Really? What made you think that?" I couldn't help being curious.

"Oh, just little things here and there." Ivy shrugged. "He'd make a comment about something you were wearing, something a guy wouldn't normally notice unless he was interested in someone. And there was a certain look he had on his face whenever he talked about you. I knew he wouldn't risk doing anything to anger my father, so he'd never have acted on it, but I'll be honest. I wasn't surprised when you told me he was Amber's father. It made perfect sense." She reached out and rubbed my arm reassuringly. "You didn't need to keep it a secret from me, you know. I wouldn't have judged you. I never loved Lucas. I barely consider him an ex – it's not like I wanted to marry him. Our marriage was a total sham, like our relationship was. If you think he'll make you happy, then you should go for it. Just…"

"What?"

"Be careful, Mills. I always thought Lucas was a decent enough guy, but he's always been good at keeping secrets. There's a reason why he's come back after all this time and it's not because he has a burning ambition to be a headmaster."

"I know, right?" I laughed. "I mean, the guy's worth millions, billions even. Why would someone like that come back here and run a school? There's something weird about it, but I have no idea what."

"Have you thought about asking him? If only you had the opportunity to get him on his own so you could persuade him to tell you everything. An opportunity like… a date?" Ivy gave me a sly look and grinned.

"Okay, okay." I rolled my eyes and shook my head. "I won't tell him I've got the plague. But you have to help me decide what to wear. I can't figure out what would say 'I'm open to being seduced but you're going to have to work hard to make up for the past five years.'"

"Hmm." Ivy surveyed the clothes strewn across my bed. "What about this?" She picked up a short black dress that barely covered my butt.

"Too short." I shook my head.

"This?"

"Too big."

"This?"

"It doesn't fit properly."

"This?"

"I don't like how my bum looks in it."

"This?"

I tried to come up with an excuse not to wear the dress Milly was holding up, but I had nothing, so I took it from her and went into the bathroom to get changed.

When I came out, Ivy wolf whistled at me.

"Looking good, girl." She grinned. "I love the colour you've used on your lips."

"It's not too much?" I hadn't been sure when I put on my makeup whether I was going too far. I'd kept my eyes light, with just a touch of green on my eyelids, but I'd gone all out with a rich, deep red on my lips, making them look even more pouty than usual.

"Not at all." Ivy came over and adjusted my dress, pulling it down a little at the front to show more cleavage. I pulled it back up again to where it was and Ivy tutted at me. "Don't be bashful, Mills. You've got a beautiful figure. You should show it off more."

"I'm showing more than enough in this, thank you." I was wearing a dark green wraparound dress which emphasised my figure. There was a slit up the front which revealed my thigh when I walked and it hugged my breasts to show them off without needing to expose too much of my cleavage. It was sexy but subtle and now that I could see myself in the full-length mirror on the door of my wardrobe, I was happy with the way I looked. I'd debated going to the hairdresser and getting a new haircut, but I'd decided against it in the end. I didn't want Lucas to think I was making too much of an effort for him. Just because I'd agreed to go on a date didn't mean I wanted him to think I was going to be an easy conquest. Not this time, anyway.

"Lucas is going to love you in this," said Ivy, as we went downstairs to wait for him to come pick me up. "He's going to kick himself for disappearing on you all those years ago. Has he said why he did that?"

"No." I shook my head. "I'm planning on asking him about it tonight. If he's serious about us building a relationship, he's got to stop being the man of mystery he seems to love being."

"Yeah, Lucas always did have things he kept to himself." Ivy went over to the fridge and pulled out the bottle of champagne she'd brought over. "But people can change and maybe he's ready to be a grown up now."

"We can hope!"

Ivy poured a glass of champagne for both us and passed one to me. "I figured we should celebrate your first date in forever. Even if it doesn't work out, I'm proud of you for finally getting yourself out there. I know you've been focused on Amber for the past few years, but it's about time you put yourself first. If it doesn't work out with Lucas, don't let this be the last date you go on, okay? There are plenty of eligible bachelors out there who'd love to get to know you better."

"I don't know." I sipped at my champagne, the alcohol giving me a little buzz and taking the edge off my nerves. "If it was anyone else, I wouldn't be going out tonight. I mean, Nigel's asked me out so many times I've lost count and I've always said no, even though he seems like a perfectly nice guy. I don't really want the complication of a man in my life. Amber and I are fine just the two of us."

"Poor Nigel." Ivy sighed. "I've seen the way he looks at you. He really likes you. How do you think he's going to react when he finds out you're dating the head?"

"I hadn't thought about it." My stomach clenched with nerves when I realised that some people might think I had an ulterior motive for dating Lucas. Nobody knew he was the father of my daughter. What if they thought I was seeing him because I was trying to further my career? "Do you think he's going to be upset? I don't want to hurt him. He's been such a good friend to me over the years."

"If he's really your friend, he'll be happy for you." Ivy shrugged. "You're entitled to a love life and you can see whoever you want."

"Mummy, you look beautiful!" Amber came running into the room, practically throwing herself into my arms. I had to jerk my arm up to stop myself from spilling champagne all over my dress.

"What are you doing down here?" I scolded. "You're meant to be in bed. I already read your story."

"I'm not sleepy," Amber protested. "I wanted to see Daddy when he got here. I wanted to give him the picture I made for him at nursery."

"You can give it to him on Saturday," I told her. "Go back to bed."

Amber looked like she was going to argue, but Ivy scooped her up.

"Come on, Amber. You're going to be a good girl for Auntie Ivy, aren't you?" she said, starting to carry her out of the room. However, the doorbell rang and Amber wriggled out of Ivy's arms and ran over to open the door.

"Amber!" I raced after her, but she'd already pulled open the door to reveal a delivery driver with a package. I grabbed Amber's arm to stop her running outside to look for Lucas, took the package and shut the door. "How many times do I have to tell you not to open the door?" I hadn't telling Amber off, but as the daughter of the Knight heir, she was a prime target for being kidnapped and I'd drummed it into her that there were things she couldn't do so I could keep her safe. "What if there had been a bad man waiting there?"

"I thought it was Daddy." Amber started crying. Normally that would have been enough to soften me, but I was nervous about the date, stressed about Amber's behaviour and not in the mood to deal with a fractious four-year-old who should have been in bed.

"Okay, Amber. Why don't you let Auntie Ivy read you another bedtime story?" Ivy came to my rescue, picking up Amber and taking her off to her room.

I went back to the kitchen where I'd left my champagne and finished off the glass in one go. My hands were shaking as I set the flute back down on the side. Until now, I hadn't realised just how nervous I was about the date. I knew I wouldn't have shouted at Amber like that normally. Sure, I would have told her off for answering the door when she knew better, but I would have taken the time to explain to her why she needed to be more careful instead of trying to scare her into behaving.

Lucas was changing my world already and not for the better it would seem.

I debated pouring myself more champagne but decided against it. I needed to keep a clear head for this date if I was going to figure out what was really going on with Lucas, because I couldn't believe that this was just a normal date. Lucas always had an ulterior motive for what he did and I was going to figure it out. If Lucas thought he could play me, he was going to discover that there were two of us in this game and I was going to win.

"She's back in bed, although she's not happy about it." Ivy came in to join me. Seeing my empty glass, she picked up the champagne bottle to refill it.

"No." I shook my head and put my hand over the glass. "I'd

better not. Lucas is going to wine and dine me, remember? It's probably best if I don't start the night out tipsy already."

"Fair enough." Ivy topped up her own glass and we went back to sit in the lounge. "You know it's okay to let your hair down once in a while, Mills? It *is* okay to enjoy yourself every now and then."

"I know," I said. "And I'm going on this date, aren't I?"

"You are, but I want you to be sure you actually have fun while you're out, even if you decide you don't want to have a relationship with Lucas."

"I'll do my best," I promised. "But it's all going to depend on Lucas, isn't it? Until I know what he's planning, I can't let down my guard."

"Maybe he's just planning on spending some time with a beautiful woman," Ivy pointed out. "Maybe he wants to get to know the mother of his child a little better. Heck, Mills, maybe he just likes you. Have you thought about that?"

"Nobody 'just likes me.'"

"That's not true," Ivy said. "Nigel does or he wouldn't be okay about the fact you keep knocking him back. I know there were plenty of guys who would love to date you, but they don't even register on your radar. You're beautiful, Milly. If you could see yourself the way others see you, you'd realise that you have plenty of choices if you wanted to get out into the world of dating."

"If you say so."

It was a discussion we'd had plenty of times, but I was saved from having to repeat myself by a knock at the door.

I went to answer. This time, it actually was Lucas. His grey eyes lit up as he looked me up and down before handing me a large bouquet of red roses.

"Thank you, Lucas. They're lovely. Do you want to come in for a moment while I put them in water?"

I turned and walked off to the kitchen without waiting for his reply.

"Hi Lucas." Ivy wiggled her fingers at her ex-husband in a little wave as he followed me into the kitchen.

"Hey, Ivy. Long time, no see. How are you doing?"

"Good, good, thanks."

"I hear that you've really revolutionised this town, dragged it kicking and screaming into the twenty-first century."

"Someone had to." Ivy shrugged modestly. "I might not be the leader of House Archaic my father wanted me to be, but I'm the leader the House needs if it's going to evolve and grow."

"Well, I've heard nothing but praise for you," Lucas told her. "And I'm glad. You deserve some happiness in your life. And what about Declan, Archer, and Romy? How are they doing?"

Was it my imagination, or was there a slight catch in his voice when he mentioned my brother?

"They're good," Ivy replied. "We have a little boy now. Louis."

"So I heard." If Lucas had any issue with Ivy's unconventional relationship, he didn't let on, as she pulled out her phone to show off some photos of her son. I know that Lucas had hoped their arranged marriage would work out, but he had underestimated the power of her feelings for the three men she lived with. Ivy had a lot of love to give, but no room in her heart for Lucas and when he realised there was no hope for the two of them, he'd been happy to sign the documents annulling their marriage. Even so, there was a part of me that wondered whether Lucas had really been looking for me that night in the club which had resulted in Amber. I knew my best friend was prettier than me, a better House leader than me, a better catch than me. Of course Lucas would rather have been with her than me.

"You seem lost in thought," said Lucas, bringing me back down to earth. "Everything okay?"

I shook my head to shake away the negativity. "Yes, fine. Shall we get going?"

"Absolutely. Lovely to see you again, Ivy."

"Likewise." Lucas waved goodbye to Ivy before offering me

his arm to escort me out to where his driver was waiting for us. The driver opened the door to the back of a stretch limo and I climbed in to find strawberries and champagne laid out.

"I thought we should start the evening with a celebration," Lucas said, as he followed me into the limo and sat next to me. "I've thought about you a lot over the years. You have no idea how happy I am that you've agreed to come out with me. This is a new beginning, for both of us."

He popped open a bottle of champagne, expertly keeping hold of the cork so it didn't go shooting off in a random direction. He poured out my second glass of champagne of the night and popped a strawberry into it before passing it to me. He did the same for himself then raised his glass.

"To new beginnings."

"New beginnings," I echoed, as we knocked our glasses together and took a large sip of champagne.

"I have to say, you look amazing, Milly," Lucas said, once again looking me up and down. "You're like a fine wine, only getting better with age. Clearly, motherhood suits you."

"Thanks. You don't look so bad yourself."

It was true. Lucas had always been attractive, but now he was approaching thirty, he was really coming into his own. He seemed larger, but the line of his suit showed off a body that was well defined as if he'd been working out a lot, filling out the wiry frame he'd had when we were at school together. He'd cut off his pony tail and the shorter cut really suited him, showing off his rugged jawline and fine features. His grey eyes were as intense as ever, and as our eyes met over the champagne glasses, I sensed a promise in them. Whether it was of a single night of passion or something more remained to be seen.

We made small talk until the limo pulled up outside the Taj Mahal, a high-end Indian restaurant on the other side of town. Although the place was usually packed out, thanks to the amazing food they served, we walked in to a completely empty room.

"I figured we could use some privacy," Lucas explained, "so, I booked every table."

Typical Lucas, I thought. *Always has to make some kind of grand gesture when just being himself would be more than enough.*

The head waiter, Dave, stepped forward to welcome us. I'd eaten here enough times that I knew all the staff and Dave was a sweetheart.

"Lovely to see you, Ivy," he beamed. "I had no idea you would be accompanying Mr Donatello this evening. Would you like your favourite table tonight? As you can tell, you can choose to sit wherever you like."

"Could we sit somewhere at the back, please, Dave?" I requested. Usually, I liked to sit by the window and people watch the passers-by, but although I knew I couldn't keep news of my date quiet for long, I wanted to keep things discrete for as long as possible.

"Of course, Ivy. Follow me." Dave made a little bow with his head and led us through the restaurant and out to a raised section in the back. He gestured to a small table tucked away behind a pillar and I gratefully took a seat where no one would be able to see me from outside. Dave lit the candle in the middle of the table and gave us both a menu.

"Would you like something to drink?" he asked.

Lucas nodded to me to choose.

"Could we get a bottle of red?" I said.

"Of course." Dave did his little bow again and went off to fetch the wine, as Lucas started to examine the menu. I didn't bother – I'd eaten here enough that I knew what I wanted.

"I can't decide between the lababdar chicken or the prawn pachranga," he said.

"Go with the chicken," I advised. "I'm having the chicken razzala. Their chicken is always divine – it just melts in your mouth."

"Chicken it is, then."

Dave came back with our wine. He poured it out for us, took our orders and left us on our own again.

"So, how are you finding it as head of the Academy?" I asked.

"Interesting," Lucas replied. "You think you know what to expect, but the Academy's unlike any other place I've ever worked."

"If you don't mind me asking, how did you end up in teaching? You never spoke about wanting to go into teaching and I had no idea this was what you wanted to do. I thought you were going to go into the Donatello family business and continue making more millions."

Lucas laughed, a little embarrassed. "It's a bit of a long story."

"That's okay. We've got all night." Intrigued, I picked up my wine glass and settled back in my chair, making it clear that I wanted to hear the story of how he ended up as head.

"After everything fell to pieces with Ivy, I *did* take up the position of CEO of Donatello Holdings," Lucas told me. "I mean, there was no reason for me to stay round here if I wasn't with Ivy and given what happened to Solomon, I figured it was better if I made myself scarce for a while. It turned out that I have a really good head for business and under my leadership, the company went from strength to strength until it was practically running on autopilot.

"But something was missing. Sure, making lots of money is great, but it wasn't enough. I wanted something more fulfilling. With all my money, I could have done anything, so in the end, I decided to set up my own Academy in Italy. We award scholarships to gifted children from deprived backgrounds who would benefit from a private education and it wasn't long before the Academy was inundated with applications. Not only did we give a first-class education to all our students, those which showed promise were given positions within Donatello Holdings, helping to grow the business with dedicated young talent."

"But didn't you need to go to university to qualify as a teacher to do that?"

"Not when it's my own school." Lucas shook his head. "Private institutions can set their own rules."

"So that's how you got the head position at King Academy?" I asked. "Despite your lack of experience?"

"That's right," Lucas confirmed. "Although they advertised for someone with more experience than me, when they saw the results I'd achieved at the Donatello Academy, as well as the fact that I was a former pupil myself, the Board decided to take a chance on me."

"And you didn't have to bribe your way into the role?"

Lucas had the good grace to look embarrassed. "I may have made a generous donation when I applied for the position."

"Jenny must absolutely hate you," I said. "I bet if you hadn't done that, she'd have been given the job, so I suppose I should be grateful."

Lucas leaned forward. "Between you and me, Jenny didn't stand a chance. Even if she was the only applicant, the Board would have found someone, *anyone*, to take her place. They thought she would step up if they gave her a chance, but Jenny managed to alienate just about every single member of staff."

"You got that right." I snorted.

"Two valuable teachers had already resigned because they didn't want to work with her and they wouldn't wait for her replacement to arrive," Lucas said. "The Board didn't want to risk losing anyone else and face having to find an entire staff at short notice. So, when I showed up, they were practically falling over themselves in relief. Jenny wasn't happy, but I pulled a few strings and got her a headship down south. Who knows? Maybe the change of scenery will inspire her to do better."

"It would be nice to think so, but something tells me she'll continue to be her annoying self," I said.

Lucas shrugged. "It doesn't really matter if she does. She's someone else's problem now."

Dave came up to us with our starters.

"One hot butter devilled shrimps for the lady." Dave put my

plate in front of me. "And a spicy squid for the gentleman. Enjoy!"

He bowed and backed away, leaving us to enjoy our meal. One bite, and Lucas closed his eyes, moaning with pleasure.

"Jeez, that's good," he said. "If this place had been open when I was living here, maybe I would have stuck around for the food."

"Yeah, Dinesh, the chef, is amazing," I said. "Apparently she used to cook for her family and never considered cooking professionally. But when Ivy was holding an event, her caterers let her down at the last minute. She couldn't find anyone at such short notice, but one of her secretaries suggested she contact her aunt and ask if she could come in. Dinesh was that aunt and she managed to work miracles with what Ivy had in her kitchen. When the night was over, Ivy insisted that Dinesh should go pro so that more people could experience her food. Dinesh's children were all grown up by that point and she'd been feeling at a loose end, so when Ivy offered to invest in a restaurant for her, Dinesh agreed. Ivy's still a silent partner in the business, but she lets Dinesh handle everything. Although most restaurants go bust within the first couple of years, this place has gone from strength to strength. People travel for miles to eat here and they're usually booked solid for weeks. They always set aside a table for Ivy, and she lets me use it when I want to come here. Not that I go out all that much. I usually get a takeaway and eat at home with Amber."

"Amber likes curry too?"

"She's an absolute fiend for it!" I laughed. "She can't get enough of the spicy stuff. But what I want to know is how you managed to get the entire restaurant to yourself when I have to pull strings to get just one table."

"It's like you said. It's all about who you know," came the enigmatic answer.

I looked pointedly at him.

"All right." Lucas shrugged sheepishly. "I got my assistant to ring round everyone who had a booking tonight and buy their table from them. People were more than happy to make a couple of grand just to stay home and enjoy a takeaway."

"So it's who you know *and* a ton of cash," I said.

"Exactly," Lucas said. "Maybe it's not the most ethical thing to have done, but I wanted to spend some quality time with you without having to deal with the noise of dozens of other people talking in the background. I heard this was the best curry house in town, so I did what I had to do so we could enjoy a night out together. I want to get to know you again, Milly, start from the beginning as if we were strangers."

"We pretty much *are* strangers," I pointed out. "When we were at school together, you were married to Ivy and aside from the occasional dance together, we didn't exactly get to talk much. That night in the club... well. Talking was the last thing on either of our minds."

"True, true."

We'd finished our starters and Dave came to whisk our empty plates away, expertly laying out the things for our next course in record time. Soon, we were alone again.

"So, if you want to start from the beginning, why don't you start by telling me what you've really been doing for the past few years?" I said. "I don't believe you've been nothing but a teacher. You're Lucas Donatello. Scheming is practically in your DNA."

Lucas laughed. "I don't blame you for being suspicious, but I promise you, I've been focused on my Academy. Most of the time."

"And there it is." I slapped the table, leaning back in my chair. "What have you been doing with the rest of the time?"

"Figuring out where I came from," was the surprising reply. "I don't know if Ivy told you, but I'm adopted. I've been trying to track down my birth mother to find out where I really come from."

"Seriously?"

Lucas nodded.

"You'd think with all the money I have, it would be easy to

find my family, but despite hiring the best detectives in the world, there's been no trace of my mother."

"Maybe there's a reason for that." I spoke gently, reaching out to put my hand on Lucas's. "Has it occurred to you that she might be…"

"Dead?" Lucas shrugged. "Of course, it's possible that's why I haven't found her. I mean, I know very little about her except that she was willing to give me away in exchange for money. Sometimes I wonder whether she spent it all on drugs and alcohol and wound up dead with a needle in her arm."

"And how would you feel if that's what happened but you could never know for sure?"

"I guess I'd just keep doing what I've always done – live with it." Lucas took a sip of his wine. "But my gut tells me that's not what happened to her. It wasn't the only fantasy I had about her, you know. Sometimes I'd imagine that she used the money to get back on her feet, started a business, became a success in her own right and the only reason she didn't come looking for me was because she didn't want to ruin my supposedly perfect life."

"Another poor little rich boy?" I arched an eyebrow, not wanting to let Lucas have an easy ride.

"Maybe that's how it was for your brothers, but life really was hell with Penelope Donatello." Lucas toyed with his cutlery, not meeting my gaze.

"Did the billionairess take parenting lessons from Joan Crawford?" I laughed, but it tailed off when I saw Lucas's expression. "Wait. Did Penelope abuse you?"

"I don't like to talk about it much," Lucas said. "In fact, the first person I ever told was Ivy. It doesn't help the Donatello brand for it to be common knowledge that I have a weakness."

"It's not a weakness to have been abused."

"If people see you as a victim, it's a weakness." Lucas clenched his jaw, still not looking at me.

"Do you want to talk about it? It might help."

Lucas said nothing for a while, but just when I was about to change the subject, he spoke up.

"Penelope adopted me when I was eight," Lucas told me. "Everyone told me how I lucky it was that I was going to be living with someone so rich, but I knew things weren't going to be as perfect as they seemed when the first thing Penelope said to me as we drove away from my foster home was that if anyone asked, I was her nephew who had moved in with her after the death of her sister in a car accident. If anyone found out the truth, she'd send me straight back to foster care – and make sure that I'd be somewhere far worse than the place I'd just left.

"Thanks to Penelope, I learned how to cry on cue, so if anyone asked me about my sister, I'd burst into tears so I wouldn't have to say anything that might give away the truth about where I came from. Fortunately, there weren't that many people around to ask. Penelope might have been rich but she wasn't exactly popular and we were so busy traveling the world that we were rarely in any one place for long enough for people to get suspicious about who I really was.

"Maybe if we'd stayed in one place longer someone would have noticed that things weren't quite right. I was always starting fights but Penelope just called it the typical Donatello spirit. I don't know if you noticed the scars on my back when we slept together."

I nodded, remembering the feeling of raised skin beneath my hands as I clung to him.

"Penelope gave those to me because I 'only' got a merit in my piano exam. She beat me so hard I had to sleep on my front for days because my back was so sore and she promised that she'd do the same again if I ever got anything less than top marks in an exam. She said I was the symbol of Donatello achievement and I was letting down the family name to be anything less than the best.

"I knew she meant what she said, and I never got less than an A after that. It's why I graduated the Academy with straight As and why I've been able to bring out the best in my students. I know how to motivate people – *without* the scars."

"I'm so sorry, Lucas." I could feel tears welling up in my eyes.

"It is what it is." Lucas leaned back in his chair, taking another sip of his wine. "Penelope's been gone a long time now and I have the freedom to do whatever I want. For all her wealth, she couldn't cheat death and I know how much she resented that in the last few months of her life. She got worse in the last year or so of her life. She resented me for my youth and the fact that I was going to take over the business she'd worked so hard to build and she would have absolutely no control over me. To be honest, I thought she would disinherit me in one final act of cruelty. When they read her will, I was expecting to hear that she'd left everything to an animal charity, but she made me sole heir – under the guidance of Solomon Archaic. He had control of my trust fund until I was 25, which is why I wound up marrying Ivy. Solomon manipulated me into believing an alliance with the Archaics was the best way to take the business forward. After his death, my trust fund was in the hands of the lawyers. They told me that they would make decisions in accordance to what they thought Penelope would have wanted, which was hilarious. They had no idea what a bitch she really was, so they didn't realise that they were being way more generous than she ever would have been! Still, when I hit 25, it was a relief to be completely in control of my life and not have to run every little decision past a man in a suit."

"So, you set up your Academy and started to look for your birth mum?"

"Exactly." Lucas nodded. "I wanted to help kids who might be suffering the way I did and looking for my mum gave me hope that maybe there was someone out there who would love me for me. I want to hear why she gave me away. If she did it because she thought I would have a better life with Penelope, I can't blame her for that, even if she made a huge mistake in going to Penelope. Maybe I'll have a connection with her, finally get the family I always wanted."

"You already have a family," I reminded him. "You've got Amber... and me." I gave him a meaningful look.

Careful, Milly. Lucas could just be playing you.

I'd promised myself I'd keep Lucas at arm's length until he'd proven that he was committed to being a proper father to Amber, but hearing his story melted my heart. If it was true – *right, Milly. If it was true!* – it explained a lot about why he was the way he was. He seemed genuine about wanting to help the students at the Academy and I knew from Ivy that he'd handled their arranged marriage with dignity and grace, never pushing her into doing something she didn't want to do.

I'd always been attracted to Lucas and now maybe, just maybe, I had the chance to do something about it.

"Would you like to see the dessert menu?" Dave came back to clear away our empty plates.

"I think I'll just have a coffee," Lucas replied. "But you're welcome to have something if you like, Mills?"

"Coffee's fine for me," I said.

"Coffee it is." Dave smiled as he took away our dinner things. Soon after he was back with two freshly made coffees. He placed them in front of us, as well as a generous slice of chocolate cake and two forks. "I know you said no dessert, but Dinesh insisted you have a piece of her cake on the house. She made it today and I can tell you from personal experience, it is to *die* for!"

"Thanks, Dave." I smiled. "And say thank you to Dinesh as well. I know how amazing her cakes are."

As Dave backed away, I picked up a fork and broke off a piece of cake. Placing it in my mouth, I closed my eyes as the creamy chocolate melted over my tongue.

"It's even better than Dave said it was," I gasped. "You *have* to try this, Lucas!"

Without thinking, I put a piece of cake on my fork and reached across the table to feed it to Lucas. As he leaned forward to take it, I realised how flirtatious a gesture it was and my heart skipped a beat. I was really enjoying our date, but I still wasn't sure whether I wanted to take things to the next level. I couldn't remember the last time I'd been out with a man and at the back of my mind, I thought about what it would be like for Amber if I started seeing her father only for it to not work out. It wasn't fair on her to put her through that.

"You look very serious all of a sudden," Lucas remarked. "I didn't realise my opinion about the cake was so important to you. If it reassures you, yes, the cake is very good."

I could feel my cheeks going red. "I was just thinking."

"What about?"

I gulped and took a deep breath. "Us. Where... *this* is going." I waved my hands around, making a circular 'you and me' gesture.

"Where do you want it to go?"

"Oh, Lucas. You always did know how to put a girl on the backfoot." I laughed nervously. "Where do *you* want it to go?"

"Well, I don't want to waste your time with a fling if that's what you're asking," he said. "I'm getting to an age where I don't want to bother with a relationship if I don't think it has a future. At the same time, you're Milly Knight and I'm Lucas Donatello. We both have to tread carefully. I don't enjoy seeing my love life splashed all over the tabloids, so if we're going to move forward, I think we should take things slow, see how we both feel. Does that work for you?"

"Yeah. Sounds great." I faked an enthusiasm I didn't feel. I couldn't help the little bit of disappointment that ran through me. Okay, maybe it was a bit much to expect for Lucas to profess his undying love for me on our first date, but I'd have thought he'd be a little more passionate and a little less calculating than this. I wanted him to be carried away with desire for me, willing to do something stupid because that's how I made him feel. I wanted him to want to take risks for me, like the Lucas who'd taken me home that night.

Maybe I was better off putting an end to this before someone got hurt, because it was obvious that that someone would be me.

As we drove home, Lucas regaled me with stories about some of the students he'd had in his Academy. I laughed at the appropriate places and made sympathetic noises when necessary, but I wasn't really fully engaged. I kept going over what Lucas had said about taking things slow. The more I thought about it, the more I realised that slow was the last thing I wanted. It had been too long. I needed a man in my life and I wanted Lucas *now*.

We pulled up outside my house.

"Thanks for a lovely evening, Lucas," I said, trying to hide my disappointment, covering it up with a frosty tone. "We must do it again sometime."

"Definitely."

Lucas leaned in to kiss me, but I wasn't in the mood and I turned my head, leading to an awkward kiss on my cheek.

"See you at work tomorrow."

I scrambled out of the car and hurried into my house before Lucas could say anything in return. If he wanted to take things slow, I was going to show him just how slowly I could go.

Chapter Seventy-Seven

Lucas

I slumped back in my seat, annoyed with how quickly an incredible night had gone south. What had I said wrong? I wanted to build a future with Milly so I'd been careful not to say anything to scare her away. Didn't all women want to hear that a man wanted to take his time with her, get to know her, lay down solid foundations so a relationship could have a long-term future?

If only she knew that I'd spent the night wondering what she looked like under that sexy dress. Motherhood suited her, making an already amazing body even more curvaceous. I wanted to run my hands all over her, make her come so many times she lost count, until she was begging for me to stop.

But I couldn't do that to her, not yet. I needed to prove to her that I meant it when I said I was in it for the long haul. Sleeping with her on our first date would undermine everything I was trying to achieve. We had a daughter together and I was determined to give her the family I never had and that could only happen if Milly and I got serious. I'd made too many mistakes in the past to risk messing this up.

So why had she acted so weird at the end of our date?

I shook my head. I didn't think I'd ever understand Milly, no matter how long I knew her, and that's what intrigued me about her. I wanted to spend the rest of my life learning all about her. She was the kind of woman a man would never get bored with.

"Take me home." I pressed the button to switch off the intercom after giving the driver his instruction. Leaning back in the seat, I closed my eyes, wondering what my next move should be. I had one chance to get this right and I was determined not to blow it.

"YOU HAVE A COUPLE OF VISITORS, LUCAS."

Liz, my secretary, buzzed through to my office where I was working on a report for the Board about how I was going to improve the Academy's grades. For the past couple of years, exam performance had been disappointing and one of the reasons they'd hired me was because my own Academy had consistently excellent results, even with students who weren't naturally academic. They wanted me to emulate that success and restore King Academy to its rightful place at the top of the league tables.

I frowned, bringing up my calendar. "I don't have any meetings booked. Who is it?"

"Ivy Archaic and Archer Knight. They say it's important."

I sighed. This visit wasn't any real surprise, but I'd thought I'd maybe get a bit more time before Ivy and her gundog came to see me. "Better show them in, Liz."

I put on my most professional face as Liz ushered in Ivy and Archer. "Would you like any coffee?" she offered.

"No thanks." Ivy shook her head. "This won't take long."

"Okay. You know where I am if you need me." Liz backed out of the room, gazing at me meaningfully. I knew she was trying to send me a psychic message that she could always call security if I needed, but that wasn't going to happen. I'd changed since the last time I'd dealt with Archer. He wasn't going to scare me away this time.

"I hear belated congratulations are in order," I said. "I hear that Louis is a cute kid. If you were worried about getting him on the waiting list for our nursery, you really don't need to be. It should be obvious that any child of yours automatically has a place with us."

"Cut the shit, Lucas," Archer snarled. "You know why we're here."

"Milly's a big girl," I said calmly. "I'm sure she wouldn't thank you for interfering. Again. Did you ever tell her why I left?"

"You left because you knew full well you were playing her. All I did was make sure you didn't have a chance to break her heart."

Ivy reached out, putting a hand on Archer's thigh to ground him. "That's enough." Her tone held an unmistakeable authority, a reminder of just whose daughter she was. She turned to me. "We didn't come here to fight, *did we*, Archer?"

"No." Archer spoke between gritted teeth.

"In fact, Archer's got something to say to you."

I arched an eyebrow, not bothering to keep the smug grin off my face as I turned my attention to Archer.

"I'm sorry."

"What was that?" I leaned forward, dramatically cupping my ear as if I couldn't hear properly. "I didn't quite get that."

"I'm. Sorry." Archer enunciated each word clearly and deliberately so there was no way I could pretend I didn't understand.

"And what are you sorry for?" Years of running schools and dealing with recalcitrant students allowed me to put just the right amount of patronising into my tone.

"I shouldn't have told you to stay away from Milly."

The truth was that Archer had done the right thing for his

sister, but I wasn't going to give him the satisfaction of telling him that.

"It's good of you to admit that." I steepled my fingers, resting my chin against them. "But I'm not so concerned about the past as I am about the future."

"Archer and I have been talking about that," Ivy said. "Milly doesn't know the reason why you left the last time and we both think it would be better if we were to keep it that way."

"Do you, now?"

"Which is why we have a proposition for you," Ivy continued. "We will let you and Milly keep dating if you don't tell her what happened before."

"You'll 'let' me, will you?" I snorted. "I think you'll find that Milly's a grown woman who can make her own decisions."

"Yes, she is," Ivy conceded. "But we all know that we could make life very difficult for you. I'm her best friend. There's plenty of things I could tell her which would end any hope you have of a future with her."

"And if that isn't enough, I know Declan and Romy would be more than happy to assist me in running you out of town," Archer added. "Not that I'd need any help. You never could see things through when push came to shove."

"Is that right?" I wasn't going to tell Archer that things had changed somewhat since we'd last met. He'd always relied on his fists to make his point, but I'd been training and if things got physical between us, he wasn't going to find it as easy as he thought to beat me into submission.

"But that's not going to be necessary, *is it*, Archer?" Ivy glared at him. Archer rolled his eyes and shook his head.

"No," he said. "As long as Lucas treats Milly and Amber with the respect they deserve we won't have any problems."

"I think I can safely say I have nothing but love and respect for both of them," I said honestly. "You don't have to worry about them. I have every intention of doing the decent thing."

"You'd better," Archer snapped. "Because if you doing anything to hurt my sister or my niece, there'll be hell to pay.

And this time when you leave town, it'll be for good, if you know what I mean."

I knew exactly what he meant. The one thing everyone knew about Archer was that he didn't make empty threats. I was sure that if I stepped out of line, Archer would make sure no one could find my body.

Fear wasn't exactly the best motivation when it came to building a relationship, though.

"I can't believe you genuinely think this is the best way to protect your sister," I said. "Don't you think she has a right to figure things out for herself? Do you really think she'd thank you for interfering in her love life? After all, isn't that the reason why you're here – so she won't find out that you're the one responsible for her becoming a single mother?"

Archer clenched his fist and slowly released it and I knew my words had hit their mark.

Ivy glanced at him before leaning forward to address me directly. "You're right, Lucas. Milly's a big girl and she has a right to make her own mistakes. Even if everyone else can see that it's a mistake. And if you do your best to make Milly happy but it doesn't work out, that's no one's fault and no one will blame you, will they, Archer?" She nudged her partner with her knee. "Will they?"

"No, they won't," he muttered. "But if Lucas turns out to still be the arsehole he always was, then I reserve the right to beat him to a pulp. Does that sound fair?"

"Fine with me." I shrugged. "I've got absolutely no intention of playing any games and my daughter deserves to know her father. I know I wish I'd had that chance."

"Then I guess we're done here." Ivy smiled and stood up, Archer following her lead. I stood up too, mirroring her body language. "It's genuinely good to see you again, Lucas." She reached over my desk to shake my hand. "You're right. Amber should get to know her father. I hope that whatever happens between you and Milly, you make sure that little girl remains the centre of your world."

"She already is," I promised.

Ivy and Archer walked out of my office without a backwards glance. I sat back in my chair, slowly swivelling from side to side. There was no way I was going to be able to work on those reports any time soon. My head was reeling with the implications of what just happened. The fact that they didn't want Milly to know they'd interfered in her love life gave me leverage.

Leverage I might just be able to use to my advantage.

Chapter Seventy-Eight

Milly

"Do you think Daddy will like my dress?" Amber came running in to the kitchen where I was sitting at the table doing some marking. It was the fourth outfit she'd put on that day and she did a little twirl, the skirt fanning out.

"I'm sure he'll love it," I said, barely glancing up from my work. If I could finish with these books in the next couple of hours, I could put my feet up and enjoy some child free time. Which would probably involve a glass of wine and a Netflix series, rather than going out anywhere exciting, but it would feel really decadent to do it in the middle of the afternoon. I might even really go for it and have a bubble bath. It would be wonderful to soak without having to get out every five minutes to deal with a screaming child.

"You're not looking Mummy."

I sighed and put down my pen and turned to see Amber's dress.

"You look beautiful," I told her. "Daddy is going to love it."

"Do you think so?" Amber's forehead wrinkled in a cute frown. "Maybe I should wear my Hello Kitty dress. It's my favourite."

"Amber, I really don't think Daddy will mind what dress you put on."

"I'm going to put my Hello Kitty dress on." Amber turned and raced off.

I rubbed my head to stave off the dull ache that was starting. It appeared that Amber had inherited my indecisiveness when it came to outfit choice. Until I had her, I had no idea just how wearing it was to have to give your opinion on every single item in someone's wardrobe. As soon as she was old enough to dress herself, she'd drive me nuts by going through ten changes of clothes in a day. I remember apologising profusely one night to Ivy for all the times I'd made her sit while I figured out what I was going to wear. She just laughed and said that's what friends were for, but I'd still tried to cut back on how long Ivy had to wait for me to decide what I was going to wear.

My date with Lucas had seen me revert back to old habits. I was beginning to think it was a mistake even considering starting something with him.

The doorbell rang, interrupting my thoughts.

"Daddeeeee!" Amber screamed and ran to the front door, any idea of changing her clothes instantly gone. Having learned her lesson, she waited by the door, impatiently jogging from one foot to another as she waited for me to catch up with her.

When I saw Lucas standing on the doorstep, my heart skipped a beat and I knew I was in trouble. Much as he drove me crazy, he had an effect on me made me want to forget about everything and drag him off to bed. It wasn't that he was wearing anything amazing – he was in jeans and a T-shirt which had a picture of a bone on it with a slogan that said 'I found this humerus.' But it was the way he wore it, the outline of his well-defined muscles visible through the shirt, and his body language reminding me of just how confident he was in bed.

"Look at my dress, Daddy!" Amber pushed herself between us and performed another little twirl. I was grateful for the distraction. It took my mind off wondering whether Lucas looked as good naked as I remembered.

"It's beautiful." Lucas leaned down and picked up Amber, carrying her inside. "Now, are you ready to have fun?"

"Yes!" Amber practically screamed the word and I winced, hoping she hadn't just deafened Lucas.

"I thought I would take you to see my house," Lucas said. "I've got lots of surprises there for you."

"Yay!" Amber scrunched up her fists and waved them in the air. She was so cute!

"Are you coming with us?" Lucas's invite took me by surprise.

"I thought you wanted to spend some quality time alone with Amber?"

"I do and I will. But I thought you might like to come along this first time, make sure that you're happy that my home is sufficiently child proofed."

I bit my lip gazing across at the stack of books I still had to work through. I really should stay behind and finish marking them. I was going to be up all night catching up otherwise and I could think of better ways of spending a Saturday evening.

At the same time, the thought of spending more time with Lucas was tempting, very tempting. I hadn't had a chance to speak to him since our date except a very brief text exchanging confirming this afternoon's play date. Maybe hanging out together doing some normal family things would be good for us.

"Okay." Lucas's face lit up and I smiled right back at him. "Just let me go get changed. I'm not exactly dressed for an afternoon playing with Amber."

"You look fine to me," Lucas said. Was it my imagination or was there a little leer in his eyes?

"I'll only be five minutes," I promised. "Why don't you take Amber out into the garden and play?"

"Okay." Lucas carried Amber off in the direction of the garden, jogging her up and down to make her laugh.

I hurried upstairs, wondering whether I should phone Ivy for advice on what to wear...

Don't be silly, Ivy. You're not going to bother Ivy over something as stupid as this!

But what did you wear for a date-not-date with your daughter's father where you wanted to look good, but not like you'd made any effort?

I pulled open drawers, tossing tops onto the bed as I rejected one after another for not being quite right. In the end, I decided to go with my favourite pair of jeans teamed with a dark blue blouse with ruffles at the neck. I loved the jeans because they hugged my bum and made me look like I had the perfect hourglass figure while the blouse meant that if we ended up doing something messy, it wouldn't show the stains too badly. The fact that it outlined my breasts in a way that was subtle yet sexy had nothing to do with my decision...

I slicked on a bit of lip gloss and mascara, quickly bundling up my hair in a messy bun. Pulling out a couple of tendrils for that tousled look, I nodded with satisfaction at my reflection in the mirror.

"Not too shabby."

I headed back downstairs and out to the garden where I found Lucas pushing Amber on the swing.

"I'm impressed." Lucas looked over his shoulder at me when he heard me coming. "You said you'd be five minutes and were only ten. That must be a record."

"Oh, shut up," I said affectionately, coming to stand next to him. Amber was loving having her dad push her on the swing and she giggled, kicking her legs as she shouted for him to push her higher.

"We need to go," Lucas said, grabbing hold of the swing and expertly bringing it to a halt.

"But I was having fun." Amber pouted. "Can't you push me a little bit more? Just a couple of pushes?"

"If I do that, there might not be enough time for me to show you everything I've got at my house for you," Lucas warned.

"Let's go!" Amber didn't need to think twice as she ran back inside as fast as her little legs would carry her.

Lucas reached for my hand and I let him take it, the pair of us walking leisurely after our child. We didn't talk. I had nothing to say and Lucas seemed content to enjoy the moment, but it felt good to feel like I was in an actual relationship with someone who wanted to do the little things like walk hand in hand together.

"What took you so long?"

Amber was standing by the front door with her coat on all ready to go, impatiently waiting for us to catch up.

"You're just too quick for me," I told her. "Mummy's old and can't walk very fast. I can't keep up with you. You know you run faster than lightning!"

"I do, don't I?" Amber said proudly, immediately mollified by the compliment.

"So are my two favourite girls ready for an afternoon of fun?" Lucas asked, as he opened the car door for Amber to get in. There was a booster seat all ready and waiting for her and he strapped her in while I got in the front passenger seat. Once he'd secured Amber in place, Lucas got behind the wheel.

"No driver today?" I asked.

"I felt like enjoying a family drive with no interference," Lucas replied, starting the engine. "Besides, it's probably a good idea that Amber experiences more normal ways of getting around in riding in limos all the time, keep her grounded, you know?"

"You're the one who drives in limos," I countered, bristling at the implication I'd spoiled her. "Amber and I very rarely use them unless it's a special occasion."

"Grandpa has a limo," said Amber from the back seat as Lucas pulled out. "He says it's the only way a Knight should travel. I like Grandpa's limo. It's got lots of sweets in it!"

"Yes, and Grandpa knows that you're not supposed to have

too many sweets," I said darkly. "If he's keeping a stash in his limo for you, I'll have to have a word with him."

"Uh-oh. Sounds like Grandpa's in trouble."

Amber laughed at Lucas's joke as we drove out of the Knight estate and headed in the direction of his house. One of the reasons why I'd agreed to come along for the afternoon was because I was curious to see where Lucas lived. The Donatellos weren't one of the Big Four families in King Town, so he didn't own any of the ancestral land which traditionally belonged to the Houses. The estates were a show of status and only the Big Four were allowed to live in the large mansions set in acres of land. While there were other impressive properties in the town, these were reserved for those who held high status within the Houses, and I hadn't heard of anyone selling any of those large homes. I couldn't see Lucas living in the suburbs, though.

I gazed out of the window, trying to guess where we might be going from the direction we were heading. We seemed to be driving towards the Archaic part of town, but that didn't make any sense. Ivy wasn't going to give her ex-husband a home on her estate. Lucas and Amber were too busy singing *The Wheels on the Bus* for me to ask him where we were going, so I watched the scenery passing by, waiting for us to arrive at wherever it was we were going.

It wasn't long before Lucas turned off the main road and went down a narrow country road. I crossed my fingers and hoped we wouldn't encounter a car coming in the opposite direction. I didn't relish the idea of having to reverse all the way back to where the road was wide enough to pass. However, the road was deserted and we followed it until it ended in a large, wrought iron gate. Lucas pressed a button on the top of the dash and the gate slowly pulled back, letting us in. Lucas slowly nudged the car forward until the gate was completely open, then he followed the road a little further until we came to a large house with a number of outbuildings. Lucas pulled into a garage next door to the house and switched off the car engine.

"Here we are," he announced. "Home sweet home."

"I had no idea this house was here," I told him. "My father pays attention to all the property sales in the area and I'm sure he would have jumped at the chance to buy something on the outskirts of Archaic land."

"Who says I bought this place?" Lucas asked, as he got out and went round to get Amber out of her seat.

Frowning, I went round to his side of the car as he lifted Amber out and set her down on the ground. She ran towards the house. "What do you mean?"

"I didn't buy this property," Lucas told me. "Solomon gave it to me. When he died, Ivy inherited the bulk of his fortune, but there were a few little secrets she didn't know about. Before he died, Solomon had told me he wanted me to have a little bolt-hole where I could keep an eye on Ivy without her knowing if our marriage ran in trouble. Very few people know this place even exists. I don't keep any staff here – the drivers collect me from the flat I have in town which is the address I use for official correspondence. This is where I come when I want some privacy. It's perfect for my time with Amber. No one knows she's here, so she's perfectly safe, but obviously, as her mother, you need to know where she is when I have her. I'd just ask that you respect my privacy and don't tell anyone about this place, for Amber's safety if nothing else."

"Your secret's safe with me," I promised. "But you don't need to worry about Amber. No one would dare do anything to the daughter of the Knight heir."

"She might be an important member of the Knight family, but she's also a Donatello," Lucas pointed out. "There are plenty of people out there who hated Penelope and think I shared her values – or rather, her lack of them. I was brought up to be paranoid about kidnappers and it was drummed into me that I should never trust anyone, even family friends. I had a code word I had to give the driver and it changed every day. Penelope would text it to me just before the driver picked me up so there was no chance that someone could find it out and trick me into going with them by knowing the word. Even with all these safeguards in place, I was very nearly snatched one time."

"Seriously?" I gasped.

"Yep." Lucas nodded grimly. "It was when I was 15. Penelope had sent me to a boarding school for a term because she thought it was important for me to mix with my peers. I always thought the real reason she sent me away was because she was fed up with being a mother and wanted a break from dealing with a teenager. Whatever the reason, that term was one of the happiest times of my life. Although I was bullied by some of the other kids, it was nothing compared to the way Penelope had treated me and I wanted to stay there until I was too old for school.

"However, one night I was woken up by a strange sound. I had a private room, so I was all by myself and I woke up to find two men standing over my bed. I cried out and one of them put a cloth over my mouth to stifle my shouts. I wasn't going to let them take me easily, so I started kicking and lashing out. Years of using my fists to make a point came in handy and I punched one of them right in the groin. He doubled over in pain and I was able to hit the panic button by my bed. An alarm sounded and the two men realised they were going to have to leave without their prize. They ran away and although the guards searched the grounds, there was no sign of them. Penelope pulled me straight out of the school of course. She said she should have known she couldn't trust anyone else to take care of me properly."

"That's awful." I couldn't help but feel for Lucas. The more I learned about his childhood, the more it made sense that he'd run out on me after our night together and it explained why he wanted to take things slow. Anyone who'd been through what he had would have commitment issues. It was going to take time for him to see he could trust me and I decided that I was going to give him that time.

Lucas shrugged. "To be honest, with all the crazy things I went through while I was living with Penelope it was pretty much normal for me. But there's no way I'm going to let my child suffer the way I did. If it means I have to be a little paranoid and hide her away from my enemies when she's with me, that's what I'll do. I'll do whatever it takes to keep her safe."

"Hurry up, Daddee!" Amber stood by the front door, jogging from one foot to the other as she waited for us to catch up with her. "I want to see my bedroom!"

"All right, munchkin." Lucas laughed as he swooped down on her, picking her up and swinging her high before setting her back down on the ground. He unlocked the front door and pushed it open. Bowing low, he gestured to Amber to go inside. "After you, milady."

Amber skipped into the house and I followed close behind, just as curious as my daughter to see what Lucas's house was like inside.

The front door opened into a short corridor with doors to the left and right of us which appeared to lead to a lounge and a dining room. After a couple of metres, it opened out into a larger reception room, with stairs to the right leading up to the first floor. There were more doors off this part of the room, but they were shut so I couldn't see what was behind them.

"Your room's on the first floor," Lucas told Amber. "It's right next door to mine."

"Can I see it?"

"Of course!"

Lucas took Amber's hand and the two of them went upstairs. I stayed where I was, wanting to look around a little more. Lucas's tastes were more conventional than I'd have expected. There were landscape paintings hung on the walls and a closer look at one confirmed my suspicions: it was an original Constable. It was the kind of place that looked understated in that way that only someone with a large amount of money could pull off, with expensive antiques and solid oak furniture.

"Mummy! Come and see my room!" Amber's voice echoed down the stairs.

"Coming!"

I walked slowly up the stairs, not sue I wanted to see how much effort Lucas had gone to to win my daughter's affections. For all his talk of wanting her to lead a normal life and not be spoiled, it was pretty clear he was willing to spend money on creating a beautiful home and he knew that the best way to a little girl's heart was to treat her like a princess.

Amber was waiting for me in the hallway outside her room. It was very clear it belonged to her because her name was spelled out on it in brightly coloured, wooden letters. She was grinning from ear to ear, clearly delighted with whatever was inside.

"You have to see this, Mummy!" She ran over and took my hand, pulling me along and into her room.

"Wow." I stopped dead in my tracks when I saw what Lucas had done. I knew he was going to do something special, but I really wasn't expecting *this*.

The room was large, larger than my own bedroom, and the walls were painted with a mural that made it look like we were in the middle of a fairy tale kingdom. There was a large four poster bed in the middle of the room with layer upon layer of netting draped over the frame to create the perfect little hiding place for a small child. There was a rocking horse to one side of the room and on the other was a huge mound of soft toys, including another large teddy bear like the one currently occupying half of Amber's bed at home.

"Isn't it amazing?" Amber ran over to the bed and climbed up on it, jumping about like it was a trampoline.

"Don't jump on the bed, Amber," I warned.

"It's okay," Lucas said. "Let her have some fun."

"Can I have a word?" I gestured to Lucas for him to follow me into the hallway.

"What do you think?" he asked, clearly seeking my approval.

"I think you've gone way overboard," I said, his face falling at my words. "It's too much, Lucas. You were the one saying that you didn't want her traveling in limos because you wanted Amber to have a normal childhood and then you go and spend goodness knows how much money hiring an artist to paint that mural."

"No, I didn't," Lucas said.

"You can't mean you painted it yourself?" I did a double take.

"Is it so hard to believe?"

"Well… yes."

"Penelope said it was important for me to have an understanding of the arts, both in theory and practice," Lucas told me. "So, she hired a number of tutors to teach me music, art, and drama. In another life, maybe I would have studied art at university instead of being sucked into House politics and an early marriage. I don't get much time to paint these days, so it was a real honour being able to paint something for Amber. It was nice to put those skills to use for a change."

"You are a dark horse," I murmured as Amber ran out and threw herself at Lucas. She squeezed his legs tightly in a bear hug.

"I *love* my bedroom, Daddy," she said. "Thank you, thank you, thank you! I want to stay in it forever and ever."

I looked at Lucas and arched an eyebrow.

"I think Mummy might have something to say about that," said Lucas. "But you can come and stay here whenever you like. And if there's anything you want me to change, you just have to tell me."

"Nope." Amber shook her head violently. "I'm never going to change a single thing."

I suspected that might change when she was a few years older, but it was sweet seeing how happy Amber was and although I was annoyed that Lucas was going back on his wish to not spoil her, I could understand why he'd done it. If it got this kind of reaction from his daughter, it made sense that Lucas would want to bond with her through interior design.

"Are you ready for your next surprise?" Lucas asked.

"What is it, Daddy?" Amber bounced up and down, clapping her hands.

"It's outside. Come and see."

Amber took Lucas's hand and the two of them ran down-stairs. "Keep up, Mummy!" Amber called over her shoulder and I dutifully hurried after them.

Lucas went through one of the closed doors in the reception room which opened into a kitchen. He went to a door opposite and unlocked it, taking Amber out into the back garden.

Her squeal of delight practically made my ears bleed.

"A *pony*??"

"Oh, you didn't." I shook my head. This was a step too far.

"Doesn't every little girl want a pony?" Lucas grinned at me.

"Yes – until that little girl discovers how much hard work they are," I pointed out. "Have you any idea how many hours those things need?"

Lucas's face fell a little. "I thought it would do Amber good to have some responsibility."

"She's *four*, Lucas. She's a bit too young for that kind of responsibility." I folded my arms.

"All right. So I'll hire someone to look after it."

"Which then means that your little secret hideaway won't be so secret anymore."

"I'll make them sign an NDA."

"Lucas, you can't keep a secret pony! It's not going to work. You're going to have to get rid of it."

"It'll break Amber's heart." Lucas gestured to where Amber was stroking the pony's nose. It was a sweet little thing, brown with a sandy coloured mane, and it seemed very friendly, content to stand at the edge of the enclosure while Amber cooed over it.

"That's not my problem, Lucas. You were the one who bought the pony. You're the one who's going to have to deal with it."

Lucas sighed and ran a hand through his hair. "I'll figure something out," he said at last. "Still, the pony's here now, so we might as well make the most of it." He raised his voice. "Hey, Amber! Do you want to go for a ride?"

Amber nodded excitedly as Lucas strode over to her. Shaking my head, I slowly followed.

Lucas talked Amber through the process of putting a bridle on the pony and how to get it to stand still for the saddle – as well as how to make sure the saddle was properly tightened so it wouldn't slide off mid ride. He'd bought a riding helmet for Amber and soon she was sitting on the back of the pony as Lucas led it round and round the paddock.

I watched the two of them, leaning against the fence of the enclosure. Lucas was giving Amber advice on how to ride and she was listening intently to his every word, doing her best to follow his instructions precisely. I wished she'd listen to me as closely, but then I was her mother. I was the one who had to say no all the time. I was the one who'd been with her for her entire life, dealing with the dirty nappies and sleepless nights. It was easy for Amber to take me for granted and push the boundaries. She knew I would always be there for her. Lucas wasn't such a sure thing, so Amber was bound to be on her best behaviour with him, at least for now.

At last, Amber had had enough of riding the pony, although not before Lucas had taken copious photos of her sitting on it. He'd taught her how to sit properly while the pony was trotting so she wouldn't be bumped about in the seat and I was impressed by how natural she looked in the saddle. Maybe Lucas was on to something after all.

"Who wants some dinner?" Lucas asked.

"Me! Me!" Amber put up her hand excitedly.

"How do you fancy… pizza!"

"Yes! Yes! Yes!"

"Okay. Let's go wash our hands and then we can start making it," Lucas said.

"We're going to *make* the pizza?" Amber frowned. "Mummy always orders it."

"Making it's the best bit," Lucas promised. "How else are you going to make sure the toppings are exactly the way you want them?"

"So I can have whatever I want on my pizza?"

"Of course you can." Lucas smiled.

"Even banana?"

"If you want banana, anchovy and pepperoni, that's completely up to you," Lucas said. "You're the one eating it."

Soon, the three of us were gathered around the large table in the middle of Lucas's kitchen. He got out some dough he'd prepared earlier and showed Amber how to stretch it out to the right size before fetching a dazzling array of possible pizza toppings. He laid them out on the table so that we could help ourselves and the three of us set to work making our pizzas. I kept mine simple – mushroom, mozzarella, and spinach with a drizzle of garlic oil – while Amber piled on handfuls of chopped ham, sweetcorn, salami, pepperoni and cheese.

"Do you want to put banana on that?" asked Lucas.

Amber looked at her pizza, her face screwed up in concentration. "Do you think there's space?" she asked.

"We can always make space if you really want that banana."

Amber thought a little more than shook her head. "I think my pizza's perfect just the way it is."

I wasn't surprised to find that Lucas had had an actual pizza oven installed in his kitchen and he helped Amber put her pizza on a large shovel and slide it in to cook.

"It won't be long before it's ready," he told her. "Shall we go and pick out a movie to watch over dinner?"

I groaned when Lucas turned on his smart TV and flicked through to the Disney channel. I knew exactly what film Amber was going to choose. She'd seen it over a hundred times already and never got bored, even if I was happy to never watch it again.

"*Moana!*" Amber beamed and sat down in the middle of the sofa as Lucas found Amber's favourite film and put it on.

"I've never seen this," he said, coming to sit next to Amber. "Is it any good?"

"It's amazing, Daddy," Amber said seriously. "You're going to love it!"

I rolled my eyes and sat on the other side of my daughter so that she was sandwiched between her two parents. Amber was so engrossed in the film, she barely noticed when a timer went off on Lucas's phone to let him know that her pizza was ready. He went off and brought it back on a tray so she could eat without interrupting the film.

He also brought with him a bottle of red wine and a couple of glasses. After he carefully putting Amber's tray on her lap so she could eat, he stepped to the side and opened the bottle. He poured two glasses, passing one to me.

"I've put your pizza on," he told me.

"Shh!" Amber scolded him. "You'll miss the best song."

"Sorry." Lucas grimaced apologetically at me. He went back to his seat on the other side of Amber. She started to eat her pizza, her eyes never leaving the screen as Moana sang about how much she loved her home and her parents but still wanted to explore the world beyond her island. I couldn't help myself mouthing along with the words. I'd heard the song so many times I could practically sing it backwards, but Amber never got tired of it and I had to warn her not to sing with her mouth full otherwise she'd have been doing her very best Chloe Auli'i Cravalho impression.

When *Moana* had finished and the pizza was all gone, Amber insisted on watching *Frozen 2*. I'd always thought it was a better film than the original, so I was glad she picked that one to show Lucas as I slouched back in the seat and closed my eyes. Another film I'd seen so often I could recreate it in my mind without needing to see the screen, I'd often used this excuse as a cover for taking a sneaky afternoon nap when Amber had worn me out, the two of us snuggling up together in my bed to watch a film together.

"You okay?"

I opened my eyes again as Lucas gently nudged my shoulder.

"Fine," I said.

"It's just that you were snoring…"

"I was not!" I looked over to see that *Frozen 2* was almost over. It was entirely possible that I had actually been asleep and I blushed.

"It's okay. Amber's out for the count so you didn't ruin her enjoyment of the show."

I looked down to see Amber curled up against Lucas, her head in his lap.

"You know you're stuck there for the next few hours, don't you?" I smiled.

"I don't mind. It's nice that she feels relaxed enough with me to do this," Lucas said. "It's the perfect end to the day. It's been good, hasn't it?"

"Yeah. It has." I could almost kid myself we were a normal family. "Even though you're going to break her heart when you tell her the pony has to go."

"Nah." Lucas shook his head. "George and me are best friends. He's not going anywhere. Besides, what I didn't tell you earlier is that he doesn't actually live here. His regular home is at a stable not far from where you live so you can take Amber to see him whenever she likes. So you see you didn't have to worry about how he was going to be taken care of. I'd already sorted it."

"You could have told me."

"I *could*... But then I wouldn't have had the fun of seeing you get all worked up in righteous indignation at the thought I would randomly buy a high maintenance animal just to impress a four-year-old."

I opened my mouth to argue then closed it again. "I suppose I deserve that," I said at last. "I'm sorry, Lucas. This is hard for me. I'm doing my best."

"I know. It's hard for me too," Lucas said. "Discovering I had a daughter I didn't know about was a real shock and the chances are high I'm going to mess up at this parenting thing more than once. That's why I need you to tell me when I get it wrong – but also cut me some slack and don't assume the worst. I'm doing my best to make this work."

"Yes. You are. And I appreciate it."

For a moment, I thought Lucas would lean over to kiss me, but Amber snorted and writhed a little in her sleep, reminding me of the child between us.

Another time.

"Look, I know it's not what we agreed, but would the two of you like to stay overnight?" Lucas asked. "I'm happy to wake Amber up and drive you both home if that's what you prefer, but it seems silly when there's a bedroom literally with her name on it upstairs. I have plenty of spare rooms you could use."

I looked down at Amber. She looked so peaceful sleeping there. Much as the sensible thing to do would be to assert my boundaries and go home, I hated the idea of disturbing her as much as Lucas seemed to.

"We'll stay," I decided.

Chapter Seventy-Nine

*L*ucas tucked Amber up in her four-poster bed. She'd barely stirred when he'd moved to pick her up and as he dropped a gentle kiss on her cheek, she smiled in her sleep but didn't open her eyes.

We tiptoed out of her room together and Lucas quietly pulled the door shut behind us. He gestured to me to follow him and he led me to a room a couple of doors down. Opening it, he revealed a simply furnished bedroom.

"This is where you'll sleep tonight. Unless..."

"Unless what?"

"You could stay in my room if you prefer."

He looked at me, trying to keep his expression neutral, but he was unable to keep the hope out of his eyes.

I could feel my heart pounding so hard I thought it might burst, but my tone was light when I replied.

"I'd like to stay with you."

Without Amber around, there was no need for Lucas to hide his leer as he reached out for my hand. I gripped his hand tightly as he took me away from the spare room and into the room at the end of the hall. He turned to me before he opened the door.

"Are you sure about this? I don't want you to feel pressured into anything or like I'm taking advantage of you."

"Lucas, I might have had a couple of glasses of wine, but I'm hardly drunk. You're not taking advantage of anyone. Now shut up and kiss me before I change my mind."

Lucas growled and pulled me to him, kissing me hungrily like he hadn't been with a woman for years. I didn't know whether that was true or not, but it had been a long time for me and the sensation of a man's arms around me fulfilled a need I'd forgotten I had.

Lucas fumbled at the door handle, pushing the door to his bedroom open. We made our way into the room together, still kissing as Lucas kicked the door shut behind him. I let him take the lead as we made our way across the room, clumsily heading towards the bed, our legs tangling with each other.

I yelped as he pushed me onto the bed, giggling as I lay there.

"You have no idea how long I've imagined this moment," he told me as he pulled off his shirt. I propped myself up on my elbows so I could enjoy a better view. Damn, he looked amazing. He'd clearly spent many hours in the gym and the past few years had seen him bulk out in a good way. I could feel myself clenching with the memory of our night together. In this moment, I didn't care about the future. Maybe this was the biggest mistake of my life, but I deserved this. I needed some happiness, the reassurance of a man's body next to mine.

I needed Lucas.

"Take the rest of your clothes off," I told him. Lucas grinned, and started to quickly undo his trousers. "*Slowly.* I want to enjoy the view."

Lucas gave me that look, the one which had got me into trouble all those years ago. He turned his back on me and looked over his shoulder as he unzipped his fly. He wriggled his butt a bit and shimmied out of his trousers to reveal buttocks closely hugged by his briefs. Tucking his hands into the waistband of his pants, he pulled them down a little to tease me with a glimpse of more before pulling them back up. He turned round to face me again and this time, he pulled them all the way down, stepping out of his pants and kicking them across the room.

He stood in front of me, his impressive cock standing to attention. I knew he was well endowed, but I'd forgotten just how big he was and I licked my lips in anticipation of the pleasure to come.

"Come here." I reached out to him and he tumbled on top of me, the pair of us lying on the bed, kissing passionately. The feel of his naked body against me while I was still fully clothed was such a turn on. I knew what was coming and my body was crying out for him to love every inch of me. it had been too long since I'd been with a man, let alone someone like Lucas who knew exactly how to please a woman.

"I think I should get a condom, don't you?" Lucas asked when we eventually broke apart.

"Yeah, that's a good idea."

He reached over to his bedside cabinet. Pulling open the drawer, he retrieved a condom and quickly slipped it on. I started to unbutton my blouse, but Lucas reached out to stop me.

"Not just yet," he said. "Let's have some fun first."

He helped me up and we stood facing each other gazing into each other's eyes. Lucas's expression was pure sex and the way he was devouring me with his eyes, I knew I was going to have a great time.

Suddenly, Lucas spun me round and pushed me forward so that I was leaning over the bed. He reached round me and undid my jeans. He pulled them down just enough to give him access to me, and he rammed into me. Leaving my jeans on meant that my movements were limited and all I could do was arch my back, angling myself towards him so that he hit me at the perfect angle to make me scream.

"You are amazing, Milly." He gasped and I could feel his cock throbbing, pulsing in that way he did right before orgasm.

I moaned, my cries mingling with his as he exploded into me before collapsing onto my back.

He lay there panting, unable to speak as he recovered from what was clearly a huge orgasm.

"I'm so sorry, Mills," he said at last, gently stroking my head, running his hand down my hair and down my back in a loving gesture. "I wanted to make it last, but it's been a while since I've been with anyone and you're just so damned sexy."

I was surprised to hear he hadn't had sex for a while. The Lucas I'd known had never been without a woman for long. After his marriage to Ivy was annulled, he'd worked his way through a number of women before leaving King Town, leaving a string of broken hearts in his wake. I'd assumed he'd continued to do that, so it was a revelation to hear he'd tamed his ways a little.

"Don't worry. You've got the rest of the night to make it up to me," I told him, glancing over my shoulder at him.

"I will. Believe me, I will," Lucas promised, as he pulled out of me. "The night is still young and I've got plenty of stamina. I'm just going to clean up a bit. Make yourself comfortable and I'll be right with you."

He dropped a quick kiss on the top of my head and padded off to the ensuite to get rid of the used condom. I heard water running as I pulled off my jeans. I undid my blouse and lay back on the bed, almost naked, as I artfully arranged my blouse so it covered my breasts but revealed enough of my body to titillate.

I put my hand between my legs, lightly playing with myself to stay turned on until Lucas came back. I was so wet, the lightest touch sent jolts of electricity through my body.

That was the effect Lucas had on me.

I wouldn't feel brave enough to lie there, touching myself in front of anyone, but he made me want to push my limits, explore the edges of my sexuality and beyond. This couldn't be just another one-night stand. It just couldn't.

"Well, hello there."

I turned my head to see Lucas coming out of the bathroom, fully erect again as he walked towards me.

"This is a sight for sore eyes." Lucas came round to stand at the bottom of the bed. I writhed a little, smiling as I opened my legs further, knowing how erotic I must look wearing my unbuttoned blouse and nothing else. "I think it's your turn to enjoy yourself."

Lucas knelt down, grabbing hold of my legs and pulling me to him so he could bury his face in my sex. He put his arms around my thighs, holding me in place as his tongue flicked out and cover my clit. I cried out, the pleasure almost too much to bear. I felt like I was too turned on to come, that I was going to go insane before I would get my release.

I reached down and gripped a handful of his hair, holding him against me as his tongue continued to work its magic. Sometimes he used the flat of his tongue to run all the way over me from bottom to top in slow, confident movements. Other times he used the tip to flit about, tracing little circles around my clit or teasing the tip, making it dance. I was completely lost, so out of my mind that I was caught my surprise when an orgasm ripped through my body. I practically screamed while Lucas continued to go down on me, wringing every drop of ecstasy out of me.

At last he broke away, a smug grin plastered across his face. "I love it when you react like that," he said. "I think we need to do it again."

"Are you kidding me?" I pretended to be horrified, but inwardly, I was delighted at the thought that Lucas wasn't anywhere near finished with me.

He walked over to the bedside cabinet to get another condom. As he put it on, I lay back on the bed, ready for another round of pleasure.

"Hmmm." Lucas frowned. "I think it's your turn to be in charge, don't you?"

He came and lay down next to me and gestured to me to

climb on top. I didn't need to be asked a second time and I mounted him, grabbing his cock and guiding it inside me. It was a good thing I was so wet because he stretched me almost to where he was too big for me to cope. Girth was not the word and he was happy to let me sit there, adjusting to the sensation of a huge cock deep inside me.

After a while, lust took over and I started to rock forwards and backwards, subtle movements having a big impact as Lucas's cock hit me in all the right places. He was more than happy to lie back and let me take charge and he gripped my thighs with his hands, letting me decide the pace.

I leaned forward, my breasts right in front of his face. He let go of my thighs and fondled my tits, taking one of my nipples in his mouth with his hand played with the other one.

He started to thrust his hips to match my movements, closing his eyes to savour the moment. We fit together so perfectly and I loved the satisfied look on his face as we became more urgent in our movements.

I sat up, feeling the need to give Lucas the ability to fuck me deeper. I bounced up and down on him, my body welcoming in every inch of his beautiful cock as it hit my G spot over and over.

It was incredible, the sex the best I'd ever had as I started to come, losing myself in multiple orgasms so intense I could barely tell when one ended and another one started.

I could feel my pussy clenching his cock tightly and he clutched at my thighs as he finally came with me, the pair of us crying out in release.

At last, we were done and our bodies slowed and stopped. I was still panting as I ran a finger down his chest, not having the words to express how I felt, but knowing that I needed to make some kind of gesture to show him how much I appreciated what we'd just done.

"Was that okay?" Lucas asked.

"Meh." I shrugged, looking away nonchalantly. "It was okay."

"Is that right?" I squealed as Lucas grabbed me and we rolled over so that I was lying underneath him. "I suppose I'll have to try harder then."

"If you must," I murmured. Lucas leaned forward to kiss me and I knew I wasn't going to get much sleep that night...

Chapter Eighty

"ummy! Where are you, Mummy?"

I was jolted awake by a panicked screaming. For a moment, I was as disoriented as Amber sounded, the sensation of waking up in someone's arms so alien I wasn't sure I wasn't still dreaming.

"What is it?" Lucas sounded half asleep, as I leaped out of bed and hurried pulled on my clothes.

"Amber needs me," I said. "You stay there. I'll deal with her."

I ran out of the room and down the hallway to where Amber was standing outside her room, rubbing her eyes and looking for me.

"What's wrong, darling?" I asked anxiously. "What's happened?"

"I thought I saw a spider in my bed."

"You know that Daddy is very good at dealing with spiders," I said, my heart sinking at the thought of having to hide my arachnophobia for long enough to rescue Amber from an eight-legged beast. All those years as a single parent meant that I'd learned to suck up my fear so Amber wouldn't see how much I hated spiders in the hope that she wouldn't be as scared of them as I was, but she'd still developed a phobia about them but didn't realise that it was just as hard for me to deal with them.

"But Daddy isn't the one who puts spiders outside. *You* are."

"Come on, then." I sighed. "Show me where this spider is and I'll tell it to stay out of your room."

I took her hand and she pulled me into her room. "It's over there." She pointed at the wall by her bed. I took a deep breath and went closer to see if I could spot it.

"Sorry, darling. There's nothing there," I said at last. "I think you must have scared it away with all your screaming."

"Is everything all right?" Lucas came into the room.

"There was a spider, Daddy," Amber told him. "It was going to eat me up!"

"Really? It must have been a big spider."

"It was *huge!*"

"Let's go get some breakfast and you can tell me all about it."

Amber and Lucas went downstairs. As I went to follow them, a huge, hairy creature skittered across the floor. I bit back a scream and fled. We were in Lucas's house. It was his problem to deal with it.

"I didn't know what you liked for breakfast, so I got a whole heap of things for you to choose from."

I walked into the kitchen to find Lucas opening up cupboards to show Amber a dizzying array of cereals, including her favourite – chocolate Cheerios. Soon she was happily munching on a large bowl piled high with chocolate cereal. I dreaded to think about what she was going to be like when the sugar rush kicked in.

"What would you like to eat?" Lucas asked me.

"Just coffee for me, thanks. I can't face food this early in the morning."

Lucas went to his coffeemaker and switched it on.

"I've been thinking," he said. "I'd like to take Amber out today, maybe over to King's Castle."

"King's Castle?" Amber gasped when she heard the name of a local farm zoo. As well as a number of animals you could pet, there were fairground rides suitable for small children and a boating lake you could ride paddle boats on. "Yay!" She started jogging up and down in her seat.

Yep. The sugar was kicking in. King's Castle was probably a good move. It was about the only she was going to be able to work it all off.

"You'd be very welcome to join us, but I was wondering how you'd feel about me taking her by myself?"

Lucas's suggestion threw me. After our night together, I'd thought he'd want to spend more time with me. I know he'd said he was inviting me as well, but he didn't seem like he wanted me there.

Fine. If he wanted to play games, he'd could play them all on his lonesome.

"Sure. You and Amber need some quality time together and it would be nice to have a bit of a break."

"That's what I thought," Lucas said. "I mean, you work hard all week. You deserve the chance to put your feet up and not have to worry about Amber for a few hours."

"Sounds great." I faked a happiness I didn't feel, but Lucas didn't seem to notice.

"Excellent! I'll drop you off at yours on the way to Kings Castle."

"Actually, could you take me to Ivy's?"

Lucas frowned a little, but quickly recovered. If he didn't think I was going to want to talk to my best friend after last night, he was an idiot.

"No problem."

We spent the next hour or so playing happy families. Anyone watching us would have thought we were a perfectly normal family. At least Amber certainly thought her parents were getting on like a house on fire, which was a testament to my acting abilities.

Inwardly, I was a mess. Lucas seemed to be behaving like

nothing had happened between us and it was driving me crazy. How could he just write off a night like that as not worth talking about?

By the time we were ready to leave, I couldn't wait to get out of there. If Lucas wanted to play things cool, he was going to discover I could be ice cold.

Chapter Eighty-One

"Is everything okay?" Lucas asked as we pulled up outside Ivy's house.

"Absolutely peachy," I said, getting out of the car.

"Milly? What's wrong? You've barely said a word all morning."

"You be a good girl for Daddy." I ignored Lucas as I went round to the back of the car and opened the door so I could give Amber a kiss goodbye.

"I will," Amber promised, her eyes wide and serious.

"We're going to have a lot of fun together, aren't we, Amber?" Lucas said.

"Yay!" Amber kicked her feet against the car seat and I slammed the car door shut. I blew a kiss at the car and waved as Lucas drive off.

The vindictive side of me hoped that Amber was an absolute nightmare in the way that only an annoying four-year-old could be, but I had a feeling she was going to be a little angel for her beloved Daddy.

It just wasn't fair.

I knocked on Ivy's door.

"Milly!" My best friend opened the door and was surprised to see me standing there.

"Hey, Ivy. It's not a bad time is it? I can go home if you want me to. Well, you'll have to let me borrow a car, but I can leave if you've got something else on."

"Of course not. Don't be silly. Come in, come in." She ushered me inside. "What's wrong? Where's Amber?"

"I agreed to let Lucas have her for the day," I said.

"So it's going well with him then?"

I looked at her. "I think I've made a big mistake."

"Let's go to the conservatory and we can talk about it." She raised her voice. "Romy! Can you deal with Louis for me? Ivy's here."

"Sure!" Romy, one of Ivy's partners, called back from somewhere in the house.

"You look like you need tea," Ivy observed. "Or something stronger. Do you want something stronger?"

"I want it but I don't think it'll be a good idea," I told her. "I'd probably end up crying into my glass."

"That bad, huh?"

"You have no idea."

We went through to the conservatory and Ivy picked up the intercom to order some tea from the kitchen. Soon there was a tray of tea things on the table while Ivy and I sat in chairs with incredible views over the Archaic estate.

"Do you want to tell me what's up?" Ivy asked. "Actually, don't. Let me guess. You slept with Lucas."

I nodded miserably.

"Oh, *Milly*. What were you thinking?"

"I wasn't really. It's been so long since I've been with anyone and I never did get closure with Lucas. One thing led to another and here we are."

"How was it?"

"The best sex of my life." I slumped back in my chair, sighing. "Lucas and I have such chemistry. He does things to me no one else ever could. If it was crap, I could probably cope. I'd feel like I'd scratched an itch and I could move on. But it was so good, I want more. The only problem is, I don't think Lucas feels the same way."

"What makes you say that?"

I glared at her. "Am I with Lucas and my daughter having a nice family day out?"

"Ah."

"You'd think I'd learn, wouldn't you?" I said. "I mean, after last time, I promised myself that I'd play hard to get, but that went out the window the second he showed me any kind of affection. I'm pathetic."

I buried my face in my hands. I could feel Ivy moving to crouch next to me, lightly rubbing my back to comfort me.

"You're not pathetic, Mills. Don't be so hard on yourself. You deserve a bit of happiness after everything you've been through. It's Lucas who's being pathetic. If he can't see how amazing you are that's his loss, not yours." She paused. "But please tell me you used protection."

I raised my face to look straight at her. "Credit me with *some* sense."

"Okay, okay." Ivy put her hands up in a gesture of direction and moved away to sit back down. "Just checking. I know how easy it is to get carried away." She blushed and I narrowed my eyes.

"Ivy, you're not..?"

"It's too early to say for sure, but I think I might be pregnant." She blushed shyly. "I haven't told the boys yet. We weren't meant to be trying for another baby until Louis was a little older, but sometimes you just have to go with the flow."

"That's wonderful news!" It was my turn to hug her. "I'm so happy for you."

"Don't tell anyone, will you? Especially not the boys. I want to be completely sure before I break the news to them."

"They're going to be so excited. They're all amazing dads. It's all I ever wanted for Amber, a proper dad who'd take her out, come to her dance recitals, be as excited as I am about everything she does. Instead, I'm stuck with Lucas Donatello."

"Lucas seems like he wants to make up for lost time with Amber, though, doesn't he?"

"For now." I glowered. "But it's Lucas. How can say how long he'll stick around before he gets bored? Heck, he was doing a pretty good job this morning of acting like someone who'd fed up with me already. It felt like he couldn't get me out of there fast enough."

"What exactly happened, Mills?"

I took a deep breath, bracing myself to share my sorry story. "Lucas invited me to spend the afternoon with him and Amber at his house yesterday."

"That's a good sign, isn't it?" Ivy said. "He could have just taken Amber and left you out. He probably wanted to reassure you that Amber was safe with him."

"Maybe. Or maybe he just wanted to show off the pony he bought Amber, try and make me look bad in front of her."

"He bought her a *pony*?" The usually unflappable Ivy raised her eyebrows, her voice squeaking.

"Yeah."

"Talk about buying his way into her affections." Ivy snorted. "Still, that's likely to bite him in the bum when Amber gets bored of the responsibility."

"That's exactly what I said. He reckons he's found a stable where they'll look after it for him."

"All right, so he made a big show of flashing his cash about. Then what happened?"

"We had a pretty good afternoon," I admitted. "It felt right for us to be together, like we were a real family. So, when Lucas invited me to stay the night, I didn't really think about it. I was just going with the flow. And it was *so* good, Ivy. But then I woke up."

"Sounds about right where Lucas is concerned." Ivy nodded, knowing all too well what Lucas was like.

"He stuffed Amber full of sugary cereal then told me he

wanted to take her to King Castle by himself. Okay, he did say I could come along if I wanted, but it was pretty obvious he didn't want me there."

"How was it obvious?"

The question took me aback. Now I thought about it, it actually wasn't all that obvious. "Well, he didn't want to spend the day with me."

"How do you know?"

"Because I'm not with him right now!" I was so frustrated I could have cried.

"But you said he did ask if you wanted to go along, right?"

I nodded.

"What exactly did he say?"

"That I deserved to have a break from Amber and put my feet up."

Ivy sucked air in between her teeth. "I hate to say it, Mills, and you know that I'm not exactly Lucas's biggest fan, but maybe he really did think that you might like to have a day off from parenting. I mean, Amber's adorable and I love her to bits, but she can be a handful. Lucas might have expressed himself badly, but it is entirely possible he was just thinking that it would be nice to spend some time bonding with his daughter while you got to relax."

"You really think so? Why?"

"Did he have to invite you along yesterday afternoon?"

"No. We'd agreed he could have Amber by himself."

"Right. So he asked you so that you could have that family time together and let you know that Amber was safe while she was with him. I bet he didn't plan for you to spend the night. He's probably feeling as confused as you are by what happened and needs a bit of space to clear his head. But he *did* ask you if you wanted to go with them. Much as I completely understand why you're feeling the way you are, I think you ought to give him the benefit of the doubt, at least this time. Yes, it was rushing it to fall into bed with him so quickly, but I don't think anyone can blame you for needing a bit of sexual relief. You've been living like a nun for the past few years!"

I smiled. "Not quite. There was that one guy a couple of years ago…"

"What, the one who lasted five seconds, rolled over, farted, and fell asleep?" We both laughed at the memory, frustrating as it had been at the time. "I don't think he really counts."

"You really think I should give Lucas a chance?"

"I think you should at least talk to him," Ivy said gently. "See how he's feeling and what he wants. He might be regretting last night – or maybe he also thinks it was the best sex he's ever had. Maybe he's even as stunned as you are by what happened and he needs a bit of time to get his thoughts together and he thought it would be a nice gesture to take Amber out for the day so you could have some space. It's not like you can have any serious discussions with Amber running around. I agree he's handled the situation badly, but then he never was much of a diplomat. I'd wait until you've had a chance to talk about things before coming to any conclusions about his motives." She shook her head. "I can't believe I'm saying this about my ex-husband, but I genuinely believe that he was actually considering your feelings by giving you a day off from Amber. Lucas is doing his best to be the good guy. He just hasn't had much practice, so he's bound to make a few mistakes along the way."

I thought about what she said, nodding slowly. "This is why I needed to come and see you," I said. "I knew you'd be able to give me a different perspective on things. You're right. I should give Lucas a chance to explain himself."

"That's my girl." Ivy smiled. "You deserve this, Mills. Even if it turns out you just had a night of mind-blowing sex and you both go your separate ways, that's got to have been worth it, wasn't it? I mean, it was mind-blowing, wasn't it?"

"Oh yes." I could feel myself getting all hot and bothered just thinking about it. "I can't believe you never slept with Lucas while you were married. You really missed out!"

"Lucas isn't my type. Besides, three men is more than

enough for me, thank you very much. I've always thought the two of you would make a cute couple though. I always felt that Lucas had a crush on you but he was too afraid of my father to do anything about it."

"Really?" I couldn't keep the tone of disbelief out of my voice.

"Oh yes. I saw the way he looked at you when he thought no one was watching. I wasn't surprised to hear he seduced you during his short visit back to King Town. The only shock was that he hadn't done it sooner."

Chatting with my best friend worked wonders on my mood and by the time Ivy called for one of her drivers to take me home, I was feeling really positive about the future. When Lucas brought Amber back, I'd ask if he wanted to stay and help put Amber to bed. After she was safely tucked up, I'd offer him a drink and we could talk about what happened and what we wanted from each other.

I daydreamed all the way home, imagining what life would be like if I was in a relationship with Lucas. I pictured us sipping champagne in my hot tub, enjoying some adult time after Amber was in bed after another day filled with family activities. Lucas would step up to his parenting duties and I wouldn't have to be alone anymore.

By the time I got back to my house, I'd created this entire fantasy around being with Lucas. Okay, I'd let my mind run wild and I knew it would be better to take things slow, but for the first time in a long time, I felt positive about my life.

All that changed when I walked through my front door to find an envelope lying on the floor. There was no stamp, so someone had hand delivered it, and someone had written my name in block capitals so I couldn't get a clue from the hand-writing who might have sent it.

A puzzled frown wrinkling my forehead, I tore open the envelope to reveal a short note with four simple words written on it:

Lucas is hiding something.

Chapter Eighty-Two

Slowly, I walked over to the sofa and sat down. I read the note again, turning it over to see if there was anything else written on the back, but there was just that short sentence in capital letters.

What could it mean? The fact that Lucas was hiding something didn't surprise me. As the heir to House Knight, I was used to dealing with people who had secrets and at this stage in our relationship, of course there were going to be things I didn't know about him. He'd been gone for years. A lot could happen in that time.

What could be so serious that someone would go out of their way to send me an anonymous note though? It had to be something they thought was important, something that would make a difference to the way I felt about Lucas.

I was so engrossed in thought, I didn't hear the doorbell at first. It was only when someone leaned on it, making the shrill bell ring constantly that I jolted out of my reverie. Quickly, I folded the note and tucked it into my jeans' back pocket. I answered the door and found Lucas and Amber waiting for me.

"There you are, Mummy." Amber skipped into the house. "What took you so long?"

"I'm sorry, sweetie. Mummy was in the middle of something. Did you have a good day?"

"It was the *best!*" Amber launched into a long, detailed description of everything she'd done, but I wasn't really paying attention. Fortunately, four-year olds don't always notice when your mind's elsewhere and the occasional "uh-huh" seemed to be enough for her to think I was listening.

Lucas wasn't so easily fooled. "What's wrong, Milly?"

"Not now." I shook my head a little, gesturing at Amber with my head to let him know we could talk once she was out of the way. That took a little longer than expected. The novelty of having her father around was far from wearing off and she insisted on having Lucas help her with everything which took twice as long as normal. Amber really knew how to milk the moment for every piece of attention possible.

By the time she was tucked up in bed and we could talk I was exhausted and in no real state to have a serious conversation. I couldn't put it off though. I had to know what the note was about.

"I don't know how you do it," Lucas said, as I put the coffeemaker on. "Amber's amazing but she's exhausting! She's non-stop energy. One day and I'm struggling. I don't know how you've managed on your own all these years."

"I'm not on my own," I said. "Claire is a huge help, and my parents will take Amber whenever I need. Yes, it was exhausting in the early years, but after a while you get used to being permanently tired and it's just your new normal. I can't imagine what life would be like without her. Heck, I can't even remember what I used to do at the weekend before Amber came along. Probably slept all day and partied all night. I look back at my younger self and I wish she'd known what I know now. I'd have done so much more with that time."

"I don't know. I think you did all right," Lucas told me. "Most people with your background would have lived off the family money, but you went and qualified as a teacher and you've spent years helping your community."

"I'd rather be in a classroom than an office," I said. "Besides, Dad thought it would be a good idea for me to get experience outside the family business. Plus he said that if I can make positive connections with other Houses by being a good teacher, it'll help me further down the line when I take over."

"He's got a good point," Lucas said. "I always thought your father was the most effective of all the House leaders. Firm but fair, he's the reason the Knights always do well in their business dealings."

"It's a lot to live up to." I sighed. "I'll be honest. There's been plenty of times I wished Archer hadn't stepped down as heir. He'd be so much better than me."

"Don't be so hard on yourself." Lucas stepped forward and cupped my face in his hands so I had to look at him. "Your father knew what he was doing. He had plenty of children to pick from and he chose you because he knew that your compassion would help you make the right decisions while your intelligence would help you keep a clear head. You might not see it yourself, but I think you'll be a better head of House than Archer could ever be."

"Thanks." I smiled thinly and turned away, breaking our contact. It was lovely having someone to make me feel better when I doubted myself, but that note had made all my past fears resurface. Lucas always had a hidden agenda. How could I believe he truly meant what he said? "I'm going to make my coffee Irish. Do you want one?"

"Sure."

The coffeemaker had worked its magic and I poured out two cups. I added a sugar and a generous splash of whiskey to them both and topped them up with cream. I passed one to Lucas then led the way to the front room, where I sat in my favourite comfy armchair. If Lucas was disappointed that I hadn't sat on the couch so we could be next to each other he didn't show it as he sat on it by myself.

I cupped my coffee in my hands, staring at the creamy topping gently swirling around. Steam curled up, creating a mesmerising effect that gave me an excuse not to look at Lucas. All this talk of taking over the business from my father only reminded me how much I still had to learn before I could be confident taking over the helm. I hated confrontation, always had, which is why I was waiting to mention the note to Lucas but putting it off was only going to make things worse.

"Milly, I-"

"There's something I-"

We laughed awkwardly as we both spoke at the same time.

"You go." I gestured to Lucas.

"No, ladies first. What were you going to say?"

I inhaled deeply, slowly exhaling through my mouth. "I need to ask you about something and I need you to be honest with me."

"Sounds ominous." Lucas smiled.

"It is," I said.

Lucas's smile faded. "Whatever it is, Milly, I promise you I'll be truthful with you."

"What does this mean?" I took the note out from my jeans pocket and gave it to him.

Lucas read it and frowned. "I have no idea."

"Really? So there's nothing you're not telling me?"

"There's lots I'm not telling you Mills, just as I'm sure there's plenty you're not telling me," Lucas said. "I mean, you have no idea about the various businesses I'm launching over the next year or two, just as I don't know what's going on within House Knight."

"Lucas, If you're going to treat this as a game, you might as well leave now and don't bother coming back."

I made to get up, but Lucas gestured at me to stay where I was. "I'm sorry, Milly. I'm so used to being on the defensive all the time, it's an automatic reflex when I'm in a difficult situation."

"So you do know what the note means?"

Lucas read it again, grimacing. "Without more details, it's hard to say. I mean, it could be about my ex-girlfriend. We broke up not long before I came back to King Town and she didn't take it well. Maybe someone thinks I'm still with her, but I promise you Milly that my relationship with Tilda is well and truly over."

"Is that the only thing you can think of?"

Lucas ran a hand through his hair, sighing. "No," he final said. "There is something else. It was something I was hoping to keep to myself, at least until I had more information to go on."

"More information about what?"

"I have a sister, Milly."

"A sister?" Of all the things he could have told me, this was the last thing I expected.

"I only found out about her recently," Lucas said. "As you know I was adopted. Even if I hadn't been old enough to remember the adoption process, Penelope never let me forget how 'lucky' I was she'd swooped in and saved from the terrible life I'd been born into. I'd always thought my mother had died when I was little, which is how I ended up in care, but after Penelope died, I found documents which showed that my mother was very much alive. She'd put me in care because she couldn't look after me and had always intended to come and get me when she'd turned her life around. Instead, Penelope Donatello gave her money in exchange for giving up any hold on me. Since I thought my mother was dead, I didn't bother asking Penelope if we could go look for her."

As he spoke, Lucas kept his gaze firmly fixed on his coffee cup, like he was ashamed to meet my eyes. "Now that Penelope's no longer here, I'm free to find my biological family, but it's proving difficult to track my mother down. However, my investigators discovered that Penelope's money helped her turn her life around, at least for a while, because she had another child, my sister. I don't know her name. I know virtually nothing about her. What I *do* know is that she's in her final year at King Academy."

"She's at the Academy?" I gasped.

"Apparently so." For the first time, Lucas looked directly at me. "You can't tell anyone this but the real reason why I took the head teacher position was so I could find my sister. As head, I have access to all the students' information. I've been working my way through them, narrowing down possibilities so I can find my sister. I have a shortlist of five names and I've been doing a more in-depth background check on all of them to see if I can prove if one of them is my sister. Milly, this could be my chance to build a real family. I've been on my own all my life. Penelope was never really a loving parent. I was more of a fashion accessory to her than a son. I moved around too much to ever make proper friends. I can't trust anyone in my business because they're all looking to stab me in the book. Suddenly, I've gone from that to having a daughter, a sister… maybe even a partner."

His eyes were filled with a hopeful innocence that melted my heart.

"Five names you say?"

Lucas nodded. "Yes. They're the only girls whose backgrounds raise the possibility of being adopted or not being who they say they are. There's a lot of reasons why that might be. We both know that subterfuge reigns in King Town and plenty of families send their children to the Academy under a false name to keep them safe. I'm convinced that one of those girls is my sister."

"Okay." I thought for a moment, drumming my fingers on the arm of my chair. "I think I know how we can get that list down to one name. How would you feel about bringing in some outside help?"

"It would depend on who that was." Lucas was cautiously optimistic.

"My father knows *everyone* in this town," I told him. "We don't have to give him the full details. We don't even have to tell him that the girl we're looking for is your sister. But I can ask him to prepare a report on each of the names on your list and I guarantee that he'll be able to find the information you need to find your sister."

"You really think he can do that?"

"I *know* he can. Do you want me to call him?"

"Yes! Yes!"

I got my phone and called my dad. He answered within the first ring.

"Hi, Milly. Are you okay?"

"Yes, fine, Dad."

"And Amber's good?"

"Yes, dad. All tucked up in bed for the night after a weekend with Lucas." I glanced over at Lucas and smiled briefly.

"That boy's behaving himself, is he?"

"He's being a perfect gentleman."

"I'm glad to hear it. Because if that man hurts you again, I'll-"

"I know, Dad." I interrupted him, rolling my eyes. I'd heard this speech so many times I could recite it in my sleep. Dad had never really accepted that his daughter had grown up and could make her own mistakes and every single time I started dating someone he gave me a lecture about all the terrible things he'd do if my new boyfriend didn't treat me right. It was little surprise that he was sceptical about me seeing Lucas given our history, but at some point he was going to have to accept that I was a grown woman and let me make my own decisions.

"So, if Lucas isn't the problem, why are you calling me on a Sunday evening? You don't usually call me at this time."

"Look, we were talking about some of my students who've been having a few issues," I lied. "Lucas suggested there might be a problem at home, but their files seem to be lacking in detail. I was wondering whether you'd be able to do some digging for me, find out the full story about the girls."

"I can," Dad said. "But wouldn't it be simpler to call in their parents for a meeting?"

"We're doing that as well." I could feel myself blushing as I dug myself deeper into the lie. Thank goodness he couldn't see my face over the phone. "But Lucas and I both feel that if we had some more information, we can really help these girls achieve the grades they deserve. It's not long before they're due to graduate and it would be awful to see them leave knowing that they could have done so much better if they only had the right support."

"You're such a sweet person," Dad said. "That's one of your best features. You're always thinking about others. All right. Let me have the names and I'll see what I can find for you."

"Thanks, Daddy! You're the best!" I hung up and beamed at Lucas. "My dad's going to help us find your sister. Let me have the names you need to research and he'll get the information back to you ASAP."

"That's incredible! I can't believe it! I'm going to find my sister and it's all thanks to you."

He got up and crossed to where I was sitting. He grabbed my face between his hands, kissing me hard. "Thank you." He kissed the top of my head. "Thank you." He kissed my left cheek. "Thank you." He kissed my right cheek. "Thank you."

He kissed me on the lips, more slowly this time. I put my hand over his, opening my mouth to let our tongues intertwine.

"Do you want to go somewhere a little more comfortable?" Lucas murmured against my mouth. I nodded. He took my hand and led the way up to my bedroom. I closed the door behind us, locking it so that Amber wouldn't be able to run in on us.

Lucas sat on the edge of my bed and took off his socks and shoes. "Come here, beautiful." He held out a hand to me. I crossed over and stood in front of him. He reached up to the top button of my blouse.

"Have I..." He undid the button, lightly teasing the bare flesh beneath it with his fingers.

"Told you..." He undid the next button, running his hand down the front of my chest.

"That I think..." Next button, exposing more of me.

"You're the most..." Next button.

"Beautiful woman…" Next button.

"I've ever seen."

He undid the last button and I pulled my blouse off. Holding it out to one side, I let it drop to the floor and stood there wearing nothing but a bra and my jeans. I pulled down my jeans' zip and quickly shimmied out of them.

"Come here." Lucas pulled me towards him and I climbed onto his lap. As we kissed, I instinctively ground against him, the gentle friction titillating me. I could feel his cock growing larger beneath me and I couldn't help smiling at the effect I had on him.

"What's that grin for?" Lucas asked.

"Oh, I'm just thinking about how good we are together," I said. "I love how you make me feel."

"And I love you."

Wait – did he just say what I thought he'd said?

I had no time to process the thought though, as Lucas wrapped his arms around me and we tumbled back onto the bed together, me on top. He kissed me deeply and I ran my hands down his chest and up his shirt, enjoying the feel of his skin. He was pure muscle, courtesy of hours spent in the gym.

I could feel his hands moving to undo his trousers, and I sat up, pushing them away.

"You undressed me. I think it's only fair that I undress you."

"Yes, ma'am."

I moved down the bed, running my hands over Lucas's groin, a thrill of excitement running through me when I felt the size of the bulge waiting to be revealed. I tugged down the zip. Lucas lifted up his hips, making it easier for me to pull down his jeans, taking them off. His erection was more obvious with nothing but a pair of pants to conceal it, his cock straining against it, waiting for me to set it free.

"Don't leave me hanging, Milly…" Lucas bucked his hips a couple of times to let me know he was becoming frustrated.

"All in good time, Lucas. All in good time."

I pulled off his pants and sat back, admiring the view. I

didn't think I'd ever get tired of how impressive he was, the length and girth of his cock promising a girl a good time no matter what he did – and Lucas knew *exactly* what to do with it.

I moved next to him where I could get easy access to him and leaned forward, running my tongue over the head of his cock before taking as much of it into my mouth as I could. One of my hands lightly gripped his thigh, massaging it as my head bobbed up and down. My other hand worked his shaft, working with my tongue to drive Lucas wild.

He moaned and I could taste the sweet precum that warned an orgasm wasn't far away.

"Much as I hate to say it, you need to stop that." Lucas sat up and pushed me away, his cock large and throbbing as if in protest at Lucas stopping the fun. "I want to make sure you get the treatment you deserve before I even think about coming. Now, let's see about getting the rest of those clothes off."

I straddled him, reaching behind me to undo my bra. Lucas put his hands under the cups, caressing my breasts as I took off my bra and tossed it across the room.

"Absolutely perfect." He lightly squeezed one of my nipples, keeping it on the right side of painful. I closed my eyes and gasped as he played with me. I could feel my pussy throbbing, clenching in anticipation. I wanted him inside me, desperately wanted him to fill me.

My body was moving practically against my will as I writhed on top of him. I had to be naked. I couldn't wait any longer.

I climbed off him, briefly wriggling around to get rid of the last of my underwear. As I stripped, Lucas retrieved his wallet from his jeans. He took out a condom and put it on. I was glad one of us was thinking clearly. The way I felt right now, I was prepared to throw caution to the wind in the name of pleasure. That was the effect Lucas had on me – he made me want to take risks I wouldn't take with anyone else.

I lay back on the bed and Lucas lay next to me. He kissed me, his hand finding its way between my legs. I spread them wider, making it easy for him to start playing with my clit. As he started rubbing me, I practically came on the spot. He kissed me, and his fingers plunged into me, thrusting up to meet my G-spot, alternating between finger fucking me and touching my clit. He knew how to read the cues my body was sending to give me the stimulation my body needed. I had to grab a pillow and hold it over my face to stifle my cries, not wanting to wake Amber sleeping nearby.

My toes clenched, my body out of control as I dissolved into an orgasm so powerful I thought I'd go insane. Lucas kept his hand between my legs, the light pressure prolonging the pleasure until I sighed and put the pillow to one side, finally under control.

"Better?" Lucas arched an eyebrow.

"Uh-huh." I nodded. "But I'll feel even better if there's more where that came from."

"That's easily arranged." Lucas rolled on top of me, his cock easily sliding inside me. We gazed into each other's eyes, the visual contact adding to the intensity of how I was feeling. He started thrusting into me and I wrapped my legs around him, angling myself so he could go even deeper.

"We fit together so perfectly." I nuzzled my head into his neck, my arms around him holding him as close as possible. We were one being and I was completely lost to him. He completed me, filling those parts of me I hadn't even known were missing.

I wanted to do this for the rest of my life. No other man could ever make me feel like this. Now I knew why it was I'd stayed single for so long. No one else could match up to Lucas. He was my soulmate and if I couldn't have him, I didn't want anyone else.

Lucas's movements became more frenzied and I bucked my hips, matching my movements to his. As he came, it pushed me over the edge and I came with him, dissolving into ecstasy.

Lucas rested his forehead against mine, his eyes closed as he waited for his breathing to return to normal. At last, he kissed me on the lips before rolling off me.

"I'll be back in a moment," he said, padding off to the ensuite to get rid of the condom.

I lay there, my mind a whirl of thoughts. Part of me wanted to simply bask in the afterglow of incredible sex, but I couldn't let go of one simple thing: Lucas had said he loved me. Did he mean it? How did I feel if he did? Or was it something he'd said in the heat of the moment and was hoping I'd forget?

Feeling cold all of a sudden, I got under the covers. I heard the sound of running water from the ensuite and a few moments later, Lucas came back out to join me.

"You look very serious," he commented. "What's on your mind?"

"Not a lot."

"Uh-huh." Lucas climbed into bed next to me. "You can't kid a kidder, Mills. What are you thinking about?"

"It was something you said earlier."

"I said a lot of things earlier."

"I'm talking about when you told me you loved me."

"Ah. That. What about it?"

"Did you mean it?"

"Did I-" Lucas shook his head before reaching out with his arm so I could snuggle into his embrace.

I cuddled up to him, grateful for the fact that it meant we could talk without my having to look at him. I didn't want to embarrass myself if I'd said something stupid.

"What would make you feel I didn't mean it?"

"Well, we were right in the middle of having sex. Plenty of people say things they don't mean just to get what they want."

"And you think I needed to say that to get you to sleep with me? Because I don't recall having to say it last night to get you into bed."

I could feel my cheeks burning. "Maybe you were over-whelmed by what was happening between us."

"I won't deny that you were making me feel pretty darned amazing, but that's not why I said it. Look at me, Milly."

I shook my head.

"Look at me." He spoke gently as he put a hand under my chin and lightly nudged me up so I had no choice but to look at him. "Of course I love you, Milly. What man wouldn't? You're sweet, loving, an amazing mum, but you've got an inner steel that means you're nobody's fool. I look at Amber and I'm in awe of you for bringing up such a cute, smart kid all by yourself. If we can create someone like Amber together, I think we can build an amazing future. I'm going to say this again so you know I mean every single word: I. Love. You."

I could feel emotional tears pricking at my eyes.

"And I love you, Lucas. I always have, even when you were with Ivy. I just didn't think I could ever have with you, so I buried my feelings and hoped they'd go away."

"Well I'm glad they didn't. Because it would kill me to think you didn't love me the way I love you."

Lucas leaned forward to kiss me deeply and my world was complete.

Chapter Eighty-Three

J was used to early mornings thanks to Amber, but it wasn't my daughter who woke me the next day. It was my boyfriend.

Boyfriend. A warm glow spread through me to think that Lucas and I were officially dating. I'd dreamed of this day for so long and now it was finally here, I felt like pinching myself to be sure it was real.

Even so, waking me up at five was enough to test the patience of the most devoted of girlfriends.

"What's wrong?" Yawning, I got out of bed and went to the ensuite where Lucas was just finishing up.

"I'm sorry. I didn't mean to wake you. Go back to bed."

"Meh." I shrugged. "I'm always being woken up by Amber, but this is earlier than I'm used to. It's barely 6."

"I figured I ought to go home and get cleaned up before going to work," Lucas explained. "I've got an image to maintain, remember?"

"Yeah, I suppose you do." I went to stand behind him, putting my hands around his waist and looking at the two of us together in the mirror. "We look good together, don't we?"

"That's why Amber's so cute." Lucas dropped a kiss on the top of my head then swivelled round in my arms so he could hug me back. "We make a great couple. But for now do you mind if we don't tell anyone?"

"Sure." I fought to keep my smile straight, not wanting to let on that his words cut through me like a knife. I should have known Lucas wasn't being serious last night. I was his dirty little secret. Always had been, always would be.

"Hey, I don't mean it like that."

"Like what?"

"You're giving me a look like a wounded puppy who's just been kicked." He put his hands on my shoulders and looked me straight in the eye. "Don't get me wrong – I don't want to keep us a secret forever. It's just that with me being the head and you being a teacher and all the House politics on top of that, it makes sense for us to wait until we can make a proper announcement. I know how malicious some people can be and I'd hate for anyone to try and hurt you because of our relationship. Between you and me, once I've found my sister I'm planning on quitting as head anyway and if your dad is as good at finding information as you say he is, I'll be gone by the end of the term and nobody can write us off as another workplace romance."

"Okay." I hoped he meant was he said, I really did, but I'd been hurt a few too many times to take him at his word.

"Listen, Milly. If you want me to, I'll make an announcement over assembly this morning. I want to shout it out across the rooftops – *I love Milly Knight!*"

I shushed him as he raised his voice. "Don't wake Amber. What will she think if she knows you stayed over?"

"Ahhh." Lucas raised an eyebrow. "See? There *are* good reasons for us to keep our relationship quiet for the time being."

"Okay. You got me."

Lucas quickly finished getting ready and we tiptoed downstairs, wanting to make sure Lucas was gone before Amber woke up.

"I'll see you at work later." Lucas quickly kissed me and left.

"Who was that, Mummy?" As I shut the front door, I jumped at the voice behind me. I whirled round to see Amber.

"Oh, it was just a delivery."

Amber frowned. "So, where's the parcel?"

I mentally kicked myself for raising a child who was so quick witted. I'd always encouraged her to question everything, including me, but it was already starting to backfire at moments like now. I didn't want her to know Lucas had stayed over until I was a little more secure in our relationship.

I thought fast. "He had the wrong house. He was looking for Uncle Archer. I gave him the right address so Uncle Archer will be able to get his delivery. Now then, little madam, rather than you asking me questions about things which are none of your business, why don't we go and get you some breakfast? You've got a big day at nursery. It's your trip to the local aquarium, remember? Do you think you're going to see a shark?"

"Oooh, yes! Sharks!"

That was it. Amber was off, happily babbling away about all the sea creatures she was going to see at the aquarium. They'd been doing a project about the sea at nursery and she was really excited about being able to meet all the fish she'd been singing songs about for weeks.

Once Amber was in her stride, she didn't really need much input from me other than the occasional grunt and 'mm-hmm,' so I was free to process the discussion Lucas and I had had that morning. While it made sense for us to keep our relationship on the downlow for the moment, the second Amber found out about us, it was going to be common knowledge. I knew from painful experience that she couldn't keep a secret and had long since learned to keep any unflattering opinions or gossip to myself if Amber was within earshot.

While I was going to respect Lucas's wishes, with Amber around, I wasn't sure how long that could last.

· · ·

"HAVE a good day at the aquarium, sweetie." I gave Amber a kiss and cuddle before she happily trotted into nursery, waving her shark-shaped lunch box at all her friends. I'd seen it in a Facebook ad a couple of weeks ago and ordered it for her as a surprise. Her face when she saw it was a picture and I could have cried with how happy she was. She was going to have the best day trip ever.

"Be good!" I called after her, but I wasn't even sure she heard me she was so caught up in talking to one of the nursery teachers about all the fish she was going to see.

"She always is." Kym, another of the teachers overheard me and smiled reassuringly. "Amber's a little angel."

"For you, maybe," I said. "If I were to take her to the aquarium, I'd spend the day running after her, trying to keep up!"

"The children know to stick together when we go out," Kym reassured me. "Amber is buddied up with Daisy. They'll be holding hands the whole time and we have a high adult/child ratio, so she'll be with one of us at all times. She'll have a ball."

"I'm sure she will. Thanks, Kym."

As I walked away from the nursery, my phone beeped with a text. I pulled it out to see that my father had messaged me.

I have the name of Lucas's sister. Come and see me after work and I'll give you all the details x

Hands shaking with excitement, I quickly tapped out a reply.

That's amazing! I'll let Lucas know. We'll come by later x

I couldn't wipe the grin off my face as I hurried over to Lucas's office. I wanted to see his face when I told him my father had done what his investigators couldn't. His door was open and I knocked on it as I walked in. Lucas was tapping away on his computer, but when he looked up to see me, he got up and came to close the door behind me.

He pulled me into his arms and kissed me deeply.

"Wow," I said when we broke apart. "What was that for?"

"It's just the effect you have on me." Lucas shrugged. "You're going to have to get used to the fact that ever time you walk into my office, I'm going to want to kiss you. In fact, I have a rather large desk and we could…" His voice trailed off as he raised his eyebrows suggestively and nodded his head towards his desk.

"No, we couldn't. I've got class in ten minutes and I need to get ready," I reminded him. "But I have some news. Dad's found your sister."

"You're kidding?" Lucas grabbed my arms, then spun away from me, biting down on his fist to contain his happy cry.

"I would never kid about something like that," I told him. "Dad said that he'll give us all the information he's got if we go and see him tonight."

"That's incredible! I can't believe he found her so soon. I'll have to do something nice for your dad to say thank you."

"Don't worry – I'm sure Dad will find a way of making sure you pay him back." Knowing my father, he'd extract a very high price from Lucas, although the way Lucas looked right now, I really didn't think he'd care.

"What's the earliest you can get out of here?" Lucas asked.

"Amber's on a field trip and they're not due back until five," I told him.

"Five?" Lucas's face fell. "Can't you get Claire to pick her up?"

"Normally I would, but she's on leave this week. There isn't enough time to get to my dad's and back before I'm due to pick her up. I'm sorry, Lucas, but you're going to have to be patient just a little while longer. You've waited this long to find your sister. A couple of hours isn't going to make any difference."

Lucas sighed. "You're right. I just really want to find my sister, you know? All this time I thought I was alone in the world and it turns out that I have a family after all, a real one. She'll be able to tell me all about my mother – she must have so many stories to tell. I can find out about where I came from. You have no idea how much it means to me to be able to learn things I never thought I'd know. I want to give my sister a big hug and tell her how much I love her, even though we've only just met."

"I get that." I smiled at Lucas. It was hard for me to under-stand what he was going through. Growing up in a large family, there were plenty of times I wished my siblings would disappear, but the truth was that I loved them all to bits and I couldn't imagine what life would be like without my family, let alone having the kind of abusive upbringing Lucas had endured.

Lucas was about to say something else, but the bell rang to indicate the start of the school day, interrupting him.

I put my finger over his lips. "Hold that thought," I said. "I'll come and see you when I've finished teaching and maybe we can kill the time checking out that desk of yours." I stood on tiptoe and dropped a quick kiss on his lips before leaving to go to my first class of the day.

"YOU LOOK HAPPY, miss. Have you got a new boyfriend?"

"N-no." I flushed at the question from Charley, one of my pupils. "What makes you think that?"

"You've just been smiling all day and you've got that far away look in your eyes." Charley exchanged a look with her friend, Maya. "We just thought you might have a boyfriend."

"And we're happy for you if you have," Maya put in. "It's about time you were with someone. You deserve to be happy. You're our favourite teacher."

"That's very sweet of you to say, but no. I don't have a new boyfriend. Now get along before you're late for your next class."

I covered my bluster by shuffling together papers on my desk as Maya and Charley slouched out of the room in that way only teenage girls can, giggling and nudging each other. Had it really been that obvious that I was seeing someone? If my pupils could tell that something was up, I wouldn't stand a chance of hiding it from my friends and family.

For the rest of the day I was like a bear with a sore head, snapping at people in an attempt to pretend I wasn't all that happy. It was exhausting – and it wasn't fair on my poor students either who really didn't deserve it. By the time the bell rang to signify the end of lessons, I wanted nothing more than to go home and put my feet up, but I had to hang around for Amber to come back from her trip.

On the upside, Lucas would still be in his office and he did have that very large desk…

Smiling, I grabbed my things and made to go over to see Lucas when my phone rang. Pulling it out, I saw someone was calling from a blocked number. Normally, I wouldn't answer if I didn't know who was calling, but some gut instinct told me this was important.

"Hello?"

"We have your daughter. Tell no one and wait for further instructions."

Chapter Eighty-Four

My blood turned to ice in my veins as I stared at the phone in my hands. It had to be a joke. A sick one, but a joke no less. I couldn't believe someone had taken my beautiful child.

My phone rang again, this time with a number I knew. Hands trembling, I swiped the screen to answer.

"Hi, Kym. Is everything okay?"

The teacher was doing her best to sound professional, but I could hear the unmistakeable tremble in her voice.

"I don't want to worry you, but we can't find Amber. We need to send the rest of the children back to school because the driver can't wait around much longer, but I'm going to stay here to help look for her. We've called the police and-"

I hung up on her. I didn't need to hear anymore. They weren't going to find my daughter. She was in the hands of some criminal gang and I had to get her back.

There was a knock on the classroom door and I looked up to see Lucas smiling at me.

"Hey. I thought I'd come and see if you fancied a coffee while we wait for Amber to come back?"

I felt like someone had stabbed me in the gut and was twisting the knife when he said our daughter's name, but the kidnappers had told me to tell no one, so I did my best to pretend nothing was wrong.

"That was Kym from nursery," I told Lucas, waving my phone at him. "Apparently there's been a bit of a delay, so it might be a while before they're back."

"Is that right?" Lucas moved towards me, wiggling his eyebrows suggestively. "Well, I can think of a good way to kill the time while we wait."

Sex was the last thing on my mind and I knew I wasn't going to fake enthusiasm, so I was glad when my phone beeped with a text, giving me an excuse to keep Lucas at arm's length. I stepped back, holding up a finger to let him know I would just be a moment while I read the text.

The last warehouse on the right. Dauphin Trading Estate. Twenty minutes. Come alone and don't be late.

Once again, the number was blocked, but this had to be where they had Amber.

"Everything all right?"

I quickly tucked my phone away so Lucas wouldn't see the message.

"Fine, fine. But I'm going to have to go. Rain check?"

"Where are you going? I'll come with you."

I thought quickly to come up with an excuse to stop him. I couldn't risk anything happening to Amber because Lucas had tagged along. He might be Amber's father, but until the kidnappers told me I could involve him, I wasn't taking any chances.

"It's Ivy," I said. "She needs to talk to me about something. It sounds serious."

"I hope everything's okay."

"So do I." I didn't need to fake the worry in my voice.

"Well, I'm not going to come between two friends when there's a crisis. Tell you what. I'll pick up Amber from the nursery and meet you back at yours if you like."

"Yeah, that would be great." I knew full well he wasn't going to be able to do that. I could only hope that he'd forgive me when he discovered what had happened.

I drove to the trading estate as fast as I dared, pushing the speed limit but not so much I'd attract any unwanted police attention. I could pull rank as Knight heir, but then they'd start asking awkward questions and I didn't have any time to spare if I was going to get to the warehouse within twenty minutes. I didn't even want to think about what would happen if I was late.

I took the turn off into the trading estate. I didn't know what types of business Romy's family housed here, but it was quiet. Too quiet.

I slowly drove through the estate, looking out for the warehouse I needed. I followed the road to its end and on the right was a large warehouse which didn't look like it was being used for anything. The lights were out, there were no vehicles parked outside and I couldn't see any sign of human activity.

Still, if I had the right building, there was something going on here all right. Some evil bastard had my daughter held captive and I was going to get her back, no matter what.

I parked in front of the warehouse and hurried inside to the reception area.

"Hello?"

My voice echoed back to me, but there was no reply. There was a desk opposite me, but it was unmanned. There was a door behind it and I went through to find had my child.

My phone beeped with another text.

You're getting warmer…

"So you like to play games, do you?" I muttered. "This is one game you're never going to win." I raised my voice. "Where's my daughter? Come out and show yourself!"

I heard a crash off in the distance and I ran in the direction of the sound. Corridors and rooms blended into one as I frantically searched for my baby. As I raced past a door, I heard another crash coming from behind it. I yanked the door open and went in.

The door slammed behind me, plunging the room into darkness. I whirled round, fumbling for the handle. When I found it, I tried to open the door again, but it was jammed shut. I was trapped!

There was a click and suddenly the room was filled with light. I turned around to see a window opposite me which looked out over another room. Amber was tied to a chair in the middle of the room, a large piece of duct tape over her mouth.

"Amber!" I screamed and ran over to the window, banging on it to smash the glass, but it was too thick. "Hold on, baby. I'm coming!" I looked to the side, trying to find another door that would let me be reunited with my daughter, but there was nothing. I couldn't see any way out of the room aside from the door I'd come in and that wasn't opening. The room was completely empty, so there wasn't even anything I could use to smash the glass.

"So you're Milly Knight. I have to say that you look even more unimpressive in person than you do in photos."

A woman I'd never seen before stepped out from the side of the glass and went to stand next to Amber, lightly resting a hand on her shoulder. Amber jerked away from her, but the woman grabbed a handful of her hair and pulled her back into place. Amber's face creased up in pain, but the duct tape muffled her cries.

"Don't hurt her, you bitch!" I pounded on the glass, hating that I couldn't protect my daughter.

"Now, now." The woman tutted and waggled a finger at me. "We'll have none of that kind of language here. Not when there's a child present. What kind of mother are you?"

"One who'll do anything to protect her child," I yelled. "And if anything happens to Amber-"

"You'll what?" the woman sneered. "What exactly are you going to do? You're trapped in that room. You can't get out unless I let you out and trust me, honey. I'm not letting you out any time soon."

"I'm going to kill you!" I banged on the window again, desperate to break through.

"No, you won't." The woman laughed. "Instead, you're going to call Lucas Donatello and tell him to get his arse over here. Because if he doesn't get here within twenty minutes, I might just have to give him a little incentive…"

She grabbed Amber's ear, twisting it painfully.

"Stop it!" I screamed banging on the glass. "I'll call Lucas, okay? Just leave Amber alone."

"And make sure you tell him to come alone and tell no one. I'll know if he does."

Hands shaking, I took out my phone and dialled his number.

Chapter Eighty-Five

Lucas

Blue lights lit up the interior of the nursery from the flashing lights on top of the police cars parked outside. Everywhere I looked there were policemen. Over to one side, Kym was struggling to keep it together as she went over her story one more time, My fingers itched to throttle her. How could she have lost my baby girl? I'd only recently found out I had a daughter but already that child was my world. If anything happened to her, I'd burn this whole town to the ground if it meant getting revenge on the person who had her.

My phone rang. My heart dropped when I saw Milly's name on the screen. How was I going to tell her that my staff had lost Amber?

"Milly? I'm so sorry but I've got some bad news."

"It'll have to wait. Are you somewhere no one will overhear you?"

"Milly, this can't wait. It's Amber. She-"

"I know. Lucas, get somewhere private."

I looked around, wondering where on earth I could go in this chaos that would give me the privacy Milly was so insistent about. In the end, I went to the children's toilets and pulled the door to.

"What's this about, Milly? How do you know about Amber?"

"I can't explain right now," she said. "I need you to trust me. You have to come out to the Dauphin Trading Estate."

"What – now? I can't do that. The police are here. They said they weren't done talking to me."

"I don't care. You have to find a way to get out of there without telling them where you're going."

"How am I going to do that, Mills? I'm the father of the child who's gone missing and the head of the school which lost her. It's going to look really suspicious if I suddenly leave."

"I don't care how it looks, Lucas. You need to leave. Now."

I was taken aback by the violence in Milly's tone. I'd never heard my mild-mannered girlfriend be so aggressive.

"Milly, you have to tell me what this is about, otherwise I've got no choice I've got to tell the police."

"I'm with Amber right now."

I could have collapsed with shock. "What do you mean, you're with Amber?"

"Look, get rid of the police. Tell them Amber's been found and it was all a misunderstanding. Tell them you forgot you'd sent your driver to collect her. I don't care. But if you don't get here *by yourself* within the next twenty minutes, she's going to hurt Amber."

"She? Who's going to hurt her."

"I don't know who she is," Milly wailed. "But she's standing right in front of me with Amber and she's going to hurt our little girl if you don't stop wasting time and get over here."

I let out a frustrated sigh, running a hand through my hair. "The Dauphin Trading Estate you say?"

"Yes. The last warehouse on the right. Hurry – she said you

had twenty minutes, but with all the talking we've been doing, she might not wait that long."

"I'll be right over," I promised, as I hung up the phone.

What the hell was I going to tell the police? They were about to go on a full-blown manhunt for Amber.

There was no other way. I was going to have to pull rank and use my name to try and talk my way out of here.

I left the toilet and almost walked straight into a police officer.

"Mr Donatello," he said. "Would you come with me? We've got a few questions for you."

"Detective. Just the man I wanted to see." I plastered a fake smile across my face. "It would appear there's been a mix up. Amber is perfectly safe and well. She's with her mother. Apparently, she didn't realise that Amber was coming back on the bus and went to the aquarium to get her. I'm so sorry for the inconvenience."

"Is that right?" The officer raised an eyebrow. "If that is the case, then we'll need to talk to Ms Knight to confirm. I'm sure you can appreciate that in a high-profile case like this, we can't just let things slide."

I pulled myself up to my full height and channelled my inner Penelope Donatello. "And *I'm* sure that *you* can appreciate that as a Donatello, I am completely within my rights to expect you to take my word for it. If I tell you that Amber is safe, Amber is safe, and given that her mother is Milly Knight, I'm sure the Knights would take exception to your implications that I'm telling you anything other than the truth. Pull your head in, call off the search and tell everyone it's been a misunderstanding. Otherwise, I'll be having words with your superior. I'm sure you'll love being busted down to traffic police."

"You can't speak to me like that," the officer blustered.

"Fine. If you won't sort this out, you leave me no choice."

I walked into the main room where the police were still questioning staff and parents. I clapped my hands. "Can I have everyone's attention please?" One of the benefits of being head was that I knew how to make people stop and take notice and the room immediately fell quiet, ready to hear the most difficult speech I was ever going to make.

"I must offer my most sincere apologies to everyone, but Amber is not missing." Out of the corner of my eye, I saw Kym gasp and practically collapse and I felt awful knowing how guilty she was feeling for losing Amber. "She is with her mother and is perfectly safe. I'm afraid I can't go into details right now, but I am very sorry for any stress this has caused you all. I'm going to give all nursery staff the day off tomorrow so they can recover from their ordeal and will be available all day to answer any questions any of you may have, including the police. Now, I'm sorry, but I'm going to have to leave. Something has come up which demands my urgent attention."

The moment I finished speaking, uproar broke out. People crowded round me, wanting to know what the hell was going on – and I didn't blame them. I was wondering exactly the same thing, but Milly had made it perfectly clear that I couldn't tell anyone what she'd told me and I trusted her to know what she was talking about.

"I'm sorry, but I'm going to have to insist you let me go. As I said, I'll answer your questions tomorrow. Feel free to email me or call my secretary to set up an appointment."

I pushed my way through the crowd and went out to my car. I fired up the engine and floored the gas, screeching out of the car park. Milly had told me I had twenty minutes to get to the industrial estate, but as I drove away, I could see in my rear-view mirror that the police were hot on my heels. I had to lose them. I didn't want to think of what might happen if I rocked on up to the warehouse with a police escort.

Gritting my teeth, I yanked the steering wheel to the left and took a sudden turn. Luckily, I knew the streets around the Academy like the back of my hand and I knew exactly where I was going to lose the cops.

I hit the button to make a hands-free call to my driver. "Theo. Bring the Suzuki to the underground carpark off Maine

Street. Be there in five." I hung up before he could answer. He'd be there. All I had to do was keep ahead of the police for long enough to meet him.

And that was going to be tricky. The cop driving the car behind me knew what he was doing and he was determined not to let me get away. I couldn't blame him. I knew full well that I was behaving suspiciously. Any police officer worth their salt would know that there was something strange going on and wasn't going to take my story at face value. Amber was a prime target for kidnapping given who her parents were. If I was the investigating officer, I'd assume my strange behaviour was an attempt to cover something up and want to know where I had to get to in such a hurry. I couldn't blame them for doing their job – but it was potentially putting my daughter's life at risk and I couldn't allow that.

I did another sharp turn, doing my best to shake my tail, but the police driver was determined. I just had to hope that my plan would work. If not, Amber was potentially in serious danger.

The car park loomed ahead and I did my best to fake over-shooting the entrance before turning off. For once, luck was on my side and the police driver fell for my ruse, forcing him to waste precious time as, tyres screeching, I raced down to the basement level of the car park where Theo was waiting for me with my Suzuki bike.

I pulled up next to him. "Quick!" I barked. "Get behind the wheel. I need you to take the police on a wild goose chase to the west side of town. Get them as far away from the Navarre district as possible."

"Got it."

Theo was one of my most loyal servants and he got behind the wheel of my car and immediately drove off. I put on the helmet he'd left on the bike seat and gave him a couple of minutes' head start so the police wouldn't guess that I was on the bike. The tinted windows of my car would conceal Theo's identity so by the time the police realised they were chasing the wrong man, I'd be at the warehouse.

Whoever had taken my daughter was going to regret it.

I pulled up alongside Milly's car. As I switched off the engine and pulled off my helmet, my phone beeped with a text from Milly.

She says well done for making it inside the deadline – just. Now come inside. Go through reception and down the corridor. Turn left at the bottom and then go through the third door on the right.

I did as I was told, running down the hallways and counting the doors until I got to where I'd been told to go. I pushed through a door, which slammed shut behind me. I turned round to open it, but there was no handle. I was trapped!

"Lucas. You are even better looking in person than I expected."

A woman's voice came across an intercom. I frowned. "Who are you? Show yourself!"

"All in good time, son. All in good time."

"No." I shook my head. "Enough game playing. I want to see Milly and Amber. I need to know they're safe."

"Suit yourself. Go through the red door."

There was a red door in the wall opposite the door where I'd come in. There was a buzzing sound and I hurried over to open it in case it locked again. I pulled it open and I found myself in a narrow room which was nothing but toughened glass on one side. On the other side of the glass I saw Amber tied to a chair and on the opposite side of the room, there was a large window through which I could see Milly. She was as much of a prisoner as the rest of us and whoever was behind this had the three of us at their mercy.

"Who's behind this? Show yourself!" I banged on the glass with my fist.

"I'm disappointed. I would have thought you'd have guessed by now." A woman stepped forward to stand next to Amber. I couldn't tell how old she was. She had the kind of wrinkled skin that resulted from years of smoking and goodness knew what other abuse, which meant she could be a lot younger than she looked. She had long, dark hair tied back in a low ponytail.

"I've never seen you before," I said.

"Now, Lucas, my boy. That's not true. I'm disappointed that you don't remember your own I mother – but then I suppose Penelope would have done her best to wipe me from your memory."

She came further into the light and I saw that her eyes were an unusual grey colour. My eyes widened as I realised she was exactly who she claimed to be. This was my birth mother!

"M-mum?" I shook my head, confused. "I don't understand. Why are you doing this?"

"I'll cut straight to the chase. I need money."

"Okay." I rolled my eyes. "So I'll give you money. You didn't need to put us through all of this. How much do you want? Ten thousand? Twenty? I'll transfer it now and we can forget all about this."

"You don't understand, Lucas." My mother tutted. "I want *all* your money. Every last penny that bitch Penelope left to you."

"This is all over some money?" Milly yelled at her from the other side of the glass. "That's your *granddaughter.* You've traumatised her for life when all you had to do was ask."

"It's so easy for the pair of you to sit there and talk about money like it's nothing," my mother said. "You've had it all your lives. You have no idea what it's like to struggle. You don't know what it's like to be a single mother, never knowing if you'll be able to feed your baby."

"You can't pretend you're a caring mother," Milly snapped. "You've hurt your granddaughter and you *sold* your son. You are not the victim here."

"Shut up!" My mother snarled and grabbed Amber. I could see her fingers digging into my daughter's delicate skin and tears ran down her face. I had to save my daughter.

"You have no idea what it was like for me," my mother went on. "You sit there in your fancy houses looking down at people like me. You play chess with people's lives with no care for the kind of devastation you leave behind. No more! It's my turn to shine. I want you to transfer the entire Donatello fortune to me, Lucas. Your girlfriend has more than enough money to support you both. You won't miss the billions you give me."

"And what happens if I don't?"

"It's pretty simple." My mother pulled out a wickedly sharp hunting knife. Its cruel blade twinkled in the light, the serrated edge capable of cutting through Amber's soft flesh like it was butter. "If you don't transfer over the money, I'll start taking pieces off your daughter. I think I'll start with a little finger. One quick movement and it'll be gone. So, Lucas, it's entirely up to you. One way or another, you'll get your daughter back. It's entirely up to you whether she's in one piece or not. Now, I've had enough of talking. You have ten seconds to make up your mind. Are you giving me my money or am I taking my pound of flesh? Ten... nine... eight..."

"Stop!" I held out my hand, hating how helpless I felt. "I'll transfer the money." I took out my mobile and opened up my mobile banking app. "Where do I send it to?"

"This is my Swiss bank account." My mother took out a piece of paper and held it up against the glass so I could see the account details. "But if you think you're going to recover the money from it after I'm gone, think again. I'll be transferring it out again immediately. Say goodbye to your money, Lucas. It's mine now."

I tapped in the account details, but I was so nervous, I kept mistyping.

"Tick tock, Lucas. Waste any more time and it's bye bye fingers."

"There!" I snapped, holding up my phone so she could see. "I've transferred everything to you."

My mother took out her phone and opened up her banking app. She nodded her approval. "Good boy. I knew you'd see sense. I wish we could have met under different circumstances, but I couldn't risk it. You've been brought up by Penelope Donatello. She'll have turned you against me."

"No, she didn't." I laughed bitterly. "Penelope never even mentioned you. You weren't important enough."

"You're a liar!" My mother hit the glass with the knife handle. "Penelope told you all about me, which is why you never tried to find me. She made you think I was a bad person for giving you up, when I didn't have any choice. You have *no* idea the mess I was in. I gave you to her to keep you safe. I loved you, and you forgot all about me."

"You're wrong." Milly surprised us both by speaking up. "Lucas always wanted to come and find you, but Penelope would have killed him if he'd tried. If you knew Penelope as well as you say, you'd know that she wouldn't want to share Lucas with anyone, especially not the woman who gave birth to him. Lucas has been looking for his family, but he thought you were dead. If he'd known you were still alive, he'd have wanted to see you, build a relationship."

"Is that right?" My mother arched an eyebrow, turning to look at me.

"Yes." I nodded. "I always wanted a proper family. I had no idea you were still alive or I'd have reached out to you. Heck, I'd have taken you in, given you a house, money, whatever you wanted."

"Stop lying." My mother shook her head, slowly at first, but then fast. "You're a Donatello now. I can't trust a word you say. No, this was the only way to get what Penelope should have given me. I'm sorry if you really did have a bad childhood like you say, but it couldn't have been that bad. Not when you had Penelope's fortune to enjoy."

"There's more to life than money," I said.

"The only people who truly believe that are the ones who've never had to worry about it." My mother smiled sadly. "All I wanted was for you to have a better life than I did. If Penelope had given me more money all those years ago maybe we wouldn't be here now."

"It wouldn't have mattered how much money she gave you." Milly spat. "Stop making excuses and let my daughter go.

You've got what you wanted. Stop making excuses and set us free."

"I'd never expect someone like you to understand," my mother said. "But you're right. I've got what I came for and I'll always keep my promises, unlike Penelope. Your door locks are on a timer. When I leave, those doors will stay locked for another thirty minutes before they open. I'll be long gone and you'll be free to go. Goodbye, Lucas. Goodbye, Amber. Granny loves you."

I couldn't believe my eyes when my mother kissed Amber tenderly on the head before she left, as if she hadn't just been holding her prisoner at knifepoint.

"That woman is so lucky Amber is here," Milly said after my mother had gone. "You have no idea what I'd say otherwise."

"I can imagine," I said. "Amber, are you okay sweet pea?"

Amber nodded, tears streaming down her cheeks.

"It won't be long before mummy and daddy will come and get you out of there," I said. "Just hold on. We'll be there as soon as we can."

"You're such a good girl," Milly added. "I'm so proud of you. You've been so brave."

It felt like an eternity before the door to my prison finally clicked open. As soon as it unlocked, I ran through, looking for the entrance to the room Amber was being held in. When I got there, Milly had already untied her and was holding her daughter tightly to her chest. The pair of them were sobbing heavily, the stress of their ordeal proving to be all too much.

"It's okay. I'm here now. I'm never going to let anything like that happen again. I promise."

I put my arms around the two most important girls in my life. I heard distant police sirens drawing closer, the cavalry coming just a little too late. My mother was long gone and I never wanted to see her again.

Chapter Eighty-Six

Lucas

One week later

"*A*re you ready?"

Milly reached out and squeezed my hand in reassurance.

"As ready as I'll ever be."

I reached up and rang the doorbell of the address Gabriel Knight had given me. Apparently, my sister lived here and this was the first time I was going to meet her properly. I'd taken a leave of absence from work following all the drama of Amber's kidnapping. Since I'd had to give all my money to my mother, I couldn't afford to pay my lawyers and the police weren't happy with how I'd handled the situation, but Milly's family had stepped in and everything was about as okay as it could be. Amber was still having nightmares and probably would for a while to come, but Milly had found an excellent child therapist and we were working together as a family to help her recover from the fact that her grandmother had threatened to chop her into tiny little pieces.

I'd never forgive my mother for that. If I ever got my hands on her, I'd do to her what she'd threatened to do to Amber, but, thanks to the massive fortune she now had, she'd disappeared like a puff of smoke. There was no trace of her anywhere and without the funds to hire competent investigators, I didn't stand a chance of tracking her down. She could be anywhere in the world by now.

Still, my mother wasn't important right now. I was here to make contact with my sister.

A young girl opened the door. She had dark hair and dark brown eyes, but there was definitely something about her face shape that reminded me of our mother.

"Sir? Miss?" She looked panicked to see us standing on her doorstep. "Have I done something wrong? Am I being expelled?"

"You haven't done anything wrong, Daisy," I reassured her. "But could we come in and speak to your parents? I've got something I need to discuss with them in private."

"O-okay. Mum! Dad! Mr Donatello and Miss Knight are here!" Daisy beckoned for us to come inside and led the way to the lounge where her mum was watching TV.

"Mr Donatello." She stood up, looking confused. "Is everything all right? What are you doing here?"

"I was hoping I could have a word with you and your husband, Mrs May."

"Is this about the bullying?" Mr May strode into the room. "It's about time the school took it seriously. The number of times Daisy's come home in floods of tears is ridiculous. We've been trying to tell her to toughen up, but she shouldn't have to deal with that in the first place."

"No, you're right. She shouldn't," I said. "And we can discuss that in a moment, but I've got something else I need to talk to you about first. Would it be possible to have a chat without Daisy in the room?"

"I can go with Daisy," Milly offered. "I can talk to her about the bullying."

Mr and Mrs May exchanged a worried glance. "Okay. Daisy – why don't you take Miss Knight to your room?",

"Okay." Daisy gestured to Milly to follow her and the two of them left. I shut the door behind them before going back to sit on the chair opposite Mr and Mrs May, who sat next to each other on the couch. Mr May took his wife's hand and they both looked at me, concerned frowns wrinkling their faces.

"There's no easy way to say it, so I'm just going to come right out with it," I said. "Does Daisy know she's adopted?"

Mrs May gasped, a hand fluttering up to cover her mouth.

"How did you know?" Mr May asked.

"Because she's my sister," I said.

"No! She can't be!" Mrs May said. "When we adopted her, we were told she had no family. The agency said her parents had died in a car crash when she was a baby and there were no surviving relatives to take her in."

"The agency may well have believed that to be true, but you were misinformed. Not only is Daisy's mother very much alive, she was the one responsible for kidnapping my daughter last week."

"I don't understand. How can this be true?" Mr May said. "We used a very reputable agency. They thoroughly vet all the children they adopt out. They only deal with children from good backgrounds, children whose parents have died leaving them with no one to look after them." He lowered his voice, even though there was no one to overhear. "You hear so many stories of children with terrible problems coming from mothers with drink and drug problems. The adoptions go horribly wrong. We wanted to make sure that our child would be perfect, just like Daisy."

"I'm really sorry, but by the sound of it, the agency you used completely lied about what they do," I told him. "My mother is a very disturbed individual who sold me to Penelope Donatello and, no doubt, sold Daisy to your agency."

"Oh my goodness!" Mrs May looked like she might faint.

"I'm sorry, Mr Donatello, but I really cannot believe that what you're saying is true," Mr May said. "Do you have any proof to back up your allegations?"

"I do." I reached into my pocket and pulled out the documents Gabriel Knight had sent me. I passed them over to the Mays. "There's a copy of Daisy's and my birth certificates, naming my mother on both of them. My mother named her Lillian after our grandmother, but the agency changed her name. There's a copy of the deed poll document there as well. If you need more evidence, I'm sure I can arrange for you to have a meeting with the investigators to go over everything, but there really isn't any doubt. Daisy is my sister."

The Mays perused the documents, looking paler by the minute as the truth of what I was telling them hit home.

"So what do we do now?" Mr May asked. "Daisy doesn't know she's adopted."

"Obviously, I don't want to do anything to upset your family," I said. "If you don't want to tell Daisy she's adopted, I'll respect that – for now. But she has a right to know she has a brother and I want to get to know my sister beyond her being one of my students. If you don't want to tell her right now, I can wait. But sooner or later she's going to find out the truth. Don't you think it would be better for her to hear it from you rather than finding it out from someone else?"

Mr and Mrs May exchanged a glance.

"We always said we'd tell her when the time was right," Mrs May said. "Maybe that time is now?"

"It might make the bullies back off if they know that Daisy's brother is the head," Mr May said. "All right. Let's tell her the truth."

She got up and went out of the room. I heard her calling up the stairs for Daisy and soon Daisy was sitting next to her parents while Milly came to sit in the chair next to me.

"Daisy, we need to tell you something." Her mother took hold of one of her hands. "We always meant to tell you, but somehow the time was never right. But we feel that you deserve to know the truth."

"That I'm adopted?" Daisy said.

"You know?"

"I've known for years." Daisy rolled her eyes. "I was looking for some paper to do a picture and I found some documents in your office. It made a lot of things made sense, but I wasn't upset about it. I figured that you chose to be my parents, which makes our relationship even more special and I thought I'd find out about my birth family when I was older."

"About that..." Mr May shuffled about uneasily. "We were told that you didn't have any family. That was why we chose you. You had no one to take care of you, no brothers or sisters, no parents or grandparents. The agency told us that your family died in a car crash. But we've just found out that that was a lie."

"That's weird." Daisy frowned. "So what did happen to them?"

Mr May looked at me, indicating that I should take over telling the story.

"I don't know about your father, but your birth mother is very much alive," I told her. "No one knows where she is right now, but I've got people look for her."

"Why would *you* do that?"

I took a deep breath. "Because I'm your brother."

Daisy's expression would have been comical if the situation wasn't so serious. Her jaw dropped and her eyes widened while her skin paled.

"My *brother?* But you're the head! You can't be my brother. You're *ancient!*"

"I'm not that old." I laughed. "But our mum was really young when she had me. I don't think she'd planned on having any more children, but when you came along, she must have figured out that she could make some more money."

"*More* money?" Daisy asked.

"She effectively sold me to Penelope Donatello," I told her. "And then she kidnapped my daughter and forced me to sign over all my money to her. I'll be honest, Mr and Mrs May. I don't think there's enough money in the world to satisfy my mother. It'll take her a while to burn through the Donatello fortune, but when she has, I wouldn't be surprised if she came after Daisy. I think the agency targeted you because they knew you were wealthy and associated with House Knight. Having taken all the Donatello money, my mother is going to want to go after the Knights."

"Well, she'll have a fight on her hand if she does," Mr May snarled, clenching his fists. "I won't let that woman get anywhere near my little girl. I don't care if she gave birth to her. Daisy's my daughter and I'll kill anyone who tries to hurt her."

"My mother's sneaky," I warned him. "She'll come after you when you're least expecting it. But we've got people looking for her and they're the best at what they do. It won't be long before we find her."

"We'll help," Mr May offered. "Anything we can do, let us know."

"But she's my mother. She wouldn't hurt me," Daisy said.

"You don't know her," I said. "She's not normal. She's had serious drink and drug problems in the past. She's had a tough life and it's twisted her. You didn't see what she did to Amber, what she was prepared to do. Anyone who is willing to hurt their young granddaughter won't think twice about harming any of their other relatives."

"Oh." Daisy gulped and looked down.

"But I didn't come here to talk about her," I said. "I want to talk about you, about us. You have no idea how happy I was to find out I had a sister. I've always wanted a family and I'd really like it if you wanted to spend some time together, get to know each other."

"That would be weird," Daisy said. "I mean, you're the head and you're dating my English teacher. How can I see you as my brother?"

"Don't tell anyone, but I don't think I'm going to be head for much longer," I told her. "I took the job because I wanted to find you. Now that I have, I don't know whether I want to stay at the Academy. Then again, with my mother running off with the content of my bank balance, maybe I'll stay on because I need the money!" I laughed, my weak joke bringing a smile to Daisy's face. "But seriously, Daisy, maybe we'll have nothing in common and we'll drift apart. But I'd really like to try to get to know each other, build some family ties, that is, if it's okay with your parents?"

"As far as I'm concerned, the more people who can watch Daisy's back, the better," Mr May said.

"I agree," Mrs May nodded. "After Amber's kidnapping, you can't be too careful. It would be good for Daisy to get to know her brother."

"Why don't you come out with us next week?" Milly offered. "We're taking Amber to the beach. It'll be a laidback day, fish and chips, candy floss, sunbathing…"

"I'd like that," Daisy said at last. "You're right. It would be good to get to know each other."

We smiled at each other and I felt like everything was going to be all right. Finally, I was going to have the family I'd always dreamed of.

Chapter Eighty-Seven

$\mathcal{M}$*illy*

One month later

"So, it's okay for me to take the A level students on a field trip to see *Anthony and Cleopatra?*" I asked Lucas.

"I'll be honest," he replied. "After what happened with Amber, I feel nervous about allowing students off campus."

"I get that," I said. "But you can't let your mother spoil the rest of your life. She's gone and she's not coming back any time soon. These are sixth formers, not nursery kids. They're a lot more street savvy. They're not going to go off with anyone. And Daisy will be on the trip. You could come with us and keep an eye on your kid sister."

"I don't know. I don't want to spoil her street cred." Lucas leaned back in his swivel chair, thinking about what I'd said. "You're right. I shouldn't let my mother affect my decisions. She's probably sunning herself on a beach in Monaco right now."

"I wish I was on a beach in Monaco." I sighed. "I think we

could all do with a holiday after everything we've been through."

"That's not a bad idea," Lucas said. "We could take Amber and ask Daisy if she'd like to come. It would be a good opportunity to have some family time."

"I'm so glad you and Daisy are getting on," I said. "She's one of my favourite students and she's growing into a lovely young woman. Amber's so lucky to have her as an aunt."

"Yes, and they get on like a house on fire," Lucas said. "I think having Amber around has made it easier for Daisy and me to build a relationship. It's not quite so awkward when you've got a small child to entertain."

"Yeah, it might have been difficult for the two of you to connect without Amber to help bridge the gap," I observed. "That ten-year age difference isn't going to matter when she's in her mid-twenties, but right now, you're just an old guy to her."

"Hey! Enough of the old!" Lucas protested. "I can still party with the best of them. If you're not careful I'm going to have to put you over my knee."

"Ooh, promises, promises." I smiled flirtatiously. "You know, we never did try out your desk."

"That's easily rectified." Lucas started to pull off his tie, coming round to my side of his desk. He leaned forward and kissed me, his hands running down the front of my blouse. I could feel my nipples tighten in anticipation and I moaned, shifting forward in my chair to get closer to him.

Knock, knock!

"Are you kidding?" I groaned, thumping the arm of my chair with frustration.

"Sorry, Mills. You're going to have to hold that thought."

We quickly tidied up our appearance as whoever it was at the door knocked again.

"Come in!" called Lucas as he sat back down in his chair.

I turned round to see who was there and I was stunned to see my father walk in.

"Gabriel!" Lucas was clearly as surprised as I was as he

stood up to extend a hand to Dad. They shook hands and Lucas gestured to the chair next to me. "Please, take a seat."

Dad sat down and nodded at me. "Milly."

"Hi, Dad."

"What can I do for you, Gabriel?" Lucas asked.

"It's more what I can do for you," Dad replied. "Have you checked your bank balance recently?"

"Not much point," Lucas said. "I know what it's going to say."

"Are you sure?"

A quizzical frown on his face, he took his phone out and logged into his bank account via the app. From the stunned expression on his face, it wasn't what he expected to see.

"I-I don't understand," Lucas said. "All the money's back – plus interest! But how?"

"It's better if you don't know," Dad said. "Plausible deniability and all that. Suffice to say that you won't be bothered by that woman ever again."

"This is incredible," Lucas breathed. "I don't know how I'm ever going to repay you."

"Just treat my daughter right." Dad looked at him meaningfully.

"Don't worry, Gabriel. I have every intention of doing that."

"Glad to hear it. Well, I can't stick around – I've got another meeting to get to. Perhaps the two of you and Amber would like to come over for dinner one night this week? I have a few business ideas I'd like to run past you."

"That would be great," Lucas said, getting up to escort my dad to the door.

"Excellent. I'll have my secretary call to set up a time."

My father left and Lucas shut the door behind him. He looked at me, delighted. "I've got my money back."

"So I gathered." I smiled. Lucas's happiness was infectious.

"Now that I'm financially independent again, I can ask you something I've been thinking about for a while," Lucas said.

"I'm intrigued."

"Look, everyone knows we're dating and that I'm Amber's dad. So why don't we be a real family? Why don't you move in with me?"

"Move in with you? That's a big step."

"Bigger than having a child together?"

"I guess not." I pretended to think about it, wanting to make Lucas sweat a little, although I'd arelady made up my mind. "All right. Let's do it. Let's move in together."

"Yes!" Lucas came and swept me off my feet, picking me up and spinning me round before setting me down on his desk. "Now then. Let's find out just how sturdy this desk is…"

Epilogue

One year later

"I'm glad we left Amber back at the hotel with Daisy. She'd never have coped with this hill." I panted as I tried to keep up with Lucas while we walked through beautiful Sri Lankan woodlands. The scenery was stunning, but we were climbing quite a steep hill and Amber had reached that stage where she complained about everything. Listening to her whining would have ruined the mood and Lucas and I deserved a bit of romantic alone time.

Lucas pulled up. "Listen. Can you hear that?"

I stopped walking and tilted my head to one side. I heard a roaring, rumbling, thundering noise. "What is that?"

"It's the reason why I wanted us to go for this walk. Come on!" He grabbed my hand and started running. Although I was tired, his enthusiasm was infectious, and I ran along with him until we reached a clearing at the top of the hill. The sight that greeted us was incredible.

"It's beautiful!" A waterfall cascaded down a rocky cliff opposite us, ending up in a brilliant blue pool.

"You can swim in the water," Lucas told me, as we started to walk down a path that went down the hill and to a clearing by the pool. "One of the hotel staff told me about this place. It's one of those hidden local gems that tourists don't tend to know about, so we should have it all to ourselves."

"A swim would be perfect," I said. "But I didn't bring my costume."

"Who says you'll need it?" Lucas cocked an eyebrow at me, giving me a challenging look. "Last one in the water's a rotten egg!" He ripped off his top and started racing towards the water.

"No fair!" I yelled chasing after him. "You cheated!"

When we reached the waterside, we stripped down to our underwear and dove into the water. It was just the right temperature, perfect to cool us down after that long walk in the sun. I flipped onto my back, floating in the water and gazing up at the sky. "This is bliss. We should have done this sooner. This break is just what I needed. It's been a tough year."

"That it has."

The two of us floated next to each other, neither of us needing to talk as we relaxed in the pool. The only sounds were the noise of the waterfall and the birds calling to each other in the trees.

I lost track of time as we swam around, but eventually, I started to feel cold and I got out, wanting to stretch out and enjoy the sun.

"This is amazing." I sighed as I made myself comfortable on a rock overlooking the water. I gazed out at the waterfall, feeling the spray of water tickle my face. "This is such a special place."

"That's why I wanted to bring you here."

Something in the tone of his voice made me turn round and I gasped when I saw him kneeling in front of me, holding an open ring box. Inside was the most stunning platinum ring, a large sapphire set in the middle of a number of diamonds.

"Milly, you are the most incredible woman I've ever met," Lucas said. "The more time I spend with you, the more in love I feel. I'd be lost without you. You keep me sane. You keep me grounded. And I want to spend the rest of my life making you happy. Milly Knight, will you marry me?"

For a moment, I was lost for words, too happy to speak.

"Come on, Mills. Don't leave me hanging!"

"Yes, of course I will!"

Happy tears ran down my cheek as Lucas got up and placed the ring on my finger. It fit perfectly like it had been made for me – and knowing Lucas, it probably had.

"What do you think – will Amber be happy to be a bridesmaid?"

"Are you kidding?" I laughed. "Given that Amber's done nothing but ask when we're getting married, I think she'll practically burst with excitement! She's got her dress picked out already and everything. She's been taking inspiration from that kids' show *Marrying Mum and Dad* and has been begging me to let her arrange our wedding."

"It's not a bad idea," Lucas said. "It could save us a fortune on a wedding planner."

"Yes – if you fancy getting married in a llama petting zoo wearing a Batman costume!"

"Are you kidding?"

"Oh no." I shook my head. "Amber's been telling me all about it. She thinks you're a superhero, so you're Batman while I get to be Wonder Woman. And since llamas are her current obsession, she wants me to arrive in a llama-drawn carriage and have a llama to carry the rings."

"Okay. So maybe we *don't* get Amber to organise things."

"Besides," I said. "I've been planning my dream wedding for years. Since I'm only going to do this once, I know exactly what I do and don't want and I *definitely* don't want any llamas!"

"No llamas. Got it." Lucas laughed and pulled me to him, kissing me deeply.

Our journey to love had been a rocky one, but now we were here, I knew that there was never really any doubt. Lucas was the one for me and always would be.

C<small>LICK</small> <small>HERE</small> <small>TO</small> <small>SUBSCRIBE</small> <small>TO</small> <small>MY</small> <small>NEWSLETTER</small> <small>FOR</small> <small>EXCLUSIVE</small> <small>BONUS</small> <small>SCENES,</small> <small>GIVEAWAYS</small> <small>AND</small> <small>MORE..</small>

Printed in Great Britain
by Amazon

21446696R10399